Praise for Joe Samuel Starnes

FALL LINE

"Of all the contemporary Southern novels today that draw comparisons to Faulkner and O'Connor, Starnes' tale may be one of the few that deserves them." —*The Atlanta Journal-Constitution*

"A novel that accrues force the way a swollen river becomes a torrent." —*TriQuarterly*

"Starnes knows his home area and its people and how to write about them with admirable authority and poetic understanding." —Jean W. Cash, *Studies in American Culture*

"Told from various viewpoints, *Fall Line* is an affectionate, eloquent story of loss and survival." —Teresa Weaver, *Atlanta Magazine*

CALLING

"An entertaining and sometimes transcendent Southern Gothic novel worthy of his literary forebear, the late Larry Brown." —*Rain Taxi*

"A top-notch novel in the tradition of Harry Crews . . . big plot turns that will keep readers turning pages." —*Athens Banner-Herald*

"A hard-to-put-down tale . . . made me think of a Frederick Buechner work, but edgier." —*The Charlotte Observer*

RED DIRT

RED DIRT

A Tennis Novel

Joe Samuel Starnes

BREAKAWAY BOOKS
HALCOTTSVILLE, NEW YORK
2015

Red Dirt: A Tennis Novel

ISBN: 978-1-62124-015-0
Library of Congress Control Number: 2014916467

Published by Breakaway Books
P.O. Box 24
Halcottsville, NY 12438
www.breakawaybooks.com

The author wishes to make clear that this is a work of fiction and that none of the action described in the novel is true. Though there are many references to actual people, the scenes are entirely fictional. Names, characters, places, and incidents either are the product of the author's imagination or are used fictitiously.

For my parents, who gave me unlimited
love, books, and tennis rackets,
and Amy, a doctor of English who
diligently reads all my drafts,
lets me play almost as much tennis as I want,
and gives me more love than I deserve.

Part One

My earliest memory of anything on this earth is a tennis match. I was three. My dad and older sisters sat on the couch watching Wimbledon, that first Borg–McEnroe final. Dad had worked early grading dirt roads for the county and returned home before noon when he started drinking a Budweiser from the can. We lived way out in the country, back in the woods about a mile from the nearest house, a half-mile from the paved road.

Dad at that time didn't give a damn about tennis, but my sisters had become interested in Björn Borg and his long blond hair and snug Fila shorts. They watched while I played with my Hot Wheels collection, racing the dense metal cars along the floor at full speed, crashing each one into our pinewood-paneled walls. When my dad became interested in the match, I crawled up into his lap. He held me and sipped his beer and we all focused on the television. Our antenna's weak reception produced grainy pictures even on clear days. The white balls they used at Wimbledon were hard to make out, but we could see on both players' faces, in their movements, that something special was happening over there.

Dad started pulling against the Swede, partly to rile up the girls, but also because he was the kind of man who would always cheer for an American, even a cocky New Yorker like John McEnroe if that was his only choice. And McEnroe was the underdog, giving Dad another reason to get in his corner—Dad always pulled for the underdogs.

We watched McEnroe dart to net and dive to hit a drop volley winner. "Look at that curly-headed boy go," Dad said. He took a swig of his beer and bounced me on his knee. Sally and Ruth scowled at both of us.

I have seen a replay on several occasions since but I vividly remember that first time, watching Borg serve for the match in the fourth set when McEnroe broke him, and then the extended tiebreaker where McEnroe saved match point after match point, seven in all. The worn grass on Wimbledon's Centre Court looked like a patch of dirt in the winter when the blades turn brown, the players' paths from the baselines to the net trod into the turf. The tiebreaker went back and forth with all of us gasping after each point. McEnroe's face was plump with sweat and blush, his eyes near tears, but Borg showed no expression. He earned that Iceman nickname. None of us knew enough about tennis to even keep score, but we didn't need numbers for the match to matter. True artistry was going on before our eyes.

McEnroe finally won the fourth set tiebreaker 18–16 when Borg netted a backhand. The New Yorker pumped his fist and did a little hop. Borg hung his head and looked like he was about to fall asleep. "*Hooo*-boy," my dad said. "That pretty boy is done for, darlin's."

My dad gripped me under the armpits and raised me up, swinging me in the air. "Hey, Jaxie boy!" He set me down on the couch and went for another beer in the kitchen where my mother was using a serving fork to mash a clump of cheddar, Miracle Whip, and diced red peppers into a creamy spread of pimento cheese. I leaned forward and watched as he looked out the window at our grassy backyard, a yard so big most folks would call it a field. He studied for a minute on his bulldozer, parked at the edge of our driveway. He popped the top of a beer and took a long pull. He smiled, nodded cheerfully, and walked back into the den and spoke to the girls. "Get your rackets ready. Y'all gonna get you a tennis court after this match is over."

He sat down and I crawled back up in his lap and he tousled my blond hair. The girls looked at him like he was crazy, and then they glared at me, scrunching up their noses, a look inherited from our mother.

My mom came into the room and passed around the plate stacked with white-breaded sandwich halves and a bowl of sweet pickles. "John? What are you talking about? A tennis court?"

"Sandy, you'll see."

She sat on the end of the couch. We ate and watched while Borg played two weak points after the tiebreaker, but much to everyone's surprise, especially McEnroe, he came charging back and broke serve early in the fifth set. McEnroe fought back, but Borg ultimately ended it 8–6 with an arcing crosscourt backhand passing shot. He knelt like he was being anointed by the gods of tennis above for winning his fifth straight Wimbledon.

The girls squealed and jumped around and hugged each other, and my mom joined them in their Björn Borg–victory dance. The women in my family always stuck together like that. But Dad's mood wasn't dampened. He seemed happy they were happy. "Get your rackets ready, girls," he said. He walked into the kitchen for another beer, and then went out the back door.

My sisters owned Wilsons, Chris Evert models, but neither one of them moved. They knew not to believe everything Dad told them on Saturday, his beer-drinking day. That match was the next-to-last Wimbledon men's finals played on a Saturday. If it had been on Sunday, like it is now, we would have been at church and I would have missed it altogether.

I followed to the screen door and watched as Dad walked out into the hot sun past the driveway and climbed up on his bulldozer and cranked the engine, the Caterpillar puffing out black smoke as the diesel began to burn and the pistons began to pump. He looked back at the house and smiled. He put the gear stick in neutral, leaving the engine running, and placed his beer beside the seat. He got down and walked toward me. "C'mon, boy." He opened the kitchen door and lifted me up. "You can help me drive."

My mom came over and stood where I had been standing, watching us through the screen door. She took a few steps into the yard and called out my dad's name but he acted like he didn't hear her. He carried me over and pulled me onto his lap in the seat atop the bulldozer and positioned me between his legs. "Hold on, now boy." I gripped my arms on his thighs. He jammed it into gear and gunned the engine and we rolled ponderously across the yard with the blade up, the giant track wheels making sharp indentations in the high thickness of the summer grass, that big motor rumbling a diesel song.

He shifted gears and the bulldozer slowed to a stop. "How about here? This is big enough, ain't it?" He pressed a lever and the enormous vehicle jolted as the iron blade dropped to the ground, knifing into the dense fescue. My mom walked into the yard and yelled at my father but he revved the engine and drowned her out. He reached for his beer, chugged the rest down, crumpled the can in one hand, and tossed it into the grass.

"Hang on good, now." He pulled me back closer to him, and I squeezed my arms tighter around his legs. He shifted into first and we lurched forward, pushing away the earth's top layer, spreading topsoil and fescue off to the side. The smell of cut grass and moist roots rose up about us. He made a long pass of about 120 feet and then turned and went back the other way, clearing another wide swath to reveal a large rectangle of virgin clay. The fresh earth shone, steaming in the hot sun. "Red dirt," he said. "Nothing like *red dirt*."

He had teased my sisters that our court was for them, but ultimately he built it for me. If we had it to do over again, as one who hit about ten million tennis balls on that court, we'd have run it north–south instead of east–west so the sun wouldn't burn into our retinas in the early mornings and late afternoons. The yellow balls came at me as though shot right out of the sun, as though the light of the universe had catapulted a ball my way. Sometimes I think it fateful that he laid the court that direction. Playing tennis with that huge ball of fire burning into my eyes helped to make me tough.

And Lord knows I had to be tough to make it as far as I did in professional tennis, running up against all these determined maniacs, men and boys from all corners of this planet who wanted to win tennis matches more than anything, men and boys who would sacrifice everything to reach the top. The pressure ruined even Borg, as resilient as he was. He vanished at the age of twenty-five after he lost for the fourth time in the finals of the U.S. Open, a tournament he could never win. Thinking about all the miles I traveled, all the losses I suffered playing into the deep half of my thirties, I can't say I blame him. Trying to climb to the highest level of this game is no way to live a sane life.

I was five when my dad put me in his red Ford pickup truck and took me to Atlanta for my first tennis lesson. It was a long drive, almost two hours. He had scheduled time with a pro whose name he had seen in the back of *The Atlanta Journal*'s sports pages. It cost forty dollars for an hour, pricey for the time, but Dad was doing well in the road business back then.

Dad drove into the Buckhead section of Atlanta looking for the club, down West Paces Ferry Road, past roads with names like Tuxedo and Habersham, thoroughfares where sloping drives led to huge homes set up on hills with manicured lawns beneath canopies of magnolias, dogwoods, and towering oaks. He pointed out the governor's mansion, the stately white columns behind a black iron fence. "That's where old Jimmy Carter got his start," he said. "Right there behind those walls."

We found the club and pulled in through the ivy-covered stone gate and he parked, the only pickup truck in the lot. He looked over at me before opening his door. "Behave yourself, now, boy." We got out and I could see him studying on all the fancy vehicles there: Mercedes and BMWs and Cadillacs, even a Porsche or two.

On the way out of Piney he had stopped at Belk's and bought me a new pair of white tennis shorts and a white shirt, both too big but still the smallest size they carried. The new shirt hung on my body like a sheet, reaching down almost to the hem of the shorts. The shorts never would have stayed up if it hadn't been for the piece of hay-baling twine that he retrieved from behind his truck seat and tied around my waist for a belt. "Don't tuck in your shirt," he said. "This ain't the most stylish belt on the boulevard. But it'll do. You'll grow into these."

He retrieved my racket from the bed of the truck and studied on it before handing it to me. He had sawed off a Jack Kramer model about six inches from the end of the handle and moved the grip up the neck. I had been using it since that day he first built the court. It would have made more sense to give me a Chris Evert model, being that those frames were lighter, but we were men and would absolutely under no circumstances ever use a racket decorated with the silhouette of a woman in a dress. And I loved that Jack Kramer, especially the golden crown of a king emblazoned on the center of the frame. "Maybe we'll get you a new racket soon, if you keep playing well and enjoy it," he said.

My dad ran a road crew and owned heavy equipment and didn't have but one blue suit that he wore on the occasions he had to attend the county commission or meet with someone from the state—his "undertaker suit" he called it. Most days he would wear jeans and a denim shirt and a black CAT diesel cap, sometimes a green John Deere cap. But this day he didn't wear a cap or any denim. He had on peach-colored Sansabelt slacks, also bought at Belk's, and a red Izod shirt with a crocodile on the breast. On his feet were leather penny loafers, and he had slicked his black hair and parted it. The only thing he couldn't change was his ruddy tan and hard-bitten fingernails on callused hands.

My dad was in his late thirties at the time. He was tall, slim, and powerful, about six-two, with long arms. He had a dark complexion and a narrow face with a long thin nose and a pointed chin with a big cleft, always slightly tinged with a touch of a five o'clock shadow. Beneath his right ear on the jawline he had a trademark scar that he got when someone jabbed him with a broken beer bottle in one of those honky-tonks along the county line when he was in his twenties. When he smiled his chin curled up and the flesh around his nose wrinkled and it gave him a very endearing, almost goofy kind of expression. His grin put you in the mind of a lanky Buddy Hackett. I look a lot more like my mother with her blond hair and blue eyes, although I have a touch of my dad's olive skin tone.

My dad took a deep breath and exhaled long and loud before we opened the door to the pro shop. A slim man minding the counter looked us up and down when we walked inside. "Can I help you?" he said. I could hear the hope in his high-pitched voice that we were just looking for directions to a cow sale or tractor pull.

My dad smiled as though the man had told a joke. "Yes sir," he said. "We've got a tennis lesson scheduled."

"Sir, you do *not* have on proper tennis attire," the man said, nodding his narrow head firmly, his eyes sharp in protest. The man looked down at my father's loafers and back up at his face.

"It ain't for me," my dad said. "It's for my boy, here." He put his rough palm on my head and walked me forward like he might present a prize calf at the county fair. I held my racket up in front of me like I was carrying a flag.

"Oh," the man said, and began busily studying an appointment book. He picked up a pencil and gnawed on the end. "He must be . . . oh, yes . . . Jax—is that—Jaxie Skinner?"

"That would be him."

The man looked up.

"What kind of name is Jaxie?"

"It's a nickname," my dad said. "For John. My name. His name."

"Okay." The man looked in his book again. "You are an hour early."

"Well. Where can we wait?"

"There are benches by the pro's court. Behind the pro shop here. I guess . . . I guess you can sit there."

My dad paid him with two crisp twenty-dollar bills and we made our way out to the courts. We sat on an open bench near the service line.

In front of us, two women, blondes, maybe late twenties or perhaps thirty, were taking a lesson. The pro was across the net with a grocery cart full of tennis balls, and behind him on the baseline was another cart, also brimming yellow. The court was covered with hundreds of balls, in the net and against the fence behind him. Never had I seen so many—at home, on our court, we had two plastic red milk crates' worth, but our entire supply of balls wouldn't even fill half of one of his baskets.

I was hypnotized by the tennis balls, but my dad was mesmerized by the women taking the lessons. They were tall and curvy with billowing hair and short white tennis skirts and thin cotton tops. They both wore visors that covered their brows, and their buoyant curls shielded their faces from the side.

The pro was a smooth talker, oscillating easy feeds to the women, each ball delivered with an encouraging comment mixed with instruction. "Get your feet ready, here you go, racket back . . . That's a great shot . . . nice ball." If it went astray, or they missed altogether, he would shift into pep-talk mode. "That's all right, Barb, keep your eyes on the ball next time." The women's gazes were riveted in the pro's direction and their body movements appeared like they were bound by invisible strings and he was the puppet master. He immediately became my dad's hero.

We sat that way for a long time, watching the tennis lesson. The pro's voice and the scuffle of the women moving their feet in the sandy Rubico—what southerners call green clay courts—and the soft thump of the balls on the rackets and the court surface were comforting. Even though we were near big highways and not far from downtown Atlanta, that country club was as peaceful as our country road at home.

After a while, one of the women mis-hit a forehand that flew over our heads. "Go get it, boy," my dad said. I scampered around the bench and fished the ball out of the patch of purple and pink begonias in an enormous flower bed behind the pro shop. I ran to the pro's side of the court and held the ball up and he looked over to me.

"Hey champ, toss it here," he said. I wound up and threw a strike at him. "Look at that arm, there, Nolan Ryan." He caught the ball on the face of his racket like it was a glove, cradling it softly and then, without ever touching his hand to the ball, flipped it three feet in the air. When it began to drop he hit an easy forehand to the woman in the ad court who hit a wild backhand against the fence. I thought the way he maneuvered the ball was the coolest thing I'd ever seen, like some magic trick.

At the end of the hour the women finished hitting with the pro and helped to collect the balls. My dad watched intently when they bent down and their skirts went up. The pro soon bid the women farewell with a joke and they giggled, and he gave them a wink and watched them walk away. He stopped at the net and toweled off and came over to us.

"Okay, champ, you must be next. What's your name?"

I told him. He patted me on the head and took a look at my racket.

"All righty, Jaxie Skinner. I'm Harry. Nice to meet y'all."

He shook my dad's hand. "Where are y'all from?" Dad told him and he seemed puzzled for a minute. "Where's that? North Alabama?"

"Almost," my dad said, "but not quite. We are just inside the Georgia line."

"Y'all have come a long way. Has your son ever played tennis before?"

My dad nodded and said I had been playing about two years, that we had a court at home. "He started hitting the ball when he was three," my dad said. "He'll be six next January."

Harry turned to me. "Okay, let's see what you got, champ. Get over there on the service line."

I ran out on the court and stopped on the T, holding my racket in front of me and bouncing around on my toes like I had seen Borg and McEnroe and Connors do on television. The green Rubico felt the same as our red dirt at home, only smoother without the lumps and puddles of our court. It had a wonderful feel under my red-clay-stained shoes.

"All righty, good stance, champ. I'm going to give you a few easy ones to see what you got."

He pulled the basket close to the net and stepped over it onto my side, only about eight feet from me. He wasn't a tall man, about five-six. "Nice and easy," he said. "Just get the ball on your strings." His fingers loosened and the ball softly released from his grip as he tossed it to me. I stepped forward and took the racket back and swung my forehand hard like I always did—I only knew one speed—and whacked it solidly down the middle. He ducked as my shot barely missed nailing him in his bushy mustache.

I was worried he would be pissed off—my sisters never found it funny when I hit the ball at them, and they had taken to either standing behind the baseline or refusing to play with me at all—but he laughed and said, "What a forehand, champ!" He pushed the net down and stepped over it and rolled the basket back a few feet and picked up his racket—he was the first person I'd ever seen with a graphite frame, that black Wilson Tony Trabert—and hit a ball to my backhand, this one with some pace on it, but I was ready and took my racket back with both hands and threw my body into the ball and hit a hard crosscourt shot that landed deep in the corner.

"Hey, little Björn, great shot," he said. He fed another ball, this one wide to my forehand. I twirled the racket to my forehand grip and charged the ball and slid with my left foot out in front of me and hit it hard down the line, about the same place in the corner where the previous shot had landed.

"Way to go, champ. My job's going to be easy." He began feeding balls from side to side. I hustled, concentrating fiercely, and hit about ten good shots in a row until I netted a forehand down the line.

He had been smiling the whole time, laughing and praising each ball. After my shot hit the tape he pushed down on the net and stepped over it to my side of the court and put his hand on my shoulder. "Son, I want you to remember something. One day when you are famous, be sure to tell them your first lesson was with Harry Crummy. That's Crummy—C-R-U-M-M-Y. Just like it sounds, you got it?"

Then he turned to my dad. "Mr. Skinner, I don't know what you've been teaching this boy, but keep it up. He is going to be one hell of a tennis player."

Dad and Harry didn't waste any time in entering me into com-petition. A month later I played in a ten-and-under tournament in Atlanta at a dogwood-dotted country club of the well heeled. Against my mother's wishes, Dad had bought an eight-year-old, cherry-red BMW, a sporty two-door model. The first day he drove the car home he affixed a green coaster-sized USTA sticker on the driver's-side edge of the windshield. We were the only family in Piney with a BMW. My mom told him he was being foolish, but through their bedroom door late one night I heard him shout that he was "almost forty god-damn years old" and he had worked hard and his business was doing well and he could afford a German luxury automobile, that he had the time to take me to tennis tournaments. "Stop your goddamn yam-mering," he'd said.

He also had bought me a new racket, the Kramer Junior model. Mom had altered my shorts so they fit without the hay-baling twine and she had found a red tennis shirt that was still too big but fit better when I tucked it into my shorts. I had a new pair of Beta tennis shoes, too, the ones with thick white soles and large rubber toe plates that evoked laughter from the kids at school who did not realize these were tennis cool, just like the ones Harry Crummy wore. Country kids never understood tennis cool.

My sisters, both teenagers by then, didn't care for my interest in tennis either, and sneered at me when I put on my outfit for the tour-nament and carried my racket out to the car. They couldn't hit the ball worth a lick and never wanted to take lessons, but they were envious of mine and Dad's trips to Atlanta.

As soon as my dad and I reached the club, I sensed the tournament's aura, a tension palpable in the expressions of the players and their parents waiting around on couches and disarrayed armchairs in the tennis clubhouse. Kids were lounging everywhere, from teens to near toddlers, like I was. Some families sat outside in folding chairs they had brought, along with coolers and bags of equipment, enough supplies to get them through a war or natural disaster. We had only my racket and a towel.

My dad sent me to check in, handing me my USTA card. I reported to the table run by several stern-eyed women in visors and two twitchy old men who bumped into each other as they searched through boxes for entry forms and pencils and draw sheets. They looked me up and down like I was too young to play. I told one of the men my name. He shouted, "What's that?" I raised my voice as loud as I could and yelled, "Jaxie Skinner. Piney, Georgia." I held my tennis identification over my head, the first piece of paper I ever possessed with my name and a number on it. They marked me off a list and returned the card to me and said they would call me when it was time for me to play. Dad and I sat down on the grass under a dogwood tree to wait.

After a while, they called me and my opponent, Larry Levenson. He was a head taller than I was, and he regarded me like I had stepped out of *The Andy Griffith Show*. He had wild curly dark hair and wore an outfit identical to the one McEnroe wore, a thick white headband with coordinated Sergio Tacchini shorts and a shirt. He had two brand-new-looking Dunlop Maxplys, both strung with expensive blue-colored gut. For some reason I can't explain, he wore rubber plugs in his nose and ears, the kind used by swimmers. I had never seen anyone like him.

Despite the snazzy attire and top-of-the-line racket, he was terrible, gangly and awkward and barely able to get his serve into play. On the first point I hit his weak serve back into the center of the court and he flailed at the ball, missing altogether. He double-faulted three times, six in a row into the bottom of the net. He turned and slung his Dunlop against the windscreen-covered fence and screamed, "Jesus—Jesus fucking Christ." He retrieved the racket and waited for me to serve. It was the first time I ever heard the F-word.

I crossed around the net but he held his ground. I knew that we were supposed to change sides after the odd games but since he was older, I returned to my side. I hit my serve, at that time simply a bloop of a shot to put it in play, and he lunged wildly at the ball and it ricocheted off the edge of his racket and over the side fence. Again he slung his racket into the windscreen, cursing words that I didn't even know yet about mothers and cocks and suckers.

He lined up for the second return and again I hit another easy serve into the box to his backhand. This shot he got back, a slow drifter down the line to my forehand, well inside the baseline. I took my racket back, rushed forward and stepped toward the net with my left foot, lowering my shoulder and throwing my whole body at the ball like I was making a tackle in football. The racket head whipped around and connected with a crisp *thwack*—there was nothing better than the sound or feel of that Jack Kramer sweet spot—and the ball rocketed crosscourt with angle and topspin over the net band and landed six inches inside the deuce court service box corner. Larry Levenson didn't move, standing there flat-footed, still admiring his weak duck of a backhand. He watched my ball go whizzing past, not bouncing a second time until almost near the fence. He turned and looked at me, mouth agape, one of the rubber plugs hanging out of his nose. He walked straight to the sideline, gathered his spare racket and yanked off his nose and earplugs and left the court, flinging the gate wide open. His mother, a short, chubby woman, tried to console him, but he slammed his rackets to the ground, the wood frames clattering on the concrete sidewalk. "Jesus, Mom," he said, and took off running toward the parking lot. She gathered up his Dunlops and ran after him, hollering, "Larry, come here, *Larry*," but he dashed through the clubhouse and was gone.

I watched this departure standing in the spot inside the baseline from where I had hit my ferocious forehand. I looked over at my dad, who had been joined by Harry for the last two points. Harry flashed me a thumbs-up sign and Dad waved at me to come off the court.

"Hey there, champ," Harry said when I got over to them, and he raised his hand. "High five."

I raised my hand and our palms smacked. I will never forget that moment, my first high five. My first victory. For the first time in my life, I felt exceptionally cool.

That very afternoon I moved on to the inevitable, my next match. No matter who you've beaten, there's always a next round or another tournament. For me it was against Allen Springer, the number two seed, a ten-year-old twice my age who stood more than a foot taller. His serve was big and he was fast and my dynamo method of hurling my body into my groundstrokes did not faze him. He toyed with me a little in the 6–0, 6–0 drubbing, pulling me to net and then lobbing over me—being that I was less than four feet tall, a highly effective strategy.

After the match Harry cheered me, saying that I played very well and that I would grow into my game. He told me not to be discouraged. I wasn't. I loved being a tennis player like nothing else before.

Or since, I guess.

My mom did not approve of my budding tennis career, and since they always took my mom's side, neither did my sisters. She never said anything about it to me, but I overheard her tell my dad many times, "He's too young, John. He's too young."

But my dad ignored her complaints. He was thrilled with the chance to drive his BMW into Atlanta and visit lush country clubs. Sometimes we roamed around the marble-floored, crisply air-conditioned malls in Atlanta to kill time between matches. We once even went to see a movie in French with subtitles. Something was percolating in his head, a desire for more than small-town life. He was bitten by the tennis bug, and when a bug bites, that's the best time to scratch it.

And Lord knows we scratched it. We scratched it a million times. Dad got me up early every morning and out onto the red clay rectangle in the yard as the sun was coming up over the scrub pines behind the court. He would stand at the net with an orange metal ball hopper and a stack of milk crates full of three hundred tennis balls and hit them all to me, running me from one side to the other. I chased after each ball like my life depended on it. He wasn't much of a tennis player—he had never hit a ball until that day he carved the court out of our yard, but he bought a Wilson T2000 like Jimmy Connors used and developed a functional forehand. He read Nick Bollettieri's book about junior tennis, so he knew enough drills to keep me busy with every shot in the game.

Sometimes the clay would be damp with dew in the morning and outright muddy if it had rained the day or night before, the ball slopping around. I didn't wear nice tennis clothes on our court, but a designated old pair of shorts, a T-shirt, and red-stained shoes. I even had two special practice rackets to keep from soiling my newer rackets. Dad would occasionally throw all the practice balls in a huge basin with soapy water and then rinse them off with the hose and run them through our clothes dryer. He would do that on a Saturday afternoon when my mom and sisters were out of the house, shopping or having their hair done or visiting friends. Hundreds of tennis balls tumbling in the dryer can make a hell of a racket, and Mom never would have stood for it. "What she don't know won't hurt her," Dad said.

People have asked me why my dad, who owned a road-paving business, didn't pave the court in our yard with asphalt. Hard courts are much more common and it certainly would have been easier to maintain. But the public courts in Piney had been a clay surface when he was a kid, and Dad had read an article about Roland Garros and figured that Georgia has red clay as famous as anywhere, so why should we not have our own clay court? My dad also resembled a short-haired Ilie Nastase, especially when he smiled. He had seen photographs of Nastase winning the French Open in 1973, and I think he identified with the Romanian rascal.

I also believe the clay was his way to rebel against the paving he did on roads all over the South. He wanted to keep something fresh and pristine, the sacred red earth exposed, much like the dirt roads on which he had grown up, before most routes were covered in hardtop. He was not a farmer, but like just about everyone in rural Georgia, an agrarian life was in his blood way on down to the roots of the family tree. His grandparents and great-grandparents had been sharecroppers, before the Depression ushered in the textile mills and ended the era of the dirt farmer. He thought that tennis, like farming, should be done in the dirt.

~

Dad would drill me for about two hours in the morning until I had to go to kindergarten. Before tennis, he had risen at five o'clock and driven his truck down our long dirt driveway to be at a road construction site gathering his workmen together by dawn. After my first lesson and tournament, he put a foreman in charge of the crew and he stayed with me from about six to eight before changing from tennis clothes into denim and leaving for work.

I warmed up in the dim morning light, running ten laps followed by one hundred jumping jacks. I took the racket and started on the service line and he moved me from side to side with easy feeds, concentrating on long smooth swings, first hitting crosscourt, and then hitting down the line. There was nothing like the sound of my feet shuffling in the clay and the smack of the ball on my strings. We did this for three hundred balls without a break. People don't believe me when I tell them that I would hit three hundred shots in a row, but I did. We picked the balls up, and I moved back onto the baseline where he hit me one hundred forehands in a row that I had to hit crosscourt, then one hundred backhands crosscourt, then repeated with down-the-line shots until we went through all of the baskets again.

Like Bollettieri's book and Harry's instructions, my dad was big on getting the ball well over the net. A ball into the net earned me a scolding, even a shot not very high over the net would get him riled up. But he wasn't a screamer. He would speak firmly, encouragingly, but also with a gentle threat. After the baskets were empty, he'd send me to the back fence to pick up the ones that had cleared, and he would count the balls I put into the net. For every twenty-five net balls, that would mean one line drill I would have to run on the court after our morning practice. That is how I developed those strong, high topspin shots, and why I'm one of the only American players other than Jim Courier to have much success on clay. I know the dirt.

I didn't mind, however, running the wind sprints. I would start at the doubles line and lunge to touch the first singles sideline and scamper back to touch the doubles line and then turn and hurry to the middle service line, touch it, and then back, running as hard as I could go, a few long strides before resuming the short-step footwork to bend down to touch the line and then pivot and run back to the far singles sideline and then the last, longest run to the far doubles sideline, my lungs about to burst.

It's crazy how much energy I had when I was a child, when tennis was new and the mornings were bright and I could run all day and swing the racket ten thousand times and never get bored with it. I was out there at six years old just busting my ass, day after day, hustling after balls that I had no business reaching and still smacking them back. Most kids slept late and ate Twinkies and watched TV for hours, but that never crossed my mind. I wanted to be great, and busting your ass is a requirement of becoming a great player.

When I'm tired and filled with doubts and need a boost, which has been very often, I think about those mornings out there on the court with my father, running down his feeds. That was the most fun I ever had, out there in those early mornings on the red clay with my dad cheering me on. It was so long ago that it barely seems real.

I still I have a recurring dream that started way back then. Every night when I go to sleep, I lie in bed and close my eyes and imagine I'm on our red dirt tennis court, hitting groundstrokes, the *thump* of the ball on the clay and the *thock* of it on my Jack Kramer, the rally persistent until the pendulum-like rhythm of the ball in constant motion eases me into sleep where my subconscious plays tennis while I slumber. Sometimes I'll jolt awake as an imaginary ball fired right at me almost hits me in the face. But immediately I resume the rally, drifting into my nightly rest.

All my life I've been having that dream.

I won my first tournament the week before I started school, about a year after my initial lesson from Harry. The Savannah Junior Invitational was a long way from our northwest Georgia home, about five hours by car. Dad's BMW had been having some problems, mainly leaking oil, and he had paid a mechanic about three hundred dollars to fix it prior to our trip. But two hours into the drive down, about thirty miles north of Macon, the engine started knocking and a row of red lights on the dash started flashing and smoke began to roll out from under the grille.

Dad pulled off Interstate 75 and stopped in the high grass along the edge of the asphalt. We walked a mile to an exit where he consulted a phone book at a pay phone in a Shoney's parking lot, cussing while thumbing through it because pages were torn or missing altogether. He had a hell of a time finding a tow truck to come get us. To cap it off he reached in the coin slot for his change and someone had spit into it, causing him to pull his hand out and shake off the hot saliva. We used the bathroom in the Shoney's and then bought Cokes and candy bars at the front counter and walked back to the car, my dad not saying a word as cars and trucks sped past.

There is nothing like the afternoon heat when you are stranded on the side of the road in August in Middle Georgia. We waited there for what must have been three hours, but it seemed longer than that. Dad was pissed off that it was taking so long for the tow truck to come. I sat on a towel beneath the shade of tall pines on the embankment while he paced back and forth from me to the car, sitting on the shoulder in the bright sun. "We got to be there at nine in the morning for your match. This truck better hurry up. We may have to rent a car."

I looked at him but didn't say anything. Sweat stains soaked his peach-colored shirt and droplets bubbled up on his forehead. "Your mama is going to get a kick out of this." He sighed and stared at the ground. "Me, running around the state in a BMW, pretending I'm a rich man at the country clubs. Oh, she's gonna howl when she hears this story. But you know what, Jaxie?" He stopped and turned around and looked down at me. I looked up into his red face, the sweat on his brow running into his eyes. "You ain't going to tell her a thing," he said, stabbing at the hot air with his finger. "You got that? Not a thing about this car breaking down."

"Yes, sir," I said.

In his youth, my dad had been a baseball star, a first baseman and pitcher, and was recruited to play at Georgia Tech. He had wanted to study engineering, so the school was a perfect fit for him. He had begun dating my mom in the spring of his senior year in high school, meeting her at the northwest region baseball tournament where she was working the concession stand. She lived an hour away, near Dalton. He drove up there almost every weekend that summer, and in the fall she often came to see him on campus in Atlanta. In the spring of his freshman year, about the time baseball season started, my mother told him that she was pregnant.

Dad finished out the semester, hitting a respectable .270 while platooning at first base. He was lit up in his one start at pitcher, allowing seven runs in only two innings. After the semester ended he returned home and took a job and married my mother. At the beginning of the next year, my oldest sister arrived. He never left Piney again.

But there was something he had left behind in Atlanta that he never told us about. My mom may have suspected something, or knew part of the story, but she never said anything to me.

My dad's secret was this: At Georgia Tech he had fallen in love with a beautiful Italian American tennis player from Savannah named Claudia Lane, or then Cipriani, her maiden name, and he had never fully gotten over it. It took me about twenty-five years to piece this together from the memory of my dad's complaining by the car and other things he said, but most of it I learned years later from a bundle of the letters I found hidden in an old toolbox.

That day beside the highway Dad cussed the Germans for building complicated cars—he worked on bulldozers, tractors, and some American automotive engines, but the BMW he found impenetrable and was reluctant to try and fix himself. After a while he spoke toward the engine as if the carburetor could hear him. "Well, shit. I guess we ain't going to make it for dinner tonight with the Lanes."

I stood behind him, watching him study the engine as if it had changed since the twenty other times he had looked at it in the past two hours. "Who are the Lanes?"

"They—well, really, just she—is an old friend of mine. They live in Savannah and were going to have us over for supper tonight. Their son plays tennis."

I nodded but said nothing. He looked down at me. "Their boy is eleven, and a pretty good player, his mama says. We'll see. I was hoping you could practice with him. I bet they ain't never seen a six-year-old hit the ball like you do."

This was all the information I got. But with hindsight I know from the memory of his downcast face and his slumped shoulders that it wasn't the broken-down car but missing this visit with these people—

this woman—that was weighing on him. I am certain that he bought that car just to impress her.

Eventually a tow truck came with two men, brothers apparently, mostly toothless, bearded, and covered in oil. They were rough-looking dudes, but they were friendly. They hooked up the BMW and asked us all sorts of questions, and were impressed that I was playing in a tennis tournament. "I think we got a little Jimmy Connors on our hands," one said.

Dad and I had to sit squeezed in between them in the cab, me in his lap, but being rescued brightened his mood and he tousled my hair. Shortly after the truck pulled out, towing that cherry-red BMW behind, there was a long pause and then Dad asked if they wanted to hear a joke. He had a running series about a redneck couple named Leroy and Linda Sue. He did various voices, and had a series of stories involving stolen and sexually compromised watermelons, chickens, and pigs, as well as extramarital liaisons and misunderstandings that always set his road crew or country boys handing around a bottle to laughing.

The joke he told the tow-truck drivers went like this: "Leroy and Linda Sue were driving fast down the road through the swamp one night, too fast for their own good, when they hit a big old pothole and the car went running wild off the road." He told these jokes slow, so you've got to imagine good long pauses and him drawing out the syllables to hear it right. "I mean they up and went end over end, just a flying through the pine trees and cypress stumps . . . the car flipped *four times*, just a going thisaway and thataway. They were both thrown from the car, like Godzilla had slung them loose with his big, scaly paws . . . they went assholes over elbows, and Linda Sue screamed, and Leroy too, he just screamed . . . they both just screamed up a storm until they landed far apart in that nasty ol' swamp, full of gators and water moccasins and God knows what else. The car smashed upside down about a hundred feet away and started to burn. There was much groaning and hollering and a *terrible* gnashing of teeth. And then, Leroy called out in the deep, dark night of the Okefenokee. 'Linda Sue, baby, where you at?' She yelled, 'I'm here, over here. And Lord, I'm hurt.' Leroy was hurt too, his legs bruised, and couldn't move too good, but he was otherwise okay. 'How bad are you hurt?' he yelled. She said, '*Bad*, Leroy, *bad*. I got a gash that stretches all the way from my ass to my belly button.' He said, 'I know that. But are you *hurt*?"

Those two dudes laughed so loud they drowned out the engine of their tow truck. It was a joke I laughed at every time—at the telling, not the content. I didn't fully comprehend the punch line until I was much older and first saw a naked woman up on all fours.

My dad became a different person when he was telling those jokes. I saw many sides to my father when I was little, and I sometimes thought that maybe this was the real him, if there was a real him, if there is a *real* any of us. There aren't many more men like him, at least not younger than my generation, and there are very few in my age bracket. And I know I've shed much of that influence, as the way I talk has changed the more I've traveled around the country and have been out of the rural South. I've become citified. Some folks would say that is a good thing, that the old southern white men, the good old boys who tell off-color jokes and spit tobacco and like a drink of hard liquor every now and then are gone or dying off. But I disagree. Not all of them are complex, but men like my dad are a lot more complicated than most understand.

What I'm trying to say is that my father was not a simpleminded hick. Not long ago I found a box of his college books, several that looked to be standard math and science texts. In the bottom, however, there was a dog-eared *Complete Works of Shakespeare*, novels by Fitzgerald, Lawrence, and Hemingway, and a book of poems and plays by T. S. Eliot.

I can't say why I did, other than I guess I had liked his poems I read in my one year of junior college, but I opened up the Eliot book and thumbed through it. There were many notes in the margins, all in pencil, in my dad's dense, neat print. On the very last page of text, beneath the Index of First Lines, he had written a long note: "We regret death or good-byes because when we leave a person we cut off a part of our personality. Leaving someone who really matters hurts so much because we are closing forever an aspect or picture of ourselves—one that we like. We are as many personalities as we know people. To lose a friend is to lose a personality. When we really love, we love the personality that the other has stimulated in us."

I don't know if he copied this from someone else or if it was his own creation. All this time I had spent with my father I never dreamed he had such thoughts. The book had been bought at the Georgia Tech bookstore on North Avenue in 1963, my dad's one and only year as a college student, a year when his future seemed wide open and limitless, back before he got my mom pregnant and carved his life's path in granite in the decade before I was born.

I won the ten-and-under division in the Savannah tournament easily, obliterating three kids in a row, all a few years older than me who played like they probably had practiced less in their lives than I did in an average week. One boy fell down at least six times when I kept hitting the ball back behind the spot from where he had hit his last shot, wrong-footing him again and again. Tennis strategy is not that complicated, especially on clay.

I also beat the eleven-year-old Lane boy in straight sets in a practice match, although in one he pushed me to a tiebreaker. He finished second in the twelve-and-unders. My dad was enormously proud, and reveled in the bragging that Mrs. Lane showered upon me, although her son didn't like it or me one bit.

It felt unbelievably good to earn that small trophy, and later to come home and have the picture my dad took of me on the front page of the *Piney Post*. Dad bought ten copies, and hung one up on the wall in our kitchen.

The next week I started school. My mom made a big deal of my first day, dressing me in a new pair of shorts with pictures of old cars on white denim and a light-blue short-sleeved, button-down shirt she had bought at Belk's. She made me pose between my sisters—the oldest, Sally, was starting her senior year in high school, and Ruth would be a sophomore. It is one of very few pictures of me and my sisters together. Sally had long blond hair and stood tall like my mother, and Ruth had my dad's dark hair but blue eyes and a blossoming figure. Hordes of boys came out to our house in those days, but my dad, instead of being overprotective, focused his energies on me and my tennis and let my mother worry about the girls.

I had gotten up early that morning like I always did and wanted to hit some with Dad but my mom didn't allow it, insisting that I take a day off from tennis and have breakfast with the family. Before he left, Dad hugged all of us and said that we made him proud. When he leaned down to me, he whispered that we would practice when I got home from school.

I went into the first grade a celebrity. The teachers had seen my picture in the paper and even the principal congratulated me on winning the Savannah tournament. Girls in the class cast their eyes my way during the first roll call, and later I overheard a few in a circle giggling about me.

The boys in my class divided into one group that admired me and a second group that wanted to kick my ass. I ruined the outfit my mom had bought me wrestling with Bubba Samson in the dirt in the playground that afternoon. He was much heavier, but I was fast and wily and tripped him and punched him twice in the nose, causing it to bleed before the janitor could separate us. I was in some ways a mean son of a bitch.

I still am, I suppose.

I won every important junior tennis tournament in Georgia by my twelfth birthday, doling out beatings in multiples. When I turned thirteen, I started hanging around the Piney city park where there were usually a few decent high school players and a handful of dudes in their thirties with knee braces and elbow bands, two or three who had played small-college tennis. Those old guys could hit the ball solid and were crafty, putting up a good fight for about an hour until they wore down.

I spent countless hours there. The three green slick hard courts played as fast as glass except on spots where the gritty, black asphalt had been exposed. A curious pattern of cracks ran through the courts, with crevices along the service lines making a good target for first serves. A ball hitting a crack either popped over the returner's head or ricocheted low and skidded beneath his racket. The nets were faded, the webbing more gray than black, and the white net cords had wrinkled from exposure to sun, rain, wind, and the occasional ice storm.

The courts bordered the city swimming pool and in the summer players had to contend with multiple distractions: announcements over the loudspeaker—"Bart Forrester, your ride is here"; music blaring from the distorted sound system such as Barry Manilow's "Copacabana" on a 45 rpm disc played over and over again; and children, of course, crying, screaming, laughing, splashing, and playing games in which they chanted in unison like angry zombies. "Mar-co!" . . . "Po-lo!"

The biggest distraction for me, though, was a lifeguard named

Wendy Crenshaw. She was two years ahead of me in school. I had maintained a crush on her from afar since the first grade when I saw her on the playground, spinning the seat of a swing so the chains wound together and then slowly unwound.

From the tennis courts I liked to watch her climb up and down the lifeguard chair ladder in her blue bikini. She was a short girl—buxom and tan with long, curly dark-brown hair that had a sun-tinged streak of blond running through it. She wore a gold ankle bracelet and a thin leather strap around her neck that dangled a silver whistle into cleavage glistening with suntan lotion and sweat.

Two senior players at Piney High School—Ricky Puckett and Ray Vazquez—were the best of the city court regulars. They were tall, hit big serves, moved well, could volley, and had strong overheads. I played them many times, and could only pull out a win if they were not at their best and I was on top of my game. The fast courts also gave them an advantage—they could hit the ball hard and often charged into net, back in the days when players tried to volley more.

Ricky played high school football, middle linebacker, and he was thick in the torso and neck and arms but was surprisingly fast for his frame, about six feet one and two hundred pounds. His game was wild but he could knock the cover off the ball. His doubles partner, Ray, had a much smoother game, long pretty strokes, a one-handed backhand that was his best shot when he rolled over it and drove it crosscourt. His forehand was steady and accurate, and he moved as efficiently as a top pro. He could hit the prettiest approach shots I have ever seen, hard slices that he could carve into or away from you.

The reason he never went farther in the game than he did was his lack of desire—he was just too nice of a dude to be a great player. He had sympathy for his opponents. When he played Ricky, for example, he could have played consistently and beaten him easily, but he never would. Against me he would take a lead and then go to sleep, making careless errors or hitting short balls I could put away. Sometimes he double-faulted inexplicably. If he had improved his serve, Ray had the game to have been a great player, maybe enough to earn some money in tournaments, perhaps winning some of the satellite events. I've seen less talented players on the ATP tour. Every player ultimately finds their own level. I saw him lose matches that he should have easily won, and he didn't even seem to mind. His problem was all in his heart—his heart just wasn't in the game. And without the heart to win, you certainly don't have the head. The head to win is the most elusive element of all.

I've thought long and hard about what it takes to make it in the pros. First of all, there is the basic talent, a natural inclination for the game. Then there is physical ability: quickness, foot speed, eyesight, coordination, and strength. You've got to be able to see the ball, to have the eyes, to move. There are many players that have these first two assets, but fewer who have the third element: heart. Heart is getting up to hit at five thirty in the morning when you are five years old and not complaining, being thrilled to be running around smacking the ball in the early-morning light. Heart is traveling to China the day after you get knocked out of U.S. Open qualifyings to play in front of as few as fifty people. Heart is Vitas Gerulaitis declaring after breaking a sixteen-match losing streak against Jimmy Connors, "*Nobody* beats Vitas Gerulaitis seventeen times in a row."

There are many players who have the first three in this equation: talent, physical ability, and heart. But then there is the head. The head is not a practice problem. Any good player can hit 1,000 balls, 950 of them great shots, but when most players get into a big match and are down 30–40 on serve, those without the head will always hit that five-percent-of-the-time shot that goes out, in the net, or a fat short ball. For some, the head is fine in early-round matches, in matches where the prize money is low, in matches that really don't have much impact. The head only comes into play when the match matters, when it's crunch time. The head is the great equalizer, the Achilles' heel that has brought many a smooth-looking tennis player down to the level where they can lose to a fat kid with a cast on his hand who hits nothing but lobs. I lost a match like that one time. For me, the head comes and goes.

I was thirteen but played up in an older division, the sixteen-and-unders, in the clay court Southern Regional in Nashville. I drew a fifteen-year-old, a fat little blond-headed boy named Tommy Knott who had a cast on his left hand. Everybody there called him Tater Tot.

The match started out reasonably well. Tater Tot made a few errors and hit a few short balls that I put away easily. I went up 3–0, breaking his serve in the second game. His backhand was weird, two-handed with the cast on top of the grip, sort of a yanking motion as though he was pulling a rope out of the ground. I started thinking about my next round, where I wanted to eat, about sitting poolside at the motel.

When he couldn't control his groundstrokes, he started hitting lobs. In spite of the cast and the fact he was chubby, he moved well and his topspin lob took a crazy aerial path, shaped something like an upside-down, italicized *U* in the sky. I stayed back and pounded my groundstrokes, figuring his weight would wear him down. It turned out to be a bad plan. His balls pushed me well behind the baseline, often all the way to the fence. I started making errors when I tried to hit winners from deep in the court.

He won four games in a row, or I should say, I *gave* him four games in a row. A moonballer never wins points; they wait for you to lose them. I started charging the net, taking the high balls in the air, hitting angled volleys to make that fat little dude run. But he was tenacious, and he anticipated well and had flawless footwork. He ran down a lot of balls and sent them on a high, slow path back to me. I was out of my game—although I didn't play the net that badly, particularly with drop volleys—I was shaky on overheads.

He led 5–4, 40–30 when I hit a hard forehand past him that landed on the baseline. He raised a finger from the hand with cast on it and shouted, "Out." He didn't make eye contact with me, but pumped his fist and skipped gleefully over to the courtside chairs and began to drink from a red-and-white thermos. I crossed to the other side and found the mark on the tape, and pointed down to it. "That ball got the line. Right there."

He came over and pointed to another spot that was at least six inches out. "That's it, I swear," he said. He looked about to cry. "It was out. I promise."

He was full of shit, but I felt I could beat him despite his cheating. I'd beaten kids before against whom I had to hit the ball a foot inside the line. I started the second set well, hitting some strong overheads with angles, and stiff volleys he couldn't reach. I took the lead and then held on through some long points to pull that set out 6–3. He went for a bathroom break and stayed in the clubhouse—this was his home club—for fifteen minutes.

The long break killed my momentum in the third set. Whenever I came to net, he lobbed even higher. I tracked what seemed like hundreds of balls across the sky, my racket in a ready position behind my back, my left hand raised and my index finger pointing at the ball, shuffling my feet under the lob, just waiting . . . waiting . . . *waiting* on the goddamned ball to come down so I could put another whack on it.

After about my fifth overhead into the net, I began to get tentative, and started to hit the overheads with less pace to ensure I would get them in the court, stroking them down the middle where he was waiting to hit another lob. On one point I must have hit at least fifty groundstrokes and twenty-five overheads—and I *still* lost the fucking point.

At deuce at 5–all, he hooked me again with a bad call, this one a winner he called wide when I could clearly see the mark on the inside edge of the tape. He pointed out another mark about a foot out. I tossed my racket against the fence, called him an asshole and left the court, marching to the tournament desk. I complained about his calls to the tournament director and they sent out a line judge for the remainder of our match.

The first thing the line judge did was to give me a warning for cursing and throwing my racket. I never recovered after that. Tater Tot played consistently and acted like a perfect gentlemen, while I made five errors in a row.

I was dumb and inexperienced, plus I was skinny, not strong enough to move in and take the high volleys and put them away or hit a powerful overhead past him, or even better, right at him, striking him in the nuts like I wanted to do. Every time I see a new draw sheet, I hope to find Tommy "Tater Tot" Knott. All these years later, I still dream of drilling him with an overhead in the gonads.

That loss is the one and only time my mother took me to a tournament. My dad had a business meeting he could not cancel, so he persuaded her to take me.

Mom never cared for tennis, had no interest in either playing or watching it. It was not because she was not athletic—before getting pregnant, she had been on the track and field team in high school, running sprints and competing in the long jump. She always kept herself in good shape, jogging and attending an aerobics class. But she wasn't competitive. She had always liked to read, and started writing poetry after my sisters left for college, about the same time she finished her bachelor's degree and started a job teaching English at the junior high school.

She didn't understand the ritual that my dad and I followed at tournaments, mostly lounging around the motel and watching TV or sitting by the pool, maybe practicing a little and then visiting the nearest mall. The day before my match she had wanted to go to an art museum in downtown Nashville, see the Parthenon and the Vanderbilt campus, and eat at a sushi restaurant a friend had recommended. She had maps and brochures and big tourist plans. I refused. I wanted to eat pasta and then come back to the room in time to watch the Braves. I told her that was what Dad and I always did.

She frowned at me, raised her voice, and said I needed to be more rounded, to learn about art and books and places, and not just care about myself and my tennis. But I did not budge. She gave me money for dinner and left me in the room while she saw the town.

I walked to the nearby mall and ate spaghetti in the food court. She didn't get back until almost midnight. I pretended I was asleep when she came in the room.

That next day I don't think she watched more than a few points of my match against Tater Tot. She stayed up by the clubhouse in the shade, reading a book of short stories. When I came off the court, she looked up at me from the pages as though she was surprised to see me. "Did you win?"

I didn't say anything at first. I was angry as hell, and I missed my dad. He would have been engrossed in every point. With his encouragement, I think I could have beaten Tater Tot. I stood there, hating her.

"Let's go home," I said.

She looked relieved. Few words passed between us on the three-hour drive back to Piney.

A year later I started high school. I had grown six inches and stood as tall as I am now, six feet one.

Unlike most pros groomed in tennis academies who have hit with excellent players every day of their lives, I suffered from a deep void of practice partners.

I abandoned the Piney city courts for the busier tennis center in Thessalonica, a larger town about thirty minutes to the north.

I often practiced with college players there, but when none were available, I hit with the resident tennis bum, a guy I knew only as Fast Eddie. Regardless of the weather, he spent most of his waking hours at the center, either on the court or sitting beside his van in the parking lot. He played well for a guy in his forties, and was willing to feed balls or do whatever I wanted for practice. Happiness for him was a tennis racket in his hand.

The coach of the Piney High School team urged me to play for the school, but I debated whether or not I should do it. The competition in our region was laughable. After easily winning my singles, I would have to play doubles with a hacker, against other hackers, on rugged public courts with cracks, moth-eaten nets, and creosote-covered posts that held lightbulbs intended for softball fields. I once ran for an angled ball on a court in Rockhaven and collided headfirst into a tar-black pine log used as a light post. I was lucky not to be paralyzed. Those courts were ten feet from the railroad tracks, and freight trains carrying cut-down trees or cotton or coal or kaolin often passed by, blowing the whistle and rattling so heavily that the hardtop surface would tremble. Ray and Ricky had told me about a school they competed against up in the mountains of northwest Georgia that had players who wore overalls and camouflage caps, their sole objective to bounce overheads into the gravel parking lot, an act that set off hooting and hollering from the locals, many who sipped tallboy Budweisers from paper sacks and smoked Marlboros or chewed Red Man, spitting juicy brown streams onto the edge of the court. My dad, and especially Harry, advised against my joining the team, wanting me instead to practice with stronger players. "This ain't going to help your game one iota," Harry said.

I knew it wouldn't help my tennis, but I thought it might be fun to play for the school. At the coach's urging, I went out there on a Saturday morning in September to practice with the team. The talent level had dropped precipitously after Ray and Ricky graduated. I hit with several of the upperclassmen and all were terrible, either football players who wanted something to do in the spring but who could not make the baseball or golf teams, or band geeks who had played just enough tennis to know which end of the racket to hold. Some of the football players could hit decent forehands and big serves, but they were not steady enough to maintain a rally.

I wondered why I was wasting my time when from the corner of my eye I spotted Wendy Crenshaw, the lifeguard I always watched, parking her car, a banged-up, red Ford Escort. That Saturday morning she walked up to the courts, carrying a tubular green aluminum Yonex racket over her shoulder. She wore a tight white tennis dress with a skirt that rose up high on her tanned but short legs, and her wild long brown hair was tied back in a ponytail that couldn't contain all her cascading curls. I knew right then and there that I very much wanted to play on the high school team.

Wendy joined a few of the other girls who were standing behind the fence talking and watching the boys practice. I went back to pick up a stray ball and she smiled at me from close range. She had rosy cheeks, green eyes, and fairly thick eyebrows, framed by that big head of hair. I went back and played one point in a daze, losing an easy point on a sloppy return of serve. I then focused on nailing forehands, keeping the ball down the middle for a few shots, overpowering the inept football wide receiver.

When we switched sides, I saw her standing behind the court, her eyes on me. I put my longest, smoothest motion on the ball and fired several hard serves, two aces out wide and then two winners into the body. One of the aces hit right against the fence in front of her, clanging on the metal support post. She jumped and then looked at a girlfriend and giggled, and then looked wide-eyed back at me.

She waited there, with a few other girls, watching my match, if you can even call it a match. I think I won the last four games without losing a point, smoking that clumsy dude. If the ball didn't come right up to his forehand in a medium-high bounce, he was helpless.

After the last point, I gathered my rackets and put them in my bag and slung it over my shoulder—I took great care to get that pose where the racket bag hung just right, like the pros, aloof and confident, strolling off the court. I snuck a glance Wendy Crenshaw's way and could tell by the look in her eye that she approved.

That Saturday night we went on our first date. I was only fourteen so she drove, picking me up at our house. My mom did not want to let me go, reminding me of my age. She said my sisters, who were both married and moved away by then, had not been allowed on dates until they were fifteen, and that I should be subjected to the same rule. My dad, however, scoffed at her, told her she was being ridiculous, that I was in high school and that she would have to get used to it. I could tell by Mom's furrowed brow and the tight-lipped look she cast my dad's way that there would be more yelling and cursing from behind their closed bedroom door.

I put on a new pair of jeans and my coolest tennis T-shirt with the U.S. Open logo and waited on the porch in the gloaming until I saw her pull up into the yard. I ran out to meet her, jumping in her small car and slamming the door.

"Hey," she said. She smiled wide and our eyes made contact.

"Hey."

She studied on our house and yard. "What's the best way to get out of here?"

"You can just back up and turn around in the front." I swiveled in my seat and pointed my arm behind her. She smelled wonderful, like flowers, but she looked so good that I would have thought chicken shit had a nice aroma if it had been rubbed on her body.

"Don't y'all have a tennis court out here? That's what everybody says at school."

"Yeah, around back."

"I would like to see it sometime."

"Okay, we can hit one day next week."

She drove down our dirt driveway and up onto the paved road.

"Do you want to go to Thessalonica?" she asked.

"Yeah, that would be cool."

On the way she told me about her classes. She asked what I was taking and I told her, and she then launched into a description of teachers—who was nice, who was weird, which of the men teachers were perverts and looked at her leeringly, as I had noticed the tennis coach doing.

She pretended she was too young to understand her sexiness, but a man would have to have been gay or dead to not want to look at her. Wendy had the kind of body that when she was walking down the street men would almost wreck their cars, the kind of shape that men with eyes for women detected from a quarter of a mile away. She couldn't have prevented the attention unless she started wearing a parka and chopped off all her hair.

She talked a blue streak on the way up to Thessalonica, and I sat watching her lips, her teeth, and the glisten on her tongue as it moved in her mouth. She had on a short-sleeved silk blouse and through a gap between the buttons I glanced at her lacy bra and flashes of skin, including a large brown freckle on a voluptuous curve. She chattered on, her voice kind of high, childish some said, but I loved it.

She drove to the mall in Thessalonica, not much to it by big-city standards, but our only choice. She circled the parking lot, looking for a space, until we saw a metallic-blue Mustang with a 96 ROCK bumper sticker. We both knew the car belonged to Dwayne Cooley, her ex-boyfriend who went by the nickname "Deranged." He was a starting defensive end and sometimes fullback, had a neck like a tree trunk. "Let's go somewhere else," she said. I agreed. She pulled away, driving faster, and onto the main road through downtown Thessalonica.

I suggested that we stop by the Dairy Queen for hamburgers and milk shakes and go to the park next to the city's big tennis center. The park had picnic tables with a nice view of a bend in the muddy river that snaked through town. I had killed a lot of time there in between tennis matches. It was the only place I knew well in Thessalonica.

Wendy and I ate and then walked along the path by the river, sucking on milk-shake straws. I had a chocolate shake and she had a grape Mr. Misty, a frozen concoction swirled with syrupy flavorings that stained her tongue purple. The trail was dark, only a few streetlights casting a silvery glisten on the river, the paved path cutting beneath high oaks still thick with leaves.

We talked, walking close together, not looking at anything but each other. She took my hand and told me about her desire to be a better tennis player, how awesome she thought I was, how she would give anything . . . *anything* . . . and as she said this she inhaled deep and sighed and her chest heaved and her shoulders rose and fell and her voice was sincere and sympathetic and come hither all at once. The trail snaked up a rocky hill, close to a graveyard on a crest of high bluffs overlooking the city, and we sat down on a bench there with a view of the main street downtown. We held hands and the conversation came easy for me. I had never been much of a talker but she asked me questions about tennis, about tournaments, and I surprised myself with stories of matches I'd played and places my father and I had been.

She told me how cool it was that I had been all over the state and beyond, going to Nashville for the regionals. It seems pretty small-time now, but my childhood was adventurous compared with most of my peers, rural folks born in Piney who would most likely die there. They rarely left the local environs except to go to Atlanta for a Braves game or Six Flags, and maybe an occasional jog down to the beaches of the Florida panhandle.

As I told her these stories, I could see her eyes shining in the otherwise dark of the riverside beneath the trees on the hill. If I had been older and wiser, I could have had sex with her right then and there. But I was naive and scared, so we only kissed, her mouth dark with the stain of the Mr. Misty, sitting and squeezing her body against mine.

Two days later she drove me home after school with plans to play tennis. It was a sunny, breezy afternoon and we had several hours of daylight. I showed her around and fixed glasses of lemonade. We sat on the bench by the court and talked for a little while and then started kissing, probing, sticky kisses, our hands rubbing each other's thighs until I worked up the courage to touch her breasts through her shirt.

"Is . . . Is anyone here?" she asked.

"No."

"When will they be back?"

"Not till late. Nine maybe, maybe later."

"Let's go to your room."

I followed her inside. Beside my bed she kicked off her shoes and stripped in front of me, shucking her jeans and shirt and panties and bra so smoothly that it seemed like one movement. She had a tangle of dark pubic hair and was full-bodied, her nipples dark and round.

I stood almost a foot taller but she seemed nine hundred feet high, looming over me like a god. I swallowed hard, had some trouble breathing, my mouth suddenly dry. She helped me out of my T-shirt and jeans and briefs, and then she lay back on my unmade bed and held my hand and pulled me to her, spreading her legs. I lay down on top of her. I didn't know exactly what to do, so she reached down and guided me inside.

It was the best feeling I'd ever felt in my life, bringing on a warm tremble that lasted all of about two seconds. When it passed, I lay my head on her chest, embarrassed. She stroked my hair and kissed the side of my face. She kept kissing me, and rolled me over on my back and rose up on her knees and leaned over me, pressing her lips all over my body, her long hair trailing against my skin.

I entered her again about fifteen minutes later, and this time it lasted a little longer, didn't seem as frightening. I watched her face as I moved on top of her, and I kissed her forehead, ears, and lips. She put her hands on my lower back and directed my movement, pulling me harder into her. "Kiss my eyes," she said, and I did. She breathed heavy and moaned softly, and I trembled again.

I barely remember hitting tennis balls to her later, half an hour before the sun went down. She shanked shots all over our yard off the frame of that lime-green Yonex, a small-headed aluminum racket with an open V throat that was ten years past its prime.

That fall my dad traveled regularly for work, my mom attended evening classes for her master's, and my sisters were grown and long gone. It was just me and the dogs and Wendy Crenshaw at our house in the afternoons, until almost nine each night before my mom got home from school. As soon as we opened the door to the house we would run to my bed. We would lie there a little while after the act and then get dressed and I would give her a tennis lesson. One day she surprised me on the court when she set her racket down and slipped off her panties from beneath her skirt and bent over and summoned me to her side of the court.

On the weekends when my parents were home, we would do it in her car on an abandoned logging road about a mile from our house. It's no easy feat having sex in a Ford Escort, but she wore tennis skirts and we managed. She loved it when I kissed her on her eyes, wet sloppy ones on her eyelids, and she asked for it when she wanted to come. She had this way of saying my name, a breathless moan she would repeat three times. "*Jaxie . . . Jaxie . . . Jaxie.*"

After a few intense few months, our relationship started to change. The weather often was rainy or too cold for tennis, so we stayed inside and started experimenting with our mouths, with blindfolds, in different spots in the house, including the shower. We tried out multiple positions she had seen in her older brothers' porn. She would suggest something weird, and I would suggest something weirder, usually something stupid like having sex in the seat of my dad's bulldozer. It got out of hand.

I had told no one about my time with Wendy Crenshaw in the bed or on the tennis court. But she had talked some. Her ex-boyfriend was a senior, and was a scary son of a bitch if there ever was one, about six feet two and 220 pounds, but quick for that size. He was handsome in sort of a gorilla-like way, his hair dark and his skin swarthy. I heard a lot of girls say that he was the best-looking dude in Piney High School. Wendy was the first girl ever to snub him. I often saw him in the halls between classes and he scowled at me, but most of the football studs had those inarticulate glares down pat. I figured he looked at everyone that way.

On the first Wednesday of December, Wendy and I headed out to my house after school. I sat in the front seat watching her drive, my hand alternately caressing the back of her neck and rubbing the top of her thigh through her blue jeans. She liked me to touch her neck, and I massaged her there, beneath the swirling brunette locks she spent hours shaping with an electric curling iron.

We were cruising along the two-lane country road, a clear and warmer-than-usual day with the leaves all turned and most fallen on the ground, when all of sudden she screamed like she had been shot. I looked around just in time to see the enormous grille of a silver Chevy tow truck ram into us. It didn't hit that hard, but it might as well have been a tank. That little Ford Escort she drove was a tiny piece of shit.

I could see her ex-boyfriend Dwayne in one of his daddy's tow trucks, high up behind the wheel, wearing a red baseball cap, cursing and pointing. A thick-necked buddy in a black ball cap rode with him.

Dwayne gestured for us to pull over. Of all places, she stopped on the narrow, two-lane bridge over Piney Creek, where there was no shoulder to the road. She almost scraped the door against the concrete railing that stood about three feet high. Even if I had wanted to get out of my door and run, I couldn't because the door would only open a few inches. I was pinned in there. I yelled at her to move up, but she turned off the engine.

Dwayne pulled alongside us and stopped. His tow truck sat enormous and high above her little car. Wendy looked over at me and with her eyes as big as golf balls. "*Go*. You've got to go. Run away from here. I can handle him. He won't hurt me—but he'll kill you."

I shimmied out of the passenger window, keeping an eye on Dwayne. I stepped out on top of the wide concrete railing of the bridge and held on to the frame of her car to keep from falling backward in the water about twenty feet below. I paused on the railing, watching him come toward me. I contemplated jumping into the creek, but the bridge was high and who knows what was under that muddy water—it was most likely shallow and could break my neck. So instead I leapt forward like I was a hurdler and stepped one foot on the front of her car near the hood ornament and propelled myself toward the asphalt in a long stride.

He lunged at me and raised his arm and threw a punch, nailing me solidly in the jaw, beneath my left ear. I spun and fell toward the bridge railing, falling sideways, but as soon as I hit the ground I bounced up and continued running. I ran past him, off the bridge and down through a swale and into a pine thicket. Dwayne chased me—he was the star defensive end, expert at chasing down quarterbacks—but when he saw me dash into the tree line, I heard the click of his boot heels on the road stop. The idiot wore a stiff pair of pointed-toe cowboy boots to administer my beating. I could have outrun him anyway, but he could never catch me in pair of roachkillers.

He yelled at me, voicing the populace of Piney's general feelings about tennis. "Hey, you pussy-ass tennis player, you better fuckin' run. Fuckin' tennis. Don't nobody but faggots and girls play tennis. Which one are you, boy? Which one are you? You fuckin' pussy."

I slowed and looked back through the trees, rubbing my jaw. My head ached from the weight of the blow. His buddy joined him on the roadside and they were glaring into the woods. I could see them through the brush, could hear them laughing. He made more jokes about tennis, and then his buddy, Donnie Denson, who most people called "Donuts," began to pantomime a limp-wristed sissy, pretending to hit shots, tiptoeing like a ballerina, poking his big ass out. "Oh *tennis* boy," Donuts hollered. "Tennis anyone? Would anyone like to give me a blow job? How about a hand job, tennis boy?"

He made a few more ridiculous lunges and pretend shots, criss-crossing the road in cowboy boots and tight jeans. Dwayne stood there, his laugh deep, until Wendy came up and screamed at them. "You no-good asshole, Dwayne! And you too, Donuts. Who in the *Sam Hell* do you think you are? I ain't your property, Dwayne. I ain't even your girlfriend no more. I told you that. Me and that boy are just friends. He needed a ride home. Sometimes he gives me tennis lessons . . . that's *all*. You two big dumbasses couldn't hit a tennis ball if your lives depended on it."

Dwayne's posture changed, and he stepped gingerly to her, his head hung down. "Do you love him?" I could barely hear him as he spoke. "You love that boy?" His voice was all choked up, on the verge of crying.

"Hell, no!" she said, and from the venom in her voice I believed her, although later I changed my mind. I think she did love me, although she never said so. She dropped her voice a few levels and looked up to Dwayne as she spoke. "He's just a friend. He is helping me to learn tennis. That boy ain't but fourteen."

This cut me deep. I was young and stupid and loved her deeply, even though I'd never told her so. I don't know why I didn't tell her. We had been naked together many an afternoon, and I knew her smells and kisses and everything about her. I thought she loved me too.

A car came down the road and they dispersed, Dwayne and Donuts getting in the tow truck and making a big loop in the road and heading back to town. Wendy waited until they turned around and then did the same, leaving me in the woods alone.

I dashed off through the pines in the direction of our house, about a mile and a half away. I came to a dove field grown high with dried millet and found my bearings. From there I crossed back over the road and ran up our driveway at full speed. I rushed inside the house and put on tennis shorts and went out onto the court and set up our ball machine and starting pounding one forehand after another, hard as I could hit, aiming at the baseline, rocketing shots off the white plastic line, trying to dig a trench with tennis balls.

I don't know what else Wendy said to Dwayne, but he left me alone after that. He glared at me whenever he passed me in the hallways at school, but the look wasn't much different from his usual caveman expression.

Wendy and I hooked up a few more times. Although we never talked about that day, things between us were not the same. I was thinking about what she said about me being only fourteen. She seemed distant and less affectionate as we went through the motions. She quit asking about tennis, and started leaving as soon as the sex was over. The last time we were together was about a week before Christmas. We didn't talk about breaking up, but I could see in her eyes that it would be our last time together.

She quit tennis the following spring. It was no loss to the game, but I sure missed her for a while.

Like Wendy, I also quit the high school team, but I threw myself even more aggressively into tennis. I practiced with college players in Atlanta that Harry recruited and I worked out much harder on my own. It helped me to get over Wendy. I had grown stronger, and with stiffer competition, my shots had matured and I developed a more complete arsenal, a kickass serve. Never again would I fall to another moonballer.

After a successful string of tournaments in the summer between my freshman and sophomore years that earned me a national ranking, I received an invitation to the Orange Bowl, one of the top junior events. Held in Miami in December, it drew players from all over the globe, including those encamped at tennis academies in Florida, Nick Bollettieri's in particular.

My dad at that time had sold his business to a larger company that hired him on as a vice president, a change that required him to travel frequently, usually to Texas. He had to ask for a week's vacation. His boss, whom Dad resented bitterly after owning his own business for so many years, gave him a hard time. Dad thought he might not be able to go, but ultimately, he worked it out. We thought about flying, but two days before he decided to drive and bought a brand-new black Lincoln Town Car with plush leather seats.

We left home about four o'clock on a cold, rainy morning, the Lincoln riding smooth on the two-lane from our house into Piney. I loved waking up early to go tournaments, that predawn light eerie through the windshield, the car cutting through the darkness.

Dad and I didn't say much. We were often quiet in the early morning on our rides. We had talked a good bit the night before, Dad sitting at the kitchen table, drinking a glass of bourbon, looking over a map of Florida, doing some laundry. My mom had stayed out late, telling Dad that she had a meeting with her poetry group after her grad school class in Thessalonica. I fell asleep before she came home, and she didn't wake up to tell us good-bye.

Dad took U.S. 27 south out of Piney, rolling out of the foothills of North Georgia toward the center of the state. He had a shoe box with cassettes from his vast collection of country music that included dozens of Johnny Cash, Willie Nelson, and Waylon Jennings albums, but instead he flicked on the radio and tuned into a classic country station on AM way down left of the dial, a low-powered outfit in Douglasville that didn't reach us at home. Roger Miller's easy tone of "King of the Road" warmed up the inside of the car. Dad tapped his thumbs on the steering wheel in rhythm with the beat.

He turned onto I-20 and headed east toward Atlanta to pick up Harry. Harry's second wife had recently divorced him—he was in his early fifties then—and he lived in an apartment in Smyrna on Atlanta's northwest side. We reached the outskirts of the city and went north up I-285 a few miles to where Dad exited and found Harry's place. The sky was still dark above us, but the streetlights and glow from the enormous apartment complex near the highway gave the night an illuminated feel, an encapsulating glow that dimmed the stars, unlike the flat-out darkness we were used to in our country house. Dad instructed me to knock on the door and tell Harry that we had a ten-hour, six-hundred-mile drive ahead of us.

I tried to shut the door of the Lincoln gently but the vacuum-like pull of that car thumped it shut. Lights were on behind Harry's blinds and I tapped twice with my fist on his painted steel door. Harry let me in as soon as I knocked. "Mornin' champ, up and at 'em," he said.

I was four inches taller than he was but he still talked to me sometimes like I was five years old. If I hadn't liked him so much, I would have scowled and given him a dose of teenage angst that most folks got from me in those days, but I couldn't do that to Harry. He was too cool of a dude.

"Come on in for a minute," he said. "I'm almost ready." He went down the hallway into the bedroom and left me there where the kitchen opened up into the living room, all beige carpet and light-cream-colored walls, his only furnishings a recliner and a black plastic TV tray in front of a large Magnavox situated on a coffee table. Where a dining room set should have been he had two orange plastic barrels full of tennis rackets, at least one hundred, all with the heads of the rackets facing up. One barrel contained old rackets with small frames, mostly wooden, models that no one used anymore, and then there was another barrel with newer rackets, black graphite and painted aluminum, many that looked like they had never been used, most unstrung. I stepped closer to the rackets but I didn't touch any.

Harry emerged from the bedroom and came down the hallway and saw me studying the rackets. "Check 'em out, champ. I got a few of those new Princes in there, some kickass sticks. Racket technology is going to change the game, my boy, and you, son, will be the benefactor."

He slung an enormous duffel bag over his shoulder, marked with the PRINCE label, and then a smaller racket bag, and we headed out the door. "You got practice balls?" he asked. I said, yes, that we'd brought a ball hopper. "I know you wouldn't leave the house without 'em," he said.

I took one look around his apartment before we went out the door and Harry paused there with me. "Yeah, son, this ain't much, but it's home. For now, anyway."

He reached out like he used to when he would tousle my hair but instead gave me a punch on my left arm, high up on the shoulder. "Don't want to hit you in the good serving arm," he said. "Now let's get on out there to that big new car your daddy was telling me about."

I climbed in the backseat and Harry, after tossing his bags in the open trunk and slamming it, slid in the front next to my dad. They shook hands, Harry always a vigorous handshaker.

My dad smiled, excited about having Harry's company on this trip. Harry and my dad always got along well, chatting before and after my lessons, and often watching my tournament matches together. A few times Harry had gone to lunch with us when we were in Atlanta for a tournament, and once we all went out for a spaghetti dinner after I won a tournament when I was twelve. But most of our contact with him had been limited to one paid hour at a time.

Dad headed south down I-285, already growing thick with taillights of cars and eighteen-wheelers before the dawn. "Only two weeks until the shortest day of the year," Dad said. "The winter solstice."

"That's right," Harry said. "But where we are headed—*My-am-uh*, Florida—they ain't got no winter. They got oranges growing in the trees under that beaming Florida sunshine."

He reached over and patted my dad on the shoulder. "John, you and I are going to have us a fine time down there, where the royal palms are tall and the ladies are lovely." He turned in his seat and looked back at me and reached for my knee. "And you, my man, are about to kick some international ass all over the court with that big serve and them deep-digging groundstrokes. This is where it all comes together for you. This is the place."

The traffic began to give way after Dad exited onto I-75 South, locking the Atlanta skyline in our rearview mirror, a dense stream of cars in the opposite lanes inching north toward the office towers of the city.

"*Whew-wee.* Look at all them poor folks, like rats in cages, rushing in to meet the work whistle," Harry said. "I worked in an office once, for six whole days. One week and a day. I'm telling you, it liked to have killed me. My first wife's old man was a stockbroker, and he hooked me up with a job. I'm telling you I've never felt so nervous or uptight after being in that big glass-and-concrete cage. I thought I should have earned a medal for making it that long. I ain't never going to get rich teaching tennis lessons, but it ain't bad. Look at me now, riding in a fine Lincoln to *My-am-uh*, with a future champion of the Orange Bowl. And I get to spend my days on the tennis courts, with people hitting balls around, many of them smiling, happy to be there. More than half of them running around in skirts and dresses. I like it. Ain't a soul on that crowded road over there smiling."

My dad had been staring at the other side of the highway. "Yep, I helped pave that road, widened it too," he said. "The wider we build 'em, the busier they get. Soon we'll have to widen it again. I'm like you. I like being outside on the job, not trapped behind some desk like most of those folks are."

About half an hour south of Atlanta, the rows of cars like ants in an ant farm lessened and the highway opened up wide with nothing but us and eighteen-wheelers and the occasional local in a pickup truck with dogs in the back. I saw a sign that said MACON 30 MILES as the sun began to peek above the horizon to the front and left of us and Dad pulled out his Ray-Ban aviators, a new pair of ninety-five-dollar glasses he'd bought in a mall in Atlanta, not the six-dollar Eckerd drugstore kind he usually wore. The highway veered east for a few moments and we drove straight into the sun for a ways, so Harry dropped down the sun shade and pulled out a white visor and put it on his head, hanging low over his eyes. He also put on a pair of cool black horn-rimmed sunglasses.

As we got on closer to Macon my dad pointed out for Harry the Shoney's near where we had broken down that time on the way to Savannah. "You remember that, boy?" He looked at me in the backseat via the rearview mirror. "That was more than nine years ago. Can you believe that?"

I nodded. Dad told Harry the whole story, about the broken-down BMW, the spit in the payphone. Harry laughed, this effusive, warm chuckle that made me want to try to tell him a joke, even though I've never been much of a joke teller like my dad.

We cruised through Macon and its sleepy imitation of a downtown with the first few inklings of morning traffic, a Mayberry compared with Atlanta. The interstate cut right through red-brick buildings and six-floor towers and green trees on the last few hills of Georgia. After Macon, the rolling Piedmont meets the Coastal Plain to form the fall line, the boundary where the state becomes flat as a pancake and the landscape takes on the shape of the ocean bottom that it was eons ago. The sun was up full but hung low in the sky like a giant fiery tennis ball.

The traffic below Macon was sparse, and Dad sped up, hitting ninety and even one hundred miles per hour. He had a new radar detector and its lights ran mostly green, occasionally turning red to warn him of a state patrolman or local sheriff's deputy with a speed gun hiding in the bushes or under an overpass.

We soon hit a patch of empty fields and swampy spots. "Damn, look at this old barren land," Harry said. "I dated a woman from South Georgia once—Berrien County, town of Eldorado. I tell everybody this story and they say, 'Boy, you are talking about Arkansas,' and I tell them, 'No, there's an Eldorado, Georgia, too.' I, of course, ain't got to tell y'all that, as y'all ain't the get-up-in-my-face-and-second-guess-me types.

"Well, I met her in Atlanta, one of those *gentlemen's* clubs"—he lowered his voice deep, pronouncing the word *gentlemen's* slowly, as though he was doing an imitation of some kind of southern Nixon.

"She was," he continued, "she was . . ."—and here he turned and looked at me, and then at my father, a mischievous smile on his tanned face, him sitting low in the seat like a frisky child—"she was a woman who danced with an enormous snake, a boa constrictor."

My dad laughed, sort of a subtle "Heh heh."

Harry smiled at him, a glint in his eye. "She would get up there and that snake would wrap around her shoulders and wriggle around, and then she would wriggle around, all sexy-like." He made a little side-to-side move sitting in the seat. "And they both had on the same amount of clothes, which was nothing. I'm talking about N-U-D-E *nude*. She was twenty-two years old, black-haired, looked like a Gypsy, stacked like a lumberyard—and she had these green cat-like eyes, probably fake contacts. I didn't know and didn't care.

"It was right after my first wife kicked me out. She had been a tennis player at the University of Florida." He turned toward me, his voice serious. "Never get involved with Gator women, son, never. They are a curse put on us by the devil." He turned back around. "So I was about thirty years old and had been married almost eight years." He swiveled again and touched my knee. "And don't get married too young, son, and by too young, I mean ever." My dad laughed, and Harry nodded. "See, your daddy knows. You just gotta pay some woman to have you a good son who can hit a tennis ball, and then you go on about your business.

"But anyway, I'm getting off track here. This woman I'm telling you about made her living, and I'm telling you what, she made a *fine living* at that, with this old boa constrictor. He was green and silver and scaly and she had a specially designed box for him that she toted around. It was painted with flames on the side. She said that snake liked music by Black Sabbath and Led Zeppelin, and that's what she danced to . . . I do not lie.

"So anyway, I went back to her place. She wanted to come to my house, but I discouraged it. I didn't have a bed, only my recliner and a sleeping bag on the shag carpet. But that's not the real reason. The truth was I didn't want that snake in my home. Not for two minutes. She was a fine-looking woman, so fine that I'd go home with her and a snake, but I had some scruples, marginal though they were. I drew the line at letting that snake into my place.

"Oh, Lord, going down there was a big mistake. Her place was wild, man, I'm telling you. She lived in this old bungalow down near downtown, around Five Points there, where everybody is either an artist or a pizza deliveryman or both. Where tattoos are more common than haircuts. I look back on it now and I was crazy at the time, I realize it, the one time in my life where I did a lot of drinking. Wild Turkey, my friends, Wild Turkey was it. I swore it off not long after that, when I met my second wife, a religious woman, a good woman too.

"Anyway, I get back to this house sitting down there on one of those strange, surprisingly steep Atlanta hills where if you weren't careful you'd tumble right out of the door and down through the yard and roll into the street. Her bedroom door was made of beads and the walls were painted black and she had six lava lamps—*six*—all red, just a-bubbling, those blobs floating and breaking off and rejoining again.

"She wasn't in the mood for talking, either. I guess dancing with a snake in front of men throwing money at her got her all riled up. Fortunately this was in the days before the diseases that would kill you came along, so I went in to the aforesaid situation without a raincoat. Like I said, I was drinking too much and not using good judgment at the time." He turned to me. "Something you should not do, boy. You got to learn from the mistakes that those of us who have gone on before you have made."

"Aw, come on, Harry," my dad said. "He's a good boy. Tell us about this woman."

"Well, my man John, she was something else. I mean a bona fide *sweet thang*. Good God almighty, I was drunk as a skunk but I remember that, the wildness of that woman. We finished and I collapsed right out on her leopard-skin sheets. I slept like a baby for who knows how long.

"The next thing I know . . ." He paused, shook his head side-to-side. "Oh, Lord, get ready . . . the next thing I know . . . I wake up and feel something heavy on my stomach, in fact, all around my middle, my back too.

"I was groggy and the room was still dark except for a speck of light coming in under her shabby old blinds. All the lava lamps were off. I tried to shift, thinking maybe I needed to shake off some indigestion, the bourbon burning in my belly, and I couldn't move. I tried to sit up and—goddamn!—that snake was double-wrapped around my middle. That sumbitch was trying to squeeze me flat in two. Its head was lying on the bed, but when I shifted it rose up and looked at me from about two feet in the air with its beady little eyes. Its forked tongue flickered at me! Most of its body was coiled around my stomach . . . and it was hard as a damn rock. And cold. Lord have mercy it was cold.

"I looked around and she wasn't even there. I thought maybe that snake had eaten her, I didn't know. I started wriggling but that snake gripped me tighter. I slid off the bed and got to my feet and tried to unwrap it but I couldn't unwind it from its hold around me. It was heavy, and was starting to hurt my midsection something fierce. I looked around the room for anything I could find—man, how I wished for an ax or a gun—but the only thing in that room was lava lamps and bottles of lotions. Love oils, I guess you call them. I grabbed this one big bottle and took off the cap and just started pouring that greasy stuff into the crevices between me and the snake. Well, I got that thing good and lubed up and pressed with my arms as hard as I could and slid it down my body, like I was rolling a rubber band off a newspaper. That thing was fighting me, squeezing as tight as it could, and hissing to beat the band. I was worried it was going to bite my pecker off.

"But that oil was too slick for it to hold me and it hit the ground like a swelling fire hose. I grabbed my britches from the floor and hit out running from the room—that goddamned snake struck at my skinny ass and just missed me as I scooted through her bedroom door. I didn't know where she was, and I didn't care. I ran out in the yard and put on my britches and walked home, seven miles. I was glad to get the hell out of there alive. Needless to say, I never saw her again."

My dad and I were laughing hard, me till my eyes watered, Dad sounding like he was gasping for air. Harry paused for a minute and shook his head from side to side. "Lord have mercy," he said. "Let that be a lesson to you, boy. Don't let them women get their snakes wrapped around you."

We'd quit chuckling for a while and then we would break into a laugh just from looking at Harry, imp-like in his seat, the brim of his visor pulled down low. After another long break Harry said, "Following that episode, I rushed back to the safety of the country club and stayed inside those chain-link fences and near the net and the service line and lived a clean life. I even married a preacher's girl and was a fine, upstanding citizen for a good long time. We almost made it twenty years. Until this past summer. That's my story—sad but true."

There was a long period of silence until my dad asked Harry if he'd ever heard any Leroy and Linda Sue stories. He said, no, but he would like to, and dad launched into his repertoire, all of which I'd heard many times before.

I leaned back on the leather seats of the Lincoln, the short night's sleep weighing on me, and I drifted off into a long nap while listening to Dad's jokes and Harry's peppery laughter.

I woke up a few hours later in North Florida, Dad driving fast and Harry quiet, the sun up high and the flatlands of scrub pines bright with the midmorning light. Dad glanced in the rearview mirror and saw me sitting up and asked if we were ready to eat. Soon we were settled in a booth at a Waffle House, a corner spot with big glass windows looking out onto the asphalt where several big rigs sat in extra-large parking spaces. A crowd of truck drivers, bikers, and random folks that looked like either they hadn't slept in days or had just woke up surrounded us. We were an oddly dressed trio compared with the rest—Harry and I in tennis clothes, my dad in a light-blue pair of Sansabelt slacks and a red polo shirt, the only three people in there not smoking. A dusty-white cloud swirled about the stained ceiling tiles.

We ate and piled back into the car and Dad pointed the big Lincoln south toward Orlando, joining on the Florida Turnpike and scooting on down the direction of the equator. We passed by the house that Mickey Mouse built and covered the last four hours from Orlando to Miami quickly, Dad driving fast. The traffic was heavier the farther south we drove, the sky dark with black clouds, swollen cumulonimbus.

We pulled into Miami in rainy afternoon traffic and found the motel, a Comfort Inn near I-95 where my dad and I shared a room. We flipped on the TV and the local news said the weather would continue all night. Despite the rain, we decided to head over to the tennis center and check out my draw.

The parking lot of the enormous public tennis complex brimmed with cars in large puddles, big droplets falling from the sky. I wasn't nervous going in the crowded clubhouse, but both my father and Harry tensed up. I had seen my dad get this way before, and I thought all the way back to that very first time he took me to see Harry for a lesson. Harry surprised me, though. His cocky strut disappeared and he became hesitant. I had never known Harry to keep his mouth shut for very long. But he walked slow and easy and let me lead the way.

I headed inside and found the registration desk. I studied the draw and located my name among the 128 players in the eighteen-and-unders. I played a Croatian, Andro Mestrovic, seeded ninth. I had never heard of him, but there were many international players unfamiliar to me, including most of the seeds.

We poked around the two-tiered clubhouse for a while, and then sat down on a mauve-colored couch beneath the peach stucco walls hung with watercolors depicting tennis scenes. Out through the rain-splattered windows I stared at the courts that spread out into the flat swampfill of South Florida. Inside I didn't see a single player I knew from Georgia, not even any from the Southern Regionals. I heard more foreign languages in that clubhouse than I'd ever heard before, thin-faced white folks speaking in strange voices dominated by words that sounded like they buzzed. We also heard Spanish by the boatload, a language I had heard from the Mexicans in Piney who worked at the chicken plant.

We milled about for another fifteen minutes until an announcement over the loudspeaker said that all play was canceled for the day, that players should check back in first thing in the morning, that matches started at nine. "All right, John, let's get on out of here and get this boy some macaroni," Harry said.

We stood under the awning for a few long moments studying the downpour until Harry looked at us and said, "Let's go!" We dashed out to the car and got drenched. I retrieved a towel from the trunk and we dried off in the car, laughing as the rain began to come down in windblown sheets.

Dad drove back to the motel, our clothes smelling of rain, the car windows foggy. We agreed with Harry's suggestion to drive out to South Beach for dinner. I changed out of my tennis shorts into a pair of jeans and put on a dry tennis shirt. I was into Fila, the clothing Björn Borg had worn. I relished the way that little F fit into the logo on the sleek white shirt with the red collar.

My dad put on a new pair of designer jeans and this sleek-looking silver buttondown shirt I had never seen him wear. He must have bought it when he was out on the road, traveling on business in Dallas or Houston.

Harry had the room next to ours, and he rapped on the side connecting door, a funny and fast rhythm. I let him in, and saw he had on a Fila shirt and jeans—the exact same outfit I did. We got a laugh out of that, and headed out to the car.

We rode out the Miami Beach Causeway in the pouring rain, admiring the fleet of cruise ships lit up bright and towering in the spotlights of the port. The sun was down and the night pitch dark with heavy clouds roiling the sky, the rain beating on the Lincoln's roof in a steady patter, the puddles along the sides of the road swooshing as Dad drove through.

We found Ocean Drive and cruised along, looking up at the neon signs of the art deco hotels there facing the beach and the Atlantic Ocean, the spot where the Gulf Stream turns and scoots north. We stopped at a hotel that advertised a restaurant. Dad surprised me by using the valet. He was usually one to do it himself and save a nickel, but he had on that new shirt and jeans and we didn't have an umbrella, so I guess he figured we would park in style. Or maybe he wanted to impress Harry.

The valet looked at us a little bit funny, and when I got inside, I saw why. I have since eaten in fancy restaurants and know what to expect from the desperate folks who crave fame and money and love the image of themselves in shiny glass. I'd seen many rich Atlantans in their fatuous glory, but I had never seen anything like this place. The front room had a long neon bar lined with models and would-be supermodels, and men sleek and dark who looked like Colombian cocaine dealers. Two old southern men and a teenage tennis player were a strange sight in this sleekly lit restaurant decorated with candles, glossy red stone, and plush leather seats. There was loud merengue music playing, a xylophone driving the sound, but not so loud that we couldn't hear one another. I had never heard a sound system that clear, and certainly not the exotic sounds of merengue.

We approached the hostess, a Latina with straight, long dark hair and a shimmering silver top that came down low on her cleavage and up high on her stomach and left her back completely naked. The entire piece of fabric was about the size of a wash cloth. I don't know how it adhered to her body. She turned her black eyes our way and brushed her hair back but didn't smile, didn't say anything. She was so good looking that she scared the hell out of all three of us. A painful moment hung in the air until Harry ended the standoff when he stepped up and said, "Three?"

She tilted her head back and said, "Yes," and grabbed menus and turned and headed down a hallway. Not a one of us moved, watching her ass in a white short skirt, until she swiveled and held up her hand and gestured for us to follow, her long red nails flashing in the soft light.

We moved along sheepishly, following her into a big room with an open space surrounded by tables, skirting the edge of the dance floor that had about twenty people on it, mostly women. The dancers were shaking every bit they had and then some, moving in high heels and spinning, their long hair flying and hips gyrating like motor-powered juggernauts.

Dad and I followed but Harry was so taken by the scene on the dance floor that he walked headfirst into a mirrored column, grunting as he did. I turned and he looked at me and laughed. He grabbed me around the shoulders and spoke loudly in my ear, "Damn, boy, what you think of *My-am-uh* now?"

The hostess gave us the menus and deposited us into a round booth, me in the middle, and we turned our attention to the dancers. "Look at that one in the red dress," Harry said. She had long, curly black hair and she was tall and her hemline was very high, just below her plentiful round ass that was moving one hundred directions seemingly all at once. "That skirt's like a sack full of cats headed for the river," Harry said.

My dad and I both laughed, and were still laughing when the waiter came along and took our drink orders. He was a short, handsome dude with too much gel on his dark hair and most likely steroids or some sort of amphetamine in his system, grinding his jaw as he spoke to us. Dad and Harry ordered bourbon, Maker's Mark, with ice, and I got a Coke.

We opened the menus—heavy-bound leather covers on a fancy sheet of parchment paper printed in a font that was almost illegible. Much of the menu was in Spanish and I tried to focus and make sense of it and find something to eat, something with pasta. The merengue ratcheted up a notch and the xylophone sounded as if it was trying to mimic a runaway car flying down a mountain in the Caribbean. I can still hear that song and see that restaurant and the dance floor and the illuminated liquor bottles behind the bar, all red and blue and golden amber in the silvery backlight of the mirrored shelves.

We all chose something that we thought we could eat. I was worried I would end up with some weird type of shellfish or octopus or some such slimy crustacean. My dad and Harry both got fish, while I ordered fettuccine with chicken and a green salad. We all pointed at the items we wanted and hoisted the menu up where our waiter could see. The waiter wrote our orders down and slunk away.

"John, Jaxie," Harry said, speaking our names without looking at us, his eyes still affixed to the dance floor. "What do you think all these women do for a living? Is it something their mamas know about?"

My dad smiled but offered no answer for Harry's question. He drained the last of the bourbon from his glass and looked over toward the waiter and gestured with the empty and held up two fingers. Then he smiled at me, a little lazy at the corners of his mouth and eyes. He reached over and tousled my hair. "Jaxie, my boy."

"*Dad*," I said, and recoiled from him, scowling, keeping my eyes down. He pulled his hand back and his smile faded.

I had been thinking about what Wendy Crenshaw might have looked like out there shaking that sexy body of hers, and that she would fit in, although she would be shorter than the others, perhaps a little thicker and not as much rhythm. And I wondered if maybe one of those women—a few looked as if they might be as young as seventeen or eighteen—would be impressed with a tennis player of my caliber and perhaps give me a chance.

Harry laughed. "John, don't embarrass the boy now. If we've got any shot with these women out there, this boy is it. Jaxie's our point man tonight, our young celebrity, playing in the Orange Bowl. Next stop, ATP tour. We'll have to settle for the castoffs."

Harry put his hand on my dad's arm and patted him, "It's all right now, John. The boy's growing up."

Harry turned toward me. "Jaxie, you can salsa dance, can't you?" Both my dad and Harry laughed, and I sat with my eyes down, sneaking furtive glances at the dance floor.

Soon after that the entrées came. The meals were tiny—even the pasta was skimpy—on square, glazed-brown plates. The food looked like sparkling pieces of art, with sauces and creams designed in fancy patterns. "I don't know if I should eat it or save it for my mantelpiece," Harry said. "Maybe hang it up in the hallway." My dad laughed again, louder this time, and reached across the table and affectionately jabbed Harry in the arm.

We scarfed down our food. Dad and Harry then had another round of drinks and we all watched the dance floor, the women spinning and shaking. The music picked up in both pace and volume, loud Spanish singing with a heavier beat. The tables around us began to fill up, all young and ferociously attractive couples except for the occasional older man with a young hottie.

The check came and Dad sent his credit card up and it came back and he signed it. He swallowed down the rest of his drink. "Jaxie, Harry, let's get the hell out of this nitshit place." He stood and we followed him out the door, Harry behind him, this time paying more attention to where he was walking, but still moving along in that funny chicken strut that was his walk.

The rain had let up and we stood on the sidewalk, waiting for the car to come around, in front of the neon-blue sign. We looked out to the Atlantic, the lights from the street gleaming low on the wet sand and reflecting faintly in the churning waters, waves kicking up high and white on the wide stretch of beach. "I finally feel like I am in

Florida," my dad said. "I don't ever feel like I'm here till I see the ocean."

"Yep," Harry said, "that's the truth. Maybe after Jaxie wins this thing, we can come over here, spend a day in the sun. He can introduce his older brothers around, let us have the second string."

Dad looked at me, and moved again like he was going to tousle my hair, but then thought better of it. I stepped back just in case he came my way. He turned to Harry, and he smiled. "Yep, he's already had the finest piece of pussy in Piney, Georgia, so no reason he can't put the moves on some of these ladies here. Just give him a little time."

I was shocked. Harry looked at me and nodded approvingly, like he knew all along. It never occurred to me that Dad knew I was screwing Wendy Crenshaw, although thinking back on it there must have been a million clues in our house—wet sheets, crumpled tissues, the fecund smells of sex.

The valet brought the car around and we climbed into the black Lincoln. It seemed like an enormous funeral boat among the Porsches, Mercedes, and other sporty cars along the street in hues of red, yellow, and even purple. Dad tipped the diminutive Cuban valet a dollar and in return got a scowl that indicated we were too cheap or too low-class for his tastes.

I sat in the backseat and stared out the window, longing for Wendy and her body and her eyes and her kisses, remembering the sweet stink of wetness between her legs. I wondered if my dad knew what I was thinking. He probably did. If you ever have to guess what a man is meditating over, it's most likely a woman or some of her parts.

On the way back to the motel Dad stopped at a liquor store and he and Harry went in and came out with a bottle in a brown paper sack. I went in our room and flipped on the TV. Dad said he and Harry were going out to sit by the pool since the rain had let up.

I changed into shorts and a T-shirt and flossed and brushed my teeth. I took the remote control to bed and clicked through the dial, watching a little bit of a dull college basketball game from the West Coast. After I while, I pulled up the sheet and thin blanket and my head relaxed into the pillow and I turned off the television. I closed my eyes and my somnolent ritual of envisioning the hypnotic back and forth of a rally began, sleep coming to me in my comforting tennis-court dream.

Despite all my years on the road sleeping in uncomfortable beds with papery sheets beneath scratchy comforters of dubious history, waking up in the middle of the night in a motel room is something I'll never get used to. For those first few moments of consciousness, it's the same whether it's Miami or Manitoba—the confrontation with the strange dark, the sharp red light of a digital alarm clock, the unfamiliar layout of furniture. I've been awakened by couples fighting in the hallways, enormous truck engines rumbling to life in parking lots, sirens blaring on city streets, and rowdy drunks arguing on sidewalks. In all cases I've taken a peek out the window, rolled over and got my bearings—remembering the critical details of who I am and what I'm doing there—and then gone back to sleep.

But that night in Miami I awoke to a noise that scared me, a startling sound that kept me awake. I heard a shout of some kind, and woke up in that very dark room draped with heavy curtains designed to fend off the Florida sunshine. The shout sounded familiar, and then it was quiet for a moment. I lay there and looked toward the window where a slice of a light cut thinly along the side of the curtain covering the sliding glass doors.

I rolled over. The clock radio read 3:25 AM. I listened, and then looked at my dad's bed. The covers had not been pulled back, and there was no sign of his dark hair on the pillow. After a few moments, I heard the familiar but unintelligible voices of my father and Harry. My dad and Harry were carrying on in Harry's room next door, talking sometimes both at once, and then Harry talking fast, sort of a soothing patter, while my dad let out another mournful sound like the one that had awakened me. It took me a while to realize that he was sobbing.

I couldn't understand a word he was saying. I could hear Harry, talking in a calming tone but with anxiousness in his voice that I'd never heard before, trying to reassure my dad, but not convincing in his delivery. My dad's cry was nothing like I'd ever heard from him. He went on for a long time, a pitiful wailing, his deep voice cracking as he spoke.

My first instinct was to jump to my feet and run in there, but I didn't. They were drunk, I reasoned, and there was nothing I could do to help them. I lay there and listened, trying to figure out what was upsetting my dad. I had seen how he and my mom had been treating each other, passing in the kitchen like ships taking a wide berth. I was young and didn't understand what was going on, but I could sense that something had been wrong for years by then, had been going wrong since I was little, maybe even about the time I started playing tennis.

I kept listening, hoping I could make sense of it, trying to decipher what they were saying. My dad rambled on and let out another sob. Most of what he said was too slurred to make out, but I did hear him say something about someone named Claudia. Years later I realized that Claudia was the college girlfriend, Mrs. Lane, the Italian American woman from Savannah he had met at Georgia Tech when her last name was Cipriani, a rich girl who married an even richer man. I didn't know that then, and I don't remember if I even knew Mrs. Lane's first name. I lay there, fully awake, wondering who in the hell Claudia was, if I was even hearing it right, and if he hadn't gone completely crazy.

He went on like that for a long time, saying the same things over and over. It upset me to hear my father moaning and jabbering like a drunken fool. I naively blamed it on the bottle, believing that it made him be someone else, that it wasn't my father there babbling and hollering and regretting his life, bemoaning the lost love of a woman I didn't even know. I figured my real dad would come back tomorrow.

Many years passed before I learned what drinking can do, how it can lay bare the soul instead of covering it up. I didn't realize that the man in the next room was my *real* dad, and that in some ways the man I knew was a veneer concealing a foundation of pain and regret. Years later, when I was in my twenties, I realized that the song about whiskey making people into fools but not liars is true.

But that night I just rolled over. I fell back to sleep, reassuring myself that I had things figured out, that it would all be fine in the morning when the liquor wore off.

The alarm went off at seven and I reached and hit the snooze. Light streamed in around the edges of the thick drapes that hung over the sliding glass doors. I closed my eyes and thought first of my match, listening for rain. I heard nothing, and figured I needed to get up because my match could be as early as nine and I wanted to warm up with Harry beforehand. We had traveled a long way and I didn't intend to be there for only one round.

Ever since I was about ten years old I've conducted a private ritual I adapted from one of Harry's motivational stories. I'll lie there and close my eyes and picture a pack of English bulldogs like Uga, the University of Georgia mascot—squat and white with thick shoulders, wrinkled, stumpy faces, and powerful jaws. I always see these dogs run across a misty green field, chasing a herd of horned Hereford cattle, and I imagine myself as one of the dogs. I watch as the dog that is me latches onto the biggest bull in the pack, a huge bovine with horns sharp and high and slashing. The dog bites into the bull's neck, chomping into the hide with a growl, and just hangs there, despite the Hereford's shaking and lowing and snorting. The dog hangs on and bites harder, cutting into muscle and the fat, crunching into the bones of the enormous bovine's shoulder and neck, all the way into the gristle of its spinal cord until the bull collapses, the dog still hanging on as the bull falls, the dog single-minded and ferocious and hell-bent on killing the giant bull even if it kills him. I lie there—even today, I do this—and think of the stumpy dog killing the enormous bull and conquering all odds in size and logic, biting into that neck and holding on until death, either of himself or his opponent. You might say it's dark, but it has worked. I never give up, no matter how outmatched I might be. When I was little, Harry told me about these bulldogs that hung on against all odds, these British dogs that kings bred to kill for sport, dogs with jaws like a vise. Once you get an image like that in your head, you never lose it.

So as weird as the night had been, hearing my father crying like a baby, I woke up with the match on my mind and rolled the internal movie of that tenacious bulldog in my brain, killing the bull in the open green field under a heavy mist. It wasn't until the alarm clock began buzzing again, nine minutes after the first alert, that I remembered my dad had been shitfaced. I looked over to his bed and it was still made, his small travel suitcase lying open on the foot of the comforter.

I got up and went to the door adjoining our rooms and knocked. I heard a grunt that sounded like Harry. I knocked again. "Yeah, Jaxie, hold on." His voice was gruff, and I heard him cough.

"Is my dad over there?"

"Yeah, he's here." Harry opened the door in white boxers and a gray Atlanta Lawn Tennis Association T-shirt and stepped into the room with me, shutting the door behind him. His eyes were red, his wiry hair askew, and his face sagged and looked sallow. "He might be out for a while. What time do you need to get down there?"

"I could play as early as nine, depending on how backed up they are from yesterday. I was hoping to hit some, get loose before we play."

Harry sighed, nodded. His breath stunk. "Yeah, you need that. I'll feed you some balls. But don't expect me to run around any. You got a feeble old man on your hands today. Two, in fact."

He forced a smile. "It'll be all right, champ. It'll be all right."

Harry and I dressed and headed out, leaving my dad to sleep it off. It struck me as very strange to see Harry behind the wheel of my dad's new Lincoln. Even though Dad had bought the car only a week before, it was unquestionably his, the way he steered that big boat, his left hand lightly on the wheel, his right resting on the seat back and reaching over behind the passenger in a gesture that ensured confidence and security.

Harry, though, struggled with the seat, trying to get it into position so his short legs could reach the gas and the brake. I never realized until that morning how short his legs were, that he was more torso than anything, and that perhaps the short pants he wore most of the time made him look taller. Harry was a head shorter than my dad and needed the seat moved or we would never get there. His being hung over didn't help, and he cursed the electronic buttons, raising the seat, pushing it farther back, even tilting it, but not getting it any closer to the pedals, where he needed it to be.

I offered to help, but he waved me away. After a few more frustrating minutes, he figured it out and the seat slid forward and we were off. He forced a laugh. "Here we go, Jaxie boy."

The morning was one of those when Florida lives up to its marketing. The sun climbed in a pristinely blue sky, and a soft sea breeze blew, almost like there was a fan turned on low out over the ocean. The warm air carried the smell of salt water and the greenness of the land, the Everglades only a dozen or so miles west of us.

Harry drove slowly, unlike my dad who had a lead foot and drove like a maniac sometimes, although he never wrecked. Dad had spent his career paving roads and operating heavy machinery, and drove fearlessly in traffic. Harry's lazy maneuvering was a disturbing change —even the oldest of the old drivers passed us. It occurred to me that Harry didn't drive much. He lived near his club in Atlanta, and teaching tennis lessons certainly didn't require getting behind the wheel of a car. The only vehicles I had ever seen him own were small sports cars—an MG convertible when we first met, later a sleek silver Porsche. I don't remember what he drove at the time we were in Florida, but I'm sure it was small and bright and had a ragtop.

I studied Harry's tanned, wrinkled face, his mustache of the style actors in 1970s car-chase movies wore, full and brown with a tinge of gray coming on. He might have looked just a little bit like Burt Reynolds but he sure as hell didn't drive like him. His lips were tense and his eyes severely bloodshot. Traffic was heavy on the four-lane city streets with the wide turning lanes.

Harry didn't say anything, but after driving down the main boulevard for a good fifteen minutes, he pulled in a McDonald's parking lot and looked around the floorboard and in the glove box. He let out a long sigh and I could smell liquor on his breath, even though the windows were open. He let off the brake and the car moved a few feet and then he pressed back down on it, looking one way and then the other down the long road gleaming with the reflection of sunlight on the line of windshields headed east. A row of enormous palm trees swayed in the breeze parallel to the street.

"Jaxie, did your dad have a map in here?"

"I don't know."

"Do you remember where he turned off this road?"

I realized we were lost, and that I had no idea where Dad had turned, what the name of the road was, what the name of the suburb even was. With the benefit of hindsight and faded newspaper clippings, I can tell you the name of the tennis center, but then I didn't know Coral Gables from Cape Cod, and could not have found either on my own.

"No, I don't."

"What was the name of that place? It had the town's name, right? Something or other racket club?"

"I don't know."

"Well, shit. Wait here."

Harry put the car into park and left the engine idling and went inside the McDonald's. I watched him walk away, moving along stiff-legged with his hands hanging lifelessly by his side. He kept his head still, like I had seen him do when teaching how to best hit volleys, this amusing routine of running around at the net with his arms and legs flailing but holding his head as still as a statue, his eyes focused on the balls coming at him. But that day there was nothing funny about his pained walk.

I waited there and thought about hearing my father's drunken crying and babbling, and I became very angry with him. I couldn't understand at that time, having never been drunk myself, what the big deal with getting drunk was, why anyone would succumb to it, and much less why they would break down and cry like a baby. I was furious that he would come all this way and miss my first match. He had been as excited as I was. I could only chalk it up to his being weak.

Harry came out with a cup of coffee and an orange juice that he gave to me. "It's back the other way. Young lady in there says we've got to get on U.S. 1, that it'll be quicker."

I made a *pffft* sound with my lips, and turned my head from him. Harry wrinkled his brow and took a long look at me. "What's gotten into you, Jaxie? I'll get you there."

"You better," I said.

He pulled the Lincoln out of the lot and worked his way down the busy street. We waited for what seemed like at least ten minutes to make a left turn that put us on a frontage road to access U.S. 1. Harry slugged along the entrance ramp and almost came to a stop before squeezing his way on, driving on the highway's shoulder for about a hundred yards before he merged into the slow lane. Cars and semitrucks passed us like we were standing still. Harry nervously checked the side mirrors and the rearview frantically, his eyes darting back and forth. He flinched when a motorcycle zipped by us, straddling the line separating two lanes, its engine roaring a high loud pitch. "This big damn car is too much," he said. He rolled up the windows as we picked up speed.

We drove on for a few miles in the middle lane and Harry started muttering to himself. "Shit. D'she say north or south? Goddamn Cubans. She probably don't know what the hell she's talking about."

He drove along for about twenty more minutes until we saw an exit for Homestead, the town that had been flattened earlier that year by Hurricane Andrew. Even I knew it was too far south of Miami, on the way to the Keys. "Damn, Harry, this is way south of Miami. We got to turn around. Get off here."

Harry's eyes twitched, scanning the mirrors. He turned the wheel to get over to the right but a fast-moving truck was coming and he swerved back into our lane and almost too far into a car in the lane to our left. Someone honked at us and he got nervous and slowed all the way down to about twenty miles per hour. Drivers tapped on their brakes and swerved around us.

The exit approached and he tried again to cut over but more cars were coming and he kept cussing but couldn't move over in time. It was a driving maneuver so easy that my dad could have done it with his eyes closed. Harry kept trying to merge into the right lane but was reluctant to make the move. As the exit approached, he cut the wheel sharply and mashed the gas and the car careened to the right as another car in the lane tried to speed up and get around us and behind that was an eighteen-wheeler bearing down. Harry drove on across the lane but we were too far past the exit to get off and he veered onto the shoulder and drove right up onto a big concrete curb, ramming it with the front right tire. The tire blew out, exploding like a gunshot, and he slammed on the brakes and we screeched to a halt on the side of the road, sparks flying from the metal rim, the car coming to rest under the overpass of the road for which we had missed the exit. "Motherfucker," Harry said, "goddamn motherfucker." He slammed his fist on the dashboard and cursed again, a string of *motherfucker*s and *son of a bitch*es.

Smoke was coming from under the tire well and the whole car smelled of burnt rubber. I got out and inspected the damage. The tire was ripped to shreds. The rest of the car, however, seemed fine. Harry took a quick look and then sat down on the asphalt and hung his head. "Damn, Jaxie, I'm sorry." He rested his face in his hands.

I realized that if I was going to get to the match on time I was going to have to take charge and change the tire and find directions and drive the car myself. I slid in behind the wheel and adjusted the seat and backed it off the curb, the tire rim screeching on the bare concrete.

I had seen my dad change a tire. I pulled the full-sized spare out of the trunk and leaned it against the back bumper. I removed the jack and wedged it under the front chassis and began to turn the handle with a tire iron, raising that big beast of an automobile on that small metal contraption.

Harry said something, but I ignored him, acting like the whooshing roar of traffic made it impossible for me to hear as I went to work turning the lug nuts. A few of the nuts were on extra tight, probably tightened by a mechanic's motor-powered wrench, and I had to strain and cuss and kick at the tire iron with my foot to get them loose. I finally did, removing the rim and setting it down by the trunk. I slung the shredded pieces of tire into the high grass by the side of the road.

I put the new tire in place and screwed on the lug nuts. I looked back at Harry, still sitting, looking like he was about to vomit. His brow was wet, and his underarms damp with sweat circles.

I tightened the nuts as best I could by hand, and gave each one an extra turn by pressing the tire iron with the heel of my shoe. I spun the jack handle and it lowered the car back to the ground, and I slid it out from under the car and put it and the tire iron back and the old rim into the Lincoln's cavernous trunk and slammed it shut.

"Let's go, Harry," I said. "I'm driving."

"Naw, Jaxie, you are not old enough."

"Harry, I got my learner's license. I'm okay . . . really. Get in the passenger side. We won't never get there with you driving. We're out of spares."

He gave me a stern look. "C'mon," I said. "I've got a match to play."

I started up the engine and scanned the rearview and the side mirrors. Dad had let me drive plenty by then, and I had no fear as I backed up for about twenty yards along the shoulder of the road, far enough so we could access the off-ramp that Harry had missed. I crossed the overpass and reentered the freeway, heading north. I drove until I saw the exit where we had gotten onto the highway and I pulled back off.

I found a 7-Eleven and studied the yellow pages in a pay-phone booth—you know you are in a well-to-do neighborhood when the phone books are not ripped to shreds or marked up with drawings of penises—and found a list of tennis centers. I recognized the name of the tournament site when I saw it, and wrote down the address and the number. I went inside and asked the store clerk there, a polite young Pakistani, where this was and he said it was very close. He produced a map and showed me that it was just two blocks away—a left at the light, and then another right, and I would see the courts.

I squealed the tires pulling into the parking lot and jumped out and ran inside the tennis center without waiting on Harry. I checked in with a wrinkle-faced woman with a dark tan and dyed-black hair and a sinister New York accent. "We've been looking for you," she said. "You are late. Another ten minutes and we would have defaulted you. Court Twenty-Nine. Your opponent is already there."

I had hoped to wash some of the grime off my hands, and maybe sneak in some practice, but instead I had to run to the court in the farthest corner of the large complex.

The court was at the end of the long walkway and had a short set of bleachers, three seats high. Waiting on me was Andro Mestrovic, one of Bollettieri's protégés, a tall seventeen-year-old Croatian, already six feet three and even slightly muscular, not one of the skinny beanpoles you see in the juniors. He must have weighed around 180, at least 25 pounds heavier than me.

We didn't speak or shake hands, simply nodded coolly at each other. We started warming up and I wished then that I had been able to practice that morning. A mild wind blew, and the green hard courts were faster than I expected. When we started hitting serves, I knew I was in trouble. A lefty, he had a huge serve, maybe 120 miles per hour. He could hit it flat or with a big kicking spin that rode into my forehand.

Mestrovic had an entourage of friends, other players from Bollettieri's camp, about eight boys and four girls, including Fiorella Santangelo, a sexy blond Italian girl with an olive complexion whose picture I'd studied closely in *Tennis* magazine—she had a racket endorsement and ad campaigns, although she was my age, only fifteen.

Mestrovic won the toss and served first. I tried moving back for my returns, but I'm not sure if it would have mattered what I did. He knocked off two big aces and one winner. I put only one ball into play, and that one he drilled with a hard crosscourt forehand past me.

I could hear some of his friends laughing after he buzzed through the first game. They only half watched, all looking off in different directions, fooling with their Sony Walkmans. Mestrovic and I changed sides and he stopped and spoke to Fiorella, some kind of wisecrack in Italian. She laughed and flashed her brown eyes at him, said "*Ciao*," and sauntered off.

In the second game, I tried to hit some big shots and missed most of my first serves. He jumped on a few of my second serves and crunched forehands, and also hit a well-placed down-the-line backhand drive. I won only one point on my serve and then he ripped through another love service game, this time with three enormous aces and a final kicker out wide. My return sailed pitifully outside of the doubles lines to give him a 3–0 lead.

The first three games had taken about six minutes. I needed to slow the pace down, to win some points. I sat down in the white plastic chair during the changeover and he stared quizzically at me as though asking, *What, are you tired? You need a rest?* I ignored him. I knew that next service game was critical. I settled down and made sure to get my first serve into his backhand, putting some balls wide in the deuce court that pressured his two-hander. One he missed wide. Another he floated back and I put it away, hitting back to his backhand as he dashed toward the other side of the court. In spite of two weak serves that he pummeled back down the middle at me, I held my serve in a two-deuce game. He cursed something gruff in Croatian, a word that sounded like it was built upon a weird combination of *d*'s and *z*'s.

He served another great service game, two aces and two winners, as though he was pissed off about not breaking my serve. He started to grunt on his serves, something he had not done earlier, and the grunts accompanied even harder balls.

We changed sides at 4–1 and again I took the full time-out. Harry had found the court by then and was sitting on the second row of the short bleachers, sipping an orange Gatorade, his posture like that of a man who had been beaten with a steel pipe. I made eye contact with him. "Let's go, Jaxie," he said, but it looked like it hurt him to say it.

It occurred to me that this match would be possibly the most important in my tennis future. If I lost in the first round, I wouldn't be invited to international or even national junior tournaments. I would return to Georgia and continue as the local champion there, maybe play small-college tennis somewhere in Alabama or South Georgia and then have to go out and get a real job and talk about the one time I went to the Orange Bowl and got smoked by a player much better than me, a dude who went on to the tour. Tennis is all about levels, moving from one to the next, and I was testing my game in an arena of players all jockeying to be pros, not simply the best Georgia players looking to get their names in the agate pages of the Atlanta newspapers.

I held my serve. Then the wind picked up and Mestrovic began to have trouble with that high toss of his. He started missing first serves. I also was getting a feel for how the ball was moving, reading his spin better. I stepped in on a second serve and caught it early and chipped it hard and low down the line to his backhand, not a customary shot for me, but one Harry had encouraged me to try on the big servers. Mestrovic is tall and gangly and tried to move and hit his two-hander but he didn't bend down low enough and sent the ball into the bottom of the net. He cursed and grumbled back up to the baseline and tried to punish the ball. He sailed a few first serves well past the service line, and then took something off his second ball to ensure he would get it into the court. I glanced over to Harry and he gestured with his hand toward the net and mouthed the words, *Come in*. The man couldn't drive or change a tire, but he knew tennis strategy as well as anyone, and having him there gave me a boost. He was on the edge of his seat, and I know he knew as well as I did that it was a crucial time in the match, the crossroads of my tennis career.

Mestrovic gritted his teeth and glared, his long hair parted in the middle, his sharp nose pointing straight at me like the sight on a gun. At 30–40, a break chance for me, he bounced the ball numerous times before going into his long service motion. He netted the first serve. I moved in a few more steps for his second serve, just to rile him up, and he glared again and bounced the ball even more, at least twenty times, and seemed to be talking to himself as he did it. I knew that if he got a strong serve in deep, I was screwed, and at best could only push the ball back to him. But I also figured, moving in that close, he would either try to knock me down with a serve or push it into the court very cautiously and I could jump on it and hit a winner. He did what I expected, he went for the big one—what almost anyone could have predicted the big goon would try to do—and sailed it long by a few inches.

He threw another fit and slung his racket into the fence. I was down 3–4, but I was back in the match with the breaker. His entourage had dwindled, but the three remaining players had been joined by Nick Bollettieri, the overly tanned coach whose compound in Florida had become an assembly line of superstars. Bollettieri had a thick black mustache and he wore very dark sunglasses and a Fila T-shirt. He was very tan and his hair had started to recede so that he looked like a turtle poking his head out of his shell.

I almost never stopped to watch the sidelines, but Bollettieri, whom I had seen on television in Andre Agassi's box at the U.S. Open, was a major big deal, the reigning king of coaches. He spoke to the oldest of the three kids, all boys, who were watching our match, and I heard him ask the score and the kid tell him I had just broken serve. He bobbed his head, tilting it backward, and—I'll never forget this—he looked toward me and pulled his sunglasses up and peered my way, as though he was trying to remember me from somewhere.

We switched sides. I turned to serve, Bollettieri on my end of the court, even with the baseline, watching. I took my time and tossed the ball slightly to my right and went up and hit a big angled serve with some kick on it hard and wide into the box. Mestrovic lunged but could only get the tip of the racket on it, deflecting the ball over the short side-court fence. The ball bounced toward Harry, who reached up for it but couldn't catch it. I watched as Harry got up slowly, moving as though it hurt his head to walk, and retrieved the ball from the base of a flower bed beside the walkway and tossed it into my side of the court.

I didn't stare but I took a quick glance over to Bollettieri, who was still watching, his eyes intent on me. I hit three more big serves, none of which Mestrovic returned, the third point in the deuce court an ace up the T when he guessed I would go wide again, and then a near ace in the ad court, again going to his forehand and surprising him at 40–love. Mestrovic burst into another round of Croatian curses, and Bollettieri looked at him and held his hands out like he was pressing on a table. "Calm down," he said.

The next game at 4–4 remains to this day one of the best I've ever played. Mestrovic had taken a long time between games, muttering, but had seemed to calm down before he stepped in to serve. I moved in tight and was anticipating a big ball into my forehand, that lefty spin riding in on me. I stepped to my right to run around my forehand and took the ball early and cleanly, driving a backhand by him down the line. I did the same with the next serve he hit me, the return coming off my racket hard and flat and skidding past him.

I hit two more winners off his first serve, surprising everyone except me. I was completely in the zone. I had one of those moments on the court when I was seeing the ball as clearly as I've ever seen it, like the tennis ball was as large as a basketball, enormous and yellow and seeming to move slow, just waiting there for me to move my racket to it and put it away cleanly. And this was off serves hit at least 120 miles per hour, maybe even 130, from a lefty, no less.

I can try to tell you what it is like to be in the zone, but I can't do it justice. It's a mysterious, elusive place. For me, the mind becomes perfectly quiet, a stillness I can't describe. Only the ball penetrates the silence, flying through the air like a bullet in slow motion that only I can see.

That day against Mestrovic was my first sign that I could be an exceptional player. I stepped up my game like never before, serving winners and nailing returns off probably the best server in the juniors, a renowned international player important enough that even Bollettieri came to watch. I remember seeing concern on the old coach's face after I took the first set 6–4. I had won five games in a row.

I was so focused that I didn't even look at Harry, although I could hear him clapping and saying "Atta boy, Jaxie." I can recall every single detail of that day, from the shots I hit, to how Mestrovic's shoes squeaked when he ran, to the way the American and Florida flags on poles in the corner of the tennis center flapped in the December breeze. A few fluffy clouds hung distant in the west, somewhere out over the Everglades where alligators flopped in the mucky water, and north of that, fresh water oozed out of Lake Okeechobee. I could see and feel it all. Only when I got up 4–0 in the second did I pause, breaking the trance for a moment when I looked at Harry and smiled. He pumped his fist and said, "Close it out, son, close it out." I hit an ace. I was on the end near Bollettieri, only a few feet from him, and I took a quick glance his way. He nodded his wrinkled, overly tanned head at me, smiling slyly.

Across the net Mestrovic had gone apoplectic, hitting every ball that came his way with as much force as he could, making a string of errors that helped me to finish out the second set at love. His cursing had continued to escalate. After match point, he smashed his racket onto the court, bashing it repeatedly until the black graphite frame, now connected only by the strings, flopped like it was made of wet spaghetti noodles. He slung the battered Prince along the court and it skittered into the far corner. He came up to shake hands and never looked me in the eye, reaching out briefly in a wet fish handshake that lasted only a millisecond.

Harry rushed over to me and shook my hand and patted me on the back, congratulating me. He said to Mestrovic, who was violently gathering his bag together, "Good match, son," and received a harsh glare in return.

Bollettieri came over to me when I came off the court and shook my hand in a vise grip. "Young man, that was an excellently played match. Congratulations."

I thanked him, and introduced him to Harry, whom he shook hands with quickly and then looked back at me. "You're from Georgia, right?" Bollettieri said. "Where do you play up there?"

I told him I was from Piney, and he asked where that was, and I told him. I said Harry had been my coach all along and that I practiced mainly with college players in Atlanta.

He looked away from me for a second when Mestrovic passed by, his gait fast in the direction of the clubhouse. Bollettieri turned and raised his finger, yelling like an army sergeant. "Andro, you wait on me." He pointed to a spot behind him. "Right there." Mestrovic, head down, stood obediently like a dog who had done wrong. Bollettieri turned back to me and Harry, his face transitioning from a grimace to a warm smile, his black mustache turning up at the tips. "Sorry, about that, son," he said. "I've got to go, but I hope to see your next match, and visit with you more later." He started off, but then turned back to Harry and said, "Nice meeting you, too, Coach."

He then faced Mestrovic and raised his finger in the air about eye level, shouting that representatives of the Nick Bollettieri Tennis Academy were required to represent "dedication, discipline, and ability" and that he, Andro Mestrovic, had failed miserably on all three counts. That he, Andro Mestrovic, had let down the academy and its other members with his poor play and "peasant-like behavior." He gestured with his pointed finger inches away from Mestrovic's face. "Go get that racket you smashed. Be at the bus in ten minutes. We'll take this up then."

Harry and I had lingered, moving away slowly, listening to him rant at Mestrovic. Harry smiled at me and his eyes seemed to laugh. "Man, I'm sorry your dad wasn't here to see that one," Harry said.

"Yeah, me too," I said. "Me too."

My dad didn't get out of bed that day until well after lunch when Harry and I returned to the motel and woke him up. He was puny that afternoon but felt better the next morning and came to the rest of my matches. Harry returned to his normal self, and he practiced with me on the following day, warming me up, as well as scouting my opponents. Both he and my dad said nothing about what had happened on that first night in Miami, and the shredded tire never came up. They didn't drink another drop while we were down there.

I won the next six matches I played in the Orange Bowl, beating three of Bollettieri's pupils, two of whom, including the aforementioned Mestrovic, went on to play on the ATP tour for several years. After my first win, we all enjoyed ourselves immensely. Harry was thrilled to be down here at the world's premier junior tournament, strutting around in a new outfit of Fila tennis clothes, cracking jokes, his head sort of bobbing on his shoulders like some sort of Alabama barnyard rooster. This also was a big time for my dad, a man who usually had coffee and sausage-biscuits for breakfast and lunches of bologna sandwiches, all on the side of a half-paved road.

In the final I played Romanian Andrei Pavel, eighteen at the time. The match went to a third-set tiebreaker in which I won with a running, down-the-line, two-handed backhand that had both enormous topspin and sidespin that brought it back into the court, gliding past his racket as he dove headlong onto the green hardtop.

My dad beamed that Sunday afternoon when I raised the winner's crystal goblet stuffed with Florida navel oranges above my head for the cameras. It's a rare and special feat to win a tournament, to be the last one standing on Sunday afternoon, especially in a tournament with such prestige. But I could tell something else was on his mind, and I could feel it when he hugged me, one of the few times in our lives that we embraced. When he put his arms around me, I detected something weighing on him, something that was heavier than he could bear. But I was young, and didn't think much about it.

Now that I am older, I realize that there were severe problems beneath his happy-go-lucky exterior. I was too immersed in my game back then to see anything else. I knew my career was about to take off like a rocket ship. And me . . . me was all I really cared about . . . selfish tennis-playing bastard that I was.

Part Two

Two and a half years later, at the age of eighteen, I stepped foot on an airplane for the very first time. Six months earlier I had won my second Orange Bowl championship. I had followed that win with trophies at professional Futures events in Atlanta and Jacksonville, and then I reached the semis of a higher-level Challenger tournament in South Carolina, earning an ATP ranking in the mid-two-hundreds. I signed with an agent who sought me out. I decided to skip college tennis altogether when I landed a spot in the men's French Open qualifyings.

No one in my family had been to Europe before. My dad wanted to travel to Paris with me, but the invitation had come very late and my mom talked him out of it. I learned later that the sale of his business a few years before had not raised nearly enough to pay off his debt.

I wanted Harry to go, but Dad said the expense was too much. That pissed off Harry, and he refused to pay his own way. He and my dad had harsh words on a phone call the week before I left, Harry calling us both "ungrateful sons of bitches" before hanging up.

If I had it to do over again, I'd have insisted we bring Harry. But I didn't know at the time that my parents were having financial problems, and it's unfair now to second-guess them. All they were doing is the best they knew how.

At the Atlanta airport my dad hugged me, the first time he had embraced me since I won that first Orange Bowl tournament. His once dark hair had started graying and he looked the thinnest I had ever seen him. "Play hard, Jaxie, play hard," he said, his eyes red and watery around the edges. "Win a few and maybe I'll get to see you on television."

I flew to JFK and changed onto a Paris-bound 747. I remember the spacious jet lifting ponderously off the runway and the vibration of the wheels tucking into the fuselage, clicking into place deep beneath my seat. I watched New York become tinier and tinier until it disappeared into dark clouds. I thumbed through an old Frommer's guide to France my father had given me, studying the pictures and reading blurbs about Parisian neighborhoods, food, and museums. I skimmed the vocabulary section, noting the recommendation to speak French to the locals even if you couldn't speak it well. I tried to sleep but couldn't, and instead sat staring at the back of the seat in front of me.

After seven fidgety hours the plane touched down in Paris. I hailed a black Mercedes-Benz taxi and showed the driver the name and address of my hotel. The taxi soon topped a hill and the suburbs fell away and the ancient city spread out enormous and vast before me like a spread in a picture book. We descended into the busy part of town where I saw a lone Labrador retriever holding an enormous loaf of bread in his mouth as he trotted casually across the street.

The Grand Pont Neuf Hotel, tucked away on an alley, was not as glamorous as its name. I entered the cramped lobby and approached the clerk, a twentyish woman peculiarly attractive in a dusky sort of way, one of those French women that I've heard described as being either very ugly or very beautiful—if only you could tell which. I stood up straight, threw my shoulders back, and tried to recall vocabulary from my guidebook. "Au revoir," I said.

She threw back her head and laughed, a bird-like chuckle, her dark eyes alive. "Yes. Good-bye to you, too." Her English was perfect. "Do you have a reservation? You must be . . ." She thumbed through a short stack of index cards. ". . . Mr. Skinner?"

I signed my name, she gave me my key, and I found my room, a narrow space with a tub but no shower and lights operated by a baffling panel of buttons. I lay down on the bed for a short nap.

I woke up in the dark and checked the time—it was eleven o'clock at night. I had slept ten hours. I sat on the bed, waking up for a while, and then went for a walk, winding my way along narrow, silent streets. I studied on dark brick buildings and painted ones, grown elegantly dingy through time, many with wrought-iron railings that encased balconies and adorned staircases.

I found my way to the Seine, and walked along the wide boulevard by the river with Notre Dame behind me and the Louvre and the Eiffel Tower up ahead. I went into an all-night café and ordered a Coke, a grilled ham and cheese sandwich, and authentic french-fried potatoes—to this day, croques-monsieur and pommes frites are my favorite French food. The waiter wasn't busy but he still took a very long time bringing me my check, and then even longer bringing me my change.

I walked past the Louvre for a view of the Arch of Triumph, traffic streaming around it. I then walked back to the Louvre and studied the illuminated glass pyramid placed in the middle of the museum's stately courtyard. The scene awed me, but I felt lonely. I wondered what my dad and Harry would say.

Back in the room I began flipping through the TV channels, only one in English, growing anxious about my visit to Roland Garros. I worried I might oversleep, so I set the hotel alarm clock as well as a travel alarm I brought with me, and I called the front desk and asked for a wake-up call. I lay awake for an hour or more until I finally drifted off to sleep when my dream of hitting tennis balls overtook my mind.

The next morning I stood curbside in my red Fila warm-up, my Wilson racket bag slung over my shoulder, wondering if Björn Borg had started out this way. A black limousine pulled up and the back window rolled down and my agent, Cathy McDermott, poked her head through. "Hi, Jaxie," she said, her Boston voice sounding like a subdued yell. "Toss your rackets in the trunk and hop in." My dad and I had met her in Miami at the Orange Bowl. Although she was loud and a bit obnoxious for our tastes, she impressed us with her energy and her record of success with young pros on the tour. She also had assured my dad that she would look after me in Paris, and most important, she required no payments up front.

The driver took my racket bag from me, tucking it in the trunk beside three others. I climbed into the couch-like seating that encircled the back half of the car. Cathy hugged me, kissing me on both cheeks. She introduced me to three other young players: an Argentine, a Serb, and a Chinese player named Min-Chi Wang. The first two didn't bother speaking or making eye contact, but Wang looked me in the eye, smiled, and reached over and shook my hand. He said it was nice to meet me.

Cathy did all the talking, describing the city to us. Soon we were in the Paris outskirts, near Bois de Boulogne, which she explained was a forested park that bordered Roland Garros. The limo whisked through a main gate and to a special players' entrance. We got out and retrieved our bags from the chauffeur and followed Cathy onto the grounds.

She led us straight into a hallway that went beneath Court Central, as the main stadium was then known. We walked down to a black door and she opened it. Goose bumps began rising on my arms and legs when light burst through and I saw that court, the sun shining bright on the distinct orange clay. We stepped out onto it and I was struck by the softness, softer by far than most of the green clay in the U.S. The pulverized brick surface was powdery and perfectly groomed. Even though my home court was much harder and grittier, this took me back to that day fifteen years earlier when my dad had scraped away the turf from our yard and my future was determined. "Nothing like red dirt," I said.

"Red dirt!" Cathy said, and laughed. "Did you hear that? Over here, they call it terre battue. But I like red dirt." Wang smiled but the other two looked at me like I was a pariah.

We walked from the corner of the court, that very corner where I'd seen players come out to play the finals, and toward the net. Only then did I look at the sixteen thousand seats there. I thought of the French Open matches I'd watched, Courier winning back-to-back tournaments only a few years before, hoisting that silver cup over his head, and of footage I'd seen of Borg, who won here an amazing six times by the age of twenty-five.

She led us out of the stadium and to the tournament administration offices where she handed us schedules with times for breakfast, lunch, practice courts, and massages. There were very few players in the locker room, and I put my racket bag away and strolled around. The deep-red carpet in there was soft, like it had a pad under it. I kept thinking about how this was the same floor on which Borg had walked, the same toilets he had pissed in, the same showers he had used.

I joined Wang in the cafeteria for breakfast. He and I sat at an empty table and talked about what tournaments we had played. He had won every junior event between Sydney and Moscow, but said that he didn't like clay and was concerned he would not do well in Paris. He didn't have a coach with him either, so I asked him what he wanted to work on, how he wanted to practice. He said he would be fine simply playing a few groundstroke games, and then some tiebreakers.

After breakfast we walked out to the far practice courts and that's where I saw Olga Polykova for the first time. I had not yet heard of her, but I couldn't pull my eyes away. Her braided blond ponytail hung down her back all the way to her waist, her skin was tanned, her legs slender but taut, and her shoulders broad but feminine. Her arms also were slender but toned with slight but rippling muscles. She wore a small pair of tight red shorts that hugged the perfect curvature of her butt, and her white top of the same material was snug, revealing the exact shape and size of her firm breasts.

Her coach was hitting her groundstrokes, moving her from side to side. She was pounding the ball, hitting as hard as I had ever seen a woman hit. A glistening sheen of sweat lathered her and she took deep breaths, bouncing on her feet, her ponytail bobbing with each move. Her face had a natural pout, and her forehead was perfectly smooth. Her eyebrows, darker than her blond hair, were furrowed and serious above big blue eyes, focused intently on the ball.

Wang and I stopped beside her court, about the service line, and watched how she stared down the ball like she wanted to either kill or seduce it. She was only sixteen, but I had never seen a woman with such a combination of tennis shots and raw sexiness. There was something supernatural about those high cheeks, her lissome body, her thick, golden hair. I was lost there on my feet, watching her move on that Parisian red clay, hitting ball after ball after ball.

When she and her coach picked up the practice balls, I hoped she might glance over our way, that I'd have a chance to smile at her, to make eye contact, but she never lifted her eyes, staring only at the red clay and the balls she balanced on her red Yonex, bending over ever so gently as she did.

I watched her practice serves for a while until Wang tapped me on the shoulder. "Maybe the draw sheets are up?" He smiled and nodded. I had forgotten he was there. I tore myself away, trying to break the hypnotic spell that she had placed on me, a spell applied without even a sideways glance.

Wang and I waited around the tournament information desk in the lobby for the draw to go up. There were about two dozen players in there, a few young European dudes about my age I recognized from the Orange Bowl, and a few older players, including Dragomir Bochinsky. I thought the old Romanian had retired long ago, and I figured he was a coach hanging around. I had seen footage of him at the U.S. Open, playing Borg no less, in the 1970s in one of those feisty New York night matches, Bochinsky's curly hair resisting his headband, his eyes bulging, and his mustache thick on his upper lip. He still had the mustache, although his hair was thinner on top and not as long. His best year on tour had been 1978, a year after I was born, when he was a finalist at Roland Garros and a semifinalist in Australia.

At ten o'clock a woman pinned up the qualifying draw on a large bulletin board. Most of the players, coaches, and other hangers-on stormed forward to get a look, shoving like wild dogs fighting for raw meat. Wang and I were stuck in the back of the pack, not close enough to read.

After the mob cleared I went up and found my name in the draw sheet—I played Dragomir Bochinsky, second match on Court One, the small, round stadium known simply to English speakers as the Bullring.

I turned and bumped into Bochinsky who had been reading the draw over my shoulder. He glared at me, his eyebrows intense. "Sorry," I said, dropping my eyes to the maroon carpet and slinking away.

A gray sky covered Paris the day of my first match at Roland Garros. Bochinsky and I were scheduled after a match between a slight, blond Czech girl of about fourteen and a bulky woman from Uzbekistan who must have been thirty-five years old. I watched from the hallway by the small locker rooms in the Bullring. The circular stadium held almost four thousand, but there were only about twenty people there, all in the front row behind the players' seats. Both players hit the ball very hard, their shots echoing in the empty stadium. The Uzbek took an early lead with her old-school serve-and-volley game, but she began to wear down while the Czech girl in a flouncy light yellow dress didn't break a sweat as she came back and won the second set easily. The little girl closed out the one-sided third set with a gorgeous dipping crosscourt passing shot and squealed with delight. The Uzbek woman waited at net, shook the girl's hand, and slid her racket into her bag and slouched off alone, down the hallway past me. I don't remember her name, but I sometimes wonder what happened to her. Did she go back to Uzbekistan and get a job teaching lessons? Is she working as a sheepherder? Nobody keeps track of the losers in the qualies—they just disappear from the game like forgotten ghosts.

There was a break between matches while the grounds crew groomed the court. The umpire, a thin Frenchman, climbed up in his chair and called out our names over the loudspeaker in a very officious although effeminate tone, "Bochinsky. Skinner. Court One, s'il vous plaît."

I walked from the locker room onto the court with my big red

Wilson bag slung over my shoulder. I set it down by my chair and shuffled through the eight Pro Staffs I'd brought with me, all freshly strung.

I thought about how in the 1970s Bochinsky had often played with spaghetti strings—a cockamamie string job that was later outlawed. It consisted of strings layered over strings, wrapped so the ball, even when hit softly, would spin wildly. I wondered what sort of bullshit head games he might try to pull on me.

His most famous psych-out was a decisive Davis Cup match he won against John Newcombe in Romania. Bochinsky was a huge underdog, but his spaghetti-strung racket imparted so much spin on the ball that his drop shots would sometimes come back over the net to him like he had the ball tied on a string. The Romanian team had soaked their red clay courts for days until the surface became so soft that their shoes sank into the soil. And with barrels of free brandy, Bochinsky had lured hundreds of shepherds and their flocks of sheep and goats from small Romanian villages into the center of the Bucharest. The drunken shepherds and their braying animals were all crammed into the open end of the national soccer stadium that had been converted for tennis. Bochinsky worked them into a frenzy by raising his hands when he wanted a commotion. Newcombe and the Australians never had a chance.

I contemplated Bochinsky's mythology, waiting there with the umpire, line judges, and ball kids. About ten minutes later Bochinsky swaggered out onto the court, wearing a purple velour warm-up suit and carrying two enormous bags of rackets, one on each arm. A cigarette with a long gray ash dangled from his lips.

He ignored me and tossed his bags down beside his chair and grumbled something in Romanian at the umpire. He sat down heavy in his chair and stared at the red clay court, smoking.

The umpire climbed down from his chair and cursorily shook my hand, and extended his hand to Bochinsky but the big Romanian refused the greeting. The umpire reached into his pocket and pulled out a coin and looked to me and asked, "Heads or tails?"

"Heads," I said, and he tossed the coin up in to the air and watched it drop to the red clay, landing flatly.

"Mr. Skinner has the honors."

"I'll serve," I said.

"Mr. Bochinsky? What side will you take?"

Bochinsky rifled through his enormous white Adidas bag, ignoring the umpire.

"Please get started," the umpire said. He climbed back up into his chair and adjusted the microphone and timidly announced, "Five-minute warm-up."

"What? You cannot start clock until we hit," Bochinsky said. "No time limit."

"Please start the warm-up," the umpire said, his voice pleading, desperate.

"This boll shit," Bochinsky said. "Boll shit."

I walked to the baseline on my side and stood there with a few balls in my hand. Bochinsky acted like he didn't even see me. He took a long drag on his cigarette and flicked the butt over the net and onto my side of the court.

"Mr. Bochinsky, if you do not begin warm-up I am going to give you a warning. After that, a penalty point, and after that, the match will be defaulted."

Bochinsky stood and glared at the umpire and then at me, his eyebrows and mustache thick and foreboding. He took off the purple velour warm-up. He was an ox, large in the shoulders, with enormous forearms and thick, hairy legs. His shirt was loose, concealing his stomach, but his shorts were comical, the old-school white ones from the '70s that were a little tight and much shorter than the baggier kind that I wore. He picked a racket out of his bag, a midsize Völkl, and strode slowly back to the baseline.

After an uninspired warm-up in which Bochinsky slapped balls haphazardly around the court, he put the Völkl away. He dug around in his racket bag and pulled out an old wooden Adidas racket with a small head, a frame that by then was like a museum piece, the light-blond wood painted with red-and-white stripes angled down the throat of the racket all the way to the grip.

The umpire called time, but Bochinsky made us wait several minutes before he took the court and lined up in the deuce side, at least fifteen feet behind the baseline. I bounced the ball, watching him prepare for the return, assuming he would come charging up when I served, but he never moved. He stood there straight-legged, holding the racket at his side, like he wasn't ready to play. I held up the ball in the traditional good-luck gesture and nodded at him. "Serve fucking boll!" he said.

I did, hitting a wide spinner to his forehand. The ball landed just inside the sideline in the service box, not deep, but spun hard at a sharp angle. He didn't move, didn't even look at the ball sliding away from him, but let it go as an ace. The umpire called the score in my favor. Bochinsky moved to the ad court and stood even farther back. With him so deep, I went for a hard ace out wide but missed it by a few inches. I tried to hit my second serve in the place I had aimed the first and missed it too.

"You idiot," I said under my breath. In the deuce court I hit another ace, a similarly good serve that he ignored, and in the ad court I double-faulted again. At 30–all, I hit the same deuce serve to the same result, another easy ace, and had a game point, a game point to win the strangest game of tennis I had ever played. This time I tried to take a big serve down the middle, right up the T, but I hit too hard and it sailed long. I decided on the second serve that whatever I was going to do, I was not going to double-fault, but make the old Romanian son of a bitch play a point.

I spun the ball into the court, squarely in the middle of the box. He stepped to his right, taking the racket back with two hands in a flamboyant backswing, arcing the racket up high over his head and then down low and when my serve arrived he took a long stroke and lunged forward, coming up under the ball in a swing half Björn Borg, half Hank Aaron. He knocked it out of the cozy stadium, and I watched it fly like an airplane into the dirty silver of the Parisian sky. He held the follow-through until the ball vanished, the racket pointing the direction of the landing place.

The crowd, perhaps one hundred people by now who'd drifted in to see Bochinsky, *ooh*ed at the satellite launch of his return of serve. He had a small entourage that burst into raucous laughter, and he turned and bowed to them. He walked to the net after the first game, his mustache curling in a self-satisfied smile.

I crossed to the other side without stopping to take a break. He sat down in his chair, taking the seat like a man in a train station not destined to leave anytime soon.

"Time," the umpire called. Bochinsky did not move.

A minute passed, and the umpire said, "Time, please, Mr. Bochinsky."

Still he did not move. Another minute passed, Bochinsky holding the old Adidas racket up in front of him, examining the strings, straightening them out.

"Warning, Bochinsky," the umpire said, timidly, and scribbled something in his notebook. "The next infraction will result in a penalty."

Bochinsky stood and cursed in Romanian, something that sounded violent and vile. He stepped up to serve and bounced the ball at least twenty times, a pause between each bounce. I was bouncing around on my toes, ready for the serve, wishing he would toss the ball and send it my way. After what seemed like an hour, he released a very low toss and hit a serve wide at my forehand, his motion a violent, quick slash at the ball. I'd never before or since seen a ball spin quite like his serve—it curved into my body, toward the forehand, and did not slice away from me as I expected. I hit the ball off the frame, near the throat, and it flew up high and well wide of the court, bouncing almost into the first row along the sideline. His entourage snickered their approval.

I trudged over to the ad court, shaking my head, trying to understand the spin I had just seen, wondering what sort of string job he was using. I kept my head down, avoiding eye contact with him, and looked at the surface, studying the mark where the ball had bounced, well inside the sideline, a foot short of the service line. I dug in for the return of serve on the ad court, standing right on top of the baseline, and saw him glaring at me. He bounced the ball only once this time and tossed it high into the air and took a long swing, snapping his wrist. I could read from his motion that it was going to be a slow kicker to my backhand. I prepared to move up and take the ball early, leaning in hard and getting my grip right and sliding the racket back to jump on the ball and drive it hard crosscourt. I lunged forward ready to pounce, but the ball hit and bounced like it was made of rubber, like one of those pink little kids' balls known as Super Balls, kicking harder and higher than I could have ever imagined. I was planning to step in and strike the ball at about four feet off the ground but it was six feet high and rising like a helium-filled balloon. I tried to adjust my stroke but again hit the ball on the frame, this one on the top side of the racket head, and again my shot flew weakly and errantly well wide of the court, landing a foot outside the doubles line.

He hit two more serves that confused me with their spins, and I made the costly mistake of trying to step in and take the ball even earlier, which on a hard court or grass might have been a good idea, but on a clay court was the wrong way to play it.

The score was 1–all. The crowd continued to increase, with maybe two hundred people by then, all Europeans out to see Bochinsky. There wasn't a single face on my side.

I served my same deuce court first serve out wide again, but this time he was there and jumped on the ball and hit a hard slice forehand down the line to my backhand. I rushed over to it and the ball stayed low, much lower than I expected, and I sailed a backhand out. On the next point, I double-faulted, then on subsequent points he hit a few more good slice returns, and then charged into net, hitting volley winners. I hit a few safe groundstrokes, just wanting to get a few balls in the court, make him play a longer point or two. On his first break point he responded with the most sinister, backspinning drop volley I have ever seen. Even if I had known he was going to hit a drop shot exactly in the place he did, I could not have gotten enough of a running start to reach that ball. It landed as if made of marshmallow.

The first set continued much this way, his serve and his volleys giving me fits. I stayed up close on the returns and started simply blocking the balls back into the court, and he was ready, either at net—he got up there surprisingly fast for an old dude—or waiting inside the baseline to hit an angled, topspin putaway.

I lost the opening set 6–2. He had run off five of six games, breaking me twice. He started to strut around, throwing back his broad shoulders, smiling, and playing to his swelling group of fans.

I sat at the changeover and thought about my future in the pro game. Would this be it for me? One and done? I took some deep breaths and then decided that I was not going to lose to this *old hacking Romanian son of a bitch motherfucker*. I had seen what Sampras and Courier had done to the old players in previous years: Sampras drilling John McEnroe and then Courier obliterating Connors when the old-school hardass had made his determined and unlikely run to the semis of the U.S. Open. I had seen how in earlier rounds Patrick McEnroe and Aaron Krickstein had let Connors have his way with them, how he got into their heads and played it up to the crowd. I was determined not to let that happen to me. I fired myself up, imagining my bulldog biting into the neck of the largest bull in the herd, knocking it to the ground and hanging on until death.

I served the first game of the second set and focused on nothing but the ball. I put my first serve in and then made him run, hitting deep angled topspin kickers, pushing him back behind the baseline. When he tried to move up, I forced him to take the ball on the short hops of dipping topspin drives. It worked and I won my serve, grinding out a hard-fought game.

We switched sides. He had started playing fast, so I dawdled a bit, making him wait. He scraped around in the clay with his Diadora shoes, his thick mustache rising and falling with his heavy breaths.

He served, and I continued to try to step in and take his serves early, but it was to no avail, the ball spinning too damn much for me to do anything with it. He charged in effectively behind each one and feasted on my weak returns. At 30–love, I did what I should have done earlier and stepped way back behind the baseline. He tried to counter with a very sharp angle wide to my forehand, this time slicing the ball and making it spin away from the court. The ball hit and rose up, spinning like a crazy yellow top, but was still hanging there when

I ran it down and nailed a hard forehand, mostly flat but with a little topspin arc down the sideline, hitting in the corner, well beyond his flailing backhand as he charged the net.

I stayed deep for my return at 30–15. This time he hit the twist, the ball jumping back toward my forehand, the serve that had been giving me so much trouble, but with the extra time to watch the flight of the ball, to let it play itself out and calculate the spin it was taking, it sat up there and I stepped back, at least ten feet behind the doubles corner, and ripped a hard inside-out forehand that crossed the net and dove down toward the red clay with extra topspin. He had charged the net and lunged for the ball, hitting a weak pop-up half volley, a blooping sitter that landed well inside the service line, hanging there for me to attack. I took the racket back for my forehand and charged, running up to the ball from well behind the baseline, my shoulder turned and my right arm in position with the racket like a deadly weapon coiled behind me, focusing on the ball although I could see in my periphery that he had stayed at the net, maybe taking a step back, ready for my shot, his wooden racket in position out in front, his knees bent. I closed in and probably could have won the point with a variety of passing shots, but I did what I had to do—I hit the hardest possible forehand I could straight at his nuts. He flinched and stumbled back into a crouch, covering his genitals, but instead of hitting him in the scrotum for which I had been aiming, the ball popped him right in his stomach as he tumbled backward onto the red clay and sprawled supine on the terre battue.

I turned and walked back to the deuce court and began to get ready for the next return. I didn't raise my racket in the feigned apology most players offer. I wasn't going to say I was sorry—I meant to hit him. He knew it. Everyone there knew it.

Bochinsky walked over to the sideline where he toweled off and changed his shirt, his dark, hairy gut making him look even burlier. After he gathered himself together and finally served at 30–all, I again waited on it and hit a hard, spinning forehand that he could not handle, even though he had stayed back this time, avoiding the net. I won the next point and that is how most of the rest of the match went, with me pummeling groundstrokes from deep behind the baseline, balls that were too hard for him to come in on and gave him trouble on groundstrokes because of his ponderous movement. He tried a few spinning drop shots but I was ready and pounced on them, and took my time putting them away. I knew every move he would make before he did.

I won the second set 6–0, and the final third 6–2. Only near the end did I falter and make a few errors, but by then the match was out of his reach.

I had been so focused that I hardly realized what I had done. I had not seen that Cathy and Wang and a few American players had showed up to watch, and had cheered me on. I don't remember anything other than hitting the ball, the feel of it on my strings.

After I hit a passing shot on the final point, the umpire called the match in my favor and I met Bochinsky at the net. I was numb with victory, still so focused that I could barely speak.

His hand was enormous and he gripped mine hard but with respect and looked me square in the eyes. His glare was gone. "You are better than most Americans I ever play. Most of you country . . . how do you say? Punks. Easy to beat on clay. But not you. Not you. You can play."

One week after beating Bochinsky I was in the first round of the French Open main draw. I had won my subsequent qualifying matches easily, both in straight sets on distant outer courts against players in their early twenties, a Spaniard and a Dane, both pros who had traveled the world but didn't have the games to crack the top one hundred. I played with a confidence unlike I'd had before or since, and I can't explain where it came from other than my affinity for the surface. I loved that crushed brick, and it called up something in me from my very earliest days of hitting tennis balls out there on that red Georgia clay in the pasture-like field that was our yard.

In the first round I had a good draw against an unseeded Swedish player who had never cracked the top fifty after six years on the tour, floating in and out of the top one hundred, his highest finish a third round at the Australian Open. I beat him easily in three straight sets, outlasting him with my heavy groundstrokes, moving him around and keeping him pinned so deep that he could do nothing but push the ball back. I moved in and took his short balls and put them away with heavy spin, running him from side to side. That angled topspin ball had been a shot Harry had worked on with me for hours, as far back as when I was seven or eight years old, encouraging me to move in and take the ball early and whip it crosscourt into the corner of the service box. Harry had placed tennis ball cans as targets in the service box corners, and I practiced that shot thousands of times. That day in Paris, it worked like a charm on the hapless Swede.

~

Reaching the second round of the French Open meant that strangers invited me to parties. Wang had also reached the second round and received the same invitations. So on a Tuesday night he and I went to a disco tucked away on a narrow side street not far from the Arch of Triumph, the door hidden so that Wang and I walked past it about three times trying to find it.

As soon as we stepped in the small dark lobby, I realized we were about as uncool as they come. Men stood around in shimmering shirts and leather pants and stylish suits, not traditional business suits, but funky cuts of all sorts with collars and plaids like I had seen once on a Rolling Stones album cover. I didn't think real people dressed this way; I thought it was only a world created for fashion shoots. We waited in a line in the hallway to check in with the bouncer, a stocky gentleman wearing sunglasses despite the near-dark of the room. I wore a collared, white tennis shirt with blue jeans and sneakers, while Wang had on a strange pair of pleated khaki slacks, high-top basketball shoes, and a tight orange T-shirt that looked like it was made for a woman. I figured we would be turned away for being geeks.

The dude at the door looked us up and down and asked us our names. He checked his list and said, "Yes, tennis professionals." He pointed to his right. "Go through that room, and then down the hallway on the other side."

I led the way past small rooms with black doors, some of which were opened to reveal plush couches and suave couples in black sitting and drinking from martini glasses. They were all lit in a translucent light that made it seem they were swimming in an aquarium. An ominous industrial dance song with a heavy drum beat blared from speakers that seemed to be everywhere. Wang's ever-present smile had disappeared, and his lips were pursed tight together.

In the green neon light at the end of this hallway I spotted Olga

Polykova. She stood there in outrageously high heels, maroon tight pants, and a silvery top that exposed part of her stomach and most of her back, her long blond hair down. I took a deep breath and looked at Wang, whose mouth was hanging half open.

She turned as we approached and recognized us as tennis players. Olga looked at me and smiled subtly. "Hullo," she said, a Russian accent heavy and sweet at the same time, her movements dismissive even as she welcomed us. I stepped up and held out my hand and spoke loudly, "Hey," I said. "I'm Jaxie. Jaxie Skinner, and this is Wang. He's from China."

She smiled bigger and took my hand and I remember thinking how cool hers was compared with mine, her touch sleek and gentle. "It sure is nice to meet you," I said. "Very nice. I'm sure Wang here feels the same way." I looked back at Wang, standing behind me. He nodded and grinned a nervous, toothy smile, but he didn't say a word.

"What is your name?" I asked, although I already knew. She'd won her way into the main draw and had upset a seeded player in the first round. Her photo had made all of the newspapers, and the French TV and BBC News broadcasts had featured her prominently.

"I am Olga," she said, enunciating the words severely, clipping each one tight.

"It's a pleasure to meet you, Olga. You look very nice tonight."

She smiled, and I stood there holding her hand. Her eyes were a lighter shade of blue than I had ever seen before, not the dark or grayish blue of the women I'd known—my mom and sisters were all blue-eyed women, and I have blue eyes myself, sort of grayish, grainy swirls of silver in the blue—but even in the dark of that room Olga's eyes were like a clear winter sky. Her long hair hung loose on her shoulders and when we finally let go she turned her head and I could see blond strands hanging way down, tickling the skin of her lower back.

She looked down the hallway and I followed her gaze and saw a dance floor, people moving around in the flickering lights in the otherwise pitch black punctuated by scattershot flashes of bright light that darted about with the heavy beat of the industrial music, not even music but something like the sound of a giant rhythmic machine. A very tall woman with an acne-scarred face and intensely dark hair approached Olga and said something in Russian without looking at me. Olga's response caused the woman to laugh and then glare at me, and the woman grabbed Olga's hand and began to pull her back down the hallway toward the dance floor. Olga looked back at me for a second and I asked, "Can we dance, later?" She smiled, nodded yes, her teeth showing and her tongue poking out a little bit so I could see its glistening pink tip.

I turned back to speak to Wang who looked at me in awe as though I had just won Wimbledon. "Do you know how to dance?" he asked.

"There's nothing to it. All you have to do is move around to the music."

Wang told me later that he had never been to any Western parties where people had danced, and what he had seen of dancing was only in Boy George videos, about whom he had wondered if he was even really even a boy at all.

Olga and the woman ran off down the hallway toward the room reserved for tennis players. Wang and I followed and watched the dance floor, a scene like many you'll see early in the night at small parties, where only the women are out and the men lurk hesitantly in the shadows. The dozen or so dancers were mostly Eastern European women players and their girlfriends, many of them dancing with one another, some awkwardly, like Olga's tall chaperone, while others were graceful, especially Olga, looking like she was in a high-dollar music video.

Olga spun around and glimpsed me for a moment, a flash in her light-blue eyes. I waited until the song, an interminable dance number, ended. I stepped out and smiled at her and she smiled back and turned toward me and then another song began and we started dancing. I moved my feet around and did this funny move I do raising my shoulders like I'm in the circus and was rolling a ball back and forth from the top of one to the other. She laughed, getting a kick out of my effort, and began to put on these long moves with her arms, like she was blending ballet and yoga and disco, and then she spun and leaned forward and I got a look at her naked back, all lean muscle under taut, tan skin. She bent farther forward and poked out her bottom, shaking it to the beat, and her long hair fell in front of her and almost touched the floor until she straightened up and spun and tossed her hair back. We smiled at each other and kept dancing until the song ended and she hugged me, her perfumed hair falling all over me, tickling my arms. Her tall chaperone danced over and said something into Olga's ear and took her hand and pulled her off the dance floor. Olga waved back at me and our eyes met one last time and she mouthed, *Good-bye*, and they were down the hallway and out the door and gone.

The next morning just before eight I was lying there half asleep, Olga in my head, waiting for my wake-up call. Wang and I had a practice court and then I had a massage scheduled and I was going to come back to the room and watch the tennis on Eurovision and relax, preparing for my second-round match the next day with Raul Fernandez, a Spanish pro who was seeded sixteenth and had been a finalist three years before. He was one of the best European dirt-ballers, a guy who lived for clay court tournaments with his topspin and passing shots and patience, a player who made his money from April through early June and then all but disappeared when the game moved on to the grass of England and then the hard courts of America.

The phone rang.

"Good morning, Jaxie," Cathy said, her voice explosive through the phone. She had a mighty set of vocal cords.

"Yeah."

"How did it go last night?"

"What do you mean?"

"I heard you were having a good time at the party."

"Yeah, it was okay."

"You didn't sleep with that Russian girl, Polykova, did you?"

This woke me up. For a second Cathy reminded me of Sally, my oldest sister, who always asked me about how I treated girls, if I was being good to them or not.

"No, of course not. I only danced with her a little while."

"Well do me one favor, Jaxie." I braced for a lecture that didn't come. "Introduce me to her, let me take you both out for dinner. I would kill to be her agent."

That afternoon Wang and I hit with two French junior players Cathy had found for us to practice with. It was a smart move, because although Wang was the nicest fellow I've ever met on tour, I wanted to practice against a different style. His flat balls were nothing like what I would see from Fernandez, the big topspin loopers he hit, as well as the devious sidespinning drop shot he possessed.

The French kids were arrogant, cocky as all get-out, as cocky as only a sixteen-year-old Paris rich kid can be. They had this attitude that Wang and I were old, has-beens already, and they hit the ball as hard as they possibly could, making a lot of errors, but when they put the ball into the court it was ferocious, hard hit with heavy topspin.

I had four wins under my belt by then, and returning the topspin burners that these kids hit was the perfect preparation for Fernandez's heavy groundstrokes. It was during that practice round that I started to feel invincible. I moved in on the bullets these kids were hitting and started stroking them back harder than they had come, sizzling groundstrokes with enough topspin to keep the ball in the court, just inside the baseline, knocking them back onto their heels. They tried to hit even harder but they couldn't hang with me. I thought, *Who is cocky now, motherfuckers? Who is cocky now?*

That night Cathy took me and Wang to an Italian restaurant on the Left Bank, nothing fancy, but excellent food, loads of pasta. She knew we were both in for tough matches, and I think in her mind this was her farewell to Paris for us because she kept saying things like how proud she was that we'd both won through the qualies and into the second round of the French, more than anyone had expected us to do. Instead of talking about our matches, she talked about the grass court season and what tournaments she had lined up. I asked, "What happens if I win tomorrow?" and she didn't even answer, just went on talking about the upcoming grass events.

At the time I thought she was being a bitch and it irritated me, but now I see it was smart, her way of trying to take the pressure off me and Wang. Because the more you think about a big match, the more you worry about it, the tighter you'll become and the worse you will play.

Although Cathy had avoided my question about what winning my second round match could mean, I lay awake that night thinking about it, clenching my teeth. It meant I would be in the third round, among the thirty-two most elite tennis players in the world, a chance to go even higher in the rankings. I had looked ahead at my draw, something that's never wise to do when you are an underdog, but I studied the sheet closely. The other high seeds in my quarter were out—Sampras and Agassi had both lost early. If I beat Fernandez, I would not have to play one of the world's top ten until the semifinals.

Before the Fernandez match I sat in the locker room in one of the stuffed side chairs, my racket bag next to me and my shoes off, watching players come and go, a men's match and two women's matches ahead of us. I sat there, trying to tune everything out, nervous as hell, thinking scattered thoughts. I tried to conjure up my bulldog but my mind wandered. I thought a lot about my dad.

Up until the French Open, my dad always had been there to wait with me, usually reading a book, perhaps a James Lee Burke novel or a western. He would never stress over the big matches, or if he did, he didn't show it. If I was nervous he might tell me about one of the characters in the books he was reading, relating a joke or passing along something dramatic, like former New Orleans cop Dave Robicheaux getting his testicles hooked up to an electric current while being questioned by an enormous, perverted Neo-Nazi. And then he would tell me how old Dave got out of it.

After several hours I got very sad, sitting there alone in that chair in the locker room in Paris, waiting on a tennis match while the world's best players and coaches swirled about me, scowls on their faces, speaking in languages I didn't understand. I felt like the loneliest man in the world, about to go on court with no one in my corner. My dad was out on a road crew somewhere in Texas, Harry was teaching lessons and not speaking to us, my mom was never into my tennis, my sisters had moved off to Atlanta, and here I was, a surprise to everyone, in the second round of the French Open. My only supporters on hand were a Chinese dude I had known for a week and an agent I had known only a few months.

I went to the bank of pay phones outside the entrance to the locker room and tried to call my dad. I dialed the number of the motel in Dallas where he was staying, reaching the front desk. He didn't pick up. I tried our home but no one answered, the answering machine off, the line just ringing and ringing. I tried Harry's tennis club, but the answering machine with the flamboyant desk clerk's funny message that Dad and I had always imitated picked up. It wasn't the least bit funny that morning—it was the saddest sound I'd ever heard. I held the earpiece of that big black phone to my head and I almost cried. I fought back the tears welling up out of the most intense loneliness I had ever felt in my life.

I stood there until Olga came by, carrying her racket bag. She wore a pink velour warm-up suit and her long blond hair was down, still wet from a shower. "I won!" she said, her English breathy. "I won! I'm into the third round! Can you believe it?"

I put the receiver down and smiled at her, her face as fresh as a newborn baby. She moved forward and put both arms around me and squeezed me tight, right there at the entrance to the locker rooms. "Oh," she said right into my ear, "I am so happy." I felt her body against mine, lean and strong but marvelously supple.

We broke the embrace after a long hug. She smiled at me, her face beaming like I've never seen anyone's, a sixteen-year-old from a Siberian village who had just reached the upper echelon of the world's best tennis players.

As soon as she and I parted, Fernandez and I were called to the Bullring and started our match. He was tough as nails but I played my best, and we split the first two sets. I had a letdown and he won the third set handily and took a lead in the fourth, but I fought back and pushed the set to 6–all.

He jumped out to a lead in the fourth-set tiebreaker but I held off a match point, hitting a running down-the-line forehand winner off a ball that everyone in the stadium, including Fernandez, was certain I could not reach. My forehand zipped over the net post with topspin and sidespin and curved just inside the sideline to the groans of the crowd that was heavily in his favor. Only a small contingent of Americans were on my side, packed into about five rows in a corner, a group of tourists who had never heard of me before then and probably don't remember me now. But they raised hell for me that day, and the support boosted me up when I needed it most.

I pumped my fist after my winner, and then glanced up toward the players' box. I saw Olga's face—so flawless was her skin that she almost glistened like a silvery Christmas ornament—her blond hair pulled back and her blue eyes looking right at me. Her pink lips curled seductively into a smile and she nodded and applauded. With the fourth-set tiebreaker tied at 6 points all, I hit one of the best returns of serve I can ever remember, a ball that pulled Fernandez way off the court. I followed it into the net. He hit a big looping forehand cross-court that I stepped in on and hit an angled drop volley back to the same corner he was rushing frantically from, anticipating me to go down the line to his backhand. My ball bounced softly three times and then began to roll until snagged by a ball boy.

I had a set point on my serve. I lined up and fired my next serve down the T, hitting it with everything I had and making smooth contact. The ball gunned down the middle and hit the center stripe about three inches short of the service line and rocketed past him flailing back at it since he had wrongly guessed I was going wide to his backhand. He dropped his head and I pumped my fist and glanced toward a standing Olga Polykova, her hands above her head, clapping.

My ace had leveled the match at two sets all, and the crowd grumbled and Fernandez complained to the umpire that the serve was wide but he found no sympathy. He slumped in his chair with a towel over his head. I sat up straight and excited, like I was just getting settled into the match, like I was unbeatable.

Despite Fernandez's will and fitness, in the fifth set he began to tire but I just kept getting stronger. His serve faltered, and on his weak second serves I was able to step in and hit aggressive forehands that kept him on the run.

I took a lead of 5–3 to serve for the match. I let my concentration lapse for a few moments and made two careless errors, and found myself down love–30. I had for a moment imagined what it would be like to call my dad and tell him I had won. I should have never done that—Yogi Berra was right about that fat lady's song. Fernandez started to get pumped up for a last stand and the crowd joined in and it felt like all of Continental Europe rallied against me, hoping I would lose my serve and let him back in the match. It was nine o'clock and shadows draped solid across the court although the sky was still blue with the evening sunlight, about thirty minutes at most before the match would have to be postponed due to darkness. A few fat clouds floated above the horizon and the evening sunlight tinted the big air-borne cotton balls with a trim of gold around the billowing white. There was an electric feeling before that point, the crowd rowdy, but as soon as I stepped up to the line in preparation to serve, almost four thousand people gathered in a circle stopped talking and sat perfectly still.

I bounced the ball a few times on the clay and stared at the white center mark. I relaxed and imagined I was back on our home court in the yard in Piney, Georgia, and tossed up the ball and hit a great serve, right into the body, and he struggled with the spin and hit a backhand wide. I then nailed an ace out wide, and at 30–all I hit a big spinner to his forehand and he hit a weak return and I put it away into the other corner.

I held a match point. The crowd buzzed, a few shouts of that "Aaaaaaa-lay-up" sound the French fans make. I thought it was some sort of soccer cheer at the time, but years later I learned it is a distorted form of the word *allez*. I bounced the ball some more, studying the seams of it as I did, that sort of Möbius-strip-like pattern of lines that is really only two number-eight-shaped pieces of felt stitched together around a core of compressed air. I was thinking about the ball at that moment, not about Fernandez and what he might do, or about the pressure that was on me, not about the money that I might win, not about the fact that my match was being carried live back in the states on ESPN and that my father was in a hotel bar in Texas cheering me on, and not even about the sexiest young woman on the planet who was also a kickass tennis player sitting up there in the players' section watching me with covetous, pale-blue eyes. All I thought about was the tennis ball as an object that I completely controlled, just the way I imagine those artists in the Louvre who paint apples and peaches and pears think of nothing but the fruit while the brush is in their hand.

I tossed the ball precisely nine and a half feet into the air and struck an ace right down the T. The smattering of American fans went berserk, chanting "U.S.A. . . . U.S.A.," a cheer that could not be more loathsome to the French. The rest of the stadium crowd applauded reluctantly, but it was the best sound I have ever heard in my life. I looked in Cathy and Wang's direction and raised my right hand and pumped my fist and walked to the net where Fernandez offered only a quick blow-off handshake and grabbed his bag and rushed to the locker room. I shook the umpire's hand and then did the move I had seen the great players do many times on TV, stepping back onto the court and waving to all four sides of the stadium, holding my racket above my head, performing soundless applause by clapping my free hand against the strings.

Cathy somehow finagled a late celebratory dinner for us with Olga, her chaperone, and her coach, a dour Russian. Cathy and I met them at a swanky place managed by some celebrity chef—I've never been able to remember the names of restaurants or cooks—and the maître d' recognized both Olga and me. He asked for our autographs and took our picture with the chef beneath a chandelier as big as a Volkswagen that hung from a pink ceiling trimmed in gold. Olga struck a pose worthy of the cover of *Vogue*.

Olga ordered an expensive bottle of champagne and gave a toast. "To my championship," she said, even though she was only in the third round. She drank two glasses and claimed that she was going to make Chris Evert and Martina Navratilova look like "been-has." Her sexy, exotic heavy voice rose to a high pitch with excitement, mixing mispronounced English with Russian, inverting common phrases. I didn't understand what she was saying half the time, but it didn't matter when she turned those blue eyes on me.

After the check, which Cathy picked up, Olga and I and her chaperone went for a walk around the Left Bank, toward her hotel, the lights of Paris artful and serene. It was late, after midnight, but I wasn't a bit sleepy. When the chaperone went into a café to buy cigarettes, Olga smiled at me, and moved close and spoke in a low voice.

"You should go . . . but come to my room in an hour, number six forty-nine, Hotel Rousseau." She leaned close and pressed herself against me, pointing ahead. "On next street." She reached around and touched the back of my neck, her fingernails lightly tickling my hairline. I nodded, and she arched her eyebrows playfully. I leaned to kiss her, but the chaperone came out of the store and Olga stepped away. I shook her hand and then Olga's and bid them both good night.

An hour later Olga answered her door wearing a plush white hotel robe and white tennis footies with little pink balls dangling from the heels. She said nothing but kissed me and guided me to a big armchair near the end of the bed and sat down in my lap and we began to consume each other in a deep kiss. After a few moments my hands began to reach through the seam in the cotton. She pushed my hand away, stood, and pulled open the robe and let it fall, throwing back her shoulders as though her body was a lost Michelangelo sculpture being revealed to an audience of thousands.

How can I describe Olga Polykova naked without sounding like a fat little mouth-breather who scrawls letters to *Penthouse Forum*? I don't think I can, because she was the true content of many a young teenage boy's wet-dream. I swear she looked exponentially better in person than she did on TV or in photographs, and she looked even better undressed than she did dressed. Olga had a beauty that cameras could not capture. Her skin, luminescent and flawless, wrapped tightly on her frame, muscles ridged and luscious in every nuanced curve, her belly tight and flat. Her breasts were not large but perfectly shaped with red, protuberant nipples. Down below she had a very narrow strip of black manicured pubic hair that contrasted with her long blond mane that fell down her back. She positioned her legs apart so that the moist pink lips of her vulva glistened in the lamplight, beckoning me.

Very soon I was on top of her on the bed, and she acted like she was overcome by a mystical trance. She moaned, so loudly at one point I wondered about the proximity of her chaperone's room, hoping it wasn't next door, and she called out in Russian words I didn't need to understand to know the meaning. The sex didn't last long, but at that intensity it didn't need to. I've never been with a woman who made more noise or who orgasmed more quickly—or at least acted like she did.

We lay on our backs catching our breath. She reached down between her legs and then extended her tongue and put two fingers wet with my semen in her mouth. She swallowed. "Ah . . . eets so good," she said.

That aroused me again and I turned toward her. "No," she said, "stay there. I tell you something." She shifted on her side and nestled in the crook of my arm, her long, blond hair trailing behind her and across the bed. My arm fit around behind her so that I could almost reach the top of her ass with my fingers. I caressed the softness of her lower back, covered in tiny, almost invisible white hairs.

She looked right at me from only inches away, her blue eyes like a deep pool of water in which I couldn't touch the bottom. Her hand moved down my stomach and began caressing my balls, and she held my stiffening penis with a western forehand grip. I could feel a few calluses on her index finger and thumb from where she held the racket.

"Have you seen . . . what you call, swings?" she asked. "With the two chains?"

"A swing set?" I gulped as she continued to move her hand on me.

"Yes. Precisely. Do you in your country when you are children go up to the swings, an individual swing, and spin it? Wrapping the chains together?"

"Yeah, ah, yes, sometimes. Kids do." I was already hard again, and her hand kept caressing.

"Do you spin it so that the chains wind together the more you spin?"

"Yeah, I have. Um, yeah, a long time ago."

"You know how force of chains starts out fast, so chains wind together and the seat spins until tight? And then unwinds, starting to unravel slowly—and then speeds up and unravels fast other way? The chains loosen for a brief moment and then spin back . . . and then chains wind together again?"

"Yeah, I know what you are talking about." I shifted a little so my fingers could reach her ass and I slid my first one into the top of her crack.

"That is what my insides feel like, those chains. Muscles deep inside me . . . they wind and unwind like chains holding up that swing . . . except they are wrapping around your penis." She leaned forward and kissed me. "It feels so good. I love your penis." She gripped me hard, and for a split second I imagined I was the racket she was holding, smacking a hard forehand.

Then she crawled on top of me, and we did it once more, the second of four times that night.

I left her room at dawn, a skip in my step despite a night of almost no sleep following a five-set match. I walked back across Pont Neuf, the river glistening and Notre Dame resplendent in the early-morning light.

That night we had planned to eat together with her mother, who was in Paris but had not wanted to go out and eat with the group Cathy assembled. Olga said she was shy and spoke no English. I met them in the lobby of their hotel. Her mom, a small fortyish woman with a short haircut and a hard face, didn't take to me at all, looking me up and down with a suspicious glare, as though she knew what I had been doing to her daughter. Olga's mother all of a sudden began berating her in Russian. Olga said to me, "Wait, Joxie." She and her mother went back up the stairs, arguing as they did, the mother continuing her fierce diatribe.

I waited there about fifteen minutes, watching tourists pass by, until Olga came back by herself and said that she was sorry, but we would not be able to have dinner together. She said this slowly, staring at the terrazzo floor of the hotel lobby, but then her eyebrows raised and she looked at me with a sly smile. "Come see me tonight. In my room, after eleven thirty."

I started sneaking into her room every night. It was insane how close we became in less than a week, one of those rare relationships where it feels like the other is the reason for which you were put on the earth. She started calling my room about every thirty minutes when we were separated, asking me things like if I thought she should wear a red skirt or a white skirt. At night she always wanted to know if I thought she was beautiful. Whatever I answered, she disagreed with. I would have to tell her she was beautiful over and over until she calmed down.

It was the truth, too. She was stunning. Nowhere on her body did her skin sag or bear imperfections, not even a blemish or a mole except for four large freckles, one about an inch below her left nipple, another one on her collarbone, and the other two on her right ass cheek, just above the curve where it met her leg, like a snakebite. She thought it hilarious when I pressed two fingernails on the freckles and made a slithering snake sound. She had never heard that one before, she said, laughing. And trust me when I tell you, there is nothing better than making the best-looking woman you've ever seen laugh when she is naked.

Although we fornicated like we were in a contest, three or four times nightly, we did in fact get some sleep when pure exhaustion began to set in, about three or four in the morning. We coiled together there on the bed in her room, until dawn crept in and I had to slink back out before her mother came to wake her up.

We won our next rounds, the first Saturday of the tournament, both reaching the round of sixteen. I had a surprisingly easy match against a Colombian player who was a clay court specialist but played an error-riddled match and double-faulted a surprising amount. It's amazing how badly even some pros can play on off days.

We continued our routines during the day of practicing, eating, resting, and then spending the nights intertwined, the relationship known to no one but us. We also continued winning, she her fourth-round match easily and then her quarterfinal match in a miraculous victory over a Spanish veteran who had won the tournament four years earlier. I won my way into quarterfinals after a four-set battle against a tough Czech player whom no one expected me to beat.

My concentration on the court was like it had never been before. I was hitting my groundstrokes as solid and as hard as ever, and players, assuming that I was an American and would be impatient and make crazy errors, that the tennis cloud I was on would eventually evaporate and my game would fall to the rugged earth, simply tried to keep the ball in play and gave me easy sitters that I attacked. I ran them ragged, from side to side to side until I finally hit the closing putaway. After beating Fernandez like I had, I felt like nothing could stop me. That and being naked with Olga Polykova for long stretches of the night, hearing her moan and listening to her breathe while she slept and being able to see every bare golden inch of her, pushed my confidence higher than the Eiffel Tower.

I had called my dad every night, about ten Paris time, near the end of his workday, to tell him about my matches and practices and everything else—everything except Olga. He had been paving roads in Texas, south of Dallas, the whole time I was in France.

After my fourth-round win, he took off from work and flew over. He said he had encouraged my mom to come with him but it was near the end of the school year and she said she could not skip out on her last week of teaching.

His plane ticket, purchased at the airport counter before boarding, cost thirty-eight hundred dollars, but with my winnings we could afford it. I wanted to ride out to the airport to meet him, but he insisted that I stay with my routine of practicing and resting.

I was lying on the bed watching American cartoons with voiceovers —to this day, nothing is funnier to me than Foghorn Leghorn speaking French—when my dad knocked on the door. "Jaxie, boy!" He hugged me, said he was proud of me.

He sat down in an armchair and I saw that he looked exhausted, his face gray and sallow. "Are you feeling all right, Dad?" I asked him. He said the flight had worn him out. He went into the bathroom and stayed in there for a while, so long that at one point I asked if he was okay.

He came out and took a nap on the bed while I watched TV. Even though I was into the quarters and guaranteed a check of at least seventy-five thousand dollars, we shared a room. We had always done it that way.

~

We had plans to meet Cathy for dinner two hours later at a restaurant near the hotel. Dad walked down the street looking around, patting me on the back of my head and neck. "Jaxie and John, two old country boys, walking through Paris." He wore a blue blazer and a buttondown shirt with seersucker slacks and docksiders. I didn't have the heart to tell him he looked like some sort of nautical Matlock.

Cathy was more than her usual excited self at dinner, the restaurant a simple spot with checkered tablecloths and candles in glass globes, telling us that she had landed my first big endorsement. Tag Heuer would pay me five thousand dollars for each match I wore one of their new wristwatches. If I made the final they would give me a bonus of twenty thousand and put an ad with me in *The New York Times* Sunday magazine.

"Does he get the watch for free?" my dad asked, laughing. Cathy said, yes, I did get to keep the watch. She pulled a black case from her purse and handed it to me. The watch sported a large gold face with a woven gold bracelet to match. I almost complained that it was too big, that I couldn't play tennis with a watch this large on my wrist, that it would be distracting and would slide around. I hit a two-handed backhand and it might interfere. But I thought about the money and didn't say anything. Cathy offered to help put it on and she tightened the clasp where it fit pretty tight, but more comfortably than I had expected. I had never worn anything other than a digital watch that cost nine dollars at Walmart.

"This calls for a toast," my dad said. He ordered the cheapest bottle of champagne on the menu. The bottle arrived and the waiter poured and my dad raised his glass and cupped the back of my head with his left hand. "This is to my boy, Jaxie, who has been the hardest-working, sweetest young boy a father could ever want. He was in my lap that day we scraped our court right out of our yard." He looked over to

Cathy and winked and said, "Next time we'll run it north–south." He turned back to me and after a pause, said, "Jaxie, son, regardless of how you do tomorrow, I couldn't be more proud of you. We've traveled a lot of miles, and these are the best miles so far." He choked up, and his eyes watered and his voice broke. I thought for a minute he was going to cry, but he held himself together and said, "I love you, son." Cathy's voice boomed out, "Hear, hear—to Jaxie," and she tipped back her champagne and so did my dad and I.

The rest of the dinner was uneventful, Cathy doing most of the talking as she usually did, my dad a little more subdued after the toast, as if something had risen up in his mind that he had temporarily forgotten about. I ate and nodded and listened to Cathy, occasionally commenting on a match I'd seen, at one point telling my dad that I was sorry my buddy Wang was not here. He had lost in the second round and gone on to England to practice on grass courts. "I bet I would have liked old Wang," my dad said.

After dinner Dad and I walked down a quiet, dark street back toward the hotel. I suggested we walk along the Seine for a look at Notre Dame. He said that I should save my legs, go straight to the room, and get a good night's sleep.

"You can have the bed," I said.

"No, son. I'll just lay out on the floor. Or maybe the hotel has a cot they can roll in for me."

"I'm not—I'm not actually staying in the room tonight. I've met this girl."

"You what?"

"I said I'm staying with this girl I met. She's in a hotel across the river."

He narrowed his eyes at me, a slight smile mixed with suspicion.

"Who is she?"

"Have you been watching any of the women's matches?"

"Yeah, some. Mainly waiting for you to come on, but I've seen a good bit of them I guess."

"Well, it's that Russian girl, Polykova."

His mouth popped open and his eyes widened. "You mean that shit-hot blonde?"

"Yeah, that's her."

"Jaxie, son, how old's that girl? She ain't but fifteen, right?"

"No, she's sixteen."

"Still, that ain't legal in Georgia. They'll lock you up for that."

"Yeah, but this ain't Piney, it's Paris. And I'm only eighteen. She's expecting me in about an hour. This way we both have a bed to sleep in."

Dad didn't say anything. We walked along for about fifty yards, and he followed my lead. We passed a brightly lit corner store crammed with crates of breads and fruits and vegetables and flowers, enormous baskets of roses spilling out the door and onto the street.

"Hold on, boy." He picked a rose from a basket on the sidewalk and went in to the cashier and paid, and then brought it back and handed it to me. "You ought to take your girl a flower. She'll like this. She won again yesterday, didn't she? She's having one hell of a tournament."

I nodded and took the flower, carrying it by my side like a tennis racket. We walked farther on and the view of Notre Dame bathed in soft light opened up to us as we came around the corner. As we walked closer, the gargoyles perched atop it came into view—squat, winged creatures with bored expressions on their stone faces, resting their chins on their palms, staring out over the city.

"Look at those, would you?" Dad said. "Those little boogers would keep any evil spirits away, I'm telling you what. We could use some of those back home. Maybe I could buy some here and take 'em with me."

"What evil spirits do you have to worry about?"

"Shoot, you don't know the half of it, Jaxie. You don't know the half of it."

I thought about asking what he meant, but I didn't say anything.

We reached the railing along the river, across from Notre Dame, and stopped to gaze on it for a while. He put his hand on my shoulder and patted the back of my head and neck, like he had been doing all my life. "I guess you better get on and see that girl." He rested his hand on my shoulder. "Be careful, and do get some sleep. You got a big match tomorrow."

"Yes sir, I will. I'll be back to the room by six or seven. We can get some breakfast, then I've got a short hit at ten. Probably won't get on the court before two . . . Wait till you see this place. It's something."

"It's nicer than John Drew Smith?"

I laughed, thinking of the many junior tournaments we had sat around in Macon with nothing to do but watch Braves games on TV or wander around a half-assed mall. "Just a little," I said. "Just a little."

It was comforting to stand there with my father. As sexy and smooth as Olga was, I really wanted to stay in the room and lie there as we drifted off to sleep with him asking me questions and telling me about something when he was a boy, or recounting one of the many tournaments I had played, talking about how crazy another player or their parents were, or how good a player somebody was, how they excelled at a particular shot. But I had promised Olga I was coming to see her.

"Dad, just go back down that street there, and then take a left on the third street, rue something-or-other. You'll find it. Just give the dude your passport and he'll give you the key."

"All right, Jaxie. Come here." He reached for me and hugged me again, this time tighter than the earlier greeting. "I'd try to talk you out of this if I thought I could. But I was eighteen once, and I know how strong the pull of a young woman can be. Especially one that good looking . . . and shit, she's famous, and I guess you are too. So I know there ain't no way I can stop you."

He paused for a few moments, shaking his head, smiling to himself as though he was thinking of some distant memory of a girl in his past. "You be careful, boy. You be careful."

I walked off along the river and crossed over Pont Neuf, headed for the Left Bank and Olga Polykova's bed. Before I turned the corner I looked back at him. He hadn't moved, had been standing there watching me go, looking at me like I was still three years old.

The next morning at six I crossed back over Pont Neuf, the river almost silvery and blue with the eastern light oozing over the horizon and glistening on the water's surface.

I tapped on the door to our room and Dad was slow getting up, answering only after I rapped a second time. His hair was disheveled and his face tired. "Hey, Jaxie." He moved slowly behind me as I entered the room.

I was tired, more tired than I should have been going into a quarterfinal. "I'm going to take a short nap, Dad. Get me up at eight."

"Okay." He sat down in the chair looking toward the television and zoned out, staring at the floor. I fell into a deep sleep. The night before, after Olga had drifted off, I had not been able to relax, lying there next to her wide awake, worrying about my father and regretting that I'd abandoned him on his first night in Paris. Two or three times I almost jumped up and put on my clothes and came back to the room, but I knew he would insist on sleeping on the floor and I didn't want that.

He woke me from my nap at eight. We ate breakfast in a café—he liked croques-monsieur as much as I did—and then we caught a car Cathy sent for us. Soon I was on the court, practicing with the one of the best French juniors, just hitting a few balls to loosen up and groove my strokes.

Dad sat on the sidelines and watched, but didn't say anything. He had been my very first coach, but my knowledge of the game had long since eclipsed his. If Harry had been there, and I wish he had been, he would have played the coach's role to the hilt, picking thoughtfully at his mustache as he walked around behind me in the back court praising me with encouraging comments.

I finished up my practice after only twenty minutes. I was hitting the ball well, and I wanted to relax. The locker room was surprisingly quiet, with all but 8 of the 128 men who had started the tournament gone, and the doubles draws nearing completion. I sat on a couch in the corner of the locker room and Dad settled into a comfortable armchair with the *International Herald Tribune*. He went through the whole thing cover-to-cover and said it was the best newspaper he had ever seen. He said he wished he could read it instead of *The Atlanta Journal*. After he finished, he went back to the front page and started reading again.

When we got on court about one, the second match of the day, I looked to him in the players' box with Cathy. He nodded and smiled wide, a happy grin, and gave me a thumbs-up.

My draw in the quarters was very opportune, pitting me against a journeyman New Zealander whose best surface was hard courts. His getting into the quarters here was almost as much of a fluke as my run. He was tired from a long five-setter that had stretched over two days. He tried to serve and volley, and when my groundstrokes passed him and my topspin lob left him immobilized, he stayed back and tried to hit winners and he missed wide or hit balls that snapped into the tape. I beat him in three easy sets.

I don't know how I was able to stay so focused in that match, but I played brilliantly. He could do nothing about my groundstrokes. I closed out the match with a long rally in which I worked him wide off the court, brought him back into net on the other side with a drop shot he barely reached, and then spun a lob over his head he could only flail at with his racket.

I raised my arms over my head and looked at my dad and Cathy. My dad's smile, always a big, friendly grin, turned up a notch as he clapped and watched me celebrate with an arm raise before shaking hands with my opponent and then the umpire. I walked over to sign a few autographs and kids pressed tight against the rail and some hollered out my name. I looked over at my dad watching me and realized that something incredible was happening, that I was only *two* matches from *winning* the French Open—not the Georgia State Open, not the Orange Bowl, not even the nationals in Kalamazoo—but one of the four biggest tennis tournaments in the world.

After my match I took a long, hot shower. I wish I'd had a coach or trainer to make me stretch, to work out the stiffness in my legs and arms that had accumulated after more than two hard weeks of tennis, but I was young and stupid, and my dad was never the kind to believe in stretching. When he played baseball, they barely even warmed up at all. Stretching to him was an alien activity, a new-age exercise reserved for hippies and the Chinese. If Wang had been there, he would have told me to stretch although I probably would have ignored him.

While waiting on my massage, I watched TV coverage of Thomas Muster—pronounced *Mooster* in a hard, German way—steamrolling Sergi Bruguera, the Spaniard baseliner who often hit moon balls. Bruguera's game was all topspin and fast feet, while Muster, an Austrian known for his great fitness, pounded the ball. His legs were thick like a soccer star's. He even had muscular arms. His hairline was receding, his head tanned from being on the courts all day, and his expression was one of hostility, an angry set jaw and fierce blue eyes, more like a linebacker than a tennis player. He was seeded fourth, and all of the sportswriters predicted him to win that year.

A locker room attendant called me into the massage room and I went in and lay facedown on the table in my boxers. The European masseuses always thought it strange that I wore boxers instead of going completely nude, but I'm just not cool with a dude, which most of them are, rubbing me down while I'm buck-ass naked. I was on the table for thirty seconds when I fell into a deep sleep, before the masseuse even got there. He woke me up when he started, but then I drifted back off.

As soon as I walked into Olga's room that night, I realized that she wasn't going through her usual disrobing routine, that her semifinal match the next day weighed heavily on her mind. She sat on the corner of the bed in black warm-up pants and a gray T-shirt. I sat on the bed next to her and massaged her shoulders. "Just relax," I said. "Don't think about it."

Her neck was stiff and her shoulder muscles tight. She resisted when I rubbed a little harder. "You are hurting me, stop. I had massage already today."

"Olga, darlin', what you've got to do is to not think about the match. When you are out there, just think about hitting the ball. Don't worry about the score. I know what you've been doing has been working wonders, but Graf has been beating everybody. You are only sixteen, your first big tourney. A qualifier, like me." I paused. She kept her eyes down on the floor.

"I'm going out against Muster without a care in the world," I said, lying. "If he beats me, fine. I've made a lot of money and probably gotten a bid into Wimbledon and then who knows what else this summer. I'm going to keep playing, win or lose. You should do the same."

She looked steely eyed at me, as though she wished I would shut up. "I want to sleep."

She slipped off her warm-up pants but kept on her black thong panties and T-shirt and turned out the lamp. She got into bed, settling under the covers and turning toward the wall. I pulled off my jeans and lay down next to her, thinking that this must be what it was like for married couples, crawling into bed to sleep without having sex.

I could feel the tension in her body next to mine, a good two feet away, and heard her short breaths. She smelled great like she always did, a fresh, flowery scent from lotions and soaps and shampoos she used all over her body and in her thick hair.

I slid over next to her and spooned against her and reached my left hand under her T-shirt, palming her flat stomach. I could never believe how smooth she was, her skin like nothing else I had ever touched.

I lay there for a moment on my side, pressed up against her, aroused. I slowly slid my hand up her belly to her breasts and held one, putting one finger on the nipple until she elbowed me with her top arm and pushed my hand away.

"*No,*" she said, "*sleep.*"

I rolled back to my side of the bed and lay there staring up into the dark at the ceiling, listening to her sharp, angry breaths.

"C'mon, darlin', not once?"

"No, not once. I sleep."

"Please?" I pressed against her again and moved my hand back to her breast. "It helps me to relax."

"No!" she said, elbowing me hard with her left arm. "Let us sleep. I need rest. You must leave very early. Mother here at seven."

I rolled over on my back. It took me a long time to drift off, but eventually I did.

I woke about seven hours later to a tightly strung Yonex hitting the side of my face. I grunted and covered my head and peeked through my elbow to see Olga's shadow and a faint strip of light cutting in through the drapes. Someone knocked violently on the door.

"Hide under bed," Olga whispered. "Ma-ma here."

She then started shouting in Russian, and her mother shouted razor-edged words back at her through the door. The knocks continued, pounding loud and hard.

I slipped under the narrow space beneath the box spring, the carpet thick with dust. She threw my clothes to me and I slid as close to the wall as I could. She then stuffed a blanket down, closing me up in there like I was in a tomb.

Olga unlocked the dead bolt and her mother charged in through the door. They shouted, sounding like they were threatening to cut off each other's heads and shit down each other's necks, spelling out in great detail of how they would do it. I heard a slap, although I'm not sure who hit whom, and then the door slammed. Olga yanked out the blanket and looked under the bed at me. "Get fuck out of here."

I dressed and hustled down the stairs, hurrying along those narrow streets and back across the Pont Neuf to our hotel, brushing dust and lint off me as I walked.

I knocked on the door to our room and woke up my father. "Morning, Jaxie," he said, forcing a smile, looking as old and tired as I had ever seen him. He sat on the edge of the bed and stared at the floor while I got ready.

Even though I was the first player out on a practice court that morning, about three hundred people lined up to watch. Before we started hitting, the junior who had been my practice partner all along asked me to pose for a photo. His parents and friends were there, and all were very respectful, even applauding when I walked out onto the court.

We started to hit, but I couldn't concentrate, going through the motions like a zombie. Every time I swung the racket I thought about

Olga swinging her Yonex down on me while I was lying there sleeping, the strings bashing against my head like I was the tennis ball.

A huge crowd was pouring onto the grounds, buzzing with the excitement of the women's semifinals. I cut the practice short and rounded up my dad and we headed out of there, eluding a few British reporters who were much more insistent than usual on talking to me. I assumed that's what happened when you reached the semis, but I wasn't in the mood to talk. I needed to rest and settle my mind before my match with Muster the next day.

Back in our hotel room, Dad and I settled down to watch Olga's match on TV. The only broadcast we received was in French, but I heard them say my name a few times in the introduction, which seemed very strange to me. Why would they be talking about me so much in the introduction of a women's match? I figured perhaps they were comparing us as unlikely semifinalists, young qualifiers out of nowhere.

I knew Olga's match was over in the very first game when Graf hit a second serve down the middle at 30–love and Olga stepped up and nailed one of her trademark two-handed flat backhands crosscourt that had overpowered previous opponents. Graf took a step forward *inside* the baseline, hit the ball early with her elegant one-handed backhand crosscourt at an angle that Olga, who had shuffled back to the middle of the court, could only watch. The ball zipped past her and lodged into red courtside geraniums.

"Damn, she might be in trouble today," Dad said.

"Yeah, I'm afraid so."

It became a women's tennis mercy killing. We didn't say much else for the rest of her match, and occasionally I would hear my own name spoken among the swirl of French. Olga's stride, normally with shoulders high, slumped, and her face looked shell-shocked. Graf blitzed her 6–0, 6–1 in only forty-two minutes.

After her match ended, my dad said he wanted to go for a walk around Paris and that I should take a nap, watch the other women's semifinal, and rest. I wanted to go with him, but he insisted I stay off my feet. He reminded me to keep drinking water and eating the bananas he had bought for me at a corner fruit stand.

I stretched out on the bed and started to drift into a nap with the mellifluous commentary turned down low. I slept for maybe twenty minutes before the phone rang. It was Olga, her voice cracking. "You, you son bitch motherfucker cocksucker."

"Hey tough match," I said. "Graf is a great player. You'll get her back one day."

"Fuck you. You headshit. You headshit. Ma-ma knows about us. Everyone does. We in London newspaper . . . pictures leaving hotel . . . us together through the window. Undressed."

"What?"

"Reporters everywhere before my match. I hate you. My mom say she will have Bratva kill you. You ruin me." She sobbed.

"I'm . . . I'm sorry."

"My father's ghost spit on you. I never speak to you again. If you see me, you cannot come within one hundred meters . . . you will be arrested."

She hung up, and I pictured her slamming down the earpiece of a pay phone, the black one right outside the locker rooms.

I sat there for a while in a daze, trying to make sense of what she said, staring blankly at the second women's semifinal.

About ten minutes later Cathy barged into our room, a newspaper in hand. "Jaxie, have you seen this?" She handed me the paper. Big red letters were splashed across the front of a British tabloid that read UNDERAGE TENNIS LOVEFEST! The period on the exclamation point was a swollen, throbbing heart. The rest of the cover was a hazy picture through a hotel window. Silhouetted in the window was the unmistakable naked back and long, blond hair of Olga Polykova, her arms raised, the motion making it obvious that she was posing for someone in the room.

"Open it up, it gets worse."

I turned to the center section to see a two-page spread, this time with my photo leaving the hotel, and then one of me on court. A smaller inset of the cover with Olga's naked back was paired next to one of her from a match raising her arms, almost the same angle, so readers could compare the two and identify her as the one in the hotel window. There was the snapshot of us posing with the chef beneath the chandelier at the restaurant. And beneath that was a photo so lewd that even a British tabloid would not put it on the cover. They ran it hazy and small in the bottom, a shot of Olga holding her hands cupped in front of her mouth, unclear as to what she was doing. But I knew, and perceptive readers could study it and figure it out—she was giving me a blow job.

I stared at the photos, Cathy chattering away, "Couldn't you have at least closed the curtains?" I ignored her and read the story headlined, PROWLING SEXY SIBERIAN PUSSYCAT ENSNARES AMERICAN REDNECK TENNIS PRO. The article held her up to be the best-looking woman on the planet and me an undeserving dipshit from the backassward American South who could hardly read. The writer presented our case as evidence to the painful ignorance of beautiful women and the ultimate demise of the appreciation of British men of letters, concluding as though our relationship had sealed the decline of Western Civilization.

"Jaxie, I'm so pissed off about this," Cathy said. "You know what this means, Jaxie? You've got to beat Muster tomorrow. You've got to beat him. You can do it. And this will show the world that you are a deserving player."

She kept talking, going on about how the British press were scoundrels, how this was an invasion of privacy and we should sue, how I could shut them all up by winning the tournament. *All* I had to do was win the tournament, she said, and then after Wimbledon I could go to America and be a great hero who could join the Davis Cup team with Sampras and Agassi.

I let her ramble for a while. I reread the article and couldn't help but admire the shots of Olga, her slender but muscular back, the way her hair fell all about her face as she went down on me. I missed her touch. I wondered if the Russian mafia would really come calling.

Cathy would not stop talking no matter how much I ignored her, so I put on my shoes and left the hotel, leaving her in the room. I walked down along the Seine and past the Louvre and up the Champs-Élysées and stared at the bright afternoon sky. People began to recognize me and point, and I realized that I was walking the streets in my tennis outfit, my white shorts and the red shirt and my Nike tennis shoes, exactly what the French public who had flipped on the television to watch my matches would have seen me wearing. I began to run. I knew it was a waste of my legs, but something just told me to run the approximately two miles back to our hotel. I kept my head down and my legs and arms pumping. I was too ashamed to look these French strangers in the face.

I ran along the path by the river, passing tourists. It felt good to run, to get out of the room where I had been sitting all afternoon. I worried about Olga and wondered if all of the shit I was into because of her was worth it. Then I thought about her body and our sex and

I knew damn well it was worth it. I wondered if it was true that she would never speak to me again.

Back in the room, my dad was there alone, the newspaper spread out on the small desk in the corner. He was sitting in the chair, watching highlights of the women's matches with the sound turned down.

He shook his head side-to-side. "Damn, Jaxie, this is a mess ain't it? I'm glad your mama ain't here."

I didn't say anything.

"I had to run Cathy out of here," he said. "She was driving me flat crazy, carrying on. She's worked up as hell, wild as a buck. Says you've got to win the tournament now. I liked that woman up until today."

"She'll be all right," I said.

"Yeah, but you . . . you need to get you some rest. I'll go out and get you some dinner later, so nobody harasses you."

"Aw, I'll be all right."

"No, you stay in tonight. I'll pick up some pasta for you. You've done been running around this afternoon. You got to save your legs."

"Shit, dad, I can't stay in this room all night. I gotta get out."

He reared up, standing and pointing his finger. "Dammit, boy, you listen to me. You've got a hell of a chance at something here, but you got to rest and stay in tonight. You're staying here."

I had seen plenty of screamer parents who yelled and complained about the smallest things. Olga's mom was that way, one who threw a fit about every detail. Ultimately her daughter ignored her and ran wild, doing whatever she wanted. But when my dad yelled, it meant something. I respected his anger.

We spent that evening in our hotel room eating pasta from Styrofoam containers, drinking water and this terrible brand of bottled iced tea that he'd found. We flipped around on the television, the potpourri of channels—French, German, English, Spanish, and Italian. The English channel was the most boring, showing either soccer news that we cared nothing about or history pieces about Churchill or sitcoms that were not funny at all, only old Brits with bad teeth making peculiar faces around a drawing room.

We kept flipping until we came upon the Italian channel showing an old video of a spring-break bikini contest from Panama City Beach, Florida. Italian voices had been dubbed over, so you would hear the voice of a buxom college girl with big hair and bigger boobs in a string bikini with a high southern accent starting to say something like, "Hi, I'm Tammy . . ." and then her voice would be blocked out and an Italian woman would come on and speak sultrily in the language that was Dante's. My dad and I thought this was the funniest thing we had ever seen. The video featured southern college girls of the kind my dad and I both knew, the kind of girls that grew up in Piney, the kind of women we had seen in Atlanta. It seemed like a validation of our own culture that the Italians, with the sexy and sophisticated women from the land of Leonardo da Vinci, would put this program together featuring the South's finest girls from Spring Break 1985 in the Redneck Riviera's capital city. To them, I guess, these country girls were international women. We laughed and laughed about this, my dad doing an imitation of the girls talking and then jumping into the Italian voiceover, mimicking the male announcer who, when the women's interviews were done and the girls went into their poses, would pronounce, "Magnifico! Fantastico!" as the camera panned slowly over their bulging body parts.

The show ended at ten and dad flicked the television off and we chuckled about it for a while longer. "All right, bedtime," he said, and he settled down to the spot on the floor he had made for himself with a pile of clothes and two extra blankets and pillows. He had taken the small, dim lamp from the desk and set it beside his spot so he could read.

"Get you some sleep, Jaxie. I'll be just fine right down here."

I drifted off surprisingly fast, my mind exhausted to the point of blankness, no time for my customary tennis rally dream.

I woke up in the morning nervous and ashamed. I didn't feel rested at all. I worried about playing Muster, and I worried about the repercussions of the story about me and Olga. I decided to skip my practice session, arriving only an hour before the match. Sitting in a corner chair in the locker room, I tried to pump myself up with visions of my bulldog, but I couldn't hold the thought.

"Jaxie . . . Skinner," I heard the attendant call. I stood, my dad patted me on the back, and I headed down the long hallway, racket bag slung over my shoulder. The blue French sky opened up wide and bright when I followed Muster out onto the court. The respectful applause they gave made me think that I could put my problems with Olga behind me, that adrenaline would take over and I could play another good match. I had beaten Bochinsky and Fernandez, masters of the clay, why could I not take out Muster? Muster, an Austrian, was unpopular with the French, so the crowd, much to my surprise, cheered for me. A few hissed when he was introduced and again when he won the coin toss.

He elected to receive and I held my serve in a game with three deuces, featuring some fierce rallies, crosscourt groundstrokes pounded at each other. I stopped to catch my breath after that long first game. I had ignored the crowd thus far, but then I looked around and I could see people courtside watching me, some snickering, talking about me and Olga, I was sure of it.

That first game was my highlight reel for the day. Muster took over and I just couldn't compete. The power and weight behind his ball was overwhelming, groundstrokes that stung my hands. I was so worn down that there was no way I could play well enough to win. He was too strong, too fit, and hit the ball too heavy for me. There was no bullying that sumbitch.

Counting the qualies, I had won eight matches in a row to reach the final four. But in spite of my miraculous run that earned me $125,000 in prize money and allowed Cathy to net another $15,000 worth of endorsements, all anybody remembers about me at that French Open is that I fucked Olga Polykova, and what happened following the Muster match.

After Muster won the last point and my run in Roland Garros was over, the crowd gave me a warm round of applause, somewhat undeserved I thought for my losing effort. I went straight back into the almost empty locker room and took a hot shower and went into the massage room and lay facedown on one of the tables and fell into a deep sleep.

I don't know how long I had been sleeping when my dad came back and woke me up, nudging my shoulder and saying my name, "Jax—ee," the long slow way he had always said it. "Jax—ee, son, get up. You gotta do your press conference."

From the fourth round on, reporters had gathered in a classroom-sized space off the locker room where I had been required to answer inane questions like "What happened out there today?" and "How do you feel?"

I had not enjoyed my first two group press conferences, the British all but accusing me of being the biggest fluke in the history of the game—all of those wankers were jealous that they didn't have a British player doing well—and that was after matches I had won. I should have known better going in there after losing to Muster. Cathy, who had thought of almost everything else, had not prepared me for interviews. I needed to keep my cool, but I was in no condition to think straight. With everything that had been in the paper about Olga and me, it would have been wise if I had just blown off the press conference and paid the ATP fine.

Instead, it got ugly.

That video has been replayed many times, my face red and yelling "Fuck you, man" at the British reporter who asked me if I was a sex criminal. He looked like he was about sixty-five years old but I charged into the row of chairs and pushed him, knocking him out of his chair, sending his horn-rimmed glasses flying.

Tournament staff seized onto me and pulled me from the melee. They hustled me out of the room and my dad got into it with an assistant director, a squirrelly little French dude who threatened to ban me from the tournament forever, yelling that I should go back to "Redneck America" and not return to Paris, that I should drive in NASCAR or play baseball or some other asinine American sport, but not tennis, and not in France. My dad shoved him to the ground and reared back his fist to hit him but the coward put his arms over his face. I would have gone ahead and let loose with the punches, but my dad was too nice of a guy.

That night my dad and Cathy and I went out for a last dinner in Paris. I could feel the eyes of everyone there looking at me, whispering and pointing. No one asked for autographs or photos, and that was fine with us. Cathy laid out the rest of the summer for me, the schedule I would play and names of practice partners. She also had already negotiated a five-thousand-dollar fine for me with the ATP and issued a public apology to the British press on my behalf.

She recommended that I hire a coach, and had set up meetings with a few prospect in London. I asked if Harry could coach me, and Dad also thought it was a good idea, but Cathy was in strong opposition to him. "He's never coached at this level," she said. "You need someone who knows the ropes, and has been out on tour."

She was staunch in her position, and we ultimately gave in and agreed with her—not out of any strong belief that she was right, but we knew we were not going to change her mind. And we were too tired to fight.

After dinner, my dad and I bid Cathy farewell. He wanted to walk back through the Left Bank and along the river and take one last look at Paris, the buildings bathed in warm glows and the wear of time tangible on everything from the wooden shutters to black wrought-iron railings. The evening was clear, a gentle breeze blowing, the sky soft and stars dim overhead.

We walked along the Seine and in the direction of the Eiffel Tower. My father declared Paris his favorite city in the world, glad that it wasn't anything like Atlanta or Dallas, the two big cities where he had spent most of his time, worlds of reflective glass and concrete where he had paved highways and spent nights in prefabricated motels overlooking busy interstates.

He in particular liked the Eiffel Tower. "Look at that thing, Jaxie, all that steel wound up and bolted together, lit up with them lights. Can't believe they were going to make it temporary. Who in their right mind would have wanted to tear that thing down?"

We stared at the tower for a while from the edge of the river, and then crossed back over and walked along the Champs-Élysées, admiring the Arch of Triumph before turning back toward the glass pyramid in the courtyard of the Louvre.

"Them fellas back then knew how to build stuff," he said. "It ain't like today . . . with the technology and the glass and the plastics, everything built on the cheap and in a few days, and then on to the next crappy project. People back then took pride in their work."

We walked around the pyramid and studied it from all angles, looking up to the grand windows over the courtyard, contemplating that inside was billions of dollars of art spanning back through all of history, everything that man could imagine stored there, either hanging on the walls or tucked away in boxes and climate-controlled rooms.

"Well, that is something else, I tell you what," my dad said. "I'm going to miss gay old *Paree*."

"Yeah, you ready to head back?" I was exhausted, ready to put France behind me.

"Okay, son, let's go. I'm flying out very early in the morning. We won't have much time to talk then. There is something I need to tell you."

"What?"

We had been walking away from the pyramid through the courtyard of the Louvre. He stopped and I did too. I moved close to hear him, and he started to say something and then paused, as though he couldn't get the words out. I noticed his eyes were getting a little misty, and he looked one hundred years old, his face quivering a little, his hair grayer than I had ever seen it.

"Your mama." Again he stopped, choking up. "Your mama and I have separated. We didn't want to tell you and get you all upset before the tournament. She's filing for divorce, and I ain't gonna fight her."

I should have seen it coming, but I was stunned by this news. I was eighteen and so wrapped up in my own tennis that it never occurred to me that my parents would divorce. Even though my mother and I were not close, my parents were the one constant in my life.

We started walking again. He began to tell me the whole story, about how this had been something my mother had wanted for years, how they had both been unfaithful, how they had sort of an unspoken understanding that once I moved out of the house and on my own that they would get divorced. He said he didn't want it, but my mother was very involved with another man, that she might just marry him and move to Atlanta. There was nothing he could do to stop her. I didn't know what to say, so I didn't say anything.

Back at the room my dad packed his suitcase methodically, and laid out his clothes for the next day. I insisted on letting him have the bed, and he took it. I didn't have to play for a few days, and could sleep all day after he was gone.

We said good night and flipped off the lamps. I had begun to drift off when he sat up on the side of the bed, and looked down at me, his face lit by a narrow streak of the hallway light shining in under the door. "I want you to know one thing, son. I'm proud of you, boy. You played like a man over here. The top four in the world you are, at least for this tournament, for this week. I knew you were good, but I never thought you'd do this well. You just got to keep your head about you. Don't let women get you into trouble. You are young. You got a bright future ahead of you—*if* you use your head."

I nodded up at him, and he continued.

"You've always been a good son to me. I can't blame you for the trouble that woman got you into. Any normal man with a pair of balls would've done the same thing. But remember, boy, women can cause you to do crazy things, to hurt yourself. So be careful. You are my boy. I love you."

"Thanks, Dad," I said, and he reached over and patted me on the head like I was three years old again.

That is the only time I remember him telling me he loved me, even though I know he always did. I didn't tell him I loved him back. But I didn't need to. He knew I did. I was his boy.

My game plunged downhill fast as I tried to transition to grass courts, a surface on which I had never played, my mind muddled with thoughts of my parents' divorce and the aftermath of Olga. It was a bad combination, the slickness of ryegrass and the emotional weight I carried on my shoulders. I wished my dad could have traveled with me, but he had work to do on a project in Texas. At least Wang and I could practice and eat together, but for the most part it was a lonely time in cold and rainy England, home of the shittiest summers on the planet.

After three days of rain delays, I lost in the first round of a small tournament to a player I had never heard of, ranked well out of the top one hundred. I returned serve like a dog. I needed to win at least one match in the final preliminary event before Wimbledon to move my ranking up high enough so I could get an automatic bid into the main draw. The coach Cathy hired didn't help me one bit. He was a know-it-all who talked too much, and I ignored him from the get-go.

Wang and I checked into a dumpy hotel on the outskirts of London near the final prelim site. After practicing and eating dinner, I went back to my tiny room and lay splayed out on the single bed, bored to death of British television, waiting for my dad to call and worrying about my match the next morning.

The phone rang.

"Hello."

There was long pause on the line, common with transatlantic calls back then.

"Dad?"

"No, Jaxie, it's your mom."

I had not talked to her since Dad told me the news of their divorce. I didn't say anything.

"Jaxie, I've got some bad news." Her voice became weak, cracking at the end of the sentence.

"What?"

"It's John, your dad. He's . . ." I heard a sob, and I went cold. "He's had a bad heart attack. In Dallas. He's in the hospital, but not conscious."

I took a deep breath.

"The girls and I are flying out this evening. You need to come see him in the hospital there. He may not . . . he may not last much longer."

I didn't say anything, and I could hear her sniffling.

"I'm sorry, Jaxie."

There was another long pause, and then she started telling me about a flight she would book for me, but I couldn't listen to the details. I hung up on her midsentence and went for a long walk in a cold, dark rain, staring down at the sidewalk, water soaking through my clothes. Three times I looked the opposite way—left when I should have looked right—and almost stepped out in front of oncoming cars that zoomed my way on the wrong side of the road.

I returned to my room after a few hours and called my mom back and jotted down the details of the flight and the hospital. Early the next morning I flew from the wet mist of London to the unrelenting sun of a Texas day in June.

The cab ride from the Dallas–Fort Worth airport to the hospital seemed to take longer than the ten-hour flight, as though it was a hundred-mile journey through flatlands with no trees, searing heat rising off the asphalt in visible waves. As mile after mile of highway rolled under me, I worried that my dad would die before I reached him.

At the hospital my mom and sisters hugged me but I couldn't reciprocate their affection. Since Dad told me the news of the divorce, I had ignored a letter from my mom and phone calls from my sisters. My dad had been unconscious since his heart attack two days before, and doctors didn't know if he would ever wake up.

I went into his room. He was flat on his back in the bed, eyes closed, a feeding tube in his mouth, wires attached to his chest and temples, an IV in his arm, screens all around monitoring his vital signs. He skin looked gray and his body weak, like someone other than my dad.

I held his hand in mine, the way you would shake someone's hand, and put my left hand on his forearm. "Dad. *Dad.* It's Jaxie."

He didn't move.

"Dad. It's me. Jaxie. I'm just back from London."

His hand was cold and I squeezed it and rubbed his arm. "Dad, I've got a good shot at getting into Wimbledon's main draw. You gotta get better, come help me deal with the British press. They're already writing about me, harassing me. I'm ignoring them best I can, but I need your help."

A nurse came into the room and stood against the wall, watching me. I didn't know what to do, so I just kept talking. I spoke louder. "Dad, you'd like London. I'm sorry you're not there. It's not as pretty as Paris. It's cold, but you'd like the newspapers. The food's not as good, but there are a lot of Italian and Chinese restaurants."

I thought I heard one of the machines beep, but figured maybe that was routine.

"The TV is terrible. No Italian channels. And I don't like the grass courts. Too slick to move. I'm having a hard time with the footing. My buddy Wang has a great game for the grass, but I don't like it. I like red dirt a lot more than grass."

I imagined my dad when he was young and vivacious, when we drove all over Georgia, chasing tennis balls.

"Red dirt is what I like. *Red dirt.* Remember that?"

One of the machines started beeping fast, and his eyes opened halfway and he turned his head just a bit to the right, a barely perceptible move, restricted by the feeding tube obstructing his mouth. I squeezed his hand. "Red dirt. You remember, Dad? Don't you?"

The machine beeped faster and I could see the lines on one of the screens rising and falling rapidly. His eyelids twitched and I saw a spark in his eyes, an acknowledgment that he heard me, that he remembered.

I turned and looked at the nurse. "Can't you get this tube out of his mouth? He wants to say something."

"I'll have to check with the doctor," she said. "It reaches all the way down to his stomach." She went out the door, and I heard her speaking in the hallway. I turned back to my dad and squeezed his hand again, rubbing his arm, but then all the machines began to beep and a red light came on and the spark in his eyes faded, becoming cold and vacant as my mom and sisters barged into the room.

I told him I loved him, but it was too late.

The service overflowed the small chapel at the funeral home in Piney, and afterward a slow procession of what seemed like every car in town followed the hearse and the limo that carried my mom, my sisters, their husbands, and me to the rural cemetery beside the Methodist church that my dad had attended as a child. His parents were long dead, but my great-aunt and -uncle still lived nearby in a white farmhouse on the edge of a cow pasture. It was only about two miles from our house by gravel roads, but I had not been over there in years.

I watched the pall bearers use ropes to lower the coffin into the bottom of the red dirt hole. The preacher said a few words—what, I don't remember—while the sun beat down and everyone fanned themselves with programs and wiped sweat off their brows.

Back at our house, the kitchen brimmed with chocolate cakes and pies and dishes of deviled eggs, potato salad, green bean casseroles, ham and biscuits, and fried catfish. People had been bringing food by since the obituary had been read over the local AM radio station, announced in church, and published in the *Piney Post*. I took off my tie and I changed into shorts and a T-shirt and sat down at the table and started to eat, ignoring our company. I ate four ham biscuits and eight deviled eggs and huge helpings of potato salad and the casserole, and then two pieces of the catfish and one piece of chocolate cake.

I sat on the couch in a daze, watching a baseball game with the sound muted. My sisters' husbands tried to talk to me about Paris and Wimbledon, but they were golfers and their knowledge of tennis could fit into a thimble. Their ignorance didn't stop them from trying to act like they knew what they were talking about, parroting whatever they had heard announcers say. They were native Atlantans and had always regarded people from Piney as simple folk—the "salt of the earth," they'd call us. My dad described them as men he wished he could buy for what they are worth and sell for what they *thought* they were worth. I just nodded as they spoke but didn't respond. I couldn't have carried on a conversation with them if I had tried.

The next day, after the lunch plates were put away, we held a family meeting around the dining room table to decide what to do with the house and my dad's property.

I sat and waited on the others to gather and looked out the window as a car came up the driveway and parked. It was a silver Mercedes convertible and the driver was a man with a full head of gray-white hair, parted on the side. He wore an expensive red golf shirt and shiny black slacks. I could see as he came closer that he wore a gold Rolex watch and also a thin gold chain around his neck.

"Who the hell's that?" I said.

"Oh, George is here," my mom said. She had been gathering some papers in the den and hadn't seen the car arrive.

"George? Did you hire a lawyer?"

She looked at me and took a deep breath. "No, Jaxie, he's my—my friend. I want you to meet him. He's going to be a part of my life. Our lives."

I felt ice cold. "I . . . I can't believe you are bringing *him* here," I said. "*One day* after we put Dad into the ground. We just covered him with dirt."

She stepped closer to me and put her hand on my shoulder, but I shrugged it away. My eyes were locked on hers. I had never been as furious in my life. I noticed that she had painted her eyelashes darker, her face had a little more color, and she wore her long blond hair down with a bit more curl than the day before.

"Jaxie, son, you know that your father and I had been estranged for a long time. You'll like George. He's very smart. He's a businessman, but he also is a playwright, and he owns a theater in Atlanta. He writes poems too. I met him in a class several years ago."

My sister Ruth's husband spoke up. "George Tolbert is a *big deal* in Atlanta, Jaxie. His firm is the largest privately owned accounting firm in America. And he owns a big insurance business. He's got a lot of pull at the state capitol too."

Ruth chimed in. "And to think he's smart and likes poetry and plays. He's perfect for Mom."

I had the urge to leap across the table and start punching, but I contained myself. I shut my eyes, clenching my fists in my lap.

My mom opened the kitchen door and her new man came in and she hugged him. I didn't get up, but kept my face turned down toward the floor.

"Jaxie," she said. "This is George."

I didn't move or say anything, barely even glanced his way. He looked to be about seventy years old, almost two decades older than my mom. He approached me, holding out a hand with manicured nails. "Jaxie, son, it's my great pleasure to meet you." His voice was deeper than I expected. "Congratulations on your tennis success."

I avoided eye contact and shook my head from side to side in a short, quick motion. I wasn't about to shake his hand.

He stepped back. "Son, I understand you are hurting. I'm sorry for your loss. I am."

I looked up at my mom. "Let's do what we have to do," I said. "I gotta get back to London."

"Well, Jaxie, I know you do, but we've got a lot to talk about." She took a seat, and George sat next to her, sitting farther back from the round oak dining room table than the rest of us. He leaned toward her and rested his hand on her back.

"It shouldn't take that long," I said. "I want the house—and the land here."

"But Jaxie, I'm moving to Atlanta and you won't be in Piney," my mom said. "I thought we'd sell it and split the money. There's a lot of land, almost two hundred acres, and it's worth a lot."

"No, we should keep it. I want it. This land has been in Dad's family for generations."

"I figured you would want to live in Atlanta, or maybe Florida. Isn't that where tennis pros go?"

"No, I want to stay here. I got my own court here."

"I don't think we can, Jaxie. We need to sell. There's a lot of debt."

"I'm not going along with that."

"We need to work it out. Let's talk about this."

They did talk about it, for at least an hour, my mom and my sisters and their husbands doing all the talking about why we should sell and pay off the debt and split what remained of the proceeds. It sounded as if they had practiced. George did not speak, but I could see him nodding his big head of hair and smiling smugly in approval at what they were saying, as though he had coached them to say it.

Mom produced a folder with paperwork: They had an Atlanta Realtor picked out, a friend of George's. I didn't know much, but I knew that I was old enough to be classified as an adult and that if I didn't sign, the house didn't sell.

"I'm going to live here," I said. "And you can't make me sign shit."

Sally's husband, a middling lawyer named Roy who often had white spittle in the corners of his lips, said there were "legal ramifications" to what I wanted to do, and that I should be careful.

I started to speak and tell him to be careful, but George leaned forward and pulled up to the table, joining our circle. His voice was deep and resonated, full of confidence, as though he was the ultimate decider. "Jaxie, son, you should listen to Roy, listen to your mother. You don't want to cause problems that will bring this into court. Families shouldn't fight with each other this way. Your father wouldn't have wanted this. I think *you*"—he raised his finger and pointed at me—"understand that."

I stood up and slapped his finger. "Don't tell me what I understand, cocksucker. And quit calling me *son*. I ain't your son, and never will be. This house will be here when I get back. I made some money, pretty good money, in fact. I can afford a lawyer if I need one. I'll buy all your asses out. So don't think you can fuck with me."

I turned and looked my mom straight in the eye.

"And you. You were leaving anyway. You were divorcing Dad. And now you have the gall to bring *him* here." I pointed at George. "He's rich. You don't need the money. And Dad would have wanted me to have the house, if that's what I wanted. And it *is* what I want. I *am* keeping it."

I left the room, packed my clothes, and drove my dad's Lincoln to the Atlanta airport. On the long flight to London, I kept my house keys in my front pocket.

Two days later I was exhausted, hitting with Wang on the wet grass of a worn practice court near Wimbledon, the day before the first round of the qualies. Despite my success in Paris, I missed Wimbledon's main draw by only a few ranking points and the All England Club was not inclined to give me a wild card because of my French Open outburst. I would have to win three qualifying matches to play the main draw. It was the first time in history a French Open semifinalist did not go straight into the tournament.

Wang and I exchanged groundstrokes, and a light drizzle started to fall. They put us on the worst court they could find, an off-site practice court in a grim neighborhood. The grass behind the baseline looked like it had been run over with a tiller. They didn't dare let me on the grounds of Wimbledon before my qualifying match would be played. Everyone says Wimbledon is so elegant and pristine and polite, but that's only if you are in the top one hundred.

I couldn't focus worth a damn, my mind numb from my father's death. I hit each shot like it meant nothing, like the game wasn't worth my time without my father there to see it. Plus, I was tired as hell from all the jet lag.

And I hated the way that grass played, especially after the slow red clay I loved. Grass was not suited to my game. Even if I had been in the perfect frame of mind, I doubt I could have had much success.

When the rain picked up, I was ready to quit, but Wang wanted to practice serving. I started to walk over to the side of the court, to cover up and sit in the chair, but I saw two photographers approaching. I wasn't about to give them a close-up.

I pulled my baseball cap down over my eyes and stood in the deuce court, bouncing on my toes to stay warm. Wang started angling balls out wide to my forehand, hard and low slices that were damn near impossible to get back.

I let a few aces go and tried to ignore the photographers snapping shots of me. The rain increased, cold on my arms and neck and legs. The fatter of the two photographers, a bearded dude in baggy jeans and a black T-shirt with a gut like a huge water balloon, walked through the gate and onto the court, standing by my racket bag at the net, snapping shots the whole time.

Wang looked at him and then at me. I gestured for Wang to keep serving. He hit a slow serve down the middle and I took a forehand and whaled on it as hard as I could, aiming at the photographer, the ball zipping over his head and clanging into the gatepost.

He ducked, but then kept moving my way, his camera snapping like soft machine-gun fire. "You better not get any closer," I said. He kept shooting, inching forward, and I could see my reflection in his enormous lens.

Wang stopped, nodded toward the side like we should go, his eyes worried.

"Come on, Wang, give me another forehand." I signaled him to bring it. He reluctantly hit another ball into the box, this one wide, a strong, spinning serve. I had to lunge for it, stepping across with my left foot and then my right, rearing back for the mightiest forehand I could muster, all of the anger and loneliness I had inside me channeled into one shot. I slipped as the racket came forward and my right foot stuck in a deep divot, the momentum of my body turn pushing me on, the bottom half of my leg immobile while my thigh and upper body kept moving. I swung wildly and fell. On the way down I heard my right knee pop, the sound like a taut cable snapping, much louder than the pop of the ball on my strings, a shot that sailed well over the photographer's head. I rolled onto my back and my knee began to throb, and then the pain roared up to my head and burned in my ears like an airplane engine. I lay crumpled on the wet ryegrass, tears gushing from my eyes, the first time I had cried since I was a baby, the camera coming closer, clicking the whole time.

Part Three

I returned to Piney and limped around for a while on a ruined knee, living like a hermit in the family home. It turned out that my father had taken out a generous life insurance policy that was enough to pay off his debt. His will specifically stated if one of the children wanted the house, it should not be sold outside the family. My lawyer worked out a deal with my mom and sisters where we sold about half the acreage to pay them what their share would be worth. The rest of the property, including the house, became mine alone. We handled it through our attorneys, and didn't talk or see each other eye-to-eye. It was a good deal for me, because the house was free and clear and I kept all my French Open winnings and endorsement money.

I endured two surgeries two months apart to repair my ACL. Driving around with my left foot was a challenge, but I managed. I cloaked myself in isolation, going for days without seeing anyone, only leaving the house to go to physical therapy appointments in Thessalonica. My agent Cathy mailed me a check with my remaining endorsement money but never called. A *Tennis* magazine with my picture on the cover in Paris arrived in the mail, but I didn't bother to read the story. Newspaper reporters called and left messages on my machine, but I never called them back. With my dad gone, my motivation to play tennis, to do anything in fact, drifted away like a cloud of smoke.

I started drinking, beer mostly, sometimes bourbon. I made some buddies at a bar up in Thessalonica where the college girls went out on Monday through Thursday nights before they headed back home for the weekend. I didn't lift a racket, didn't hit a single tennis ball. I got very good at shooting pool.

Almost ten years passed by this way. Those years seemed like a dream during a long afternoon nap that ends about dusk, leaving you confused when you wake as to whether it's morning or night.

My only real friends in that lost decade were my dogs. I had a big black one named Brutus, an enormous mutt whose father had been a black Lab, and Buck, this dog that looked like a keeshond, the thickest fur you've ever seen. Both had been stray puppies that somebody dumped at the end of our driveway. They ran up into the yard one morning a few months after my dad passed. Those dogs showing up was the only good thing that had happened to me in those years.

I eventually enrolled in community college, but I couldn't get into it. I hated the math and science classes. Although I enjoyed the readings assigned in literature and history, I didn't attend regularly enough to pass, nor did I turn in any of the papers.

The one smart thing I did in all that time was physical therapy. I went through rehab for my knee, getting stretched three times a week, and then riding an exercise bike. At first I limped like crazy, but then it got stronger. To tell the truth, I did the PT because I was bored as hell. I had no job, no place to go, no close friends, and the bar didn't open until four o'clock. I got up around noon, so there was a lot of time to kill before I could get down there and shoot some pool. Besides, there was a good-looking physical therapist who liked me. She was the main reason I kept going back, long after my knee healed.

When I met her, Mary McCallister was twenty-nine, married with two kids, but she was fine looking. She was one of those brunettes who may have been a little thin and nerdy as a teen, perhaps even awkward in college, but turned sexy in her late twenties after having kids. Her boys were ten and seven and her husband was a lieutenant for the Georgia State Patrol, gone from the house for long stretches.

She was a small-town woman who when she neared the age of thirty realized she had missed a lot in life and wanted to make up for lost time before she got too old. She also was deep down a good soul who took pity on me living alone as I did.

We flirted for almost a year during my appointments. I invited her to come down to the bar several times before she finally took me up on my invitation. I taught her how to shoot pool, putting my arms around her to show her how to hold the stick. "Here, let me show you how it feels. There, that's right, put it in the hole."

We began screwing in the back of my dad's old Lincoln in the park near the river and tennis center during her breaks, and when she got off work early she'd come down to my house. She was insatiable. During my physical therapy, I had to try to act like there was nothing between us when she was stretching and massaging my leg, and it wasn't easy, splayed out on that table. I thought people didn't notice our affair, but I was an idiot. There's no hiding an affair in a small town, especially when we saw each other mostly in the light of day. We carried on like that for *nine* years. It's hard to believe, but it was that long. Sometimes we hit a few lulls, or she was too busy with family to see me, but we saw each other at least once every two weeks. I think one of the keys to our relationship lasting so long is that we didn't see each other all that much. She spent nights home with her family and I went to the bar, occasionally picking up college girls. Fridays and Saturdays were the nights I was most likely to go home alone, since most students went back to their parents on the weekends and the housewives had plans with their husbands.

Late one Friday night after another bout of sitting at the bar until closing time, I drove home, pulling the car off the two-lane paved road and onto our long dirt driveway. It was early October and the air was cool and the leaves just beginning to change when I guided the wide Lincoln that had been my dad's through the pines and sapling oaks. In some curves the vines and brambles that stretched out over the drive scraped against the sides. Weeds had grown up and the only clear part of the road was where my tires mashed down the growth twice a day, once in the afternoon when I left the house and again after midnight whenever I slunk back home. Big potholes had appeared in some low spots, and the Lincoln bottomed out once or twice since the road had gotten so bad. That car had taken a beating in the years since my dad drove it to Miami for the Orange Bowl.

All the years we lived there my dad had kept a gate up, blocking the driveway at the entrance to the house where the woods ended and our enormous yard began. I had quit shutting it a few years back, bored of the slow ritual of parking and getting out and opening it up every time I left and returned home. The gate hung wide open, the red metal rusting, just one of many things I had let go.

The condition of the house was another neglected case: The roof in the front was starting to leak, the azaleas and other shrubs in the front had not been trimmed in years, and the old yellow bulldozer that had been my father's was left just sitting in the front yard, rust bubbling up on the frame, the black seat faded and cracked from exposure to sun and rain. I should have sold it, or at least given it away.

I pulled up the hill to the house and wondered why the dogs had not come out barking at me, running down to my car and expressing their gratitude that I had come home like they always did. Those mutts constitued the only appreciation of my existence in the world.

I parked in a spot in the grass near the door and flipped off the engine and the headlights. It was a nice night, cool, about fifty-five degrees, the sky sharp and clear, with no moon, so that the stars sparkled their brightest. Nothing can compare to being out in the country and looking up at the sky when the night is a dark one and there is not another house light for at least a mile. I sat there drunk in the Lincoln and looked up through the windshield and thought about nothing in particular.

When I opened the car door, Bobby McCallister stepped out of the shadows and grabbed me in a headlock. He held me with one arm and a sawed-off shotgun in the other. He was a big man, maybe six feet three, at least 250 pounds of muscle and gut, like the big offensive lineman he had been in high school. My blurry thoughts that had been swirling around like a stray half peanut in a glass of stale beer snapped into focus: I distinctly remember thinking that he intended to kill me right then and there with that sawed-off 12-gauge. There was a lot of open land out there and if he buried me up on the wooded hill, where the leaves were beginning to fall, the grave would have soon been covered with detritus that would spend all year decaying until the spring began. In early February there might be a few mushrooms sprouted up over me. No one would find my final resting place, a six-by-three hole hidden on our overgrown acreage. Maybe a bloodhound could have found me, but the only cops around there who had access to bloodhounds were the state patrolman like Bobby McCallister.

I thought, *If he kills me, who will miss me? Will anyone know that I am gone?* Mary would, but she couldn't hunt me down. A few bartenders might wonder where I went but would ultimately shrug their shoulders and go on about their business of tapping kegs and pouring liquor shots. I was already dead to my mother and sisters.

Bobby McCallister dragged me by the collar of my flannel shirt and dropped me on my back in the grass and lined up and kicked me hard in the side of the ribs with his pointy-toed cowboy boot. The kick hurt like hell, and he kicked me again. He stood over me and held that stubby sawed-off shotgun down on my face, the two barrels like enormous nostrils of a bear hovering over me. "You know who I am, don'tcha, boy?"

"Yeah." Of course I knew who he was. Mary had occasionally talked about him, worried he might be suspicious. The past few years she had talked about leaving him and coming to live with me. She said she loved me and we should be together. I don't know what gave her the idea that I wanted her to do that.

"Tonight," Bobby McCallister said, "I'm your worst fucking nightmare." He jabbed me in the face with the snub nose of the cut-down shotgun, and then pulled back the hammer and it clicked, ready for the pin to strike the shell. I thought back to all the places I'd been and things I'd done and the sharp lines of tennis courts I'd seen all over the Southeast, especially that big red one in Paris where I had been a star for two brief weeks. I thought of my dad and all he had done for me and how I was sorry that he was gone and also sorry of what had become of me, a has-been bum, a philandering drunkard with one French Open semifinal to my name. I was about to die only ten yards or so from the tennis court he built for me.

Bobby McCallister held that ragged gun on my face for what seemed like an eternity—and eternity is where I thought I was headed. But then he yanked the gun to the side and fired it overhead, the explosion of 12-gauge buckshot echoing through the dark foothills that surrounded us, fading out like a distant sonic boom. I know this is crazy, but the sound of that gunshot echo brought to mind the pleasing sounds that tennis balls make bouncing on clay and hitting the racket.

Why a shot from a sawed-off 12-gauge that seconds before had been jammed against my upper lip made me think of the sounds of tennis balls, I'll never understand. But it did. And it made me miss the game of tennis. Those years were the only time in my life post-diapers where I did not play. I had ignored the sport that had been my meal ticket, my occupation, a game that had defined the whole of my very existence. I was adrift, a nothing without the game that had defined me.

Bobby McCallister stood up straight, his cowboy boots straddling me, and he fired the gun again, this time in the direction of the Lincoln. Buckshot pellets ripped holes in the driver's-side doors. He opened the breech and the smoking, spent shells popped out onto the ground and he pulled two more from his pocket and reloaded and clicked the gun back together. "You lucky I ain't gonna kill you. But you ain't never gonna fuck no more women in this here nigger mobile."

He moved toward the Lincoln, and from only six feet away he fired into the hood, ripping an enormous hole, and then he fired into the windshield, shattering the glass. I watched all this from the spot in the yard where he had drop-kicked me.

"Goddammit," he said after firing the last shot, picking at his arm where a pellet had ricocheted back into him. He walked around to the other side of the house and I lost track of him for a moment, hoping that maybe he was gone, thinking perhaps I could sneak inside and get my dad's old pistol and shoot his ass, but almost immediately he came back with a small towel and a gas can. He came over to the Lincoln and unscrewed the fuel tank cap and poured gas from the can onto the towel and then stuffed the towel into the tank with a broken pine branch he found on the ground.

He looked over at me and said, "You stay the hell away from my wife. You go near her again, I know boys that will kill you for me. Won't nobody ever hear of your pussy, tennis-playing ass again."

He took a lighter from his pocket and sparked the wheel. He held the small flame to the towel and it caught and he ran away, to the other side of the house. The flame took hold and a fireball whooshed from beneath the Lincoln in the shape of a mushroom cloud and the whole thing rocked with an explosion deep beneath the chassis and it burned in an inferno that lit up the yard like a fireworks show. I was close enough to it to feel the heat on my skin, lying there sore in the ribs on the browning fescue of that yard, wondering if I needed to get the hose to keep it from spreading into the dry grass, the trees, and the house. It had been a dry fall, and I knew how wildfires could spread rapidly up the pine trees and across the road, scorching everything the flames touched.

I heard his truck from back behind the house, and he drove through the yard and onto the driveway and was gone. I stood and my ribs hurt more than I expected. I was hopeful that no one would call the volunteer county fire department and get them up here with deputies asking questions of me. But I lived so far out in the country there that most likely no one would respond.

I went back to the far side of the house where we had kept three hundred feet of hose in a wooden storage box that my dad had built. I had not even bothered to use the hose for anything, not to wash my car or water any plants, certainly not to water a dusty red clay tennis court that at one time had been ideal for hitting tennis balls.

My dad had built the whitewashed wood box for the hose one afternoon when the court was fairly new. I was about five, I guess, and remember him setting up his tools, running the extension cord out the window for the power saw, a pencil behind his ear as he cut the boards. He listened while he worked to an old country radio station from across the state line in Alabama. That station had been off the air for years, and that box was warped and the paint faded from days in the sun. I opened the lid and that long, green hose was still wound tightly in there. I reached in and started pulling it out, a stiff whopper, six fifty-foot hoses linked together. Many a day when I was little I had gone out and watered that clay court when it was dusty to keep it soft and from blowing away, bit by bit, grain by grain.

I struggled to pull the hose out and stretch it. I connected one end of the hose to the spigot, and then lifted the big wound loop of the rest of the hose out and found the other end. I turned on the water. The water took a while to push its way through the long piece of dry tubing, but it did, although it was very leaky. I dragged the hose over to my burning Lincoln, the seats and the plastic and fiberglass smoldering, a stinky chemical smell. I hosed it down, wetting the ground around it.

I thought of my dogs and a chill ran through me. I feared that maybe he had shot them or run over them. I turned off the water and began calling their names, "*Buck. Brutus.* Here boys! Buck! Brutus!"

I called their names over and over, walking around the yard, getting more scared, until I reached the front part of the house down near the well. In the distance through the woods I heard a yowling that sounded like Buck, and then the heavy bark from Brutus, his deep-throated voice, loud and gruff. I half ran that way, moving fast despite the dark, my ribs hurting, and followed the sound of their barks. I passed by the well and into the brushy field where my dad had once kept a few heifers, toward the tree line over by a cow pond that had never held water for very long, really only a pond in the wettest of months when the ground was saturated.

I found them tied up to a big pine tree, a rope through their collars. I don't know who was happier to see whom, me or them, and I dropped down on my knees and hugged them and they reciprocated with sloppy wet licks from their giant tongues. They had mighty bad breath, but I didn't care, I was so glad to find them alive. I should have known that a country boy like Bobby McCallister would not be the kind to shoot someone's dogs. He wasn't a bad dude, I hear, a deacon in the Second Baptist Church of Thessalonica. I can't blame him for threatening to kill me, screwing his wife and the mother of his children as I had been, and doing it in the backseat of my car in the park not far from his house.

Shit, to tell you the truth, I deserved killing back then.

The very next day I got up and started restoring our old tennis court that had become littered with debris and overgrown with grass and weeds and even some small oak and pine saplings that had sprouted. I ignored the soreness in my ribs and worked hard removing the growth, some by muscle and the rest by weed killer. Once the court was clean, I rolled and plowed and then rolled the court again, striving to soften it like the terre battue of Roland Garros.

It took several weeks to work it into playing shape. The only time I left the house was to go to the store for food and once to Atlanta to buy a new net and practice balls. I didn't drink a drop of alcohol, swearing it off for the first time in years.

The court was more than ready and the pain in my ribs gone when I decided to hit a tennis ball again. I got one of my rackets from under my bed and filled my old ball hopper with brand-new Wilsons. I put on an old red Fila warm-up suit that I had worn around when I was in Paris, fitting a little tighter than it had then, and went out onto the court, carrying the ball hopper in my right hand and the racket in my left. The dogs ran around me, thinking that this was a game for them. I shooed them away and stepped up to the baseline. They crouched together on the side of the court, watching at exactly same angle as a line judge calling foot faults.

I bounced the ball on the groomed red clay. I liked the comforting sound of that ball hitting the court, that familiar *thunk*, but I felt scared to toss it up, to hit it across the court into the dilapidated fence behind the baseline, to cross back over the line into the game I had left behind. I looked at the dogs and smiled. "Good boys," I said, and bounced the ball twice more, studying hard on the Wilson 3 script as it came up off the clay. I caught the ball and held my arms out and touched it to the strings in front of me, the bow-like motion that signals the serve is to begin. I arced the racket down and then back and tossed the ball perfectly above me, nine and a half feet high and about a foot in front of me and to my left. The racket moved back and up without me telling myself what to do. My elbow and shoulder knew the routine. I stepped up and into the ball as the racket head slid down my back and then ratcheted up and unwound into a full stretch and the strings met the ball and I hit a crisp serve right down the T. The ball kicked off the red clay and propelled into the back of the chicken-wire fence.

It felt so good to hit a serve again—I couldn't forget how to hit a tennis ball if I tried. I served the whole bucket, not straining, but taking nice, easy fluid strokes, banging one serve after another into the box. The dogs gave me those happy dog smiles that said they approved. When I hit the last ball out of the basket, I walked over and petted them on the head and they licked my hand gratefully.

The ball hopper refilled, I stood on the baseline and alternated hitting forehands and backhands, trying to get some topspin on the ball. The shots looked awesome with no one there to retrieve them, well-struck groundstrokes deep into both corners, parabolas spanning the net and then arcing down into the court.

My knee felt good, too, the right knee I had injured, and it didn't tweak with pain or even feel weak when I stepped up to hit backhands, the shot that forced me to lead with my right leg.

I hit a few more buckets of balls and then went into the house, zipped up my warm-up jacket, found the keys to my dad's old pickup truck, and headed for the city courts in Thessalonica.

~

Thessalonica's eight public courts next to the high school football stadium were often busy on weekends and after school, but noon on that Wednesday the place was dead, one empty court next to another. I knew, however, there was always one person there I could hit with. Fast Eddie by then was a fiftyish tennis bum who hung out in the parking lot, always looking for a match. He wore white zinc cream all over his nose, and aviator sunglasses that he strapped to his head with a twirl of rubber bands. He had a very dark, leathery tan, but the tan only reached his arms and legs and his neck and face, stopping at his white V-neck T-shirts. I saw him changing his shirt once and his skinny chest reflected sunlight like a white sheet.

Fast Eddie would hit with anybody—kids, high school players, old women—and sometimes he would just stand out there by himself and hit serves. If he wasn't out on the court, he would be sitting beside his van in his beach lounger chair, reading a book, usually about tennis. And his van was something to see: a late-1980s black Chevy Astro conversion model with orange flames painted on the hood and trailing back along the door panels.

He was reading that day I pulled up in my truck and hopped out with a bag of rackets and headed toward him. I had not seen him in years, but he acted like we saw each other every day.

"Hey, Jaxie. Where you been? I hear all you do is sit around in that bar down there on the alley. I wondered when you were going to come around and play some tennis, or if you ever would. You wanna hit?"

"Yeah, Fast Eddie, let's do it."

"I got some new balls."

I followed him onto the court. He had these wild hustling movements even when he walked slow, elbows and knees working at crazy angles, his head jutting forward as though to follow his big nose. He had an enormous honker, his schnozz he called it.

He opened two cans, that pneumatic slicing sound of the air pressure releasing the balls, and stuck three in the enormous pockets of his shorts, a funny striped pair like Sampras had worn when he was young, baggy britches that looked almost like pajama shorts. We took our spots on the baselines and he fed me a ball right down the middle and I stepped back to my left and turned sideways and moved my left foot out front and hit a solid forehand right back at him, the ball taking some topspin and kicking up on the slow hard courts.

Fast Eddie smiled, and hit the ball back to me, a perfectly flat groundstroke. His shots were old school, like a lot of the old dudes who learned to play in the 1950s and '60s, strictly flat or underspin, a Jack Kramer to Arthur Ashe to Jimmy Connors lineage, before Björn Borg came along and changed the way everyone played, looping over the ball with topspin. Fast Eddie had very economical groundstrokes, not a single wasted motion. He used one of those enormous Prince rackets with a snowshoe-sized face that could hit the ball two hundred miles per hour if swung hard enough. As long as contact was made somewhere on the racket the ball came off strong, so he did what smart players do, especially the older smart players, and let the racket do the work.

I hit another forehand, and we continued like that, exchanging solid shots right down the middle to each other, each ball struck cleanly in the center of the strings, back and forth, like a three-part metronome: he and his racket, me and my racket, and the ball. Neither of us was trying to kill the ball or gain an advantage, we just took pleasure in that sweet feel of the yellow-felt-covered rubber in the center of the racket, the ping of the ball on the strings. He smiled like it was the best sex he'd ever had. I did too.

If I had wanted, I could have easily moved him from side to side, put a little more pop on my groundstrokes and overpowered him, but there was no point in that. I wanted to get my strokes back, and even though I was hitting the ball pretty damn good for someone who had not played in almost ten years, I was aware that a strong player would wear me down. I also got tired pretty quick. I could feel tension coming on in my forearms and hands and even my back, and my legs were getting tired. Fast Eddie kept firing balls back at me like he was a wiry ball machine. I started working on hitting some backhands, alternating from forehands to backhands to forehands again. We hit like this for about half an hour, until I waved my hand and said that was enough for me.

We walked up to the net post and he shook my hand, said it was an honor. I hadn't noticed while we were hitting, but about ten people had stopped to watch. I overheard a man in a tie telling his ten-year-old son that I had been a pro, that I had reached the semifinals of the French Open in the '90s. He said he had often wondered whatever happened to me.

The next day I ached. My shins hurt and my wrist and forearm and even my shoulder were tender. What's worse, the right knee that had felt fine was very stiff, cracking when I flexed it. It was the first time in my life I had ever experienced such stiffness from playing tennis. My inactivity had let some of my more toned and conditioned tennis muscles atrophy. The strands of tissue that bound the body together and made it run where you wanted and swing when you wanted had softened. It would take time for me to get my fitness back together. I jogged around on the court at home, trying to loosen up.

After lunch I went back to the Thessalonica courts. Fast Eddie sat in his lawn chair in the far end of the big parking lot, reading. When he saw my truck, he jumped up and bookmarked his page and grabbed his rackets and his ball hopper and hustled my way.

"Hey, Jaxie, I was hoping you'd show up."

"Yeah, Fast Eddie, I'm here. But I'm sore."

"Man, you've got to stretch. Before and after, but especially after. Don't they teach you anything out there on the ATP tour?"

"I wasn't on it that long."

"That was a shame, Jaxie. I was thinking you'd go far. You think you'll try to get back out there? You are still a young man."

"I doubt it, Eddie, this knee and all."

"Well shit, man, you've got to try. It's probably all right, being that you've rested it so long. Come up here every day and I'll feed you all the balls you want. I'll even run some wind sprints with you. You got a gift, Jaxie, you can't let it go to waste."

"I don't know what I want, Eddie. I just want to hit the ball. I doubt I'll ever get back on the tour."

"Damn, Jaxie, don't rule it out. You got the game, man. You got the game."

We went out on Court Eight, the far one on the end. A light breeze blew, not a cloud in the sky, still early in the afternoon. We were the only ones at the whole tennis center, the other seven courts quiet. School didn't get out until three, and it was Thursday, so none of the ladies' leagues were playing, or maybe they were off at one of the private country clubs, playing on groomed clay. The only noise was the occasional car or truck passing down the side street that led to the courts. Across the parking lot and through the football stadium I could see the busy road, a line of school buses on the way to the high school. I stood out there and slid my racket out of my bag and looked across the empty courts, all identical with their net posts and white net straps and the black webbings below, all diametrically perfect and rectangular green boxes inlaid on a canvas of deep red. I had played at one time or another on every single one of those courts, junior tournament matches, many times when I was little, and would be matched up with an older kid who I beat mercilessly. I had doled out some serious ass-whippings on these courts, especially in my early years. I won the men's Thessalonica City Championship easily when I was fifteen, the summer before my first Orange Bowl win, when everyone was talking about me and my future in the game, asking me when I was going to turn pro even though I was only in the tenth grade.

All the history on those courts rose up inside me and I could see myself winning match points as a kid, that cocky walk I had, that arrogance to think I could beat anyone, and then go out and actually do it. Those years in junior tennis seemed so long ago, like another lifetime, as though another person had been running around in my skin and with my face.

I never have been one to let emotions overtake me, but in that moment all of the tennis I had blocked out, all of the memories of my father that I had ignored, these visions all came flooding back over me like a heavy wall of water. I stood there, stone cold in the October sun. I realized that all of these memories added up to who I was as a person. The man who had been sitting in the bar and playing pool—that wasn't me. The real *me* was out on the tennis court.

Fast Eddie had been knotting, untying, and reknotting the laces on his Tretorns while I had zoned out. He stood and said something to me and I went back on the baseline and he fed me a ball. I tried to block the thoughts from my mind, tried to ignore the pain in my body. I focused on hitting, watching the yellow sphere so closely that I could read the name of the manufacturer and the number on the ball, an almost self-hypnotic trick.

My mind quieted and I saw the ball Eddie hit me clearly, my eyes as sharp as ever.

~

Fast Eddie and I practiced every day right up through Christmas, hitting groundstrokes and playing serve-and-volley games, the first one to twenty-five points. It was a warm fall, and even December stayed sunny and clear. Georgia that year was going through one of its frequent droughts, a long, dry spell that was bad for farmers and reservoirs but great for tennis. Only at the very end of the year did it turn cold and damp.

I stayed home on New Year's Eve and Day, watching college football bowl games for two straight days, not drinking a drop. I had bought an exercise bike and rode it for an hour at a time in the morning and the evening, and I stretched diligently. By the third day the good games were over and I was a little stir-crazy and wanted out of the house.

I drove my dad's old pickup truck around on country roads, listening to some of his music, Willie Nelson, Waylon Jennings, and Conway Twitty and the Twitty Birds. The rain had let up but it was frigid, not more than twenty-five degrees, the coldest day we'd had all year by far.

Most of the leaves had fallen from the hardwoods, although some of the hills still looked a little green because of all the pines, except in a few spots near the Alabama line between Piney and Thessalonica where pulpwooders had cleared trees for thousands of acres. The landscape with the trees gone looked like a mangy dog's bare ass.

I drove into Thessalonica and it was one of those Fridays that falls the day after a holiday, so there wasn't any school traffic, although the mall had a parking lot full of cars. I hate the mall when it is crowded, so I drove over toward the tennis courts for the hell of it. I wondered if Fast Eddie would be there on a day like this, cold and dry, but too damn cold to play tennis outdoors. Nothing I hated more than playing in temperatures below fifty, and certainly wouldn't do it below freezing. Ice-cold tennis balls feel like hitting rocks.

Fast Eddie's black van with the red and orange flames painted on the front and sides was there, smoke puffing softly out of the tailpipe. I parked and saw his face peek out the little porthole on the back of the van. He was looking out that window, hoping somebody would drive up and want to play some tennis.

He opened the door and ran over to me, waving. He wore a black Russian woodsman-type hat with a bright red warm-up suit, and it looked as though he had three warm-up suits on under that one, and big black gloves, and, of course, his trademark white Tretorns. I have never seen him without those shoes.

I rolled down my truck window a crack. "Jaxie, come on in the van." His breath made a cloud in the gray air of the day. "I got a TV and some videos of old matches. Wimbledons, French Opens. That crazy McEnroe–Nastase spat at the U.S. Open."

I was relieved that he didn't want to try to drag me out onto the court. I was so bored, I would have done it. I knew I would be miserably cold, but I also knew that I either needed to get out and play some tennis or I would end up sitting back down there at the bar, playing pool and drinking and talking to whatever sweet young things—or the closest approximation of sweet young things—who came around. Even a mean old thing would have made do, as lonely as I was then.

I turned off my engine and got out and hustled over through frigid air. Those raw Georgia days are the coldest of all when they bump up against the warm days that have come before that softened your senses and lulled you into believing winter was easy. Three days before it had been sixty-five degrees and I had played tennis in shorts and a T-shirt.

Inside Fast Eddie's van was surprisingly comfortable. He had two director's chairs and on one side of the van he had built pinewood shelves with a small collection of tennis books. In the middle of the shelves was a space big enough for a nineteen-inch TV screen, a Sony, that fit comfortably. He was watching that 1980 Borg–McEnroe final, the one that formed my earliest memory and had inspired my father to climb aboard his bulldozer and claim our court from the earth. It takes me back every time I see that match, as though I'm witnessing my own birth. "Isn't this great?" Fast Eddie said. "I bought it on the Internet. The BBC has been putting out videos with all sorts of great matches."

I nodded, not taking my eyes from the screen.

"McEnroe is about to force that famous tiebreaker here," he said. We watched McEnroe dive and hit a remarkable drop volley cross-court winner that even the lightning-fast Borg had no chance to reach. "Look at that shot, will you?"

"That's something else," I said.

"You want some hot chocolate?"

I nodded, and he heated up some water in the microwave and made me a cup, serving it in a ceramic tennis mug, the handle in the shape of a racket frame. We watched the rest of that match, that tiebreaker where the championship hung in the balance for seven amazing points. That match may be McEnroe's ultimate performance, even though he lost. Borg was not from this planet, as Nastase said, and to come back from losing the thirty-four-point tiebreaker and pull out the fifth set was and still is truly unbelievable. No wonder Borg got bored with tennis, and into drugs and women. After that match, there was nothing more that he could do on a tennis court.

Fast Eddie was talking up a storm. He was the same age as Connors, and said he had beaten him once in a junior tournament in Chicago when they were both eleven years old. He said by having a win over Connors, he had indirect wins over just about everyone in the world, including me. His logic went like this: Connors had beaten McEnroe, who had beaten Thomas Muster, to whom I had lost. "Indirect win, only two players between us," he said. He was serious. He said he had a diagrammed chart of all his indirect wins if I wanted to see it, and started looking through a row of three-ring binders on the bottom shelf.

I laughed, and said no thanks, I didn't need documentation. I was enjoying myself, sitting there, talking with him.

"Do you ever watch any of your old matches?" he asked me.

"No, I actually haven't ever seen them."

"You've got to be kidding me? You haven't seen those French Open matches?"

"Nope, not a single time. I saw myself on the news, the highlights in Paris, but only a few points."

"Well, damn, Jaxie, I taped them. I've still got a tape of you. I watched it again back in the fall, when you first started coming around."

He began digging through the videocassettes stacked on the bottom shelf on the side of the van.

"Hey, here you go." He took the tape out of the case, and I could see he had written on it, JAXIE SKINNER . . . PINEY, GA, BOY . . . FRENCH OPEN, 1995.

I started to freeze up at the prospect of this. I knew that I had been on television, that the whole world who cared anything about tennis had seen me, but it didn't bother me then. In fact, I'd never thought much about it. But the prospect of sitting there in the tight confines of a van with the local tennis lunatic and watching myself ten years before when I had all the promise in the world scared me in a way I still can't explain.

He popped in the tape and hit REWIND. The little reels caught and the sound of it spinning backward hummed. I took a nervous sip of the hot chocolate.

"Yeah, I got some of the Fernandez match, parts of the others you won easy—they didn't show all of those on the air, but all of the Muster match."

The tape finished rewinding and he hit PLAY and the red courts of Roland Garros filled up the small screen. I leaned in closer and there I was, in a red Fila shirt and white shorts, tan and thin and young looking, skinny as a damn beanpole, although my legs were muscular.

I felt like I was peering back into history in some crystal ball, some time beyond the Middle Ages. It was spooky. I looked so young, so naive. I had a bowl haircut and my skin was tan and my hair bleached blond from the sun. The tape started with the Fernandez match, that was the first one of mine that made it on TV. My expression was so intense, my eyes narrowed and shooting daggers at the ground, at the ball, at anything at which I looked, almost as if I was in some sort of trance.

My shots looked smooth, long, graceful groundstrokes that really popped, balls driven deep against the powerful Spaniard. I moved effortlessly around the court, like I was one of the great South American or European dirtballers, players like Borg or Vilas or Gustavo Kuerten. Fast Eddie fell uncharacteristically quiet, perhaps because he saw how amazed I was to see myself on the NBC coverage of the French Open. I heard the announcers talking but I didn't comprehend a word they said.

We watched several points, including one of the longest rallies I had ever played in a tournament, fifty shots at least. I watched as I won the point with a drop shot and a warm feeling flowed over me. Without Fast Eddie's videotape I might not have remembered that point. It had been lost in my head somewhere with all those past vaporous remembrances, wherever they go.

How could I have forgotten that point? After recalling it, I was back in that match. I remembered the ball boys, the linesmen, the umpire, and the warm temperature of that day and clear sky and the exact spot where Olga Polykova had been sitting in the players' box. Before a match point against me in the fourth set, I leaned over to Eddie. "This one, this is the shot of my life," I said.

"I know . . . who thought it could get any better than that long rally you ended with that drop shot?"

I watched as Fernandez hit a crosscourt volley that looked to be a winner, angled well off the court, but I had guessed right and ran with all my might and nailed a forehand passing shot down the line to stay alive. I followed the momentum of my fierce sprint to the sidewall and pumped my fist once and opened my mouth in a plain and simple yell of joy. Joy, pure and unadulterated joy, is the only way to describe that shot. "The shot of my life," I said. "That was it. No way was I losing that match then. Or he winning it."

Fast Eddie reached over and punched me in the arm, and said, "High five, brother." I raised my hand and the dry skin of our palms slapped in the front of the TV.

I leaned over toward the small porthole window and looked out the side of his van at the open courts of the Thessalonica Tennis Center. "Let's get out on there and hit some balls," I said.

"I'm with you, Jaxie," Fast Eddie said. "I'm with you, buddy."

Six months later I was ready to make my comeback. I had been training and practicing very hard, working out with Eddie almost every day. I also bought a new ball machine and hit thousands of shots on my court at home, and I honed my serve with hours of practice buckets. I played practice matches with college players and a few strong juniors in Thessalonica, winning most of the time.

I also had developed one other routine that was key to rebuilding my strength and stamina and shedding twenty pounds. Piney's biggest textile mill had closed down in the 1980s, but it remained standing, surrounded by a large asphalt lot. One side was a flat brick wall with no windows. On a cold Monday afternoon in early January when I got serious about playing again, I took two rackets over there and a can of new balls and slid through an opening in the chain-link fence that surrounded the shuttered mill. I started hitting against the wall, grooving my groundstrokes, one after another. The asphalt was slightly coarse with tiny black pebbles but the size of the space was perfect, fifty feet by fifty feet, and the brick wall was high, at least three stories, and smooth, so it offered a true return of the ball.

The mill was across a creek from a neighborhood now occupied by mostly Mexican immigrants. I often saw people looking out their windows at me, and I imagined them saying something in Spanish about a lunatic out hitting tennis balls in cold weather. But hitting balls against a wall, when you are hitting them hard, is work, and soon I warmed up under the old gray warm-up suit I wore, breaking a sweat and breathing hard, my labored exhalations forming large moisture clouds in the chilly air. I can't tell you how good it felt to stand there and hit the ball into that wall as hard as I could, the bam of the yellow felt orb against the bricks of that mill falling into a regular rhythm, a three-cycle sound: *wham* against the wall, a softer *thock* when it came back and bounced on the asphalt, and then a sweet *whack* of the ball on my strings. *Wham, thock, whack . . . wham, thock, whack . . . wham, thock, whack.* The only other sound I heard was the slight scuffing of my tennis shoes on the black hardtop below my feet, my front foot stepping forward into each shot, and then getting back in position only to repeat the pattern again. I hit for thirty minutes without stopping, alternating between long series of backhands and forehands until I finished with a series of crosscourts, alternating wings, and giving myself a little more of a push with the running from side to side. Thirty minutes of hitting against a wall is one hell of a workout.

Regardless of how much I had played during the day, I started driving down there every evening to bang balls against that wall before sunset. One hundred forehands, then one hundred backhands, and then repeat. I built up to the point where I could do this for an hour at a time. On my second visit there I took a piece of chalk and marked off a line for the net and a few round targets on the wall. Beyond those targets I envisioned another part of the court there, a court just like center court at Roland Garros, and other days I imagined Flushing Meadows. It's amazing if you stare at a wall how much you can see into it. This was supposedly how Ivan Lendl developed his game in Czechoslovakia, before he escaped the Communists, by hitting on a wall over and over and over again, targeting spots that became more than a wall to him.

My textile mill bricks became more than a wall to me, too. My arms became stronger than they had ever been, so that my grip on the racket felt like an oarlock. My legs grew lean and flexible from the hours on the bike and stretching and the fast footwork during the wall sessions. I learned a great deal about myself, hitting alone, just me and the ball and the racket and that enormous stack of mortar and bricks.

At home at night I studied the schedule for the Challenger and Futures circuits, the minor leagues of tennis. I printed the tournament calendar and taped it to my bedroom wall, drawing thick black circles around several clay court tournaments. I put a star by Tunica, Mississippi, which would be my first big test on the clay, and later in the year I thought about venturing down to play in South America.

I was worried about the economics of the venture. With food, gasoline, and other sundry expenses, living on the road was not cheap, and the motel bills are the highest of all. Even if I could find places that were forty-nine dollars per night, most motels tacked on a tourist tax that added about ten bucks. I thought about the coziness of Fast Eddie's van, and decided I could live on the road in a van of my own while making my comeback. Although I had lived cheaply and sold off more of our acreage over the years to generate some income, I was afraid of burning through what was left of my money. A van would be the only way I could afford to travel.

I knew that a lot of the players on the low-level tours often stayed for free with host families, rich folks who were tennis-crazy and hoped to have brushes with greatness in the making. But I didn't want to be a charity case, and I didn't want to have to go through the obligatory bullshit small talk. I'd rather sleep on the side of the road than have to appease some family that would distract me from my tennis with inane questions or, even worse, ask me to hit with their kid and give free pointers. A van would allow me my much-needed solitude.

The next day I drove up to Thessalonica and found Fast Eddie, and we hit for about an hour. After, we sat in folding chairs and I told him about my desire to buy a van. He leaned forward, his eyes excited. "Jaxie, there's a great tradition of American tennis players and vans. I'll help you find the perfect one. I've learned a lot about van engines over the years, and have done all the maintenance on this one myself."

I nodded.

"In fact, you've got to come down to Savannah with me in two weeks. That's the place to buy one. There's a big vanner convention there. All sorts of vans for sale, at great prices. We'll take our rackets and get in some matches. Great clay courts down there too."

We left early on a Friday morning for the Southeastern Vanner's Association Convention, held each year on Tybee Island near Savannah. We planned to return home late Sunday night, possibly Monday if we were having a particularly good time. I met him at the tennis center and left my truck there for the weekend.

Fast Eddie had bought us bottles of orange juice, cups of coffee, and bran muffins—he was a health food freak, although it seemed to me like his skinny frame could have benefited from eating a box of Krispy Kremes every now and then. He pointed his big van southeast and we headed from the Appalachian foothills for Georgia's coastline, the large engine humming smoothly.

I realized sitting up in that cozy seat in the front of his van that I had known him most of my life but really knew very little about him other than he spent almost all of his waking hours hanging around the tennis courts. I would have all those gaps filled in and more. "I was born in Dayton, Ohio," he said, and went on to tell me about growing up there and playing tennis as a child. He said he peaked at the age of twelve, and never got much better, despite playing all through high school.

He quit playing tennis when he moved to Athens, Georgia, where he went to college and then stayed for veterinary school. "The biggest regret of my life," he said, "is that I gave the game up for so long. But I just couldn't get any better. I was nowhere near your level."

I started to tell him that I thought he hit the ball rather well, but he didn't give me a chance to get a word in edgewise. He was full of coffee and he was driving his van down the road and talking as fast as he could go.

After graduation, Fast Eddie became a veterinarian, got married, and lived in Dalton, Georgia, for about eight years until his wife left him and he lost his practice due to a dishonest partner. It was then that he began playing tennis again, devoting himself to the game. Since the age of thirty-three, he had lived in an efficiency apartment in Thessalonica and hung around the tennis courts every day, rain or shine. He hated small animals of all kinds, and eschewed marriage as well.

I tried to steer the conversation back to tennis. He told me in specific detail about the 4.5 team he had played on that won the Southern championships and went to Nationals about ten years back, losing in the semifinals to a team from California that was stacked with more ringers than his team had been. He had played the two and three lines of doubles, back when he was younger, before his body inevitably began to break down and injuries plagued his feet and ankles and elbows and shoulders and the worst of all, his lower back. Every ache and pain he'd ever had on a tennis court I think he told me about.

We arrived at the beach about lunchtime. The Tybee Island van gathering wasn't nearly as big or as wild as I had expected. I'm not sure what I thought it would be like, but I guess I was imagining some sort of Hell's Angels–like debauchery with strippers and snakes and tattooed women in leather. I should have known that wasn't Fast Eddie's style.

The vans numbered about one hundred and were five rows deep along a thick, hard gray beach, set back maybe seventy-five yards from the water. Fast Eddie checked in with the guard at a gate where the vans drove out onto the sand, and parked in his designated spot. He began setting up a tent beside our van while I got out and stretched my legs and checked out the scene.

Along the back row there were twenty vans for sale, and that's where I saw a big white van with bright orange flames painted on the front and flickering along the sides. It was enormous, a 1988 Ford E-150 conversion van, one of the last years Ford made vans this big, a throwback to the days when gasoline was cheap and Reagan-era Americans didn't worry about road wear or running out of oil or any such inconvenience as global warming or small parking spaces. The white paint on the outside was dulled, almost chalky, but the orange flames seemed to have been touched up with a bright, glossy paint. The way the flames started on the grille and flickered back along the fenders and the side put me in the mind of a rocket shooting into space at fifty-five miles per hour. I dubbed the van Flaming Whitey the minute I saw it.

It was the kind of van that mainly appealed to old southern hippies—not a contemporary vegan, yoga West Coast hippie, but the kind who grows his own weed and eats steaks and carries a .357 magnum, the kind of dude who likes nothing better than to kick back and hear some Skynyrd.

The inside of the van was spacious, with two plush, removable chairs and a single bed folded onto the wall. The other side had a counter with a small TV on a stand. It had two big windows on the driver's side and one on the passenger side, but they were tinted dark and the inside had gray velvet curtains that blocked the light out even on the brightest days. The owner, this very tall dude from Texas who tied his silver hair back in a ponytail, let me get in there and shut all the doors and close the curtains. It was as black as a tomb even on the bright sunny beach.

The Texan wanted eight thousand dollars, and that sounded good to me, but I wanted Fast Eddie to take a look under the hood for me before I committed. He got his toolbox out of the back of his van and came over and inspected the engine thoroughly, taking off the air filter and looking down in the carburetor and listening closely to the smooth rhythm of the pistons and the rods. He called me over and began explaining all the parts, how they worked, and I was impressed with his knowledge of the motor. "Let's take this thing for a ride," he said.

I drove and we cruised up and down the main drag there in Tybee, an island less fancy than many of the vacation spots dotting the coasts, what some call a redneck beach. The van rode like a dream, and Fast Eddie agreed that it was a good deal. I think he was a little jealous that I might have a better van than the one he was driving.

I went back and shook hands with the owner, paying him four hundred dollars cash for a deposit. Fast Eddie and I then took the van and went in search of a bank where I could get a certified check to cover the rest. There were no branches of my bank on the island so we drove into Savannah in my soon-to-be new van and turned toward the main part of town. That's where we saw Bacon Park, one of those sprawling Savannah parks, and this one had a tennis center with sixteen Rubico courts. There were a few folks milling around, and Fast Eddie suggested I pull in to see if we could find a match. I didn't realize he had brought rackets until I looked into the backseat and saw his bag, two of my Wilsons sticking out of it.

That van turned heads. I parked right near the walkway to the courts so everyone could see it, and players on every court stopped and stared at that ponderous but pretty machine that would soon be mine. Fast Eddie and I got out and we walked into the tennis center, checking out the matches in progress, a mix mostly of kids on a few courts and women's doubles on others, but one court had two college-aged looking dudes who were hitting the ball well.

We stopped and watched a tall white boy lose a set to an Asian player who had ferocious topspin groundstrokes. They sat down on the bench by the net posts and Fast Eddie walked over and stood behind them. "You guys want to play my partner and me one set for a hundred bucks?"

I was shocked at this, especially since I hadn't seen Fast Eddie play an actual set in years. I was worried they would recognize me, and if he had asked me beforehand, I would have declined. I pulled my Atlanta Braves baseball cap down lower over my eyes. I didn't want to back out after he had laid down his challenge, but I didn't even have on a jock strap.

The Asian kid, I think he was Chinese, looked back at Fast Eddie, and said, "You off your rocker, old man?"

"Why don't you play us and see?"

The white kid turned and looked at Fast Eddie, and then at me, and said, "Come on, Lee, let's do it. I got money on me."

The Asian kid nodded and the white boy reached into his tennis bag and found his wallet and pulled out five twenties. He held the money up where Eddie could see, and said, "Let's see yours, old man."

Fast Eddie reached into his front pocket of his tennis shorts and pulled out a money clip and flashed a one-hundred-dollar bill. "Let's do this," he said.

We got our rackets and warmed up with these dudes. Fast Eddie said he wanted the ad court and that I should serve first and stay back on the baseline and nail my groundstrokes, and he would cover the net and poach. It was his one hundred dollars on the line, so I did what he said.

Fast Eddie played like a champ. He volleyed every ball he touched, angling low balls that if these kids reached them at all they hit wildly into the back fence or the net or threw up a sitter that Fast Eddie picked off. His returns of serves were like well-placed darts, and neither of these kids could volley very well and wanted to play doubles about like they would a singles match, just standing on the baseline smashing forehands.

Fast Eddie played so well that I sat back and hit solid but not my best groundstrokes, keeping the ball deep until he could pick it off at net. He anticipated their shots brilliantly and moved much faster than I ever would have expected.

We won the set easily, 6–2. We shook hands and the white kid paid up. Fast Eddie pocketed their twenties, and the white boy asked, "Who are you?"

"I'm nobody," Fast Eddie said, "but Jaxie here made it to the semis of the French Open a few years back."

I nodded, and they both stood there slack-jawed.

"I thought you looked familiar," the white kid said. He asked me my name and I told him. "Can I have your autograph?"

I signed a white tennis cap he had in his bag and we were on our way.

Driving back to the van convention, I asked Fast Eddie, "How did you play so well? I haven't seen you play a match in years. Your volleys are dead-on crisp."

"Jaxie, I'll never lose it. I think about tennis, I meditate, I practice on the wall and run wind sprints five times a week. I don't eat unhealthy food except once a year, and that's today, at the opening-night barbecue."

I realized then how much he and I were alike, devoted solely to the game. We had isolated ourselves from human contact, from friends and family, simply to pursue a yellow ball.

"And Jaxie, I want to tell you something. I couldn't be happier that you are going to make another run at the big time. You can do it. I'll do all the maintenance on your van, and take care of it when you are home. I've got you covered there. Don't worry about it, but focus on your tennis. Your game will come back. It's going to take time, but you've got a game like no one else I've ever known. Sometimes I think you haven't even scratched the surface of what you can accomplish."

I thought about his statement all the way home, following him in my new van on the long flat highway through the Georgia pines, driving the vehicle that would take me on the road across two continents in search of my lost tennis glory.

Fast Eddie didn't travel very often, but he was eager to go with me to hit practice balls and chart my matches at my first match in Tunica.

We left early the day before the tournament started, our two vans forming a mini convoy, the road ahead of us lit softly from the big ball of fire climbing over the horizon behind our back. We followed the two-lane state highways that cut through Alabama and Mississippi towns with names like Rodentown and Boaz, through and near larger towns like Huntsville and Florence and Corinth and Tupelo, small places not any bigger than Thessalonica, towns just barely big enough to have two McDonald's, although it didn't seem both were needed.

Our vans cruised by muffler shops and lumberyards and boiled peanut stands and shade-tree mechanic shops. I saw wild dogs with tongues hanging low, an occasional bloated deer carcass on the roadside, and thought about how tough this tournament was going to be. Tunica was a Challenger event, the highest level of the satellite tour, and this event was noted for being a drawing card for young studs from South America hoping to earn enough ranking points to make the French Open. It was held at a resort casino with a tennis club and golf course.

We crossed into Mississippi and made the rest of the drive in good time, arriving early afternoon at the strip of casinos clustered along the Mississippi River, about sixty miles south of Memphis. There was plenty of parking in the lot, a vast stretch of asphalt spreading away from the casino hotel on a flat spread of black Delta soil.

Fast Eddie and I got our racket bags and a ball hopper full of practice balls and headed into the front entrance of the casino. Slot machine bells were ringing and people crowded everywhere on the impossibly loud carpet, the middle of a Monday afternoon. We garnered some pretty funny stares wandering around the card games and roulette wheels looking for the courts. A multitude of sunburned, chubby-faced white dudes lined the craps and blackjack tables, many of them chewing on cigars, looking like they had just come off the golf course. On down toward the quarter, nickel, and even penny slot machines, the demographics changed to mostly black women, many obscenely wide in girth, a few in curlers and one in a bathrobe and slippers.

I asked a woman at a change booth where the tennis courts were. She said she didn't know, but pointed me to the information desk near the front entrance. An old man there drew a long line on a map with a shaky pen that led back through the full length of the casino and then down a series of long hallways. He circled the tennis center on the most distant spot of the complex.

Fifteen minutes and at least half a mile later, Fast Eddie and I arrived at the pro shop. A pimply teenage kid in headphones minded the front desk, playing a handheld video game and holding his mouth in some crazy position like he was getting his prostate checked for the first time, his fingers skittering on the keys of the small contraption.

"We're here for the tournament," I said. "We'd like to get a practice court."

"Tournament? What tournament?"

"The Challenger event this weekend."

"Never heard of it. Do you have a reservation?"

"No. Do I need one? You don't look busy."

"Ah, yeah. You gotta have a reservation." The kid threw back his shoulders and looked at me like he could kick my ass. "Are you a guest of the hotel?"

"Yes," I lied.

He shoved forward a reservation form that said courts were fifty dollars per hour. I wrote my name and made up a room number and filled it out and he never looked at it.

"If your tennis pro comes in, tell him Jaxie Skinner is here."

Fast Eddie and I went to a far court and hit for about an hour. After, he sat in a courtside chair and talked about matches past while I put a big towel down on the court and stretched. We sat there for a long time, enjoying the warm Mississippi spring day. Eventually the pro came out and spoke to us. I introduced myself.

"Oh yeah, I saw your name on the draw," he said. "I'm so glad you're playing in this tournament. How's your room?"

"Actually, Fast Eddie and I here," I said, and paused while Fast Eddie and the pro nodded a hello to one another, "each have a van of our own we sleep in. Mighty comfortable. A lot cheaper out on the road. You know these events don't pay much."

He laughed. "Hey, well let me comp you a room here. I probably can only get one, but I'll get you one with two beds."

Fast Eddie stepped forward. "No, I'm better sleeping in my van," he said. "You just get him a big suite, king-sized bed and all."

The pro said he would be right back, that we should wait for him. He went into the pro shop. Through the window we could see him pick up the phone. We sat back down.

"Let's hope the court time is free," I said.

"Yeah, no joking," Fast Eddie said.

The pro hung up the phone and left the shop. About five minutes later I heard footsteps behind us and turned to see a man in a maroon blazer and black slacks, a sixtyish dude with artificially dark hair parted on the side and sweeping across the top of his head. He had ruddy skin, a big bulbous nose, and dark eyebrows. His jacket was cheap polyester and the slacks weren't much better. The penny loafers he wore were the kind that easily pulled onto and off of your feet without much effort. He walked with a stride of great confidence, and the closer he came the bigger I could see he was, about six feet three and 250 pounds. He had enormous hands with thick meaty fingers, and he wore a huge University of Alabama class ring with a crimson stone.

"Hey there, now," he said. "How y'all doing?"

I nodded back to him. "We're all right. Just fine. And you?"

"Well, I'm doing good." He stepped onto the court in front of us and stuck out his hand. "I'm Gordy. Nice to meet you."

I stood up and shook, told him my name, and introduced him to Fast Eddie, whom I called by his full name, Eddie Kobeleski.

"I know who you are," Gordy said to me, smiling. "You playing in this tournament here, ain't you?"

"Yes sir."

"Well, we don't get many players of your caliber out this way."

"I ain't what I used to be. I've been off the tour a long time."

"I bet you still got it. But there's some good players in this draw, especially some of these South Americans. They say that boy from Uruguay should make it to Paris."

Fast Eddie stood and asked, "Are you in the tennis business?"

The man smiled.

"Yes sir, I guess you can say I am. I'm into all sports businesses. Why don't y'all let me take you to dinner tonight? I've got a membership to the VIP room of a club y'all will enjoy—the Kitty Kat Palace up around Memphis. You can enjoy yourself and good up there."

I'll be honest and say that the thought of taking this stranger up on the visit to a strip club crossed my mind. I had been living a monk-like existence for six months, avoiding bars and keeping my head down and my nose clean, but impure thoughts of women had been creeping into my head late at night when I flipped through the TV or thumbed through a magazine.

But I also knew that those strippers shaking it in my face and the liquor and the cold beers they would pour down me there would drain my wallet, and I would be tired and hung over tomorrow. I was thinking it over, weighing the risk versus reward, when Fast Eddie spoke up. "I don't want any part of that," he said. "We got a tennis tournament to play." He grabbed his racket bag and stormed off through the pro shop.

I looked up at Gordy's smiling face, his gray-blue eyes exaggerated beneath caterpillar-like eyebrows, his moist forehead reminding me of a shiny cut of meat. "What you think, son? It'll be a fine time."

"What is it you want with me?" I asked. I knew, but I wanted to hear it from him.

"Son, we can talk about it in more detail tonight."

"I can't make it tonight. I need to rest. I get off in one of those places, it will be bad for my game."

"Well, son, what I want you to do, your game doesn't need to be at its best."

"No sir," I said. "I'm not interested. I'm here to win. This, I hope, is going to be my big comeback."

"Well, take my card, son"—he handed me one—"if you change your mind."

I stuck his card in my pocket and headed toward the pro shop. The pro had returned and gave me a key to a room, and asked if I met Gordy. I nodded, returned the key to him, and said, no thanks, I would stay in my van.

It's disturbing that people all over the globe can go on the Internet and bet on a first-round singles match in a low-profile event in Tunica,

Mississippi, a match that no one will bother to come see. It makes greyhound racing seem humane. I could have made some good money over the years if I had been willing to throw matches. But I was never willing to lose. Never.

I had applied for the main draw at Tunica based on my past success in the French Open, and they gave me a wild card because my ranking points had long since expired. In the first round I drew a Hungarian I had never heard of named Janos Szucs, ranked 276 in the world.

Fast Eddie went to the casino's business center and looked him up online, finding a few short articles about him in Florida newspapers. Like most international players on the tour, Szucs had not lived in his home country for years but kept his passport for tax purposes and the possibility of playing Davis Cup for Hungary one day. He was five years younger than me, and had moved to Florida in his midteens to train. He had played one year of college tennis in Orlando, and then he had been slogging it out on the Futures and Challenger circuits for four years, never rising above the high two hundreds.

I am not sure how to pronounce his last name. I've always said it the way I heard it called by the tottering Mississippi woman on the tournament help desk who intoned over the loudspeaker. "*Ja* Nose . . . Su . . . *Sucks*?" He didn't correct her, but dutifully appeared with a racket bag slung over his low, sloping shoulders.

In the warm-up I asked myself how this guy had made it to as high as he had in the world rankings. He was a brooding, swarthy dude of not more than five-seven with ripped arms and muscular thighs. He hit two-handed on both sides, a style you rarely see beyond Monica Seles and the ten-and-unders, and often with underspin, even on the forehand, much like Fabrice Santoro. That should have been a sign I was in trouble, because Santoro was one tough player, but I didn't see it that way then because Szucs's motion was so unorthodox. He never even came to net for a single volley or overhead, and his serve was a herky-jerky slash that looped the ball into play. I looked over at Fast Eddie during our warm-up—he was the only person there for our match, one of only about six spectators in the whole tennis center that day—and shrugged. I couldn't believe that dude's game. I figured I would beat him easily.

He won the toss, but let me serve first. *This dude has really got some balls*, I thought. I hit several strong first serves, but much to my surprise Szucs moved inside the baseline and hit hard returns down the lines, taking the ball insanely early and pushing me back on my heels. My responses, mostly short balls, he angled away for winners. I won one point on an outright ace, but other than that he broke my serve easily.

I figured on the changeover that I could jump on his serve, that he must have deferred for a reason, and eagerly leaned forward when he threw his first toss in the air. His weak warm-up serves must have been for show, however, because the first serve he hit was hard and flat right to my backhand. I hit the ball into the bottom of the net. He then hit a crazy angle out wide that aced me. In the deuce court at 30–love he spun me far off the court to my forehand side, and when I ran it down, he played a deft angled drop shot back to my backhand to win the point.

He totally perplexed me. It's agonizing to lose to a player you know you should beat—one whose style of play shouldn't cause you the problems it does—but it humiliates you nonetheless. Nothing moves faster than losing eight of nine points. I panicked, and instead of sticking with my game and being patient, I did what most strong, young, but unwise players do, and that was to hit the ball even harder, and, of course, that brought on many more errors than it did winners. I might have been older than when I played my last tournament match, but I wasn't any wiser. I lost the first set 6–1.

The second set didn't go any better. I couldn't push him back, and trying to hit the ball hard enough to drive him deeper caused me to make more errors. Down 3–1, I dialed it back a little and kept the ball in play, but it seemed he couldn't miss, angling balls away from me that he took on the rise, making contact almost as soon as the ball came off the clay.

He won the final point with a devastating drop shot that I had no chance to get, closing out the second set 6–2. I left the ball rolling softly and hurried to net and shook hands with him and tossed my rackets into my bag. I hustled off the court and through the tennis center and casino, Fast Eddie pursuing right behind. It seemed like the match had lasted about ninety seconds.

I had much to think about while driving that van drive back to Georgia. It was the first of the many moments in my long comeback when I questioned the sanity of tennis for my livelihood. Driving six hours down the sleepy roads through Mississippi and Alabama in my used van, the red clay of Roland Garros seemed another lifetime away, like some distant dream. Did I really have a chance to get back to the pros, where my time had been so fleeting? Was there any way to undo the damage I had done to my body and my brain with all the drinking and time off? I had a million miles to go if I was going to get my game back.

Over the next decade I played about two hundred small-time pro tournaments, averaging about twenty a year. Ten long years on the road. I played everywhere from Miami to Vancouver to Argentina, anywhere that I could drive. I slept in my van in parking lots across two continents, showering and shaving in tennis center locker rooms. My goal always was to crack the top one hundred so I could play in the Grand Slams, especially the U.S. Open, but I could never get near it, losing as much as I won. I didn't give up, however. I clung to the dream because there was nothing else for me to cling to.

I drove all the way to Buenos Aires one time. Guess who I lost to in the second round? Janos Szucs. He became my nemesis. It was the fifth time I played him, and the fourth time I had lost to him. My only victory against this little fireplug son of a bitch came in Dallas, on a fast, indoor carpet. But on the clay, where most of our matches took place, he ate my game up.

I can't overstate how much this little Hungarian tormented me. I drew him everywhere. It seemed like an angry higher power had sent him to knock me out of tournaments with his unorthodox game, those ugly groundstrokes that he could do so much with, those drop shots like yo-yos that he jerked around the court. I often defeated players better than him, young players who had enough power to knock him off the court, but I couldn't beat him. If I tried to hit too hard, to do him like the young studs did, I made too many mistakes. My age had made me a smarter player, much more tactical and a more consistent returner of serve, and these traits gave me an advantage on the younger players who stood back on the baseline and did nothing but launch rockets until the ball didn't come back or they missed. Those kids were all heart and muscles but no head, but many of them could beat Szucs while I couldn't. That son of a bitch almost drove me into retirement several times. I think I gave him enough ranking points to keep his career afloat.

Szucs and I were like everyone in minor-league tennis, riding the cusp, scrambling for a ranking, just a few big wins from the next level, from the ATP circuit where you can go from Rome to Monte Carlo to Paris to London, making good money, instead of the low-budget pig trail that runs through Lubbock, Texas, and Joplin, Missouri. I never could string enough big wins together to make the move.

One year I played twenty-eight tournaments, and in *eleven* of them I lost to the little Hungarian son of a bitch, five of those losses coming in a South American swing: Puebla, Mexico; Buenos Aires; Quito, Ecuador; Medellin, Colombia; and Caracas, Venezuela. He cost me at least a hundred ranking points, points that would have elevated me to 150 in the world and would have made my life much easier. Instead I hovered around three hundred, a level where you don't get into the qualifying draws for the Grand Slams, a level where you are lucky if you can get into the Challenger draws. My goal was to rise high enough to reach the U.S. Open qualies, but he stood in my way at every turn.

A bothersome thought began to eat at me: Perhaps my French Open run was just luck. Maybe I had played over my head for those three weeks, running off wins against players whom I should not have been able to beat. Was it possible that I was undeserving of those eight victories in Paris? That I had an easy draw with the exception of beating Fernandez in the second round? Was I a fluke? I know many tennis insiders believe that was the case. This notion began to consume me, and it still persists.

I never considered throwing matches for gamblers, and there were more offers through the years, but I did consider cheating another way. I seriously debated taking steroids and human growth hormones. I know other players on the tours were using, ripped as they were. Often edgy and irritable, they were strong as horses, never injured. I needed the drugs too, in my late twenties and then my thirties, playing kids a decade younger. My knee often stiffened up after matches, and despite regular stretching and working out, I knew was vulnerable physically. My shoulder began to feel tired, and for a while I fought tendonitis in it. Another time I badly sprained my ankle and had to take off three months while it healed.

Shortly after the ankle injury, about the time I turned thirty-three, I bought ten vials of liquid human growth hormone, known as HGH, from a personal trainer in Florida recommended by a player I knew. He gave me instructions on how to inject it into the fatty tissue on my stomach, assuring me that the formula would not show up if I had to take a drug test. "We test it regularly, to make sure it's not detectable," he said. "You'll be as strong as a bull in no time."

I went into a toilet stall in the locker room and pulled off my shirt and primed the needle and watched the drops come up on the tip. I pinched a spot on my stomach but then I heard my father say, "Don't do it. If you have to cheat to win, it's not worth it. It's not winning, it's cheating."

I threw the unused vials and the syringe into the trash.

Money became a big worry for me. If you are the five-hundredth best baseball player in the world, you are on a major-league roster, earning a minimum salary of five hundred thousand dollars, most likely more. If you are five hundredth in the world in tennis, you don't make shit. I have won less than thirty thousand annually in all but two of the years I played the various minor-league circuits. My average tax return is on par with temporary workers and substitute school-teachers.

My tax accountant, an old friend of my father and local attorney in Piney who also handles wills, divorces, and the occasional lawn mower repair from his home office out by the new lake, has saved me a lot of dough. He helped me manage and invest my money, and most years he pushed my taxable wages down so low against my travel expenses that my income was negative. But near the end of this long streak, it didn't matter what he did with my taxes. I had burned through most of my savings. The money I won in Paris and profits I made from selling off parcels of land was almost all gone.

For a while I earned a small income from a few college students who rented rooms in my house. I needed someone there while I was on the road, to keep an eye on the house, and to feed my dogs. After a while, they moved away except for one kid named Randy, a good boy who was the son of a man who had worked for my father years ago. Randy stayed on after college. For a while he had this very sexy live-in girlfriend, a Costa Rican exchange student who liked tennis. Her name was Gabriella. They kept the court in good shape, and in return I let them live there for free. I liked him, and fought the powerful urge to fool around with his girlfriend. The opportunity to go to bed with her presented itself more than a few times, but I never touched her. It wasn't easy restraining myself, but I did it. I liked Randy too much to do that to him.

Randy always asked about how my tournaments were going. The more time passed, though, the worse things went and the less good news I had to report. The year I turned thirty-seven, I lost in the first round of thirteen consecutive tournaments and my ranking fell way down in the eight hundreds. If you are in the eight hundreds and you are in your late thirties, even the Futures tournaments don't call you back. It was also my direst straights financially, because losing in the first round of a Challenger pays only $580, but then I fell out of eligibility for the Challengers and had to play the qualies. Losing in the qualies, you don't get paid shit, not even a penny. Then I started losing in the first rounds of the Futures, losing to much younger players, earning nothing.

I thought about quitting all the time, about finding a job teaching lessons, as abhorrent as that seemed to me. I've never liked teaching the game, being a robot feeding balls to people, one after another, a country-club version of factory work. The dread of becoming a teaching pro, of standing on a court giving lessons eight hours a day, stoked my desire to keep competing.

Then my serve got the yips. That had never happened to me in all my years of playing tennis, but my timing went completely off kilter. Losing the serve was like a bodily function had gone awry. I sought out lessons from a well-known teaching pro in Birmingham, but he couldn't help me.

I still had not built up the courage to talk to Harry. All those years I tiptoed around Atlanta like a bad memory, ashamed to show my face where people remembered the great player that I had once been. I also worried I might run into my mom or sisters over there.

Despite my slump, I kept playing. I begged a tournament director I was friendly with for a spot in the qualifying draw of a Challenger tournament in Tallahassee. He reluctantly agreed, knowing full well I didn't deserve it.

My match was scheduled for eight in the morning, so I drove down the night before from Piney, a five-hour trip. I parked in the lot of the public tennis center there about dusk, under a patch of pine trees in the far corner next to a trio of softball fields. The neighborhood was rough around the edges, the tennis center one of the USTA's efforts to develop inner-city tennis.

I hoped that no police officers would run me off. I had seen a truck stop on Interstate 10 where I could go spend the night if needed. I thought about turning back, but then figured I would be okay where I was. There were no cops in sight. I'd been doing this sort of thing for years.

I still avoided staying with host families, but on that hot-as-hell night sleeping in a stranger's air-conditioned house it didn't sound half bad. I cursed when I found out the tennis clubhouse there had closed at seven, despite two good hours of light. I walked over to the bathrooms by the softball field and used those odorous facilities, washing my face and brushing my teeth in the filthy sink, getting some strange stares from a few young kids and their father.

Back in the van I stretched out on the single mattress and thumbed through an old *Sports Illustrated*, reading by the light of a low-wattage flashlight. The mattress took up one side, but I had room for a small but comfortable padded chair and ottoman, a big cooler stocked with ice, and a bookshelf with a thirteen-inch television on top and a compact boombox radio and CD player on the bottom shelf. When I was able to stay places with easy access to an outdoor electrical outlet, I ran an extension cord from the van and turned on a brighter lamp and a small but powerful oscillating fan. It made the place mighty homey.

But this night there was no free electricity. I had to use a tiny battery-powered fan I had picked up in a dollar store. Its cooling effect was almost nil.

I opened the van's front windows and vented the sides and back. It didn't matter, there was no breeze at all on that night, and the humidity must have been about eighty-five percent and the temperature about as high.

I drank ice water from a gallon jug I had frozen before the trip that was about half melted, and I poured some of it on a hand towel and held it to my forehead. I thought about checking into a motel, but my credit card had a ten-thousand-dollar limit, and I was about fifty bucks shy of maxing out. I debated going back to the truck stop and hooking up to an electrical outlet.

But then I started to drift off, the sound and visions of a tennis ball in motion in my mind. I slept for I don't know how long, waking up to loud laughter, voices going back and forth, not far from the van. I sat up, and listened. They sounded harmless, just a few drunks out in the park in the middle of the night.

I tried to go back to sleep but they kept carrying on. One of them was funny, singing "Sitting on the Dock of the Bay" in a very deep voice, and then trying pathetically to whistle the part at the song's end. I chuckled about this for a while. Later they began to argue about their need for more beer and how to pay for it, eventually drifting away, walking off into the trees toward the softball fields.

After a long period of silence except for the occasional car going down the street, I fell asleep again, this time pretty deep. I dreamed of playing on pristine red clay courts in the south of France, the Mediterranean spreading out crystal blue as far as the eye could see. I was hitting the ball well, feeling young and strong and fast. Watching my every move were young women with names like Giulietta and Dominique, all olive-skinned with big brown eyes and long dark hair, sexy bodies squeezed into tight sundresses.

The dream ended with a harsh blow, a ball hitting me right in the face and the sun flashing in my eyes. I woke up in darkness with a pistol against my forehead, a man on top of me, his knees pressing into my chest. He smelled like piss and shit and sweat. He pulled back the small revolver's hammer, the ominous click of the pin ready to hit the shell, the muzzle against my skin. He leaned down over me, his coal-dark face only inches from mine.

"What the fuck you doing?" His voice was deep, and his breath smelled like rotting meat. I gasped with his knees on my chest.

"Tennis tournament . . . Playing in a tennis tournament tomorrow."

"A what?" He laughed, a deep grumble. "A tennis tournament?"

"Yeah."

"Goddamn." He laughed again.

"You can have my wallet . . . The TV . . . That's all I got worth anything."

"Nope, you gonna give me the keys, motherfucker. And then you going to get the fuck out." He moved the pistol from my forehead and jammed it into my ear. "Where the keys?"

"Top of the TV."

He eased the hammer of the pistol down, and then reached over and picked up the keys and put them in his pocket. He nudged me in the ear again with the gun.

"All right. Get out."

He eased back on my chest with his knees and pulled the gun from my head, although he kept it pointed at me.

"Hey," I said. "Let me have my rackets. Please."

"What they worth?"

"They ain't worth much. They're old, used."

"Lemme see 'em."

"The bag . . . behind the passenger seat."

He crawled off me and sat in the chair and turned and looked at the racket bag, keeping the gun pointed at my head.

"Goddamn, motherfucker. That's a big-ass bag. How many you got?"

"Twelve."

"Twelve? What does a motherfucker need with twelve tennis rackets? You outfitting a football team?"

"They're all mine."

"Shit. Twelve tennis rackets. You don't need no twelve tennis rackets."

"No, please, I do. Please let me keep 'em. I'm . . . I'm at the end of my rope." I swallowed hard, aware of my voice sounding whiny, pitiful, but I went on. "I used to be a top pro . . . I'm trying like hell to get it back, to make one last run. If you got any sympathy at all . . . you'll let me have that. You can have my van, all my money."

I thought about my watch, the Tag Heuer from Paris, worth maybe three thousand dollars. It was stuffed into a side pocket in the racket bag. Other than my house and van and rackets, it was the only thing I still owned with any value.

"Shit. You must love this damn game."

"Yeah . . . I do. I do. Just let me take my rackets. Please."

He moved over and I could see him better, shifting into a dim light coming into the open back door. His eyes were red and bloodshot, his skin sweaty beneath a wild scraggly beard, his Afro unkempt beneath a tattered baseball cap. He shook his head, smiling, looking at me like I was the biggest freak he'd ever seen.

"I got a gun on your ass . . . and you're begging me for tennis rackets."

"Yeah, please. Please. Gimme a break. Lemme have 'em."

He stood up, bent over in the van, looking at my rackets, and then lifted the bag and slung it toward the back door. It bumped against the van ceiling on the way out and then hit the pavement with a thud. "Get yo' ass out of here before I shoot you."

Three hours later, I got my ass kicked, *1-and-1*, barely better than the dreaded double bagel. I played like shit, but no worse than I had played during the six months previous. I couldn't get a decent serve in the court and resorted to spinning pitiful second balls just to start the point, weak offerings that my nineteen-year-old opponent annihilated.

I shook hands with him and shoved my racket in my bag and walked straight from the court out to the road, ashamed to face the tournament director. I walked about a mile to a convenience store near the highway. I called Fast Eddie collect. He said he would come pick me up and carry me home.

I sat on the curb and waited, head down in the heat, thinking that this was no way for a thirty-seven-year-old to live. By the time he got there five hours later the smell of exhaust fumes had started to make me nauseous. "I'm quitting tennis," I said. "This is it."

"No you're not," Fast Eddie said. "No you're not. Let's get you on home. I'm sorry about the van, but there're more vans in the world. We can get you another one."

I didn't say much of anything, just stared out the windshield at the pine trees and the wiregrass prairie passing by. I looked at my wrist to check the time and started to wonder how much that gold Tag Heuer they had given me to wear in the French Open was really worth.

Two days later I drove my dad's old pickup truck to an Atlanta jewelry store on Peachtree Road north of Buckhead where the fancy malls of Lenox and Phipps Plaza straddled the boulevard named for the famous Georgia fruit. I sold the watch for seventeen hundred dollars, a stack of one-hundred dollar bills, crisp greens with that engraving of Ben Franklin's bald head. I had hoped for more but I'm certain I would have made less at the Thessalonica pawnshop that carried glass eyes. The payoff was more than I had won from playing in a tennis tournament in three years.

I cruised south down Peachtree, amazed at the enormous new buildings that had gone up in Atlanta, black and blue gleaming towers surrounding the busy intersection of Piedmont and Peachtree roads. I turned right on Piedmont and followed it out toward Wieuca Road, back into the residential area and toward the country club where Harry had taught lessons. It had been nineteen years since I'd spoken to him, and even though I had gone to Atlanta with only the intention of picking up some fast cash, I soon found myself on a mission to see Harry, to tell him about my problems with my serve. If anybody could help me with it, he could. If he couldn't, and if I couldn't get the ball in the air and hit it smoothly and hard and accurately and consistently, I would be done with competitive tennis, resigned to the lesson court for the rest of my days.

When I was five and my father took me to that elegant country club back off Wieuca Road with its sloping driveway down through perfectly manicured hedges, the place had seemed enormous and magnificent, like a grand city unto itself with its own terrain and landscape tucked in a fortress of perfectly planted trees and shrubs, safe from the hustle and madness of Atlanta. But three decades and hundreds of tennis clubs later, it seemed mediocre, an average facility at best.

I drove through the big parking lot down to the tennis pro shop and the eight clay courts. It was a Wednesday afternoon in late June, an absolutely great summer day, not too hot, maybe low eighties, and the air was dry with a soft breeze, weather about as good as you could want for playing tennis. But despite the perfect conditions there was no one on the tennis courts, not even a single car in the parking lot by the tennis pro shop. Up the sloping hill, there were many Mercedes and Jaguars and enormous SUVs, pairs of fat men loading their clubs onto golf carts in the asphalt lot.

The tennis pro shop had not changed. The room was as still as an empty library, the lights dim and the dark wood paneling elegant in a 1950s kind of way that blocked out the sun and made it seem gloomy even on the brightest days. No attendant was on duty. A black rotary dial telephone sat on the white Formica countertop in a light patina of dust. On the walls hung the familiar framed pictures of old tennis stars, Pancho Gonzalez looking suave and handsome and tall and only a touch Mexican, holding the Wimbledon trophy, and Jack Kramer in a plain white T-shirt diving for a volley in loose-fitting short pants. To the back was the wall of plaques with rows of small nameplates marking the club's adult and junior champions back to the late 1950s, the updates stopping about twelve years prior. I studied the junior winners of the mid-1980s and early 1990s, players I had beaten easily. I wondered what happened to all these people. My name was not there because I was never eligible to play the club tournament since we were not members. I chuckled at a few of the names, not from remembering the people themselves but the preposterous labels of some of these rich country-club snobs: Tippy Gordimer, Howard Cullingham IV, Dinky Gilstrap, and my all-time favorite ridiculous name, Horvath Horvath McGraw.

I remembered that there used to be pictures of Harry and an assistant teaching pro beside the plaques honoring the tournament winners, but that section of the wall was blank. I could still see the small nail holes where Harry's picture had hung and a faint outline where the frame had protected part of the oak paneling from light.

I walked out the back door to the empty courts, paired off in twos with low side fences. If the courts had been full, like they often had been, you could follow eight matches at once. I walked out onto the pro court and could feel it hard as a rock under my feet. It had been a dry summer. Clay courts need water to keep them soft, to make them slow, otherwise they'll become hard and will play fast and the ball will bounce like it hit concrete. I figured there was no point in watering if there was no one to play there. I went over and sat on the side bleachers, three short rows lined up along what had been Harry's lesson court.

I looked at that court and my eyes teared up thinking back over the years about how cool I thought Harry was, how he had called me champ and encouraged me in the game of tennis, giving me confidence and belief just by throwing a high-five my way and treating me like I was a stud when I was only five years old, nothing but a scrawny kid from the sticks of Piney, Georgia. I needed to find him, wherever he was, and make up for the wrong that I had done—really, that my dad had done, but he didn't mean it—the time we dumped him when I went to the French Open.

I turned to leave when two men in their seventies emerged from the pro shop, one a chubby, tall bald-headed fellow with an enormous Prince racket, and the other a short, wrinkled old man with thick hair and gnarled posture in tennis whites carrying, of all rackets, a Head Professional, the small aluminum one with the red throat piece in the frame. I had not seen someone playing with a Red Head since the late 1980s, maybe longer. That racket had a sweet spot about the size of a quarter.

The little man scrunched up his face and homed in on me like I was a burglar. “Did you sign in? You’ve got to sign in at the clubhouse. I’ve never seen you before. What’s your member number?”

All I could do was shake my head and laugh. It was either smile or throttle the old son of a bitch, and I needed no legal problems with a rich old dude. Every country club has a few pricks like this who view their clubs as primeval estates that are always under attack by heathens who do not obey the rules, by visitors who do not register, by the hoi polloi who do not keep to their place on the other side of the tracks. “I was looking for Harry Crummy,” I said.

“What? You a bill collector? He hadn’t paid his alimony again? He hasn’t worked here for ten years. That imposter retired a long time ago.”

“Where is he now?”

“I don’t know and I don’t care,” he said. “But let me tell you one thing, son. Here at *the club*—” He paused to let the word linger in the air and he took a deep breath from the exertion he had expended in saying it. “—we do not let visitors just gallivant around our facilities.”

“Fuck you, old man,” I said. “This dumpy place was lucky to have Harry Crummy. It’s not worth a shit without him. And those courts are in sorry condition. I wouldn’t want my dog pissing on these courts.”

I walked through the pro shop and toward my dad’s old truck as the old man rushed to the telephone, summoning the security guard. Shitheads like that guy were the reason I could never be a club pro. I drove out of the parking lot, squealing the tires. When I was a safe distance away, I pulled off to the side of the road in front of someone’s long driveway, a huge brick home painted white and flanked by large oaks in a vast green yard rising up a hill. I dug my cell phone out of my pocket and called information and asked for the number for Harry Crummy.

The operator chuckled. "What was the last name again?"

"Crummy. C-R-U-M-M-Y. Just like it sounds."

She gave me his number and connected me. It rang several times before an older woman with a pronounced southern accent answered.

"Is Harry there?" I said.

"Who's calling, please?" she said, dragging out the "pl-ease" in two long syllables.

I told her and she said, "Just a moment, please," and set the phone down. My cell connection was clear and I could hear her say, "Jaxie Skinner is on the phone for you." I heard Harry in the room with her, his voice crackly. "Really? Jaxie Skinner?"

It was only a second or two before he was on the phone. "Jaxie, boy, is that you?"

"Yes sir. It's me, Harry. How are you?"

"Boy, I'm getting old. Don't teach tennis lessons at all anymore . . . I'm living near Bitsy Grant. Go over there and sit on the bleachers and watch people play. Even go to the junior tournaments and watch. I was telling somebody about you the other day. Told 'em you were the best student I ever had. It's good to hear from you, son . . . Where are you?"

"I'm in Atlanta right now. Not too far from Bitsy Grant."

"Well damn, boy, come on over and see me."

"Hang on, Harry. Let me get something to write with."

I choked up. I fought the tears from my eyes, and looked for a pen that wasn't dried out from sitting in the truck for years. I found four, all of them dry, until I dug up an old carpenter's pencil and a weathered Georgia map from the glove compartment. I struggled to keep it together. "Okay, Harry, I'm on Wieuca Road, near the club." He laughed hard, that raspy chuckle of his, and said, "Damn, boy, I ain't good with directions, but I know that route." He gave me the address and told me how to find him. I scribbled a note on the margin of the map and told him I would be there in a minute.

Harry's cottage-style brick house sat near a small park where the yuppies who lived in the area jogged, only a few hundred yards across Northside Drive from the Bobby Jones Golf Course, a once prestigious loop that had become a goat track under city management.

I parked in the driveway and he came out to meet me. He looked much older, his hair thick but solid gray, his mustache silver as well, although he wore his hair in the style he always had, a little long in the back. He was still trim except for a small paunch, and his face had weathered and wrinkled more. He had been in his midfifties when I last saw him. Although nineteen years isn't that much in some ways, it's a long time for a man passing from the end of a career into retirement. I couldn't picture Harry retired with all his restless energy, sitting around the house, talking back to the television all day long.

He waved and grinned, his bushy mustache curling up, his face more ruddy red than the deep tan he'd always had. "I remember this old truck," he said, and laughed. "How you doing, Jaxie?"

I opened the door and stepped out and extended my hand to shake but instead he came at me with both arms and hugged me. There was a little water in his eyes, and a tremble in his voice for a minute.

I hugged him back, and it seemed like the most natural thing in the world.

"Damn, Jaxie, where you been? I looked for your name in *Tennis* magazine all these years."

I told him the short version of my story, standing in his driveway. I apologized for not taking him to Paris, that it was my biggest regret, that it was my dad's doings and we were hurting for money, and that my family had all sorts of other problems.

"How is your dad?" he asked. I told him.

He slumped his shoulders and looked at his shoes. "He was a good man. I'm sorry to hear about his passing. I know he didn't mean anything bad toward me. I was too proud a fool to call."

We'd been standing there talking, me doing most of it, for I don't know how long, when a silver-haired woman came out through the garage. "Jaxie, this is my wife, Suzette."

She smiled and we shook hands, and I told her it was nice to meet her. "Harry talks about you just about every day," she said. She turned to Harry. "Don't ya'll want to come inside? Or sit out on the patio? I can get you some coffee or lemonade if you want?"

"Lemonade's good," he said.

He put his arm on my shoulder and guided me up the driveway and through his garage and into the kitchen, the house immaculate and meticulously decorated like something out of *Southern Living* magazine. We went onto his back patio and I sat there barely touching the lemonade and told him most everything I've already told you. He listened, asking questions here and there, but I did most of the talking. I brought the story of my life up to the present and told him of being thirty-seven years old and losing my serve. "The goddamn yips," he said. "Happens to the best sometimes."

The next thing I know he had his hand on my arm and was guiding me back out to the driveway and we got in an old car he had bought, a vintage red Karmann Ghia, the kind with the engine in the back that rode very low to the ground. He drove, and he still drove slow as hell, even in his own neighborhood. I realized that I didn't have my rackets nor did we have any balls. "Don't worry, boy, I've got a trunk full of rackets. The pro is a buddy of mine and will loan us some practice balls.

We are going to get that serve of yours fixed up, and fast."

He led me out onto a court at Bitsy Grant, a soft pad of Rubico, and I couldn't help but feel like I was five years old again. "Let's get warmed up, Jaxie boy." He pulled the basket on his side of the court and stood about the service line and started feeding me groundstrokes, just lobbing them over to me. I took my time and stroked the ball deep into the corners. "Those are the groundstrokes I know." He was smiling; I was too.

After about twenty balls he began putting a little more pace on the feeds. We ran through the basket and I was working up a sweat. The sun had started to go down behind the clubhouse that sits atop a concrete bank of bleachers, and the plate glass windows reflected red and orange and fiery pink.

Harry held up the last three balls in his hand, and even though I hadn't worked out with him in almost twenty years, I knew his gesture meant that he was going to run my ass off on these shots, to get ready. He went from my backhand corner to my forehand corner on the first two before tapping a very short drop shot on my backhand side. I raced from the deepest corner of the court toward the net post and got there just in time to slice it crosscourt at an absurd angle so that it skidded on the white plastic sideline tape, a shot that would be an outright winner against anyone on the planet. "Atta boy, Jaxie. That one's almost better than a wet dream I had about Evonne Goolagong . . . but not quite." He winked at me, his face beaming, that big gray mustache curling up in punctuation. "Let's pick 'em up."

I took the ball hopper from Harry and pressed down on the scattered practice balls, each one squeezing through the metal bars and into the basket, that sliding sort of thump they make comforting in a way that's hard to explain. The courts around us were busy, and I was glad to see that somewhere people went out and played tennis on such beautiful summer days, unlike the quiet desperation of lonely tennis courts I'd seen over at Harry's old club.

He came over to my side. "All right, Jaxie. Your groundstrokes look damn good. What's going on with your serve?"

I told him about the serves that I tried to hit with power sailing on me, and then when I tried to pull the ball down with some spin how all I could do was hit pitiful second serves that seemed they wouldn't even reach the net in the air. "My rhythm is all gone," I said. "I just can't get the timing right. Sometimes I try to slow it down, and that might help for a ball or two. Then it goes on me again, and I feel like I'm too slow. If I speed it up, it all goes to hell."

"Hit a few for me, champ," he said. "Let me take a look at it." He gave me some room, moving back to where the baseline met the singles sideline.

I stood there and bounced the ball repeatedly, thinking, afraid to begin. Thoughts were running through my mind and I must have bounced it twenty times.

"Jaxie, I can see your first problem. You are bouncing the ball too damn much. Let that thing loose in the air and hit it."

I tossed the ball into the air and hit a serve, feeling as clumsy as an offensive lineman hitting a tackling dummy. The serve sailed almost two feet long.

"Do it again, Jaxie. Hit a bunch of them for me."

I hit one after another, hitting a few good ones but then it turned bad, shots flying well long until I tried to correct the errors and the serves started dropping into the net.

"Son." Harry put his arm around my shoulder. "It's all in the ball toss, boy. It's all in the toss. It's going to take some work, but we can fix it. Yes sir, we can fix it right up."

I started working out every day with Harry. He recruited players for me to hit with, and he watched every practice match. He said he wanted no payment; he was just glad to have something to do.

I drove all the way back and forth to Piney the first few days until he suggested that I stay at their house. "I don't want to do that, Harry, to put y'all out."

"Son, Suzette and I'd be glad to have you. You'll get you some mighty fine meals, too. She suggested it. We want you here."

So for most of the summer I was their guest, staying right across the hall from their master bedroom. My room was so close to theirs at night I could hear them snoring, and about every three days I would hear the springs squeaking a little. It made me happy to think that even into his seventies Harry could still get it up.

The room had a very comfortable single bed and the nightstand had a well-placed reading light that gave off a warm glow. Harry and Suzette went to bed at nine every night, so I would lie there reading for about two hours before going to sleep. I had plucked the first volume of Shelby Foote's Civil War histories from their shelf in the front room, books Harry and Suzette encouraged me to read. I had never been much of a reader before, but I really started getting into it. I took solace in the futility of the battle the South was fighting, inspired by the effort that the Confederates kept up in the face of an army superior in size and supplies.

I woke up about seven each morning to the smell and the sound of sizzling sausage patties, the clatter of pots and pans being shuffled in the kitchen while Suzette made eggs or pancakes or French toast or waffles. Sometimes she would sing old country songs like "Blue Eyes Crying in the Rain." When she did sing Harry would come in and sing "Whiskey River" or "Mamas Don't Let Your Babies Grow Up to Be Cowboys," his scratchy voice way out of tune and high-pitched.

I don't know if I could have changed my ways, even my outlook on the world, without those breakfasts that Suzette made. After just a few days under their roof, I realized that I did not need to set the alarm clock but would wake with the sun beaming through the sheer white curtain and the smells and sounds of the kitchen. It was such a joy to be around two people who were so happy, content to wake up and eat and relish life's simple pleasures, pleasures like exceptionally fluffy biscuits and gravy and sweet but spicy sausage patties. I had not eaten much of a breakfast in years. If anything, all I usually had was a bowl of cereal or maybe some Pop-Tarts.

I know it sounds like Suzette's meals, delicious though they were, were not healthy, and that someone at the age of thirty-seven trying to make one last stand as a professional tennis player and crack that elusive top one hundred should not be eating southern-fried meals of eggs and biscuits soaked in gravy or sausage patties. When I was home or on the road I was into bran muffins and fruit and oatmeal and healthy cereals, and when I played in a tournament in Atlanta, I requested she make whole wheat pancakes, and of course Suzette obliged. But there was a heart to those meals that nothing could equal. And not everything she made was terrible for you. Her pancakes were light and she used lots of bananas and put out strawberries and other fruits like sweet, fresh cantaloupe.

In the morning I worked on my game with Harry, and in the afternoons, I played practice matches against local college players and the best juniors that Harry and a friend of his could find. I struggled some at first, losing a few to inferior players, but by August I fixed my serve and my game returned and my confidence soared. I began drilling before everyone I played.

I was back. By Labor Day, it was time to hit the road again.

This time, I did not try to do the small tours in a van. It was cost-effective, but I was kidding myself when I was out on the road sleeping in the back of a roomy Ford Econoline. Fast Eddie seemed disappointed when I told him, but I needed a real bed and a good night's sleep and somewhere to take a piss and a dump and running water with which to brush my teeth, especially before playing a series of grueling tennis matches. Harry loaned me five thousand dollars to buy a used Hyundai Elantra, a small but reliable car that was great on gas mileage.

Harry also found me a prospective sponsor, a tennis-crazy old man in Atlanta who owned a construction company and a chain of lumberyards. He took me by to see Winston Culpepper IV at his Buckhead home on Tuxedo Road, his house an antebellum-style mansion built in the 1940s that had been added onto so much it was as big as a school. His butler, a smooth-faced black man whose age was hard to guess, met us and asked us to wait on an overstuffed love seat in the spacious foyer where a huge curving staircase went up and around to a second level that was sectioned off in ornate railings. It was cold in that house with the blood-red walls and Persian rugs as big as a service box. Mahogany and cherrywood furniture filled the rooms, not to mention enormous oil paintings on the wall, mostly of hunting scenes and bird dogs and raccoons. I watched the stairs as if Scarlett O'Hara would emerge, but instead the butler came in from a side hallway, pushing Mr. Culpepper in a wheelchair. He was thin and wrinkled and had a red Georgia Bulldog blanket over his lap despite it being August and above ninety degrees outside.

The old man greeted Harry who bent down and shook his old bony hand, and then Harry introduced me. "Mr. Skinner," Mr. Culpepper said, his accent so pronounced that it took about four seconds to get my name out. He stuck out his hand and I shook it. It was dry and cold, but he squeezed surprisingly hard. "Harry here tells me great things about your game, the way you have been playing."

"Yes, sir, I've been working hard at it." I looked at his thin face beneath a thick head of hair for such an old man. He reminded me of an old southern politician behind horn-rimmed glasses. I figured he probably knew George Tolbert, my mom's second husband, but I sure as hell wasn't going to bring them up.

"Well, son, Harry says you have a chance to get back to the big time. I remember that French Open, watched it on TV. I used to go to Roland Garros every year in the '60s and '70s, saw everyone from Laver through Borg. That was a time, let me tell you. I don't get out as much as I used to. To be honest, I don't much like what I see in the game here today . . . these rackets are more like rocket launchers. It's all power and punch and not much spin and panache, but only *boom, boom, boom*," he said, smacking his fist against his palm.

Harry spoke up. "Jaxie here's got a complete game, Mr. Culpepper. He hits the ball with a lot of spin sometimes. He's playing smarter than ever. He's been working hard. I think he moves like a player still in his early twenties. Next year he'll have a shot to get back on the ATP tour for a few events, maybe even try qualifying at the U.S. Open. He possibly even could go back to the French or play Wimbledon."

The old man looked me up and down as though he was thinking about buying me. "You know what I told Jimmy Connors one time?"

"No, sir," I said.

"I said, 'Jimmy, if your dick was as big as you act like it is, you'd need a truck to haul that thing around with you.'"

He laughed, and Harry and I did too.

"Let's go into the drawing room," Mr. Culpepper said. His butler pushed him down the hallway and we followed, entering an enormous room with large windows looking back over a sloping yard at least two acres in size. Down the hill I could see a clay tennis court, and near that was a swimming pool and a cinder-block pool house with a cupola.

Harry and I sat on plush brown leather couches and Mr. Culpepper told us about seeing Borg and McEnroe and Vilas and Nastase, mixing in great details of the matches with stories about where he stayed and what he wore and what he had to eat and drink—he liked mainly gin and tonics, and fish sandwiches, but his favorite was lobster. He attended all of the Grand Slams of the 1970s and said he was there for the 1980 Wimbledon final between Borg and McEnroe. That had been his last time at Wimbledon, but he figured tennis couldn't get any better.

"I started playing tennis after that match," I said. "It is my earliest memory of anything on this earth. I was three. My family watched it on TV. Then my dad went out and built a tennis court in our yard."

"He built it himself?"

"Yes, sir. He was in the road business, and scraped it right off with a bulldozer. Red clay. Red dirt, really. That's where I first played."

"Why didn't he ever pave it? Put down some DecoTurf or something? If he was in the road business?" The old man's eyes twitched kind of funny.

"I guess we just always liked it. He could have paved it, but never did. He liked that red dirt."

"Ha, red dirt. Well, I'll be damned." He reached over and patted me on the leg. He turned and looked at Harry. "This boy's all right," he said.

He turned his head and yelled, "Johnny, would you bring out those shirts?"

The butler returned, this time carrying a large cardboard box, about four feet high and wide, his arms just long enough to grip it. The box blocked his vision and we couldn't see his head, only arms and cardboard coming our way.

"Set it down here," Mr. Culpepper said. The butler put it on the floor next to him. The old man leaned over the box and pulled out two white cotton tennis shirts. They were wrapped in plastic but I could see they had a collar and a big logo that said 75 LUMBER on the left breast, the spot where most players had either an alligator, a Fila F, or the Nike swoosh.

He tossed one to me and then one to Harry. "I'll give you ten thousand dollars for wearing these out on tour for one year—twelve months, that is, starting today."

I thought about how the tour I was on rarely had any fans, that most matches, with the exception of the semis and finals, wouldn't make the sports pages of even the local newspapers, and there would rarely be any photographs published. Most matches I would play were witnessed by only a few people, if any, perhaps a girlfriend or coach had who made the trip, people who had never even thought about buying a two-by-four in their life. But I didn't say anything when the butler brought him his bank book and he starting writing the check. He stuck his old tongue out of the corner of his mouth as he concentrated on his penmanship.

He signed the check and handed it to the butler and looked at me. "Let me see how the shirts look on you."

"Should I change here?"

"You can go back in the bathroom. First door on the right."

I put on the shirt and looked at myself in the mirror. The logo stood out, the big red rectangle and a white 75 inside the red, the number puffed up like it was filled with air, and beneath the red rectangle in a heavy black font was lettering that said LUMBER. It is a good thing I never cared much about fashion, because these shirts were flat-out ugly and I knew that the cotton would be heavy when it got sweaty. But I didn't complain. I was getting ten thousand dollars, and that would fund me for at least a year of tournaments if I stayed in cheap hotels and ate frugally.

I went back into the hallway beneath a huge chandelier and modeled the shirt for Harry and Mr. Culpepper. "That's sharp looking, son, sharp looking," Mr. Culpepper said.

"Thank you, sir, I appreciate your support." I shook his dry, cold hand and the butler handed me the check.

For most Americans, the tennis season ends when the finals of the U.S. Open are played one week after Labor Day, matches overshadowed by the beginning of football season. But September of that year is when my comeback truly began.

I had to go all the way to California to play, and it's not a bad place to be if you are on vacation or if you are rich, but if you are traveling in a Hyundai Elantra and staying in the cheapest motels you can find, it doesn't matter if you are in California, Oklahoma, or South Carolina, the only difference is the weather and maybe the landscape as seen from a distance, big mountains versus flat plains versus a murky swamp. Up close the pasta bar at the Olive Garden or the check-in desk at the Red Roof Inn is all the same.

I set my sights on Claremont, a town about thirty miles east of Los Angeles, not far off I-10. I started driving west early in the morning, shooting through the pinelands of Alabama, Mississippi, Arkansas, Oklahoma, and into the dust of the Texas panhandle.

I stopped in Amarillo when I could no longer stay awake. I slept in a dumpy motel called the Scotsman's Inn—run by a family from Mumbai. There was a muck on the floor you couldn't see but I could feel when my bare feet touched the carpet. Not having been on the road for a while I'd left my flip-flops behind, having forgotten the most critical rule of staying in dive motels: Never let your bare feet touch the floor because who knows what has gone on before you in a slimy cubbyhole of a room where thousands have stayed and spilled their germs onto the comforters and bounced their twisted dreams against the greasy walls.

I drove another eighteen hours the next day. The place in Claremont, when I finally got there, was not bad, a Red Roof Inn, sixty-nine dollars a night, a steal for Southern California, but clean and the free breakfast included a few choices of cereal, lukewarm skim milk, orange juice made from concentrate, and best of all bananas. I always felt lucky when I got free bananas.

I was far and away the oldest player in the Southern California Futures tournaments. The Futures are primarily for young players on the way up, juniors who have turned pro or graduating college players who want to take a shot at the big time before they beat a retreat back home to teach lessons at their local country club or join the world of suits and ties and weekly reports.

I had to qualify in Claremont. The eighteen-year-olds I played had not been born when I made my run at the French, so none of them had ever heard of me. Even the dudes in their midtwenties were hazy on who I was. Most of these players were Southern California kids and had never been big on tennis history, or any kind of history for that matter. Ancient days in their minds consisted of *Brady Bunch* reruns.

Take Chip McCourt, for example. He was twenty-two, had played the number four spot at USC. I remember sitting outside the clubhouse there in a comfortable green mesh chair, watching his car pull up in the parking lot, a silver, high-number BMW convertible with the top down. I didn't know who he was, and I wouldn't have cared, but I paid attention to the woman who was with him, a longhaired blonde in a tight white skirt and blue tight top that hugged a slender but curvy body. She wore dark sunglasses and sandals with enormous heels and followed him into the tennis center, talking on the phone and carrying a poodle, one of those designer dogs. She had that look that many of those USC Trojan cheerleaders do. The dog was dressed in a crimson-and-gold body suit with a matching bow.

McCourt carried a Babolat bag and wore Lacoste clothes and stepped up to the registration desk as though he was the new club president and expected a butler to come along and grab his bag and offer him something to drink. "Hello, I'm Chip McCourt."

The old woman at the desk checked him off a list and said, "You'll be going out on Court Four." She reached under the table and pulled out a can of tennis balls and handed it to him. He turned and smiled at the girlfriend who was still talking on the phone. She held up her hand to him in a way that said, *Not now*, and he stepped off to the side, waiting for his chance to speak to her.

I went out to the court—the old woman had forgotten about me altogether, but I knew who I was playing, so I didn't need her to call my name. I was there stretching when McCourt sauntered up. He had this funny way of walking, and I could tell before we started that this would be an easy match. It's funny how some rich people walk, these big goofy steps like they expect the red carpet to be there but it's not so they tread as though each step could be dangerous to their soft, pampered feet. He shook my hand in a strong, proud grip and looked me in the eyes. Up close I realized he was taller than I thought, maybe six-three, with long arms and a high tan forehead beneath golden hair. He looked down at the 75 LUMBER logo on my shirt and smiled like he had heard a joke. That pissed me off. I could tell that this guy had not played on the tour, because when you meet somebody who has been traveling around like I had been, they glare and let you know that you are the enemy and they are going to put you down. This guy was approaching the match like it was a fun Sunday afternoon, and I was his buddy. Nobody whose tennis career is dependent on the match to be played does that. We all glare at one another like vigilantes at a bus stop in the worst part of town.

Most casual tennis observers might have thought from the warm-up that he was the better player, but I could tell from the second ball that the match would be a breeze. He had classic groundstrokes, smooth and long, and this one-handed backhand that looked like it could have been useful at Wimbledon in 1955, a graceful stroke on the ball, almost like you might see in a Bill Tilden newsreel. He was one of those perfectly trained tennis players who knew how to look good handling the racket but wasn't adept at hitting the ball. He was more about the method than the result. When the match started I moved him around the court, from side to side, and mixed up big topspinning balls with some low spinners. A player like he was, so smooth and perfect but ultimately mechanical, you throw off his rhythm and he has no chance at all. They'll make the prettiest mistakes. His appearance and his money are why he had one of the best-looking women I've ever seen trailing him around. His tennis was the epitome of modern-day America, especially California: If you can't be good at something, at least you can look good doing it.

I beat him 0 and 2, and I could have bageled him if I had been determined, but I knew that I wouldn't lose to this guy, so I tried out some other shots for practice. I served and volleyed and chipped and charged the last part of the match to work on my net play and lost a few games in the process when I missed some approach shots and volleys. He hit three nice passing shots, including one of the best running one-handed backhands you will ever see. His girlfriend even put down her cell phone and her poodle and clapped. It was a gorgeous shot, but it was only one point. Like they say in golf: It ain't pictures, it's numbers.

When I finally served it out, he shook my hand and smiled like I was his uncle and I had just hired him into our family business. I figured he had played in this event to say that he had played on the tour, that he had tried the pro ranks before retreating into an easy trust-fund life.

I rolled on through the Claremont tournament, easily winning three matches in the qualies, and then three in a row in the main draw, seven matches in seven days. I lost in the finals to a young stud who had been the number one player his freshman year at San Diego State, a Chilean kid who had a great game, a huge serve and groundstrokes off both sides that I could do nothing with. He was as strong as a horse, slim but with tight biceps and quads that rippled when he walked. I'd bet a big bill that he was on the juice, probably some type of human growth hormone. I could see it in his eyes and in the way he walked around between points, ramped up, grinding his teeth.

I could have used some performance enhancers myself. I was one tired dude, having played a week straight, and even though only one of the matches went three sets, when you hit your late thirties and you play every day on a hard court laid over some of that asphalt like the hardtop my father used to spread over highways, your body feels the pounding.

Tired though I was physically, I was stoked getting to the finals after my first tournament back in three months. I had been talking to Harry every night, calling him on my cell phone and telling him about my matches, taking him through every game with the step-by-step detail that I used to tell my father. He loved hearing about it too, and enjoyed my rendition of the characters, the variety of Californian Chip McCourt types I had played, and the South American studs who strutted around the court whether they had the game to match it or not. Every story I told him would usually generate a story of his own, a player that he remembered, a match he was proud of or one he had dumped. His voice crackled alive on that phone. I wished that he could have been out there with me, but we couldn't afford it and he didn't like to travel and wouldn't abandon Suzette. I wouldn't have wanted to leave her cooking either.

A good thing about finishing second in the Claremont tournament was that I earned a check for fifteen hundred dollars. That more than covered my expenses for the drive out and the week in the Red Roof Inn and my food, mainly turkey sandwiches for lunch from a deli and pasta from an Olive Garden one stop down the interstate.

But the best thing about getting to the finals was that I could enter into the main draw of the next Futures tournament the following week without playing the qualifiers. If I'd had to make another run through the qualies, matches that pay nothing for winning them, and then into another main draw, I would have been hurting and could have not gotten very far. But with four full days off before playing my first round in Costa Mesa, only about an hour from Claremont, the second tournament of the four Futures events in Southern California, I liked my chances. From what I had seen, I could play a steadier and smarter game than most of these big-hitting young dudes. Even though the Chilean kid beat me, I knew I would have had a better chance with more rest in my legs.

I lived like a monk when I wasn't on the court, staying in my motel room except to get breakfast, lunch, and dinner. I stretched a good bit and read, having brought with me the final volume of the Civil War trilogy, and also a few of Shelby Foote's novels. I got to where I could read for four or five hours at a sitting, and I think it's as much a testament to Shelby Foote's skills as a storyteller as it is my reading ability. During the heat of the day I would stay inside and stretch out in my boxers and a T-shirt on the bed and read, perhaps taking a nap after lunch. In the late afternoon when it cooled down, I went outside and sat by the pool and enjoyed that soft Golden State air. Even as far inland as I was, I could feel the salt and wetness in the breeze from the Pacific, the world's biggest ocean casting a whiff of its moisture over the dusty red mainland.

It's amazing how winning a few matches, playing well and steady and showing promise again, can affect your mental attitude. I was not in the least bit bored that week, resting up for the tournament to come, stretching, and not practicing until the day before the Costa Mesa tournament when I went down to check out the surface there and hit with a qualifier who was hanging around.

I went on to win Costa Mesa. The following week, I won Laguna Nigel. The next week I lost in the semis of Huntington Beach. My ranking jumped high enough to put me into the qualifiers for some Challenger events in late October and early November. I had a little money in the bank, and I set my sights on the biggest of the Challengers in Hawaii in early January.

I thought then that the way I was playing and feeling, that maybe, just maybe, I could gear it up enough so that I could get back to qualifying for the French Open in May, possibly Wimbledon, and definitely the U.S. Open at the end of the year, a tournament I had always dreamed about. These were things Harry and I discussed every afternoon. With someone to tell, it seemed like a realistic goal, more than just a crazy dream.

I busted my ass the entire winter, playing well and earning enough ranking points to establish me in the Challenger events, one step beneath the big tour. A sore ankle slowed me down, so I didn't rise high enough to make the French Open or Wimbledon qualies, but I felt like the way I was playing I had a legitimate shot of reaching the U.S. Open qualifyings at the end of summer if I stayed healthy. At the age of thirty-eight, I had found my game again.

The spring tour brought me back to the South after eight months on the road. I drove up the red dirt driveway and smiled when I saw my dogs Brutus and Buck running out to meet me.

Randy, no longer a college kid although he still lived like one, continued to look after the house and dogs for me. He had been there seven years now, the last half of it moping about his lost Costa Rican love who had departed a few years before. I've known several dudes like this, dudes who would hang on to a lost love like it was a religion, thinking about it all the time, in fact, unable to think about anything else, going through the day like a goddamn zombie.

On my first night back Randy cooked out, had laid in a supply of chicken and ribs before I even got there, and we sipped a few beers and we talked and watched the Braves on TV. He moved on to bourbon and got a little drunk and started talking about Gabriella, his old girl, wondering where she was, if he could ever get her back.

"What you need is to find another woman," I said. "You need you a slump buster. Have you been with a woman since she left?'

"No, I can't," he said, his eyes almost in tears. "No one else would be the same."

"Goddamn, boy. You got to put that woman behind you."

"I don't know," he said.

"What's it been? Two years?"

"Four and a half."

"Dude. That's a long time. I bet she's gotten fat, or has the clap. Probably slept with about half the dudes in New York by now."

"Shut up, Jaxie." He slammed his fist on the arm of the recliner. "Shut the fuck up, goddammit." I had never seen him mad at me, but he was drunk. And I was hitting him in a soft spot.

"Sorry, man." I patted him on the back. "Just kidding you. Let's go up to Thessalonica. It's Thursday night, ain't it?"

"Yeah."

"We'll let's go find some college women. Tonight's the night they go buck wild, ain't it?"

"I don't know."

"C'mon, dude. Put on a clean T-shirt. We are going to find you a woman. I'm driving."

It had been almost ten years since I had been a drinker and lived in Piney full-time, running up to the bar in Thessalonica six days a week. Nothing had changed other than the bar's name and that the pool table had new felt, red instead of green. Even some of the bartenders were the same, a little grayer, a little balder, a little thicker around the middle. The jukebox was still the same too, with its heavy dose of Skynyrd and Bad Company, although somebody strange must have established tenure as a few mournful Smiths records made it onto the playlist.

The bar was packed full of college students, a few lookers hovering. Randy and I sat at the bar and I bought him a shot of bourbon and a

Budweiser and I got a light beer and we looked around. The pool table was open and just beyond it I saw two blondes, one with a big nose and bigger cleavage, too much blue eye shadow, sitting near the pool table, checking the screen of her smartphone. The other one was a slender girl with less makeup and a head of very long, dirty-blond hair. I led Randy over there toward them and told him to put some coins in the pool table.

"Hey, y'all want to play some pool?" I asked.

The girls looked at each other and grinned.

"C'mon now, it's my buddy's birthday. He's Randy." I pointed to him. "And I'm Jaxie."

I don't know why it is, but good-looking girls are almost always sympathetic to a man when you tell them it is his birthday.

"Happy birthday," the big-breasted blonde said to Randy, giving him a hug. After she hugged him, she turned to me and shook my hand. "I'm Tina, and this is Jessica, my cousin, from New York."

Jessica did not bother to stand up. I looked more closely at her and realized she wasn't who I thought she was. She was young, very early twenties, but she had this cool nod, a look on her face that implied she was smart. Her eyes were a touch smoky, and she sort of half smiled at me, and said, "How are you doing?" in a voice that was clearly not from around here. I thought maybe Tina, who was as country as honeybee syrup, was joking about New York, but she wasn't.

Jessica's voice surprised me, but I liked it. I held my hand out to her and she shook it, her small fingers cool and smooth in mine. "Hey, I'm good," I said. "You know I've been to New York before." She didn't seem impressed by this, letting go of my hand. "I hated it," I said. "Too many damn people all over the place. And too expensive. I like living out in the country, a mile from my next neighbor."

She laughed. "Yeah. I'm really from suburbs, but went to school in the city. I like it down here. My family always comes down here in the summer. Tina's father and my mama are siblings."

"She"—I pointed over at Tina, who had taken a liking to Randy—"has Yankee blood in her?"

"Hell, naw," Jessica said, putting on a good drawl here for my amusement, smiling after she did. "My mother went to New York for college. She married a New Yorker and never came back, except to visit in the summertime."

"What do you do? Are you in college?"

"Yeah. I graduate next year."

"What are you going to do then?"

"I don't know. Grad school, most likely."

"What's your major?" I felt like an idiot as soon as I said this, a dumb freshman trying to chat up a hot girl.

"American studies. I'm studying country music from the late '50s to the early '70s."

"No shit?"

"Seriously."

"I didn't know you could study such a thing in college."

"Yeah, beats hell out of econ or statistics, don't it?" Again she did the southern voice, but she was good at it, funny, and it didn't strike me the wrong way. I usually resent it when Yankees mock my speech by talking slow.

"Who's your favorite?"

"Willie Nelson and Johnny Cash."

"You ought to come see my dad's old record collection. It's quite a stash. Has lots of eight-tracks, too."

"Now I know you are bullshitting me."

"No, seriously. You can come out tonight and see them if you want. He must have five hundred old albums and eight-tracks if you put them all together."

"Really? I love eight-tracks, and have collected them. I was even thinking about writing my senior thesis about lost old country eight-tracks. There are some albums that were eight-track only, never made it onto vinyl."

"He might have some. You are welcome to look through them. You can have the ones you want."

"Hmm," she said, and chewed her lips like she was thinking. She looked over at Tina. Randy had his hand on her shoulder and was telling her a story. I hoped for his sake that he wasn't carrying on about his old flame. "I'll be right back," she said.

She stood up and she was taller than I thought she'd be. She whispered something in Tina's ear and they walked off to the bathroom together. She had on jeans that were tight without being obscene and a light orange T-shirt that conformed to her trim, athletic body.

I tapped Randy on the shoulder. "How's it going, partner?"

"I think I'm in love," he said.

"Yeah, well, take your time. Don't get too carried away and scare her off."

"Okay."

"Let's take them back to the house, if they'll go."

"Shit, you think they will?"

"Yeah, let me do the talking. How much beer we got back there. And liquor?"

"We got plenty. I laid in a big stash when you told me you were coming home."

"You're a good man, Randy."

"Shit, dude, you've been good to me."

He was drunk and reached over and hugged me, something I would normally resent, but I appreciated it. I, who have done very little for anybody in my life, felt glad that someone had benefited from my act of kindness. I had gotten into the relationship with Randy strictly because I needed someone I could trust to stay in my house, to take care of my dogs. I was glad I was able to return the favor, to help him out in some way.

The girls walked out of the bathroom. Jessica had a tall slim figure, breasts sort of small, but a flat stomach and narrow waist. Her long, dirty-blond hair hung down well past her shoulders, like she had stood in the bathroom and tossed it around to give it a sexy look. I pictured how she would look in the morning, her tousled hair all over her pillow.

Tina was a heavier girl with a curvy figure, blond hair, blue eyes, and a warm country-girl smile. She was not my type, but I could tell she looked mighty good to Randy. She put her hand on his shoulder and said, "You are cute."

Jessica rolled her eyes and looked at me.

"Where do you live?"

"In Piney, only about fifteen miles south of here. Out in the country. We've got plenty of beer, and some food too if y'all are hungry."

"Why don't we follow you?"

"You can ride with us."

"No," Jessica said. "What if we want to leave? I need to get home tonight . . . and Tina's daddy is a sheriff's deputy." She smirked when she said this, the threat hanging in the air.

"All right," I said. "We can leave our car here and ride back with you. I'm plenty sober enough to drive your car. Randy can drive me up here tomorrow for mine."

"That's fine with me," Tina said.

Jessica sat up front with me and I drove Tina's car, while she and Randy sat in the back and giggled at each other.

Jessica took a deep breath next to me but kept her distance. We rode listening to Tina and Randy's conversation and the radio softly playing some bad commercial country music. I turned off on Booger Holler Road and Jessica pointed at the sign and laughed. "I've seen that road before. I even tried to write a poem about it."

"A poem?"

"Yeah, the 'Ballad of Booger Holler.' But I could never get it right."

"Sounds like a good country song."

"Yeah, it could have been."

"I like driving down these two-lane country roads," I said. "I wish we were doing it in a truck with an eight-track player, listening to one of the old country ones like Conway Twitty."

"*Oooo*. I love Conway Twitty," she said, her voice, which was sort of deep, rising high on this occasion and cracking a little bit. "He's amazing. There's nobody that sings with such lust in his heart like he does. It's as pure and raw as it gets."

"I thought most women think he's a pig."

"Oh, he is. But a lovable pig. He's sincere. Too sincere for most."

I smiled at her and she gave me a wistful smile back, the sort of smile where you know things are going well, where you are connecting with her on a lot of levels. I realized that she was one cool chick, and had a lot going on upstairs. I worried that maybe she was too smart for me.

We drove along and didn't say anything for a mile or two, and I appreciated that, a woman who didn't have to be talking constantly, every minute filled with words, like most women I've met do. There is something to be said for silence, shooting along that dark two-lane country road late at night, the trees in some spots so thick and green in this part of the summer that it was like a canopy of leaves over the narrow, empty road.

I pulled off on my driveway, the dirt path winding through a cow pasture and then a stand of trees before it rose up the hill to my house. "What's this?" Jessica asked, sitting up rigid.

"Don't worry," I said. "It's my driveway."

"Driveway? This is not a driveway. This is a wild country road."

"You'll see. It's a half mile long. I don't guess you have any of these in New York."

"Wow, you really are out in the country."

"Yep. Have been all my life."

"Are you a farmer?"

"Nope."

"What do you do then?"

"I'm a tennis player."

"A what?"

"A tennis player. I play professionally, on the satellite tours. Was on the ATP tour once, trying to get back."

She tensed her lips and looked out the window with a scowl.

I pulled up to the house and parked, the headlights panning across the porch and front door. I had let the paint and the shrubs go. It looked decrepit and creepy in the night. I flipped off the lights and turned off the engine.

"Seriously," she said. "What do you do?"

"Just because I live in an old house in the boondocks doesn't mean I'm not a tennis player."

She scoffed but didn't make eye contact. I opened the door and got out of the car and out of habit took the keys from the ignition.

"Leave me those," she said. I handed her the keys. "Tina." She turned in the backseat, as Tina was getting out of the car, and Randy too. "I think we should go."

"Hey, not yet," Randy said. "What's wrong?"

"Randy," I said. "What do I do for a living?"

"You're a tennis player."

Tina piped up, her country voice loud. "Hey! Jessica plays too. She's great, plays for her college team."

"Really?" I said.

"Yeah," Jessica said, but she didn't look at me.

Randy spoke up, laughing. "I bet you can't get a game off Jaxie. He almost won the French Open."

"Okay, that's it," Jessica said. "Tina, we are leaving. You can go on a date with him tomorrow night, or something. But we've got to get home. I'm not going to stay here and listen to this bullshit."

"Hold on," Randy said. "Wait right here." He ran into the house.

Tina and Jessica stayed in the car, whispering to each other. I shut the driver's door and the interior light went off. I walked over and sat on the front steps and looked up at the stars above and listened to the songs of crickets and the tree frogs.

Randy returned with the July 1995 *Tennis* magazine that had pictures of me at Roland Garros. I had never shown that to Randy, thought the copies I had were well hidden in my bedroom closet, but I guess I had no secrets from him, living as he had in my house for all those years.

He opened it to my picture and handed it through the passenger window to Jessica, who took it skeptically, and opened a car door to turn on the interior light. She looked puzzled for a minute, back toward me, and then studied the picture some more. She started reading the article about the French Open. Her mouth was agape, and then she read a little more and then looked at me again.

She got out of the car. Tina, who had been flirting with Randy while Jessica read, asked her what the article was about. Jessica ignored Tina and came over to me and sheepishly started to hand me the magazine.

"Keep it," I said.

"You were in the French Open? The semis?"

"Yeah. Almost twenty years ago."

"That's unreal."

"Thanks."

"I'm sorry I doubted you, but I didn't think . . . being out in the country in this house and all . . . I was with a tennis star."

"That's all right. I'm not a star now. Haven't been in a long time."

"You know, I do play college tennis. I'll never be good enough to go pro, though. I peaked in high school."

"We've got a court in the back. Red clay. It's not in the best of shape, but I still use it."

"Red clay, huh?" she said. "I'd love to hit with you sometime, if you don't mind."

"We should try tomorrow. I'd be glad to."

Randy and Tina had by this time taken a seat on the front steps of the porch, and he whispered something in her ear.

Jessica and I turned toward them and took a few steps.

"So we are staying, right?" Tina shouted, and Jessica said yes.

"Yeah heh!" Randy said. "Who wants a drink?"

We went into the kitchen and had variations of bourbon. Tina mixed hers with a Coke, while Randy took a sip straight from the bottle and chased it with a beer. Jessica and I each took some in a glass with a piece of ice.

"Do you want to see the eight-tracks?"

"Yes, but later. Right now, I want to see your tennis court."

"Come on, I'll show you." We left Randy and Tina inside. They had made their way to the couch and were already starting to make out. I was happy for him how this night had ended up. It was probably some of the first moments in years that he hadn't thought about Gabriella. I hoped he had put her out of his mind, and wasn't closing his eyes and imagining her there in his arms.

Out back the summer night was peaceful and moonless, the clear sky lit with a thousand stars, the twinkling patterns of other galaxies. Randy had cut the grass a day or two before, and in the dark it looked like a smooth, green carpet. We stood there in the driveway for a minute or two to let our eyes adjust, and I wondered how it looked to her. I could see it in the dark because I had seen it thousands of times before, this big backyard with the tennis court and the pasture before it ran into the pine trees and then up the hill where the hardwoods grew. Once you see something you love, you always know it is there, even in darkness or if you are a thousand miles away.

"Is that the court there?" She pointed at the net, sort of squinting.

"Yeah, let me get a blanket and we can go sit out there . . . look up at the stars."

I stepped inside and grabbed an old comforter from the closet in the hall, and went back out, my eyes having to adjust all over again.

I took her hand when I returned and she reciprocated, her fingers and palm smooth and cool in mine, caressing my thumb. It was a tender gesture, and I liked it. She had soft, small hands, not the kind you might expect of a tennis player.

We walked across the grass, fescue that smelled good from being freshly cut, a little wet with the dew of the night coming on, and onto the tennis court. I spread the comforter out over the T of the service line, on the west end, the higher side of the court, and we sat down.

"When I was little," I said, "my dad and I would come out here, sometimes my sisters and mom too, and we'd look up at the stars and study on them."

"Where are they all now?"

"My dad's dead. I . . . I lost touch with my mom and sisters. They've all moved away." I didn't say it, but I thought that the women in my family might as well be dead.

"I'm sorry."

"It's okay. I'm all right."

But it must have been something about the way I said it, a loneliness in my voice that caused her to reach over and touch my face, and then kiss me. I kissed her back. Her lips were soft and moist and her mouth had a smoky, bourbon flavor that doesn't sound that great, but was very appealing.

The conversation, in between kissing her, was easy, and she told me about her family and her junior tennis career, a career like so many others that had shown promise but never quite achieved what she had hoped. She was by this point in her life sick of tennis, burned out, still playing only because she had committed to the college team. She couldn't wait until her after her senior year was done when she could to grad school and put the rackets away.

I told her about my efforts to make the U.S. Open draw, that this would be my last year to take a shot at it, that after that I would be too old. I even told her about my troubles back in Paris with Olga and then my knee injury and how I lived like a bum. I liked talking to her. Most women I've been with before, the relationships were not about talking, but talking was the exercise I had to endure until I could slip off their clothes and get them into bed.

But Jessica was different. Lying there next to her on that comforter on the court where I had learned to play tennis, it felt natural telling her my story, and listening to hers. We stayed out there on that court talking and kissing until dawn when the sun began to rise up over the bank of pines to the east, the dark sky turning to orange in a thin line before the clouds raged pink and orange around the edges when the sun rose up over the trees and it began to turn into daylight. "This was about the time of day my dad and I would get out here and practice before school," I said. "I would always take that end, with the sun in my eyes. Dad said it would make me tough . . . would make me immune to balls coming out of the sun, and that I would never complain about being blinded on a serve or during a point with an overhead."

"That's harsh."

"He only did it because he loved me . . . he wanted to make me a great player. Too many people coddle their children. They think it's because they love them, but in reality it's because they are too weak to do what's best for them. I have never been bothered by the sun in my eyes . . . it was good for me."

"Did you like practicing when you were little?"

"I loved it. I absolutely loved it, hitting the ball again and again. I still do. I love to just hit the ball, to just line it up and smack with all I've got."

"I used to feel the same way. I don't know what it is anymore, but I'm so sick of playing. It seems like I can't get any better, that the game is just so boring, that the ball doesn't have the same feel on the strings that it used to have for me. I wish I could get it back."

"I'll hit with you later today, if you want. We can hit here."

"I love the red clay," she said. "I haven't played on it many times."

"Yeah, well let me roll it out. It's an old court, really just red Georgia dirt, but it doesn't play too bad."

She smiled, the early-morning sun lighting her face and hair.

"We should probably go," she said. "Tina's daddy is going to freak out. But I'm sure she'll have a story for him. She's a daddy's girl . . . he'll believe anything."

"Didn't you say your parents are down here too?"

"Yeah, it's a family trip. But they are cool."

We got up and she picked up the comforter and shook it off and folded it neatly and handed it to me.

"You didn't have to do that."

"It's okay."

I smiled at her.

"I was right about your hair."

"What do you mean?"

"I imagined it would look really beautiful in the morning, all tousled and long like it is."

She blushed, and stood up on her tiptoes and gave me a kiss.

In the house the door to Randy's room was closed and I started to tap on it but heard moving, a rhythmic shake of the mattress, low grunting, and heavy breaths. I smiled. I knew this would do the boy some good, and I hoped he would see her again. It was a great sign that they were at it first thing in the morning.

I walked back out into the kitchen to Jessica. "We better give them a little time."

"What? Is she sick?"

"No. Far from it."

"Oh." She smiled sheepishly.

"Want some coffee?"

"Yeah, that sounds good."

I started the coffee and the warm aroma of the roasted grounds filled the kitchen. She sat in one of the high-backed chairs at the table and I sat across from her while the coffee brewed.

The coffee machine beeped and I got up and poured us cups. "You take anything in it?"

"Nope, black is the way I like it."

I put some sugar in mine and sat across from her and we sipped our coffee. We didn't say anything for a good five minutes. It wasn't awkward, but comfortable, just being there together, occasionally smiling or making eyes, but not having to run our mouths every minute. We had talked all night long, but never forced the conversation. I liked that she looked so pretty in the morning despite having not slept, and wearing almost no makeup. She had very white skin and a roundish sort of face that was cute as a button, that made her look young, despite the long wild dirty-blond hair that framed her head and shoulders.

"What are you doing today?" I said.

"Sleeping, mostly. I don't really have any big plans otherwise. Visit with relatives. We head back to New York on Sunday."

"That soon?"

"Yeah."

"Do you want to go to dinner with me tonight?" I asked.

"Yeah, I'd love to. And when do we get to play tennis? I want to see you in action."

"We can tonight, before dinner, if you want."

"Okay. But I need to borrow a racket."

"Don't worry. I have several dozen for you to choose from."

Randy's bedroom door opened and he came out in nothing but boxers, smiling like I hadn't seen in years.

"Good morning, sunshine," I said.

"Hey Jaxie. Hey Jessica. Good morning. Is there enough coffee for us?"

"Yeah, of course."

He got two cups out of the pantry and filled them, taking great pains to measure large doses of cream and sugar in one for Tina. "We'll be out in a little while," he said.

I grinned at Jessica and shook my head. I almost started to tell her about how much Randy needed this, and how happy I was for him to find another girl, but I didn't say anything.

Instead, I sat there and looked across the table at her. "I'm really sorry you are leaving so soon," I said.

"Yeah, me too." She reached across the table and put her hand on mine. "But you'll be going out on tour before too long. You need to practice, no distractions, right?"

I shrugged, thinking I could use a good distraction if she was it.

"But we've got a few days," she said. She grinned and her eyes flashed as she caressed my forearm. "I'll see you tonight."

I was sweeping the court when Tina and Jessica drove up. Jessica got out of the car in a short white tennis dress, some of the best legs I'd ever seen, lean but muscular thighs and shapely calves. She had her dirty-blond hair pulled back in a ponytail, a contrast with her dark eyebrows.

She walked across the yard, a big smile on her face. She knew she looked good in that tight tennis dress, not anything really fancy, but the right fabric to accentuate her body. I walked from the court and hugged her, and we exchanged a quick kiss on the lips. I liked this girl, the down-to-earth New Yorker, a smart girl who studied at a good university. I wondered what she would think of my reading habits. I liked the way my hand felt on her back, the skin taut on her slender muscles and sturdy lithe frame. "Are you ready to hit some?" I asked.

"Yes, let's do it. Go easy on me, though."

I got two rackets, picking for her one of my newest ones that hadn't had the grip built up yet, and a basket of balls. I had this fear that she would be terrible, that maybe she had ugly groundstrokes, that she had lied about playing tennis for her college team, or maybe it was one of those schools that fielded terrible players. There really are some awful college players in the Northeast, players who shouldn't be rated 4.5 on their best days.

Would it have ruined our relationship if she had been terrible? If she had that hacker backhand that leads with the elbow, the sharp joint pointing straight at the target, and then unbending like some sort of weird mechanical lever, slapping violently at the ball? I don't know for sure, but it might have. I can't stand people who lie about their tennis abilities, claiming to be good players when ultimately all they can do is hack. Men are worse lying about their golf skills, but there is no end to the things that men will lie about.

Fortunately, Jessica had very nice strokes, a long easy backswing with an elegant follow-through, especially on her forehand. She gripped the racket loosely and let the frame do the work, barely exerting much effort. Her backhand was two-handed, sort of like mine in a way, with a loopy backswing and a low follow-through, but still a solid shot, not a herky-jerky motion like you see from a lot of players with weak two-handers. I enjoyed watching her run around the court, her brow furrowed as she followed the flight of the ball, her ponytail flopping when she ran. She moved elegantly, although with very long strides, not ideal footwork for a match. I could see how an aggressive player or someone who hit the ball with a lot of spin would give her trouble, disrupting her slow rhythmic windup.

We hit the ball smoothly back and forth. From the look of concentration on her face, she was trying really hard to hit the ball well and impress me. I took it easy. I didn't want to hit my best groundstrokes, balls that would kick up too high and hard for her to handle, so I guided them back to her at a pace she could manage. Randy and Tina came out of the house with beers in their hands and he carried two lawn chairs with him. I was glad there was someone to sit with him other than me. The dogs, Brutus and Buck, followed them out and sat beside them. Tina petted Brutus on the head and cooed to him, the cooing doing more for Randy than it did Brutus.

After twenty minutes of nice, easy rallies, Randy shouted, "Why don't you play a set?" I shook my head no, that it would not be a good idea.

"Aw, c'mon," Tina said. "You ain't scared of her, are you?"

Jessica smiled and said, "I don't mind. Let's play a few games at least."

I sighed, and said, "All right, you can serve." I tapped the three balls over the net to her.

Her serve had the same problem that afflicts many good female players. I'm not sure why this is, but so many women, even on the pro tour, have a motion that is much too complicated. Her ball toss was too high and she took the racket back too fast and exerted a great amount of effort for a fairly weak shot. At least she got it in the court. I patted it back to her down the middle and she ran around her backhand and hit one of the prettiest inside-out forehand winners you'll ever see from an amateur player, rocketing the ball to my backhand side at an angle I couldn't reach.

Randy clapped and Tina hooted and hollered. "Way to go Jessie girl," she yelled, and put her hand up to her mouth with her thumb in one corner and her ring finger in the other and whistled.

"Nice shot," I said, and looked at Jessica. She smiled, but it wasn't her warm smile. I could see a competitive fire in her eyes, as though she thought this might be a close match, that maybe she could even win it.

I couldn't afford to let this charade continue. I decided to turn up my game, to show her what I could do.

The next serve she hit I stepped in and took it early with my backhand and blasted it crosscourt with such pace and topspin it was by her before she even recovered from her service motion.

She shook her head, as though she was disgusted at hitting a weak serve and I didn't have anything to do with her losing the point. In the deuce court she hit her best serve yet, a medium-hard ball wide to my forehand, and for an average college woman player, it would have been a tough return. But it was the kind of serve a male pro annihilates. I took two quick steps forward and one to the right and nailed it, catching it high in the air and driving it down the line like it had been shot out of a gun.

I looked to see her expression, and thought maybe she would get my point and call off the match, but she twisted her mouth into a scowl. I noticed as she came up to get a ball out of the net that she was almost chewing on her lips, a wild motion of concentration. She was not giving in one inch.

The lip chewing must have gotten to her because on the next point she double-faulted. At 15–40, she hit another good serve out to my forehand. This one I hit crosscourt with a hard underspin and attacked the net. She got a good jump on the ball and wound up that big windmill forehand of hers and tried to pass me down the line but I saw it coming before she even knew where she was going to hit it and I knocked off an easy volley winner. "Yeah, Jaxie! Woof, woof, woof!" Randy shouted. Both Tina and Jessica gave him a dirty look.

"Okay, 0–1," she said. She started to change sides.

"Stay over there. The sun's in your eyes on this side."

She kept coming. "I don't want to be coddled." She strode around the net post insistently.

At first her competitive fire had ticked me off a little bit, but then something about the look on her face, the way her shoulders were up high and she walked back and dug in on the baseline to return my serve, determined as all get-out, appealed to me. She was a real player, and real players hate to lose to anyone, even professionals when they know they shouldn't have a shot. I also realized I was obligated to give her my best, to hit the ball as hard as I could and let her see who she was up against. She deserved nothing less, this woman who just the night before had refused to believe I was a pro.

"Did you want to take a few?" she asked.

"No, these are good."

I decided to serve and volley on the first ball. I hit a serve wide with a lot of spin and charged in behind it. She barely reached the ball and nicked it off the frame into the yard. On the next two points I lined up and hit big aces right down the middle of the court, blasting them off the T. Both serves, in fact, hit right about the same spot, on the center line, about two inches inside service line, so hard and fast and well placed that she couldn't touch them.

"Forty–love," I said. I noticed that her competitive expression had relaxed, that she had realized that her thoughts of possibly competing with me were delusional, and that she wanted to find a way to end this gracefully. She was starting to look at me with this glow of admiration and awe. I must say, I enjoyed every second of it.

I bounced the ball in preparation for my serve to the ad court and she backed way up this time, almost ten feet behind the baseline, a truly ridiculous distance. I could have angled a serve out wide and it would have been a forty-foot run to the ball, an impossible distance for anyone slower than Rafael Nadal to cover. But instead I went with what can be considered either a great joke shot, or sometimes the ultimate insult. I released the ball about knee-high and hit an enormous under- and sidespinning right-to-left forehand drop shot that just cleared the net.

I expected this ball to be so far from her that she would just let it go and laugh and not even bother to play anymore. I hoped she would take it as a joke and we could end this match and have a drink and spend some time together. I wondered if she brought a change of clothes with her, if she wanted to shower here, and I thought of maybe what that would lead to.

But she didn't give up. She took off running, her long legs hustling and her left arm pumping wildly and the racket reaching out in front of her. She had no chance of reaching the ball, in fact, she was probably twenty feet away when it bounced and the spin kicked it farther off the court and it bounced again, but she lunged and fell. To avoid landing face-first, she twisted and went down hard on her side and dropped the racket, her ponytail flopping as she rolled over on her back and ended up supine on the red clay. "Hey," I said, and started to run around to her. "I'm sorry. You all right?"

She popped up fast, like a tackled football player who wants it known that he's not intimidated. Her eyes were excited but I could tell she was okay, only dirty with clay clinging to the back of her tennis dress. She had a nervous edge to her lips, chewing them again, and she laughed, a nervous laughter. "That was a dirty trick," she said.

"I'm sorry. I didn't think you'd try so hard to get it."

"I can't help it," she said.

Randy and Tina walked out onto the court. "You okay, sugar?" Tina said. Jessica nodded that she was fine.

"Is the car unlocked?" she asked Tina. Tina said it was.

"You probably want a shower," I said. "I can wash that dress."

She smiled at me warmly this time, and held out her hand. "Nice match, Mr. Skinner," she said, feigning a British accent.

I returned the handshake, and started to say something, but she leaned over and pulled me to her with one hand and gave me a kiss, slipping me a taste of her tongue.

We headed up through the yard and toward the house. She got her bag out of the trunk and I rushed in ahead to see if the bathroom was clean. It had not occurred to me to clean it, but fortunately Randy was a thoughtful dude and had already done it.

I found a clean towel and met her at the door and took her bag. "Let me show you the facilities, young lady," I said, doing my best southern train porter imitation. She had a sultry laugh.

"Here is the master bedroom and the master bathroom," I said.

"Can I be the master?" she asked.

"Yes, you can be anything you'd like."

I gave her the towel and said I'd be in the kitchen if she needed me, just to holler.

I was in there about two minutes, studying the beer in the refrigerator, wishing that I had bought some champagne, when she called to me. "Jaxie, can you come help me for a moment?"

She stood in the bathroom doorway, her shoes and socks off and her hair loose from the ponytail, wild and tousled on her shoulders and down the front, covering much of her face, still in the white tennis dress stained with splotches of red dirt.

I approached her and she turned. "Can you unzip me?"

Rare is the tennis dress these days with a zipper, but I was glad for this one. I pulled it halfway down her back. "Lower," she said, softly, a little breathily. "All the way down."

I unzipped down to the bottom, near her waist. She didn't have on a bra—it was one of those dresses that didn't need it—but she did have on a silky orange thong with a heart-shaped white ribbon at the top. With the dress loose, she wiggled a little and the body-hugging fabric fell to the floor and I got a look at the best ass I have ever seen. I ran my fingertip lightly down her back and touched the heart of ribbons, soft cool material, and then she turned around to face me.

We spent the next two days and nights together, and then she went back to New York. My tennis got better and better. Four months after that first weekend with Jessica, following a strong run in the Challenger tournaments, I was in position to push my ranking high enough to make the U.S. Open qualies if I could reach the quarterfinals of a tournament in Binghamton, New York. This tournament was my last shot to make the Open. Of course, to do this I had to beat none other than Janos Szucs. He too was on a comeback run after having been away with injuries. I had not seen his name in a draw sheet all spring or summer. I thought, had hoped, had prayed that he had retired or died. It gave me a chill when I looked at the draw there in Binghamton and saw his name on it, in my half, no less. If I was going to get to the U.S. Open, I had to beat him.

Szucs had won his way through the qualies in Binghamton, the determined bastard. I watched his progress as I made my own way through the main draw, praying that someone would knock him out, but there he was, like some sort of stumpy-legged creature from deep in the Hungarian night who stalked me. I knew like I know my own name that I would end up playing him.

I was by myself in Binghamton when I ran into Szucs. With the financial support and a little success, I had been able to fly to tournaments and rent a car and stay in motels. I talked to Harry every day, giving him reports on my matches. The occasional serving and volleying he implemented had added a great new wrinkle to my game, and I often used it as a surprise, to keep my opponents guessing. I was amazed at how many service return errors opponents made when I went charging into the net. When I approached, I could see my opponents take their eyes off the ball, wondering what I was about to do. Janos Szucs had not seen me in a few years, so I hoped that I could surprise him on big points, if I got down, and the going got rough, which I was sure it would. It occurred to me that the U.S. Open was special, a sacred American trust in the game of tennis, the championship of my country. If I couldn't beat Janos Szucs, I didn't deserve to go.

The biggest change in my life was that I had been talking to Jessica on the phone, twice a day on most days, sometimes in the evening for as long as an hour. This was a dramatic turn for me. I've always hated to talk on the phone for very long. My dad was the same way.

But talking with Jessica was great. We talked about everything, about my tennis matches, and sometimes I would take her through an almost point-by-point breakdown of a match from earlier in the day. She not only listened, she seemed excited by the discussion, and asked knowledgeable questions: "Did he have a good drop shot on his forehand side, too? Did you have any trouble with overheads in the wind?" She is easily the most knowledgeable woman about tennis I've ever known, but maybe that's because I've known very few. It's not that they don't exist—it's just that I've never reached out to any of them, living like a hermit as I have.

After we talked tennis, which we usually did in the beginning of our conversations, Jessica and I would move on to music and books and sometimes movies. For twenty-two years old, that girl seemed to know about everything there was to be known, or at least it seemed that way to me. She was on a combined reading kick of Faulkner and country music biographies, talking about how great Willie Nelson's recent biography was, and also carrying on about how much she loved Faulkner's *Light in August*, a book she had read and then as soon as she was done with it, went back to the front and read it again.

On these phone conversations, short ones in the morning when I first woke up and called her at her internship in New York—she was working at a fashion magazine and hating every minute of it—and the long ones at night when she was back in her little East Village apartment that she shared with two girls, and me in a cheap motel somewhere, stretched out on the bed, the scratchy comforter tossed onto the floor, I relaxed and did more talking and listening in the space of a week than I had done in the previous year.

I started the tournament at Recreation Park in Binghamton, New York, ranked 258 in the world. It was held in July, less than a month before the qualifying at the U.S. Open. With a win against Szucs, I'd pick up enough ranking points to move me up high enough to earn an automatic bid to the qualies.

It all came down to beating Janos Szucs. The match, with about twelve people casually watching, would determine my future in the game, or maybe it would be the place where I retired. I didn't know if I missed the Open if I had the heart or desire to go out on tour again, traveling by myself, living like a monk, chasing a dead-end dream. Even if I wanted to, which I probably did, I'm not sure I could be as successful as I had been earlier in the summer. Every year I get a little older, a little slower, a little weaker, while another crop of eighteen-year-olds rise up into the pro game.

Before the match I was desperately nervous, feeling jittery in the warm-up, my body sort of stiff despite all the stretching I had been doing, the good care I had been taking of myself. I had been eating well and getting lots of rest, almost twelve hours a night. But the concerns I had now were not about my body, but about how my mind would handle the pressure. I wish there was a drug for the tennis brain.

That I would willingly take. Sooner or later someone will come along with the mind-enhancing equivalent of steroids, and then just wait until how good the tennis you see is going to be.

I started the match with a nice hard serve that Szucs barely reached, hitting it into the net when he tried to go down the line with his funky-ass two-handed forehand. That a short little bastard like him could even try that shot, much less pull it off more often than not, is a flat-out tennis miracle. I should probably give him his due, because he wasn't physically gifted by any means, and he had hung in there into his early thirties with a game teaching pros would discourage anyone from emulating.

But I was not letting myself feel any admiration or respect for him at that moment. When you get into a match, you've got to be as focused as a Ninja on amphetamines, flat-out looking to kill everything that opposes you. I think dudes who read and re-read that *Art of War* book are a little foolish—especially, say, if they sell cars or tax-preparation services—but there's some truth to the war metaphor in tennis. Any pity in your heart and you'll end up a loser. I was there by myself and didn't want to go home alone in defeat.

I lined up to serve the second point and bounced the ball a few times and then stopped. I raised my head to look at Szucs, to see how close in he might be preparing to hit his return and I thought I saw Jessica on the sideline near his end. I stopped and looked closer and it was her, wearing flip-flops, white shorts, and a tight pink tank top and this nifty, small white hat that framed her smiling face. She waved and then clapped and said, "C'mon, Jaxie," getting a chuckle out of the small crowd. I smiled and bounced the ball a few more times.

Jessica had asked me on the phone about coming up to see me, Binghamton being about a three-hour drive from New York. I had been vague on what I wanted in our phone conversations, saying I didn't think she should come—she didn't own a car and would have to rent or borrow one, and she would have to call in sick to her internship—and I had such a precise routine I didn't want it disturbed. But I had told her much about my rivalry with the stumpy Hungarian and how much was riding on this match.

I was thrilled she was there, that she had woken up early and arranged to find a car and come all that way to see me play. I started bouncing the ball again, and thought of that first day with Jessica on my tennis court at home, in my shower, in my bed, and everything clicked for me. I started out playing my old-style game, the hard serves and the big forehands and backhands looping the ball deep to Szucs, the game of mine he knew. I was serving so well that I held my serve easily, one of those beautiful serving days when the toss of the ball feels like it floats straight up out of your hand and the racket goes back and down and comes up and hits the ball with the least amount of effort and the ball rockets into the corners, occasionally one deep in the box right at him into the body, a good play as close as he stood to return inside of the baseline. My serve can be almost celestial, following the rotation of planets or stars or moons or whatever, and that day, the sun and the earth and the moon were all aligned and I was blasting the ball, my arm loose and limber and not straining but whipping the ball into place. I knew the way I was hitting my serve that he would not break me.

But Szucs was serving well, too, well enough to keep me back on the baseline and then make his trademark move of stepping into the court a few feet and taking the ball early and hitting it at a sharp angle out of my reach. He was like a tall fireplug planted squarely on the baseline who could hit the ball only inches after it bounced. A freak of nature he was. I knew that he would not give me anything. That bastard made you work for every point.

At 2–all, on his serve, I did something I should have done seven years before, the first time I ever saw the sawed-off son of a bitch. I moved inside the baseline and took his serve, which was hard and low with a sort of sidespin, and chipped it and charged, hitting a hard slice down the line and coming into net. It worked, worked so beautifully that I could hardly believe it. Taking away that split second that he gained from me returning deep in the court forced him to scramble to the ball and he was not able to put much pace on his shots while on the run. With the hard chip he had to stretch and put the ball back into the court with much less velocity than he usually did when he was leaning forward. I knocked off a sharp-angled volley back to the other side that he could only scowl at as it went by out of reach. I saw his face express emotion for the first time, sort of a dropping of his cheeks, and his mouth hung a little slack-jawed and I could see the dark crevices on his bad teeth. He sighed deep and hit another serve and again I attacked, chipping a hard backhand down the line to his forehand, and he hustled over but had to resort to a one-handed forehand—he usually hit with two—and again I knocked off a volley that his short little legs could bring him nowhere near. On the next point he tried a lob, a well-hit topspin ball, but I anticipated it and crushed an overhead back at him that he couldn't handle. After all these years and many losses, I had finally figured that son of a bitch out.

I won the next point with another overhead, breaking his serve at love to go up 3–2. I kept serving well myself, this time charging in and volleying like I had been doing it all my life. I maintained my focus, not looking over at Jessica, but I could hear her clap and give an occasional shout of encouragement. I didn't want to break the trance I was in, or slow the momentum, or do anything different.

I won sixteen points in a row, and the first set 6–2. The best part of all was I saw him slump his shoulders sitting in the chair at the break. He was beaten and he knew it. I had never, ever seen him discouraged.

After the first set, I allowed myself one glance at Jessica, her green eyes twinkling and her sort of pouty lips pink and smiling, absolutely beautiful.

But then I put my focus back on Janos Szucs. I won the second set without dropping a game, losing only four or five points. Never have I been so proud of a win.

Jessica hugged me when I came off the court, just as Szucs squeezed by us, a dejected little man on the way out of competitive tennis. She gave me a big kiss, and said she was proud of me.

It didn't matter to me that the eleven other fans watching had long since sauntered away to see if a better match was taking place somewhere else with a player they might recognize.

Jessica was there, and she was all I needed.

Part Four

The taxi from LaGuardia sped through the Midtown Tunnel and dropped me off at a hotel on Seventh Avenue, just a few blocks north of Times Square. From the sidewalk I looked down into the canyon of neon signs and billboards all awhirl.

The USTA had held a block of rooms at the hotel for participants in the qualies at a "special" players' rate of $229 a night, which I realize for a nice hotel at that time of year in New York was a discount, but for me still added up to a pretty penny. I didn't dwell on it. I was in the qualifying of the U.S. Open, a chance to make the tournament for the first time in my career. If ever I was going to spend money on lodging, this was it.

Jessica had invited me to stay with her, but after Binghamton I had visited her sweat box of an apartment in the East Village, a two-bedroom place that couldn't have been more than six hundred square feet, the third roommate sleeping on a fold-out couch in the tight confines of a living room in which I could stand in the middle and reach my arms out and touch opposite walls. The kitchen sink and the shower were so close I worried I might accidentally wash my ass with the dishrag. I told her I needed a room of my own.

I called her before she got off work and she asked me to meet her at a bar not far from where she lived. She said it was a favorite place of hers, a dive with a pool table in the back.

"I . . . I don't want to go to a bar," I said. "I'm playing my first match tomorrow."

"Oh, I'm an idiot—of course," she said, but I detected disappointment in her voice.

I had to remind myself that she was young, and although she did sound very excited to see me, I knew that it would be a bad idea to see her before I played. I sure as hell wasn't going to go down to Greenwich Village and sit in some dark bar and drink. I wanted to remind her that I had been hustling my ass off for years, playing tennis tournaments from New York to Buenos Aires, in places like Waco, Texas, and Winnetka, Illinois, often sleeping in my van. I was hitting the ball as well as I had in years, and I had overcome Janos Szucs after years of miserable losses. But I didn't feel I should have to explain myself. All I said was, "Hey, I can't see you tonight. I've got to rest, get ready for my match."

"Oh, ah, okay. Can I stop by and say hello?"

"Well, no, I don't think so. I'm sorry, but I've got to get ready. This is my big chance, my last chance. I don't mean anything against you. I want to spend some time with you. If I win my three qualies matches, I'll have some time Friday night to relax." I almost told her I loved her, but I wasn't ready for that yet.

"Do you want me to come see your matches?"

"Yes, of course. I'll probably go on court about five tomorrow. But it could be later."

"Are you sure? What's wrong?"

"Nothing's wrong, darlin'. I just have the biggest match of my life. I've got to be ready."

"Okay," she said. I didn't think she believed me. She was probably thinking I had another woman lined up, that maybe she should be leery of a thirty-eight-year-old tennis pro who had never married.

"I'll see you tomorrow, then, at my match? We can talk some after it is over, but if I win, I can't visit that long. I'll have to get ready to play again the next day."

"Okay," she said. "I'll see you then. Good luck."

I hung up the phone and went to the window and looked down forty-one stories below. I watched the flow of cars and the mob of pedestrians, intersecting, pausing, letting one another pass, then bumping, and jostling, hurrying to wherever the hell it was they had to be.

I raised my eyes and looked into an ugly black steel office building across the way. I saw a floor full of people working in cubicles, talking on the phones, some sitting around a conference table, others in big offices with a menagerie of knickknacks and framed poster-sized photos.

Beyond the office tower I had a view of 53rd Street West all the way to the Hudson River, and on the right I could see the marquee of the *Late Show*, its golden-yellow text on a blue background. All the way at the end of the street where the river met the road, a line of cars crept by on the highway.

My phone rang, and it was Harry. "Hey Jaxie, I'm calling you from a smartphone, can you believe that?"

"Did Suzette show you how to use it?

"Of course," he said. "In fact, she was the one who dialed the number for me. But I figured out on my own which side of this little booger to talk into."

"Are you here?"

"We just got off the plane in Newark," he said. "Do you know who you play yet?"

"Yeah, Ronnie Nguyen, a kid from Louisiana, only seventeen. He finished second in the juniors last year."

"Shit, boy, seventeen. I remember when you were seventeen. He's half your age."

"Not even quite half, Harry. I'm thirty-eight."

"Well, you might be old, but you can beat some young punk. You know anything about his game?"

"Yeah, I heard a little. The kid is all forehand and fast feet. He supposedly's got an amazing forehand, but it's wild."

"You are a smart player now, boy. Not like you used to be. You used to be sort of the same way."

"Yeah," I said.

"You know what to do, right? Make his ass work. Make him hit some balls. You've seen big forehands before."

"Yeah, you're right. It ain't that complicated."

"He'll be nervous, and will make some mistakes."

"I hope so."

"Shit boy, if he doesn't, you start beating on that backhand, and get into net. Mix it up on him. These juniors ain't seen the likes of you."

"I hope."

"Hey, anyway," he said. "Suzette is getting tickets to go see a play tonight, *The Lion King*. Do you want to go?"

"No, thanks, Harry. I'm going to get some food from room service, and then take it easy tonight. I have to rest. I'm giving away twenty-one years to this boy tomorrow."

"You don't want to wait and have dinner with us?"

"No, I'm hungry now. It's already after six. I want to eat and get to bed early."

"All right. I guess I'll see you in the morning, bright and squirrelly. What time did you want to meet?"

"Just come by my room, about eight. We can order something up."

"You sure you don't want to go out?"

"Nope, let's stay in. All I want to do is get ready for my matches. Save my legs."

"All right, you got it, champ."

I ordered dinner from room service. The dude who took my order was rude and acted like I was bothering him. Explaining that I wanted whole wheat pasta without the Alfredo sauce was an ordeal. You would have thought I was telling him how to perform heart surgery.

The food arrived about the time an Atlanta Braves game on TV was starting. I sat on the end of the bed and ate, drinking water and sipping the iced tea, watching my Braves when strong nostalgic feelings began to come over me, thinking about my dad. He would have had some funny things to say about the outrageous prices on the menu, I'm sure, and the jokes I made in my mind he would have liked. There would have been nothing better for him than to travel to New York to watch me play in the U.S. Open, to sit and have dinner with me in my hotel room. My last nights with him were in the hotel in Paris. That was so long ago it seemed like a dream, like another lifetime, like it was not me who had lived through it, but someone else.

The next day, Harry and I headed for Flushing Meadows. I had considered calling a car service, but I decided instead to take the inexpensive route and ride the subway. He wore tennis whites like he was ready to step onto the court—Tacchini, like McEnroe had worn in the early 1980s—and carried a straw hat with him.

After a forty-five-minute ride with dozens of stops, we piled off the No. 7 train and headed down the stairs from the platform and back up another set of stairs to the long walkway to the Billie Jean King National Tennis Center. I walked through those gates and looked up at that giant concrete-and-brick bowl that is the Arthur Ashe Stadium, the world's largest arena devoted solely to tennis, a twenty-three-thousand-seat colossus used only once a year for fourteen days. It towers over the Louis Armstrong Court that was the main stadium until Ashe opened in 1997. Jessica told me that she'd once had a seat in the top level of Ashe that was so high that she felt like she was watching the match from an airplane.

I had hoped they would give the qualifiers the run of the locker room deep in the bowels of the stadium. I should have known better. They crammed all 128 of us into the front section where there were only thirty-two lockers. They assigned lockers only to the seeded players in the qualifying draw, and said any unseeded player who beat a seeded player or who won their first two matches would get a locker later in the week.

There was a velvet rope between the depths of the locker room and the qualifiers. A security guard, a beefy dude who could have been an extra on *The Sopranos*, was stationed to make sure we didn't cross that line to where the top players would be housed. I guess the USTA worried that some qualifier might try to sniff Roger Federer's jock strap.

Players crowded into the accessible section of the locker room, some of them so young they looked like they should be in high school, gangly and acne-faced, staring daggers with hate-filled eyes. I sighed and sat down on a bench, while Harry excitedly bounced around on his toes, jabbering to players and their coaches.

It was about as desperate a room of tennis players as you'll ever see, 128 men, many of them still boys, competing for sixteen spots in the main draw. I saw young American kids I had seen before and a few I had played out on the Challengers and Futures, but I also saw many more I didn't know, a handful of college players, as well as hordes of foreigners, more South Americans and Spaniards than I could count.

I was easily the oldest player there, older even than many of the coaches. I should have been the most experienced, the cagiest, the calmest, the one who knew how to handle the pressure. Every player in the qualifying, whether eighteen or thirty-eight, knew it could be their last time at this level. I should have been ready, but instead I was nervous as hell. Thoughts bounced around in my mind like loose tennis balls in the trunk of a car, a whole ball hopper sprung loose, rolling and thumping. "Hey boy, let's take a walk," Harry said, "maybe go sit out by the practice court until it's your turn."

We walked through the tennis center there, more than forty courts, and every court had either a match in progress or someone practicing, with many courts doubled up. That's as busy as you'll ever see the USTA National Tennis Center, on the qualifying day when all 128 men and 128 women who are invited play their first qualifying round, and you know that half of the players who arrived in New York with high hopes will be going home after that first day, while the other 128 start getting nervous about their next match. They all know that losing in the qualies sucks, that it pays no money and for the next two weeks they'll be sitting around listening to John McEnroe and Mary Carillo carry on about who is the greatest this or that of all time, while all they can do is practice and exercise and lick their wounds, getting ready for a trip to California or Mexico or China or wherever the next stop might be on the never-ending circuit that is the minor-league tennis tour.

I was assigned to the east-side practice area, about as far as you can get from the premier courts. These courts were so far away they were practically off the grounds, about halfway back to the subway it seemed. We walked out there and I threw my rackets down under a tree. I stretched and mumbled to myself, doubtful of all my goals. I thought about Jessica, wondered if she was pissed at me.

Harry had made arrangements with some young teaching pros for me to practice with, and they came along and we went through that metal gate onto our court and pulled out our rackets and they took turns hitting with me. With the ball in motion, every stray thought fell away from my mind. Shots felt solid on my strings. I was seeing the ball good, watching it from racket to racket, arcing over the net and onto the court. My legs felt limber, my arms loose, and that reverberation of the ball on the sweet spot emanated through my body like it had ten million times before. It was good to be in motion, thinking about nothing but hitting the ball.

My face didn't show it, but I was worried as hell that first day of the qualifying, paired up against Ronnie Nguyen, the seventeen-year-old from Metairie, Louisiana, one of the kids the USTA perennially proclaims as the coming savior of American men's tennis. He must have been more nervous than I was, because the errors poured out of him. I dug in on the pristine DecoTurf, the Open's trademark blue-and-green hard court surface, smooth and hot in the sun, and played solid. I won easily, 6–2, 6–2. Jessica and Harry and Suzette clapped whenever I hit a winner, but I didn't hit many, only a few volleys I knocked off when, after a litany of errors, he started pushing the ball to keep it in the court. The last three games I attacked the net on every ball, something I never in my life dreamed I would do. We didn't have a rally that lasted more than four shots.

My match the following day I had expected to be much tougher, against Eduardo Arguello, a rising Spaniard who stood six feet two inches tall and weighed 180 pounds with big biceps, shiny black hair, straight white teeth, and dark brown eyes. He had been hovering near the cutoff for the main draw, and many were surprised he didn't get a wild card bid. *Tennis* magazine had included him in an article in their U.S. Open preview issue about up-and-coming stars to watch, and I'm sure when they wrote it, they never dreamed that he would be forced to qualify, slumming with the players well out of the top one hundred, which is where his ranking had fallen to due to a poor second half of the summer on hard courts.

Arguello dressed resplendently, a red silk Nike bandanna tied around his head, white shoes with a matching red swoosh, and his shorts and shirt the same strong dark red. I served one of the best matches of my life, knocking out eight aces and more winners. He cursed and smashed one racket—for some reason the umpire didn't give him a warning—but then after I won the first set 6–2 and went up 2–0 in the second he became sullen and for all practical purposes gave up, hitting every ball as hard as he could, most well beyond the baseline. You've never heard any crowd as quiet as that one became in that match, the Spaniards stunned. My contingent, knowing they were outnumbered and also a tennis-courteous bunch who would not applaud errors in a blowout, only meekly applauded when I hit an ace or a winner. But I could feel them smiling on me. I didn't look to them, and I didn't look at anything except what was on the court right in front of me until that last backhand of his went into the bottom of the net and the umpire announced, "Game, Set, Match, Skinner, 6–2, 6–1."

My dad had sometimes told me this funny story about a gorilla who played golf, who could drive the ball 485 yards to within an inch of the hole, but when it came time to approach the ball and putt, he would hit it another 485 yards, unable to use finesse. I stood there on the court and thought of my dad's story about the gorilla, and how he used to tell me that story and laugh. I never really understood it until that day. He had been trying to teach me through the metaphor of the gorilla that I should be able to do more than crush the ball.

I sat down in my chair by my racket bag and closed my eyes for a second and thought about my dad. I would be lying if I said I'm a religious person, but I wondered about his soul. I hoped he could see me, one win away from playing in the U.S. Open.

These two easy wins didn't tire me out, a great advantage in the third and final qualifying match, the match that anyone who has spent any time on the tour knows is the most difficult to win. The pressure is tremendous. Win, you are in the Grand Slam, the main draw, and guaranteed to earn at least twenty thousand dollars and take home a bunch of ranking points; lose, you go home with nothing.

I played Anatoly Orlov, a twenty-eight-year-old Russian who had once been in the top twenty and was trying to climb back up the ladder after injuries. He stood about six feet and weighed a muscled 175 pounds, his blond hair in a short buzz cut. His expression never changed, simply a stern gaze of disdain was all he offered, his blue eyes severe and unfriendly. Harry had scouted him and told me that if I kept going at his backhand, mixing up the pace against him and coming in behind deep approach shots, this wing, picturesque though it was, would break down.

We started at eleven, the hot New York August sun beating down, and the very first point was a battle: I hit him a big serve down the T and attacked the net; he hit a one-handed backhand return very solidly, a hard, flat ball back down the middle at my feet; I scooped the ball up with an awkward forehand half volley, just happy to get the racket cleanly on it, and it went short to his forehand and I moved tight into the net, anticipating that he might pass me down the line; he ran forward but instead of hitting the passing shot I expected he flicked a crosscourt lob over my head, just out of my reach if I tried to jump for it; I didn't jump, however, but turned and took off running and barely caught up to the ball on my forehand side and threw up a very high, defensive lob; he had closed into the net and backed up, his hand pointing up at the ball, waiting on it to fall, letting it bounce and hitting a safe overhead down the middle from about ten feet behind his service line; I had positioned myself just behind the baseline and was able to hit a solid forehand groundstroke down the middle; he had moved back to the baseline and stepped around his backhand and responded to my forehand with a harder forehand with some topspin down the middle, slightly crosscourt; we exchanged about ten crosscourt groundstrokes this way, five forehands apiece, until I changed direction and took the ball down the line to his backhand; he responded with a beautifully struck crosscourt backhand, his one-handed form as pretty as you'd see in a tennis instruction book, coming over the ball with topspin and power; his backhand sent me scuffling off the court to catch up to it and all I could do was stretch as far as my arm would go and float the ball back into the court; he had moved into net, anticipating my weak duck of a return, and when he saw the floater I offered he moved in tight and took a swinging forehand volley and knocked off a winner to the open court, a shot I could do nothing about but watch. I was down love–15.

We went on to hit the ball about four hundred times in that very first service game of mine, both of us having about five ad points each to win it, but neither able to close it out until I finally did. Each of us played better, more determined, when our backs were against the wall. He went on to win the first set 7–5, and I came back and won the second set in a tiebreaker by a score of 9–7 with a running backhand slice passing shot down the line from far off the court, evoking a curse from him in Russian, his one and only exhortation of the day.

The third set was another battle, both of us fighting to hold serve all the way to the final tiebreaker. After eleven hard-fought points, both of us slugging it out from the baseline, looking for a short ball to try to hit for a winner or an approach shot, he had a match point at 6–5. I hit one of my best serves of the day, a hard angle out to his backhand that he could barely reach, and he put the ball into the net. At 6-points-all in the deuce court, I changed the pace and hit a slow, sidespin serve that moved into his body and aggravated that smooth backhand stroke of his. He took an awkward chop at the ball that floated it back. I charged the net and drove a solid volley down the backhand side, just as he guessed forehand and ran the other way to the empty court, the ball scooting to the backstop behind him.

That made it match point for me. One point from the U.S. Open main draw. I was so focused then that I didn't think about what I sometimes think about on match points—the matches I have blown after having a match point to win, the worst feeling there is in tennis. But that day I didn't think about my many past failures; instead I concentrated on winning the point at hand. If he had suffered any problems at all that day, his serve had started to decline in the second set, and he never quite recovered it. He changed his strategy to simply placing the balls deep in the service box with a little bit of spin. Most of his serves were too deep for me to chip and charge and his passing shots were top-notch. I didn't dare try to sneak into net against him except on the best of serves or approach shots. That's how I lost my serve in the first set, and why I had to fight for so many tough games simply to hold.

But three hours after that first point I had a match point to move on, to place myself in the big draw, in the bright lights of America's biggest tennis tournament. He scared me when he tried to hit a big serve down the T to my forehand, surprising me, but fortunately the ball was just wide. I moved in a step or two, and knew as well as he did that he would try to hit a second serve with some spin deep in the wide corner of the box to make me hit a backhand. As soon as his ball toss reached its apex I started moving back and to my left, my forehand grip strong and the racket going back as I watched his topspin serve come my way, exactly where I had anticipated it, and not with too much pace. I took the racket back in a loop and readied my feet beyond the doubles line and stepped forward onto my left foot as my racket began to come around and my shoulder opened and I made contact with the ball slightly out in front of me and hit it hard and just over the net with topspin. I drove the ball a foot beyond the service line on his ad court side, the side from which he had served, and he had followed the serve into the court and took a step back to the middle but instead had to lunge back at the ball that I blasted. As soon as I hit the ball it felt like a winner but I worried that maybe, just maybe, I had pushed it too far wide and it would be out, but it flew, this inside-out forehand, over the net strap at a ferocious angle and came down just beyond the service line, landing on the sideline. I'm glad that day we had an umpire and line judges who both saw the ball as I did and called it good because in many tennis matches where you call your own lines all it would have taken is for my opponent to extend the index finger up, although Orlov was not the kind of player to cheat, a straight-up serious Russian he was who did not take to American chicanery. He knew he was beat when the ball came down on that white line and then angled off into the short side fence and ricocheted into the corner by the small digital scoreboard where it bounced a few times before coming to rest.

I raised my hands over my head and closed my eyes, a waterfall of relief washing over me as the stress fell away. I shook hands with Orlov and the umpire and stepped through the small side gate. Harry hugged me, jumping up and down on his toes, shouting, "That's my boy," again and again. I went to Jessica, hugging and kissing her. She didn't mind that I was sweaty. Her mouth tasted sweet, sort of minty, mixing with the citrusy lemon-lime Powerade flavor in mine.

We ended the kiss but I held her and looked into those pretty green eyes of hers and started to tell her I was glad she was there but she spoke first. "That was a great match," she said. "You played so smart and so well, especially on the big points."

"Thanks," I said, and kissed her again.

Two hours later Jessica and I lay sprawled on the sheets in my hotel room with a bottle of champagne. I had only half a glass, but she drank two glasses and started on a talking jag about my match, about how my serve was amazing and the sliced returns I mixed in with top-spin shots were unlike anything she had ever seen. "You're going to win this whole thing," she said.

"Hush." I put my index finger to her lips, and she playfully bit it. "You'll . . . You'll jinx me." We made love a second time, and then drifted off into naps, her head in the crook of my arm.

I woke up about an hour later and Jessica turned her attention to dinner reservations, pulling a *New York* magazine and her smartphone into the bed. She made about a dozen phone calls, but all of the places she wanted to go were booked.

"We could go to Applebee's," I said. "It's only a block away. Harry and Suzette had dinner there earlier this week. They said it's good."

"No! Are you crazy? I *am not* going to Applebee's. There are thousands of great restaurants in this city. Just give me a little time. It's Friday night. A lot of them are full." She kept calling until she found an Italian place in Greenwich Village that could accommodate us at eight.

She then got out of the bed and stood in front of the mirror naked and started brushing her long hair, her slim white figure luminescent in the lamplight, her nipples as pink as cotton candy. I would have eaten in any restaurant in the world where she wanted to go.

We met Harry and Suzette in the hotel lobby at seven thirty. They had dressed like they were going to church, Harry in a blue blazer with a red tie and khaki slacks, and Suzette in a light-blue skirt and matching top and black pumps, her gray hair smelling of hair spray. I laughed at seeing Harry dressed up, something Suzette made him do, but then they reminded me of my long-dead grandparents when I was very young, how they would dress up for the annual dinner on the grounds, an enormous lunch at their country church, the white A-frame sanctuary by the road, the church's graveyard where they knew they would one day lie on the hill rising up to the tree line where the open space ended and the Georgia woods began, the same graveyard where my father was buried. I felt guilty for forcing Harry and Suzette out late into the New York City night, where after a muggy August day the city stank of garbage, sweat, piss, vomit, and exhaust fumes.

They were very sweet to Jessica. She hugged both Harry and Suzette, kissing them on the cheek, startling them a little. The way she did it was sincere, not like most people in New York who perfunctorily hug and kiss you regardless of whether they care if you lived or died. I could tell that Harry and Suzette liked her, and their approval was important to me. We followed her outside and she led us to the taxi line and after about a ten-minute wait, we finally got a cab.

I tipped the bellman a dollar and he held the door as we piled into a taxi. Harry, Suzette, and I sat in the back and Jessica in the front seat, turning her head and smiling at us through the open sliding window in the bulletproof glass.

The taxi shot down Seventh Avenue into the swirl of traffic around Times Square, stopping and starting in a mass of honking cars, until the driver turned to get on the West Side Highway and scooted on down toward Greenwich Village. Harry and Suzette held hands and didn't say a word. Jessica tried to talk, but it was noisy and hard to hear, so she gave up on conversation.

The car was moving at a pretty good clip when my smartphone

rang. I pulled it out of my pocket and looked down at the illuminated screen, a number I didn't recognize. I answered and heard a voice that sounded like a twelve-year-old girl. I couldn't understand a word she said. I put my hand over my right ear and squeezed the phone to my left. "What's that?"

"Hi, can you hear me?" the juvenile voice said. I thought maybe it was a prank call.

"Yes, I can hear you, but just barely."

"This is Ashley Michenfelder." She sounded like she was straining to yell, but it still wasn't very loud. "I'm an intern for the U.S. Open. I wanted to let you know when your first-round match is."

"Okay, when?"

"Monday night."

I knew right then my draw could not be good. Only the top seeds are scheduled for the night sessions on the Ashe Stadium court. I let out a deep sigh, almost a groan. I hoped that I wouldn't run up against Federer, Nadal, Djokovic, or Murray, the foursome who had been dominating the game. I had hoped maybe to get lucky and end up against an unseeded player, maybe either another qualifier in the first round. But hearing the Monday-night time slot, my immediate hope was that I would get one of the American stars, either Andy Roddick, who had come out of retirement earlier this year, or John Isner, whose game was starting to fade. I had planned that Friday night to not even think about the draw, but to wait until Saturday when I practiced to see who I would be playing. I wanted to take one night off from obsessing about tennis, to put it out of my mind, and to enjoy Jessica's company, to celebrate with Harry, and just revel in the fact that I had made the main draw of the U.S. Open. But of course, the USTA had assigned this intern, probably some rich prep school kid, to call me and spoil my one night of relaxation.

"Are you still there?" she said.

"Yes, I'm here."

"Do you want to know who you play?"

I closed my eyes and had visions of the USTA committee giggling as they spread the draw out on a big mahogany table, slotting me into line number two, right below Novak Djokovic.

I groaned again, and thought about saying no, don't tell me, but now she had piqued my curiosity. "Yes, okay, tell me."

"You play . . ." And here she paused, as though she was going back to double-check the draw. "You play a wild card"—and I knew it was Roddick before she said it.

She told me and I let out a little "Yep" and thanked her and clicked off the phone.

"Who was that, boy? Who do you play?"

"Andy Roddick," I said. I nodded and smiled. "Monday night, prime time, Arthur Ashe Stadium. Are you ready for some *football*?"

Harry's eyes lit up, and he bounced in his seat and patted me on the knee. "I'm ready, Jaxie. Baby, I'm ready. And you are ready too, so let's do it!"

The next day the USTA allotted me thirty minutes to go onto the Arthur Ashe Stadium court to practice. Although I had been hanging around the tennis center all week for the qualies, and had been through the hallways and in and out of locker room, I had not poked my head out into that enormous arena. I had avoided it as though seeing it before I was assigned to play there would be some kind of jinx.

I thought I was prepared for Ashe's colossal size but when I stepped onto the court, it really blew me away how big it was. The most dramatic thing about the Ashe Stadium was how it shrank the court. In the context of rows upon rows of seats, enough for twenty-three thousand in all, the three thousand square feet of the singles court seemed but an insignificant, confined rectangle. With the seats empty, the ball echoed in the cavernous stadium as though we were at the bottom of a gorge, the Wilsons bouncing on the court sounding like hoof steps in a deep canyon.

My practice partners teamed up and hit against me, running me some, and then working on my groundstrokes for about twenty minutes. Harry watched from behind me, praising my good shots. After I got into the rallies, the immensity of the stands fell away and I was able to concentrate. I didn't want to tire myself out, but wanted to hit just enough to stay sharp, to get a feel for the sightlines in that place. I practiced hitting returns of serve. Harry asked one of the players to move about ten feet inside the baseline and pop the ball as hard as he could in order to prepare me for Roddick's big serve, still one of the fastest in the game even though he was almost thirty-four and had been off the tour for two years during his temporary retirement. The Ashe court was faster than the exterior courts where I had played, but I had expected that. The USTA had quickened the surface, trying to do whatever it could to help out Roddick and John Isner and the rest of the big-serving young Americans. If I could get Roddick's serve back in play, I would have a chance to win points, and get a break. I finished with some service practice of my own, working on knifing the ball into the backhand side, tight serves that kept it away from his lethal forehand. I left thinking that I was ready for the big stage.

I woke up at seven on Monday morning, the day of my match, to a ringing telephone, a few hours before I had planned to get up. "Hello," I said, my mouth dry, first words of the day.

"Jaxie Skinner?" The hard-edged voice of a New York man.

"This is he."

"I'm Ronald Womblatt of the *New York Post*. I was hoping I could—"

I put the phone back in its cradle—I didn't slam it, but just let it rest on the clicker. Harry had taken to reading the *Post* from cover to cover every day, and I had seen enough headlines—RING A ZING ZING for Donald Trump's new Zambian girlfriend, or BONER-RAMA, about an osteopath and his one-legged nurse mistress—to know that I didn't want any part of whatever they were writing about me. I hadn't set the phone down for two seconds—it was only seven and I had hoped to sleep until nine—when it rang again. I lay there for about six rings before I decided to answer it.

"Mr. Skinner," a British voice said this time, that pompous airy way some of them have of talking as though emitting the words is an enormous strain. "I am . . ." and I didn't even wait for it, I just put my finger on the clicker and turned off the call. I didn't care if he was from the BBC, *The Guardian*, or the *Piney Post*. I sat up on the edge of the bed and reached behind the nightstand and unplugged it from the wall. As soon as I lay back down, the phone in the bathroom rang, sounding like fire alarm bells clattering. Why anyone in a two-hundred-square-foot hotel room needs a phone in the bathroom is beyond me.

I got up and unhooked the bathroom phone and went back to sleep, napping restlessly until about ten. I ordered a room service breakfast and called Harry and Jessica on my cell phone, telling them I didn't want to get to the tennis center until about six. I spent the rest of the day lounging in the room, the DO NOT DISTURB tag on the door, doing some light stretching, napping and watching TV, and for a while re-reading the opening of the first volume of Shelby Foote's *The Civil War*. Twice I ignored when reporters knocked, tempted though I was to go out and punch them in the face.

I had decided over the weekend that I would not speak to the press. I was going to keep as low a profile as possible and play tennis and worry about nothing else. Whatever they said about me, favorable or not, it wouldn't affect how I played on the court if I didn't bother to read or watch it. I couldn't, however, completely block out of my mind why a few reporters were so eager to talk to me. I assumed it was a few who had gotten off their asses and done a little research and unearthed the tale of my relationship with Olga Polykova, whom I had neither seen nor spoken to since that time in Paris. She had since blazed a trail of celebrity lovers, from hockey players to Latin heartthrobs, so many that I was long forgotten. She was now married to a Brazilian sugar plantation millionaire and occasionally played World Team Tennis and modeled for a clothing company. And like every attractive person ever to play professional tennis, she had a contract to promote expensive watches. She had retired from the tour ten years ago, but in spite of that she got more news coverage than many of the active players. *Sports Illustrated* and *Tennis* magazine were compelled to do "where-is-she-now?" stories every two or three years, and had celebrated her thirtieth birthday as a cultural sporting watermark. And there must be about nine million pictures of her on the Internet, the most popular being that famous photo of her cleaning sand out of her tiny red bikini bottom.

How could I have even begun to explain myself to a reporter? The press and bloggers would write what they wanted to write anyway. So much meaning and metaphor and confused intent becomes attached to words, and that's maybe the reason I have no desire to do any interviews with anyone. Whatever I said would be distorted; I figured they could make up the stories they wanted to write without my help. I don't really care what anyone in America believes about me, and even if I did, I don't know what I could do to change it. Who I am is not that simple.

Part of me just wanted to pack up and go home and live way out in the woods behind a big fence with guns and dogs. I lay on the sheets in my boxers with the air-conditioning cranking and I began to realize that I was regretting the very thing I had been working toward for years. I pondered everything in my tennis life, and I thought a lot more about my father, how he would be proud of me for sticking it out and finally fighting my way into the tournament. I could hear him saying, *Boy, if you can overcome that damn Janos Szucs and beat him, you can do anything you want. You can do anything you put your mind to if you work hard enough.*

At five, the car I had hired drove Harry, Suzette, Jessica, and me out to Flushing Meadows. I warmed up on a distant practice court for about twenty minutes, mainly practicing returns hit off serves fired from about ten feet inside the baseline, and then took a shower and waited in the farthest corner of the locker room. Thank God that the Open doesn't allow reporters in there, like they do in some sports. I can't imagine why other sports do. I could see some nosy reporter coming along and try to ask me questions while I was taking a dump or something.

The only distraction I had was the required drug test an hour before the match was scheduled to take the court. A humorless French man from the International Tennis Federation walked into the bathroom with me and stood at the side and watched me pee. I had submitted urine samples before at Challenger events, but never with someone standing there staring at my pecker while I produced it. I guess the higher you go up in levels, the stricter they become on the testing.

After the piss test, I sat back in my spot. I could try to tell you that I wasn't nervous, that I sat there and bullshitted with Harry, but that would be a lie. My stomach was dancing around, and my spine and arms had this weird sort of tingle. What made it worse was that Harry was nervous too, and his attempts at making small talk, bullshitting about other matches or the Braves or the meal we had eaten Friday night, were all wooden, awkward conversation. I could hear the tension in his voice, see the jumpiness in his expression.

I sat in a chair and leaned my head back against the wall and closed my eyes, forcing myself to think about my bulldog. I imagined him running across a green, misty field somewhere mysterious in Europe or the African Serengeti, taking down a big black bull with a running leap, biting his teeth into the enormous neck. That white little bloodthirsty booger writhed and growled, his jaws gritting with gristle and bone and leather cowhide. "Hold on, goddammit," I said. "Hold on."

I sat there a good two and a half hours. The USTA staff didn't call me until almost nine thirty, and not because Serena Williams needed extra time to win, but due to the bloated opening ceremony that had lasted about an hour and a half. The first night of the U.S. Open is somewhat of a circus, with dancers and singers and bureaucratic bullshit, sort of a cross between a Broadway musical and a session at the UN.

A young man in designer glasses and very intense black eyebrows that appeared to be enhanced with makeup was assigned to be my handler. "Mr. Skinner, right this way, please," he said in that Mr. Rogers way of speaking that afflicts so many young men nowadays. He reached out to take my arm, as though I needed an escort, but I pulled back and sort of glared at him, to let him know not to touch me. I don't like anyone randomly putting their hands on me, especially not dudes like this dubious joker with the glistening eyebrows and a tube of gel in his short hair. And I certainly don't want anyone taking me by the arm when I am as nervous as I was before that match. "Okay," he said, as condescending as possible. "We'll go through these tunnels, and then you'll do a quick interview and then onto the court."

I had watched hundreds of televised U.S. Open matches over the years, but I had forgotten that they interview players before going on court in prime time. Never in the history of these discussions has any player said anything insightful, but they still insist on doing the interviews.

We traipsed through the maze of hallways and turned the final corner and the camera lights hit me. The obsequious pledge stepped away and a cookie-cutter reporter in a suit with blow-dried hair angled toward me and I stopped next to him. He held the microphone up and said, "Jaxie Skinner, *twenty years* since your last Grand Slam. You reached the semifinals of the French Open at eighteen. You haven't played an ATP tour match since. How does it feel to be back at another slam—your first U.S. Open—at the age of thirty-eight?"

The cameraman, a dude with a huge beer gut and a long ponytail, lumbered my way and directed the white light from a sharp bulb right above the camera directly at my face, as though he was about to bash me on the head with the lens. I winced a little and looked down at my feet as I answered.

"You know . . . all I want to say is that I'm just sorry that my father can't be here to see this. I want to thank my coach, Harry Crummy, for sticking by me after all these years." With my next thought, I raised my head and looked at the lens, and smiled a little. "And I want to say hello to Jessica." I almost told her I loved her, but I didn't want to be too cheesy.

Fortunately, the reporter didn't think I was worth more than one question. Two more frantic handlers waved me to the doorway that opened onto the court. I waited there as Roddick came down the hallway, the white-boy gangsta rap strut that he has, decked out in his Lacoste clothes that he gets something like one million dollars a year for wearing.

His interview was from the school of athletic media training, quips like, "I'm happy to be back here. I'm going to take it one match at a time." He popped some fluorescent-lime-green gum while asked another question, something about would this be his last U.S. Open. "It might be," he said. "But you never know. I've already retired once."

And then they were done and he walked my way and a grim-faced young woman with a clipboard in her hand and a pencil tied into the knot of brown hair on top of her head motioned frantically for me to go out onto the court, mouthing *Go* as though there was a fire under my feet.

I heard my name over the loudspeaker and stepped out onto that blue-and-green DecoTurf and walked toward the net posts, keeping my head down, trying to make myself think about my determined bulldog but mesmerized by thousands of voices all jabbering at once, the overlay of many vocal cords, some cheering for me, but mainly for Roddick, as he followed about ten feet behind me onto the court and waved. Flashbulbs by the thousands were going off.

I looked up at the crowd just as the cameras fixed their lenses on me, projecting my image onto the Jumbotron. I had trouble breathing and my arms and legs tingled. I felt like every eye in the place was bearing down on me. That's a powerful thing, about twenty thousand people or so, all of them staring at you, a total of forty thousand eyeballs, some in the first row and some in the last, all focusing on me, Jaxie Skinner, a dude who has done the best I could and am trying to make right for the bad deeds I've done, to recover some of the talent I wasted. I saw a big camera swivel, its enormous glass lens following me, and I imagined billions camped around their TV sets. I believed everyone in the world could see me, could look into my eyes, that they knew about all the mistakes I had made in my life, could list all the things I had done wrong.

Soon, though, we were summoned to stand by the net posts while the umpire, a diminutive French woman, made a big deal of introducing herself and telling us the rules of the match, as though this was our first time playing tennis. Roddick won the toss, they took our picture together, and then we went back to the baseline to warm up.

It felt good to get the ball into play, to concentrate on the shots. My groundstrokes felt smooth. I stared at the ball like my life depended on it, and everything else fell away.

The match started like many Roddick matches do, with quick games, him holding serve easily with big bombs, and me holding serve with steady play and him making errors. Although he has been one of the greatest players in the world, a career top ten guy and for thirteen short weeks the world's number one, he is really only a few points here and there better than someone ranked 250.

The first eight games whizzed by until we reached a crucial stage in the first set. At 4–all, 15–all he tossed the ball into the air and as the yellow Wilson reached its apex and he wound up and began that mighty ball-crushing swing of his, when the twenty thousand bloodthirsty fans were salivating for an ace, a toddler in the third row across the court from the umpire screamed, "WAAAAAAAAAAAAAAAAAAAAA!" Nothing can convey the volume of this piercing noise, especially when it first started. Roddick was too late into the serve to stop his motion and went ahead, hitting the ball off the top of his frame, shanking it about thirty rows up. The fans, as though they were confronted with peculiar and surprising news, laughed tentatively, chuckling, and collectively it added up to a minor roar. I even laughed a little myself and smiled, but Roddick was not amused.

He looked at the umpire as though to ask for a let and she leaned into her microphone and said, "Second serve." Roddick scowled at her and crimped his shoulders, narrowing his already beady eyes, and then he turned to the source of the wailing. The stumpy child of about three was sitting on the armrest between his two parents, both of whom were turned to him. He looked like a miniature John McEnroe, circa 1980, dressed in a red, white, and blue headband. As Roddick stared him down the little bastard cut loose once more, this time with a "*MAAAAA-MAAAAA*." His mother, a short but buxom dark-haired woman, tried to comfort him, but I could tell she had no control and was the kind who would not dole out the force the little bastard so desperately needed. I could hear her trying to reason with him. "Jared, now be a good boy, okay, Jared? . . . *Jared . . . Jared.*"

Roddick looked back to the umpire. She leaned forward and spoke timidly into her microphone. "Quiet, please. Second serve." Roddick shook his head and then looked across the net at me. He shrugged his shoulders and held up the ball, asking me could he have a first serve. I hadn't come this far to give one of the world's top players any breaks. I glared back at him and readied for a return.

He talked to himself more and bounced the ball repeatedly before dumping it into the net for a double fault. The crowd started to buzz, that dubious hum you never want to hear if you just hit a shot. Roddick shouted "Goddammit" and bounced his racket onto the frame and I thought I heard it crack, but it was hard to tell with all the noise.

"Warning, racket abuse," the umpire said. Roddick stormed up to her chair and complained, accusing her of being "the lead clown in amateur hour."

I tried to stay loose and bounced around on my toes to focus while he continued griping. I was playing well, serving particularly strong, and I knew all I needed was a couple of service breaks in this match and it would be mine. I looked around, back at the screaming kid, who was now up in his father's lap, a dark-haired man with smart-looking wire-rimmed glasses, and chubby, like his child. The mother was leaning over and comforting the little boy, kissing his forehead and caressing his legs. The kid was smiling, but his plump beet-red face was stained with tears.

Roddick complained to the umpire for a little longer, and then dug around in his bag looking for a new racket. I stared up at my box, where Harry, Suzette, and Jessica were, and smiled at them. Jessica looked right at me, and she looked great, like she had put on some extra eye makeup that brought out her green eyes even more. Her hair was long and fell down on her shoulders and the straps of a white sundress she wore.

I smiled back as subtly as I could, and nodded. I turned to see Roddick back at the baseline, bouncing the ball, preparing to serve into the ad court. I steeled my resolve, because I knew I desperately needed to win the first set. Roddick is the kind of player who can get on a roll, and if he gains some confidence is very hard to beat.

Of course, as soon as Roddick tossed the ball up for his first serve, that little son of a bitch courtside screamed again, almost as if on cue, but this time Roddick had enough time to stop his serve and catch the ball toss. He glared at the umpire again, and she asked the crowd, "Quiet, please." This time the crowd got into the act and emitted a guttural buzz.

Then the crowd calmed down. Before Roddick could serve, however, the kid went berserk, screaming as though his toenails were being plucked one by one. I can't imagine anyone, child or adult, screaming that loud without being tortured. He must have been near a court microphone, because his cries echoed throughout the stadium. The crowd started to boo, and this provoked the ire of the mother, a buxom fireplug of a woman who started cursing at an old man two rows in front of her who had yelled for the kid to shut up. The old man started yelling back, and I could hear lots of venomous New York "fuck you," "asshole," and "son of a bitch" aspersions being tossed back and forth, until the old man called her a "stupid cunt" and the little boy's father went down the aisle two rows to confront him.

The old fellow was one of those dudes who has not accepted the fact that he is in his seventies, the kind of old man who wants to go out swinging even though his rotator cuff muscles atrophied years ago. He threw a big roundhouse punch at the boy's father, a punch that never connected because the father, one of those types who acts tough but has always been carpooled and well schooled and has a bigger mouth than he does balls, stumbled toward him and they fell in tandem. As they went down, the old man bent his elbow and brought it crashing down on the father's face, breaking his glasses and his nose. I heard it crack, a snap very much like the sound of Roddick's racket when he had smashed the graphite frame onto the court.

The mother ran down and pulled out the only weapon she had at her disposal, an enormous designer purse, the kind Jessica later told me cost something like thirty thousand dollars. She wound up her short little stubby arms and swung that fine bag of red leather with all her might at the old man who had jumped up to his feet. The old man was reveling in his knockout when the mother's windmill of a purse swing struck him square in the face before he could even get his hands up, knocking him ass over elbows. The cameraman at the net post had captured all of this and it was broadcast on the huge video screens towering over both ends of the court. Everyone in the crowd screamed and laughed. A dozen security guards in yellow shirts and two paramedics converged down the aisle. An enormous black security guard hoisted up the mother, and she wildly swung her short little legs in the air, kicking out at anyone near her and screaming, while the paramedics began checking out the two felled men, getting them to their feet, the younger man's nose gushing blood.

During the melee, the little boy had crawled under the seats, hollering the whole time. When a security guard tried to subdue him, he climbed over the short sidewall and scurried onto my side of the court, his stubby feet flying. He ran face-first into the net and then fell backward. It looked like he hit his head pretty hard, but that crazy little New York son of a bitch was not to be stopped. I moved back to the wall, wanting no part of him. He hopped up, and a ball boy and a ball girl tried to subdue him, but he was hard to catch and ran from them. They were able to keep up, but when they caught him they could not hold on to him as he simultaneously scratched and kicked and punched and bit and spit and screamed—a whirlwind of appendages and teeth, his vocal cords running full blast. The ball girl grabbed him up and he bit her on the arm and neck, and she dropped him, and he was off again. He ran to the umpire's chair and began to climb it, grabbing on to her shoe and screaming bloody murder, trying to bite her foot.

A gray-haired New York City cop finally grabbed the little boy by the hair on his head and got him under control, losing him for a moment when the kid squirmed away and ran screaming across the court. The second time the cop caught up to him he used plastic wrist ties to bind the little boy's hands and feet together and carried him away hog-tied, keeping the kid's gnashing teeth a safe distance from his body. His mother's screams of "Jared! Jared! Jared!" echoed throughout the stadium as security led her away, also in plastic handcuffs, while the paramedics guided the two wounded men for the exit.

The crowd hooted and hollered, transformed into a rowdy mob. Something about the spectacle turned the Monday-night crowd in Arthur Ashe Stadium against Roddick, producing a bloodthirsty pack ready to see me, the obscure, forgotten journeyman, beat the best American player of the last decade. It was late by this point, ten thirty, and some of the fans were good and drunk on nine-dollar Heinekens, ready to raise some hell.

Once the melee was cleared and the perpetrators were ushered away, the umpire tried multiple times to silence the crowd. "Quiet, please," she said ten times if she said it once. But a soft French voice asking twenty thousand New Yorkers to be quiet was not very effective. The rumble continued.

So at 15–30, after about a fifteen-minute break, Roddick finally served, the crowd still buzzing. Roddick was rattled, and he double-faulted again, missing a spinning kick serve wildly for the second. At 15–40, he tried to crush an ace that scalded the bottom of the net, and then he pushed a second serve so slow into the court that was such a sitter I could hardly believe it. I stepped up and nailed a crosscourt forehand into the corner, easily past him for a break of serve. I saw Roddick's mind go, he just lost it, and I could see the rage in his face, his anger at not just the kid and this match, but all the tough losses he had suffered during his years on the tour. I think he must have been questioning the wisdom of trying to make a comeback, wondering why he wasn't out spending the evening with his swimsuit model wife instead of me.

I held my serve with ease, taking the first set. I came back out in the second and was able to focus on nothing but the ball. And I mean, absolutely nothing but the ball. I didn't look at my box to see Jessica and Harry and Suzette. I didn't scan the crowd for celebrities, and I ignored the bevies of good-looking women in tight dresses and blouses and skirts, with long, expensive hair treatments and diamond jewelry, all texting on fashionable smartphones, phones with special covers that change to match the clothes and shoes they were wearing and the handbags they were carrying. I'm telling you all this now but I didn't think about any of it then. I thought about the ball and the ball only, not what Roddick was doing, not where he was missing, but just hitting the ball solidly.

I won fairly easily, 6–4, 6–3, 6–3, getting one break of serve in each of the sets, just enough to carry me through to victory. I played about as flawlessly as I could on my serve, getting seventy-six percent of my first balls in, and charging the net about forty percent of the time, keeping him guessing.

I was in the zone, and what a time for it. I did just what I needed to do and nothing else, not even really thinking about the score, just letting my subconscious take over and hit the ball, hitting it as solidly as I could, like I was alone hitting against a brick wall. It wasn't until I hit my last serve, a big ball down the T to his forehand that he sailed long, that I reflected. I raised my arms over my head and the crowd let out an overwhelming cheer.

I hit a ball as high up as I could toward the Jumbotron and watched as a pack of kids, probably all twelve or so, scrambled for it in the emptying rows of the upper deck. I shook hands with Roddick at the net and he didn't have anything to say, going with a more traditional shake instead of the gangsta rap grip he usually adopted when he won. As I went over to the umpire I saw kids by the hundreds jammed down at the end of the aisles, crying my name, "Jaxie!" like they had known who I was all their lives, many of them holding those souvenir tennis balls that are bigger than basketballs. Some hollered for Roddick, but he slung his bag over his shoulder and hustled out of there, head down, giving only a single wave to the fans who cheered him halfheartedly as he departed.

I felt like I was waking up out of some sort of dream to see all those kids there, kids who three hours ago didn't even know who the hell I was. It doesn't take but one night in America to become adored by kids and adults alike. We had finished the match at midnight, and fortunately, because it was so late, ESPN wanted to forgo the on-court interviews, a decision that was fine with me.

A USTA staffer handed me a Sharpie and I went to the front row and started signing my name like crazy. I signed autographs for every little bastard there, until they all had my big cursive *Jaxie* as a keepsake.

Jessica, Harry, Suzette, and I rode back to the hotel in a limousine. I kissed Jessica good night and instructed the driver to take her to her East Village apartment. "I'm so proud of you," she said. The long black car slid into the street and she leaned out the side window and waved, mouthing the words *I love you*, the first time she'd ever said that to me. I had thought about asking her to stay, but I needed rest and solitude to prepare for my next opponent.

I watched the limo disappear with her into the bright lights of Times Square south of the hotel. When I turned to go inside, I noticed a few people in the street pointing at me, and when I walked into the lobby a small crowd had gathered. Somebody yelled my name and the whole group, about twenty, applauded. A few women came out of the hotel bar to ask for photos and autographs and I obliged, including one very hot blonde with big blue eyes who was a little drunk and a lot willing. I wrote my name big on the scrap of paper she provided, trying not to stare at her breasts spilling out of a tight, low-cut black blouse. She then hugged me and handed me a note that I stuck in my pocket. She lingered there to talk, putting her hand on my arm, but I excused myself and slipped away.

I glanced at her as she walked with a friend back to the bar—she was extremely sexy in body-hugging white shorts and high heels. On the huge TVs in there I could see replays of my match with Roddick. A close-up of my face, intense with concentration, flashed across the screen.

A bellhop told me I had a stack of messages waiting at the front desk. All were from people I didn't know, most of them reporters. I turned on my cell phone and there were multiple voice mails, including one from Fast Eddie. I also got a voice message from Wendy Crenshaw who said she had seen the match on television and wanted to wish me well. I hadn't spoken to her in almost two decades. I don't know how she got my number.

This instant fame, however, was not settling well. I didn't like the obvious phoniness of people who hadn't given two shits about me who all of a sudden wanted to be my friend. I realized that there is a high price to pay for being famous, and I had wanted to win at this level all along but I didn't know if I wanted what went with it. Fast Eddie and Harry and my dad were the only men who had ever given a damn about me. I thought about Fast Eddie. He had always been my friend, regardless of where my life was. If you loved and played tennis, you were Fast Eddie's friend. He had even done free maintenance on my van for almost ten years! I thought about how I should have called him more often. I would have called him right then, but I knew that he always went to bed early.

Harry rode up in the elevator with me and hugged me good night before he got off, his gray mustache curled up in his trademark grin. He held the elevator door and told me this was the greatest treat he could ever have imagined, that this was to him like a dream, to coach a player in the U.S. Open, one whom he had brought up from the very first lesson.

In the room I put my rackets down. I reached into my pocket for the note the blonde had given me and opened it. *Hi, I'm Cindy, great match! I'd love to meet you, spend some time with you! I think you are awesome! I'm in room 1845, and my cell is 972-458-9555. My friend likes you two. We are adventurous! Open to anything!*

I held the slip of paper in my hand and thought seriously about calling her, knocking on her door, and how that would go. She was hot, and I was keyed up and wide awake, and this woman was a short elevator ride away. I tried to remember what her friend looked like. I had never been with two girls at once. I wondered if this is what it meant to be a star, and if I should take what I had earned and enjoy myself. But then I thought about Jessica, how sweet she was. I thought about the man I had been in my life, and the man I wanted to become. I crumpled up the note and threw it in the trash. I took a long hot shower, and then stretched some in hopes that I could go to sleep.

I got into bed and thought about flipping on the television but then decided that would keep me awake. Instead I called Jessica. We talked for a little while and I told her I was happy that she had been in my box for me on this night, that I missed her and wished that she was in the bed with me right then, and that it wouldn't be long before we could spend lots of nights together. I told her I loved her, the first time I'd said so—in fact, it was the first time I'd told *any* woman I loved her. She told me she felt the same, that she loved me too. After I hung up, I was very relaxed and quickly fell asleep.

I dreamed about being out on the road in a motel somewhere. It was one of those weird dream sequences, a conglomeration of the random memories and images that embed themselves in your brain and come out bouncing around in your skull in the middle of the night when you least expect it. I dreamed of a dingy motel room, a place where the sheets were so thin and papery it was like sleeping under a large newspaper. The carpet was a deep blood red and the comforter on the bed was like the old quilt that my parents had used when I was a child. Outside of the room, I could hear my dogs barking, Brutus and Buck, their throaty deep voices carrying on, gruff and loud. When I opened the door to the hallway, they were gone.

I walked down the hallway and it was not the hallway to a motel as I expected but the tunnel deep in the Arthur Ashe Stadium, the tunnel I had walked down for the first time earlier that night to play my match against Roddick. It's a lonesome walk, and the nerves of getting ready to play make it seem even longer. In the dream, I looked around frantically for my father, and walked down the hallway fast and alone, and started calling out, "Dad, Dad," but I didn't see him. The hallway seemed endless, and I was convinced in the dream that he was there somewhere, in one of the rooms, and I began opening the numerous doorways along that claustrophobic hall, and each door was a surprise. The rooms were scenes from my life, including the first one that was like our den when I was little where we watched that Borg–McEnroe final at Wimbledon. There were many more rooms, more than I could remember, and many of them occupied by the women I had slept with in my life, some of them on the bed summoning me, and others sitting in chairs crying or watching TV and reading magazines. I shut each door quickly, as though I had accidentally walked into the wrong room.

I kept going, looking for my father. I came to a room at the end of the hallway that was enormous, not really a room at all but a space opening into the yard where our red clay court was, the backyard where I had hit five million tennis balls. I stepped through that door and into the yard and called for my father, shouting at the top of my lungs "Dad! Dad! Where are you?"

I woke up, startled, and gasped to catch my breath, sitting upright. I was cool and clammy, sweating despite the chilly air in the room. I stood and looked down onto Seventh and 53rd, yellow cabs still racing for position, some folks walking around in the street in the middle of the night.

I stared out the window for a long time, looking at the taxis and the people in the street forty stories below, the New York buildings high and lit up in the late-summer darkness, and even a glimpse of New Jersey in the distance. I replayed the dream and those scattershot images of my life that had been thrown back up at me, trying to remember every detail.

I lay there awhile and noticed that my shoulder felt a little sore. I also could feel fatigue in my right knee, the one injured all those years ago, and my ankle hurt a little bit from the pounding on the hard court. I was too old to be doing what I was doing.

I went into the bathroom and stood in front of the mirror. I'm a good-looking dude for thirty-eight years old, and if you met me on the street or saw me on a tennis court in some public park and didn't know who I was you might guess I was only twenty-eight.

To tell how old I really am you would have to get closer to see my face, to look into my eyes, to see the miles I have traveled, the wrinkles starting to come up in my brow, the dark circles around my eyes, flanked by crow's-feet, the sun-dried cheeks and neck that have spent too many days out on a tennis court in the sun, so many days that the strongest SPF in the world can't save me from the damage doled out by that big ball of fire our earth circles, the flaming tennis ball that provides all the power in our solar system. The exercise and the eating right have kept my body young, my muscles and bones and ligaments strong, but the wear of time can't be prevented on my face. You could look at me up close, from maybe eight to ten feet away, and see that I had traveled some hard miles and made some dumb decisions along the road that unfurled behind me.

I lay down on the bed, pulling the sheet up over me, and my mind wandered. I thought about how good that blonde looked, the rare possibility of a ménage à trois and that her number was still in the trash can, but then I tried to right my mind. All of a sudden I was on fire with thoughts about tennis. I started talking out loud. "Come on, now, Jaxie. Think straight, boy. You got a job to do." And it was funny how I talked to myself then, sort of in my father's voice, the way he would give me little pep talks before matches, just a few sentences, a plainspoken seriousness that helped me to get ready.

And it worked. I thought about my best shots against Roddick, the serves I hit and how mixing up every shot, from the topspin to underspin to serving and volleying to staying back and waiting for a short ball, produced success. I allowed myself to enjoy the match, laughing about the crazy little bastard kid that had run across the court, complimenting myself on the way I had held it together under the enormous distractions. Some poor teaching pro was going to have that wild little son of a bitch in a children's clinic before too long. I smiled for a moment, and then I thought about playing again. I had seen the Spaniard I would play next on TV, in a match at the French Open, grinding it out with heavy groundstrokes and an awesome spin serve.

I started my pre-sleep routine of putting myself in a rally with him, both of us on the Ashe court. We were warming up, the *thock* of the ball on the court and the *ping* of it on the strings, the machine-like rhythm of a warm-up rally between two good players. If there's one thing I love the most in tennis, it's the sound of the ball on the court and the strings.

I kept this up for what seemed like a long time but I didn't fall asleep. After the long visions of warming up, I imagined a few points, the Spaniard's big serve coming in hard and kicking up high, and me taking it on the rise and slicing it back hard to his backhand. I knew playing him it was going to be critical to exploit his backhand on the crucial points or in the moments in a rally when I had gotten into trouble.

I thought of something that Fast Eddie told me once, about playing the backhand but not overplaying it. Play it, he said, when you need the point the most, when your back is up against the wall and your opponent is bearing down and has pressure on him. I could picture Fast Eddie sitting in that folding chair that he had webbed himself with the wide plastic ribbons, a style of chair that was popular in the 1970s but that you don't see as much anymore. He kept two of those chairs in his van, and I was there talking with him, sitting in the parking lot at the Thessalonica Tennis Center, just the two of us, at the beginning of my comeback, on a warm winter afternoon, one of those January days you can get in Georgia when the thermometer rises into the sixties. He leaned forward, his narrowly set blue eyes stern and serious. "Sometimes, in a match," he said, "I've seen it a thousand times, a player will go out with the strategy of banging a player's backhand and start right out of the gate, ball after ball, to the backhand. But what very often will happen is that the player with the weak backhand gets a hundred or so balls to practice on in the first few games, and by that repetition . . . of hitting backhand after backhand . . . they get better. So start with the strength, and break it down if you can."

He went on in my mind like this, providing long details of matches he had played and matches he had seen, in person and on television, to back up this point. I was there with every word, this vision of Fast Eddie. I could hear his intense voice, his storytelling style, his detailed description of matches and points and the most specific minutiae of a tennis shot you can imagine. I forgot that I was lying in a bed in a New York hotel, but was transported to the gravel of that parking lot that looked onto the red-and-green courts of the Thessalonica Tennis Center. "I've got to call Fast Eddie," I said. I sat up and looked at the mirror on the dresser. "I've got to bring him up here to see my matches, to hang out."

It was seven o'clock. I called Delta Air Lines and checked to see what time flights came to LaGuardia, and bought a one-way ticket in his name with my credit card for six hundred dollars. I didn't check with him first. I knew he was probably already done with his breakfast and was about to drive over to the courts and start hanging around, beginning his day like he did most days. I knew this would make him happy beyond his wildest dreams, and damned if I don't believe he didn't know as much about tennis as anybody I knew. All of these top-flight teaching pros that get all the publicity and coach the best players, they don't have any secrets that the rest of us don't have. Arguably the best coach of all time, Bollettieri, has made his fortune on the simple mantra of practice, practice, practice. He was an army paratrooper, not even close to being good enough to play professionally. He seems like a damn cool dude, although many of his best pupils, particularly Agassi and Seles, turned on him as they grew up, probably because he was taking too much of the credit. But who wouldn't take credit for those players if they started them young and coached them to eighteen? He coached ten world number ones. He deserves more credit than anyone gives him.

Yet the only difference between Fast Eddie and Nick Bollettieri is that Bollettieri had the unyielding ambition and dedication and outgoing personality to take the tennis world by storm, devoting himself to it fully and without compromise, bringing junior players to live in his house, to eat, breathe, sleep, shit, shower, and play tennis, twenty-four/seven, 365 days a year. Fast Eddie also approached tennis not as a game, certainly not a business, but as a religion and a way of life. He, however, never had the organizational skills or the outgoing personality, and he got started too late and suffered a few bad breaks along the way. But inside that van of his sitting in the parking lot of the Thessalonica Tennis Center was a world of tennis knowledge, a lifetime of the game's finer points stored in his skinny, pointed noggin.

I called Fast Eddie. He was thrilled to hear from me, and raved about how well I had played. "I always knew you were great, Jaxie, but I never expected this. Man, I've taped the match and plan to watch it again today. Everyone here in Thessalonica is talking about you . . . about all the matches they saw you play."

"Hey, well, Ed, I've got something for you. I bought you a plane ticket, leaving from Atlanta about one, getting here later this afternoon. Take a taxi to Flushing Meadows and go to the players' gate. I'll leave you a pass. You can find me on the practice courts."

There was a long pause on the line.

"Ed, you there?" I asked.

"I can't afford it, Jaxie. New York's too expensive."

"Dude, I got you covered. I'm paying your way. I'll get you a room. You can be one of my coaches. You helped me when I was down and out. I can never repay you for all you've done, taking care of my van and practicing with me like you did. I want you here. Bring your rackets."

I heard him breathing, but he didn't say anything.

"C'mon, now Eddie. I know you don't like to fly, but it's a short flight." I gave him the confirmation number and told him to use it and his driver's license to check in at the airport. He had told me once that he hadn't been on an airplane since he was in college.

"Jaxie, I don't know what to say."

"Well, there's a first time for everything. Just get on up here. I'll see you this afternoon."

With Fast Eddie in my box, I won my next two rounds. I had a very fortunate draw that pitted me against unseeded journeymen. I rose to the occasion, playing the best tennis of my life, especially in the close games and the tiebreakers, dominating the points that really mattered.

My fourth-round opponent, Stanislas Snedeker, was an Eastern European rich kid. His father was a Slovakian billionaire, the wealthiest man ever in the history of Bratislava, and he had his hands in so many businesses there after the Iron Curtain fell on what had been Czechoslovakia that the list didn't fit on one page. I read about him in a *Fortune* magazine that Fast Eddie brought me the day before I played him, listing his father's major business interests as insurance, banking, timber, electric utilities, manufacturing, and a company that was hugely profitable for inventing a machine that produced a higher quality of compressed air. I'm not shitting you. Compressed air. It's always the things you would never imagine that make the most money.

I had been avoiding reading all newspaper articles except for the things that Harry and Fast Eddie thought would fire me up. They told me about but didn't show me a profile *The New York Times* wrote after I won my second-round match that focused on how Fast Eddie and I had traveled in a van to Mississippi, and how I had lived in my van for years when playing the Futures and Challenger tours. They said the article made it sound like I had lived my whole life in a van, and that I was still residing in it. I thought it was funny as hell. While

I had refused to talk to the reporters, Fast Eddie and Harry blabbered all about me. If you ever make it to the U.S. Open, that's the way to do it. Get some talking heads out in front of you and don't talk to anyone yourself. They fed so many stories about me, most of them true, that the press could barely fit even two percent of what they heard into print. Here's an example of what I overhead when Harry talked to a reporter from a London newspaper:

Reporter: How much did Jaxie's relationship with Olga Polykova, when she was only sixteen, affect his play? His career?

Harry: I don't know, but you should have seen him when he was six years old, that boy could hit a forehand like a gun shoots a bullet. I knew he was going to be great even then.

Reporter: Yes, but if he's so great, why has his career been so spotty?

Harry: You call being in the fourth round of the U.S. Open spotty? Well then, Nigel, I'll settle for spotty any day. I never made it to Forest Hills, and I feel like I had a fine career in tennis. What level are you? How's your backhand? Never mind. I was great, but not as great as Jaxie. Okay, so he's not Roger Federer, but then who is? I tell you who is always the best in my book, and that's Rod Laver . . .

And on he went. Harry and Fast Eddie talked their heads off, something they love to do. I didn't read a word of it except for the very few things Harry and Fast Eddie filtered out. One piece was a magazine story about Snedeker that really got me going. It talked about how he had taken his father's private plane to juniors and Futures tournaments, how he had two full-time coaches, including now-retired Thomas Muster, as well as a trainer, a sports psychiatrist, and a physiotherapist—whatever the hell that is.

Snedeker also did a lot of advertisements, everything from watches to grip tape to racket vibration dampeners, those little rubber devices that are shaped like either donuts, smiley faces, or decorated triangles that you stick in the base of the strings to absorb some of the shock of hitting the ball. Fast Eddie bought one with Snedeker's picture on the packaging and his name printed in a cute little circle around the black plastic loop, about the diameter of a quarter but much thicker. The evening before my match he tossed it on my bed, where I was lying there watching *SportsCenter*. I picked it up and studied on it. "I can't believe this damn thing," I said. "Rich little shit—like he needs the money. He's going to need a vibration dampener for his ass after I get through kicking it."

And kick it I did. I stayed aggressive, mixing up the serving and volleying and keeping him guessing, even beating him in the baseline rallies with my forehand. On one key point I hit the hardest forehand I've ever hit. It was a zone moment except I didn't have the spaced-out feeling, but I was there in every second of the action, conscious and clear and strong. Every ball I had hit over the past thirty-five years led up to this, and there was no stopping me. I drubbed that rich son of a bitch 6–1, 6–2, 6–2. The games he won were meaningless holds of serve after I had taken early breaks. I was into the U.S. Open quarterfinals, one of eight men left standing.

In the quarterfinals I played Will Gardner, the only other American left in the draw. Gardner, who stood the same height as Michael Jordan, was like a long line of tall Americans over the past decade, lanky hard-serving players who could hit the ball 140 miles per hour but had limited mobility on the court, and with the exception of a great forehand usually had shaky groundstrokes. He had been a tennis standout at Stanford, winning the NCAA tournament twice, before going out on tour earlier this summer. He had done well, reaching the third round at Wimbledon, the semis in the hard court tournament in Cincinnati a few weeks back, and had become the darling of the American media with his dark-haired good looks and his smiley disposition. I liked what I had seen of him. Despite the fact he too was a rich kid—his father a technology executive from North Carolina who had made a fortune during the Internet boom of the 1990s when he wisely sold his web business that distributed pharmaceuticals for pets—he didn't act like he owned every place he went.

But I could afford no respect for his game when we were on the court. I had played enough matches in my life by then to pick out what would beat him. I was playing a very cerebral game, thinking about how to break the players down, just as willing to take an error from my opponent as I was to hit a winner. As tall as he was, very low balls would give him a lot of trouble. No matter how much you bend your knees, if you are six feet seven inches, it is hard to cover underspin shots that don't rise.

I went through my monastic pre-match routine, ignoring my cell phone. The voice mail filled up with messages from the press, as well as PR flacks from the USTA and ATP who insisted I do news conferences. What were they going to do, default me from the tournament for not talking to the press? Fast Eddie pointed out to me that shunning the media was even winning me fans, some of whom wrote on blogs about how they were glad to have an American player who did what he wanted to do, someone not hypnotized by the Nike media training where their answers were carefully cooked like grilled salmon and a side of pasta—never completely bland, but rarely exciting.

The person who pissed me off the most was John McEnroe. His great tennis on that day thirty-five years ago at Wimbledon is one reason I chose to play tennis. But on the night before my quarterfinal match with Gardner, I was lying on my bed with the air-conditioning turned on full blast, Fast Eddie and Harry sitting around in chairs, and we were watching the coverage of the Open. McEnroe, in what seems like one of the endless talk shows they broadcast instead of showing actual tennis, went on a diatribe, condemning me and accusing me of insulting the USTA, the media, and all of America for refusing to do press conferences or interviews. He essentially called me a hacker who was a fluke in the French Open in 1995 and a player who also was a fluke here, a lucky player who really deserved my very low ranking. He said my win against Roddick happened only because of the poorly behaved child in a big service game. He recounted my dismal record in the Challengers and Futures and even dug up my lopsided match statistics against Janos Szucs, certainly the only time Szucs ever received a national broadcast mention.

When he had started talking about me, Harry got up to change the channel, but I told him I wanted to hear it. "Honestly, Jaxie Skinner is not good enough to be this far into our nation's biggest tournament," McEnroe said. "He is a disgrace."

McEnroe continued, predicting that Gardner would beat me easily. He said I couldn't handle the pressure of playing another late match in the Ashe Stadium. I think he knew that his running me down would get the crowd fired up, that of the crowd that would fill Ashe, many would be a little drunk, some a lot drunk, and that many of them believed everything that the great John McEnroe said.

He was trying to goad me into responding, to flush me out of hiding to do the interviews he and everyone else in tennis officialdom thought I should do. But I wasn't going to rise to take the bait. "I'm gonna prove myself with my racket," I told Harry and Fast Eddie. "Fuck this son of a bitch."

"Damn right, boy," Harry said, patting me on the back. "Damn right."

Walking out onto the Ashe Stadium when it is full on a big night match is like nothing else I've ever experienced. The sold-out crowd was lubed up and wild, a coherent mob, a big beast-like organism. Flashbulbs went off when we walked out and people cheered and jeered and screamed, making my adrenaline rush.

Gardner was cool, smiling and waving to the fans, while I kept my head down. He was even polite, and shook my hand before the match and wished me good luck and looked me in the eye, and it was sincere. I hope he goes far and is America's next great champion, but I doubt he will because you've got to be a mean son of a bitch to rise to the top.

I will always remember walking out onto that court and setting my racket bag down by the chair, the crowd abuzz and noisy, the chatter of twenty-three thousand voices all at once, excited about the tennis match they were about to see, many of them having traveled long distances and excited with the energy that is New York and the last great tennis tournament of the year before summer falls away and autumn rolls in with brown leaves and the impending threat of the winter. I picked out my racket, a freshly strung Wilson Blade, and pinged it on the strings of another freshly strung frame. A Wilson rep had given me ten brand-new rackets just for the match, said there were plenty more if I needed them.

I stood there, waiting on Gardner, a slow-going, easy-does-it type of dude when the ball wasn't in play, to get ready to make his move to the court so we could warm up when a huge 747 Delta jet rocketed above, the black nose of that big red, white, and blue bird nosing over the enormous scoreboard on the south end of the stadium, followed by the massive heft of that big steel tube with wings. It seemed like the plane was crawling across the sky at a pace of five miles an hour, the way it hovered there and you saw it before you heard it, and then the sound of the big engines on each wing growled in a deep roar, drowning out the edgy crowd.

I thought about those airplane route maps in the back of airline magazines where you can see the almost infinite number of flight paths that connect the cities of America to the rest of the world. I thought about my old dog-eared atlas, the road map I'd used thousands of times. I thought of my dirt road at home, and all the other roads I've traveled in my life. I relaxed, thinking that this match was either meant to be or not meant to be, and that I just needed to do my part and hit the ball, to mix up my shots, and everything would fall into place.

I won the toss and served first. I stepped to the baseline and the umpire said "quiet please" and I bounced the ball a few times as the crowd, many of whom were rushing back to their seats, settled down. I held up the ball to Gardner and he nodded, that smile of his, and we had that unspoken acknowledgment of good players who are wishing each other, if not luck, at least respect. I bounced the ball a few more times and it thumped on the court below, the DecoTurf surface that is really a thick base of concrete, a few feet deep, settled onto the foundation, and then covered over with a rubberized, paint-like, oil-based substance that gives it a grittier, softer feel, and then topped with the blue inner court and green back court and white paint on the lines. The ball bounced straight up, a *thump, thump, thump*.

I must have bounced the ball twenty times, concentrating, until the crowd grew deathly silent. I looked up at Gardner and he was hopping on his toes. I tossed the ball and hit a big serve out wide to his forehand and charged the net. He got over to it quickly and nailed a very hard forehand down the line at a beautiful angle. I had guessed he would go there and reached across my body for a backhand volley and stretched out as much as I could and lunged and caught the ball just before it would have hit the court by the service line and hit a volley winner back across court at a sharp angle that even the world's fastest player could not have reached. He gave the traditional tennis applause, pretending to clap with his racket on the strings, and the crowd gasped approval. I wanted to turn up to McEnroe's booth and yell, *Yeah, fuck you, John*, but I didn't.

Gardner and I both played as well as we could possibly play, one of those rare tennis matches when two of the most talented in the world play at their best. I felt the ball on my strings that night almost like I had supernatural powers, like every shot was a dialed-in precision swing, the ball striking as cleanly in the center of the racket as was humanly possible. I also know that Gardner must have felt the same way, that his shots were as hard and crisp as any balls that have ever come at me. His serve that night—he ended with forty-nine aces—was about as good a night serving as anyone has ever had in the history of tennis. If it wasn't for tiebreakers, it is possible we would still be playing. As it was, we played two tiebreakers in the first two sets and he won both by scores of 7–5.

I was down two sets to none, but I didn't give up. There were no breaks of serve until the third set at 5–all when I cracked several forehand winners, and then laid a beautiful backhand crosscourt when he guessed down the line. That shot, if I do say so myself, was a thing of beauty. I held serve, and we were on to the fourth set.

I was still down, however, two sets to one, but I felt great, even though it was already eleven o'clock. We had won over the crowd with the quality of the tennis. I looked over at Gardner and he was maybe a little tired, and down at not winning the third set. He had played a few tough matches already, including a five-set win over a Thai player in the fourth round.

I was ready to go, and nothing could break my concentration. I didn't look up into the stands, not even my box, even once. According to the news reports, Olga Polykova was in attendance, and the TV cameras often focused on her, but I never knew. I stared at the court, thought about that airplane and how my fate was sealed like a gift waiting for me to open it. I played the best tennis I could possibly play, but I still didn't know if it would be good enough.

There is nothing like a close match that runs late on a weeknight at the U.S. Open, when it is past eleven and the clocks record the match time—three hours and two minutes after the third set—and the crowd works up into a frenzy. When the points are well played and the ball being cleanly struck and errors are few and winners are high, the crowd settles into an almost church-like reverence and respectfully falls silent with every point. It also depends much on how the players behave, and both of us that night were strictly dialed in and kept our mouths shut for the most part, not speaking but letting our rackets do the talking. When a feisty player starts tossing his racket around, running his mouth, complaining to the umpire, and grunting unnecessarily loud, it's almost like a message to the crowd to raise a little hell, to get noisy during the points, to yell out to the players. But neither Gardner or I did anything to rile up the fans, instead treating them to an almost flawlessly played tennis match.

His serve that night was colossal, and he hit an average of almost ten aces per set. The time I broke him I think he missed two first serves, and I was able to hit some great and also a little bit lucky returns. But in the fourth set he stepped in and served the first game, banging four consecutive aces, one in each corner of the service boxes, nary a ball I touched. I had never seen a serve this fast and so smooth, his long motion so elegant it looked like he was hitting the ball easily, but often registering well above the 140-mile-per-hour mark.

After the opening game of the fourth set in which he hit the four straight aces, I served an unsteady game and found myself down 30–40. He danced around on his toes with a break point, practically match points the way he was serving. One break of serve would be all it would take for him to then hold serve the rest of the match and put me away. I bounced the ball before my serve and dug deep and hit a hard first serve into his backhand and charged the net. He hit a weak return and I nailed a volley winner back down the line, right on the line in fact. The line judge, there, however raised her hand, calling it out. I have never been a fan of the video replay challenge system because only the show courts get to use it and players farther down the rankings like me go without. This was only the third match in my career I had ever played where I could use it. But losing my serve probably would have been the end of the night for me, so I raised up my racket. I was certain the ball was good.

"Mr. Skinner is challenging the call," the umpire said. "The ball was called out." Everyone in attendance looked up at one of the two big Jumbotron screens at either end of the Ashe Stadium and watched that blue and white and yellow silhouette of the court as the ball came into the picture and flew until it hit squarely on the line. The word IN appeared in big letters.

"Deuce," the umpire called, and the crowd cheered and even Gardner nodded his head, and I nodded back at him.

I stepped up and served a ball with some slice, spinning it into his body on the backhand side, and he tried to step around and take a forehand, but he put it in the net. I had stayed back on this serve, but saw him look up quickly as he hit his shot, trying to see if I was attacking. My plan to keep him off balance was working. I went on to hold serve and then we both went on a run of holding serve, not giving up more than two points in any game.

Soon it was six games all, and we started a tiebreaker. He served almost immaculately, hitting some aces and winners, while I put my serves into play and grinded out some rallies, moving him around the court. He was slowing down, so on my serve when he was up 4–3 in the tiebreaker he went for winners on his returns and was successful both times: Once on a backhand he stepped in and chipped a ball down the line hard and low that I could reach but couldn't get into play; in the deuce court he stepped back and around his backhand and nailed a hard crosscourt forehand past me, a brilliant zooming shot that had just enough topspin to pull it down on the sideline. That put him up 6–3 in the tiebreaker, giving him three match points, two of them on his serving racket.

If he hit a winner or I missed one more time I was done. He tried to hit an ace and missed his first serve, and then tried to crush a second serve, popping it into the net for a double fault. The crowd all gasped, twenty-three thousand of them at the same time, *aww* . . .

Four–six. In the deuce court he took a little off the first serve and spun it out wide on my forehand, and his ball had a lot of kick and it rose up high and I had the millisecond decision to either back up or move forward. I backed up, knowing that he wasn't going to charge the net, and took a swing at a hard topspin forehand crosscourt, hoping to wrong-foot him. He got back to the forehand and hit another ball crosscourt to me, this one a shorter ball, bouncing about the service line. I moved in and sliced a forehand low with hard backspin down the line to his backhand and charged the net. He was so tall and gangly that bending his knees and getting down to hit a two-handed backhand on those fast courts was hard for him, and he was tiring, and also very nervous. He pushed an easy ball back up the line to my forehand and I moved in and smacked a volley hard and crosscourt for a winner.

Five–six. He still had a match point, although I was serving, and I felt as confident then as I had the whole match. I took a quick look back at all my past matches, then at every serve I had hit to Gardner, and it occurred to me that I had hit very few big serves with slicing spin down the T, instead going more and more to his backhand every serve into the ad court. If I wanted to make a strong statement, an ace down the middle, right up the T, with spin going away from his forehand would be the way to do it. I could almost see him edging toward his backhand, ready to jump on that ball, or if he was lucky he could run around the backhand and crush an inside-out forehand. I made sure to toss the ball the same way I had been, and not give away my shot before I hit it, but after I took the racket back I swiveled hard and brought it up on more of a roundabout trajectory that hit it farther to the side of my body and directed it bomb-style down the T and fooled him completely for my twelfth ace of the match, my first one of the fourth set. The crowd cheered wildly, although I know it was more for their desire to see a fifth set than it was to see me win.

In fact, I think probably eighty percent of that crowd wanted Gardner to win, the handsome young American with so much promise, although there were many men above thirty who pulled for me, who felt some camaraderie for a fellow old dude.

Six–all. I had held off three match points, but was still only two points from losing. I was serving again, and this time I figured wrongly that I could ace him twice. I hit a big hard serve out to his forehand but this time he was ready for it and he stepped into the court and with those long arms of his lined up a forehand that was as much out of anger and frustration and adrenaline and fear, banging it so hard down the line past my backhand that by the time I had moved it thudded into the backstop, sending the line judge there diving for safety as she put her hands down in the "good" position.

Six–seven. Another match point against me. And he was serving. I wish I could say I thought back to that Borg–McEnroe Wimbledon match and drew some inspiration from it, but I didn't. Besides, McEnroe had held off seven match points in the fourth set but still lost in the fifth. All I thought about was watching the ball, moving my feet, and getting the racket ready. I didn't think it in words, but in that unconscious mindset that is the tennis zone, a place where words have no place.

I had a choice to make. There are two ways to return a great big serve: Stand way back, and hope that it is not angled too greatly for you to reach, but run it down and send it high and deep back into play, a safe bet as long as your opponent is not serving and volleying, which he was not; or stand up tight and take a very short backswing and use the power of the ball as it rockets off the court to send it back hard and fast, hopefully catching the server still recovering from their violent stroke. Perhaps you saw Federer do this to Roddick, including once in the tiebreaker of their U.S. Open quarterfinal match in 2007 in which Roddick hit a 140-mile-an-hour serve and Federer nailed a one-handed backhand return at Roddick's feet that nearly knocked him out of his shoes.

I had been going with option one most of the match. I was at heart a clay courter and standing back was my style, but it worked only the one time I broke his serve in the third set, and that was when I was going for broke and got a little lucky. This time I stepped in tight, a foot inside the baseline, and it was like teasing a lion, coming this close. I saw him grimace, a face that said *I'm going to hit the ball so hard it's going to knock you down.* I was glad to see it, because I knew that increased his chances of missing. He hit a first serve that was at least a foot out. On the second serve I crept in even tighter, and I knew it would bring one of two things—an easy serve I could jump on, or an attempt at another big bomb. He was nervous, and had already double-faulted once, so he spun the ball lazily into my backhand and I went with a hard slice and chipped it crosscourt with backspin and charged the net. I didn't get the ball as deep or as wide as I had hoped, because that angled return is a dangerous shot and I didn't want to float it wide. He seemed ready for my return, moving forward with his racket back and ready to drive a passing shot by me. I knew before he hit it that I had to guess one way or the other—down the line or crosscourt—if I was going to have any chance to cover the ball. As soon as he started to hit it I moved toward the line and he came that way and I was right there and I knocked off the volley crosscourt at a hard pace with lots of angle for which he had no hope of reaching. If I had not guessed right, either waiting to see which way he hit it before moving or guessing crosscourt, the match would have been over and we would be shaking hands and I would have been on my way back to Georgia.

Seven–all. I studied on him after that point, and he was really starting to drag. He went back and got his towel from a ball girl and wiped his face. He leaned over and panted and tried to catch his breath. I was calm and felt as strong as I had the whole match. He hit a big serve to my forehand but I just sliced it down the line to his backhand and stayed back. He hit crosscourt and I drew him into a long baseline rally, not trying to hit winners but to just make him hit ball after ball. Perhaps he was nervous and didn't know what to do and he settled into a pattern of shot after shot crosscourt. I decided to grind this one out. I didn't count the shots at the time—once a ball's hit, it doesn't pay to count it—but the newspaper article Fast Eddie read to me the next day said it was a forty-eight-ball rally that lasted about seventy seconds. I ended that rally with a deft drop shot to his backhand that he chased down and lunged for, ending up sprawling onto the ground as he hit the ball into the bottom of the net. The point drew my life's one and only all-out standing ovation, a feeling I'll always remember. I felt like the king of New York for a few moments. I thought that maybe this kind of adoration is what turns some great players into such assholes.

Eight–seven. After he got up and toweled off and recovered from his fall, I lined up and hit an ace down the T that he could barely offer at, and took the fourth set by the score of 9–7 in the tiebreaker. The crowd roared and hooted and hollered. It was ten minutes after midnight, and we had a fifth set to play.

But he was spent. I broke his serve in the first game of the fifth and didn't look back. He never recovered, and I played it out to an anticlimactic 6–2 ending, delivering myself to the U.S. Open semifinals at the age of thirty-eight.

I raised my arms over my head, and looked up into the New York night sky and thought about my dad. He would have been mighty proud.

The quiet of the locker room on Super Saturday is remarkable when only four men use the enormous space. I kicked back on a plush blue couch to await my semifinal match. We were first on court before the much-anticipated showdown between Federer and Djokovic.

I was scheduled to play a relatively unknown young Argentine who of all things upset Rafael Nadal in the quarterfinals, a remarkable match that went five sets with this kid hitting winner after winner from the back court, a twenty-one-year-old who out-groundstroked the king of the groundstrokers. I watched it with Harry and Fast Eddie and it was astounding, scary, in fact, to think that I have to play this dude. But you're never going to run across any pussies in the semifinals of the U.S. Open.

It was amazing to think that six months before I couldn't beat Janos Szucs, and here I was one match away from playing either Federer or Djokovic, two of the greatest of all time, in *the final.* It was hard to get my mind around that.

Harry and Fast Eddie, however, were right. I shouldn't have thought for one second about the final, but instead needed to focus on the Argentine. One match at a time, remember? But it was hard not to think about the possibility of playing Federer or Djokovic in front of all those people, etching my name in tennis history. Most of the great players—everyone from Tilden to Budge to Kramer to Gonzalez to Laver to Connors to Borg to McEnroe to Lendl to Wilander to Sampras to Agassi to Federer and Nadal—have played against surprise opponents in the finals of majors, players who are remembered only in the context of the legends' biographies: Manuel Orantes against Borg in the French Open final; Cédric Pioline against Sampras in both the U.S. Open and Wimbledon finals; Rainer Schüttler in the Australian Open final against Agassi. All were pounded, and their names became lines in the record books as minor characters in the stories of the greatest players to play the game. I had the chance for that to be me, Jaxie Skinner, in the "def" line by either Federer's or Djokovic's name. I could be happy with that. A year before I had dwelled on quitting and had considered taking a job teaching lessons or doing something else, maybe even going to truck-driving school or starting a catfish farm.

And I knew that soon I would have to do something else. Maybe with the semifinal money I earned I can go back to college, and actually learn something, focus on something other than my game, my restricted life inside the subdivided rectangle that is a tennis court.

All these thoughts bounced around in my head while sitting on that couch in the locker room. What I should have been doing is relaxing and thinking about how I could take the Argentine out of his rhythm, how I could keep his groundstrokes off kilter and win some points in transition, with spins, at net. I knew I needed to mix up my shots. But I couldn't focus. I couldn't keep my mind still because of the dream I had very early that morning.

It started the same way as it did the night after I beat Roddick. I dreamed I woke in a dingy motel room and I got up and went down a long hallway, like the one in the Ashe Stadium, opening each door, except this time instead of all the women I've been with, the rooms were moments out of my childhood: I saw meals my mother had made on the table; classrooms from the schools I had attended; one room set up like the Sunday school class in First Baptist Church of

Piney, with the white pine ladder-back chairs in a circle, young kids with heads down praying; tennis clubhouses everywhere where I had waited for my matches to start; and then my sisters' rooms, and my parents' bedroom, with them in it, in the early morning, starting to wake up. It shook the hell out of me to see that.

The final room is the one that got to me, that still gets to me. It was our den that morning of the 1980 Wimbledon, my dad and sisters sitting around the TV set, the ball like a white blur on that worn out grass court. I lingered in front of that door in the dream for a long time, just looking at them sitting there, as though I was studying mannequins in a department store window. I wanted to go into the room and talk to them, to join them, but it was one of those dreams where I wanted to move but couldn't. I tried to move my mouth to speak but the words would not flow. I wanted to reach out and embrace my family, my people, gone from me for so long, but I was frozen. The dream would not let me. I watched my mother come in with the pimento-cheese sandwiches, and I watched as they ate while focused on the match.

I turned and looked at the bright sunshine that was pouring in through an open door at the very end of the long hallway. I walked down and looked through the door frame that opened into our yard as it was when I was five years old, the red clay of the tennis court damp in the morning dew. I realized I had a racket in my hand. I went toward the court and my dad was there with the milk crates full of tennis balls and his T2000.

He was young, dark-haired, and handsome, like he looked when he had built that court. He gestured for me to take the baseline and started feeding balls to me. I charged into my routine, one hundred forehands down the line, one hundred crosscourt, and then one hundred backhands down the line, one hundred crosscourt. My dad was smiling the whole time, encouraging me, always complimenting a very good shot, nodding on the mediocre ones, and not letting me get too down on the occasional one into the net, saying "That's all right, get the next one up."

I wanted to say something back, but I couldn't talk, so I just kept hitting shots. I can't tell you how long that part of the dream lasted. I had loved those sessions. Even when we went three hours, it barely seemed like any time at all had passed. Eventually, he ran out of balls and said, "That's good, son, now come up here." I went up to the net to speak with him. He looked at me and put his hand on my shoulder. I thought he was going to say something about my success at the U.S. Open, about how he was proud of me for persevering and showing the world what a great player I am. In my dream that's what I expected. But that's not what he said at all. He said, "Boy, you need to call your mama. And your sisters."

I tried to say something in the dream, about how Mom had wanted to divorce him, but the words would not come. I could not speak. He could read my face, though. "I know, things ended hard," he said. "I know, but they are family. And time has passed . . . a long time. Y'all are blood. You should remember all the good times you had, all the fun things y'all did. You are a man, and a man's got to forgive, otherwise, you'll go crazy. Call your mama, boy. Call your mama. I don't hate her . . . I love her. We had a good long time together, just grew apart at the end. You might think the end can ruin the whole story, but the end is only the end. It don't change the beginning and the middle. Those were good times."

He put his hand on top of my head and tousled my hair. His eyes gleamed with promise and youth and energy, the vigor he once had. "Call your mama, boy, set things right."

~

I woke up sweating in a cold room, dark in the middle of a New York night. It had been the most vivid dream I've ever had, and I've always been a vivid dreamer. I can still see in my mind that dream, the color of the clay, the heavy green of the pines behind the court, the grass of the lawn, the brown and black dogs running around in the yard, my father's dark hair, the yellow tennis balls, and the blue sky.

I lay there thinking about the dream, about everything I'd seen, and then I thought about what my dad said to me, that I should reconnect and make good with my mother and sisters. It was something I never thought I would do, and to me, it was like they had been dead, more dead to me than my father, my father who really was in the ground, having been buried for twenty years in that little churchyard where he had grown up.

I must have lain there for an hour before I got up and drank some water and looked out on the street and thought about my life. I wasn't the least bit sleepy. It was five o'clock but I got an urge to call Jessica, to tell her about everything. I dialed her number. She was groggy at first but sounded happy to hear from me. I told her about the dream and she listened as I recounted every detail. It felt good to talk about it, to let it all out.

I realized as we talked that my parents' bed where Jessica and I had made love for the first time was the bed in which I had been conceived. I thought about all these things as my story poured out and my love for Jessica became palpable. I almost proposed to her then, but I didn't want to do it over the phone, and I reminded myself that I shouldn't get too much on my mind before my match.

Jessica listened to me, for at least an hour. Relief washed over me as I told her family stories I'd never told anyone before, details about my dad's death and the estrangement from my mother and sisters. I told her what my father had said in my dream about reconciling. "I don't know," I said. "What do you think?"

"Jaxie, I think he's right," she said. "Once you get through this weekend, you should try to make up with them. I would like to meet them, too, if you want. I'll be there for you, any way I can help. I love you, Jaxie. I want you to be happy."

I knew then that I would propose to her, soon, when the time was right. And I will do it. She is a smart girl and I sense that my mother and sisters will like her. I want to make sure I'm not rushing it, be sure that she wants to marry me, and figure out where we will live. She has a year of college left and then grad school, so probably I will end up teaching lessons wherever she goes, or maybe, who knows, I'll be motivated to stay out on tour and make a little money while I have the chance. But at my age, it won't be long.

I sat in the Ashe locker room, all this on my mind, until something clicked and I settled down. I realized that winning a tennis match is nothing more or nothing less than winning a tennis match. I play tennis because I can, because I'm good at it, but after it's over, no one really cares a week or a month and certainly not a few years later if I won or lost. My name will be just two words consisting of twelve letters on lists in a few record books and on the Internet.

Even as recently as few months before, I would have been a nervous disaster, playing in the semis, worried about how I would do, thinking about the money. But I had learned a lot more about myself, about life, about my future, and I began to take it in stride. Thinking over my whole life was good for me. It helped me to gain perspective on my role in the world, something I've never had before.

I have a long way to go. Maybe not in tennis—certainly not on the tour—but in life. I realized that winning or losing that match would not bring me peace of mind. Peace of mind is something I have to find on my own, away from the rectangles of tennis courts.

Did it matter to me if I won? Of course. You know how it turned out. Regardless, I viewed myself as a winner. Winning is perception, not reality, because in reality, we all are eventually going to lose to an upcoming opponent, to illness, to death. In reality we are all losers, sooner or later. You have to know that, and accept it, and hope that there is something better coming next. On the other side of my tennis career, I believe there is something better for me.

After a while my thoughts in the locker room were interrupted when they called my name. I walked down the long hallway and did my interview and went out onto the Ashe court to the Super Saturday mob. The crowd cheered as we took the court, roaring when my name was announced. I waved a gesture of thanks. I looked over in my box and saw Harry and Suzette there, Randy and Tina, and, of course, Fast Eddie. Jessica, my wife-to-be, I hope, and her parents, were all there. I realized that I am one blessed dude. If I can work things out like I did, can recover from the bad luck and even more bad decisions I made, there is hope for us all, I think. Yes, there is hope for us all, the tennis- and non-tennis-playing alike.

I pulled a new racket with fresh strings out of my bag. We posed for a pre-match picture, and the umpire flipped the coin and I won and elected to serve. We started warming up. After some groundstrokes, I moved into net and hit a few volleys and then I gestured for him to hit me a few lobs.

He lofted a high one up into the blue sky. I pointed at it with my left hand and took my racket back and looked directly into the roundness of the sun, that ball of fire ninety-three million miles away. The brightness burned into my eyes, searing, almost blinding light, but I had seen it before. My dad built a tennis court when I was little that ran the wrong way, and playing into the sun's light had made me tough. I stroked through my overhead, hitting it solid in the center of the strings, my follow-through as smooth as melted butter. I watched the yellow ball thump into the backstop and then I looked up, awaiting another lob to float up toward the sun.

Acknowledgements

I spent a languid summer afternoon nine years ago at the Sewanee Writers' Conference in Tennessee in the company of the great writer Barry Hannah. He had read early drafts of *Fall Line,* my second novel that was in progress, and he talked about the crowded, talented field of southern fiction writers. We also discussed tennis, a lifetime passion we shared. He no longer played, but said if he did not have neuropathy in his legs he would "kick my ass."

I told him about my idea to write a novel about a tennis player from rural Georgia, something that had been on my mind for five years by then. He encouraged me, saying that while there was much literary traffic on the South's red dirt roads, there were very few good novels about tennis. (He did not mention it, but he had written one of the few, *The Tennis Handsome,* from 1983.)

Write your tennis novel, he said.

So I did.

It took a year to finish an insanely long draft, a year to revise it, and then another year to find super agent Scott Miller, executive vice president at Trident Media Group, who read it and gave invaluable advice on shaping the manuscript. He was the only one in this mercenary business—where everyone believes that a tennis book not written by the likes of Andre Agassi will sell only a scintilla of what golf and baseball books do—willing to take it on.

After working it very hard, however, even an agent as talented as Scott could not find a home for it until four years later when we stumbled upon Garth Battista's press, Breakaway Books. I'm greatly indebted to Garth for falling in love with the novel and giving it an excellent home. I might not have found him had it not been for my friend Jonathan Green, a marvelous British nonfiction writer now living in the states. When I told Jonathan about my novel's long search for a home, he recommend I talk to his friend, Mary Bisbee-Beek, a publicist and literary marketing consultant who knows the business as well as anyone I've met. She generously offered to read part of the novel, said to try Garth, and that's the key link that led to the book you are reading now. I can't thank Scott, Garth, Jonathan, and Mary enough.

Earlier in the writing process, my longtime friend and talented writer Kevin Catalano read the sprawling manuscript very closely, giving me excellent suggestions and answering my numerous questions. I also appreciate friends and writers David Stevens, Tenaya Darlington, and Tom Coyne for reading early drafts and offering insightful feedback. My wife, Amy Woodworth, read several versions throughout the long process, providing invaluable support and editing as she always does.

I also want to thank Peter Bodo at *Tennis* magazine, not simply for returning a random phone call and agreeing in less than one day to publish an article I wrote about searching for Bill Tilden's grave in Philadelphia, but for his continued encouragement and the great body of tennis writing he has produced for four decades.

I also must thank my family and many friends who have spent time with me on tennis courts. My parents and I hit many thousands of balls on the asphalt court in our backyard when I was young. My dad drove me to many junior tennis tournaments, some of which I played like a zombie, but he kept taking me. My mom, who could not be more different from the fictional mother in this novel, loves the game passionately and is a fierce competitor. We won the Cedartown Open mixed doubles in the early eighties, and much later in life traveled to see U.S. Open and Davis Cup matches, including the 2007 championship in Portland won by the team led by Andy Roddick, her all-time favorite player. My late uncle, Grady Starnes, and my cousin, Gary, also provided much tennis encouragement in my youth. My high school doubles partner Brian Robinson and I won many more matches than we lost—and I'm certain we had more fun off the court than our opponents. After not playing for a dozen years, I met Bobby Dowlen and Harold Graham on the hard courts of Houston. Both helped me enjoy the game again and shared fantastic tennis stories. I was very fortunate eight years ago to find the nine clay courts of the Green Valley Tennis Club in Haddon Township, New Jersey, a mere mile from where I now make my home. I have there the best group of friends on and off the court that a tennis player could hope to meet.

Photo by Amy Jean Woodworth

Joe Samuel "Sam" Starnes was born in Alabama, grew up in Cedartown, Georgia, and has lived in either New Jersey or Philadelphia since 2000. *Red Dirt* is his third novel. His first novel, *Calling*, was published in 2005, and was reissued in 2014 as an e-book by Mysterious Press.com/Open Road. NewSouth Books published his novel *Fall Line* in November 2011, and it was selected to *The Atlanta Journal-Constitution*'s "Best of the South" list. He has had journalism appear in *The New York Times, The Washington Post, The Philadelphia Inquirer,* and various magazines, as well as essays, short stories, and poems in literary journals. He holds a bachelor's degree in journalism from the University of Georgia, an MA in English from Rutgers University in Newark, and an MFA in Creative Nonfiction from Goucher College. He was awarded a fellowship to the 2006 Sewanee Writers' Conference. He works in the administration at Widener University and has taught writing courses at Widener, Rowan University, and Saint Joseph's University.

For more, visit www.joesamuelstarnes.com or follow him on Twitter @jsamuelstarnes

CAPTURED

The Corporate Infiltration of American Democracy

Senator Sheldon Whitehouse

with Melanie Wachtell Stinnett

NEW YORK
LONDON

First published in the United States by The New Press, New York, 2017
This paperback edition published by the New Press, 2019
Distributed by Two Rivers Distribution

ISBN 978-1-62097-476-6 (pb)

Library of Congress Cataloging-in-Publication Data

Names: Whitehouse, Sheldon, 1955– author.
Title: Captured : the corporate infiltration of American democracy /
Sheldon Whitehouse with Melanie Wachtell Stinnett.
Description: New York : The New Press, 2017. | Includes
bibliographical references and index.
Identifiers: LCCN 2016045845 | ISBN 9781620972076 (hardback)
Subjects: LCSH: Business and politics—United States. | Corporations—Political
activity—United States. | Democracy—United States. | BISAC: POLITICAL
SCIENCE / Political Process / Elections.
Classification: LCC JK467 .W54 2017 | DDC 322/.30973—dc23
LC record available at https://lccn.loc.gov/2016045845

The New Press publishes books that promote and enrich public discussion and understanding of the issues vital to our democracy and to a more equitable world. These books are made possible by the enthusiasm of our readers; the support of a committed group of donors, large and small; the collaboration of our many partners in the independent media and the not-for-profit sector; booksellers, who often hand-sell New Press books; librarians; and above all by our authors.

www.thenewpress.com

Composition by dix!
This book was set in Electra

Printed in the United States of America

2 4 6 8 10 9 7 5 3 1

To my family. Please know how grateful I am to you for putting
up with my choices, for standing by me through the ups
and downs, and for always being there when I needed you.
In particular, you've helped me keep my head on straight
with your irreverence and good humor about my foibles.
Such humility as I have is thanks to you.
I love you, and I am grateful.

—S.W.

To my husband and my daughter: thank you.

—M.W.S.

There are more instances of the abridgement of the freedom of the people by gradual and silent encroachments of those in power than by violent and sudden usurpations.

—James Madison

Contents

Preface to the Paperback Edition

AS THE FIRST EDITION OF THIS BOOK WAS published, Trump had just been elected. In the postscript I wrote back then, I expressed the hope that he might be somewhat independent, possibly working with both sides, possibly even disruptive in some good ways; I had hopes he might be honest and fearless. Boy, was I wrong.

We have seen from the Trump administration stunning levels of corruption, flagrant and constant lying, and low appeals to racism and hatred. Our country stands for lasting principles, but is tarnished by Trump as a messenger of our own principles. Our ambassadors are ashamed to challenge misbehavior in foreign governments, with such flagrant misbehavior in our own.

But even when—in the fullness of time—we are rid of Trump and his whole comic opera of misrule, we will still face the problem described in this book: the insidious creep of special-interest influence throughout our government. In fact, inchoate public frustration with the government's capture by those interests may well have led to Trump.

Not every corporation or industry is involved in this scheme. Many want no part of it. But the big influencers who are working to quietly capture American government, particularly those in highly regulated or polluting industries, have been disturbingly successful.

This insidious power crept in on many separate fronts:

- the steady, years-long effort by Republican appointees on the Supreme Court to give corporate interests a dominating role in our politics;

- the legislative lobbying dominance of corporate and industry interests, who outgun all other comers in Congress by massive multiples of spending;
- the evil of unlimited and dark money now dominating our elections (thanks to the *Citizens United* decision by five Republican appointees on the Court);
- the overwhelming advantage in administrative agencies of the regulated industry, leading to the well-researched (and oft-experienced) problem of "agency capture" when an industry dominates its regulatory agency;
- the growth of a complex web of industry-funded, false-front organizations who inject deliberate streams of falsehood and anti-science propaganda into popular debate;
- the slow strangulation of the civil jury, to spare big influencers accustomed to dominance in other branches of government the indignity of equal treatment in a courtroom; and
- the steady partisan packing of the judicial branch with judges who will reliably rule in favor of gun interests, polluting interests, corporate interests, dark money, voter suppression, and a far-right social agenda (they may call themselves "conservatives" but this has nothing to do with being judicially conservative and everything to do with wins for big-donor interests).

There's one additional power that has become more notable: the power of weaponized fake news to manipulate the public. Not too long ago, fake news was for fun: the *National Enquirer* announcing that JFK and Marilyn Monroe's secret love child was living in a salt cave in Utah, or that aliens ran a grocery store in Idaho. Weaponized fake news is different; weaponized fake news is the election day cover of the *National Enquirer* screaming, "HILLARY: Corrupt Racist Criminal."

This vast armada of influence can be deployed quietly, covertly, surreptitiously. The control of government by wealthy influencers is camouflaged behind webs of phony front groups and deployed through channels of anonymized dark money. Spending big money to support this apparatus is not an issue; for these big interests, the work of secret influence is a hugely profitable enterprise. The result is a campaign finance system described as "even more ethically unmoored than the one obtained before Watergate." *

We are now closing in on one billion dollars in dark money spent in our politics since *Citizens United.* That's a lot of powerful political artillery, packing a lot of influence. And understand this: it's not just the dark money spending. Surrounding the direct impact of that political spending artillery is an even darker zone of influence, where the mere threat or promise of a spending barrage can achieve the desired political result. There's not even the vague trail of an anonymous media buy to chronicle the deployment of that influence. This is the dark money double whammy: both secret spending and secret threats or promises.

It's big, and it's wildly unbalanced in favor of big Republican interests. The three largest dark-money operations are run by the Republican U.S. Chamber of Commerce, Karl Rove's Crossroads GPS, and the Koch brothers' Americans for Prosperity. A recent report by the bipartisan reform group Issue One shows them spending $130 million, $110 million, and $59 million, respectively, since *Citizens United.* The top Democratic operation comes in at $18 million.

I'm what you'd call a climate hawk. I saw years of Senate climate bipartisanship before *Citizens United.* Now I see these immensely powerful, climate-denying, dark-money front groups, all likely funded by fossil-fuel interests. And I see no Republican senator willing to cross them. It reeks.

Look also at how dark- and unlimited money can influence party leadership. Consider the 2016 contest for the Senate. Three Democratic Senate candidates stood a good early chance of winning Republican-held seats in 2016: Russ Feingold, a former senator, in Wisconsin; Ted Strickland, a former governor, in Ohio; and Evan Bayh, a former senator and governor, in Indiana. All were solid, experienced candidates; all were ahead in early polling. But then the big influencers came in, early and hard.

The attack on Feingold began with $700,000 spent against him between July and September of 2015—more than a year before the

* Thomas B. Edsall, "After Citizens United, a Vicious Cycle of Corruption," *New York Times*, December 6, 2018.

election. That's like strafing the other side's fighter planes while they're still on the airfield. Feingold got through his primary in April of 2016; over $2 million more in TV and digital spending was launched that month against him. From October up to election day, the bombardment was $11 million more.

In August of 2015, the barrage began against Ted Strickland, to the tune of over $1.3 million—again, well more than a year before the election. When he won his primary in March 2016, another $1.7 million was launched, and from April to June more than $9 million more bombarded him. A further bombardment of nearly $13 million came in from July to September.

Evan Bayh declared late, in July of 2016; in the next two quarters, $24.35 million bombarded him. The total "outside group" spending against these three Democratic candidates totaled almost exactly $70 million. All three lost their races. Their losses made the difference for Republicans to retain majority control of the Senate.

So back to leadership. If you are the Senate majority leader because big influencers spent $70 million—often very early in the races—well, you won't forget that. And you will certainly be aware of what that means for the future. I cannot prove the majority leader coordinated that 2016 bombardment to protect his majority, but it is by far the likeliest scenario. If that's true, it creates a Senate leadership deeply beholden to the interests behind that bombardment, particularly if the leadership team believes that bombardment can be called in again whenever needed. That $70-million-on-demand alliance buys influence for those donors, perhaps even controlling influence. Perhaps even climate-change-denying influence.

This is happening mostly behind the scenes. All the public sees is a Congress that won't even consider addressing climate change, or fair pharmaceutical pricing, or banning dark money, or investigating whatever financial ties our president has to foreign interests, but that will pass sleazy midnight tax bills that pour money to big political donors.

Think I'm kidding? The recent Republican "donor rewards program" tax bill added $1.5 trillion to our national debt and showered the bulk of it on wealthy and corporate interests of the sort most likely behind those hundreds of millions in dark money. That's a big payback.

Republican mega-donor Sheldon Adelson gave a $30 million political check; his interests received a reported $700 million windfall from the tax bill. A Texas oil refinery company gave $1.5 million; it received a reported $1.9 billion tax windfall. These two small examples in a flood of donor payback represent what one academic researcher calls "a vicious cycle in which growing economic and political inequality are mutually reinforcing."* You use your money to buy the power to loot your country to get more money to buy more power to loot your country more . . .

The people of America from coast to coast smell that something is out of whack; we smell a rat. So this machinery then plays a game of misdirection, to focus elsewhere those well-founded resentments. We are led down paths of anger, division, resentment, and scapegoating. And that gives us Trump.

Getting rid of Trump and his creepy minions will help heal our body politic from the injury the Trumps have done to our country. But heal that injury, and this virus of surreptitious influence will still lurk, and will still cause frustration and mischief, until we also cure that disease. Like a patient with both a wound and a virus, our democracy will not return to good health until both the injury is healed and the disease is cured.

The disease isn't new.

For as long as there have been governments, powerful private forces have tried to bend the power of government to their purposes. We think now of great political battles as Republican versus Democrat, or progressive versus conservative. We think of specific fights: polluters versus environmentalists; security hawks versus civil libertarians; tax cutters versus big spenders. But threaded through and behind those familiar fights is the long, quiet, persistent effort by forces who seek to turn the power of government to their own private advantage. When they succeed, their victim is the non-predatory majority who just want to go about their business without being robbed through their own government.

Distracted by Trumpian theatrics, or by the clash of specific fights,

* Martin Gilens, *Affluence and Influence: Economic Inequality and Political Power in America* (Princeton, NJ: Princeton University Press, 2012).

we pay too little attention to this battle over government itself. Distraction is just what the big influencers want for us. They want to win this battle silently; no end-zone antics by them when they capture another agency or judge or policy. They just want the lucrative proceeds of winning.

And they have been doing a lot of winning lately.

My thesis in this book is that many of the things that frustrate Americans today about our government are the result of losing this ancient contest to the modern big influencers. This is not new. It is as old as corruption. It's just the latest inning in a long, long game, and now it's "game on" for us to fight back.

Understand the problem. Get mad. Join the fight. We need a gentle revolution now in this country, because if the distraction, corruption, connivance, and misrule continue, we will get a not-so-gentle one later.

Senator Sheldon Whitehouse
December 2018

Introduction

IN THE SENATE, I SEE EVERY DAY how power works in the political sphere. I see who's got it. I see who uses it. I see how they use it. I see the devices by which that power is applied. I see the schemes used to obscure who's pulling the strings. I see the smokescreens put up to distract people so they don't notice the string-pulling. This is my world; it is the ecosystem I inhabit as a United States senator.

The legendary, Pulitzer Prize–winning author William S. White observed, "A senator of the United States is an ambulant converging point for pressures and counter-pressures of high, medium and low purposes."[1] What I see all around me these days is immense pressure deployed by the corporate sector in our government. Some of this corporate power is deployed in traditional ways. For as long as there has been government, there have been efforts by powerful forces to bend government to their private advantage, and to evade or prevent government oversight. For as long as there have been legislatures, there have been efforts to acquire influence over them. For as long as there has been regulation of industries, there have been efforts to control the regulators and to condition them to the interests of the industries they are designed to regulate.

But some of what I see is new. I've had a close-up look at government—as a prosecutor, as a regulator, as a government staffer, as a reformer, as a candidate, and as an elected official. Never in my life have I seen such influence in our elections from corporations and their managers and billionaire owners. Their presence in American elections has exploded, indeed become dominant, as the campaign finance world has become virtually lawless.

Never in my life have I seen such a complex web of front groups sowing deliberate deceit to create public confusion about issues that should be clear. The corporate propaganda machinery is of unprecedented size and sophistication.

Never in my life have I seen our third branch of government, our courts, the place in our governmental system that is supposed to be most immune from politics, under such political sway. The track record of the Supreme Court in particular shows patterns that are completely inconsistent with disinterested neutrality.

It's always been tough to go up against the big guys. But for most of my life I felt we had a fighting chance. American politics has deep traditions of honor. There were always pockets of government that could be counted on to do the right thing. And there was such wisdom and safety in our American system of separated powers that corrupting influences could never take over completely. As a lawyer, and as a student of our Constitution, I believed that our American system would always protect us—maybe not right away, maybe not every time, but ultimately and for sure.

I'm no longer so sure.

Huge segments of the American public think things have gone badly wrong. Indeed, nearly three of every four Americans—71 percent—reported in a February 2016 poll that they were "dissatisfied with the way things are going in the United States at this time."[2] We see these numbers in action as voters across the political spectrum offer enthusiastic support to candidates pledging to change the status quo.

How could this be? We've persevered through a revolutionary war, a civil war, and two world wars. We've endured massive expansions and great depressions. We've overturned slavery, brought women well toward full equality, pushed racism back, and recognized gay relationships. We invented automobiles, airplanes, telephones, TV, the atom bomb, and the Internet. Ours has been a tumultuous 240 years. What now, after all that tumult, has gone wrong?

Abraham Lincoln reminded us at Gettysburg, over a field that covered the decaying remains of thousands of soldiers, both Union and Confederate, that it was our American destiny, and the prize of our Civil War sacrifice, that "government of the people, by the people, and for the people shall not perish from this earth."[3] The thing that has changed the most in our government, and the thing that to me best explains what has gone wrong, is that our politics is no longer "of the people, by the people, and for the people."

Corporations of vast wealth and remorseless staying power have moved into our politics, to seize for themselves advantages that can be seized only by control over government. Organizations of mysterious identity have moved into our politics, as screens for the anonymous power and "dark money" behind them. Political campaigns are now run by new and alien organizations, super PACs and 501(c)(4)s, bizarre creatures unknown to our politics until recently.

When I speak of corporate power in politics, let me be very clear: I do not mean just the activities of the incorporated entities themselves. The billionaire owners of corporations are often actively engaged in battle to expand the influence of the corporations that give them their power and their wealth. Front groups and lobbying groups are often the ground troops when corporate powers don't want to get their own hands dirty or when they want to institutionalize their influence. So-called philanthropic foundations are often the proxies for billionaire families who want influence and who launch these tools to professionalize their influence-seeking.

I count them all as faces of corporate power—just as they do themselves. The internal coordination behind the scenes between the politically active corporate entities, the billionaire funders, the right-wing "philanthropies," the front groups, and the lobbying organizations is constant. The structure of this enterprise, with common funders, interlocking directorates, and overlapping staff, is emerging as a result of academic and investigative studies. From my perch in the Senate, I see it all as one coordinated beast. That is how it behaves, and that is how I'm going to treat it in this book. This apparatus may seem like a very complicated and unwieldy way for corporations to exert influence, but it allows them to give the public the old razzle-dazzle, running intricate plays with what appear to be many independent voices. It's smart strategy.

These forces are everywhere, and they are dominant in every area where their influence on government can be brought to bear. They are right now, as a practical matter, our unseen ruling class. When you are running for office, they can quietly back you—or your opponent—with literally unlimited funds, depending on how comfortable they are with how you'll vote. (The cudgel of secret spending need not even be swung to have its desired effect; merely brandishing it can be enough to get the attention, and obedience, of a politician.) Once you're elected and in office, corporate influence comes in the form of corporate lobbying—the behemoth on the legislative stage, drowning out all other lobbying competition by a spending ratio of more than thirty to one.[4]

As a bill moves through Congress, corporate lobbyists exploit procedural opportunities to accomplish the industry's purposes out of view of the public. Once a bill becomes law, relentless industry pressure is brought to bear on the agencies charged with enforcement: appointment of industry-friendly administrators; visible industry "caretaking" of friendly administrators when they depart their posts (and visible "freezes" on those who weren't so friendly); heavy lawyering of the rulemaking and enforcement processes, often as simple brute pressure to cause delay and cost; and sometimes direct kickbacks. All these avenues give special interests undue influence over administrative agencies, to the point of outright capture of the agency.

When there is a legal challenge to corporate behavior, or a legal challenge to the way a law is administered, having business-friendly courts to hear the case becomes important. Here corporate influence in the selection of judges is brought to bear, business-friendly "training" for judges at luxurious resorts is offered, and corporate-funded entities that are not traditional litigants appear in court, sometimes in flocks, to amplify the corporate message. The Supreme Court can do more than tilt the balance in business-related cases: the Court can change the very ground rules of democracy in favor of corporate interests. And corporate forces are hard at work using their power to fix the judicial system to seize more power.

Civil juries, the Constitution's designated check on outsized power in the private sphere, have had their place in government shrunk to a vestige of their intended role, leaving corporate forces free to wheel and deal with the established, repeat players in government who are most amenable to their influence.

Meanwhile, a vast corporate enterprise is busy constructing and marketing a pro-corporate "alternate reality": climate change is an illusion; tobacco is not really that bad for you; lead paint only hurts poor children with negligent mothers; the ozone hole isn't being caused by chemicals; various products' association with cancer is unproven; pollution controls will cost way too much and hurt the economy; consumers should be free not to live in a "nanny state." Corporations have become less willing to say these things themselves, so over the years they have outsourced the crafting and selling of this alternate reality to an array of dozens of front groups with innocent-seeming, respectable-sounding names.

And corporate forces have acquired influence in an increasingly compliant and even corporate-owned media. What better way to propagandize the American public than through the "news"?

It all adds up to massive tentacles of corporate power—particularly emanating from a few highly regulated sectors, including finance and fossil fuels—that are usually invisible or obscured but which are quietly and steadily having their way with government. Small wonder people are angry about a nonresponsive democracy. Contrary to the popular sentiment that government isn't working anymore, government is working fine; it's just working for the corporations.

Congress today is working great at helping polluters; it's working great at protecting hedge fund billionaires' low tax rates; it's working great at helping corporations offshore jobs, at letting chemicals and genetically modified stuff into your food, at creating tax and safety loopholes for industry. Congress is also working great at ignoring corporate misbehavior—until after a crisis has hurt or killed a lot of people. Even then, Congress has worked great at having taxpayers bail out the industry that caused the harm.

And worst of all, government is now working great, in a vicious cycle, to change its own ground rules and lock in the control over government by big special-influence operators.

People can feel like they are in a car that won't respond to them, that the car is dangerously out of control, that the car is broken. But the problem isn't the car; the problem is who's now driving it. Regular people are no longer in the driver's seat of American democracy.

A corporation is not an inherently bad thing. In proper circumstances and within proper bounds, the corporate form is an immensely valuable proposition. But the economic ability to amass money can spawn a political desire to amass power. And at a certain level of political power, corporate forces can upshift into political overdrive and use their power to change the political system itself. Beyond just improving outcomes for their industry from the political system, they can make changes to the political system itself that lock in lasting advantages for them and protect their dominance. That overdrive is the most worrisome use of power. That's where I believe we are now, and why I'm writing this book.

Today there is virtually no element of the political landscape into which corporate influence has not intruded, and it is usually the strongest political force arrayed in any part of that landscape. You may not see it, because it is bad strategy for the purveyors of corporate influence to herald their victories; they are better off quietly pocketing their winnings than bragging about them, and they'd rather you not know how effectively they have rigged the game. But, visibly or not, our government has been captured. The "gradual and silent encroachments" that James Madison warned of have come in a corporate guise that Madison and his compatriots did not foresee and were not able to preempt.[5]

The big corporate interests now in control would like you to give up on government. The better solution is not to give up on the American government that generations of Americans fought, bled, and died to leave to us. The better solution is to take it back and put it to work for us. It will be a battle. Even if you do not now see a clean path to victory, remember the admonition of Rabbi Tarfon: "It may not be up to us to complete the work, but neither are we free to desist from it." As citizens, this must be our work.

CAPTURED

CHAPTER ONE

The Constitution's Blind Spot

AMERICA WAS FOUNDED AS AN EXPERIMENT. It was not an easy one. No one anywhere had successfully created our dream: a popular government, without kings and crowns, without aristocracy and class privileges, and safe from military rule by force of arms. Trusting common people with uncommon power—the power to govern themselves—was the great cause of our liberty.

The Founders knew the threats that they were up against. Experienced politicians, they had a keen sense of how easily things could go wrong. They had seen how selfish pressures and popular passions could overwhelm a government, and they knew government power could be captured or perverted to a wrongful purpose. Protecting against these threats, so that a popular government could prevail against them, was the great task of the Constitution. We are all familiar with the renowned system of "checks and balances" the Founders created to preempt the threat that any one branch of government would become too powerful. Yet even with all of the Constitution's precautions, there was at least one major threat that the Founders failed to foresee.

The Founding Fathers were learning on the fly—this truly was an experiment. They had Locke and Montesquieu and other Enlightenment thinkers to give them a general conceptual structure, but their experiment was a more challenging task than penning philosophical principles. They had to adapt those high-minded principles to the pressures of politics and the practicalities of governing. They had to make the theories work amid the dust and drama and passion of real-life politics. This was a new frontier.

The Founders' first effort at a constitution was designed to address the threats to democracy that they perceived. We know what those threats were, because they were the topic of the Federalist Papers. Published in various newspapers in 1787 and 1788 under the pen name "Publius," the Federalist Papers were written by Alexander Hamilton, James Madison, and John Jay to sell the new constitution to skeptical voters across the colonies. The arguments in the Federalist Papers signal to us the concerns of the time.

The predominant concerns were these: how the Constitution would protect the individual from the power of government, how it would protect society from the dangers of faction, and how it would protect the new democracy against the emergence of a new aristocracy or a new royalty. When it came into effect in 1789, the Constitution erected its defense against these threats primarily through its careful separation of powers.

But the Constitution wasn't enough. The American people were not satisfied. They wanted still more assurances about their role and rights as citizens of this new Republic. So the Founders went back and drew up the Bill of Rights. The Bill of Rights did two key things: it buttressed the public rights of the Constitution with an array of hard-and-fast individual rights, and it provided specific defenses of those rights in areas such as free speech, criminal process, and access to a jury.

Getting this done was a long and exhausting process. The Declaration of Independence was signed in 1776; the Bill of Rights wasn't adopted until 1791. A passionate running dialogue lit up that fifteen-year period—a dialogue among brilliant individual Founders, between rival states, between federalists and anti-federalists, and throughout a new American citizenry. They thought deeply and argued fiercely about this new democratic form of government.

And they were proud. Their American achievement reverberated throughout the world. The revolutionary Americans who had pledged "our lives, our fortunes and our sacred honor" to the cause yearned to prove that this experiment was worth all their blood and hope and sacrifice.[1] They felt a keen obligation to history to get this right, and getting it right meant building into this new Constitution defenses against all the threats they perceived. They threw their hearts and souls into building those defenses.

But they overlooked one threat. They overlooked the corporation.

At the time, they overlooked it with reason. The first corporations in America bore no resemblance to big, modern, for-profit entities. Originally, incorporated entities were mostly cities, schools, and charities. They usually had a public purpose or carried out quasi-governmental tasks. By the 1790s, business corporations began to emerge in America, but at the outset they were few. These corporations were usually specific in purpose, and the business purpose was still usually quasi-governmental—to build a toll road or a canal, for instance. They were often given a temporary monopoly, and they often closed up once the corporate purpose was achieved.[2]

The few corporations that existed were fully the legal creatures of state legislatures, and they existed under close local political control. A specific legislative charter spelled out everything from the corporation's capitalization and life span to its functions and operations. If a corporation in some way misbehaved or became politically aggressive, its charter could be revoked or modified, and that ended that. Nothing about corporations looked like a threat. No American megacorporation marauded through the Founders' political landscape.

On our American continent, the big British corporations threatened no harm. The Hudson's Bay Company (or, more formally, the Governor and Company of Adventurers of England Trading into Hudson's Bay) was operating far away in Canada and not interfering in the American colonies.[3] The Massachusetts Bay Company was long gone; in fact, it had lost its charter even before the colony it founded fought its way to independence.[4]

Had the Founders given more attention to corporations, and foreseen that corporations might slip their bounds of public purpose and public control, every indication is that they would have been skeptical and suspicious of a political role for them. The experience of the great British corporations in the mother country would have been cautionary. The British East India Company notoriously corrupted the English Parliament and foreign governments; its "nabobs" were officers who had enriched themselves enormously in India, returned to

England, and bought themselves seats in Parliament, threatening to turn England into "a sink of Indian wealth."[5] The South Sea Company collapsed in a spectacular bubble, in a rancid combination of what Sir Isaac Newton reportedly called "the madness of a multitude"[6] and what parliamentary investigation called the "most notorious, dangerous and infamous corruption."[7]

The Founders may have thought that determining a political role for corporations was an issue for another day. Were Congress ever to charter a national corporation, safety measures could then be addressed in the charter. (When Congress did charter a national bank in 1791, the debate agitated our politics for fifty years.)[8] They may have attributed the power of those English corporations to the rotten political system in England, which the Founders were rejecting to build a better world. In any event, these scandals were far enough away that they did not provoke the Founders' concern and caution in the drafting of the Constitution.

The Founding Fathers saw no specific threat to our government from corporate entities, so they built in no specific defenses to protect against them. Nowhere in our Constitution or in our Bill of Rights does the word "corporation" even appear. In the eighty-five lengthy articles that together constituted the Federalist Papers, the word "corporation" appeared only three times, one of those times referring to municipal corporations.[9]

We have one pretty solid way to deduce how the Founders would have felt about a political role for corporate entities, had they considered that at the Founding: we know what two of the principal Founders said and wrote about corporations afterward. The genius of the Founding Fathers was perhaps most concentrated in the tiny form of James Madison and in the lanky frame of Thomas Jefferson, and their views are likely illustrative of what might have happened had the Constitution addressed the problem of corporations in our politics.

James Madison grew to see the dangers of corporations by 1817. That was far too late for our Constitution, but Madison's warning of two hundred years ago is plain: "There is an evil which ought to be guarded against in the indefinite accumulation of property from the capacity of holding it in perpetuity by ecclesiastical corporations. The power of all corporations ought to be limited in this respect. The growing wealth acquired by them never fails to be a source of abuses."[10] Similarly, in 1816, Thomas Jefferson had urged that we "crush in its birth the aristocracy of our monied corporations which dare already to challenge our government to a trial of strength, and bid defiance to the laws of our country."[11]

Twenty-five years earlier, when our great American constitutional effort concluded with the Bill of Rights, that threat to our country of a "trial of strength" was not yet present. As corporations blossomed in the booming 1790s, the traditional road, bridge, and canal monopolies remained of little concern.[12] But the 1790s also brought banking corporations.[13] These new entities caused new concerns, and the Founders' worries about them are instructive. Banking corporations were beyond the familiar mold for American corporations. They had no fixed, tangible purpose, and there were no obvious limits to their wealth or power, their reach, or their duration—they had no natural end. These characteristics rang alarm bells in the Founders' minds.

Looking back on this time through the lens of scholarly history, Supreme Court justice John Paul Stevens summed up the Founders' dim view of the corporation: "Members of the founding generation held a cautious view of corporate power and a narrow view of corporate rights."[14] And it was not just the Founders who came to see these new, emboldened corporations as a threat to popular self-governance if unleashed in the political arena. The American people long have as well. As Justice Stevens wrote, Americans "have recognized a need to prevent corporations from undermining self-government since the founding" and "have fought against the distinctive corrupting potential of corporate electioneering since the days of Theodore Roosevelt."[15] Indeed, at the Founding, most states prohibited any political contribution by a corporation, and punished it as a criminal offense.[16] The early restrictions on corporations in the nineteenth century were so limiting that building major enterprises such as Standard Oil required quite a bit of lawyerly ingenuity. The Rockefeller trust, for example, was created to work around laws restricting corporations from holding stock in other entities. That's why it was "trusts" that had to be busted.[17]

Economically, a corporation can be a great boon. The business corporation aggregates capital with unprecedented efficiency of both cost and purpose. Neither death nor illness interrupts it. It allocates liability and risk in ways that encourage investment. It is probably safe to say that the corporate form has allowed the creation of more wealth than any other invention. As an economic actor, it is without peer.

As a political actor, however, the corporation is a dangerous entity. The valuable characteristics of the corporate form as an economic tool are dangerous when pitted against humans in the political sphere. It was these characteristics of a modern for-profit corporation that members of the Founding generation came to perceive with such distress.

First, for-profit corporations are dedicated exclusively to profit-making, by law. That is their solemn and *sole* duty to their shareholders.[18] In business, this is an estimable characteristic, ensuring loyalty and diligence. In politics, where moral issues and public goods are so often at stake, such single-mindedness is a flaw.

Second, corporations have no soul or conscience. Courts have said they "have no personal attributes"[19]; a corporation is "without either mental or moral powers,"[20] is "without power to think, speak, or act, except as live sentient human beings may think, speak, and act for it,"[21] and "lacks capacity for numerous abilities of a natural person."[22] An artificial being without conscience or remorse, it is kept from misconduct not by an internal moral compass but by specific laws or by the adverse business prospect of gaining so bad a reputation as to interfere with its profit-making.

Third, corporations have no loyalty to any flag or nation. Mostly this is true of modern multinational corporations, which move assets, jobs, and intellectual property around the globe at will. Exxon's former CEO is quoted as saying, "I'm not a U.S. company and I don't make decisions based on what is good for the U.S."[23] They have only a simple fiduciary loyalty to their shareholders. Some have revenues that exceed those of countries in which they operate.

Fourth, corporations do not rest, retire, or die. They are persistent and unrelenting. The legal term is "perpetual succession," meaning "artificial life extending beyond the natural lives of the incorporators, directors, and officers."[24] A corporation "does not die in the sense that a person dies."[25] Nor does it rest in the sense that a person rests.

Fifth, there is no natural limit to corporations' size; they can hold preposterous sums of money. In politics, where "money is the mother's milk,"[26] those sums can be used to acquire influence for the corporation, so as to promote policies that enrich the corporation well beyond the cost of buying that influence. Indeed, given the corporation's fiduciary obligation, it has some natural economic obligation to use its power to that end.

Finally, there is no natural limit to their appetite. No corporation says, "You know, I think I've made enough money," and pushes back from the table. No corporate lobby says, "You know, I think I've acquired enough political influence," and goes out to play with the grandchildren.

The continuity, single-mindedness, relentlessness, and efficiency that these characteristics permit are valuable qualities in economic enterprise. In the political arena, they present risks, which become acute if a corporation makes the fateful decision to pursue political influence as a moneymaking strategy. It is a voracious spiral: the more money the corporate entity can make through political influence, the more money it can justify spending to acquire that influence. The more money it spends, the greater its influence, the more it can use that influence to make more money, and so on, once acquiring political influence becomes a corporate profit-making strategy.

Rare is the human being who desires to pursue, or is capable of pursuing, this influence-purchasing enterprise with such relentless and single-minded determination. We humans ordinarily have families and churches, illnesses and distractions, hobbies and responsibilities of various kinds that get in the way. We may be passionate about our politics, but we need our sleep.

The United States Supreme Court of the twentieth century summed up the political role indicated by these corporate characteristics thus: "That invisible, intangible, and artificial being, that mere legal entity, a corporation aggregate, is certainly not a citizen."[27] As described by legal scholar Burt Neuborne, the "for-profit business corporation [is] an artificial state-created legal fiction vested with unlimited life, entity shielding, limited shareholder liability, negotiable shares, and highly favorable rules encouraging the acquisition, accumulation, and retention of other people's money."[28] Supreme Court justice John Paul Stevens reminded us that "corporations are different from human beings," because unlike us, corporations "have no consciences, no beliefs, no feelings, no thoughts, no desires."[29] Putting these observations into a political context, Justice Stevens noted that corporations are not "members of 'We the People' by whom and for whom our Constitution was established."[30] "Certainly not a citizen," "different from human beings," not "members of 'We the People'"—all these descriptors imply little or no political role for corporations.

Once let loose in the political sphere, however, the sum of these corporate characteristics is a political creature with momentous natural advantages over its human competitors. The Framers simply would not recognize the constitutional alien that is the modern corporation operating in our democracy; of course they didn't design limits on the political activities of an entity they couldn't even imagine.

Add to these characteristics the twentieth-century advertising and marketing skills corporations have developed to sell their products, which apply well to the task of manipulating human voters. Add on size sufficient to dwarf many sovereign nations, and the massive profit that political ventures can provide. Then add the twenty-first-century technologies of constant communication. Finally, add secrecy. The result is a power that could turn our popular democracy into high-tech corporate feudalism if we don't learn how to restrain it.

This book addresses how corporations have grown to a size and power and political role unimaginable to the Founders of our country; how the modern corporation has exploited the gap in the Founders' constitutional foresight; how corporations now win the "trial of strength" against our democracy that Jefferson warned about; and what political prizes are sought and seized by corporate power through its political victories in that "trial of strength." Finally, this book looks at the restraints the Founders *did* build into the system, from the civil court system to an independent press to citizens' right to vote—restraints that can and must be employed to reclaim and reinvigorate our American popular democracy and restore to its proper preeminence the office of "citizen," the one office all Americans occupy.

James Madison is said to have warned that "the day will come when our Republic will be an impossibility. It will be an impossibility because wealth will be concentrated in the hands of a few. A republic can not stand upon bayonets, and when that day comes, when the wealth of the nation will be in the hands of a few, then we must rely upon the wisdom of the best elements in the country to readjust the laws of the nation to the changed conditions."[31] I believe that the day has come, and that readjustment is needed to reclaim the power that has slipped away from the hands of regular American citizens and into the grasp of corporate concentrated wealth.

The big, politically active corporations love having us sit on the couch watching ads paid for by their front groups and deciding which of those ads appeal most to our opinions, fears, and prejudices. But that is being a consumer of their political product, not being a citizen. A citizen is more than a consumer. However much the tentacles of corporate political interference may coil around and through our democracy, at the end of the day the survival of our democratic experiment depends on the active participation of the people. Citizens need to get up off the couch and set things right.

We've gotten off the couch before.

When the Cuyahoga River in Ohio caught fire, Americans woke up to the environmental damage we were doing, started Earth Day, and passed a wealth of environmental laws that have made American life better and safer: the Clean Air Act, the Clean Water Act, hazardous waste laws, chemical safety laws, and laws protecting endangered species.[32] What had happened? The creeping reach of pollution's effects on all of us had reached a point where it sparked a reaction. Our reaction changed the country and made it a much healthier place to live.

When we realized our diets were killing us, many Americans left behind the Wonder Bread, the canned vegetables, and the TV dinners. When I was young, a health food store was a rarity, even an oddity. In 2015, Americans spent an estimated $37 billion on organic food.[33] We are living nearly ten years longer now than when I was born. What happened? The creeping effects of an all-processed-foods diet reached a point for us where it sparked a reaction. Our reaction changed our diets and made us a healthier and more vigorous people.

A similar reaction is due with respect to our democracy. Too much of our democratic debate today is the political equivalent of pollution and junk food. Other generations solved other problems; it's our turn to solve this one.

We can take example and heart from the fighting spirit of the bipartisan Roosevelts. Democrat Franklin D. Roosevelt saw the powerful forces of "organized money" (as dangerous, he said, as an "organized mob") arrayed against him.[34] Here is how he responded to what he had called "this resolute enemy within our gates"[35] in an address to the nation: "Never before in all our history have these forces been so united against one candidate as they stand today. They are unanimous in their hate for me—and I welcome their hatred. I should like to have it said of my first Administration that in it the forces of selfishness and of lust for power met their match. I should like to have it said of my second Administration that in it these forces met their master."[36]

Republican Teddy Roosevelt saw a similar enemy: "Behind the ostensible government sits enthroned an invisible government owing no allegiance and acknowledging no responsibility to the people. To destroy this invisible government, to dissolve the unholy alliance between corrupt business and corrupt politics, is the first task of the statesmanship of the day."[37] His call was clear: "Our government, National and State, must be freed from the sinister influence or control of special interests. . . . We must drive the special interests out of politics. . . . The citizens of the United States must effectively control the mighty commercial forces which they have called into being. There can be no effective control of corporations while their political activity remains."[38] Ever the optimist in a fight, Teddy Roosevelt concluded: "To put an end to it will be neither a short nor an easy task, but it can be done."[39]

CHAPTER TWO

The Growth of Corporate Power

BEN COHEN, FOUNDER OF BEN & JERRY'S, has observed: "Unfortunately, the greatest collaboration in history has been between money and politics, which helps only the rich."[1] The corporate form has been a great facilitator of that collaboration. History shows that corporations have created immense economic value. History also shows that this value has constantly been accompanied by a political threat to popular democracy. Generation after generation has noticed; at times, this contest between corporate power and popular democracy has been the defining public issue of the day. And the key lesson of this history is that in this contest, democracy has won big victories against the tide of corporate influence. Brave Americans have stood up, fought back, and won against corporate political power.

Even at their very beginning in ancient Rome, corporations were seen as rivals to government. Sources as diverse as Blackstone's famous *Commentaries*, from the 1760s, and the 1917 *Fletcher Cyclopedia of the Law of Corporations* describe the antagonism thousands of years ago between corporations and government. According to *Fletcher*, "The development of corporations in Rome was gradual, and for a long period, in the face of more or less pronounced governmental hostility. From the time of the Twelve Tables until the days of the emperors, corporate activity was closely hedged about by restrictions, and decrees denouncing as illicit those corporations that had started upon their careers without authority, or had transgressed in any way, occurred frequently."[2] Through medieval times and guilds, the *Fletcher Cyclopedia* describes the great trading corporations of England as being "looked upon as public agencies, to which had been entrusted the duty of regulating foreign trade."[3] These English corporations had the natural political limit that they "could be created only by the will of Parliament or of the Crown" and were subject to government's direct supervision.[4]

In early America, *Fletcher* reports, "there was a distrust or disfavor of private corporations," and this "cloud of disfavor" persisted through the Founding period. This distrust can be seen in the very limited number of corporations chartered in eighteenth-century America: *Fletcher* notes that "during the colonial period of American history, there were only six purely native-born business corporations." Nor was there much corporate activity between the Declaration of Independence and the drafting of the Constitution: "only 20 were added to this list during the 13-year period preceding the adoption of the federal Constitution." Though corporations were not mentioned in the text of the Constitution and their future political power was not foreseen, "misgivings respecting the power of Congress to form corporations" colored the ratification of the Constitution by the states, according to *Fletcher*. Even after ratification, in the last eleven years of the eighteenth century, "the total number of charters granted did not exceed 200"—there was growth, but not the explosion that was to follow.[5]

The United States Supreme Court's first famous and consequential case dealing with corporations concerned Dartmouth College, an early corporation, in 1819. The case was a superficially simple fight for control over the power to appoint the board of trustees.[6] New Hampshire asserted the right of the legislature to pass a law changing the appointments, Dartmouth's trustees resisted, and Daniel Webster—a leading senator of the day, two-time secretary of state, and renowned orator—argued on behalf of the college.

Chief Justice John Marshall's decision described the corporation in the traditional way, as "an artificial being, invisible, intangible, and existing only in contemplation of law. Being the mere creature of law," he continued, "it possesses only those properties which the charter of its creation confers upon it either expressly or as incidental to its very existence."[7] This is a recurring theme in American law. Various courts over the years have described corporations as "a mere creature of the law, invisible, intangible, and incorporeal,"[8] "a mere conception of the legislative mind,"[9] and "a purely artificial body created by law, [which] can act only in accordance with the law of its creation."[10] A corporation, one court said, is "but a convenience, a facility, only possessing the powers conferred by the creator upon it and subject to the valid, appropriate measures of control, surveillance, and regulation governments may impose."[11] (From my perch in the Senate, I would interject, it seems that it is corporate political power that now seeks to impose its "measures of control, surveillance and regulation" upon our democracy, not vice versa.)

But Marshall decided the case for the college, espousing a new theory that legislative control over a corporate charter was not absolute. The Supreme Court determined that, once created, a corporation had certain rights against its own creator.[12] This was a fateful decision, whose dimensions have been litigated ever since.

In 1839, only twenty years after the Dartmouth College decision, Congressman Charles Jared Ingersoll of Pennsylvania gave a speech significant enough that it was published verbatim as an appendix to the January edition of the *United States Magazine and Democratic Review*, a famous anti-aristocratic periodical of the day. His speech warned that in government, "corporation power is now an overshadowing influence," and called for the "restoration of public supremacy," without which, he said, "banks are government, and the very worst government."[13]

It was the banking corporations, in particular, that concerned Ingersoll, and with good reason. As banking corporations had multiplied in number and size, so did their corrupt dealings with the legislators who had final say over which banks received charters and which did not. When the Bank of the United States's charter expired in 1812, bankers pursued a charter for what would be the country's largest bank through such corrupt means that several of their lobbyists were indicted for bribery—though none was ultimately convicted. In the 1820s, a politician from New York—future president Martin Van Buren—infamously dominated banking policy by doling out charters to friends and systematically blocking foes.[14] The corruption ran both ways: the more legislators used such power to pick and choose the winners in finance, the more incentive bankers had to lobby—and bribe—those legislators.

As Ingersoll put it, banking corporations had by then become "political engines of peculiar magnitude and moment," creating what he called "our present government by corporate supremacy." Corporations, Ingersoll said, "at this moment absolutely govern this commonwealth and this union of commonwealths with more sway than even its legitimate institutions." Ingersoll went on to describe the new banking corporations as "a novelty wholly unforeseen by the constitutions; a vast fungus grown upon government,"[15] and harked back to Jefferson's concern about what would happen in the "trial of strength" between government and "the aristocracy of our monied corporations."[16] Before long, it would be more than banking corporations that had Americans concerned.

Great and wealthy industrial corporations appeared suddenly as the nineteenth century drew to a close. Famed organizational sociologist Charles Perrow relates: "Until the 1890s there were only a few large [corporations], in textiles and railroads and the steel and locomotive industries. Then there was a spurt at the turn of the century."[17] There were thirty thousand corporations in 1860; by 1915 there were three hundred thousand.[18] Within only five years at the turn of the century, most of the two hundred biggest corporations of the time were established, many of which, according to Perrow, "still rule their industries."[19]

Bear in mind the novelty of these great beasts, too. As economists Jessica Hennessey and John Wallis observe in *Corporations and American Democracy*, "The only comparably large organizations historically were governments, armies or churches."[20] The suddenness of the emergence of these new corporate entities, coupled with their size, made them "profoundly controversial."[21] As historian H.W. Brands put it in *American Colossus*: "Capitalism threatened to eclipse democracy."[22]

Immense economic value has come to America via human effort organized through the corporate form; particularly in the industrial era, this was vital to our nation's development. As law professor Daniel Crane describes the unique benefits of the corporate structure, "[t]he mechanized processes, infrastructure investments, and enormous fixed costs that characterized the railroads, factories, mills, refineries and pipelines of the late nineteenth century required unprecedented aggregations of capital, to which the newly accessible corporate form lent a ready hand."[23] Though often producing conditions that were hellish for workers, the corporate form was an economic blessing for the country.

The mistake was to let these economic actors intrude into politics. Corporations would inevitably become brutal political players, because, as sociologist Edward A. Ross has observed, "the force devoted to wresting government from the people will correspond to the magnitude of the pecuniary interest at stake."[24] These new aggregators of capital had enormous pecuniary interests at stake, and were motivated to wrest power with a force not seen before.

This was the era of Upton Sinclair's *The Jungle*, published in 1906 to expose the horrendous conditions in the meatpacking industry, where a few mega-corporations had consolidated power. And it was the era of muckrakers including Ida Tarbell, Lincoln Steffens, and Ray Baker, who together produced a 1903 issue of the famous *McClure's Magazine* exposing the corruption that corporate power brought to the financial and political systems of the day.[25] Tarbell dove deep into the rise of John D. Rockefeller, cataloging how he aggregated power to control the means of oil production and distribution across the country, and abused it, to build Standard Oil into a monolith of unmatched proportions. A summary by historian Doris Kearns Goodwin, quoting Tarbell, captured Rockefeller's efforts to manipulate the economic system in the 1870s and 1880s to accumulate wealth and power. It stands as a warning of the dangerous ambitions corporate power can harbor, and it serves as a reminder that other businesses and enterprises are often the victims of those ambitions.

> He began his ascent by flouting the common law to secure favorable rates from the railroads, allowing him to drive his rivals out. "At the same time he worked with the railroads to prevent other people getting oil to manufacture, or if they got it he worked with the railroads to prevent the shipment of the product. If it reached a dealer, he did his utmost to bully or wheedle him to countermand his order. If he failed in that, he undersold until the dealer, losing on his purchase, was glad enough to buy thereafter of Mr. Rockefeller." In the end, "every great campaign against rival interests which the Standard Oil Company has

carried on has been inaugurated, not to save its life, but to build up and sustain a monopoly in the oil industry."[26]

Historian William Novak has noted, "though concern about public corruption was as old as the republic, what was new at the turn of the 20th century was an acute awareness of the unprecedented threat *to the polity* posed by the arrival of large scale business and corporate interests in rail, oil, meatpacking, and insurance, whose corruptions were cataloged in a seemingly endless series of reports and even fictional portrayals."[27]

State legislators across America had seen corporations gaining enormous financial and political power in the late nineteenth century, and they had tried to contain the growing threat. The general rule, according to the *Fletcher Cyclopedia*, was to restrict a corporation's powers to those "only as were expressly granted to it by its enabling act."[28] This put controlling power in the people's representatives to "enable" the corporation or not by legislative act, as the state legislatures saw fit. Corporations were denied the automatic right to do all things that a natural person could do and instead were limited to specifically granted powers. That restriction was important to allay public suspicions of this enormous new force.[29]

California offers one example. California's 1879 state constitution was designed specifically to protect against corporate power. The California Supreme Court, in a decision decades later looking back on the state's founding period, noted that the California constitution was drafted "to guard against . . . actual or potential danger existing or foreshadowed in that marvelous expansion of corporate growth in varied and widening fields of activity which mark that epoch in our state and national history." The safeguards included restrictions within the state constitution, "covering many pages thereof," including "limitations upon corporate powers, definitions of corporate liabilities and restrictions upon the otherwise unlimited right of the legislature to unduly extend the one or to remove or qualify the other."[30]

Why would Californians thus restrict even their own elected legislature? The only logical reason is that Californians sensed the danger of corporate influence over their legislature and desired to build into the state's constitution some protection from what corporate power could do if it were to control legislative power and upend the natural order.

California was not alone in seeing corporate menace: *Fletcher* reports that the development of state constitutions in the mid- to late nineteenth century was characterized by "an attitude of suspicion and fear toward the corporate mechanism."[31] The result was restrictions, lots of them. At first, as Justice Louis Brandeis later recounted, "corporations could be formed under the general laws only for a limited number of purposes. . . . Permission to incorporate for 'any lawful purpose' was not common until 1875; and until that time the duration of corporate franchises was generally limited to a period of 20, 30 or 50 years. . . . The powers which the corporation might exercise in carrying out its purposes were sparingly conferred and strictly construed."[32]

By the time the industrial boom of the late nineteenth century reached its apex, however, many of these restrictions on corporate activity were more honored in the breach than the observance; the regulatory system set up by state governments to limit corporate power had essentially collapsed. This was not because Americans felt safe, or because the restrictions had proved unwise. It was, as Justice Brandeis concluded, because of "the conviction that it was futile" for states to continue to insist upon restrictions on the size and powers of business corporations, as local restrictions in one state "would be circumvented by foreign incorporation" in another state.[33] In other words, corporations had created a race to the bottom among the states.

New Jersey was first to break from the others, with its Holding Company Act of 1891, which allowed corporations to own stocks in other firms and thus enabled the major trusts to grow and expand.[34] This move earned New Jersey the contemporary nickname the "Traitor State."[35] New Jersey benefited mightily from being the first to fold, to the tune of a nearly $3 million surplus in its treasury in incorporation-related fees. Regulation followed. As historian Daniel Crane notes, "It was little wonder that, despite grumbling about the 'traitor state,' most other states soon followed suit."[36]

Decades later, the Supreme Court would describe America during the Gilded Age as deeply suspicious of corporations. Justice John

Harlan reflected: "All who recall the condition of the country in 1890 will remember that there was everywhere, among the people generally, a deep feeling of unrest. . . . [T]he conviction was universal that the country was in real danger from another kind of slavery sought to be fastened on the American people; namely, the slavery that would result from aggregations of capital in the hands of a few individuals and corporations controlling, for their own profit and advantage exclusively, the entire business of the country, including the production and sale of the necessaries of life."[37] Justice Brandeis wrote, "There was a sense of some insidious menace inherent in large aggregations of capital, particularly when held by corporations."[38]

Another such voice was Thomas Cooley, a distinguished lawyer, chief justice of the Michigan Supreme Court, and the first chairman of the Interstate Commerce Commission. In 1874, he had warned that "the most enormous and threatening powers in our country have been created; some of the great and wealthy corporations [have] greater influence in the country at large and upon the legislation of the country than the States to which they owe their corporate existence."[39] The legendary progressive journalist William Allen White described the Senate during this period as a place where senators represented not states but "principalities and powers in business. One Senator . . . represents the Union Pacific Railway System; another the New York Central; still another the insurance interests of New York and New Jersey."[40] Charles Francis Adams Jr. looked at state legislatures and saw them "now universally becoming a species of irregular board of railroad direction."[41] Historian George Thayer, looking back at the Gilded Age, concluded, "Never has the American political process been so corrupt. No office was too high to purchase, no man too pure to bribe, no principle too sacred to destroy, no law too fundamental to break."[42]

The effect on the public of what historian Doris Kearns Goodwin refers to as a "web of corruption" between corporations and government was to shake popular confidence in American democracy.[43] Even thoughtful leaders of the establishment held that view. No one was more establishment than Elihu Root, a distinguished New York corporate lawyer before becoming secretary of war and secretary of state under Teddy Roosevelt. Root in 1894 described corporate influence as "the constantly growing evil in our political affairs, which has, in my judgment, done more to shake the confidence of the plain people of small means in our political institutions, than any other practice which has ever obtained since the foundation of our government."[44] The very non-establishment muckraker Ray Baker concurred, and wrote in 1906, "Men were questioning the fundamentals of democracy, inquiring whether we truly had self-government in America, or whether it had been corrupted by selfish interests."[45] As the nineteenth century closed, corruption-fighting President Grover Cleveland warned: "Corporations, which should be the carefully restrained creatures of the law and the servants of the people, are fast becoming the people's masters."[46]

At the end of the nineteenth century, however, while corporate power had met politicians smart enough to fear it, it had not yet met the force that could tame it, and meaningful restraint of the great railroads, monopolies, and other industrial powers was far from the order of the day. As legal historian Adam Winkler relates, it took scandals for the public to understand the true extent of corporate meddling in politics, such as a headline-grabbing insurance scandal that exposed corporate executives using policyholder funds to throw extravagant parties in New York. The investigation that followed showed life insurance companies not only abusing corporate funds but directly contributing to candidates running for office. The investigation pulled back the curtain on corporate political power for all to see.[47]

Corporations back then corrupted politics because they could, and because corrupting our politics brought them such lavish financial rewards. Indeed, it was in this era that President William McKinley's political operative Mark Hanna famously quipped, "There are two things that are important in politics. The first is money, and I can not remember what the other one is."[48] The big corporations were gushers of money. With no natural limit on the corporate effort to corrupt, American citizens had to push back, and they did. The shaken confidence of what Root called the "plain people of small means" moved the country to action.[49] And what Root memorably described as "the economic capture of representative government" brought the emergence, at the turn of the century, of the Progressive movement.[50]

The 1896 presidential race may have been the straw that broke the back of public tolerance for corporate corruption. Democrat William

Jennings Bryan had run as a reformer, "railing against railroads, big banks, the gold standard, and the concentration of economic and political power."[51] Yet he stood no real chance against his opponent, Republican William McKinley, the candidate of the wealthy whose famed political strategist, Mark Hanna, actually assessed banks at 0.25 percent of their capital to directly fund McKinley's campaign.[52] The subsequent influence of these banks in the McKinley administration was unavoidable; after all, they had paid for the campaign.

The president who carried on the fight to contain corporate political power with the greatest gusto and effect was McKinley's vice president and (after McKinley's assassination) his successor: the indomitable Teddy Roosevelt. To Roosevelt, Jefferson's concern about a "trial of strength" between corporate and government power was at hand: "the great special business interests," he said in his famous 1910 "New Nationalism" speech, "too often control and corrupt the men and methods of government for their own profit."[53] Roosevelt saw the plain difference between corporate economic activity and corporate political activity: "The Constitution guarantees protection of property, and we must make that promise good. But it does not give the right of suffrage to any corporation."[54]

To Roosevelt, the very survival of our democracy depended on whether power was held by the people or by the special interests. He wrote in a 1911 essay: "The existence of this Nation has no real significance . . . unless it means the rule of the people. . . . Unless this is in very truth a government of, by, and for the people, then both historically and in world interest our National existence loses most of its point."[55]

What he called a "matter of necessity" brought out Teddy Roosevelt's competitive spirit. Roosevelt's enemies were big, but this did not confound him; as he said in a 1912 speech, "It is imperative to exercise over big business a control and supervision which is unnecessary as regards small business. . . . a wicked big interest is necessarily more dangerous to the community than a wicked little interest."[56] As put at the time by a staffer at the muckraking *McClure's Magazine*, taking on the big corporations and titans of industry who controlled them was "a challenge such as his nature would never ignore."[57]

In this contest for power, Roosevelt made subordination of business to government a conservative cause: "The true friend of property, the true conservative, is he who insists that property shall be the servant and not the master of the commonwealth. . . . The citizens of the United States must effectively control the mighty commercial forces which they themselves have called into being."[58]

Roosevelt's solution to the corrupting influence of corporate money in elections was legislative. Focusing on "a law prohibiting all corporations from contributing to the campaign expenses of any party," Roosevelt decreed in his 1906 State of the Union address: "Let individuals contribute as they desire; but let us prohibit in effective fashion all corporations from making contributions for any political purpose, directly or indirectly."[59] With that challenge, the battle over what was to be called the Tillman Act was joined.

In a 2016 speech at the Brookings Institution, Trevor Potter, former chairman of the Federal Election Commission, called the Tillman Act "one of the first major laws geared toward reducing the corrupting influence of big money on American politics." Describing the act's impetus, Potter noted, "More and more citizens felt that government had become a tool of campaign contributors rather than responsive to average voters. State legislatures and Congress were seen as 'in the pockets' of economic interests who perverted legislation to serve private purposes rather than the public good."[60]

In opposing the Tillman Act, early twentieth-century corporate forces tried to wrap themselves in the flag of freedom and the mantle of the Constitution. Roosevelt wasn't buying it. His position foreshadowed that of his cousin FDR, who some years later referred to "the economic royalists" who "complain that we seek to overthrow the institutions of America." In his acceptance speech for renomination for the presidency in 1936, FDR wrote: "What they really complain of is that we seek to take away their power. Our allegiance to American institutions requires the overthrow of this kind of power. In vain they seek to hide behind the flag and the Constitution. In their blindness they forget what the flag and the Constitution stand for. Now, as always, they stand for democracy, not tyranny; for freedom, not subjection; and against a dictatorship by mob rule and the over-privileged alike."[61]

In the battle between big corporations and government, Teddy

Roosevelt was a government man. As he said in his Annual Message to Congress in 1907, "The fortunes amassed through corporate organization are now so large, and vest such power in those that wield them, as to make it a matter of necessity to give to the sovereign—that is, to the Government, which represents the people as a whole—some effective power of supervision over their corporate use. In order to insure a healthy social and industrial life, every big corporation should be held responsible by, and be accountable to, some sovereign strong enough to control its conduct."[62]

Corporations were deeply entrenched in America's elections at the time of the Tillman Act (even Theodore Roosevelt's campaign took corporate contributions in 1904). But when Roosevelt set his sights on getting corporate money out of politics, he homed in and fought hard. And with the tools of the presidency and its bully pulpit at his disposal, he won.

The evil of corporate money in political elections was so apparent in that era that the Senate committee working on the Tillman Act deemed it unnecessary to make an expansive legislative record in support of the law—it was too obvious. They had seen too much corruption up close. The Senate report on the bill simply stated: "The evils of the use of [corporate] money in connection with political elections are so generally recognized that the committee deems it unnecessary to make any argument in favor of the general purpose of this measure. It is in the interest of good government and calculated to promote purity in the selection of public officials."[63]

It is a noteworthy sidebar that the final version of the Tillman Act, passed in 1907, did not require proof of corrupt intent by the corporation. Corporate corruption of politics was so self-evident that the mere contribution of corporate funds to politicians sufficed to establish "corruption," as the term was used in the Act.[64] When Roosevelt said, "Corporate expenditures for political purposes . . . have supplied one of the principal sources of corruption in our political affairs," the bill he championed proved that he did not mean corporate political spending was *potentially* corrupting.[65] Corporate political spending *was* corruption, plain and simple (a view that contrasts with that of the five Supreme Court justices who gave us the *Citizens United* decision a century later).

Various loopholes have come and gone since, but the principle embodied in the Tillman Act more than a hundred years ago—that inanimate business corporations are not free to spend corporate dollars to influence our campaigns for elected office—has long been an admirable and indispensable cornerstone of our political system.

CHAPTER THREE

Where We Are Now

MORE THAN A CENTURY AGO, FOLLOWING A BRUISING battle, Theodore Roosevelt and the United States Congress succeeded in taming the beast of corporate political power. With the Tillman Act in place, corporations were prohibited from contributing to federal elections and, consequently, our democracy was protected from this form of corrupting corporate influence.

The following decades saw laws enacted to target various problems in the broader campaign finance system: the 1925 Federal Corrupt Practices Act increased disclosure requirements and limits on spending; the 1939 Hatch Act regulated primary elections, protected the civil service from political demands, and established contribution and spending limits for Congressional elections; and the 1947 Taft-Hartley Act extended the Tillman Act by banning both corporations and unions from contributing to or spending on federal elections.[1] However, while the ban on corporate election spending held, the broader system was inadequate. According to the Federal Election Commission's own account, prior to the 1970s "the campaign finance provisions of all of these laws were largely ignored . . . because none provided an institutional framework to administer their provisions effectively."[2] It wasn't until the Watergate break-in and election financing scandals reached the front page that a comprehensive system was put in place.

The discovery of five burglars breaking into Democratic campaign headquarters, funded with money contributed to Nixon's reelection campaign (the Committee to Re-Elect the President, with its apt acronym CREEP), led to the Federal Elections Campaign Act of 1971 and its subsequent amendments. Together, these provisions formed the basis of our modern campaign finance system. FECA, as it is known, limited both contributions and expenditures in federal campaigns, required significant disclosure, and established the Federal Election Commission (FEC), among other things.[3]

That's not to say that corporate power ran amok during the first three-quarters of the twentieth century. The ban on corporate campaign contributions from the Tillman Act held, and corporate political power on the lobbying side was just a shadow of what we see today. In his book *The Business of America Is Lobbying*, Lee Drutman notes that before the 1970s relatively few companies even had their own Washington lobbyists, and corporate lobbying was "sparse and mostly defensive"[4]—that is, a company would come in to fight a particular bill here or there. Lobbying was not yet seen as a strategic investment, a way for corporations to increase profits by political control. Lewis Powell, later to become a Supreme Court justice, summed the situation up in 1971, the same year FECA was passed, observing, "As every business executive knows, few elements of American society today have as little influence in government as the American businessman."[5]

But just a few years later, in 1978, an FEC advisory opinion created a loophole that allowed the political parties to accept much larger contributions in what became known as "soft money," which could pay for "issue ads" around election time and, in turn, access to grateful politicians. (An issue ad is like an attack ad, except the punch line is not "Vote for Congressman Snooks's opponent" but "Call Congressman Snooks and ask him why he hates America and wants to kill American jobs.") As the legendary Washington, D.C., correspondent Elizabeth Drew describes the impact of the loophole: "In effect, the parties act[ed] as laundries for money that [wasn't] supposed to be used in federal elections."[6]

The explosion of soft money spurred the McCain-Feingold reform efforts of the late 1990s, which were doggedly opposed by incumbents in both parties and both houses of Congress. As Drew writes of Senator John McCain, "His Senate colleagues ripped into him because he had accurately called the current system corrupt."[7] After a fierce and prolonged legislative battle, the reform effort prevailed, and the Bipartisan Campaign Reform Act of 2002 (BCRA, often known as the

McCain-Feingold Act) became law, significantly limiting soft money contributions and, among other things, prohibiting corporate-funded campaign commercials within thirty days of a presidential primary. McCain said at the time that he hoped the reforms would help "change the public's widespread belief that politicians have no greater purpose than our own reelection. And to that end, [that] we will respond disproportionately to the needs of those interests that can best finance our ambition, even if those interests conflict with the public interest."[8]

With the various provisions of these two acts (1971's FECA and 2002's BCRA), Congress took many steps toward reestablishing the public's trust in our democracy as representing the interests of the people, not whichever corporation or wealthy donor could fund a winning campaign. However, many of the restrictions Congress built up in this area were torn down by a conservative, business-friendly Supreme Court, based on a premise that corporate money is speech under the First Amendment. How this came to pass, we will consider in Chapter Five. For now, it suffices to know that this was a novel theory, which today remains controversial.

Back and forth it went. Legislators in Congress approached the problem at the practical level and tried to catch up to and regulate both contributions and outside spending in support of campaigns; the Supreme Court would then strike or water down those limits. As part of this decades-old dance, in 2008 a narrow statutory provision came before the Supreme Court—the McCain-Feingold ban on corporate-funded campaign commercials within thirty days of a presidential primary. As Chapter Seven describes in detail, the Court struck down this ban in the *Citizens United* decision of 2010 and did away with the entire ban on corporate spending in place since Teddy Roosevelt's Tillman Act.

Consequently, our democracy is today once again darkened by the shadow of corporate political influence, vulnerable to its grip not only in our elections but throughout the functioning of our government as well. In the recurring "trial of strength" between corporate power and government, corporate power has been given devastating new political artillery.

The power of modern multinational corporations to wield that artillery has grown dramatically as the wealth of mega-corporations has grown. Their scale is massive. In his book *Power, Inc.*, about these massive multinational corporations, David Rothkopf reports that "the total number of people dependent on these multinationals may have been between one and two billion in 2000, a third of the world's population."[9] And the biggest corporations today are truly enormous. Rothkopf estimates that just the top three hundred companies "control over a quarter of the earth's productive capacity."[10] Walmart alone has more than two million employees.

According to Rothkopf, the financial world's largest asset manager, BlackRock, "controls assets worth almost as much as the total currency reserves of the number-one and number-two countries, China and Japan, combined. BlackRock has $3.3 trillion under management; China and Japan's combined reserves are $3.6 trillion. BlackRock controls twenty-five times the assets that the United States has in its national currency reserves."[11] The number of countries in the world that hold hard currency reserves worth over $100 billion is twenty; by Rothkopf's accounting, "the top 125 asset managers each control the same amount."[12]

Consider a comparison of the annual revenue of the largest corporations in the world to the gross domestic product (GDP) of sovereign countries—countries with armies and currencies of their own.[13]

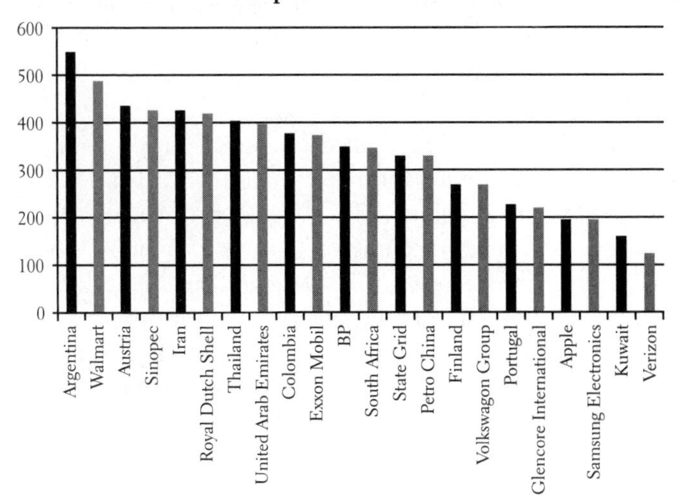

GDP/revenue in billions US$ for 2014

(Chart adapted from Worldbank.org and Corporationsandhealth.org)

Rothkopf's comparisons between Sweden and ExxonMobil are instructive: Sweden's 2009 GDP was $406 billion versus Exxon's 2009 sales of $442 billion, and Exxon's 2006 budgeted expenditures were more than $400 billion versus Sweden's of less than one-third that amount.[14] Rothkopf goes on to note that Sweden had a vote at the Kyoto Protocol meeting on climate change, but that "ExxonMobil, as it turned out, had a veto."[15]

As I have said, there is nothing inherently wrong with economic activity by corporations, even very large corporations. Corporate money dominating our politics is another thing altogether. That is where the democratic crisis lies, and that is the crisis sparked by *Citizens United*. Specifically, corporations can now spend unlimited general treasury funds to support or oppose a candidate (as long as the money doesn't go to the campaign directly). Corporations can also give unlimited amounts to super PACs (technically "independent expenditure-only committees"), and these groups can spend unlimited sums to overtly advocate for or against political candidates, as long as their spending is not "coordinated" with that of the candidates they benefit. Corporations can also give unlimited amounts to 501(c)(4) nonprofits, which (unlike super PACs) do not have to disclose their donors; the 501(c)(4) then spends that corporate "dark money" on political activity, such as political advertisements during election season. In sum, *Citizens United* gave corporations a menu of avenues of influence over who is elected in America.

The result has been staggering. In the 2012 election cycle, super PACs and other nonprofit organizations unleashed by *Citizens United* spent upward of $840 million.[16] The nonpartisan Center for Responsive Politics estimated that 69 percent of this spending was by conservative groups, 28 percent by liberal groups, and the remainder by other organizations.[17] In 2012, Republican presidential nominee Mitt Romney reaped the greatest benefit of the new flow of cash: of the $450 million in outside spending dedicated to the presidential candidates, Romney received approximately $350 million, while President Barack Obama received an estimated $100 million.[18]

Four years later, the numbers continue to rise. As of March 7, 2016, more than two thousand groups organized as super PACs reported total receipts of over $540 million and total independent expenditures of over $240 million in the 2016 cycle. The Koch brothers—through their own billions, through Koch Industries, and through a network of front groups they fund—are probably the most active corporate meddlers in our politics today. Their network alone initially pledged to spend $889 million in the 2016 presidential election.[19] Super PACs supporting presidential candidates banked more than $250 million just through June 30, 2015 (about seventeen times more than at that point in the 2012 cycle).[20] And our politics is awash with "dark money" from anonymous donors (dark to us, of course; you can bet the candidates know).

The impact of super PACs has been truly seismic for our democracy. For example, Americans for Prosperity, a Koch brothers venture, disclosed election spending of $6.4 million to the Federal Election Commission for the 2014 midterm elections.[21] But that group's own officials have boasted that they in fact intended to spend as much as $125 million—an enormous and unprecedented amount to be spent in just one election by just one group.[22] Taken together, Americans for Prosperity and the Kochs' other major nonprofit, Freedom Partners, ultimately spent over $220 million in 2014.[23] Koch Industries' reported lobbying expenditure for that year was $13.7 million, a huge number but nothing like the elections expenditure of its front groups.[24] Their 2014 election spending was just an opening bid. The Koch network initially announced a plan to raise and spend $889 million (and then adjusted it to $750 million) for the 2016 elections.[25] Their 2015 spending was right on track: In January 2016, the *New York Times* reported that the Koch network had spent $400 million in 2015.[26]

The Koch brothers' sophisticated electioneering capacity now rivals or exceeds that of the Republican National Committee.[27] As one scholarly article concludes, "a network of conservative mega-donors (led by the Koch brothers) has created a shadow GOP."[28] Yes, a few very wealthy individuals in the fossil-fuel business—huge polluters—are now such big players in our politics that they rival our national political parties. Their extravagant spending has bought the Koch brothers and their corporate empire a vast political network, with platoons of employees in critical swing states, with voter databases cross-linked to your consumer data, with advertising and media buying specialists, with an intelligence-gathering operation staffed by former CIA operatives[29]—and with no limit on what they can spend. *Politico* has reported former Republican National Committee chair Michael Steele conceding that "the Koch network and other deep-pocketed outside groups have found legal ways to do most of the other things that were once the party's sole province."[30] And some new things—I'm not aware of political parties using former intelligence personnel to do their spook work against political adversaries. Unlimited money can do unlimited things.

Since *Citizens United* the large fossil-fuel polluters and their network of interests have become among the biggest spenders, relying heavily on undisclosed, untraceable dark money. According to the Center for American Progress, oil, gas, and coal companies and electric utilities alone reported *directly* spending more than $84 million on the 2014 elections—and that's just what they report.[31] Super PACs are required to disclose their donors; by contrast, the industry's undisclosed spending on so-called issue ads through groups that are not required to disclose their donors, and for "grassroots organizing," which is not subject to any reporting at all, is estimated to be in the hundreds of millions of dollars.[32] Money talks, and in politics it talks plenty loud: $100 million has a lot to say. Asked about raising hundreds of millions of dollars for conservative, corporatist causes, Charles Koch himself said, "I expect something in return."[33]

Remember that this new corporate spending on elections rides on top of all the corporate lobbying special interests do in Washington, D.C. As described by political scientist Lee Drutman in a 2015 article in *The Atlantic*, corporations spent $2.6 billion a year sending lobbyists to Washington to push their agendas in the halls of Congress; some corporations have more than a hundred lobbyists *each*. Members of Congress get plenty of attention. According to Zephyr Teachout, "private interests spent about $12.5 million on lobbying in 2012 for every member of Congress."[34] Corporate interests are by far the most powerful: "For every dollar spent on lobbying by labor unions and public interest groups together, large corporations and their associations now spend $34. Of the 100 organizations that spend the most on lobbying, 95 consistently represent business."[35] It's a blowout.

The focus of this book is not on traditional, reported lobbying so much as on the new, less well-known, and secret means of influence. Yet corporate lobbying continues to be an enormous and enormously corrosive force, as you would imagine of any force that dwarfs all opposition by a ratio of more than thirty to one. The bipartisan campaign finance group ReFormers Caucus reports that the lobbying enterprise in 1960 occupied the effort of 3,414 registered lobbyists who spent just over $30 million lobbying Congress. By 2014 the number of lobbyists had swollen to 11,781 and their lobbying expenditures for Congress had exploded more than a hundredfold, to $3.23 billion.[36]

Administrative agencies get lots of attention from lobbyists too. Long-standing corporate lobbying efforts continue to turn watchdogs into lapdogs in a practice known as "regulatory capture" that has gone on for as long as there have been regulatory agencies to capture.

And the price of political access is going up, as money floods the system. ReFormers reports that the average cost of winning a Senate seat from 1986 to 2012 grew more than threefold to $10.4 million, and a House seat more than fourfold to $1.6 million (the truly contested races, of course, cost far more).[37] Before *Citizens United*, individuals could give a maximum of $30,400 to a national party.[38] In 2016, according to the *New York Times*, "top-tier Republican donors will pay $1.34 million per couple for the privilege of being treated as party insiders, while the Democratic Party will charge about $1.6 million."[39] The higher the price of admission, the more selective the group admitted, and the more selective the group, the more likely they are to be either big corporations or very high-income people who reflect the views of the corporate structure that provided them their vast personal wealth. One percent of the 1 percent, fewer than 32,000 people, contributed $1.18 billion in political contributions during the 2014 elections.[40] By the end of 2015, the biggest one hundred political donors had spent more to influence politics in the 2016 election than the two million smallest donors combined.[41] As the *Times* concludes, "More big money can only leave less hope for voters concerned that the richest donors are buying ever more influence over politicians, with favoritism and corruption an inevitable result."[42]

Although America is home to about 120 million families, nearly half of all the money contributed through the spring of 2016 in the 2016 presidential contest came from just 150 families, most of them with corporate connections; and most contributed secretly, through super PACs and 501(c)(4)s.[43] The *Washington Post* has chronicled our politics for 140 years; its editorial board recently warned that "campaign finance in the United States has . . . fallen into an era dominated by 'dark money,' with donors hiding in the shadows and hundreds of millions of dollars in contributions flowing through politics without a trace of who gave it or why."[44] While our new status quo of unlimited dark money may work to benefit some politicians for some period of time, in the long run it will hurt all Americans, regardless of party. Unlimited money is not a force that anyone can hope to control, and unlimited secret money is even more dangerous.

If money is power, then big spenders hold the keys to the kingdom. And if that weren't bad enough, the American people often don't even know who the new kingmakers are. The game has changed. Not long ago, campaigns were waged by candidates and parties fighting over ideas. If you saw an ad, at least you knew who'd put it on the air. Campaigns are now waged by shadowy political attack groups posing as social welfare organizations, run by political operatives, and fueled by millions of undisclosed dollars from secret special interests. When these secret special interests ramp up their shouting in our elections this way, it inevitably drowns out the voices of regular individual Americans.

This can matter a lot. Special interests don't much need the pillars of a strong middle class, such as Medicare, Social Security, and Pell Grants. Big corporations don't get sick and need a doctor's care. Big corporations don't retire. Big corporations don't have to educate their kids. It would be in their financial interest to see that spending moved elsewhere—say, to offset corporate income taxes.

These government programs help a lot of families to have far better lives and have paved the way for generations to achieve the American dream. But they have always been the target of special interests with different, corporate, priorities. If you like Medicare, Social Security, and Pell Grants, and if you want to be heard in their defense, then having your voice drowned out by an anonymous billionaire or corporate CEO at election time is a lot more than some abstract exercise in political science. And anonymity opens up attacks on such popular programs by forces that don't want their fingerprints on such attacks but will go for it if masked.

Another measure of growing corporate political influence may be the declining corporate share of America's tax revenues. When I was born, America's corporations, through income and excise taxes, were contributing nearly half of the nation's revenue, with individual income tax and payroll tax making up the other half.[45] That has gradually shifted, as corporate taxes have produced steadily lower revenues. By 2013, the individual income tax and payroll tax together provided over 80 percent of the nation's revenue.[46] America's revenue is more and more being supplied by individuals, and less and less by corporations. (Of course, corporations contribute to payroll taxes, but many economists say that contribution comes out of salary the company otherwise would have paid, so ultimately it's still on the individual either way.) When Congress has the chance to fix this, it doesn't. The *New York Times* pointed out in an August 30, 2016, editorial that "Congress . . . sat idly by as American corporations have indulged in increasingly intricate forms of tax avoidance made possible by the interplay of an outmoded corporate tax code and modern globalized finance."[47] We could have done something, but that would have stopped the corporate tax-avoidance payday, and politicians bought and paid for with corporate money are not about to start reforming the corporate tax code.

This increasing corporate political power is increasingly anonymous. In 2012, at least two-thirds of election ad spending through July from groups other than candidates or parties came from secretive corporations and billionaires whose names and agendas the voters may never know.[48] The *Washington Post* has reported that at least 31 percent of all independent spending in the 2014 elections—which were the most expensive midterm elections in our history—came from groups that are not required to disclose their donors. And this does not even include so-called issue ads, whose donors are also not disclosed.[49] By the end of 2015, dark-money spending was up more than 5,000 percent just since 2004, according to ReFormers.[50]

In 2010, Karl Rove was one of the first to set up a dark-money group, obliquely called Crossroads GPS. One measure of the explosion in such dark-money spending is a study by the Wesleyan Media Project and the Center for Responsive Politics, examining the actual number of political advertisements run with dark-money.[51] Presidential-year dark-money ads jumped from fewer than 160,000 in 2008 to over 380,000 in 2012. Off-year dark-money advertisements jumped from around 15,000 in 2006 to well over 100,000 ads in 2010, to over 200,000 ads in 2014. Karl Rove's Crossroads GPS aired the most dark-money ads, exceeding even the heavyweight business lobby, the U.S. Chamber of Commerce. The Center for Responsive Politics' investigator said, "the lack of oversight of these groups . . . has allowed nonprofit groups to be a much more tantalizing vehicle for people who want to hide their political spending."[52] When the top two ad-runners are Karl Rove and the U.S. Chamber, you can guess who those "people" are.

As the *New York Times* wrote in a 2012 editorial, "Corporations love the secrecy provided by Mr. Rove's group because it protects them from scrutiny by nosy shareholders and consumers."[53] They want a big influence on elections but without leaving any tracks. An unnamed corporate lobbyist confirmed to *Politico* in 2016 that "nondisclosure is always preferred" by corporate donors.[54]

Why is it preferred? Because it makes it so much harder for the public, the press, and law enforcement to connect the dots—to track down the corrupting influence of the money these corporations spend in elections. As legal scholar Burt Neuborne has written, "Lobbyists treat elected officials as wholly owned subsidiaries, and rivers of money flowing from secret sources have turned our elections into silent auctions."[55] We often don't even know who the winning bidder is, thanks to secrecy.

As if all this weren't enough, the use of corporate "shields," such as limited liability companies, to further conceal donors' identities from the public is exploding. Super PACs must disclose their donors to the FEC, but if the donor is a limited liability company, the actual people behind the company may legally remain unknown. In 2015, the *Wall Street Journal* reported, "more than 200 limited liability companies . . . donated almost $11 million to super PACs backing six presidential candidates."[56]

The special interests putting in their bids have big motives to spend this kind of big money. If those motives were good for America and would be welcomed and accepted by the average American voter, the big donors wouldn't need to keep them secret. We need to ask ourselves: What are they hiding? Why do they demand secrecy? Whatever the answer, one thing is clear: Americans who worry that Washington is overly beholden to special interests need to be more concerned than ever.

With no identity, there is no accountability; and with no accountability, there is no limit to what people will say. One restraint on the vitriol and the filth that is often part of American political debate is that candidates have to stand by their ads. If someone says something awful, if he engages in relentless negative attacks, voters may charge him a price for that. They may say, "Wow, he's not very nice. I'm not voting for him." That is the reason political ads are required to have that tagline at the end, "I'm Congressman Snooks and I approved this message." Now the tagline is likely to be, "This message approved by Americans for Puppies and Prosperity." Who the hell is that? No one knows. A little inquiry, and you might get a lawyer's name. Restraint, of course, disappears when the name behind the ad is just a sham entity, a phony, a shell. Joe Hagan memorably described the result in a *New York Magazine* article as a "tsunami of slime."[57]

How has this tsunami of slime worked out? Not well for an informed American public. An April 2012 study found that about 70 percent of ads up to that date in the 2012 election cycle were negative, up from 9 percent of ads in that time period in 2008.[58] If you think you're seeing more negative advertising after *Citizens United* than you used to see, it's because you are. By a lot. It's not that we are worse people; to quote renowned political analyst E.J. Dionne, "structural changes in our politics are making campaigns more mean and personal."[59] Of course it's easier to throw slime from behind a mask. As Mike Huckabee has said, the dark money unleashed by *Citizens United* is "killing any sense of civility in politics because of the cheap shots that can be made from the trees by snipers that you can never identify."[60]

It's also easier to lie. And lying has exploded. A study by the Annenberg Public Policy Center looked at the four top-spending political 501(c)(4) organizations—which don't have to disclose their donors—over a six-month period in 2012. It turns out that an estimated 85 percent of their election spending went to ads that the Annenberg Center determined to contain deceptions.[61] So not only are 70 percent of the ads out there negative, but at least during parts of the election cycle, the big spenders were putting 85 percent of their money toward deceptive advertising.

That is what five corporate-friendly justices on the Supreme Court have wrought: campaign practice since *Citizens United* is a dark web of unknown spending by unknown groups with unknown funding sources, with who knows what conversations happening in secret.

The "transparency" the five justices foresaw was supposed to have happened when people saw the corporate-funded ads on TV and could identify the interest behind the spending: "We're ExxonMobil and we approved this message." But such clear identification of the real money behind those ads never occurs. Unfortunately, the justices built in no safety checks to ensure that there would in fact be the transparency they assumed would exist (one must ask how much they really cared), and they have taken no interest since the decision in correcting their error when the transparency they foresaw did not show up. They completely misunderstood how the regulatory regime they left standing would operate (or they did not care, having achieved their objective).

A sense of what this secrecy may do in real life comes readily to anyone who has ever investigated or prosecuted public corruption (none of the five *Citizens United* justices ever had) or who has ever run for elective office (none of the justices on the Court ever had—indeed, this is the first Supreme Court in American history that has no former elected official among the justices).[62] The special-interest lobbyist tells a fellow political operative to let the congressman's campaign manager know that if the congressman doesn't "get right" on issue X, they're in against him, big-time. The congressman will never see it coming, because the ads will be from Americans for Puppies and Prosperity or some other bogus front group, and the money will have been laundered through DonorsTrust or a similar identity-laundering organization (more on them later) or simply hidden behind shell corporations and lawyers. It will just be *POW! No fingerprints.*

What does the sudden, anonymous political attack look like in practice? On the very morning I was presenting the DISCLOSE Act—my bill to ban dark-money contributions—on the Senate floor in 2012, the *New York Times* ran an article describing an organization called the Commission on Hope, Growth and Opportunity. (In this upside-down environment, you know an organization with a smarmy name like that has to be bad.) Funded with "a single $4 million donation from an anonymous benefactor," the *Times* reported, "the group kicked off a multimillion-dollar campaign against 11 Democratic candidates, declining to report any of its political spending to the Federal Election Commission, maintaining to the IRS that it did not do any political spending at all, and failing to register as a political committee required to disclose the names of its donors. Then, faced with multiple election commission and IRS complaints, the group went out of business."[63] Done and gone. No fingerprints. The group's registered lawyer told an inquiring reporter from NPR, "You're not going to get anything out of me, so let's just end this right now."[64] Citizens for Responsibility and Ethics called this episode "the political equivalent of a hit and run."[65] Another entity, ironically named the Government Integrity Fund, popped up and spent more than $5 million in the 2012 election, mostly against my Senate colleague Sherrod Brown. Its attorney refused to name its donors, citing attorney-client privilege. They can strike out of nowhere, without limits and anonymously.[66] *Citizens United* is inherently corrupting because it empowers that threat.

And the power of the *threat* to spend money is the second major problem with this sort of secrecy. We will get more into this in Chapter Seven, where we take a close look at *Citizens United*. For now, it is enough to realize one very obvious real-life fact: what you allow big corporate or billionaire spenders to do, you also allow them to threaten or promise to do. If you're allowed to drop a $5 million campaign attack into a congressional race, you can just as easily threaten or promise to drop a $5 million campaign attack into a congressional race. And if the threat works, you save the $5 million. Anyone with an ounce of political common sense should have foreseen the problem of secret threats and promises, which remains a gaping hole in the logic of *Citizens United*. But more on that later.

In the early stages of the 2016 Republican presidential primary, the new, creepy vehicles of corporate and billionaire funding—the "affiliated" super PAC and nonprofit 501(c)(4) entities—have exploded. (Hillary Clinton had her own super PAC, so the sins are bipartisan, but in the 2016 election, the primary action was mostly on the Republican side.) In September 2015 the *New York Times* reported: "A super PAC backing Jeb Bush will spend $37 million on ads through February."[67] New Hampshire alone was slated for $22 million of that spending. Jeb Bush was not the only one; as the *Times* reported, "Rival super PACs and allied groups are also set to run TV ads primarily in early voting states for Gov. Chris Christie of New Jersey ($11.4 million), Senator Marco Rubio of Florida ($15 million) and Gov. Bobby Jindal of Louisiana ($5 million)."[68] That's nearly $70 million just for these candidates, just in that period. The total, according to the *Times*, is $106 million, of which "super PACs and other outside groups account for 82 percent."[69] And this was just the warm-up. The article continues: "TV spending in the 2016 elections is projected to reach $4.4 billion."[70]

Where does all this come from? As Eric Lichtblau reported in the *Times* in October 2015, "This rise of the 'super PAC,' which can raise unlimited donations from individuals and corporations, has put a premium on billionaire donors who can give once-unimaginable sums to support their preferred candidates."[71] Super PAC money comes not only from corporations but also from billionaires who have amassed their fortunes through the corporate form, such as Maurice "Hank" Greenberg, the former chairman and CEO of AIG, the largest life insurance corporation in the world, who gave $10 million to Jeb Bush's PAC.[72]

It's a flood of big money. An Associated Press investigation in the summer of 2015 found that "nearly 60 donations of a million dollars or more accounted for about a third of the more than $380 million brought in so far for the 2016 presidential election."[73] By August of 2015, seven donors who each gave $1 million or more made up nearly half of the funding for Hillary Clinton's Priorities USA Action super PAC.[74] Contributions of $100,000 or more made up about half of all donations to all the candidates and to their super PACs.[75] To ordinary citizens $100,000 is a huge amount; it's even a lot to candidates. But it's chump change to the big donors.

Citizens United, of course, said this would all be fine because it would all be "independent" of the candidates (whatever that meant).[76] But even if that made sense, it's just not true. As Trevor Potter, former Republican chairman of the Federal Election Commission, has said, "The theory is that super PACs are independent groups, so it's not corrupting for them to take large sums of money. Reality is that they are now joined at the hip with the candidate."[77] Indeed, they are often "affiliated" with a particular candidate.

Let's start with Jeb Bush, who began his campaign with a long, phony "pre-campaign" period. (Why do I say phony? During this time he told Mitt Romney he was "all in" on the presidential race.[78]) Not formally declaring allowed Bush to raise more than $100 million for his own super PAC without violating the rule against super PACs "coordinating" with campaigns—there was no campaign yet to coordinate with! Candidates including Jeb Bush, Carly Fiorina, and John Kasich shot film for their super PACs before they formally declared, allowing them to raise the money to film and air political ads without respect for funding limits, because they were not yet declared candidates under the election laws—a dodge if there ever was one.[79] Really? Jeb Bush wasn't sure whether he was running? Please.

Then he declared. But even after declaring, Bush could still show up for his super PAC events. The *Wall Street Journal* reports that candidates Jeb Bush, Scott Walker, Chris Christie, and Marco Rubio "all attended events organized by their affiliated super PACs after declaring their candidacy."[80] In the case of Jeb Bush, the *Journal* reports, "Mr. Bush's super PAC fundraisers are often scheduled immediately after campaign receptions at nearby homes or in different rooms in the same hotel."[81] And as is true with all of the "affiliated" super PACs, Jeb Bush's "affiliated" super PAC was specific to one candidate only: Jeb Bush. Some independence. (When did "affiliation" become "independence" anyway? That doesn't even pass the dictionary test.)

Carly Fiorina's campaign was called Carly for President; her super PAC was called CARLY for America. CARLY for America ran and paid for campaign events where Carly Fiorina showed up running for president.[82] The "biggest donor by far" to the Carly Fiorina super PAC, according to Eric Lichtblau in the *New York Times*, was a reclusive California billionaire who at one point had contributed about half of her super PAC's money.[83]

As she campaigned through South Carolina, the *New York Times* reported, Fiorina "traveled with a few campaign aides who squeezed into a white sport utility vehicle, while a team of at least seven people from the super PAC swooped in, often hours ahead, at each stop to stage her backdrops, set up sign-up tables and arrange stacks of posters and placards." Said Fiorina, "We are not coordinating."[84] One has to wonder what coordinating would look like.

Oh, and by the way, there's a Federal Election Commission regulation that prohibits using the candidate's name in the super PAC's name. No problem. "CARLY" in CARLY for America actually means "Conservative, Authentic, Responsive Leadership for You," they say.[85] (Never mind that this makes the super PAC's actual name "Conservative, Authentic, Responsive Leadership for You for America.")

How about Marco Rubio? He went beyond even that. According to reports from the Associated Press, "the Florida senator benefit[ted] in unprecedented ways from a non-profit group funded by anonymous donors."[86] As of October 2015, "every pro-Rubio television commercial so far in the early primary states of Iowa, New Hampshire and South Carolina has been paid for not by his campaign or even by a super PAC that identifies its donors, but instead by a nonprofit called Conservative Solutions Project."[87]

What Marco Rubio *said* at a town hall meeting to a voter who asked about the rise of money in politics is: "Full disclosure and sunlight into all these expenditures is critical."[88] He said it is important that "you know who's behind the money and how much they're giving."[89] What Marco Rubio *did* in his campaign for president, according to the *New York Times*, as of October 2015, was to have "all the television advertisements aired in support of the Florida senator so far this year—$5.5 million worth . . . [flow] through a political nonprofit group called the Conservative Solutions Project . . . which has raised more than $18 million [and] will never be required to disclose anything about its donors."[90] At least we know the identity of the auto dealer who gave $5 million to Rubio's super PAC. We'll never know who gave the $18 million to the Conservative Solutions Project.

Of course, the nonprofit claimed to be independent. It said it was "created . . . to help the conservative movement."[91] In fact, as the *New York Times* reported, "the group's commercials all focus on Mr. Rubio. The senator's picture is prominently displayed on its website, and a video featuring Mr. Rubio speaking is the first thing shown to the site's visitors."[92] As the *Times* went on to document, the nonprofit shared its name with the Rubio super PAC, Conservative Solutions PAC; it was run by a political operative from Rubio's Senate campaign; and the super PAC and the nonprofit used the same fundraiser. The pro-Rubio nonprofit did not even seek the approval of the Internal Revenue Service, "which means its political activities will not face the possibility of agency review"—and potential denial by the agency as a phony nonprofit—"until after the group files its next tax return, probably long after the Republican primary season is over."[93]

This combination of big money, anonymity, and connections to the candidate, taken together, powers the "tsunami of slime" Americans see in our elections. Americans know this is new, and they are disgusted. Fred Wertheimer, a respected campaign finance reform advocate, said about 2016, "We have never seen an election like this, in which the wealthiest people in America are dominating the financing of the presidential election and as a consequence are creating enormous debts and obligations from the candidates who are receiving this financial support."[94]

I see a real effect on our politics. Money isn't decisive: it can't cure the problems of a candidacy such as Jeb Bush's. But it makes a difference. It is a big advantage to have money. As Trevor Potter said in his 4th of July speech to the Chatauqua Institution in 2016: "Money and power. Power attracts money, and money maintains power. Money and power in Washington have become a closed circle."[95] Money matters.

And two things stand out. One, virtually all the candidates had a billionaire in their pocket. When one candidate told me he was going to run, he said: "Now I'm going to have to find my billionaire." Two, the money is driving the content of campaigns. No Republican will talk about climate change, because of where their money comes from. No Republican will talk about legendary Omaha investor Warren Buffett's plan for fairer taxes on Wall Street, because of where their money comes from. Indeed, as Wall Street money flowed into Marco Rubio's campaign (in the last half of 2015, about over half of his super PAC money came from financial industry donors[96]) he announced he was for Wall Street paying not just lower taxes, but no taxes at all on income they can treat as capital gains.[97] As Fred Wertheimer has said, "Who wins and loses elections is very important, but even more important is the question of what kind of policy results it buys. We have hedge fund managers who put huge amounts into our campaigns; they have the most unjustifiable tax break in our tax system."[98]

This new corporate political effort is not limited to choosing between the candidates the parties produce and driving the candidates to (or away from) a certain agenda. The Koch brothers' political enterprise has begun finding and growing its own political candidates. This is done through a variety of corporate screens, so first meet the players. One is Freedom Partners Chamber of Commerce, which has been described in *Politico* as "the central group in the increasingly powerful network of conservative public policy and political groups helmed by the billionaire brothers."[99] This outfit raised more than $160 million in the run-up to the 2014 elections.[100] We don't know from whom that money came, because this is one of the bogus nonprofits operating under a provision of the tax code known as Section 501(c)(4) that requires no donor disclosure (but also in theory requires the nonprofit to stay out of elections). Another player was called Trees of Liberty, described by the website Conservative Transparency as a "short-lived 501(c)(4) front group funded by the Koch brothers' 'secret bank,' Freedom Partners."[101] A third is called Freedom Partners Action Fund, a "candidate-affiliated" (but not "coordinated"—big difference, right?) super PAC.[102]

In 2013, Joni Ernst was an Iowa state senator with single-digit name recognition around the state. But the Kochs liked her politics as a United States Senate candidate and invited her to their secretive political gathering of wealthy conservative donors that August. A report from *Politico* describes what happened. First, the short-lived Trees of Liberty group popped up and went to work in the Iowa Republican primary.[103] With $400,000 from Freedom Partners Chamber of Commerce, Trees of Liberty began attacking Ernst's Republican primary opponent. Behind the scenes, *Politico* reported, Freedom Partners had what was needed to make Trees of Liberty's attacks effective: a $13 million payroll, nearly $2 million for focus groups, over $1 million for ad production, $1.5 million for messaging experts, and $1.4 million for a direct mail firm.[104] (This was a Koch brothers operation, so it is no surprise that the specific attack on Ernst's opponent slammed him for having supported a restriction on carbon emissions.)

The Trees of Liberty attack campaign was designed to obscure the source of the money behind it. As *Politico* reported, "Trees of Liberty carefully tailored its ad campaign to avoid triggering rules that would have required more financial disclosure during the campaign. It pulled down the television ads just before the calendar reached the one-month election countdown. Had the ad aired within that month, Trees of Liberty would have been required to report its spending—but not its donors—to the Federal Election Commission."[105] As *Politico* also disclosed, Trees of Liberty reported to the IRS, under oath, that it did not "engage in direct or indirect political campaign activities on behalf of or in opposition to candidates for public office."[106] (More on this requirement in Chapter Eight.) Ernst won the Republican primary and went on to the general election.

That's where Freedom Partners Action Fund kicked in. Even before Ernst had won her primary, the super PAC Freedom Partners Action Fund had begun what became a $1 million-plus ad barrage against her Democratic adversary, funded by $693,000 from Freedom Partners Chamber of Commerce.[107] Again, Ernst won.

As *Politico* concluded about the Koch brothers' political enterprise: "They're building a muscular political machine capable of electing the right politicians and ensuring they implement the right policies," and "they're well on their way to achieving that goal."[108] From the candidate's point of view, anyone who will spend this kind of money is a force to be reckoned with. On one hand, there's the gratitude due. On the other, there's the recognition that if you don't stay in line, the stealth spending may be for your opponent next time. (As I have said, the sins are bipartisan. The *Washington Post* reported on the mysterious entity DE First Holdings, incorporated in Delaware. The day after its creation, it gave $1 million to a super PAC tied to a New Jersey Democratic officeholder. Its owner, according to the *Post*, "remains unknown."[109])

And as I describe in Chapter Eleven, the effect of the *Citizens United* decision has been particularly villainous with respect to the climate change debate in Congress. Indeed, it has been disabling—exactly as the big corporate spenders want. *Citizens United* did not add to America's policy debate; it gave big special interests a weapon to suppress debate, with political threats and bullying they did not have the power to use before. But more on that later.

Here, it's perhaps worth addressing the elephant in the room: does the surprising strength of Donald Trump's "self-funded" campaign prove that the super PACs and corporate money unleashed by *Citizens United* have no bearing on our elections? No, quite the opposite. One way to understand Trump's popularity among Republican voters is as an expression of anger at this post–*Citizens United* system—the system that is serving the powerful, not the people. Yet as we have seen, the true source of the system's dysfunction is not immigrants and foreigners, as Trump would like voters to believe. It is forces of corporate power that have infiltrated our democracy, leaving ordinary Americans out.

The irony, of course, is that the embrace of Trump was an embrace of the very same corporate power machine that is shutting Americans out of their own democracy. Trump could not have accumulated his wealth without the power of the corporation and the favorable tax and regulatory environment corporate lobbying has secured. As a real estate magnate, he may pay no taxes at all. Like a magician waving a bright scarf in one hand while he sneaks a rabbit into the hat with the other, Trump has effectively focused voters on anyone he can easily scapegoat, while himself benefiting from and perpetuating the real menace: a system that persistently serves corporations and the rich. And it's hardly throwing open the doors of democracy to say that you don't have to *have* a billionaire to win, it's enough that you can *be* a billionaire.

Even where a candidate campaigns on being outside of money in politics, the system of political money tends to seep in, sooner or later. Unsurprisingly, it didn't take Trump long after securing the nomination to turn to super PACs and their multimillion-dollar contributions for support. In fact, the day *before* Trump's acceptance speech at the Republican National Convention *Politico*'s headline read: "Trump Blesses Major Super PAC Effort."[110] *Politico* then reported on August 7, 2016 ("Trump's Economic Advisers Are Also His Biggest Donors"), that of the thirteen men Donald Trump announced as his economic advisory council, "five are major donors whose families combined to give Trump's campaign and his joint fundraising account with the Republican Party more than $2 million."[111] Trevor Potter noted of Trump that this was "the path he has said was corrupt: raising large sums of money and then giving donors special access."[112] The inevitable switcheroo pulled a fast one on Trump's primary voters, who were "an easy mark for a P.T. Barnum con man," said right-wing Iowa radio host Steve Deace.[113]

Americans of all political stripes are disgusted by the influence of unlimited, anonymous corporate cash in our elections and by campaigns that can succeed or fail depending on how many billionaires the candidate has in his pocket (or vice versa, perhaps: how many candidates the billionaire has in his pocket).[114] More and more, people feel their government responds only to wealthy and corporate interests, and they are right.[115] Indeed, there is even scientific documentation of this: a 2014 report by political scientists Martin Gilens and Benjamin Page, looking at data even before the worst effects of *Citizens United*, attempted to answer the questions, "Who governs? Who really rules? To what extent is the broad body of U.S. citizens sovereign, semi-sovereign, or largely powerless?"[116] The unhappy conclusion of the report was this: "The central point that emerges from our research is that economic elites and organized groups representing business interests have substantial independent impacts on U.S. government policy, while mass-based interest groups and average citizens have little or no independent influence."[117] The report notes the "impediments to majority rule that were deliberately built into the U.S. political system—federalism, separation of powers, bicameralism," which give the American political system a built-in "substantial status quo bias."[118] They understood that the Founders deliberately made it a somewhat uphill struggle to get things done in Washington. But this is different. "When a majority of citizens disagrees with economic elites or with organized interests, they generally lose."[119]

This is more than just a matter of ordinary people not getting what they want from government, say the authors: "we believe that if policymaking is dominated by powerful business organizations and a small number of affluent Americans, then America's claims to being a democratic society are seriously threatened."[120] And America's example as a democratic society matters a lot in a dangerous world, as I argue in Chapter Twelve.

* * *

While today's Congress can't make much progress on many problems facing the country, from gun control to the climate crisis, the Senate can be remarkably efficient in tackling obscure items important only to the corporate lobby. For example, on October 22, 2015, senators were summoned to the floor regarding an ambassador's nomination. I walked up to the two desks on the Senate floor in front of the parliamentarians and clerks, one for each party, where during a vote there is a piece of paper on each desk describing the subject of the vote, along with leadership's position on the vote (sometimes also the name of the lead senator in opposition, if there is one). I looked at the paper to see what appointment was important enough to call the full Senate to the floor and saw that the subject at hand was the confirmation of our ambassador to the tiny, corrupt nation of Equatorial Guinea. You've probably never heard of the place; if you have, you've probably heard nothing good.

Equatorial Guinea has been described by scholars and writers as "one of the few African countries that 'can be correctly classified as a criminal state'"[121] and as a "mafia state in which power and wealth are tightly controlled by a brutal gang family and a small number of cronies and enforcers."[122] The U.S. Department of Justice has sued to seize assets of the ruling family, alleging the assets were the product of extortion, misappropriation, theft, and embezzlement. Allegations of torture abound. I knew a bit about the country because years ago my family was posted in nearby Guinea. Of all the things to be called over for, Equatorial Guinea?

At the time of this vote in 2015, there was a de facto blockade in the Senate of the president's nominees to State Department and Defense Department civilian positions. The executive calendar had more than fifty nominations pending, including the State Department's lawyer and ambassadors to Norway and Sweden. So why did we call up for a vote on the ambassador to this nasty little country?

The one noteworthy thing about Equatorial Guinea beyond its corruption is that oil was discovered there about twenty years ago, so much that little Equatorial Guinea has been referred to as the "Kuwait of Africa."[123] Big oil and gas concessions went to American companies. A 2004 Senate report into money laundering by the ruling clan chronicled these unsavory business ties, and as Ken Silverstein's *The Secret World of Oil* reports, "U.S. oil companies remain the bulwark of Equatorial Guinea's economy."[124] Clearly, the oil and gas industry wanted a Senate-confirmed ambassador to assist their dealings with this regime.

Was it bad to confirm the ambassador? Of course not. Do I know exactly why that ambassador's nomination made it to the floor that day for a vote? I don't. But with fifty other nominees waiting on the calendar, it's a reflection of whose priorities matter in Congress when the one that gets the recorded vote is the ambassador to the "Kuwait of Africa."

CHAPTER FOUR

What the Corporate Political Machine Wants: Four Short Case Studies

THE FORCES OF CORPORATE POWER ARE MURKY. They seek to be obscure. It can be hard to identify what they really hope to achieve. Moreover, their public relations messaging is usually designed to hide rather than clarify what they really want to achieve. There is no shopping list posted anywhere for us to examine. They often don't want us to know.

But we can drill a few core samples and extract some data to form at least a general idea. Four quick samples—the regulations corporations don't want, the taxes corporations don't want, the extreme policies the Kochs do want, and the differences in what the wealthy want—provide important clues as to the goals and possible effects of corporate power as it is deployed in the political arena.

On October 6, 2015, Senator Ted Cruz held a hearing in the Judiciary Subcommittee on Oversight, Agency Action, Federal Rights and Federal Courts.[1] The focus of the hearing was "overregulation." He called as one of his witnesses a small-business owner from Chicago, Sabina Loving, who runs a tax preparation service. The purpose of Loving's testimony was to decry the burden of a federal regulation that required her to obtain a license before preparing other people's tax returns. The thrust of the hearing was to make the case that regulations in general were burdensome on commerce, interfered with people's livelihoods, and were annoying. Loving was a nice person and an appealing witness.

But here is what was interesting: Senator Cruz had never filed a bill seeking to overturn that regulation. The Congressional Review

Act allows Congress to overturn agency regulations. It wasn't used. A review of the record shows that no senator had made any legislative effort to repeal or correct that regulation.[2] While we've seen more than a hundred legislative attacks and votes trying to repeal environmental protections per year since the Republicans took control of the House of Representatives in 2010[3] and repeated votes trying to undo the Dodd-Frank bill's restraints on Wall Street that were put in place after the Great Recession caused by Wall Street in 2008,[4] not once did anyone force a vote on Loving's little license regulation problem.

The reason I point this out is that there is a specific agenda behind a lot of the corporate mischief in Congress, and behind the generalized concern we often hear over "burdensome regulations." The Koch brothers' political groups, for instance, love to say that "burdensome and costly regulations are sucking the life out of our economy"[5] and that "Americans are suffering under the crushing burden of overregulation."[6] Oh my.

If that's so, where's the package of burdensome regulations we in Congress might well agree to repeal if they really didn't make sense? Regulations do get obsolete. The need for regulation can be affected by new technologies. Practice can show that particular regulations are ineffective. There's plenty of room for bipartisan work to clean that up. But this is never about those situations.

The corporate groups will talk generally about burdensome regulations, but what they want specifically is for Congress to help the usual suspects. Pull back the curtain marked "Burdensome Regulation" and you see some very familiar Rottweilers: Wall Street and the big polluters. The Koch brothers and Koch Industries, for instance, one of the top producers of toxic waste in the United States year after year, are the pointy tip of the corporate political spear.

A Wall Street billionaire saying he didn't want regulations on his financial schemes would not be a very appealing witness, especially after the big Wall Street meltdown and resulting bailout. Neither would a major polluter seeking relief from environmental regulations. So nice Sabina Loving is marched in to testify, although even on the Republican side there had been zero effort to do anything about the regulation she cared about. She was a prop. The real political energy is always behind Wall Street and the big polluters. That's where the big money is.

Indeed, as I was writing this section, a headline in *Politico* said: "GOP Targets Dodd-Frank, EPA for End-of-Year Fight."[7] Well, well.

Noteworthy too in this deregulation tale is the effort by big utility polluters to reregulate themselves. When it looked like state and federal regulators were restraining their profits, electric utility deregulation was their mantra.[8] Now that the cost of wind and solar power is undercutting their big coal-burning plants, various utilities are trying to reregulate themselves in order to get paid for power plants the market may not support. Some of these companies charged their ratepayers for these power plants, and then in the deregulated environment they were able to mark up prices and get consumers to pay again through that system; now, as they face "stranded costs," they are trying to get their customers, or even people using wind and solar, to pay them yet again.[9] In one happy story, the Atlanta Tea Party and Sierra Club chapters joined together to form the Green Tea Coalition. They beat back utility-sponsored legislation that would have put a tax on rooftop solar with the money going to the big polluting utilities.[10]

The lesson from this particular core sample is not to be duped by the sound of appealing generalities. Who the hell is *not* for getting rid of obsolete or useless "burdensome regulations"? But when you hear the refrain about "burdensome regulations," look out for your wallet, and for your lungs, because in practice it's almost always a cover for the deregulatory agenda of two narrow interests: Wall Street and the big corporate polluters.

Next let's drill into corporate tax priorities. More than anything, the right pursues eliminating the estate tax, which only about 0.2 percent of the very wealthiest Americans—those whose estates are worth more than $5.45 million—will ever have to pay.[11] In my time in the Senate, estate tax repeal seems to come up more frequently than any other proposed tax reduction or repeal. Over and over, when the Senate budget process opens the floor to amendments (in the process known irreverently as "vote-a-rama"), Republicans insist on votes on repealing the estate tax. In my experience, the degree of Congress's political interest in tax reform corresponds directly to the wealth of the beneficiaries of that tax reform: the wealthier the beneficiaries, the more ardent the repeal effort.

During one of these mostly symbolic budget vote exercises, there was a tie vote on an estate tax repeal amendment, and the vice president of the United States, Dick Cheney, rushed in his motorcade to the Capitol so that the vote could be retaken and won by the repeal proponents. Cheney ejected Senator Jon Tester, who was presiding, from the chair (the vice president, serving also as the president of the Senate under the Constitution, has the right at any time to claim the chair and preside in the Senate, and his vote is then added to break a tie), and the vote was retaken. Such was the distaste for Cheney in the chamber that the measure actually got *fewer* votes. But the episode shows the political energy behind estate tax repeal. As a budget amendment in the "vote-a-rama," the measure wouldn't even have changed the actual law; yet the vice president of the United States came tearing up to the Senate for that vote.

Tax cuts add to the national debt. When senators express concern about the national debt, they will often suggest that the very survival of the Republic depends upon reducing the national debt. All things considered, this is an admirable goal. But those same senators will often fight tenaciously against repealing even the worst special-interest tax breaks, even when the revenues from the repeal would reduce the deficit. Many want *still more* special-interest tax breaks. It is a contradiction.

Contributing to a national debt that "risks the survival of the country" are massive subsidies for the big multinational oil companies, who make the largest profits the world has ever seen. Corporate welfare for big oil companies should be the last place in the world to waste tax subsidies, yet even in the name of debt reduction, repealing this subsidy is a nonstarter with senators beholden to corporate interests.

Another classic is the "carried interest" tax rule, which allows hedge fund billionaires to treat great chunks of their income as if it were a less taxable long-term capital gain—a long-term capital gain that just happens to occur every year.[12] Because of this loophole, some of the most highly paid people in the world, with incomes that can run into the hundreds of millions of dollars in a single year, pay lower tax rates than a truck driver or a bricklayer.[13] There is no scheme of reason, nor any notion of justice, that could make sense of so massive a tax break. Some of these corporate highfliers make so much money they don't even notice the last million dollars they make in a year—in economic terms, that last million dollars has near-zero marginal utility to them. Yet we tax more heavily the income of people who need their earnings to pay the rent and the heat bill every month, people for whom even a hundred dollars makes a real difference.

One startling example of this special-influence tax policy at work, highlighted by economist Martin A. Sullivan, is a luxury residential building on Park Avenue in New York City so big that it has its own zip code. Since the IRS reports taxpayer information by zip code, we know, on average, what the people in this zip-code-sized luxury building make each year, and we know, on average, what they pay in taxes. The IRS reports for 2007 show that the adjusted gross income declared by the residents in this building averaged $1.2 million per household per year. The average federal tax rate paid by the residents in this building was 14.7 percent.[14]

By way of comparison, the Department of Labor reports the wage and tax rates for security guards and janitors in New York City. Security guards reportedly average a little over $27,500 in annual income, and janitors a little over $33,000. At those salaries, the statutory tax rates are 23.8 percent and 24.9 percent, respectively.[15] Thus the doorman holding the umbrella up in the rain in front of this building is likely paying a higher federal tax rate than the hedge-fund mogul climbing out of his limo under the doorman's sheltering umbrella. This disgraceful state of affairs—not reducing the national debt—is what the corporate lobby fights to protect. If they truly cared about reducing the national debt, corporate America and its high-paid denizens could pay their fair share of taxes, and fight to see that it went to reducing the debt. Fat chance.

The moral to be drawn from this core sample into the tax debate is that the political power of very highly paid corporate executives and investors, as that power gets deployed in Congress, is dedicated often to protecting the well-being of very highly paid executives and investors. In this case, it protects them from the indignity of having to pay taxes like regular working people.

Oh, did I forget to mention? That building in New York City is the Helmsley Building, as in Leona Helmsley, famously quoted as saying, "Only the little people pay taxes."[16]

* * *

We return to the Koch brothers for our third effort to seek out the true agendas of the corporate elite and the politicians they fund. This core sample drills back in time to the official platform of David Koch of Koch Industries, when he was the vice presidential candidate in 1980 for the Libertarian Party. Yes, that Koch, of those Koch brothers, once ran for vice president of the United States, and his political platform of thirty-five years ago reveals volumes about the Koch brothers' actual priorities. Right-wing operative Grover Norquist has said, "David Koch ran in '80 to go against the campaign finance rules. By being a candidate he could give as much as he wanted."[17] But Koch wanted to do more than give money. Time may have mellowed his views since then, or he may just have learned to keep these parts of his agenda from the public, but the platform below is just some of what David Koch actually campaigned on as vice-presidential candidate. Buckle up, because it's quite a ride.

> We specifically oppose laws requiring an individual to buy or use so-called "self-protection" equipment such as safety belts, air bags, or crash helmets.
>
> We advocate the abolition of the Federal Aviation Administration.
>
> We advocate the abolition of the Food and Drug Administration.
>
> We call for the repeal of the Occupational Safety and Health Act.
>
> We oppose all so-called "consumer protection" legislation . . . and call for the abolition of the Consumer Product Safety Commission.
>
> We propose the abolition of the governmental Postal Service. The present system, in addition to being inefficient, encourages governmental surveillance of private correspondence. Pending

abolition, we call for an end to the monopoly system and for allowing free competition in all aspects of postal service.

We advocate the complete separation of education and State. Government schools lead to the indoctrination of children and interfere with the free choice of individuals. Government ownership, operation, regulation, and subsidy of schools and colleges should be ended.

[We] call for the dissolution of all government agencies concerned with transportation, including the Department of Transportation, the Civil Aeronautics Board, the Federal Maritime Commission, Conrail and Amtrak.

We demand the return of America's railroad system to private ownership. We call for the privatization of the public roads and national highway system.

We condemn compulsory education laws, which spawn prison-like schools with many of the problems associated with prisons, and we call for the immediate repeal of such laws.

We call for the privatization of the inland waterways, and of the distribution system that brings water to industry, agriculture and households.

We support repeal of all laws which impede the ability of any person to find employment, such as minimum wage laws.

We support an end to all subsidies for child-bearing built into our present laws, including all welfare plans and the provision of tax-supported services for children.

We oppose all government welfare, relief projects, and "aid to the poor" programs. All these government programs are privacy-invading, paternalistic, demeaning, and inefficient.

> The proper source of help for such persons is the voluntary efforts of private groups and individuals.
>
> We favor the abolition of Medicare and Medicaid programs.
>
> We favor the repeal of the fraudulent, virtually bankrupt, and increasingly oppressive Social Security system. Pending that repeal, participation in Social Security should be made voluntary.
>
> We oppose all personal and corporate income taxation, including capital gains taxes.
>
> [We] support the eventual repeal of all taxation. . . . As an interim measure, all criminal and civil sanctions against tax evasion should be terminated immediately.
>
> [We] support the abolition of the Environmental Protection Agency.
>
> We support abolition of the Department of Energy.
>
> We urge the repeal of federal campaign finance laws, and the immediate abolition of the despotic Federal Election Commission.[18]

Wow. This is obviously not the agenda of all corporate America, but it shows the antigovernment extremism of one of corporate America's most politically active voices. And, together, the Koch brothers are perhaps America's most politically active corporate voice. Indeed, with their private political operation said to exceed the capability of the Republican National Committee, their goals and intentions matter.

And don't be fooled by the Koch brothers' public statements against "corporate welfare." It's all part of a carefully orchestrated campaign to rebuild their image, following so much unwelcome disclosure by author Jane Mayer and others of their behind-the-scenes scheming in recent elections. The Kochs fight for every kind of corporate welfare that helps them: low corporate taxes, low tax rates on money earned as capital gains from corporate stock, offshoring of American jobs and profits, and of course deregulation. The Kochs' top political operative, Richard Fink, has conceded: "We want to decrease regulations. Why? It's because we can make more profit, okay? Yeah, and cut government spending so we don't have to pay so much taxes."[19]

But that's not the big one. The business that made the Koch brothers into billionaires has been called the biggest toxic waste emitter in the country. The fossil-fuel industry with which they are entwined is the biggest polluter on the planet. And they particularly want the biggest piece of corporate welfare that exists: the ability to privatize their profits but socialize their costs (yes, the Kochs are fine socialists when it comes to the costs they impose on humanity—"share the wealth" is anathema to them, but "share the pollution" is their business model).

As a quick sidebar, I recently ran across one of their efforts to clean up their reputation and found a particularly cynical trick. I was a co-author of a criminal sentencing reform moving along in the Senate Judiciary Committee. The Kochs and their political operation made a big splash when they decided to support criminal sentencing reform; the news media loved the "strange bedfellows" aspect of their alliance with liberal and minority groups, and the Kochs' usually surreptitious efforts were all at once unusually noisy.[20] I'll confess, I smelled a rat.

Sure enough, after the sentencing bill was negotiated and ready to pass out of the Senate Judiciary Committee, there came a sudden fuss from Republicans about how "mens rea reform" had to be added: an amendment to add the new mens rea provision was unexpectedly brought up in the Judiciary Committee when we voted on sentencing reform, and a committee hearing was suddenly held on mens rea reform right afterward, House members started threatening that our Senate bill would be dead without mens rea reform, right-wing groups began to insist on adding mens rea reform when the bill was taken up on the Senate floor, and the ever-obedient *Wall Street Journal* editorial page began editorializing for "mens rea reform."[21]

Well, "mens rea" is a legal term—Latin for "guilty mind"—and the "reform" was to make the government have to prove knowing, criminal intent in order to prosecute wrongdoing. While criminal intent has long been a component of trials for crimes such as murder or manslaughter, it has not been a factor in regulatory offenses. The purpose of regulatory statutes is safety, and the method is deterrence: where safety violations would be dangerous, the idea is "to require a degree of diligence for the protection of the public which shall render violation impossible."[22] Forget about intent; just don't do it.

In such public danger cases, corporate polluters are often the defendants. Moreover, since a corporation is an artificial legal entity without a soul or mind, forcing prosecutors to prove a culpable state of mind on the part of the corporation, and not just the criminal act by the corporation, opens up a field of mischief for corporate defense attorneys and adds another snarl for prosecutors to have to untangle. So mens rea reform is a corporate payday.

If you were the biggest toxic waste emitter in the country and you could hobble the forces of government that were prosecuting you for your pollution and safety violations, wouldn't that be ideal? Such a loophole wouldn't be likely to pass on its own, though. But maybe if you snuggled up to a criminal sentencing reform effort and got in with that, you could turn it into a Trojan horse with your mens rea reform tucked inside. And in the meantime, you could get all that good publicity for looking like a nice guy as you helped build the Trojan horse.

The Koch brothers themselves of course denied this was all part of their scheme, and said they'd be happy to have criminal sentencing reform pass without adding the corporation-protecting mens rea reform. But at the same time, Koch-funded groups were the ones demanding mens rea reform as part of sentencing reform, and Koch lawyer Mark Holden has conceded they were motivated by a twenty-million-dollar settlement they paid arising out of a Department of Justice prosecution under the Clean Air Act after carcinogenic benzene releases at a Koch refinery.[23] Great combo, if you can get it: mens rea reform to help out your corporations, clean hands for the Kochs. The fronts for the Kochs in the criminal sentencing reform effort were Holden of the Koch Foundation and Edwin Meese III, the former U.S. attorney general (you may recall he was forced to resign in a swirl of ethics problems). Later, before the Judiciary Committee, Meese was actually the lead witness for mens rea reform, there representing the right-wing

Heritage Foundation, which is supported by the Koch Foundation. Subtle as a brick.

If you think there must be some reasonable boundary around this corporate agenda, think again. The extremism of David Koch's vice presidential platform shows how unrestrained and even reckless some corporate-sector voices are about uprooting programs that ordinary Americans count on for their health, their retirement, their safety, and their prosperity. This set of policies would re-create the law of the jungle in our economy. (I guess if you were born a very big cat, the jungle may not seem like such a bad place.)

America is full of responsible corporate leaders as horrified as you and I are by this vision of America. So let me be clear: there is a small but powerful segment of corporate America driven by self-interest and ideology to seek power in politics. Their priorities drive what I describe as the "corporate agenda." This agenda reflects the views of a minority of CEOs, but it is the loudest, strongest, and most persistent corporate voice in my world, in Congress. It is the voice we hear.

Other corporations come in and dabble in trade, intellectual property, or tax issues of the moment. Different sectors of the economy have their industry concerns. Their worst sin, and it is a mild one, is to crowd out other interests and other issues that don't have their lobbying clout as they jostle to get their issue resolved. The defense establishment, for instance—which is well funded and powerful—focuses intensely on defense programs and the defense budget. So every year in the Senate we do a defense bill, even if we never get to student loans.

The hard core is different from corporate America at large. The Kochs are different. This tiny group of corporations and corporate leaders has made the determination that intense engagement in politics, and particularly intense *hidden* engagement in politics, is a very rewarding business strategy. It has embraced the new political artillery that *Citizens United* provided. It manages a fleet of front groups to obscure its role. It engages in super PAC and 501(c)(4) politics on an unprecedented scale. Its impact is outsized. I feel comfortable calling what it seeks the corporate agenda, even if it's not the agenda of all or even most corporations, because it is the corporate agenda we most see and feel in Congress.

It's worth noting that, from my perspective in Congress, I've seen that the agenda of a CEO and of the corporation employing her may diverge considerably. A CEO may be honorable and fair, but the corporation itself may not prioritize her fair and honorable views when lobbying Congress. Indeed, those fair and honorable views may be left entirely on the cutting room floor by the time the corporation's government affairs folks and lobbyists communicate to Congress. The industry's trade association may then exacerbate this, representing the worst, most selfish views among the various players in the industry. The trade association's lobbying will then focus on the sketchiest industry priorities, those furthest from the public interest—such as eliminating limits on air pollution or protections from extreme risk-taking by big banks. The result is that the happy talk from an honorable and fair CEO up in the executive suite may be almost completely transformed by the time the lobbying rubber has hit the road in Congress. We in Congress will usually see the worst face of the industry.

Senator Elizabeth Warren and I did a report on the U.S. Chamber of Commerce, for instance, which has lobbying positions on tobacco and climate change that are significantly different from the public positions of the corporate directors on the Chamber's board.[24] A few corporations left the Chamber over its extreme positions, but most took no action at all.[25] The result was one set of policies in the executive suites, but a completely different push from their lobbying muscle in Congress.

And my experience is that even the very best American companies won't push back against their industry's nefarious fringe. Corporate CEOs who are sincere about climate change and effective at driving sustainability still won't lobby Congress for a serious climate bill or push back against the fossil-fuel industry. Yes, if they think something big is coming, they will rush in to make sure they get their share, as they did in the cap-and-trade bill, which would have limited overall emissions and allowed polluters to "trade" carbon allowances. But regular corporate America ordinarily won't dissociate itself from the most disgraceful lobbying, the dark political rough stuff by the hard core of corporate activists. Not when the rough bunch takes over industry associations like the U.S. Chamber of Commerce. Not even when they say things that are known to be false.

While this book is a general warning about the infiltration of corporate forces into our democracy, it is worth highlighting again that the corporate forces exerting themselves in our politics are not always representative of the larger business community. The exercise of political power by corporate forces tends to grow with the size of the corporation. The big boys dominate. Moreover, the desire to exercise political power tends mostly to animate a few highly regulated sectors, particularly finance and fossil fuels, but also insurance, pharmaceuticals, chemical manufacturing, and, to a lesser degree, defense. These industries monopolize the deployment of corporate power in our government, and do so to such an extent that small businesses, and even big businesses in other sectors, may be as much the victims of hidden corporate power as regular human citizens are. Many—perhaps even most—corporations should actually have common cause with regular citizens in resisting these hidden forces as they exert themselves in our politics.

My last core sample of "what the corporate political machine wants" explores the policy preferences of the wealthy compared to the general public to reveal just how much the priorities of individuals with great wealth diverge from those of regular citizens. Big CEOs now earn on average three hundred times the average wage of a worker in their company, so those CEOs, in addition to representing their corporate interests, also reflect personal views that are associated with great wealth and increasingly are out of step with the realities and wishes of modern Americans.[26]

A 2011 study by Benjamin Page, Larry Bartels, and Jason Seawright showed stark differences between the opinions of the very wealthy and those of other Americans on America's economic needs.[27] Polls consistently show that Americans care much more about job creation and economic growth than they do about reducing the deficit.[28] In contrast, the study found that high-wealth interviewees' top concern was "budget deficits or excessive government spending"; this was mentioned far more than any other issue.[29] Unemployment and education "ranked a distant second and third to budget deficits among the concerns of wealthy Americans."[30]

The 2011 study showed this pattern repeated again and again. Should "the government in Washington . . . see to it that everyone who wants to work can find a job"? Sixty-eight percent of the general public thinks so, but only 19 percent of wealthy respondents agreed. Should "the federal government . . . provide jobs for everyone able and willing to work who cannot find a job in private employment"? A majority (53 percent) of the general public says yes, compared to only 8 percent of wealthy respondents. What about a minimum wage "high enough that no family with a full-time worker falls below the official poverty line"? Seventy-eight percent of the public are in support, whereas only 40 percent of the wealthy agree. As for spending on Social Security, food stamps, and health care, the wealthy favor cutting such spending, whereas most Americans would like to see it expanded.[31]

The study extracted these policy views from a highly affluent group of Americans corresponding roughly to the top 1 percent.[32] It provides some key lessons. One is that the rich are indeed different, as F. Scott Fitzgerald observed. Because they are different, they don't make good proxies for the public. Because these very wealthy Americans have very different views than the public at large, there is actually a disenfranchisement that occurs when their views carry outsized political weight in our democracy. In other words, we can't delegate running the country to them and trust them to deliver results we will want.

One specific difference is that the very rich will not fight for middle-class employment and for social programs that support and sustain the middle class. When the interests of the rich control the political process, the central pillars of American middle-class security are in peril. To use a phrase from my childhood, they're the "pull up the ladder, Jack, I'm on board" crowd. As the talented writer Peggy Noonan has said, "The donor class . . . [i]nevitably . . . see to their own enthusiasms and policy priorities."[33]

There are undoubtedly other core samples that could be drilled into the complex geology of corporate political influence, but I would wager that almost all of them would confirm the following principles: (1) when you pull back the curtain, the interests of Wall Street and the big polluters will always be at the forefront of the deregulatory agenda (other business interests, look out—you may be being suckered!); (2) the very well-off will usually fight for the economic interests of the very well-off even if the result is plainly unfair to those who are less well-off; (3) for some of the most powerful corporate voices, there is no end to the law-of-the-jungle extremes they have championed publicly as their goals; and (4) the very rich are indeed different, and see things so differently that consolidating power in their hands will disenfranchise ordinary Americans.

As Americans careen into levels of income inequality not seen since the Gilded Age, when robber barons ruled the roost, these core samples suggest a link between all this hidden corporate political power and worsening income inequality. The corporate chokehold on Congress certainly contributes to our inability to do anything about our widening income inequality. And the forces of corporate power have been on the winning economic side of the income inequality divide. At a minimum, they don't feel its injury. At worst, they are lapping it up.

CHAPTER FIVE

The Powell Memo and the Corporate Strategy

IN 1906, THE UNITED STATES SENATE proclaimed that the evils of corporate money in politics were "so generally recognized" that the threat was deemed too obvious to need to discuss.[1] In 2010, five corporate-minded Supreme Court justices ruled that corporations had a constitutional right to spend unlimited amounts of money to influence elections, and that this would pose no possible threat of corruption. Such a dramatic change could not, and did not, happen by accident. Rather, a coordinated, deliberate strategy by corporate and conservative interests built a system that, over time, allowed big business to have its way.

The sea change is often said to have begun with a corporate lawyer named Lewis Powell and a 1971 memo that he wrote, now known as the "Powell Memo."[2] Shortly after writing the memo, Lewis Powell would be appointed to the Supreme Court by President Richard Nixon. Once on the Court, Justice Powell laid the legal groundwork for corporate political rights.

Powell was a Virginian, educated and trained for the law at Washington and Lee University. He became a prominent partner in Virginia's biggest corporate law firm. He was active in the American Bar Association, ultimately becoming its president. He was both a lawyer for and board member of Virginia tobacco companies. He was courtly and polite, the ultimate "establishment lawyer." Indeed, Powell was so established that when in 1969 Nixon first offered him a seat on the United States Supreme Court, Powell turned the president down.[3]

Beneath Powell's establishment gloss lay a sharper edge: Powell was a member of right-wing billionaire Richard Mellon Scaife's League to Save Carthage, described by Jane Mayer in her book *Dark Money* as "an informal network of influential, die-hard American conservatives."[4]

Lewis Powell wrote his 1971 memorandum at the request of the United States Chamber of Commerce.[5] The Chamber of Commerce was then a less partisan organization than it is now. Today the U.S. Chamber of Commerce supports virtually only Republican candidates. It is usually more representative of multinational than American corporate interests; in a 2010 letter to the Senate opposing a bill that sought to prevent offshoring of American jobs, the Chamber actually wrote to us, "Replacing a job that is based in another country with a domestic job does not stimulate economic growth or enhance the competitiveness of American worldwide companies."[6] And among American corporate interests, it is dominated by fossil-fuel interests and Wall Street.[7] Indeed, one might say that the U.S. Chamber of Commerce has been captured by these particular narrow interests.

The 1960s were an anxious time for the business establishment. Long-haired sons and bell-bottom-wearing daughters openly scorned a CEO dad's straitlaced corporate world. The wildly popular movie *The Graduate* famously mocked "plastics." Napalm symbolized American productive capacity gone morally adrift. Tectonic forces in the antiwar and civil rights movements were shaking our social consensus.

In this turbulence, the late 1960s and early 1970s saw a surge of new regulation, including the establishment of major new agencies, including the Department of Transportation (1967), the Environmental Protection Agency (1970), and the Consumer Product Safety Commission (1972). As political scientist Lee Drutman puts it, American businesses were "reeling from a remarkable expansion of government regulation and a general rise in anti-business sentiment."[8] In the wake of this new regulatory activity, the Chamber sought advice from Powell on how to increase the influence and power of its big business clients. Powell laid out "possible avenues of action" to aid American big business.[9] His recommendations ranged from enhancing corporate public relations departments to promoting pro-corporate faculty at universities and textbooks in schools. The strategy's centerpiece, however, was a new focus on government. "Business must learn the lesson . . . that political power is necessary," Powell instructed.[10]

The quest for political power in the Powell Memo did not just focus on business interests' traditional regulatory and lobbying influence in the administrative agencies and the executive and legislative branches. Powell included in his recommendations a section entitled "Neglected Opportunity in the Courts." It was not enough to have your lobbyists prowling the legislature and executive agencies. "Under our constitutional system," Powell argued, "especially with an activist-minded Supreme Court, the judiciary may be the most important instrument for social, economic and political change."[11] Powell called on the Chamber of Commerce to assemble "a highly competent staff of lawyers" and hire "lawyers of national standing and reputation" to file amicus briefs in the Supreme Court.[12]

Powell had in mind a sophisticated strategy of what we now call "impact litigation," litigation where the purpose is not so much to represent the client as to change the law. In keeping with this direction, in 1998 the Chamber launched its Institute for Legal Reform, which has described itself as a "national legal reform advocate . . . working to change the laws, [and] also changing the legal climate."[13] Impact litigation had a distinguished history in the civil rights and environmental movements. *Brown v. Board of Education*, the decision desegregating America's schools, could be said to be public-interest impact litigation. But Powell was going to turn those public-interest strategies in a new direction having little to do with the public good.

Powell sent his memo to the Chamber on August 23, 1971. President Nixon announced Powell's appointment to the Supreme Court on October 21 of that same year.[14] It is unclear whether Powell knew when he turned in the memo that he would be the president's next appointee to the Court. (There must have been considerable discussion prior to the October announcement, particularly within the Powell family, because Powell biographer John Calvin Jeffries reports that at Powell's swearing-in, Powell's wife, Josephine, said, "This is the worst day of my life. I am about to cry."[15])

The business community responded quickly to the recommendations of the Powell Memo. As I've mentioned, Lee Drutman, author of *The Business of America Is Lobbying*, has pointed out that scarcely any Washington lobbyists were deployed by corporations prior to the 1970s. That changed fast. Political scientists Jacob Hacker and Paul Pierson have reported, "The organizational counterattack of business in the 1970s was swift and sweeping—a domestic version of Shock and Awe. The number of corporations with public affairs offices in Washington grew from 100 in 1968 to over 500 in 1978. In 1971, only 175 firms had registered lobbyists in Washington, but by 1982, nearly 2,500 did. The number of corporate PACs increased from under 300 in 1976 to over 1,200 by the middle of 1980. On every dimension of corporate political activity, the numbers reveal a dramatic, rapid mobilization of business resources in the mid-1970s."[16]

In the 1970s, the Chamber doubled its membership and tripled its budget; its fellow lobby group, the National Federation of Independent Businesses, doubled its membership; and the CEO lobby group the Business Roundtable was formed.[17] Corporate political spending ramped up, as well. According to Hacker and Pierson, "From the late 1970s to the late 1980s, corporate PACs increased their expenditures in congressional races nearly fivefold."[18] These were expansions of existing activities, so it is not surprising they would happen quickly.

But some of Powell's ideas were novel. In particular, his call for mobilizing in the courts was inconsistent with the common view that courts were neutral places where decisions were handed down dispassionately and corporate influence would have little role.

In 1978, now a Supreme Court justice, Powell delivered a decision that kicked wide open a whole new realm of opportunity for corporate America. Contrary to prior Court precedent, Powell wrote in the case of *First National Bank of Boston v. Bellotti* that the First Amendment protects corporate speech in political discourse.[19] With that decision, two things happened. First, a new front was opened for corporate political engagement under the umbrella of protected speech, a front that corporate power would explore and expand for decades to come, leading the Court ultimately to the profoundly misguided *Citizens United* decision. And second, Justice Powell presented to the corporate community a living example of what can be accomplished through aggressive efforts to build an "activist Court" with like-minded judges. If the Chamber hadn't fully believed his memo about the prospects of judicial activism on behalf of corporations, they certainly did after they saw his decision. He had delivered a prize, proven the potential of an activist Court, and illuminated the pathway.

The business community and the conservative movement got the message from Powell and the Chamber and began to build a sophisticated legal infrastructure. In 1982, for instance, the Federalist Society, a conservative, pro-corporate legal organization, opened its doors at prestigious law schools. Legal historian Steven Teles has described the role of the Federalist Society in the Reagan administration:

> [Federalist] Society membership was a valuable signal for an administration eager to hire true-believers for bureaucratic hand-to-hand combat. In addition, by hiring the Society's entire founding cadre the Reagan administration and its judicial appointees sent a very powerful message that the terms of advancement associated with political ambition were being set on their head: clear ideological positioning, not cautiousness, was now an affirmative qualification for appointed office.[20]

The Federalist Society provided a means of signaling the ideological bona fides of ambitious conservative and pro-corporate lawyers, but it was only one of many such legal organizations. Some were created with the explicit goal of grooming and vetting the ideological purity of foot soldiers in the conservative movement. Others were created to look for opportunities to systematically and strategically advance conservative and pro-corporate legal theories. I ran across one of these advocacy institutions as attorney general of my state.

When I became Rhode Island's attorney general in 1999, I inherited a long-standing regulatory quarrel over a small parcel of land on the shores of Winnapaug Pond, along our southern coast. The parcel was owned by a gentleman named Anthony Palazzolo, who was something of a local character. Mr. Palazzolo's parcel of land was mostly tidal wetlands, which made the parcel not buildable under Rhode Island's centuries-old "public trust" doctrine. After several of his proposals to develop the property were denied, he filed a lawsuit against the state asserting that the Rhode Island Coastal Resources Management Council's effort to protect coastal wetlands rendered his property worthless and was thus an unconstitutional "taking" without just compensation. Palazzolo's case came up through the state's coastal regulatory body, and from there into the state courts, as a small and unassuming part of the great flood of business of the Department of Attorney General. But this small case would soon take me to the litigant's podium of the United States Supreme Court.

To understand how that came to pass, it's helpful to have some background on the takings clause of the United States Constitution. The takings clause, reasonably, requires the government to pay you if it condemns your land for a highway, for instance. Corporate interests, however, have long argued that it also requires the government to pay you if a government regulation reduces the value of your property from its "highest and best use"—for instance, if you can no longer build a shopping mall or nuclear power plant on it. In part this is a property rights movement ("Who are you to tell me what I can and cannot do with property I own?"), and in part this is a corporate effort to make it harder for regulators to regulate. Corporations have a powerful tool when they can threaten litigation and ultimately perhaps even demand a money judgment against a little state regulatory agency by claiming that a regulatory restriction violates their constitutionally protected property rights under the takings clause. On the front lines of this battle lie corporate-funded legal organizations, exactly as suggested in the Powell Memo, which troll through court records and news reports for cases that they think can be useful in this cause.

Anthony Palazzolo's case was noticed from across the country by an entity in Sacramento, California, called the Pacific Legal Foundation. This is a corporate-funded entity whose employees read case reports from lower courts around the country all day long, looking for platforms to advance their pro-corporate, pro-property-rights argument.

Someone in Sacramento read legal reports about Mr. Palazzolo's little lot on Winnapaug Pond and thought it would make a good case for impact litigation. So they swooped in, became Palazzolo's attorney of record, and took over the case. Unlike the usual situation of a client choosing a lawyer, this law group chose its client from across the country, and next thing you know we're in the U.S. Supreme Court.

As it turned out, the property rights movement gained no ground in that particular effort in the Supreme Court. We held them off. There was a technical error in the state court's decision, so the case was sent back to the state court.[21] From the Pacific Legal Foundation's perspective, the Supreme Court case ended with a whimper, not a bang.

With no prospect remaining of any national impact, the Pacific Legal Foundation declined to represent Palazzolo in the subsequent state proceedings. Nothing has been built on the lot to date, and Mr. Palazzolo has since passed away.

Corporate America has these kinds of front groups on duty every day, actively looking for litigation that will advance their causes. The front groups don't represent real clients in the ordinary course; they swoop into existing litigation and offer to litigate for free to make their point, then vanish once they have. And the Pacific Legal Foundation is not alone—these front groups have become endemic. The docket of the United States Supreme Court is riddled with parties, intervenors, and "friends of the court" that are corporate-backed "advocacy advocates," rather than regular lawyers advocating for regular clients in the ordinary course of litigation.

These entities are the new buckled-and-feathered corporate courtiers of the Supreme Court, seeking "impact" exactly as the Powell memo prescribed. They have made the Supreme Court an arena for political combat. It is not uncommon to find five or six of these groups filing amicus briefs on matters before the court, parroting each other's arguments and providing the conservative justices an instructive and reassuring right-wing echo chamber. (Indeed, there were five such briefs in the Palazzolo case.)[22]

Let's be clear: these are not public interest organizations taking key civil liberties cases through the courts to vindicate the rights of ordinary American citizens. These are well-funded corporate front groups that have co-opted a strategy pioneered by the great advocates of the civil rights movement, and put it to the service of special interests. The goal is not to give voice in court to citizens whose voices are all too often not heard; it is to manipulate courts in the service of corporate power and wealth. These corporate-funded groups masquerade as independent organizations, but they are tools of a self-serving corporate network.

Again, I will take the liberty of calling these groups corporate-funded, whether the funding comes directly from big corporations, has been contributed by individuals who have amassed huge wealth through corporate activity, or derives from trusts or front groups set up by such individuals and corporations. All these roads lead to Rome, and Rome is the pro-corporate agenda.

As if this "impact" machinery were not bad enough on its own, a not-so-subtle signaling system has emerged between the conservative judges and these entities, sending the groups hints as to which cases and arguments the conservative justices would like to have come before them. One recent example of this signaling was described by the *New York Times*. It involves a pet peeve of the union-busting right wing and the corporate sector: a decision from 1977 called *Abood v. Detroit Board of Education* that allows unions to collect dues from nonmembers whom they represent in collective bargaining. If *Abood* were reversed, unions would lose the revenues they now get from the fees of nonmember employees, employees would be encouraged to become "free riders" and get the benefit of union membership without paying, and the balance of power between corporations and unions would shift further toward corporations. As Supreme Court reporter Adam Liptak tells the story in the *Times*:

> In making a minor adjustment to how public unions must issue notifications about their political spending, Justice Alito digressed to raise questions about the constitutionality of requiring workers who are not members of public unions to pay fees for the unions' work on their behalf. . . .
>
> Justice Sonia Sotomayor saw what was going on. "To cast serious doubt on longstanding precedent," she wrote in a concurrence, "is a step we historically take only with the greatest caution and reticence. To do so, as the majority does, on our own invitation and without adversarial presentation is both unfair and unwise."
>
> Michael A. Carvin, a leading conservative lawyer, also saw what was going on. He and the Center for Individual Rights, a libertarian group, promptly filed the challenge Justice Alito had sketched out. Indeed, Mr. Carvin asked the lower courts to rule against his clients, a Christian education group and 10 California teachers, so they could high-tail it to the Supreme Court.

(A brief interruption here to underscore that the conservative impact litigation outfit wanted to *lose* the case, to get more quickly to the forum they really wanted: the U.S. Supreme Court, where they anticipated a welcoming audience. Now back to the *Times* story.)

> Last year, Justice Alito wrote a second majority opinion attacking the central precedent in the area, a 1975 decision called Abood v. Detroit Board of Education. But the majority in the new case, Harris v. Quinn, stopped short of overruling Abood.
>
> By now everyone saw what was going on. "Readers of today's decision will know that Abood does not rank on the majority's top-ten list of favorite precedents—and that the majority could not restrain itself from saying (and saying and saying) so," Justice Elena Kagan wrote in dissent.
>
> Last week, the court agreed to hear Mr. Carvin's case, Friedrichs v. California Education Association, No. 14-915, and it may soon complete the project Justice Alito began in 2012, that of overruling Abood.[23]

The Supreme Court heard oral argument in *Friedrichs* in January 2016, and it certainly looked like another 5–4 decision in favor of corporate interests was coming down the pike. It was only the unexpected death of Justice Antonin Scalia in February that took history on a different course. A tie vote on March 29 effectively left the Ninth Circuit Court of Appeals decision in place, upholding the long-standing precedent.[24]

The extent of the planning and expectations between the conservative justices and the corporate world is displayed in the reactions in major newspapers—the *Wall Street Journal*, the *Washington Post*, and the *New York Times*—to Justice Scalia's death. "Corporate America had high hopes," the *Journal* said, because "the Supreme Court appeared poised to deliver long-sought conservative victories," in the form of "body blow[s] that business had sought against consumer and worker plaintiffs."[25] The cases "had been carefully developed by activists to capitalize on the court's rightward tilt," including " 'test cases tailor-made for a court including Justice Scalia.' "[26]

The *Post* noted that each of the "cases and causes that had the right so excited at the beginning of the term" was " 'an attempt to push the law sharply to the right.'"[27] "Conservatives . . . welcomed a new docket in October studded with cases that seemed poised to move the law to the right," said the *Times*, a new docket that included "a half-dozen potential blockbusters."[28] "Conservative advocacy groups hoped," the *Times* continued, that these cases "would help business interests and Republican politicians, while dealing setbacks to public unions, colleges with racial admissions preferences and abortion providers."[29]

But "things soon changed," noted the *Times*.[30] "Conservative hopes for a transformational term at the Supreme Court ended with Justice Antonin Scalia's death," said the *Post*, quoting law professor Pamela Karlan, who noted that an "era of aggressive conservative legislation and litigation at the Supreme Court may largely be over."[31] Concluded the *Journal* after Scalia's death: "The court frustrated conservative expectations."[32]

In the corporate effort to influence the judiciary, a cottage industry has even cropped up of conservative, pro-corporate organizations hosting "continuing legal education" sessions for judges at luxurious resorts where, between the golf and fishing outings, they can hear from "experts" in pro-corporate legal theories. An investigative report by the Community Rights Counsel, now the Constitutional Accountability Center, examined this practice and concluded that the groups hosting these events are "run by ideologues and funded by special interests."[33] One such group actually bragged of its intention in these sessions "to serve the interests of its contributors effectively."[34]

The retreats are free to the judges, since they are bankrolled by oil, timber, and other corporate interests, and they are so luxurious that the judges often bring their spouses along to enjoy the occasion.[35] The locales have included Amelia Island and Sea Pines plantations, Florida beach resorts, Arizona golfing destinations, and private ranches out west.[36] Another investigation found that "the seminars take place at truly plush resorts (many of them the same used by ALEC [the American Legislative Exchange Council] for their annual meetings involving legislators) during all expense [paid] trips provided to the judges by a number of conservative funded organizations."[37] (Focused on state legislators, ALEC is also in the business of saturating decision-makers with pro-corporate, conservative ideology.)

This is no small effort. One group gloated that "more than one-third of the sitting federal judiciary" had attended its retreats.[38] At one time, about 10 percent of the federal judiciary was attending one of the various retreats each year, reaching by one count an overall total of 40 percent of the federal judiciary.[39] The nonpartisan Center for Public Integrity has estimated the attendance count at around 185 federal judges from 2008 to 2012.[40] The partisan nature of this effort is apparent, too; for one group, Republican-appointed judges accounted for 97 percent of the guests[41]—at which point it becomes sort of a right-wing judicial jamboree and team-building exercise. The judges who were listed as having attended the most retreats were all appointed by Presidents Reagan or George H.W. Bush.[42]

The sponsors get value for their money, as the investigative report described: "Imagine one wealthy foundation, interested in shaping the law in a conservative, anti-regulatory fashion. That foundation decides on a strategy, which has two parts. First, fund groups that are going to litigate. Second, fund seminars that will try to persuade judges."[43] And sure enough, the report showed, sponsors funding these retreats "are simultaneously bankrolling litigation in federal courts to limit environmental regulation, often before the same judges."[44]

Not surprisingly, the report found "no balance whatsoever" in the presentations.[45] Presenters include former oil company CEOs and "Free Marketeers," people who "weave together . . . doctrines from economics and political science to attack federal environmental laws."[46] A more recent report by the Voters Legislative Transparency Project summarized: "These junkets are designed to provide attending judges with an ultra-conservative, pro-corporate outlook on key issues. During these free trips judges attend daily seminars provided by purported scientists, corporate executives and others advancing a one-sided, pro-corporate, free-market conservative ideology."[47]

The materials provided to the judges are pretty extreme. A "Desk Reference for Federal Judges" prepared by one group for conference attendees says this about air pollution: "The first step is to realize that an external cost is not simply a cost produced by the polluter and borne by the victim. In almost all cases, the cost is a result of decisions by both parties. I would not be coughing if your steel mill were not pouring out sulfur dioxide. But your steel mill would do no damage if

I (and other people) did not happen to live downstream of it."[48] Darn me for living downwind and having these pesky lungs.

Activism is a desired result. One instructor at these seminars is an advocate for "unabashed activism."[49] He has complained that "the Reagan revolution will come to nothing as these judges sit on their hands in the name of a simplistic theory of judicial restraint."[50] He applauds judges who depart from Supreme Court precedent in the service of a "libertarian Constitution."[51]

And the strategy has worked. The report found a "remarkable correlation between seminar attendance and judicial activism."[52] "In case after case, the judges writing the opinions that strike down environmental statutes have attended [these groups'] seminars."[53] This should come as no surprise, given who's funding them and what they want: "The seminars offer something that is more helpful to a conservative judge and more dangerous to the independence of our judicial system: the tools to reach the results conservatives favor as a matter of politics or ideology."[54] And no wonder: as a recent Voters Legislative Transparency Project report disclosed, "six of the seven [groups] providing such judicial trips are funded with money from one or more of the Koch-controlled family foundations. In addition many known conservative foundations also fund these trips and seminars for judges, including: John M. Olin Foundation, Inc., M.J. Murdock Charitable Trust, Castle Rock Foundation, Claude Lambe Foundation (Koch controlled) and the Lynde and Harry Bradley Foundation."[55]

Many of the judges did not even disclose on their mandatory ethics reports that they attend these corporate-funded retreats. I don't know what would be worse if you are a party litigating an environmental claim—knowing your judge was being indoctrinated at partisan seminars paid for by your adversary, or having the judge keep it a secret from you. Either way, litigants may well see justice perverted by both the indoctrination and the secrecy.

Does this have a bad odor to you? You are not alone. One newspaper editorialized that it "creates an egregious ethical conflict of interest, bordering on wholly improper out-of-court communication with special-interest lobbyists or representatives of people who have filed lawsuits."[56] Another said it looks like "an interest group has put part of the federal judiciary in its saddle."[57] A third said, "The conflict is clear, and the judges' participation is mind-boggling."[58] And lest you think I've gone to liberal, elitist, Yankee publications for these quotes, every one comes from a newspaper below the Mason-Dixon Line. Northerners were tough, too: one writer described these junkets as "popular free vacations for judges, a cross between Maoist cultural reeducation camps and Club Med."[59]

Another task of the conservative legal groups has been to create an aura of academic legitimacy around the pro-corporate cause. Seminars, publications, and societies have sprouted, and traditional law reviews have been barraged with submissions. Some of these submissions are highly strategic, even targeting specific cases.

I ran into this too as attorney general, in a civil action I brought against the lead paint industry seeking a remedy for lead paint having poisoned so many children in Rhode Island. It was a big case. Our state's assistant medical director for the Department of Health had said lead poisoning was "Rhode Island's number 1 children's environmental health problem."[60] The lead paint defendants lawyered up massively: dozens of lawyers appeared for them at court proceedings, and more than a hundred lawyers were involved in various stages of the proceedings. I remember looking across the courtroom at one point and guesstimating that the companies were burning more than $10,000 per hour in legal fees just from the lawyers present that day.

The companies really began to panic when we won the case at trial, before a Rhode Island jury. Cleaning up the trail of poison from their product in buildings across Rhode Island was not going to be cheap, and the case could point the way for other, bigger decisions in other, bigger states. So they pulled out the stops in their appeal of our trial victory to the state supreme court.

One tactic they used was to have their own paid consultants write "articles" purporting to be regular scholarly work, but which were in fact written during the pendency of the case to be cited as legal authority by the lawyers for the big corporations in the case. It worked. The Rhode Island supreme court's decision overturning our jury verdict relied in part on a law review article in the *University of Cincinnati Law Review* written by a professor of law at the University of Maryland School of Law who was also a paid consultant to the lead paint companies.[61] It appears that the Rhode Island supreme court was unaware while citing the "article" that it was a piece planted mid-litigation by a paid advisor to the lead paint companies.

My consolation was having put the Lead Industries Association, the industry's front group, out of business. They closed up shop rather than answer questions under oath.

The corporate effort runs broad as well as deep. Do the phrases "runaway jury" or "frivolous litigation" ring a bell? Planting those phrases in your consciousness is the work of this enterprise. If the phrase "burdensome regulation" resonates with you, that's the work of this enterprise, too.

Of course, all the argument and indoctrination in the world might be unavailing without, as Lewis Powell observed before stepping onto the Court himself, "an activist-minded Supreme Court"—one that is willing to make the judiciary "the most important instrument for social, economic and political change."[62] That task appears to have been accomplished as well, judging from the direction in which five conservative, pro-corporate justices took the Court in recent years.

The steady march of the activist right-wing bloc on the Supreme Court to establish its political priorities as the law of the land should come as no surprise. It represents the fruits of a long-standing and often very public effort to turn the law and the Constitution to the advantage of special interest groups and conservative activists. It is the realization of the "activist-minded Supreme Court" that Lewis Powell originally dreamed about in his memo.

The results of this meld of political ambition, ideological positioning, and activist judicial appointments have been terrible. What were once fringe conservative ideas—hostility to our nation's civil rights, environmental protection, and consumer protection laws—have been steadily dripped into the legal mainstream by endless repetition. The mainstream of American law has been shifted steadily to the right by the force of this effort, backed by seemingly endless corporate funds. This new "rights movement"—for the rights of corporations, the rich, the powerful, and the fortunate—has been aggressive and explicit.

CHAPTER SIX

Capture of the Court

FOLLOWING A DECADES-LONG CAMPAIGN FOR INFLUENCE over the Supreme Court, the corporate effort, under Chief Justice John Roberts, reached a pinnacle.[1] During his confirmation hearings, Chief Justice Roberts had cast himself as an "umpire," promising that he would just call "balls and strikes."[2] Yet a study by law professors Lee Epstein and William Landes and Judge Richard Posner analyzed more than two thousand cases argued before the Supreme Court between 1946 and 2011 and found that the Roberts Court's decisions have been, as reported by the *New York Times*, "far friendlier to business than those of any Court since at least World War II."[3] As described by renowned law professor Arthur Miller to the *Times*: "The upshot . . . is that businesses are free to run their operations without fear of liability for the harm they cause to consumers, employees and people injured by their products."[4] And, as Jeffrey Toobin noted in the *New Yorker*, this pattern of decisions "has served the interests, and reflected the values, of the contemporary Republican Party."[5] The strike zone has been moved.

Activism is not the Supreme Court's proper role. Justice Felix Frankfurter once noted that "it is not the business of this Court to pronounce policy. It must observe a fastidious regard for limitations on its own power, and this precludes the Court's giving effect to its own notions of what is wise or politic."[6] The conservative bloc on today's Supreme Court has done nothing of the kind; instead it has blatantly used its power, while it had a five-vote majority, to promote an agenda.

Corporate and conservative interests provided powerful support for the conservative justices' nominations; and it appears, to paraphrase the old song, that those judges were determined to "dance with the guys that brung them." The dance even included, for Justices Antonin Scalia and Clarence Thomas, attending the Koch brothers' secretive annual political conference.

This may sound like a harsh indictment. However, taking a fair look at the patterns of the Court's decisions during the power period of the five conservatives, and considering the strategies employed to achieve their results, it is difficult not to see the hand of activism at work. Over and over, the conservative justices ignored traditional, conservative judicial principles when those principles obstructed a political result favorable to corporations. Over and over, the conservative justices laid groundwork in one decision to shape pro-business policy in later decisions. Over and over, given the choice between achieving consensus and attaining the most ideological result, even if they had to get there by a narrow 5–4 decision, Chief Justice Roberts and the conservative bloc repeatedly chose to max out their agenda in 5–4 decisions. In those 5–4 decisions, the chief justice was amazingly reliable, taking the conservative side of the case 85 percent of the time.[7] A recent study co-authored by conservative Seventh Circuit judge Richard Posner found not only that the Roberts Court was more favorable to business interests than its predecessors but also that all five members of the recent corporatist bloc were among the top ten most business-friendly justices in the past sixty-five years—with Chief Justice Roberts number one and Justice Samuel Alito number two.[8]

There remains an unmistakable pattern suggesting intentionality and purposefulness here. The clear beneficiaries of the conservative justices' agenda were corporate and conservative interests, winning in the Supreme Court at an unprecedented rate. The role the five justices played in implementing a robust corporate agenda was far from conservative in the judicial sense; they were aggressive activists with a purpose. They were, clearly, the corporate, big-business bloc.

Concern over the Roberts Court's activism is not limited to lawyers, advocacy groups, and those in the partisan fray in Washington. Recent polling shows that less than one-third of Americans have confidence in the Supreme Court.[9] By two to one, Americans think the justices often let political considerations and personal views influence their decisions.[10] Americans massively oppose the *Citizens United* decision

(80 percent against, with 71 percent "strongly" opposed).[11] And, most tellingly, by a ratio of nine to one, Americans now believe the Court treats corporations more favorably than individuals. This sentiment is true even of Americans who identify themselves as "conservative Republicans." They agree by a four-to-one margin.[12]

While Americans across the political spectrum are disillusioned with the Court's apparent lack of neutrality, a nexus clearly exists on the Court's right wing between politically conservative ideology, the corporate agenda, and the Republican Party's interests. The five corporatist justices seemed also to rule in favor of the ideology and the party whenever they could. Even renowned *New York Times* reporter Linda Greenhouse, who had long resisted labeling those justices partisan ideologues, ultimately wrote that she found it "impossible to avoid the conclusion that the Republican-appointed majority is committed to harnessing the Supreme Court to an ideological agenda."[13] Other noted Court watchers such as Norm Ornstein at the conservative American Enterprise Institute and the *New Yorker*'s Jeffrey Toobin had long before reached a similar conclusion.[14] *Washington Post* columnist Dana Milbank observed wryly of a recent decision: "The Roberts Court has found yet another way to stack the deck in favor of the rich."[15]

The obvious retort to these arguments is the "Obamacare" decision.[16] It may seem that the Court's decision upholding the Affordable Care Act disproves any accusation that the Court has been politicized by the conservative movement. But the Obamacare decision was predictable—and anticipated by many of us—under a "politicized Court" theory. It was actually the smart play for the chief justice and his fellow conservatives.

First, being against Obamacare was a big conservative rallying effort; why should the Court deprive the party of such a unifying cause? Second, if the Court had actually ruled the Affordable Care Act unconstitutional, then what? The Republican Party would own the resulting mess, and the party had no plan whatsoever to offer as an alternative. Like the dog chasing the car, there was the problem of what they'd do if they caught it. Third, the health insurance industry needed Obamacare. However things turned out, one thing was clear: there was no going back to letting the insurance industry deny insurance coverage for preexisting conditions. To do that would have been political Kryptonite. If there were no Obamacare (which stabilized the insurance industry with the "tax" on uninsured individuals) and also no way to avoid covering preexisting conditions, the health insurance industry would be imperiled by what it calls "adverse selection." Undoing Obamacare would have been a nightmare for the insurance industry, and the corporatists on the Court would not want that.

Finally, under cover of the decision allowing Obamacare, the Court could provide some big conservative deliverables—and it did. Rhetorically, the Court could call the program a "tax" (providing a very successful conservative talking point to the right).[17] Further, the conservative justices could and did narrow the scope of the commerce clause (thereby narrowing federal legislative power).[18] And on top of that, the chief justice invented a new "dragooning" theory limiting Congress's ability to attach conditions to federal spending programs.[19] Those latter two constitutional novelties would have been the subject of much notice ordinarily, but they were drowned out in the "Supreme Court Upholds Obamacare" headlines.

A governor I once worked for, Bruce Sundlun, liked to say, "If you have a disadvantage, make use of it." The five conservatives made great use of the Obamacare decision.

Usually, political efforts to "capture" great public institutions come, as it were, in sheep's clothing. But the conservative takeover of the Supreme Court came as a wolf. Consider the official Republican Party platform of 2000, which "applaud[ed] Governor Bush's pledge to name only judges who have demonstrated that they share his conservative beliefs and respect the Constitution."[20] They didn't just have to share those beliefs; they had to be willing to impose them too.

The political deal that leads to this result is not complicated. America's big corporate interests fund Republican candidates for office. Those corporate interests want those Republicans to help them. That is as old as politics. So Republicans make it a priority to appoint judges who also want to help—judges who may in their confirmation proceedings pay obligatory lip service to opposing "judicial activism" but who, once on the bench, will actually deliver on core Republican political interests. When Republican appointees to the Court have not adequately delivered on the corporate agenda, the *Wall Street Journal* editorial page has accused them of "political betrayal."[21]

A series of landmark Supreme Court decisions in the second half of the twentieth century provided fertile soil from which the rage of the Republican voter base has grown. *Brown v. Board of Education* ended the segregation of schools across the South, infuriating southern conservatives, who came out for "massive resistance" to it.[22] *Roe v. Wade* recognized a woman's right to decide to have an abortion in the first trimester of a pregnancy, infuriating conservatives and fundamentalists.[23] The Court created rights including Miranda warnings ("you have the right to remain silent . . .") for arrested suspects, infuriating the law-and-order crowd.[24] And the Court said that burning the American flag as a form of protest was protected by the First Amendment.[25] The Republican "base" was mad as hell about these decisions and others.

Elements of the modern Republican Party base thus saw judicial appointments as a vital means of political action to unwind those decisions. A Republican can raise far more money than a Democrat can from a fundraising email railing about "activist judges." The baseline Republican voter cares a lot more about judicial appointments than the baseline Democratic voter does.[26] With the "base" ginned up about appointing conservative judges, adding a pro-corporate payload to help the big donors out was as natural as cake with ice cream. And if election laws too can be made favorable to Republican political strategies, that's a cherry on top.

Despite the Court's professed political neutrality, election decisions of the Court's recent Republican-appointed majority always seemed to come down on the side that helped the election prospects of the Republican Party. The sockdolager of political decisions, of course, is *Bush v. Gore*, in which five conservative justices determined who the next President of the United States would be. Constitutional law scholar and Yale Law School professor Akhil Amar has described the ironies of that decision this way:

> Justices who claim to respect states savage state judges. Jurists who condemn new rules make up rules of breathtaking novelty in application. A court that purports to frown on ad hoc,

> after-the-fact decision making gives us a case limited to its facts. A court that claims it is defending the prerogatives of the Florida Legislature in fact unravels its statutory scheme vesting power in state judges and permitting geographic variations. . . . The case that bears the name of a professed strict constructionist is as activist a decision as I know.[27]

Principles galore were trampled to achieve that decision's result.

More recently the Court intervened in voting rights in a way virtually guaranteed to help the Republican Party at the polls. Access to the polls for minority voters is facilitated by the aptly named Voting Rights Act, a federal law that was a key victory in America's civil rights struggle. Section IV of the Voting Rights Act is the act's preventative mechanism to protect minority access to the ballot from local laws designed to restrict that access; this section operates only in those states that had long histories of discriminating against minority voters. The conservative majority's 5–4 *Shelby County* decision in 2013 fired a torpedo into that section. Minority voters tend to vote Democratic, so sinking the section that proactively safeguarded their ballot access tipped the balance at the polls to Republicans.[28]

With the safeguard gutted, there came swift enactment in many of those states of a raft of voter-identification laws, cuts to early voting, bans on same-day registration, and voter-roll purges.[29] Voter suppression laws such as these, freed up by *Shelby County*, work exclusively in favor of Republicans. In January 2016, the *Washington Post* described the "surgical precision with which North Carolina Republicans approved certain forms of photo IDs for voting and excluded others"—"passports, motor vehicle department IDs, expired IDs for those over age 70, and veteran and military IDs" were in, while "student IDs, government employee IDs, and . . . public assistance IDs" were out.[30] Ultimately, a federal appeals court saw through the ruse in North Carolina, declaring in July 2016 that the restrictions "target African Americans with almost surgical precision" (in an echo of the *Post*) and striking down the law.[31] Of course, the law had been in place since 2013; Republicans still enjoyed the benefit of fewer Democrats in the electorate during the time it took to litigate this blatant voter-suppression strategy.

Notably, the conservative justices ignored a voluminous bipartisan congressional record that supported the preclearance requirement. The Court's disrespect for Congress in this matter is odd, because the Fifteenth Amendment to the Constitution gives Congress a vital role in enforcing the voting rights of racial minorities (it explicitly gives "Congress . . . power to enforce this article by appropriate legislation"),[32] yet the conservative justices trampled over this express power. The late Justice Scalia even suggested during oral argument that the overwhelming bipartisan support within Congress for reauthorization of the Voting Rights Act in 2006 actually made the statute more suspect.[33]

A closer look at *Shelby County* suggests that the conservative justices were determined to disable Section IV, and planned, years in advance, to achieve that outcome. Four years before *Shelby County*, in 2009, Chief Justice Roberts, writing for the conservative majority in a decision called *Northwest Austin Municipal Utility District No. 1 v. Holder*, criticized Section IV of the Voting Rights Act and announced a doctrine of the "equal sovereignty" of all states.[34] Later, in *Shelby County*, he relied on his *Northwest Austin* "equal sovereignty" concept to disable Section IV, gutting the "preclearance" safeguard provisions of the Act.[35] Far from just "calling balls and strikes,"[36] it looks like the chief justice (to switch sports metaphors) actually "teed himself up" in *Northwest Austin* for the later decision he rendered in *Shelby County*.

Federal appeals court judge Richard Posner, in an essay about *Shelby County* tellingly titled "The Voting Rights Act Ruling Is About the Conservative Imagination," noted: "There is no doctrine of equal sovereignty. The opinion rests on air."[37]

The conservative justices' decisions on gerrymandering gave a second election boon to Republicans. Gerrymandering is the political technique of designing the shape of a legislative district to make sure a legislator has a friendly electorate. In the early nineteenth century, a salamander-shaped district, designed at the behest of Massachusetts governor Elbridge Gerry to shape a state senate district he needed to protect, was described by Massachusetts newspapers as a "Gerry-mander," which gave us this word.[38]

Gerrymandering has been seized on by Republicans as a way to enhance their legislative power in the U.S. Congress. One notable example of how this has succeeded comes from Pennsylvania. In the 2012 elections, Pennsylvania voted statewide to reelect President Obama. Pennsylvania also voted statewide to reelect my Senate colleague Bob Casey, a Democrat. You'd think that would have made Pennsylvania a Democratic state in its House delegation, too. But Pennsylvania in that same election sent thirteen Republicans and five Democrats to Congress from its eighteen congressional districts.[39]

How is that possible? A new and clever form of gerrymandering has emerged. Old-school gerrymandering helps a friendly congressman by shaping his district to make sure he wins. Nasty gerrymandering takes on an undesirable incumbent by reshaping his district to make sure he loses. Modern "bulk" gerrymandering is more strategic and looks at a state's whole congressional delegation. Such bulk gerrymandering isolates Democrats into heavily (80 percent or more) Democratic political districts, "wasting" Democratic votes, and constructs 60/40-majority Republican districts out of the remainder of the state. It thus delivers congressional delegations that don't reflect the state's popular vote.

These diagrams give a good illustration of how this "bulk" gerrymandering works:

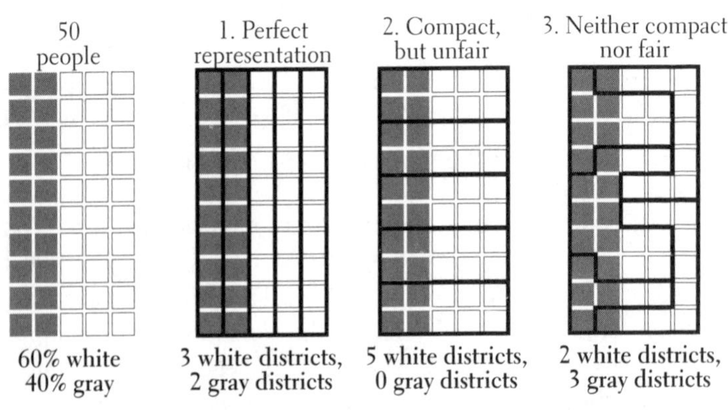

(Chart adapted from Stephen Nass)

To lay the groundwork for acquiring this power in Congress, Republicans launched the Redistricting Majority Project (REDMAP). They spent more than $30 million—much of it dark money—to help elect majorities in state legislatures in battleground states including Ohio, Michigan, North Carolina, Pennsylvania, and Wisconsin.[40] Winning those state legislatures was the key that opened the door to redistricting the federal congressional delegations, since it's state legislatures that usually draw those maps. In Pennsylvania, REDMAP spent nearly $1 million to win three state representative races, helping Republicans take over the Pennsylvania House of Representatives.[41] It seems like a lot of money for three state representative races, unless you see the bigger prize.

Sure enough, when voters in Pennsylvania came to the polls in 2012, a total of 2.79 million voters statewide voted for Democratic candidates for Congress.[42] Only 2.71 million voters statewide voted for Republican candidates for Congress.[43] It was close, but Democrats won—83,000 more people in Pennsylvania voted for Democratic candidates for Congress than voted for Republican candidates for Congress.[44] Yet although Democrats won more votes overall, Pennsylvania sent a delegation to Congress that year of five Democrats and thirteen Republicans, as we have seen.[45] Because of the supersaturated Democratic voting districts that had been created, Democratic members of Congress averaged over 76 percent of the vote in their districts, with one district over 89 percent! Republicans averaged 59 percent, winning more districts by smaller margins.[46]

This was not just a Pennsylvania fluke. Ohio in 2012 voted for Barack Obama for president and returned my Democratic colleague Sherrod Brown to the Senate in the statewide vote, but on the same day Ohio elected twelve Republican congressmen and only four Democrats. Wisconsin voted for Obama in 2012 and elected Tammy Baldwin, a progressive, to the Senate; yet Wisconsin sent a delegation of five Republicans and three Democrats to Congress.[47]

Across the country in that 2012 election, 1.59 million more Americans voted for Democratic candidates for Congress than voted for Republican candidates for Congress.[48] Yet the ensuing Congress fell into Republican hands by a majority of thirty-three seats.[49] It was gerrymandering that won the Republicans control of Congress, not winning more votes. And the strategy was plainly admitted.[50] Indeed, the Republican organization behind REDMAP sent out a memo bragging of its achievements:

> Farther down-ballot, aggregated numbers show voters pulled the lever for Republicans only 49 percent of the time in congressional races, suggesting that 2012 could have been a repeat of 2008, when voters gave control of the White House and both chambers of Congress to Democrats. But, as we see today, that was not the case. Instead, Republicans enjoy a 33-seat margin in the U.S. House seated yesterday in the 113th Congress, having endured Democratic successes atop the ticket and over one million more votes cast for Democratic House candidates than Republicans.[51]

In 2004, in a gerrymandering case called *Vieth v. Jubelirer*, a group of Pennsylvania Democrats objected to gerrymandering by the Republican-controlled Pennsylvania legislature.[52] The case went all the way to the U.S. Supreme Court. The Republican-appointed judges on the U.S. Supreme Court held, in simplified terms (and again with a 5–4 vote), that the question of gerrymandering was just too hard to agree how to decide, so they wouldn't try to decide it. Four Republican justices announced in their decision that they would no longer even try to determine if gerrymandering interfered with any constitutional voting rights; one, Justice Anthony Kennedy, left a glimmer of light. But the effect was open season for gerrymandering, no matter how crass or obvious the political motive, and no matter how strong the evidence of partisan strategy in the redistricting. The American Bar Association's publication on redistricting law now states: "The Court's recent decisions appear to give legislators leeway to preserve partisan advantage as zealously as they like when drawing district lines."[53] As we have seen, Republicans took full advantage, and by 2012 had seized Pennsylvania's, Ohio's, and Wisconsin's congressional delegations with a minority of voters.

For a Court that regularly addresses vague and challenging constitutional doctrines such as "due process of law" and "equal protection of the laws," to say that this was too hard seemed like a very convenient admission of defeat. It was also dishonest: because of the protected status of race under the Constitution, when districts are gerrymandered for race rather than for politics, the Court must grapple with the hard questions of gerrymandering, so evidently gerrymandering presents problems that, while difficult, are not impossible to resolve.

* * *

A series of campaign finance decisions has also helped tip the political balance toward big donors (who tend to be corporate entities, front groups, and super-wealthy individuals), with the predictable result—proven out since in practice—that this would tend to help the Republican Party. The most notable of these is *Citizens United*. That decision (again 5–4) is so extraordinary that it merits its own chapter (which follows this one). But a constellation of decisions surrounds *Citizens United*, beginning with United States Supreme Court justice (you guessed it) Lewis Powell's original decision opening up political rights for corporations.

The notion that the First Amendment protects political activity by corporations as if it were free speech by humans traces back to Powell's 1978 opinion in *First National Bank of Boston v. Bellotti*.[54] In a (guess what) 5–4 vote, the Court gave First Amendment protection to corporations' political expenditures and recognized a corporate constitutional right to influence the political process. A direct line can be drawn from Powell's reasoning in *Bellotti*, through cases like *Buckley v. Valeo*, to the outcome in the Court's 2010 ruling in *Citizens United*. Indeed, Justice Kennedy's majority opinion in *Citizens United* referenced *Bellotti* twenty-four times. In the wake of his own memo urging more corporate political activity, Powell gave corporations the tools for that activity once he was on the Court.

Thus Attorney Powell's memo providing a strategy to enhance the political power of corporations begat Justice Powell's opinion recognizing a corporate constitutional right to political influence, and that in turn begat *Citizens United*, which forbids any limitations on corporate use of campaign spending to acquire political influence.

What merits noting before we move on is that even speech is not always protected "speech" under the First Amendment. Courts over the years have affirmed that the First Amendment doesn't protect the yelling of "Fire!" in a crowded theater and that it doesn't protect fraudulent statements. Some language we utter is libelous and can be punished in civil proceedings. Treasonous statements, criminal threats, and certain other acts of speaking are prosecutable crimes. Offering a bribe is not protected speech. Conspiring to fix an election is done using speech, but it's not protected. Commercial speech by corporations may be regulated to protect the integrity of markets and the expectations of consumers.

So if all actual speech isn't even protected "speech," it makes little sense to think that all corporate spending in politics is necessarily protected "speech." Corporate money is a selfish and driven force with few natural limits in the hydraulic pressures and counterpressures of our politics. It selectively amplifies the voices of a corporate CEO class, giving that class precedence over everyone else. Corporate money in politics can be used for bullying; it can be used for propagandizing falsehoods; it can be used to drown out other voices and deafen the electorate; it can be used for buying political loyalty or punishing political disobedience; it can be the bait on a hook; it can be artillery; it can be blandishment; it can be a "tsunami of slime."[55]

In a country that has made such effort to create a meaningful and open democracy, it is both wrong and simple-minded to refuse to grapple with all the mischievous effects of massive money let loose in politics, to just say it's "speech," and to walk away wiping your hands. It is both wrong and simple-minded to equate corporations, as political actors, with human citizens; they are very different creatures. This ignorance is the price we pay for having the first Supreme Court in America's history with not one justice with any political experience. This ignorance and an associated rashness rushing in to unleash the forces of money have done enormous damage to our democracy—damage that we see all around us.

The Court also has a proclivity in favor of the conservative agenda on social issues, from prayer to abortion to gun control. Curiously, to get to the politically conservative result, the judges will often violate judicially conservative doctrines.

A politically conservative result is something political conservatives want, as an end result, like laws that are pro-gun or anti-gay-marriage, pro-prayer or anti-choice, pro-fossil-fuel or anti-undocumented-immigrant. A judicially conservative doctrine is a theory of jurisprudence, usually a principle that will discourage change in the law and more closely tie the law to the past. It is a conservative *means*, not a conservative end. It is conservative in that it is steadying, prizes continuity, and resists change. (William F. Buckley is said to have observed: "A conservative is someone who stands athwart history, yelling 'Stop.'")[56]

For example, the principle of originalism, or faithfulness to the original meaning of the Constitution, is a conservative judicial doctrine. Some scholars and lawyers believe that the drafters of the Constitution launched in that document very general principles, which they articulated as best they could, but which they left to future generations to define anew as society developed, in what has been described as a "living Constitution." Originalism is the conservative counter to that argument, tying constitutional theory much more closely to the manners and the mores of the Founding era. A "living Constitution" could find the death penalty unconstitutional as "cruel or unusual" or inconsistent with "due process of law"; originalism would scoff at the notion that the states, which all executed criminals during the Founding era, could possibly have sent to the Continental Congress men who wrote a document that could be read to ban the practice. More generally, filtering constitutional theory through the eyes of well-off, eighteenth-century white men is not very likely to lead to dramatic change.

But originalism became inconvenient to the conservatives in the *District of Columbia v. Heller* case about gun control.[57] The Second Amendment had always in prior precedent been tied up with the idea of local militias. In a radical decision, the Court entirely recast the Second Amendment, implying for the first time in our history that the Second Amendment protects an individual right to keep and bear arms for self-defense. The individual right had no Court precedent. As recently as 1991 this doctrine was such a fringe theory that it was described by retired chief justice Warren Burger as "one of the greatest pieces of fraud, I repeat the word 'fraud,' on the American public by special interest groups that I have ever seen in my lifetime."[58] U.S. Appeals Court judge Richard Posner has noted wryly that "the true springs of the *Heller* decision must be sought elsewhere than in the majority's declared commitment to originalism."[59]

The result of the *Heller* decision was the long-sought dream of the National Rifle Association (NRA), the gun industry, and the right wing: recognition of an individual right to bear arms. As Amanda Hollis-Brusky noted in *Ideas with Consequences*, the role of the right-wing legal infrastructure was profound: "With the properly framed case brought by Federalist Society–affiliated litigators and with intellectual capital nurtured and supported through the Federalist Society network, five Justices on the Supreme Court were able to reinterpret, by some standards radically, the Second Amendment's right to keep and bear arms as a personal, not a collective right in *Heller*."[60] Standing right behind the Federalist Society was the NRA, and standing right behind the NRA were the gun manufacturers.

In order to give the gun industry its win, the conservative judges also cast aside the conservative judicial principle of respect for precedent. The Latin name of this doctrine is *stare decisis*, or "it stands decided." If you do not favor change in the law, you want to respect existing precedents from past decisions. Those precedents are an anchor against modernity and change, and a stabilizing influence protecting settled expectations against new ideas. Again, that all became inconvenient in *Heller*. No Supreme Court in history had ever found an individual right to gun ownership in the Second Amendment; hence the former chief justice's comment that the idea was a "fraud." But the NRA wanted it, the right wing wanted it, and the gun manufacturers wanted it—and that was that. Right-wing Justice Alito has since said of *stare decisis*, "It is a Latin phrase. It means 'to leave things decided when it suits our purposes.'"[61]

Alito's dismissal of *stare decisis* may have been tongue-in-cheek, but Chief Justice Roberts has gone further, announcing that he evaluates precedent in light of whether his bloc of justices objects to it. He is surprisingly up front about this: "*Stare decisis* effect is . . . diminished . . . when the precedent's validity is so hotly contested that it cannot reliably function as a basis for decision in future cases."[62] He continues, "The simple fact that one of our decisions remains controversial . . . does undermine the precedent's ability to contribute to the stable and orderly development of the law."[63] As anybody looking at this can see, this is a completely self-fulfilling theory. It allows the right-wing bloc on the Court, like sappers, to gradually undermine a settled precedent simply by "hotly contesting" it—until the day comes when they can blow it up.

A Court with five conservative justices who would tip America's politics toward one party in voting rights, gerrymandering, and campaign finance cases (toward the party that appointed them, if it need be said), and who would deliver conservative social policy victories to the party that appointed them (even though these decisions run against traditional conservative legal doctrine), should also have no trouble delivering the substantive goods on legal issues important to the corporate hierarchy backing that party. And the conservative five had no trouble at all with that.

According to the Constitutional Accountability Center, between 2006 and 2015 the Roberts Court supported the legal position of the United States Chamber of Commerce (by then the Chamber had become a de facto organ of the national Republican Party—or vice versa) 69 percent of the time.[64] The Chamber's side had won 56 percent of the time during the Rehnquist Court and 43 percent of the time during the Burger Court.[65] If it was Lewis Powell's dream to have the Chamber actively litigating before an "activist" Court, it has been Justice Roberts's achievement to provide them that Court.

The Chamber's impressive "win" rate in the Roberts Court is itself an understatement of the pro-corporate direction of the Court. An aggressive, confident Chamber, knowing it had an active conservative majority on the Court, could file cases where it expected a win would have "impact" and move the law in its direction. A "loss" in a case like that meant no more than that the status quo remained intact. An opportunity may be lost, but if the status quo remains, no actual harm is done to corporate interests.

Many Chamber victories have been significant. In the *Ledbetter* case, the Court overturned a verdict of employment discrimination, concluding that an employer could not be held liable if it successfully hid the discriminatory treatment from the victim long enough—that is, after decades of unequal pay, the plaintiff could recover damages for only the single paycheck received within the 180-day window allowed for filing a complaint.[66] In the *Leegin* case, the Court reversed precedent that had long prohibited manufacturers and distributors from setting minimum prices for the sale of retail goods to consumers.[67] In the *Janus* case, the Court limited the ability of mutual fund investors to recover for securities fraud, holding that fund advisors cannot be found liable for knowingly including misstatements of others in the documents they prepare.[68] And in the *Gross* case, the Court overturned a jury decision in favor of a victim of age discrimination in the workplace.[69] Each of these cases was decided by a 5–4 margin, with the five Republican appointees voting as a bloc in support of the corporate position.

Corporations have also won a series of cases that make it harder for people, and groups of people, to bring them to court for wrongdoing. As we'll discuss in detail later, big corporations hate being hauled into court and having to face juries, and the Supreme Court has protected them from this equalizing mechanism of justice in several ways. Through the *Iqbal* and *Twombly* decisions, corporations benefit from heightened pleading standards—meaning that the bar is now higher for plaintiffs who want to take a defendant such as a big corporation to court.[70] They have won rulings pushing disputes into corporation-favoring arbitration, as in *Rent-A-Center, West, Inc. v. Jackson*.[71] They have won rulings making it harder for injured Americans to band together to press cases of large-scale corporate wrongdoing, such as in *Wal-Mart v. Dukes* and *AT&T v. Concepcion*.[72] They recently won a two-fer ruling that pushed disputes into corporation-favoring arbitration *and* made it harder for injured Americans to band together.[73] They won *Vance v. Ball State University*, in which the Court made it more difficult for workers to hold their employers accountable for harassment in the workplace under the 1964 Civil Rights Act; *Mutual Pharmaceutical Co. v. Bartlett*, in which the Court made it harder for consumers who experience serious side effects from medications to sue drug companies; and *Comcast v. Behrend*, where the Court made it even harder for consumers to bring class actions.[74] They won *Hobby Lobby*, where the Court put the religious rights of corporate entities over the rights of those entities' employees (corporations, being people, can have religion, I guess), and *Harris*, already discussed, in which the Court not only dealt a significant blow to the political and economic clout of unions but issued an invitation to come and take another slug at them.[75]

It is highly improbable that corporate interests have prevailed so often and so reliably by mere happenstance, by neutral calling of "balls and strikes."[76] When you add in the rate at which Republican election interests have prevailed and the rate at which conservative social positions have prevailed, the case for happenstance becomes even more remote.

CHAPTER SEVEN

Capture of Elections

Citizens United

IN DECISION AFTER DECISION, the five-man conservative bloc that dominated the Roberts Court found a way to hold in favor of corporate and conservative interests with alarming predictability. Given the Court's corporate bent—in areas from civil procedure to workers' rights—perhaps it should not have been surprising when, in 2010, the Court unleashed unlimited corporate spending in our elections. Nevertheless, to court-watchers and Congress alike, *Citizens United* came as a shock. It was once the opinion of the United States Supreme Court that "to subject the state governments to the combined capital of wealthy corporations [would] produce universal corruption."[1] No more.

Citizens United, another 5–4 decision, marked the crowning victory for corporate interests. It opened the floodgates for unlimited, anonymous corporate cash in our elections, causing the "tsunami of slime" that we have seen in recent election cycles. *Citizens United* granted inanimate corporations and their special-interest fronts new power in our elections, not just through the corrupting ability to buy elections for favored candidates but also through the corrupting but less visible ability to threaten officeholders with a barrage of negative attack ads if they fail to cast a pro-corporate vote.

Such a dominant role for corporations in our government would shock our Founding Fathers, who foresaw no important role in our republic for the corporations of the time. They certainly did not foresee today's massive agglomerations of corporate wealth, nor the corporations' now-unlimited power to deploy that wealth in our elections. I believe they would be disgusted.

The *Citizens United* decision was wrongly handled jurisprudentially, wrongly managed procedurally, wrongly founded factually, and wrongly decided substantively. Even for the Roberts Court, with its near-explicit support for the corporate agenda, the decision was extreme, a rare kind of error-plagued and mischief-riddled legal monstrosity.

To unleash that corporate power in our elections, the conservative justices had to go through remarkable contortions.[2] I will discuss those contortions shortly. For now, let's just say it was a dirty business. And it has produced lamentable results.

The Founders worked hard setting up the Constitution to protect against the emergence of a new aristocracy. It is therefore saddening to see the five conservative justices create a new political aristocracy with the stroke of a pen. But they did.

We each bring to our American democracy our own voice, and we each bring to it our own pocketbook. Some of us may have a more compelling or thoughtful voice than others, and some may have a bigger or more free-spending pocketbook, but fundamentally we Americans have all historically been equal with one another in the respect that it was our own voices and pocketbooks we brought to politics. First the Founders, and then the leaders of our great civil rights movements, fought hard to make it so.

After *Citizens United*, that is no longer true. After *Citizens United*, if you are in America's corporate elite, you have been given a super-empowered voice and pocketbook to put to work in politics, on top of your own. In addition to their own voices, corporate leaders now have the megaphone voices of the corporations they command. In addition to their own pocketbooks, corporate leaders now have the vast treasuries of the corporations they control.

Unleashing corporate power into elections thus super-empowered the men and women who command those corporations. They already had the advantage of greater-than-average voices through the network of influence their corporate position provided to them (and their corporate lobbyists and PACs). They also already had the advantage of greater-than-average pocketbooks, through the generous incomes their corporate positions provided them. So they would do just fine in our democracy on their own. Corporate CEOs were not a hurting, beleaguered class.

But on top of that, they have now been given the voices and pocketbooks of the corporations they command. They are "double-decker" citizens now: once through themselves, and once through the enormous constitutional aliens the corporatist justices have brought to such robust political life. And this state of affairs has produced a massive deformation of American politics.

Elections are the lifeblood of democracy. The U.S. Constitution is established by and for "We the People of the United States." Humans are clearly different from artificial legal fictions called corporations. And nothing in the Constitution gives CEOs the right to amplify their voices over all of ours through the corporations they control. The activist bloc that drove the Supreme Court to *Citizens United* did not seem to appreciate this foundational, commonsense principle of our republic.

Our government is intended to be "of the people, by the people, and for the people." By refusing to distinguish between people and corporations, the Court allowed CEOs special privileged status and unleashed a foreign force into our politics against which the Constitution provided no adequate protections. We can remind ourselves that the Founders never imagined that such a power would emerge, and that they would never have wanted such a power to intrude into our political life.

We are not alone in that thought. The decision's nightmarish consequences have been recognized by leaders of all stripes. Senator John McCain, Republican of Arizona, has called *Citizens United* "one of the worst decisions in history." Due to the Court's "absolute ignorance of what happens in politics," he said, they created a "flood of money into campaigns, not transparent, unaccounted for."[3] Richard Posner, the conservative legal scholar and federal judge, put it even more bluntly: "Our political system is pervasively corrupt due to our Supreme Court taking away campaign-contribution restrictions on the basis of the First Amendment."[4] And as Senator Chuck Schumer, a Democrat of New York, said in 2010 about *Citizens United*: "The Supreme Court has just predetermined the winners of next November's elections. It won't be the Republicans or the Democrats and it won't be the American people; it will be corporate America."[5]

Republican former officeholders are just as dismayed. Former senator Alan Simpson of Wyoming has written: "Ending the tyranny of big money corruption isn't partisan—it's patriotic. It's essential to preserving the most deeply held values and beliefs we share."[6] Former congresswoman Connie Morella of Maryland has written: "Democracy requires constant vigilance. When the interests of major campaign donors and their allies are favored over the needs of ordinary citizens, we all pay the price."[7] President George W. Bush's political advisor Mark McKinnon has said, "Money in politics is . . . discordant with a free market philosophy because currently our public policy markets are not free—they are hostage to crony interests that pay for what they get."[8] We now live in a country where the conversation intended to be between American citizens and their candidates for public office has instead been overwhelmed by unlimited spending by corporate power: spending by corporations themselves, by the front groups they have established, and by the billionaires they have heaved up.

Corporations, as Justice Stevens has reminded us, are "invisible," "intangible," "artificial," "mere creature[s] of the law,"[9] with "no consciences, no beliefs, no feelings, no thoughts, no desires."[10] Unsurprisingly, the corporate power unleashed by *Citizens United* has turned things into a mess. As legal scholar Burt Neuborne summarized:

> Billionaire oligarchs have a First Amendment stranglehold on the electoral process. Wealthy ideologues on the left and right dominate the electoral agenda. Huge for-profit corporations are guaranteed the power to pour unlimited sums into buying political influence. Public officials and candidates spend most of their time trolling for support from wealthy donors, who often view campaign contributions as economic investments. Political investors can now choose whether to buy influence directly, with checks to specific leaders, or indirectly, as independent spenders. Election winners repay their wealthy supporters with excessive political influence; election losers mortgage their souls trying to persuade investors to bankroll their comebacks. Giant loopholes in the disclosure rules let wealthy individuals and corporations

> spend huge sums in secret to manipulate unwitting voters, and well-meaning legislators are forbidden to break the economic stranglehold of the rich by using the most efficient form of campaign subsidy—matching public funds tailored to the sums raised by privately funded opponents.[11]

This unbalances our politics. As legendary investor and CEO Warren Buffett has said, "They say it's free speech, but someone can speak 20 or 30 million times and my cleaning lady can't speak at all."[12]

The Supreme Court's 2010 decision in *Citizens United* was a shocking assault on the electoral system in our democracy. The *New York Times* called it "a sharp doctrinal shift."[13] One defeated congressman described *Citizens United* as "the polluters['] triumph." He told the *New Yorker*'s Jane Mayer: "There was a huge change after *Citizens United.* When anyone could spend any amount of money without revealing who they were, by hiding behind amorphous-named organizations, the floodgates opened. The Supreme Court made a huge mistake. There is no accountability. Zero."[14] By unleashing corporate money and the money of corporate billionaires and front groups, much of it now anonymous or laundered through intermediary organizations, the Court let loose into our political discourse waves of out-of-control spending, anonymous corporate influence, negative and false advertising, and unpunished lying. The American public is understandably disgusted and disillusioned. It seems like madness.

My point here is that there was method in the madness. *Citizens United* was cast by the conservative justices as being about the rights of individuals—in this case, the all-important right to hear more corporate speech.[15] Seriously, that's the way they framed it: our individual right to hear unlimited corporate speech. Burt Neuborne's *Madison's Music* describes it thus: "The Court allows the corporate speaker to borrow the hearer's First Amendment rights to receive the information."[16] Notwithstanding that "right" supposedly of ours, the decision's practical effect was to benefit corporations—Big Oil, pharmaceutical companies, debt collection agencies, health insurance companies, credit card companies, banks, coal barons, tobacco companies.

Unfortunately, the public doesn't know the half of it. The true impact of *Citizens United* on our elections and our policy making can be understood only by taking a closer look at the ins and outs of politics. I see that impact every day in the Senate. Let's have a look at some of its practical effects.

Months prior to the *Citizens United* decision, the U.S. Chamber of Commerce already had announced in the fall of 2009 "a massive effort to support pro-business candidates."[17] *Citizens United* enabled the Chamber's spending on this effort to be both limitless and faceless. By 2014, the Chamber was the single largest dark-money spender in the midterm elections and the single largest dark-money spender in twenty-eight of the thirty-five individual races in which it was involved.[18] The corporate lobby was now free to attack political candidates from behind a cloak of anonymity. The response from Republicans to *Citizens United*, as reported by the *Washington Post*, should come as no surprise: "Republican leaders . . . cheered the ruling as a victory for free speech and predicted a surge in corporate support for GOP candidates in November's midterm elections."[19] A team of economists has since "found that *Citizens United* shifted the odds of electoral success detectably and in a clear direction: from Democratic to Republican candidates."[20]

Since the Court took the fateful step of forbidding any limits on corporate spending, nothing now prevents corporate polluters under investigation by the Department of Justice from arranging unlimited ads supporting a more sympathetic presidential candidate who'll tell his attorney general to go easy. Nothing prevents financial services companies from spending their vast wealth to defeat members of Congress who are tired of the way business is done on Wall Street and dare to become a thorn in Wall Street's side. Nothing prevents big defense contractors from overwhelming candidates who might dare question a multibillion-dollar weapons program that they build.

But the problem runs far deeper than corporate interests spending their money. More insidious, corporations (and their front groups and billionaires) can now *threaten* to spend their money. Put simply, what big money can do, big money can threaten to do, or promise to do. And those threats and promises are very likely to be private. There's nothing "independent" or "transparent" about private threats and promises in a back room. The public will never know of the secret threats and promises, and corruption will inevitably follow. It doesn't take a constitutional scholar to figure that out.

The *Citizens United* decision opened this avenue to corruption, while pretending corruption was impossible.[21] Pretending that political corruption through corporate campaign spending is impossible is a notion that is laughable on its face, but even that laughable conclusion overlooks the problem that limitless untraceable political money doesn't actually have to be spent to corrupt our democracy. It can corrupt through the threat of spending it, or through the promise of spending it. And although the public won't see those back-room corporate threats and promises, or be aware of the deals that result, the candidate will know, and the special-interest dealmaker will know. Just the public will be left in the dark.

A well-funded super PAC can now make a single giant expenditure—or just threaten to make one—and have a major impact on a race. The overwhelming influence of outside money and dark money is particularly significant in congressional races with smaller media markets and campaign budgets than a presidential race or most Senate and gubernatorial races. In my state, members of Congress can run a $2 million race for reelection and feel they spent a lot of money. Spending $5 million would be a huge election effort. But $5 million is play money to big corporate interests when big money—perhaps tens of billions of dollars—is at stake in Congress.

Voltaire made a famous wry remark about the Royal Navy hanging Admiral Byng, saying that every once in a while the English have to hang an admiral "to encourage the others."[22] A similar effect can be had by picking off a particularly vexing member of Congress, or one whom colleagues in Congress look to for leadership on an issue. Take Bob Inglis, for example: a conservative Republican South Carolina congressman whose respect for science and love of his children caused him to take up the issue of global warming. He traveled to Antarctica to hear from the scientists directly. His children told him, "Dad, you're going to have to clean up your act on the environment." So he took the plunge and tried to make a conservative, faith-based case for taking on climate change. The response was immediate. Bombarded by outside money in his next primary, he was crushed by a margin of two to one, the kind of beating it usually takes an indictment to produce. Republicans in Congress got the message: Inglis says that for a time after that, his name "became a verb" in political circles—to be "Inglissed."

Corporate power doesn't have to hang all the admirals: hang one, and all the others will get the message. The smart strategy for a corporate-funded political attack would not be to fund massive attacks against everyone; it would be to make an example of someone. The efficiency of that strategy makes the threat all the more real, because it makes so much sense to attack for the sake of example. It's such a bargain.

That reality gives politicians an incentive not to be the example—not to be the admiral the corporate powers want to hang "to encourage all the others." So the overall message this threat conveys to members of Congress is to pull in your horns, be docile, don't be an annoyance, and perhaps you won't become a target. What a bargain for big special interests, if just having the *capability* to attack is enough to "encourage" everyone! You don't actually have to spend the money at all.

And that's the gift five pro-corporate justices gave the big special interests.

The threat of an attack doesn't even have to be specific to one particular candidate to be politically effective. Threats that are general, that are more in the nature of an announcement and that would never qualify in court as criminal bribery or extortion, can nevertheless ping loudly on the political radar of candidates and campaigns and influence political behavior in corrupting ways.

A sense of what that might look like comes from the actual warnings some special interests have issued. The climate-change-denying, Koch-backed campaign group Americans for Prosperity (a helpful name at letting the public know who is really behind it, for sure) within months made two big announcements: one, that the group was going to raise and spend $889 million in the 2016 election (since adjusted downward to merely $750 million); and two, as Carol Davenport reported in the *New York Times*, that the group would put anyone who crossed them on climate change at a "severe disadvantage."[23] Later, as reported by Davenport, the group warned that supporting a price on carbon pollution would be a "political loser."[24] According to an article in *Politico*, they bragged of the "political peril" that would result for those who crossed them.[25] You can practically imagine a big brute walking into some campaign office in a black trench coat, slapping a bat into his palm. "Nice little campaign you got going here, bub, be a shame to see it 'severely disadvantaged' . . . oh, and by the way, what're you doing on climate change?" Smack, smack.

If you want another example of how special interest politics works in Washington, read *Politico*'s story, "Drug Lobby Plans Counterattack on Prices," from August 4, 2016: the plot of the story is that PhRMA, "a sleeping giant, which routinely spends more on lobbying than any other health care group and took in more than $200 million in member dues in 2014," is "gearing up to spend hundreds of millions of dollars on a post-election ad war," seeking "to reassert its dominance in Washington after several years in which it has taken a public shellacking over prices." The punch line of the story: "Targeting politicians is not part of the initial plan, but lobbyists say the organization is prepared to do so if members of Congress or the executive branch push agendas that are seen as detrimental to the industry."[26] *Citizens United* has made all the difference in targeting politicians, and it's not for nothing that the opening bid is lobbyists telegraphing the threat before the money has to be spent.

There is an equation in political threats: size times intensity equals danger. If someone is furious at you and is going to go all in for your opponent and give them $200, the intensity may be high but the size of the threat is low, and the threat is not particularly acute. An anxious congressman can still go about his job of representing the many. If there's a billionaire in your state, one not particularly interested in politics, a prudent congresswoman may want to steer around him, since the size of his fortune is a political threat. But if he's not intensely engaged, his threat is not particularly acute. However, mark the size of the threat at $889 million (or $750 million) to be spent all in one election, and mark the intensity at "you'll be 'severely disadvantaged' if you cross us," and a very big warning beacon pings very loudly on the radar of every campaign and candidate.

Before the flood, a corporate CEO could threaten to host a fundraiser for your opponent, he could put his support for your opponent in the employee newsletter, or he could send your opponent a $10,000

PAC check, and that was about it. And he'd have to do it all publicly. It was a crime, for instance, for the CEO to launder a donation through an employee, friend, or family member to boost his giving clout or hide his role. Now the corporate CEO (or more likely his political operatives, as he probably doesn't want to get his hands too dirty with the new "wet work" of politics) simply has to approve a dollar number and unleash the new apparatus. Since corporations regularly seek benefits in Washington worth many billions of dollars for their industry, the natural limit on the dollar number it makes economic sense for the CEO to unleash is very, very high.

One example is when hedge fund CEO Robert Mercer took umbrage at a proposed federal transaction tax by Oregon's Representative Peter DeFazio that would have taxed hyper-fast "flash trades" of the type done by the hedge fund. As *Time* reported, Mercer retaliated in force: the "hedge-fund boss has financed challenges to the Oregon Democrat for four election cycles running. 'DeFazio pissed him off,' says a Republican consultant who has worked with Mercer." Showing bipartisan spirit, the hedge-fund magnate also went after John McCain for participating in a Senate hearing investigating an accounting maneuver used by the hedge fund to avoid nearly $7 billion in taxes. Again from *Time*: "with McCain locked in a primary fight, the financier cut a $200,000 check to a group supporting McCain's right-wing challenger. 'We issued a scathing report about this guy evading taxes—his firm. I'm sure there's no connection,' McCain quipped."[27] While McCain and DeFazio did not quail, lesser members of Congress certainly could have; and for a $7 billion dollar tax dodge, the political attacks and related threats could easily get into enormous numbers.

In areas where the Supreme Court actually has some experience and some idea of what it's talking about—say, with respect to the buying of judges—it has been somewhat less generous to the big special interests. In the case of *Caperton v. A.T. Massey Coal Co.*, an elected West Virginia Supreme Court of Appeals justice had been the beneficiary of more than $3 million in election support through a nonprofit started and funded by the owner of Massey Coal and through that owner's independent expenditures.[28] The money was raised and spent for the state supreme court judge's election while a case involving Massey

Coal—in which the coal company lost a $50 million trial verdict—was coming up through the West Virginia courts. The coal company owner's nonprofit political group ended up spending three times more money on the judge's election than the judge's own campaign spent. (Rather like today's candidate-specific super PACs that spend more than the campaigns.)

Obviously, the coal company owner wanted a friendly court for the appeal of a $50 million loss, whether Riviera vacations or campaign contributions were the inducement. (Another judge on the court had been photographed vacationing on the French Riviera with the same coal company owner, but that judge prudently recused himself from the case.) The judge whose election was funded by Massey Coal's owner turned out to be the swing vote in favor of the coal company when the appeal was decided, and the $50 million verdict was overturned.

When the case went up to the United States Supreme Court in 2009, this was all too smelly for Justice Kennedy, who wrote the majority opinion for the Court, stating, "We conclude that there is a serious risk of actual bias—based on objective and reasonable perceptions—when a person with a personal stake in a particular case had a significant and disproportionate influence in placing the judge on the case by raising funds or directing the judge's election campaign when the case was pending or imminent."[29] So from now on, if a litigant before a judge has such massive influence over the judge hearing his case, the remedy must be recusal of the judge—at least if the case is pending or imminent when the influence is acquired. (Otherwise, maybe the influence is okay; who knows?) No similar remedy is available for members of Congress, no matter how "significant and disproportionate" the influence acquired by a big interest through campaign spending.

(Stunningly, the other four hard-core members of the Supreme Court's pro-corporate bloc all dissented from the majority decision in the *Massey Coal* case. Even this level of corporate influence-buying through campaign spending, even in the election of a judge actually hearing the coal company's case, even when that judge was the swing vote in the company's favor, was not too much for them. Corporate money can do no wrong.)

* * *

As noted, this is the first Supreme Court in American history to have no justice with experience running for or holding elective office. With that experience gap on the Court, many people believe the decision in *Citizens United* by the five conservative justices was the product of ignorance and error. Trevor Potter is a well-respected and thoughtful campaign lawyer who has represented both John McCain's presidential campaign and Stephen Colbert's tongue-in-cheek super PAC, and has also served as chairman of the Federal Election Commission. He says, "The conservatives on the court seem to fail to understand what leads to corruption or the appearance of corruption." He considers them "out of their depth" in campaign finance law, yet "forging ahead without understanding the consequences." He notes that the conservatives completely blew their forecast of what would happen in the wake of their decision, in the way of transparency of donors and independence from campaigns. Contrary to their expectations, he says, "what we got was a tsunami of money in the 2012 elections from tax-exempt groups that did not disclose their donors and from supposedly independent super PACs run by candidates' former top aides, close friends and family members. This was easy to predict. But the five justices who signed the majority opinion didn't see it."[30] Similarly, former Federal Election Commission chairman (and current commissioner) Ann Ravel says that the justices "did not understand what the implications were going to be of what they did."[31] Maybe.

There is another theory: that the conservatives specifically wanted to open the floodgates of corporate spending, and went through elaborate machinations and contortions to accomplish their purpose. They may have been ignorant of how badly it would work out, but they had a plan.

To explore that possibility, we now move from what's bad *about* the *Citizens United* decision, to what's bad *within* the *Citizens United* decision.

Unleashing the corporate power *Citizens United* set loose in our elections required the conservative justices to go through some pretty remarkable contortions: reversing previous decisions by the Court that had said the opposite, making up facts that are demonstrably flat-out wrong, creating a make-believe world of "independence" and "transparency" in election spending, and maneuvering their own judicial procedures to prevent a factual record that would belie those facts they were making up. Each of the contortions was unusual, objectionable, wrong, or all of the above.

The sins of *Citizens United* are many, but the most venal is the strategy that links them. Let's look at the individual sins of *Citizens United*, and then at the strategy. Together, these make abundantly clear that the conservative corporatists on the Court got exactly the results they were shooting for from the get-go.

Let's start with their "facts." Despite more than a century of warnings by the elected branches of government about the real dangers of corporate political corruption, despite harsh experience of corporate-funded corruption that had led to those warnings, despite recent precedents from the Court itself protecting against corporate corruption in elections, despite extensive records on corporate corruption developed in those prior precedents, and despite 100 years of settled law from Congress, the conservative justices used their bare 5–4 majority to make the fateful (many would say fanciful) finding of fact that "independent expenditures, including those made by corporations, do not give rise to corruption or the appearance of corruption."[32] They didn't stop there. They went on to find that "the appearance of influence or access, furthermore, will not cause the electorate to lose faith in our democracy."[33] These assertions in *Citizens United* stood on nothing. They were bald assertions, in air.

As you wonder about these puzzling assertions, remember something else: there is a well-established judicial principle that courts of appeal, and especially the Supreme Court, *do not make findings of fact*. That is the job of trial courts and juries. In our judicial system, the fact-finding is done by those who take the testimony and hear the witnesses. Appellate courts seek errors of law and simply take the facts as found for them by the trial courts. From its earliest days, the Supreme Court has defined its job as deciding "what the law is."[34] So it is not just weird that the *Citizens United* justices made up *bad* facts; it's weird that they made up facts *at all*.

This was no small thing. The rule against higher courts' fact-finding is one way the American system of separated powers restrains courts from gallivanting off into policy making. Courts don't get to pick the topics they want to rule on; they have to wait for cases to come to them in the ordinary course of litigation. And they can't meddle with the facts of the case as it comes to them. The appellate courts are thus tethered to the facts as the lower courts have found them. In a government based on separated powers, this limitation on the free-range wanderings of higher courts is not an idle principle; it's a key one. A judge "is not a knight-errant, roaming at will in pursuit of his own ideal," to borrow Justice Benjamin Cardozo's words, and tethering appellate courts to the facts in the case is an important judicial constraint against such roaming.[35] Here, that principle simply went out the window. Why? Read on.

The Supreme Court usually has a factual record presented to it and then must interpret the law based on that factual record. Here, the case *had no factual record* on the fundamental question of corrupt corporate political influence. As Justice Stevens objected in dissent: "In this case, the record is not simply incomplete or unsatisfactory; it is nonexistent."[36] In this respect *Citizens United* differed from the cases it overruled, which had voluminous records on the danger of corporate corruption—including the hundred-year-old Senate finding that the dangers of corporate corruption of elections were too obvious to need elaboration. Having no record, in a case of this magnitude, was unusual.

It was unusual that there was no factual record on this question, but it was no accident. There was no factual record because of a procedural maneuver pulled by the Court itself. Every case that goes to argument in the United States Supreme Court has a "question presented" that confirms what the case is about. The briefs that parties file in the Court are required to have a section stating the "question presented"—it is one of the Court's formalities. It makes sure everyone knows what the issues before the Court are. In a very unusual procedural maneuver, in the *Citizens United* case the chief justice late in the proceedings *changed* its "question presented."[37]

Citizens United was initially an extremely narrow case challenging whether the McCain-Feingold campaign finance law prohibited, in the thirty days before primary elections, airing an on-demand cable video critical of a candidate—Hillary Clinton, in this case.[38] Late in the proceedings, after the legal briefs were in and oral arguments by all the parties were done, the Court issued a *new* "question presented," which reframed the case as a broad challenge to the government's power to regulate corporate spending on elections. In dissent, Justice Stevens aptly explained, "five Justices were unhappy with the limited nature of the case before us, so they changed the case to give themselves an opportunity to change the law."[39] Balls and strikes, indeed.

By changing the question presented so late in the proceedings, they also gave themselves an opportunity to change the law *without a record*. An extensive legislative record or trial court record concerning corruption from corporate political activity would ordinarily have been developed in the preceding stages of a case of such magnitude. Past experience from similar cases shows what such a record would have revealed: a massive, reeking, obvious, and persistent threat of political corruption by corporate forces. Without any record, however, the conservatives conveniently avoided that obstacle to the ruling they were pursuing.

In sum, changing the "question presented" late in the case was an unusual procedural maneuver. That maneuver created the unusual circumstance of the Court not having a full record on the new question it had presented itself, but it was necessary to have no record in order to open the way for that equally unusual assertion of fact about corruption.

Without a record to the contrary, the justices were free to break the "no fact-finding" rule, take that one little fact-finding liberty, and pretend that corporate money, even spent in unlimited amounts, can't corrupt politics or even create the appearance of corruption. To use their exact phrase, it would "not give rise to corruption or the appearance of corruption." This finding, made in that exact language, was more than just an observation; it was a key.

The last piece of the *Citizens United* puzzle to understand is a basic principle of First Amendment law that limits free speech rights under the First Amendment. Free speech rights must be weighed against the government's efforts to police corruption, or even the appearance of corruption, in elections—and if the efforts to control corruption are reasonable ones, the right to speech must yield.[40] For instance, conspiring to fix an election likely involves talking, but it's not protected free speech. The test is whether the government is reasonably protecting against "corruption or the appearance of corruption."[41] The Court's puzzling finding of fact that "independent expenditures, including those made by corporations, do not give rise to corruption or the appearance of corruption," suddenly comes into focus.[42] It synchronizes exactly to this core principle of First Amendment law, even matching its language. It was the key to turn this lock.

If it was their goal from the outset to open up unlimited corporate spending in elections, the five justices knew they *had* to find that corporate political spending was not corrupting. Otherwise their First Amendment rationale for allowing unlimited corporate political spending would flop. The factual assertion by the justices may have been ludicrous, but it was *necessary*. Without it, the corporate "First Amendment right" they wished to create would lose to the government's legitimate interest in protecting the integrity of elections. That governmental interest in fair and honest elections, and in protecting against "corruption, or the appearance of corruption," would be an insurmountable barrier without that precisely matching finding that corporate money in elections *can't cause corruption*. That door had to be opened to get to the desired result, and this key turned the lock.

And then on you go through the rest of the scheme. To make the findings of fact you need in order to knock aside the political corruption concern, you have to break the rules about appellate courts making findings of fact. To make the specific findings of fact that turn the lock, you also have to keep out of the case any factual record, since the records established in previous cases show that a factual record on this question would blow your imaginary facts out of the water. To avoid having a factual record on the question, you have to fiddle with the question presented late in the proceedings, when the time for creating a troublesome record is long past. And, of course, you have to make the laughable findings of fact.

Each of these is an error, but they are not separate errors. They link together in a chain of necessity to form the only avenue to the decision's result. And that result was a massive explosion of corporate political power and influence.

When all the effort and craft it took to link these steps is deconstructed, only one rational conclusion can be drawn: that the five pro-corporate justices were bound and determined from the very start to unleash corporate power into our elections—to deliver that political boost to those big corporate interests willing and able to spend big political money.

And that line about how "the appearance of influence or access, furthermore, will not cause the electorate to lose faith in our democracy"? Like other "factual" findings in *Citizens United*, this just ain't factual. An independent poll conducted in 2012 by the Brennan Center for Justice found that approximately 70 percent of Americans believe super PAC spending leads to corruption.[43] In the same survey, 75 percent of Republicans and 78 percent of Democrats agreed that there would be less corruption if there were limits on how much could be given to super PACs.[44] A June 2015 *New York Times*/CBS News poll found that more than four out of five Americans believe money plays too great a role in political campaigns, while two-thirds say that the wealthy have a greater chance of influencing the electoral process than other Americans.[45] In a November 2015 *Washington Post* column titled "Americans See a Government of, by and for the Rich," Harold Meyerson described within the American public "one area of remarkable agreement: Across party lines, Americans believe that our economic system is rigged to favor the wealthy and big corporations, and that our political system is, too." Indeed, he notes that "by nearly a 2-to-1 margin (64 percent to 36 percent), Americans believe their 'vote does not matter because of the influence that wealthy individuals and big corporations have on the electoral process.' "[46]

That is new since *Citizens United*. People are mad: 69 percent of poll respondents recently confirmed that they "feel angry because our political system seems to only be working for the insiders with money and power, like those on Wall Street or in Washington, rather than working to help everyday people get ahead."[47] And eight out of ten Americans disapprove of *Citizens United*.[48]

Aside from the peculiar method the Court needed to get to its result in *Citizens United*, the path to that result ran right over several judicial principles usually thought of as conservative principles. One collateral casualty on the road to the *Citizens United* decision was the conservative judicial doctrine called "originalism," discussed in Chapter Six. Originalism is seen as a conservative principle because conservative judges favor it and because its approach to constitutional interpretation focuses on the original intent of the Founders. If your touchstone is the mores and prejudices of property-holding white men of the late eighteenth century, you have a pretty good conservative weapon against modern readings of the Constitution.

In *Citizens United* the five justices made the leap that corporations are people and that money is speech. Thus they were able to give corporate money First Amendment protection as speech. They went a more roundabout route than that, but that's effectively where they ended up. And that's quite a leap when you think how suspicious the Founding Fathers were of corporations, and when you consider that there is no mention whatever of corporations in the Constitution. The conservative justices' fidelity to "originalism" is inconstant, and *Citizens United* is another case in which the conservatives ignored this principle in getting to their desired result.

In *Citizens United*, the only thorough discussion of the Founders' "original intent" appears in Justice Stevens's dissent, not in the majority opinion or in Justice Scalia's concurrence. Justice Stevens correctly explains the Founding Fathers' dim view of corporations. They were suspicious of corporations. They considered corporations prone to abuse and scandal. And, as discussed, the corporations that did exist at the time of the Founding were largely creatures of the States. They bore little resemblance to enormous contemporary corporations, and had no lawful role in electioneering.[49]

Justice Stevens rightly describes it as "implausible that the Framers believed 'the freedom of speech' would extend equally to all corporate speakers, much less that it would preclude legislatures from taking limited measures to guard against corporate capture of elections."[50] Avoiding any discussion of originalism, the *Citizens United* majority reached a result that would have astounded the Founding Fathers: unlimited corporate spending in American elections, with big corporations in a more robust political position than human persons.

Another core judicial doctrine abandoned in the *Citizens United* decision is respect for precedent, for previous decisions of the Court. As noted, respect for precedent gives the law stability, and is usually seen as a conservative judicial doctrine. To treat corporations as people and money as speech, the conservative justices had to throw over previous Supreme Court decisions that had said the exact opposite, upending a century of law, including *McConnell v. Federal Election Commission*, decided in 2003, and *Austin v. Michigan Chamber of Commerce*, decided in 1990.[51] Justice Stevens recognized in his dissent that the principle of *stare decisis*—"it stands decided"—ensures that our Nation's "bedrock principles are founded in the law rather than in the proclivities of individuals."[52] The conservative bloc undid these judicial precedents with almost no hesitation. Justice Stevens reviewed those recent prior precedents of the Court that had gone the opposite way, and noted that since those precedents "the only relevant thing that has changed . . . is the composition of this Court."[53]

The big winners of *Citizens United* were the forces of corporate power; the justices' ruling tipped the balance of power in their favor. The Republican Party was a direct beneficiary of *Citizens United*. For example, the largest corporate lobbying group in America is the U.S. Chamber Committee. The Chamber virtually exclusively supports Republican candidates and spends big money for them, to the point where the boundary between the Chamber and the Republican Party has become nearly indistinguishable. Beyond the Chamber, super PACs and other nonprofit organizations unleashed by *Citizens United* spent upward of $450 million in the 2012 election cycle to support Republicans or attack President Obama.[54] At one stage in the 2016 election cycle, PACs and super PACs supporting Republicans had raised 93 percent of all outside political donations.[55]

Citizens United fits the pattern of the conservative justices favoring Republican interests in election cases, and it also fits the pattern of the Roberts Court favoring corporate interests. Americans have noticed these patterns. Now by a ratio of nine to one, Americans doubt the Supreme Court will give an individual a fair shake against a corporation.[56]

Less than a decade after the *Citizens United* decision, the two premises on which it rests—that all this corporate election spending would be "transparent" to the public, and that it would be "independent" of the candidates[57]—have both proven to be false. The notion was that if big corporations were just out there on their own saying their piece ("We like free trade so we support Congressman Snooks"), and if it were clear to everyone who they were ("We're Mammoth Corporation and we approved this message"), then they wouldn't collude with candidates for favors, and they would be accountable for what they were saying and doing. It is brutally evident in the decision's aftermath that neither premise is even close to true. The current system is rotten with collusion and bereft of accountability. Yet, despite repeated opportunities, the conservatives have taken no action to correct for those errors or to police the slime they have created.

They had the chance in a case that came to them out of Montana, *American Tradition Partnership v. Bullock*.[58] Since 1912, Montana state law had prohibited corporate political spending, be it for or against a candidate. When the law was challenged based on *Citizens United*, the Montana Supreme Court upheld the ban as constitutional.[59]

A few things were different in the *Bullock* case than in *Citizens United*. First, there was an extensive factual record in Montana, based on Montana's long history of political corruption by mining interests.[60] The political corruption by corporate interests in Montana's history was almost theatrical. For one instance, in the early 1900s, Montana copper baron William Andrews Clark famously bought himself a U.S. Senate seat, bribing state legislators at a time when U.S. senators were still picked by state legislatures.[61] He was unrepentant, saying, "I never bought a man who wasn't for sale."[62]

A second difference was that the law in question was a state law, not a federal law. The Court had the chance to reconsider whether as a matter of "states rights" state legislatures in states with an abundant local history of corrupt corporate political influence could act locally, though Congress couldn't act nationally.[63]

Third, by the time the Montana case came to the Supreme Court in 2011, it was already evident that neither the "transparency" nor the "independence" premise of *Citizens United* was true in the real world. The world the five justices had dreamed was not the world as it was. This new decision gave them the chance to correct for those errors.

In a bipartisan brief to the Court, Senator John McCain and I argued all these points, and also argued that *Citizens United* had failed to consider the problem of private threats and promises in its evaluation of how noncorrupting this corporate campaign spending was all going to be.[64]

The Supreme Court didn't even give the case a hearing. The

Montana legislature had passed this law a century earlier. The Montana Supreme Court had carefully distinguished Montana's circumstances from those present in *Citizens United*. Montana had a rich historic record of local corporate political corruption. Montana's attorney general defended the Montana law before the Supreme Court.[65] None of that mattered. The five pro-corporate justices summarily dismissed the case in a terse order, again 5–4.[66]

Later on, another campaign finance case called *McCutcheon* reached the Court, challenging a campaign finance law that had survived *Citizens United*: the aggregate limits on the amount of money individuals could contribute in total to candidates, parties, and committees in one election cycle.[67] Once again, the five conservatives relied on their own "facts" about corruption, transparency, and independence, even after these had been so thoroughly disproven in practice.[68] Again they turned down the opportunity to correct their plain errors, instead throwing out another protection put in place by Congress to safeguard the integrity of our elections. It seems they were happy with the way *Citizens United* had worked out. Mission accomplished. Money unleashed.

But the horror of *Citizens United*'s effects is so great that some glimmers of regret are appearing. Justice Kennedy has said that it's "not working the way it should."[69] Justice Scalia before he passed away was more defensive, saying, "If the system seems crazy to you, don't blame it on the Court."[70] Actually, I blame it squarely on the Court.

In the end, our faith in the Supreme Court is founded on its constitutional role as a neutral arbiter of our laws. I submit that *Citizens United* does not merit that faith. Corporate power helped get that conservative majority onto the Supreme Court. In return, the conservative majority on the Supreme Court very deliberately opened American democracy to massive, unprecedented levels of corporate political power and influence.

It's a disgrace for the Court.

CHAPTER EIGHT

Capture of Regulatory Agencies

I GREW UP IN FARAWAY PLACES, AMONG AMERICAN families who had left behind the safety and comforts of home to serve their country. These families were willing to face risks and discomforts to represent the United States in grim and dangerous places overseas. They inspired me.

As a United States attorney and as my state's attorney general, I worked with lawyers and prosecutors who could have doubled their salary in private practice, but they loved the work and service, and they stayed. I've worked with first responders who go out at all hours and in all weather, and who are required in the course of their duties to see things that we would never want to see, things that would dwell on in our nightmares. I have watched talented men and women throw themselves energetically into solving the big problems that only government can solve, working appalling hours week after week without complaint. I've seen our armed forces and intelligence agencies doing their duty bravely in areas of conflict far away. I've admired the work of government scientists who are defining the cutting edge of knowledge in areas such as cyber technology and disease research. These government employees are admirable, principled, talented, hardworking people. I know there are petty bureaucrats out there, and government workers who are "retired in place." But that, in my experience at both the state and federal levels, is the exception, not the rule.

So there is my bias. I confess it. I admire hardworking government people. I'm also a fan of the mechanisms government uses—rules and regulations—to help us live together in a civilized way. I've seen overseas how desperate life can be in countries where government regulation has failed. We are very lucky to live in America.

I accept that some rules and regulations are hard to understand. Arrival to Washington, D.C., for instance, is through Union Station, where you walk from your train through the soaring great hall of the station out to a long sidewalk where fifty taxis may be waiting, with fifty people waiting for taxis. Someone decided that it would be a good idea to make a rule that only one person could be loaded into a taxi at a time, creating a completely artificial wait. You could load all the people into all the taxis in about three minutes if the linekeeper just went away, or better yet helped those travelers who need assistance. But that sort of time-wasting regulation for regulation's sake is, in my experience, the exception in America and not the rule. (In less developed and more corrupt societies these artificial gateways can be created just to provide an opportunity for someone to collect a little fee to get you through the gateway, but that's a whole different issue.)

In the private sector, I've also seen plenty of time-wasting, incompetence, and worse. I've seen big banks ruin people's lives making decisions so dumb the decisions hurt the bank itself as well as the beleaguered homeowner. I've spent frustrating hours trying to get through corporate phone trees that seem designed to exhaust rather than help you. Pick the company that has annoyed you most. You cannot convince me that government has a monopoly on incompetence and the private sector a monopoly on efficiency. At the extremes of private sector misconduct, I've over and over had to clean up in the courtroom after instances of corporate fraud, corporate crime, and corporate pollution.

I'm not arguing that government should run everything, or even most things. Corporate competition on a fair playing field is often not only the right course but a fantastic blessing for humanity. All I ask is that you remember, when you hear about the evils of "bureaucrats" and "big government," the "trial of strength" Jefferson warned us of. Big corporations are in a contest against government as their only real rival for power. If they can convince you that all corporate activity is good and efficient and helpful and that all government activity is bad and wasteful and interfering, they win an advantage in their "trial of strength." Whipping up scorn for government is very convenient in the corporate contest for political power. So take whatever side you wish in that contest, but at least be aware that there's a contest under way.

Clearly, some government regulations are ill-advised, some are stale, and some are overly broad. But look at the safety that regulation provides. Medicines are not snake-oil mysteries any longer. People are rarely burned or killed nowadays in boiler explosions. Automobiles have airbags. Smokestacks mostly have pollution controls. Stock jobbers have a harder time suckering innocent investors. Most insurance policies actually pay when the insured risk occurs. Quacks can't be doctors and barbers can't be surgeons. We take for granted the safety and reliability that a regulated world has built.

We also take for granted how regulation helps advance our economic progress. Regulation helps channel America's competitive enterprise into good and helpful innovations instead of into new tricks and traps for consumers, or new ways of cutting safety corners, or new ways of conning gullible buyers. Confidence in our industries grows when consumers know they can count on the safety and reliability of the product. Ask yourself: would the American pharmaceutical industry be a world powerhouse if patent medicine hucksters were still allowed to operate? Regulation sets a positive frame for our economic progress. Just as the solution to medical malpractice is not to get rid of medicine, so the solution to bad regulations is not to get rid of regulation.

In his book *The War on Science*, Shawn Otto makes an interesting point about regulation and freedom. Our initial reaction might be to think that regulations constrain freedom, which is certainly the narrative that big, regulated industries want to sell about regulation. But that is not necessarily true. "[W]e accept limitations on our individual freedoms to gain greater freedom," Otto argues. This greater freedom comes through "regulations that reduce smog, acid rain, ozone destruction, the use of DDT, backyard burning of garbage, driving while intoxicated, noise pollution, lead in paint and gasoline, certain carcinogens, water pollution—and more recently, exposure to secondhand smoke, injuries caused by not wearing seat belts, and texting while driving." As he describes it, the freedom we gain from these regulations is "the freedom they provide from the tyranny of others' stupid decisions," freedom from "a tyranny of trash—of ignorance."[1] Of course, to the creators of the trash and the purveyors of the ignorance, regulation is indeed a constraint; but it's one that delivers freedoms the rest of us enjoy.

Over the past fifty years, Congress has tasked an alphabet soup of regulatory agencies—the EPA, NHTSA, FDA, SEC, and countless others—with protecting the public interest. These agencies have been given the job of enforcing laws that ensure the safety of the water we drink, the air we breathe, the cars we drive, the medications we take, and the markets we invest in for our retirement and our children's future. These regulatory agencies have vast and vital responsibilities to Congress and the American people.

The incentive of regulated industries to work mischief with these regulatory agencies is equally vast and vital. Big corporate interests do not overlook the administrative agencies. Lobbying legislatures, securing agreeable appointments to the Supreme Court, pouring money into politics, and trying to elect a friendly president are all important priorities of the corporate political effort. But over the long haul, influence over regulatory agencies can be an equally valuable proposition.

As we've seen too often, wealthy and powerful industries can acquire excessive influence over regulatory agencies. When they do, the consequences can be grave. The basic tactic to control a regulatory agency has been in place for as long as there have been regulatory agencies, and the phenomenon of a regulated industry seizing control over its regulator is widely known as "regulatory capture."[2] When a regulatory agency is captured, it becomes the industry's tool, overlooking errors and misdeeds, setting rules that favor the industry, and keeping out competition that might challenge the big incumbents. That's when regulatory agencies stop working for us and become pawns of the industry they were supposed to regulate.

Two recent catastrophes—BP's *Deepwater Horizon* oil spill in the Gulf of Mexico and the giant 2008 Wall Street financial meltdown—I see as direct results of regulatory capture. They offer powerful examples of what happens when regulatory agencies come under the influence of corporations and industry.

* * *

Responsibility for regulating oil and gas drilling in the Gulf at the time of the *Deepwater Horizon* disaster fell to the U.S. Department of Interior's Minerals Management Service (MMS). But the relationship between MMS and the oil and gas industry had become completely toxic. Agency staff failed to collect millions of dollars in royalties owed to the American people.[3] MMS district managers were documented telling their investigators, "Obviously we are all oil industry."[4] Agency employees accepted gifts from regulated companies: trips to the Peach Bowl on a private airplane, skeet shooting contests, hunting and fishing trips, and golf tournaments.[5] Social events hosted by industry for MMS representatives involved illegal drug use and sex.[6] An MMS inspector inspected the oil drilling platforms of a company with which he had a job application pending[7]—yes, while they were considering whether to hire him, he was inspecting their oil drilling rigs. It should come as no surprise that he found no violations.[8]

The *Wall Street Journal* published an opinion piece about the Gulf oil spill, saying: "By all accounts, MMS operated as a rubber stamp for BP. It is a striking example of regulatory capture: Agencies tasked with protecting the public interest come to identify with the regulated industry and protect its interests against that of the public. The result: Government fails to protect the public."[9] Even my hometown paper, the *Providence Journal*, editorialized trenchantly about the role of MMS in the Gulf disaster: "The Deepwater Horizon accident has made it painfully clear that, in its current form, MMS is a pathetic public guardian. Neither it nor BP was prepared for a disaster of this magnitude, and MMS's cozy relationship with industry is a big reason why."[10]

The regulatory failures at the Securities and Exchange Commission (SEC) in the run-up to the Wall Street meltdown were less pungent, but still extraordinarily painful and damaging for America. Led on by Wall Street, the SEC, which should have been regulating the financial industry stringently and limiting the amount of debt any one institution took on, instead allowed "leverage ratios" of up to thirty to one, meaning that for every dollar a bank had in equity, it could hold $30 in debt.[11] If you're an ambitious Wall Street speculator, leverage is a beautiful thing. If you're in a deal at thirty-to-one leverage and the deal doubles the investment made, you earn thirty times your investment, less whatever you paid the lenders you brought into the deal. If you're a bank using depositors' money on which you pay 4 percent annual interest, they share your risk but you keep the big payday.

Do the math. You put your $1 and your depositors' $29 into the kitty, and you get $60 when the deal pays back double the investment. You return the $29 you borrowed plus 4 percent (if the deal took a year, that would be $1.16 in interest), and you win a $28.84 payday on your $1 investment. What's not to love?

Until one of the deals blows up. If it's a total loss, on your own $1 gamble you've got nothing, and you still owe your depositors their $29 and their $1.16 in interest. That's where leverage can hurt. And it will particularly hurt if it happens widely, if a whole market turns sour and lots of bets fail at once. Maybe paying back the $29 to the depositors wipes out the capital of the bank entirely. If the whole bank can't stay solvent, then the government has to step in to provide any money still owed to the depositors (the government guarantees those deposits up to $250,000 per account). The government may even have to bail out the banks themselves if it looks like their collapse will take down the whole economy, which is more or less the story of the Great Wall Street Meltdown at the end of George W. Bush's presidency.

Regulatory capture has been around for a long time, with discussions of it all over economic treatises and administrative law textbooks. In a column in the *Wall Street Journal*, Thomas Frank told a fascinating early tale of regulatory capture involving the Interstate Commerce Commission (ICC) at the very inception of federal regulatory agencies in the 1880s. The ICC was designed to regulate railroad freight rates. Grover Cleveland's attorney general, Richard Olney, had been a prominent railroad lawyer. When Olney's former boss at the railroad corporation asked Olney to get rid of the regulatory agency completely, Olney replied, "The Commission . . . is, or can be made, of great use to the railroads. It satisfies the popular clamor for a government supervision of the railroads, at the same time that that supervision is almost entirely nominal. Further, the older such a commission gets to be, the more inclined it will be found to take the business and railroad view of things. . . . The part of wisdom is not to destroy the Commission, but to utilize it."[12]

That remains the recurring goal of regulated industries: to tame and "utilize" the regulator. And regulatory agencies are often not very good at pushing back against that corporate pressure.

In 1913, the year he was inaugurated as president, Woodrow Wilson wrote: "If the government is to tell big business men how to run their business, then don't you see that big business men have to get closer to the government even than they are now? Don't you see that they must capture the government, in order not to be restrained too much by it?"[13]

The first dean of Princeton's Woodrow Wilson School of Public and International Affairs, Marver Bernstein, wrote more than half a century ago of the pattern that regulators tend over time to "[become] more concerned with the general health of the industry," even to try "to prevent changes which adversely affect" the industry; and ultimately to "surrender," when the regulatory agency "finally becomes a captive of the regulated groups."[14] He noted that this problem of regulators captured by industry "is a problem of ethics and morality as well as administrative method."[15] He properly pointed out that this ethical failure is also "a blow to democratic government."[16] After all, it is democratic government that is cheated when an agency of the government is secretly working for the industry and not the people.

A regulatory agency is constantly engaged with the regulated industry. The industry is pushing on it all the time. The industry has lawyers and lobbyists working the agency. The industry threatens lawsuits if it gets regulations it does not like, and is accommodating and friendly when it gets regulations it does like. The industry often twirls a revolving door: nice jobs for regulators who have been good to the industry, or industry operatives cycled into regulatory positions and then taken care of when they return to the private sector.

Regulated entities have a strong incentive to gain influence over the drafting and enforcement of regulations. The Food and Drug Administration, for instance, regulates industries that represent a trillion-dollar market.[17] The bank robber Willie Sutton is said to have once explained that he robbed banks "because that's where the money is."[18]

When it comes to why regulated entities seek influence with regulators, the answer is the same: that's where the money is. In the high-stakes derivatives market—derivatives are financial contracts that "derive" from real assets, such as a "futures contract" to buy or sell an asset at a given price at a future date—the notional value of derivative products alone is more than thirty times greater than the gross domestic product of the United States.[19] That's a lot of incentive.

It's the same reason powerful interests spend millions of dollars to lobby Congress. In the Eisenhower era, Senator Everett Dirksen was rumored to have commented about a congressional appropriation, "A billion here, a billion there, and pretty soon you're talking real money."[20] With regard to drugs, derivatives, and other massive industries, the billions are approaching trillions. So while the big bucks spent to influence decision making may seem amazing, the money spent is actually trivial compared with the stakes. These are well-placed political "investments."

With such large rewards, industry ends up at a major organizational and resource advantage compared with the more diffuse public interest. In a volume of articles dedicated to examining regulatory capture, law professor and economics blogger James Kwak notes that while industry resources can focus with great precision and persistence, public interest groups are "likely to lack the organizational infrastructure and staying power to knock on regulators' doors month in, month out on issue after issue."[21] Intensity of interest matters in the regulatory as well as the political world. And the intensity of industry interest in regulatory decision making is difficult to match.

On the side of the public interest, nonprofit groups are ordinarily spending down scarce resources with no reasonable expectation of financial profit from their regulatory exertions. Corporate influence machinery can be self-perpetuating and pay for itself, where the public interest machinery requires constant replenishment. Up against corporate influence, the public interest is the eroding seawall holding back the ocean.

This mess is made worse because so much regulatory decision making and oversight occurs outside of public attention. Figuring out where capture has occurred is not easy. Regulatory capture is notoriously difficult to detect. Little-known agencies are often the target. Rarely does a corporate entity plant its flag victoriously over a regulatory agency, to announce that the agency has been successfully captured. By its nature, regulatory capture is a stealth operation.

Corporate interests have the patience and resources to play the long game. The revolving door between industry and government is an example. University of Chicago economist Luigi Zingales explains that "this form of regulatory capture does not require an explicit quid pro quo between regulators and regulated, where a job is offered in exchange for a favorable decision."[22] It's not necessary or smart to be that obvious. The implicit prospect of a high-paying industry job may sufficiently induce a regulator to favor industry as he thinks about moving on. He may notice how well the industry's friends do when they leave the agency, compared to how coldly consumer-oriented members are treated. Zingales describes this subtle pressure as "much more legitimate" and thus "quite pervasive."[23]

Regulatory capture can cause terrible damage. We often hear how high the cost of burdensome regulation is, but the cost of inadequate regulation can be catastrophic. I will never forget the families of the men killed on the *Deepwater Horizon* rig, who came to Congress asking for help and answers after lax enforcement of regulations led to conditions on the rig that a judge later characterized as "reckless" and "grossly negligent."[24] I will never forget the hardworking Rhode Islanders who lost their jobs when the Wall Street meltdown shattered our economy and who then lost their homes to foreclosure—after having worked honestly all their lives in good jobs and done nothing wrong. They were the collateral damage of the government agencies failing to regulate Wall Street. And I'm sure the families let down by the Mine Safety and Health Administration who lost loved ones in the Sago Mine and other mining disasters bear from that loss an incalculable agony. News stories describing the agency as a "meek watchdog" with a revolving door of industry appointees must have come as bitter solace.[25]

There's another, more general harm, too: agency capture assaults democratic government. "We the People" pass laws through a democratic and open legislative process. We then pay public representatives with public funds to take on public responsibilities in our administrative agencies and enforce those laws. Those administrative agencies craft regulations to enforce the laws and to protect the public interest. All is well until industries co-opt and control those regulatory agencies. When they do, the agencies are pried out of the matrix of our government of laws to become silent corporate servants. The public's voice is lost. The "trial of strength" in that arena is won by industry.

In the Senate, I held a hearing on regulatory capture that revealed bipartisan agreement across all the witnesses on all these points:[26]

> First, agency capture is a real problem, and a threat to the integrity of government.
>
> Second, the enormous stakes for regulated entities give them an incentive to gain influence over regulators.
>
> Third, regulated entities usually have organizational and resource advantages in the regulatory process compared to public interest groups.
>
> Fourth, regulatory procedures can be gamed by regulated entities in their quest for influence over regulation.
>
> Fifth, regulatory capture by its nature happens in the dark, as invisibly as possible.
>
> Sixth, the potential damage to the public from agency capture is enormous.

The takeaway from that hearing was best summarized by one of the witnesses, administrative law professor Nicholas Bagley, who said, "The core point that I would want to take away from our testimony today is that when you talk about agency capture, you are talking about a complex of problems whereby well-organized, well-heeled interest groups are likely to be able to bring a lot of pressure to bear on agencies under the cover of darkness."[27]

Madison and Jefferson left us warnings about corporate power. They also left us advice useful in considering regulatory capture. Thinking of the revolving doors from the regulator to industry reminds me of

Jefferson: “Whenever a man has cast a longing eye on offices, a rottenness begins in his conduct.”[28] Madison saw conflicting interests, such as those between the industry and the public, as questions of “faction.” Though he felt “the causes of faction cannot be removed,” he still found hope “in the means of controlling its effects.”[29]

On June 10, 1999, two ten-year-old boys, Wade King and Stephen Tsiorvas, went out to play in a field near Whatcom Creek in Bellingham, Washington. They were fourth graders at Roosevelt Elementary School. An eighteen-year-old boy, Liam Wood, who had just graduated from high school a few days before, was fishing in the creek not far away.[30] They did not know that Olympic Pipe Line Company had a poorly maintained, leaking gasoline pipe nearby that was gushing over 200,000 gallons of gasoline into the creek.[31] Excavations years earlier had damaged the pipe, the damage was never corrected, and that afternoon a pressure surge over 1,400 pounds per square inch ruptured the pipe at the site of one of the gouges.[32]

Liam was overcome by gasoline fumes and collapsed. Incapacitated, he drowned, and his body was later found partly submerged in the creek.[33] His autopsy report later stated that he had been “overcome by volatile hydrocarbon fumes, lost consciousness and died from hypoxia by freshwater drowning.”[34] A spark of some kind ignited the gasoline spill, sending a smoke and fire column miles into the air. “It looked,” said one witness, “like the explosion of Mt. St. Helens.”[35] Rescue personnel responding to the explosion found Wade and Stephen. They had suffered what the official accident report described as “extensive second and third degree thermal burn injuries of the head, trunk and extremities (80 to 90 percent body surface area).”[36] The boys were rushed to St. Joseph’s Hospital in Bellingham, and then by air ambulance to a burn unit at Harborview Medical Center in Seattle.[37] Both boys died the next day.[38] The gasoline fire raged for over an hour, and it took days to finish putting out brush fires. Twenty-five acres were burned. The county fire chief said, “I’ve been here 30 years, and I’ve never seen anything like this before.”[39]

In the investigations that followed, blame settled on a regulatory agency, the Office of Pipeline Safety. The head of the National Transportation Safety Board (NTSB) faulted every aspect of the agency: “its regulations, its inspections, its assets, its staffing and its spirit."[40] The Pipeline Accident Report from the NTSB listed as one of the "major safety issues identified during this investigation" the "adequacy of Federal regulations regarding the testing of relief valves used in the protection of pipeline systems."[41]

Criticism of the agency went way beyond the Bellingham disaster. A state pipeline safety official, disappointed by his federal counterparts, said, "From the get-go, the regulations get watered down. There's not a lot of teeth behind them."[42] A *Politico* investigation found "gaping holes in pipeline safety regulations" and an agency "that grants the industry it regulates significant power to influence the rule-making process, and that has stubbornly failed to take a more aggressive regulatory role, even when ordered by Congress to do so."[43] One frustrated congressman, Peter DeFazio, ranking member on the House Transportation and Infrastructure Committee, complained to *Politico*, "They only seem to act when confronted by and forced by Congress to act. And even then, they don't act."[44] Even those laws from Congress, the Bellingham disaster victims' families thought, had been "watered down by those who pay homage to the powerful oil and gas lobbyists."[45]

In the wake of the Bellingham disaster, the agency's name was changed to the Pipeline and Hazardous Materials Safety Administration, or PHMSA. Not much else changed. As one practitioner reported to *Politico*, "With PHMSA, there's only one wind, and it blows from the industry."[46]

These obscure agencies are ripe for regulatory capture. The public takes little interest, until something goes horribly wrong; the industry attends to the agency day in and day out. Revolving doors spin—the last head of PHMSA was a former pipeline industry lawyer who had to recuse herself in a major spill inquiry because of conflict of interest.[47] Safety and environment groups struggle to hold their own against industry, particularly an industry that consists of behemoths such as ExxonMobil. A judge described the efforts of one public interest group to go up against the oil pipeline industry as "Bambi taking on Godzilla."[48] And no part of the federal government anywhere has as its task to systematically seek out and flag instances of regulatory capture, nor even to identify warning signs. There is no "regulatory capture cop" on the beat.[49]

As Representative DeFazio told *Politico*, this isn't just cost/benefit, dollars and cents: "This is life or death. Pipelines blow up and people die."[50] When Wade King died, the local paper reported, his parents "shut the door to his room and left it closed." There was simply too much pain. His mother said afterward, "The first three years were a fog. I look back and I don't know how we got through those days. It was hell. It was like waking up every day in hell."[51] As the tenth anniversary of Wade's death approached, she was asked about Olympic Pipe Line Company and all the mistakes that were made. "If I go down that road," she said, "it's with a lot of hostility. I don't forgive any of it."[52]

Regulatory capture plays a role in the massive corporate intrusion into America's elections. Here the stories of regulatory capture and corporate election mischief converge, in the now virtually lawless area of campaign finance regulation.

The Federal Election Commission is supposed to regulate federal elections. It is supposed to enforce the Federal Election Campaign Act.[53] In that law, Congress defined an "independent expenditure" as one "not made in concert or cooperation with or at the request or suggestion of such candidate, the candidate's authorized political committee, or their agents, or a political party committee or its agents."[54] This is the law meant to ensure that super PACs are independent of candidates and never coordinated with their campaigns.

In one actual case a supposedly "independent" super PAC, which supported one candidate, and one candidate only (again, how plausible is it that a super PAC set up to support one candidate only is an "independent" organization?), was founded by the candidate's former campaign lawyer, and employed the same consulting company the candidate's campaign uses. Not enough? The consulting company's founder was a former strategist for the candidate's campaign, and married to a current campaign advisor to the candidate.[55] In another actual case, a super PAC was run by the candidate's mother.[56] Are we really to believe that these super PACs are "independent"?

Larry Noble, a witness at a Senate hearing I held on this mess, is now general counsel of the Campaign Legal Center and was formerly general counsel at the FEC. He blames the FEC for not enforcing the law against coordination between super PACs and political campaigns:

"The FEC narrowed the coordination rules over time to the point where they were seen as totally ineffective."[57] The rules against coordination between super PACs and campaigns are now "narrowed" to the point where candidates now customarily post campaign ad footage online so that super PACs supporting them can incorporate the candidate's own campaign footage directly into the super PAC's ads.[58] Hard to get more "totally ineffective" than that.

At the "totally ineffective" FEC, regulations pertaining to disclosure fare no better. Disclosure of who's behind political spending is also supposedly the law of the land, believe it or not. Even that grotesque Supreme Court decision, *Citizens United*, recognized the importance of political spending disclosure to proper democratic citizenship.[59] The Federal Election Campaign Act states that groups making independent expenditures must disclose "each person who made a contribution in excess of $200 . . . made for the purpose of furthering an independent expenditure."[60] That seems pretty straightforward, no? The FEC is supposed to enforce it.

Yet the three Republican commissioners at the FEC, using their power to deadlock the six-member commission's votes 3–3, have narrowed their interpretation of the law to say that it applies only to funds the donor explicitly gives to fund a specific advertisement.[61] If the contribution is intended to fund the general effort to elect or defeat a candidate and the donor's check can't be tied to a specific advertisement, the law does not apply, says the regulator.[62]

Giving money to a campaign to fund a specific advertisement? Who does that? Money usually comes in to a campaign before ads are scripted and produced. How would an early donor ever know what ad he would like to have his money fund? The ad wasn't yet produced when he cut the check. It's ridiculous. The law is defanged, and lawlessness is the result.

Another clear federal statute prohibits giving a contribution "in the name of another."[63] Yet in the 2012 elections, we saw blatant use of shell corporations to conceal multimillion-dollar contributions to super PACs.[64] The FEC has been unwilling even to investigate.[65] One shell company appeared, contributed $5 million to a super PAC supporting a presidential candidate, and then dissolved shortly thereafter. A complaint was filed, but no official inquiry appears to have emerged from the FEC deadlock.[66] No one knows who gave the money—except, of course, the donor, and very likely the candidate.

One type of organization need not disclose its donors: an entity registered with the Internal Revenue Service under Section 501(c)(4) of the federal tax code as a "social welfare" group.[67] Groups that want to hide the identities of their donors so the donors can support candidates anonymously love this status. It's a political operator's dream.

But there's a rub. Section 501(c)(4) of the Internal Revenue Code is only for "civic leagues or organizations not organized for profit but operated exclusively for the promotion of social welfare,"[68] and IRS regulations had long made it clear that spending money in political campaigns does not constitute "promotion of social welfare."[69]

See the word "exclusively" in the law? Rather than enforce the law on those terms, the IRS began to allow organizations to spend money in campaigns as long as that was not their "primary" activity. "Exclusively" came to mean "primarily."[70] The dark-money groups seized on this and began using 49 percent of their spending on political expenditures.[71] If big money is at stake but the donor wants anonymity, the donor would in effect pay a 51 percent fee to put up anonymous political ads, with the other 49 percent funding the ads.

But folks got even cleverer. Dark-money groups began using the other 51 percent to run "issue ads."[72] These are just thinly veiled political attack ads, but they exploit yet another loophole by not "expressly" advocating election or defeat of the candidate. Instead they just urge that the viewer call the candidate and ask him why he hates America, or prosperity, or puppies (I exaggerate, but not very much).

Then the dark-money groups tried sending the 51 percent to *other* organizations that spend money on political ads. They got away with that, too. So now "exclusively," the standard set in law by Congress, comes to mean in IRS regulatory practice "virtually not at all." Where the FEC was blockaded by three commissioners who refuse to act, the IRS has been terrorized by relentless Congressional hearings, budget attacks, and threats to impeach the IRS commissioner. It is an agency curled up in a fetal crouch.

There's one more wrinkle. Even in the midst of this no-regulatory Dodge City of lawlessness, there are federal forms that need to be filed. Drill down into those federal forms, and you find groups filing IRS forms to acquire that much-treasured 501(c)(4) status. Remember, even a super PAC can't hide its donors; becoming a 501(c)(4) is what allows secrecy. Those IRS forms, filed under penalty of perjury, require the organizations to affirm that they are spending no money to influence elections, or explain what they are spending. Whatever percentage of their money they may be spending, many do not bother to explain; they just affirm that they are spending no money to influence elections. Back at the Federal Election Commission, those very same groups then report, again under penalty of perjury, that they spent millions of dollars on elections. Yes, the same groups file conflicting forms at different agencies, both under penalty of perjury.

Let me be specific. The IRS initial application form for 501(c)(4) status includes question 15: "Has the organization spent or does it plan to spend any money attempting to influence the selection, nomination, election, or appointment of any person to any Federal, state, or local public office or to an office in a political organization?" The filer is instructed to state "no" or explain.

Clear enough? I sure don't see much wiggle room there.

In addition to the initial application, a 501(c)(4) entity has to file every year the IRS Form 990 tax return for tax-exempt organizations, which asks: "Did the organization engage in direct or indirect political campaign activities on behalf of or in opposition to candidates for public office?"[73] Answer "no" or explain. Again, seems clear enough.

But organizations answer "no" to these questions and then go out and spend millions of dollars in election advertising. One organization answered "no" to these questions while sending more than $33 million to other affiliated groups explicitly for the purpose of spending in elections.[74] In one investigation, ProPublica, a Pulitzer Prize–winning nonprofit news organization, found thirty-two organizations that answered "no" to question 15 and then went out and spent money in political races. And that was out of seventy-two IRS filings ProPublica reviewed.[75] By that measure, nearly half were false, one could reasonably conclude. Some organizations had political ads running on the day they mailed their filings in with the answer "no"; some had run their ads beforehand.[76] Some spent millions on political ads.[77]

Starting from another angle, the ProPublica investigation found

104 organizations that had told state or federal elections officials in 2010 that they'd spent money on candidate-specific political ads, what the FEC calls "electioneering" communications. When ProPublica cross-referenced these with the forms these same groups had filed with the IRS, thirty-two of them had said they spent no money to influence elections.[78] That's about a one-in-three rate of discrepancy.

Even when some information is provided on these forms, the information often looks false. One organization said it would spend 50 percent of its effort on a website and 30 percent on conferences. Investigation showed its website consisted of one photograph and one paragraph, with no sign of any conferences. The same group declared it would take contributions "from individuals only" and then took $2 million from PhRMA, the big pharmaceutical lobby.[79] Another declared to the IRS it had spent $5 million on political activities, but told the FEC it had spent $19 million on political ads.[80] A third pledged that its political spending would be "limited in amount and will not constitute the organization's primary purpose," and then went out and spent $70 million on ads and robocalls in one election season.[81]

Some entities never even apply. They just start spending and file a tax return after the fact, potentially as their last act before they disband. That way they're gone before the mail brings their filing to the IRS, and before anyone can come around to ask nosy questions. One never filed the IRS tax form at all, not even after the fact.[82]

No federal enforcement action has been taken against anyone, as far as anyone knows. As Melanie Sloan, former executive director of Citizens for Responsibility and Ethics in Washington, has said, "You can go into business and violate the law and then go out of business. And what's ever going to happen about that? There's no consequence."[83]

One news article described the reaction of a state election official, Ann Ravel (who later went on to become an FEC commissioner), when she was asked about a particular 501(c)(4) group that had been active in electioneering in her state and had been the subject of her agency's scrutiny: "When ProPublica read the group's description of its activities on its IRS application to Ann Ravel, [then-]chairwoman of the California Fair Political Practices Commission, she laughed. 'Wow,' she said, upon hearing that the group said it would not try to influence elections. 'That's simply false.'"[84]

Despite her best efforts, Ravel has had little luck reviving the Federal Election Commission. Indeed, as its chairwoman, she declared it dead: "The likelihood of the laws being enforced is slim," she has said. "It's worse than dysfunctional."[85] Well-regarded Republican campaign finance lawyer Jan Baran agrees: "The agency is just not providing any legal guidance on what the rules are in the aftermath of all these momentous court decisions. That's the job of the FEC, and it hasn't done its job."[86] The *Los Angeles Times* recently headlined an editorial "The Federal Election Commission Is Worse Than Useless."[87]

At the regulatory agencies, lawlessness is the rule.

That brings us to the Department of Justice. It is a federal crime under 18 U.S.C. § 1001 to make any material false statement on federal filings like these. It is also a specific federal crime under 26 U.S.C. § 7206 to make a material false statement on an IRS form. Yet exactly zero groups have been referred by the FEC or by the IRS to the Department of Justice for investigation into whether any of these conflicting answers were false.[88]

False statement cases are bread-and-butter cases for DOJ. I did them as U.S. Attorney. Yet there has evidently not been any FBI or grand jury investigation into the apparently false statements on these forms. Perhaps there is a legitimate explanation. But when an entity declares millions of dollars in election spending under oath on one form, and then answers "no" under oath on another form to the question "Has the organization spent or does it plan to spend any money attempting to influence the selection, nomination, election, or appointment of any person to any Federal, state, or local public office?," isn't it worth investigating? Shouldn't such an apparent falsehood merit a question or two to see if there is a legitimate explanation? Is it not the DOJ's duty to examine the records to see if there has been unlawful conduct?

If there's a good explanation, great. Everybody can go home. If not, well, lying like that is a federal crime.

The "hot potato" phenomenon likely explains this multiagency failure by the IRS, the FEC, and DOJ. The forces behind the dark-money flood are powerful, intimidating, and vindictive. With responsibility shared among three agencies, each was likely happy to leave to the others the responsibility for acting, and happy to keep itself out of harm's way. When all three said, "Not me," the ball fell plop between the fielders, and we now have this disgraceful spectacle.

This has been regulatory capture of a peculiar sort. Regulatory capture can come through revolving doors with industry, through favors and perquisites from industry, or through actual encroachment of the regulated industry into the regulatory agency. But it can also come from plain old fear of the regulated industry—in this case the corporate political front groups—hectoring and bullying and pillorying the regulator. And it can come from political appointees on a commission whose very purpose in serving is to disable the commission's operations.

Whatever the method of its capture, a captured regulator fails the public it was sworn to serve. And we have been failed. These examples from the campaign finance context illustrate the importance of getting regulations right and the importance of creating responsive enforcement regimes. They also illustrate the importance of independent prosecutors willing to step in when timorous regulators, buffaloed by forces they are supposed to regulate, fear to do their jobs. We've been failed there too.

CHAPTER NINE

Capture of the Civil Jury

UNSHACKLED FROM THE CHAINS of campaign finance limits, corporate power marauds across our politics. That power has set its sights on bending a wide range of policies to its advantage, everything from corporate taxes to safety regulation. It has also set its sights on a target that is one of the fundamental constitutional pillars of our government: the civil jury.[1]

The civil jury has a unique role in our uniquely American constitutional system. In the United States, a civil jury determines the facts and decides fault in non-criminal trials, ranging from property disputes between neighbors to multimillion-dollar class-action lawsuits against corporate behemoths. The Founders deliberately built this institution into the system of government established by our Constitution and Bill of Rights. Alexis de Tocqueville, in his *Democracy in America*, observed that the jury should be understood as a "political institution" and "one form of the sovereignty of the people."[2] It gives ordinary citizens direct exercise of an American constitutional power.[3] It is the element in our constitutional system most dedicated to protecting ordinary citizens from the wealthy and powerful. Corporate political machinery, by seeking to undermine the civil jury and change the very structure of our system of government, shows the extent of its ambitions.

You may think of the civil jury as an annoyance. You may think of jury duty, and what a bother a jury summons can be. But consider why the Founders prized the institution of the civil jury so highly and defended it so fiercely.

The earliest tendrils of the jury system appeared in England way back in the twelfth century.[4] By the fifteenth century, civil juries had blossomed into their modern form: independent persons who gathered together and heard witness testimony presented by opposing counsel, and then had the power of decision.[5] It was an original form of "power to the people" and local decision making. When the earliest colonial settlers came from England to this land, they transplanted juries here: by 1624, juries were established in Virginia; by 1628, in Massachusetts; by 1677, in New Jersey; and by 1682, in Pennsylvania.[6]

Civil juries provided a treasured means of self-governance to colonial Americans as they chafed under British rule.[7] Efforts by the British government to interfere with American juries helped foment the American Revolution.[8] We know those early American forefathers cared about this, because they said so. In the Declaration of Independence itself, when the Founders protested Britain's "history of repeated injuries and usurpations, all having in direct object the establishment of an absolute Tyranny over these States," they singled out that Britain had been "depriving us in many cases, of the benefits of Trial by Jury."[9]

When our original Constitution was silent on the civil jury, Americans sounded the alarm and the Seventh Amendment, putting the civil jury right into the Constitution, was promptly sent to the states in the Bill of Rights.[10] Alexander Hamilton described the importance of juries in Federalist No. 83: "The friends and adversaries of the plan of the convention, if they agree in nothing else, concur at least in the value they set upon the trial by jury; or if there is any difference between them it consists in this: the former regard it as a valuable safeguard to liberty; the latter represent it as the very palladium of free government."[11] "Representative government and trial by jury are the heart and lungs of liberty," wrote John Adams.[12] The jury was a big deal to the Founding generation.

Sir William Blackstone was the best-known jurist in England and America at the time of the Revolution and the author of *Commentaries on the Laws of England*, probably the most widely available legal text in the colonies (still often cited today by American courts). Blackstone gave the two major arguments for trial by jury in one sentence: trial by jury, he said, "preserves in the hands of the people that share which they ought to have in the administration of public justice, and prevents the encroachments of the more powerful and wealthy citizens."[13]

Let's start with the first argument. Colonial Americans understood the civil jury to be a means of directing power to the people and recognized Sir William Blackstone's 1768 warning that "every new tribunal erected, for the decision of facts, without the intervention of a jury . . . is a step towards establishing aristocracy, the most oppressive of absolute governments."[14] The Founders intended the civil jury to serve as an institutional check by giving ordinary American people direct control over one vital element of government—giving them, in Blackstone's words, "that share which they ought to have" in the administration of justice.[15] The civil jury serves the constitutional purpose of dividing and disaggregating governmental power. And it does so in an immediate way, putting the people themselves as the decision makers.

On the second argument, in a Constitution largely devoted to protecting the individual against the power of the state, the civil jury is unique in that it is also designed to protect the individual against the power of other individuals. Wealth, power, and connections can give unfair advantage. Wealth, power, and connections can also influence officials in the performance of their duty. The remedy for this was to let an independent group of randomly selected members of the community decide whether someone was being treated unfairly, or in violation of law.

Because each jury is new—"a rotating cast of laypeople," as law professor Nathan Chapman puts it[16]—it is hard to put in an institutional fix. To amplify this protection, we have made it a crime even to try: it's a criminal act to "tamper" with a jury.[17] Contact by an interested party with a juror, unless approved by the judge in charge of the case, is forbidden. Thus does the jury prevent the "encroachments of the more powerful and wealthy citizens" who can wield influence so effectively in other arenas.[18] In the jury, our Founders set ordinary people as our Constitution's watchman against encroachments by the powerful and wealthy.

Corporations now have become the most powerful and wealthy entities in our society, and it is often corporations whose encroachments a jury will thwart. Thus, the civil jury has become the target of sustained corporate attack. The immediate corporate wish is to reduce liability exposure. But that's only part of it. As law professor David Marcus notes, "When juries decide cases, elites lose their stranglehold on legal power"[19]—and big corporations don't much care for institutions where an ordinary American citizen can have an equal voice and equal standing.

Big, wealthy, powerful corporations are accustomed to the benefit of enormous special influence, whether acquired through campaign contributions, traditional lobbying, regulatory capture, or the big political spending unleashed by *Citizens United*. They bring this influence to bear on executive officials. They bring this influence to bear on administrative agencies. They bring it to bear on elected legislatures. They even bring it to bear on judges.

But big corporations lose the advantage of all that special influence in front of a jury. Tampering with executive, legislative, and administrative agencies is a licensed activity of special interests under our lobbying and campaign finance laws. Tampering with a jury is a crime.

The civil jury can be a potent political institution. It fosters civic engagement. It educates citizens about the workings of their government. It knits together people from all walks of life. It devolves power down to the people. It offers a final check on abuse when other institutions of government are compromised by influence. But the jury trial is now close to vanishing.

When the federal Civil Rules of Procedure were adopted in 1938, about 20 percent of federal cases were resolved by either a jury or a bench trial.[20] Now, less than 2 percent of federal civil cases reach a jury or a bench trial.[21] Most litigants do not have a reasonable prospect of presenting their claims to a jury of their peers. The chief judge of my home state's federal court recently told me he had not seen a civil jury trial in his courtroom for three years.

Some reasons for this trend are practical. The economics of modern legal practice press litigants into early settlement. Judges add to this pressure their desire to manage and expedite their dockets. Jury trials are work; signing off on a settlement is easy. The growing practice of judges tolerating "paper blizzard" defense strategies rewards defendants who can bankroll aggressive and imaginative defense pretrial strategies until the plaintiff simply collapses from lack of resources before getting near a jury.

One example of this blizzard defense practice occurred in a case I brought as attorney general, where the industry defendants gave us a witness list of a hundred names. That required us to go all around the country to take these witnesses' pretrial depositions. Knowing what the other side's witnesses will say is an essential part of trial preparation, so we had no choice. At trial, the defendants called exactly zero of these witnesses. The witness list was a sham, a wild-goose chase thrown into the works of that case to waste our time and money. They got away with it.

Other changes diminishing the jury's role came via the Federal Rules of Civil Procedure. It starts with getting through the courthouse door. Corporations want this to be more difficult, and the Supreme Court as it has defined these rules has helped their cause. The Supreme Court has made it far easier for corporate defendants to dismiss cases and has helped them limit plaintiffs from gathering facts through "discovery" and from presenting their case to the jury. Recent amendments and interpretations governing how civil trials work—pleading standards, motions to dismiss, class-action standards, summary judgment, and case management procedures—have also narrowed the gateway to a jury trial. All of these changes are to the benefit of those with money and power who tend to be defendants in civil trials, namely, corporations.

Let's say a consumer believes she was harmed by a chemical and sues the corporation that made the chemical. Before a string of corporate-friendly Supreme Court decisions over the past few decades, the consumer could file a complaint in court and would likely have the opportunity to review any evidence necessary to make her case (that's called "discovery") and then present this case to a jury. After the Supreme Court tilted the playing field in favor of civil defendants—often corporations—it is more likely that the consumer's case would be thrown out before her attorneys ever had a chance to review documents and depose witnesses. If she did make it to that point, her case would be more easily thrown out by a judge for being insufficiently persuasive before it ever reaches a jury of her peers. As Justice Stevens reminded us in his dissent in one of these decisions, the rules of federal civil procedure were intended "not to keep litigants out of court but rather to keep them in."[22] More and more, the trend in judicial interpretation of those rules is to keep litigants out.

Class actions are a key tool for citizens to join together to sue a corporation. Small-denomination, large-scale frauds are the stuff of class actions. A company cheats a hundred thousand people out of a hundred dollars each, and it makes a bundle. But it's not worth it for the victims to bring hundred-dollar lawsuits one by one. Hence the class action, which provides a path to a group remedy for such frauds. The Roberts Court has made it far more difficult for individual citizens who had been injured in these low-dollar, large-scale frauds to join together, bring their case before a jury, and hold corporate wrongdoers accountable.[23]

Even where a case does get filed and begins to proceed toward a trial before a jury, a summary judgment can stop it in its tracks. In the 1980s, the Rehnquist Court issued a game-changing trio of decisions known in legal circles as the "Celotex trilogy."[24] Traditionally, defendants had to meet a high bar to get the case thrown out at this stage, but the Celotex trilogy shifted that burden toward the plaintiff, making it much more likely that a case would get thrown out by a judge far before reaching a jury.

Courts took notice. Federal courts have cited this trilogy in astounding numbers: *Anderson* has been cited more than 204,000 times, *Celotex* more than 190,000 times, and *Matsushita* more than 98,000 times.[25] Vast numbers of plaintiffs were left unable to reach a jury of their peers.

Another trend undercutting the civil jury is the addition by big corporations of arbitration clauses into consumer contracts. We consumers never bother to read the fine print, but in the contract you signed for your cellphone, for your credit card, for your bank account, and for many other services, you likely gave away your right to a jury trial. Parallel to this trend has been a series of Supreme Court decisions through which the five conservative justices approved these contracts, again and again allowing consumer claims to be forced out of the civil courts and into arbitration.

Dissenting in the most recent of these anti-consumer Supreme

Court cases, Justice Ruth Bader Ginsburg noted: "These decisions have predictably resulted in the deprivation of consumers' rights to seek redress for losses, and, turning the coin, they have insulated powerful economic interests from liability for violations of consumer-protection laws."[26] She cited a recent series of *New York Times* articles exposing the severity of this problem and the intensity of the corporate effort to keep cases out of the civil court system. As Jessica Silver-Greenberg and Robert Gebeloff reported in the *Times*, "By inserting individual arbitration clauses into a soaring number of consumer and employment contracts, companies [have] devised a way to circumvent the courts and bar people from joining together in class-action lawsuits, realistically the only tool citizens have to fight illegal or deceitful business practices."[27]

There are two big problems with these forced arbitration provisions. First, giving up your jury right is not a fairly bargained choice. Credit cards and cellphones are necessities in our economy, and the contracts for those services are what lawyers would call "contracts of adhesion," contracts in which the weaker party has no real choice—take it or leave it. Second, the arbitration process lends itself to bias: it's always one-sided, big corporation against individual, and the corporation is usually a repeat player in arbitrated disputes, while each individual is usually new to the process, a one-timer. The arbitrators—very often corporate lawyers—will not want to displease the corporation, lest they not be selected for more arbitrations. So a bias emerges. State attorneys general came together and shut down the consumer arbitration work of one firm—the National Arbitration Forum—because it had become such a racket of pro-corporate bias. Before the attorneys general shuttered its practice, the firm had managed more than 214,000 consumer debt-collection claims in 2006 alone.[28]

The corporate lust for arbitration even reaches into our international trade policy. Big corporations and industries have secured "investor-state dispute settlement" (ISDS) provisions in trade deals like NAFTA. These provisions give corporations the ability to sue nations not in court but rather before panels of arbitrators who are mostly corporate lawyers. Multinational corporations use these clauses to fight health, environmental, and safety standards established by sovereign nations that could hurt the corporate bottom line. Big nations such as the United States and Canada and Australia have all been sued.[29] Little nations such as tiny Togo, a sliver of a nation on the West African coast, have been threatened—in the case of Togo by the tobacco industry, whose revenues are more than six times Togo's entire gross domestic product.[30]

A recent *BuzzFeed* investigation, "The Court That Rules the World," released August 28, 2016, looked at "the secret operations of these [ISDS] tribunals, and the ways that business has co-opted them to bring sovereign nations to heel."[31] "ISDS has morphed . . . into a powerful tool that corporations brandish ever more frequently, often against broad public policies that they claim crimp profits." The investigation noted "the potential use of ISDS by corporations to roll back public-interest laws, such as those banning the use of hazardous chemicals or raising the minimum wage," and as a "shield for the criminal and the corrupt."[32] There is no similar tribunal in which environmental groups or labor unions can sue when things go the other way. The revolving door spins freely, as lawyers who negotiate the ISDS measures in treaties on behalf of the U.S. Trade Representative then go and practice law as ISDS litigators. One is the head of his firm's ISDS practice. Why would you cut back on the opportunities for your future corporate clients, who will pay you to bring the ISDS cases whose way you paved while in government?

The gradual suffocation of the American civil jury is neither random nor coincidental. Supreme Court justice Abe Fortas once noted, "Procedure is the bone structure of a democratic society."[33] Corporations know this. They know that procedure is power. And undermining the civil jury is a power grab. Blackstone warned that the civil jury would be a thorn in the side of the wealthy and powerful, and an annoyance to those who are used to special treatment. And it's true. There, in front of the civil jury, the wealthy and powerful have to stand annoyingly equal before the law. Their assiduously acquired influence breaks, against the hard, square corners of the jury box. As a body that "prevents the encroachments of the more powerful and wealthy,"[34] the civil jury inevitably provokes their enmity.

It should be no surprise, then, that corporations spread a mythology of greedy trial lawyers, runaway juries, abusive discovery, and preposterous verdicts, and push for "tort reform" to further insulate corporations from lawsuits for wrongdoing. It should be no surprise that corporations seek the appointment of "business-friendly" judges. And it should thus be no surprise that an already business-friendly Congress and those business-friendly judges steadily whittle away at this vital and historic American institution, the civil jury.

The cost of this institution vanishing is high. Again, you may think this is fine; what the hell, no more jury duty. But remember what we Americans lose if an institution such as this goes away. Juries are a check on political might—they disband after making their decision in a case, and consequently are hard to subject to political pressure. Juries are designed to be indifferent to wealth and power—they are made up of random people with nothing to gain from their decision. Juries are the last hope of lost causes when other elements of government, compromised by influence, become bulwarks of well-kept indifference. Juries can blow the status quo to smithereens if they don't think it's fair. They don't care if some fat ox gets gored; their job is to do justice in the one case before them. Period. That quality is not only important in the particular case the jury is deciding; it also sends a powerful message through the whole rest of the political system.

Think about it from the big special interest's point of view. If the special interest can put the fix in everywhere in government, that offers a big prize, and that prize encourages putting in the fix. But if that prize of control can't be seized because the jury stands out there as a lonely sentinel of resistance, immune to that pressure, then the whole exercise of putting the fix in elsewhere in government becomes less alluring. If a jury can blow up the special-interest fix in government, that dials back the special interests' incentive to fix those other elements of government that yield more readily to power and wealth. It doesn't cure it, but it dials it back.

When we reflect on America and the jury, we should think about the word "corruption." The Founding Fathers thought about it a lot. Noted historian (and fellow Rhode Islander) Gordon Wood has written that, according to the republican ideals of the Founders, corruption was "a technical term of political science" of the Founding era. Americans then saw as corruption things such as "monarchical instruments of personal influence and patronage" and "attempts by great men and their power-hungry minions to promote their private interests at the expense of the public good."[35] Corruption had a broad political meaning to the Founders. "Any loss of independence and virtue was corruption."[36] Corruption was the opposite of virtue, because it yielded to selfishness; it was the opposite of egalitarianism, because it allowed undue influence by some over others; and it was the opposite of independence, because it made government dependent on influence. Political dependency, writes Lawrence Lessig in *Republic, Lost*, was seen by the Framers as "dependence corruption."[37]

Hamilton, writing in the Federalist Papers, discussed the "business of corruption," worried about influences "corrupting the body of the people," and warned of "instruments of foreign corruption."[38] In their writings, the term "corruption" makes sense only if it is read as meaning far more than the simple transaction of a specific bribe. Corruption was a state of political disease; the antithesis of "corruption" was not just an absence of bribery but a "free and independent nation." "By corruption," historian Zephyr Teachout has observed, "the early generations meant excessive private interests influencing the exercise of public power."[39]

This generous meaning has collapsed in our era. The Supreme Court has in recent decades narrowed the meaning of the term down to where "corruption" means only a specific trade of a specific gift or benefit for a specific official favor or service. Now it means only what the Court calls "quid pro quo" corruption: tit for tat, precisely. The rest of the work of influence, the Court pretends, is free speech.[40] It just happens to be the kind of free speech that can be practiced only by the big influencers, who in our day and age tend to be the big politically active corporations, their front groups, and their billionaire owners. And the collapse just happens to be led by the corporatists on the Court.

This is new. Legal historian Bill Novak talks about how the classical tradition running from Aristotle through Montesquieu, the sage of the Founders, had a "preoccupation" with corruption, meaning "the private capture of the public sphere."[41] He reminds us of Socrates's definition of corruption: when "the guardians of the laws and of the government are only seemingly and not real guardians."[42] Teachout, in her book *Corruption in America*, writes of how *any* secret influence was viewed as virtually per se corruption, and how courts once read lobbying contracts with a sharp eye to the health of the public sphere. "Courts routinely held that it was not necessary to find that the parties agreed to some 'corrupt' or 'secret' action. Instead, the question was whether the 'contract tends directly to those results.' A contract was problematic when,'" to quote a decision in a Supreme Court case from 1869, it "'furnishes a temptation to the plaintiff, to resort to corrupt means or improper devices, to influence legislative action.'"[43]

Justice William O. Douglas expressed a similar view, placing corruption squarely in the context of the health of the public sphere, indeed describing it as a form of "pollution" of politics: "Free and honest elections are the very foundation of our republican form of government. . . . The fact that a particular form of pollution has only an indirect effect on the final election is immaterial. . . . [T]he Constitution should be read as to give Congress an expansive implied power to place beyond the pale acts which, in their direct or indirect effects, impair the integrity of Congressional elections. For when corruption enters, the election is no longer free, the choice of the people is affected."[44]

The current Court's dramatic narrowing of the definition of "corruption" has had a number of effects. The Court has stripped Congress of its power to protect elections by narrowing the definition of what it could protect against. That in turn unleashed forces of secret influence to operate with greater impunity. It also stripped prosecutors of their ability to bring corruption before a jury, absent an obvious quid pro quo bribe. Ultimately, the new, narrow definition elevated the private interest of influencers above the public interest in a healthy public sphere.

There is an eternal contest in government, between big, motivated private influencers who want a government that will yield its prizes readily to their influence and, on the other side, the public who want a government that will not yield so readily; between the players and those who just don't want to be played. This is not a new thought. Centuries ago, Niccolò Machiavelli spoke of "two distinct parties" in a governed society: one, "the nobles [who] wish to rule and oppress the people," and two, "the people [who] do not wish to be ruled nor oppressed by the nobles." The people's object is the more "righteous," he said, for they "only desire not to be oppressed."[45] More recently, and in our land, President Andrew Jackson's veto message regarding the rechartering of the Bank of the United States distinguished between "the rich and powerful [who] too often bend the acts of government to their selfish purposes" and "the humble members of society—the farmers, mechanics and laborers—who have neither the time nor the means of securing like favors to themselves."[46] In our times, we see the contest less colored by class or occupation. The contest is simple: between those who want to influence, and therefore want a government that will be amenable to influence, and those who just want to go about their own lives, and would like a government that resists influence on its own so they don't have to defend themselves constantly against the influencers.

In this contest, the big influencers don't need help. They are fully motivated by greed and reward. Instead, they need restraining. The public interest in a government free of their improper influence has no similarly motivated champion—the public has "neither the time nor the means" for that. The public interest doesn't need restraint, it needs protecting. By narrowing the restraint on improper influence down to its most precise, rash, and solitary transaction—a direct "quid pro quo" bribe—the Supreme Court took the side of the influencers. They opened up to the power of influencers space in the political sphere that was once occupied by that concept of a "free and independent nation." Indeed, the Court is so blind to this distinction that in a campaign finance decision it spoke of the importance of "unreserved communication" between a politician and his "constituents"[47]—by which they meant not the actual constituents in the politician's district, but his donors. As a failure to appreciate the difference between the influencer class and regular citizens, that's hard to top.

The narrow quid pro quo standard gives a particular boon to those big influencers who are a constant presence in government. Those frequent fliers can now create "dependence corruption" within government to advance their interests, so long as they avoid tying any particular favor at any particular time to any particular vote. Frequent fliers have to be very stupid if they can't structure their work of influence around the quid pro quo restriction.

The one-time actor coming to Washington seeking to influence a single vote has no such advantage. As a prosecutor who has led political corruption investigations, I know how often it's the stupid, sad-sack defendant who gets clobbered, not the big interests that have learned how to work the system. In the grand scheme of things, these sad sacks are defendants with minuscule political might compared to the big forces exerting their will day to day over government. The public is still humored with the odd corruption prosecution, but the really powerful and constant interests operate undisturbed.

The definition of "corruption" had historically in America been a jury question, and against this background, one can see why. The jury, as the Constitution's watchman against "encroachments of the more powerful and wealthy citizens," is well suited to bring its popular common sense to the definition of corruption. It is the "more powerful and wealthy" who are most likely to be the big influencers, the corrupters. So placing the jury as our public sentinel over corruption sends a powerful signal to the political class. When juries are deciding what sort of influence is honest and acceptable versus what sort of influence is excessive and against the public good, that call is in the hands of regular people. Juries are the arbitrators least likely to be either in the pocket of industry or subject to the worldview of the political class. And that's a good thing, sending a shiver of caution into the influencer class.

The Supreme Court has narrowed the field of vision of civil juries when they do hear cases involving corruption. Back when horses were the common mode of transport, leather pads called "blinkers" were often attached to the bridles beside the horses' eyes, to narrow their field of view to only what was right in front of them. By narrowing the legal definition of corruption to an explicit quid pro quo transaction, the Supreme Court narrowed the role of the jury. If the jury is our constitutional watchman, the Court has in effect blinkered the watchman.

The Court considered one case in which a trade association made a series of gifts to a lawmaker—expensive luggage, tickets to sporting events, and more—during a time when the lawmaker had direct influence over two matters affecting the association. In an opinion by Justice Scalia, the Court held that these gifts were not illegal, even if they were intended to "buy favor or generalized goodwill" and the official was "*in a position to act* favorably to the giver's interests."[48] It's not at all clear that a jury of ordinary people would agree. A jury might well think that buying ongoing influence with a lawmaker through many gifts is just as pernicious as giving one big gift in exchange for one big favor. If the Court hadn't ruled as it did, the influencer class might have to worry a bit about what a group of regular people sitting on a jury might think about a trade association, corporation, or wealthy individual buying the "favor or generalized goodwill" of a politician, and the result might be a good thing for America.

But a jury will no longer make that decision. This decision was made instead by five conservative justices, who seemed much in thrall to business interests, whose lives are remote from the daily cares and struggles of Americans, and who are profoundly ignorant of politics. Their decision has damaged the health of the public sphere in its enduring battle with private influence. I don't think America is a better place because a group of justices gave the influencer class the ability to "buy favor or generalized goodwill" with gifts of expensive luggage and tickets to sporting events.

The Supreme Court did not just narrow corruption to direct quid pro quo exchanges, they also have narrowed what official acts they will deem bribe-worthy. Recently, the Supreme Court unanimously overturned a jury's conviction of Virginia's former governor, Bob McDonnell, who with his family accepted an array of gifts and loans, including a Rolex watch, vacations, and a big payment for his daughter's wedding, from a Richmond businessman. In one instance, the Court reported, the businessman "took Mrs. McDonnell on a shopping trip and bought her $20,000 worth of designer clothing."[49] The *Washington Post*, long a witness to corruption in Washington, D.C., recently described McDonnell's case as "as hackneyed as any in America's lurid history of political graft" and his actions as "what any layman would recognize as bribery."[50]

Beyond the quid pro quo distinction, the Court's McDonnell decision held that certain official acts didn't even count as "quids" or "quos." The businessman had wanted Virginia's state universities to perform tests on a company product. Because the governor did not formally direct such tests, the court held it was not an "official act" for the governor to help the businessman in other ways that signaled gubernatorial favor, such as summoning university executives and researchers for meetings about the product. "In sum," Justice Roberts wrote, "an 'official act' is a decision or action on a 'question, matter, cause, suit, proceeding or controversy.' . . . Setting up a meeting, talking to another official, or organizing an event (or agreeing to do so)—without more—does not fit that definition of 'official act.'"[51] The *Washington Post* described the ruling in plainer terms: "the court's crabbed definition of official corruption . . . provides comfort for future sticky-fingered politicians, who will find it easier to line their pockets while leading supplicants and suitors by the nose."[52] As put by Democracy 21 president Fred Wertheimer, the decision "belies reality. If you show the facts in the case to any citizen, the citizen will conclude that the public official has sold his office for personal, financial gain."[53]

I'm with Wertheimer. In my experience working for a governor (who did not accept Rolexes or shopping sprees), those signals of gubernatorial favor indeed make a difference. Decision makers in state agencies want pictures with the governor, they want face time with the governor, and for sure they want goodwill with the governor at budget time. When the governor's office calls or sets up the meeting, it has impact. When the governor puts people face-to-face and asks them to work something out, it has impact. The idea that you're not selling your services when you're a governor who takes a Rolex for setting up such meetings is just false. It is indeed an "act," the act of showing gubernatorial favor in an arena where gubernatorial favor can be expected to have an impact. Obviously the problem isn't setting up the meeting or exerting the influence, because that's what governors do. It's accepting the damned Rolex and the damned shopping spree. Just accepting the damned Rolex looks reasonably enough like private influence-buying at work, done to acquire and reward the governor's official influence, that a jury ought to be allowed to make the call. Letting the big influencers and those politicians who accept their gifts run right to the chalk line, indeed to a line that looks morally out of bounds to many, is a significant (and in my view wrong) decision about the basic standards of our democracy.

Clearly, the public's trust in a political system where governors can receive Rolexes for setting up meetings, conduct that even the Court said was "tawdry" and "distasteful," was not a priority in this decision.[54] In the age-old political contest between big influencers, who want a system to maneuver in that is amenable to their influence, and the general public, who just want to be left alone in a system they can trust to resist such tawdry influence, yet another blow was struck for the big influencers. As Fred Wertheimer said, "The court forgot about the public."[55] And the jury's authority to draw those lines on behalf of the public was further chopped away.

While the Founders did not foresee the vast wealth, power, and influence of the modern mega-corporation and its armada of influencers, they did foresee dangerous concentrations of wealth, power, and influence. I believe they also foresaw that virtually every element of government could be subject to influence, and even foresaw the possibility that *all* the great powers of government—the presidency, the Senate, and the House of Representatives—could together fall under the sway of a very powerful influence. I am confident that this grim prospect was part of their reason for protecting the jury, that last sentinel, in the Bill of Rights.

If you think this talk about influence is just a lot of political science hooey and doesn't matter in your real life, think about what is happening in Congress. Look first at whose priorities get attention. The things that matter a lot to regular people are pretty clear: student loans and the massive debt that results; getting something done on climate change before it's too late; cleaning up our nasty campaign finance system; stopping jobs going offshore and offshore tax-dodging schemes; fixing a still-broken health care system; getting a handle on the debt; and having a fair tax system where taxes are not just "for the little people." But these things don't matter much to most big corporations—certainly not as their lobbying presence is felt in Congress—and as a result, none of those things is getting done. It's not a coincidence. The big corporate stuff, like defense spending and extending corporate tax benefits, somehow gets done every year. And in any direct conflict between corporate and public interests, in Congress the advantage is almost always with corporations. For instance, almost every measure passed or ventured by Republicans on the House or Senate floor recently on clean air, clean water, and climate change was an effort to roll back public protections. The House has taken more than a hundred runs at the EPA[56]—this in a country where the public water in Flint, Michigan, was unsafe to drink.

In a nutshell: when you shrink the definition of corruption and take it away from the jury, you degrade the health of the public sphere and you empower the big, constant corporate influencers. Power shifts to the influencers and away from the public, and the agenda and possibilities in Congress shift accordingly. People then lose confidence in the health of the public sphere and become disaffected and suspicious, and the great enterprise of American democracy suffers and falters. The only happy customers are the influencers, and we end where we began this chapter—with the "great men and their power-hungry minions who promote their private interests at the expense of the public good."[57] The jury is a small and often overlooked institution, but damaging it—blinkering the watchman—has big consequences.

Of course, juries can be bothersome to some, and can sometimes be inconvenient. They do take effort. They require care and feeding, both figuratively and literally. But the jury is an institution that makes popular sovereignty real; an institution that checks the encroachments of the wealthy and powerful; an institution that will listen when the ears of the other branches of government are deaf to you; and an institution that brings ordinary Americans together to make important decisions in their community. The jury is a little institution with a big, big role.

CHAPTER TEN

The Denial Machine

WE HAVE DISCUSSED VARIOUS WAYS that giant corporations and their minions exert power over our democracy—flooding our elections with cash intended to buy results, pushing the Supreme Court to promote the corporate agenda, capturing administrative agencies, and even trying to undermine the civil jury to meet their needs. But wait, as the TV ads say, there's more.

As we have seen, corporate money and influence are flowing into our politics through secret funding organizations. But it doesn't end there. On major issues where the facts are against them, the corporate lobby has developed a very complex system to do a very simple thing: to lie. To lie so persistently, so smoothly, and with such craft that plain truth is distorted, obscured, and sometimes demonized. This system—call it the "denial machine"—has been carefully built over the past several decades to deceive the public about the scientific facts at the heart of major political debates.

The denial machine fills a useful purpose for its corporate masters. In Edward Bernays's seminal 1928 book *Propaganda*, he wrote of twentieth-century society: "We are governed, our minds are molded, our tastes formed, our ideas suggested, largely by men we have never heard of." After the Nazis gave the word "propaganda" a bad name, Bernays gave a new name to his chosen field: "public relations." He described public relations as the "conscious and intelligent manipulation of the organized habits and opinions of the masses." Bernays described this manipulation as "an important element in democratic society. Those who manipulate this unseen mechanism of society constitute an invisible government which is the true ruling power of our country." The elite can use the power of public relations to steer democracy in ways unseen, or unappreciated, by the general public. "In almost every act of our daily lives, whether in the sphere of politics or business, in our social conduct or our ethical thinking, we are dominated by the relatively small number of persons . . . who understand the mental processes and social patterns of the masses. It is they who pull the wires which control the public mind."[1] What better way to control democracy, if you are a very big industry, than to pull those wires controlling the public mind?

The machine did not spring up at once, full-grown, like Athena from the brow of Zeus. It grew, over time, in industry-fueled campaigns to obscure risks the public faced: the dangers of cigarette smoke, the hazard to children of lead paint, the environmental harm of ozone depletion, and the health effects of chemicals. This machine has as its purpose to deceive the public, to give cover to politicians in the pockets of industry, and to thwart or delay laws and policies that warn or protect people against the dangers. Even in the earliest days of environmental PR crisis management, industry counterattacks "used emotional appeals, scientific misinformation, front groups, extensive mailings to the media and opinion leaders, and the recruitment of doctors and scientists as 'objective' third party defenders."[2]

Built up for the tobacco battles, expanded for the pollution debates of the 1980s and 1990s, and presently at work to fight climate action, the denial machine is big and artfully constructed: organizations designed to look and sound like they're real, messages honed by public relations experts to sound like they're reasonable, compromised scientists whom industry can trot out when they're needed, and the whole organism so vast and multifaceted that when you see its parts you could be fooled into thinking it's not all the same beast. But it is. Just like the mythological Hydra: many heads, same beast.

One of the frustrations of countering this denial apparatus is that over the years it has gotten so clever and so big. Robert Brulle, professor of sociology and environmental science at Drexel University, has tracked well over a hundred entities now engaged in this network.[3] By contrast to what's going on now, the attempts of the tobacco companies to fool everyone about the hazards of their cigarettes feel like the good old days. Yes, they created an entity to be their corporate front and called it the Tobacco Institute—almost quaint. In the realm of corporate subterfuge, the Tobacco Institute is a hallmark of an earlier time, like an old flivver you have to hand-crank to start, or a biplane with stretched-canvas wings. I guess the cigarette industry thought calling it an "institute" would make the Tobacco Institute sound scientific and neutral.

The Tobacco Institute might not have been the zenith of corporate subterfuge, but its work was wicked enough, along with the mischief of the tobacco companies themselves, that it earned them all a verdict in federal court as "racketeers" under the federal Racketeer Influenced and Corrupt Organizations (RICO) Act for their fraudulent misrepresentations of the health risks of tobacco.[4] Back to Bernays again: "Propaganda becomes vicious and reprehensive . . . when its authors consciously and deliberately disseminate what they know to be lies, or when they aim at effects which they know to be prejudicial to the common good."[5] The tobacco industry's propaganda effort was indeed wicked and reprehensible.

The method behind their wicked work, however, did not disappear with the verdict. Big industries regularly face the foreseeable predicament that scientists might someday find hazards in their product. They need a mechanism to deploy when that happens.

And there it is, ready to go: Big Tobacco's strategy, which worked for decades. As Steve Coll reported, the tobacco industry's example showed "how industry funding and purposeful, subtle campaigning could profitably delay a legal reckoning for a dangerous product through the manipulation of public opinion, government policy, and scientific discourse."[6] It wasn't a complicated game plan. It required some money, sure, but when really big money is at stake—selling cigarettes, for instance, or emitting megatons of CO_2—money comes easily. The machinery has gotten much better at obscuring itself, but the game plan is still pretty much the same.

So what is this game plan?

First you create counterfeit science, paid science, "science" that looks like real science but comes to the conclusions that industry wants. The great advantage to industry in this "counterfeit science" game is that the counterfeit scientists don't need to defeat the real scientists; they just need to sow enough doubt about the real science among the uninformed and sometimes gullible public to forestall action. As one tobacco memo said: "Doubt is our product."[7] To manufacture that doubt, you need a stable of agreeable "scientists" at your disposal.

Second, you need a mouthpiece, an entity with a name that sounds more neutral and dispassionate than your corporation. If you say, "This is ExxonMobil, or Peabody Coal, and we're here to tell you climate change isn't real," well, you will probably have a little credibility problem. They do have the American Petroleum Institute out there, but that's not much of an improvement over the Tobacco Institute—it's old-school stuff. If you really want to trick the public today, you've got to do way better than that. And they do.

Third, you need to fund this apparatus. That creates a little problem. Not the money—there's plenty of money available when big money is at stake—but the money *trail*. Since even front organizations often have to reveal their donors, industry money leaves obvious fingerprints that can embarrass a front organization, and that doesn't help create the desired confusion. Thus there has emerged a way to launder the money, to scrub it of its corporate identity, so it doesn't come through with a corporate name on it.

One, two, three: it's not all that complicated, considering the stakes. You might call it Big Tobacco 2.0. As Brulle reports, "Some of the same people and some of the same organizations that were involved in the tobacco issue are also involved in climate change,"[8] with the fossil-fuel industry now waging an extremely well-funded, well-organized effort to "delegitimate the science that supports . . . mandatory limits on carbon emissions."[9]

Let's look at this machinery in its most active modern role, denying the science that shows how carbon emissions are causing climate and ocean changes. First, there is the counterfeit science and the "scientists" who front for the climate denial apparatus. The same names crop up over and over again, a few ubiquitous performers. That's because (here's a good thing) there are not many people who are actually willing to do what these individuals do, even for money. So the fossil-fuel industry has to go repeatedly to their same stable of agreeable climate "scientists."

Many of the "scientists" who front for the climate denial apparatus are hired hands. The funding of one of them was unearthed recently by the *New York Times*, which disclosed that this one scientist had been paid by the fossil-fuel industry to the tune of over a million dollars.[10] According to the *Times*, he also cleared his work in advance with his industry patrons. Obviously, in real science, that would be objectionable. This, however, is public relations in a lab coat. And in public relations, the product is cleared with the client.

One recent academic study of this phenomenon described climate change deniers' reliance on "researchers who are relatively inactive in their field and focus on favorable reports isolated from larger bodies of research in order to justify their positions, clearly contradicting decades of consensus within the climate-science community regarding anthropogenic global warming." As a result, the claims of climate deniers "lack evidence considered acceptable by the standards of the international scientific community," but they do "give insight into the political and rhetorical strategies of organized climate change denial."[11]

Many of the "scientists" who front for the climate denial apparatus are merely talk-show performers. Their work rarely appears in actual scientific journals, where real scientific debate takes place. In those scientific journals, their far-fetched schemes and baloney theories would have to face stiff scientific peer review. As former vice president Al Gore pointed out in his "Inconvenient Truth" presentation, out of more than nine hundred peer-reviewed scientific journal articles addressing climate change, exactly zero deny the science connecting man-made carbon emissions to climate change.[12] (To be exact, Professor Naomi Oreskes's peer-reviewed article in *Science* magazine, titled "The Scientific Consensus on Climate Change," puts the precise score at 928–0.)[13] Peer review is a tough standard for deniers; it requires authors to subject their work to the scrutiny of objective experts in their field.

Anyway, if you're in the counterfeit science business, real scientists are not your target audience. They don't count. You're in the public relations business, and the public is your audience. So instead of wasting time in peer-reviewed academic journals, industry "scientists" are out on Fox News and talk radio, where they don't face peer review and can address their target audience directly. Out there, the listeners are not experts in the science, they're an uninformed public ripe for the counterfeit scientists' mischief.

The "scientists" who front for the climate denial apparatus also tend to be selective. They rarely talk about the warming of the oceans, which you can measure with a thermometer. They rarely talk about the resulting sea level rise, because the law of thermal expansion is a little too obvious to deny, even for a "scientist." They rarely address ocean acidification, because you can put sea water and carbon dioxide together in a high school chemistry lab and watch the pH change. The "scientists" who front for the climate denial apparatus tend to focus on things such as atmospheric modeling, where the complexity of computer projections leaves more room for their mischief. Industries that want to sow doubt focus their efforts on areas where complexity or uncertainty create an atmosphere more conducive to deception.

This focus on creating uncertainty is intentional. Yale professor Justin Farrell describes the climate denial apparatus as "a complex network of think tanks, foundations, public relations firms, trade associations and *ad hoc* groups" that operate "complex counter-movement efforts that foster intractable uncertainty"[14] about real climate science. Their other goal is "to create ideological polarization around climate change."[15] Why polarization? Because it is "well understood that polarization is an effective strategy for creating controversy and delaying policy progress, particularly around environmental issues."[16] You can mask old special-interest special pleading as a partisan or cultural battle, and distract the public and the media from the smelly special interest in the corner.

Of course, it's not enough for the fossil-fuel industry to have its stable of "scientists." It also needs mouthpieces to publish climate denial op-eds, hold climate denial conferences, produce climate denial witnesses for hearings, and release climate denial articles (rarely peer-reviewed ones, of course). The machinery for propagating counterfeit science into public debate has become increasingly sophisticated since the days of the Tobacco Institute or the American Petroleum Institute. Now industry front organizations come with names like the Heartland Institute (they're the ones who notoriously compared scientists who believe in climate change to the Unabomber),[17] the Heritage

Foundation, the Cato Institute, the Mercatus Center, and the Annapolis Council. All take fossil-fuel money; all deny climate change. Most galling, perhaps, are the John Locke Institute for Public Policy (Locke and Montesquieu were the two great social scientists behind the ideals of our American Revolution), the Franklin Center for Government and Public Integrity (with a nice profile of Ben Franklin on its logo), the James Madison Institute for Public Policy (our Founding Father), and the George C. Marshall Institute for Public Policy (George C. Marshall was the architect of our military victory in Europe in World War II, described by British prime minister Winston Churchill as "the organizer of victory"[18]). Co-opting these great names for mouthpieces in this corporate-funded denial operation shows how low these interests will stoop to paste on themselves a veneer of credibility—a veneer that makes the think tank, in Jane Mayer's memorable phrase, a "disguised political weapon."[19]

Brulle describes the purpose of this network of front groups today as "a deliberate and organized effort to misdirect the public discussion and distort the public's understanding of climate change."[20] The coordinated tactics of this network, his report shows, "span a wide range of activities, including political lobbying, contributions to political candidates, and a large number of communication and media efforts that aim at undermining climate science."[21]

In *The War on Science*, Shawn Otto describes a recurring pattern as technologies emerge: discovery and application of the new technology; development of industries to manufacture and sell it; discovery of harmful side effects; battle between industry and science over that harm; crisis when the harm becomes too clear to overlook; and adaptation as society ultimately shifts to mitigate the harm.[22] His description of the "battle" phase is instructive: "vested economic interests sense a potentially lethal blow to their production systems and fight the proposed changes by denying the environmental effects, maligning and impeaching witnesses, questioning the science, attacking or impugning the scientists, and/or arguing that other factors are causing the mounting disaster." In this battle, "science becomes a rhetorical tool and facts are cherry-picked to win arguments, pitting real science against clever public relations campaigns, with the public unsure about what or whom to believe."[23] Otto breaks the industry strategy in this battle phase into seven steps. "Step one . . . starts with phony science,"[24] using scientists "who supply a steady stream of pseudoscience that can be used by foot soldiers to sway the public debate."[25] "Step two follows with slanted press materials spoon-fed to journalists by industry-affiliated nonprofits and bloggers."[26] Then comes "the third step: building and financing industry-aligned front groups (fake public-interest organizations) and astroturf groups (fake grassroots organizations)."[27] "Step four is to proselytize the intelligentsia who fund political campaigns and shape opinions in the press."[28] Step five pushes the materials out to "industry-aligned, or otherwise sympathetic talk-radio and cable-news purveyors, who reference these mainstream sources, react with outrage, and call for policy action."[29] Next is "the sixth stage of the attack: legislative or other policy action by partisan allies in government."[30] Last comes "the seventh and final stage. Now seemingly supported by science, the press, the government, the public, [and] business and professional opinion leaders, . . . industry representatives can step safely out from behind the curtain . . . and plead their case."[31]

Behind the network of climate denial fronts lurks the fossil-fuel industry. It takes big money to fund all these front organizations. And big money is what they've got. Brulle's report chronicles, from 2003 to 2010, "140 foundations making grants totaling $558 million to 91 organizations" that actively oppose climate action—more than half a billion dollars distributed over seven years.[32] Jane Mayer has reported Greenpeace investigators' discovery that the Kochs alone, from 2005 to 2008, "poured almost $25 million into dozens of different organizations fighting climate reform," outspending even ExxonMobil.[33]

The War on Science describes the political logic of this spending. "The shifting—or as economists say, the externalizing—of private costs onto the commons takes from everyone, and in fact reduces wealth throughout the economy."[34] Of course, it "takes from everyone" in order to transfer wealth to the special interest, and it "reduces wealth throughout the economy" in order to increase wealth in that special-interest sector of the economy. This fails a test of civilization quoted by Otto, enunciated by John Hubble (father of Edwin of Hubble Telescope fame): "'The best definition we have found for civilization is that a civilized man does what is best for all, while the savage does what is best for himself.'"[35] By this standard, the fossil-fuel sector behaves as a savage in its climate denial, not as a civilized social force.

Some simple math explains the economic logic of the fossil-fuel sector's creating such a big, expensive machine just to propagate climate denial. The EPA has estimated U.S. combustion of fossil fuels in 2011 to have emitted over 6.8 billion metric tons of carbon dioxide.[36] The federal Office of Management and Budget recently set the social cost of carbon—the economic and health costs of carbon pollution that the polluters inflict on the rest of society—at $45 per metric ton of CO_2 emitted.[37] So do the math: 6.9 billion metric tons of carbon at $45 of social cost per metric ton means that just one year's carbon emissions costs the public over $310 billion. The price would be pretty high for the polluters if they were to be forced by the government to make up for the harm that they're causing.

A properly working market economy would put those "negative externalities," as economists call them, into the price of the product, so that the correct market signal was sent through the price about the true costs. Even very conservative economists agree with that. Our failure to do this amounts to a massive subsidy, worth at least $310 billion per year in the United States alone. The International Monetary Fund's effort to calculate the "effective subsidy" yielded a much higher number: $700 billion, every year, to the benefit of the fossil-fuel industry in the United States.[38] That's a subsidy worth fighting for.

Spending half a billion dollars over seven years to get away with $310 billion (or even $700 billion) of harm every year? It's the best bargain on the planet. It's a better than a thousand-to-one return on investment. We talk in ten-year budget cycles in the Senate; over a ten-year Senate budget cycle the $700 billion IMF number becomes $7 trillion. Can you imagine what mischief people might be willing to make for $7 trillion? So money is not a problem for the polluters.

The last element of paying for this racket is funding the network of climate denial fronts without leaving too many dirty, telltale, fossil-fuel fingerprints. And the industry has set up just the thing: an organization called DonorsTrust and its related Donors Capital Fund. Fossil-fuel corporations can put their money in the front end of DonorsTrust, and out the back end comes laundered, identity-free money that can go exactly where you direct, with no fingerprints. DonorsTrust has no business purpose except to launder the identities of donors who want to fund groups without attribution. It is an identity-laundering machine.

And it's a great big machine. Jane Mayer calculates that as much as $750 million was redistributed through DonorsTrust to various conservative causes.[39] DonorsTrust alone has provided about a quarter of the funding for what Brulle's report calls the "climate change countermovement,"[40] and what I call the climate denial machine or network. More than a third of the organizations examined in the Brulle report get over 90 percent of their money from hidden sources.[41]

DonorsTrust/Donors Capital Fund is by far the biggest source of funding in that climate denial web. These twin entities reported giving a combined $78 million specifically to climate denier groups between 2003 and 2010. According to Brulle's report, the DonorsTrust/Donors Capital Fund operation does double duty both as the "central component" and "predominant funder" of the denier apparatus and as the "black box that conceals the identity of contributors."[42]

This anonymous funding has grown as disclosed funding from fossil-fuel polluters has declined, with DonorsTrust/Donors Capital Fund donations to the denial network jumping from 3 percent of all foundation funding in 2003 to over 23 percent in 2010.[43] At the same time, disclosed donations from foundations affiliated with the Koch brothers declined from 9 percent of all foundation funding to the climate denier network in 2006 down to 2 percent by 2010, and ExxonMobil Foundation wound down its disclosed funding of organizations in the climate denier network, basically zeroing out by 2008, according to Brulle.[44]

It's working. As Professor Farrell at Yale has observed: "Academic researchers have had a very difficult time tracking flows of economic resources between members of this network, especially in recent years because of foundations like DonorsTrust, which enables contributors to give to specific causes while at the same time shielding the identity of the donor. Reliably assessing the influence of corporate benefactors has thus been extremely difficult."[45] Similarly, the Brulle report finds that "most funding for denial efforts is untraceable. Despite extensive data compilation and analyses, only a fraction of the hundreds of millions in contributions to climate change denying organizations can be specifically accounted for from public records. Approximately 75 percent of the income of these organizations comes from unidentifiable sources."[46] All this secrecy helps the string-pullers manipulate public opinion, and in a democracy that's a dangerous place to go.

If the fossil-fuel industry weren't up to something fishy, why all this effort to conceal? Why the commandeering of respected men's names when the people are dead and can't disassociate themselves? Why the identity laundering? And why make the scheme so big and complex?

Perhaps for $7 trillion.

But how could this intricate web of lies get by a free and independent media? Aren't they supposed to blow the whistle on this kind of stuff? Well, some have. Indeed, some have been heroic. But not all. Certain elements of the press have even been complicit—there is no gentler way to put it—in building and running the denial machine. And with corporate ownership of large parts of the media, it's perhaps no surprise that some outlets have gone over to the corporate side.

We count on the press in America to report faithfully and accurately on our changing world, and to alert the public to looming threats. Our Constitution gives the press special, vital rights so that they can perform this special, vital role. But what happens when the press fails in this role? What happens when elements of the press stop being independent, when press outlets climb into bed with special interests? The Latin phrase "Quis custodiet ipsos custodes?"—who will watch the watchmen themselves?—then becomes the question. The press is supposed to scrutinize all of us. Who watches them when they fail at their independent role?

It is assuredly an industry strategy to work the refs, trying to get their message out through legitimate media channels. Otto's *The War on Science* describes this as "[t]he industry and public-relations front, financed by corporations and conducted by PR experts, shills, and front groups, who take advantage of journalists' naiveté about objectivity and truth in order to manipulate the media, thereby shaping public opinion using 'uncertainties,' deception, personal attacks, and outrage to move public policy toward an antiscience position that supports the funders' business objectives."[47] They also seek to control their own outlets, as they have great success with people who "have drifted under the influence of slanted conservative commercial media."[48]

The editorial page of one of our nation's leading publications, the *Wall Street Journal*, is a case study in how complicit parts of the news media can be in the denial network. The *Wall Street Journal* is one of America's great newspapers. It is a paragon in journalism—right up to the editorial page, which opens to a chasm of polluter sludge. When a harmful industrial pollutant is the issue, this editorial page will misleadingly deny the scientific consensus and ignore its own excellent news pages' actual reporting, all helping the industry campaign to manufacture doubt, and delay remedial action.

As outlined in an excellent and far-reaching report by Media Matters, a deniers' playbook is visible in the pattern of the *Wall Street Journal*'s commentary on acid rain, on the ozone layer, and now—most pronouncedly—on climate change.[49] The pattern is simple: deny the science, question the motives, and exaggerate the costs. Call it the polluting industries' 1-2-3 step.

Let's start in the 1970s, when chlorofluorocarbons (CFCs) were used in everything from aerosol cans to refrigerators. Scientists warned that CFCs could create a hole in the ozone layer, putting human beings at heightened risk of cancer from exposure to the sun's ultraviolet rays. The *Wall Street Journal*'s editorial page for more than twenty-five years doggedly printed editorials devaluing the science and attacking any regulation of CFCs.[50]

As Media Matters lays it out:

> A January 1976 editorial said the connection between CFCs and ozone depletion "is only a theory and will remain only that until further efforts are made to test its validity in the atmosphere itself."[51] . . . A May 1979 editorial said that scientists "still don't know to what extent, if any, mankind's activities have altered the ozone barrier or whether the possibly harmful effects of these activities aren't offset by natural processes. . . . Thus, it now appears the excitement over the threat to the ozone layer was founded on scanty scientific evidence."[52] A March 1984 editorial said that concerns about ozone depletion were based on "premature scientific evidence" and claim[ed] that "new evidence

> shows that the ozone layer isn't vanishing after all; it may even be increasing."[53] . . . A March 1989 editorial called for more research on the "questionable theory that CFCs cause depletion of the ozone layer," calling on scientists to "continue to study the sky until we know enough to make a sound decision regarding the phasing out of our best refrigerants."[54]

Predictably, the page also attacked the motives of reformers. A February 1992 editorial, insinuating other motives, stated: "It is simply not clear to us that real science drives policy in this area."[55]

And—playbook step 3—they warned that action to slow ozone depletion would be costly. Again, from Media Matters:

> A March 1984 editorial claimed that banning CFCs "cost the economy some $1.52 billion in forgone profits and product-change expenses" and 8,700 jobs.[56] An August 1990 editorial warned that banning CFCs would lead to "a dramatic increase in air-conditioning and refrigeration costs."[57] It added: The likely substitute for the most popular banned refrigerant costs 30 times as much and will itself be banned by the year 2015. The economy will have to shoulder at least $10 billion to $15 billion a year in added refrigeration costs by the year 2000."[58] A February 1992 editorial warned that accelerating the phaseout of CFCs "almost surely will translate into big price increases on many consumer products."[59]

Despite the protests of the *Wall Street Journal* editorial page, Americans actually listened to the science. Congress took action, banning these refrigerants, protecting the ozone layer and protecting the public's health, and the economy prospered. The ozone hole is healing. What about all those costs that the *Journal* claimed? Looking back, we see that action to slow ozone depletion in fact saved money. According to the EPA's 1999 progress report on the Clean Air Act, "[e]very dollar invested in ozone protection provides $20 of societal health benefits in the United States."[60] One dollar spent, twenty dollars saved. The *Journal*'s response? Silence. They just stopped talking about it.

When scientists began reporting that acid rain was falling on most of the northeastern United States the *Journal* followed a nearly identical pattern. Again, according to the Media Matters report, out came the playbook: saying "data are not conclusive and more studies are needed"; arguing that "nature, not industry, is the primary source of acid rain"; claiming "the scientific case for acid rain is dying"; and charging "that politics, not nature, is the primary force driving the theory's biggest boosters." At the same time, President Reagan's panel on the issue warned that failing to act on acid rain would risk "irreversible damage."[61]

Now, as told by Media Matters, the *Journal* is using the same old polluter playbook against climate change. First, they deny the science:

> 1993—*WSJ* claims there is "growing evidence that global warming just isn't happening" . . . 1999—*WSJ*: "Serious scientists" call global warming "one of the greatest hoaxes of all time." . . . 2005—*WSJ* says the link between fossil fuels and global warming has "become even more doubtful." . . . A December 2011 editorial said that the global warming debate requires "more definitive evidence."[62]

The polluter playbook then produced the usual inflate-the-costs warning that solving climate change would "make the world poorer than it would otherwise be."[63] This "world poorer" piece actually hit the full polluter-playbook trifecta in just one editorial, also questioning motives of the "political actors" they claim are out to gain economic control and denying the science, saying "global surface temperatures have remained essentially flat."[64] If only the editorial page writers at the *Wall Street Journal* would read the actual news their own paper reports on climate change.

Climate Nexus did a more recent analysis of the *Wall Street Journal* editorial page and concluded that the page "overwhelmingly ignores the science, champions doubt and denial of both the science and effectiveness of action, and leaves readers misinformed about the consensus of science and of the risks of the threat . . . consistently ignoring or ridiculing the scientific consensus on the reality and urgency of climate change." Specifically, Climate Nexus found that of 201 editorials relating to climate science or policy "dating back to 1997, none explicitly acknowledges that fossil fuels cause climate change"; out of 279 op-eds published since 1995, a paltry 14 percent "reflect mainstream climate science"; and out of 122 columns published since 1997, just "four accepted as fact that fossil fuels cause climate change, or endorse a policy to reduce emissions." Between April 2015 and May 2016, as global heat records were broken monthly, the *Journal* published one hundred climate-related op-eds, columns, and editorials; ninety-six failed to acknowledge the link between human activity and climate change. The report concluded that the *Wall Street Journal*'s posture "consistently highlights voices of those with vested interests in fossil fuels . . . presenting only the dismissive side of the climate discussion," and is "a failure of journalistic responsibility."[65]

"Those who corrupt the public mind are just as evil as those who steal from the public purse," said Adlai Stevenson in a speech on September 12, 1952.[66] The big polluters aren't just polluting our atmosphere and oceans; they are polluting our democracy, with misinformation and money. They are doing it purposely. The *Wall Street Journal* editorial page, and the whole denial apparatus, has been wrong every time they've gone down this road: wrong about tobacco, wrong about lead paint, wrong about acid rain, wrong about mercury, wrong about the ozone layer, and now wrong about climate change. Yet they keep going there. Being wrong over and over doesn't seem to bother them. If being right mattered to them, or to the corporate interests behind them, they'd reassess what they do. So you have to wonder if they don't mind being wrong. Maybe it's not their intention to be right. Maybe it's much more cynical than that. Maybe the point simply is to create doubt, buy time, and maximize profits.

When the inevitable happens and climate change really starts to hit home, people will want to know why we didn't take proper steps in time. It's not as if there isn't enough scientific evidence out there for us to act. This denial machine will likely go down as one of our great American scandals, like Watergate or Teapot Dome—a deliberate, complex scheme of lies and propaganda that caused real harm to the American people, our country, and the world, all so that a small group of powerful corporations could make more money a little longer. Thank God that a small group of dogged investigators, academics and journalists is gradually exposing this rancid network, even if elements of the press have joined the other side.

I will close this chapter with a recent example I ran into of this denial apparatus at work. I had the nerve to write an op-ed piece suggesting a legal investigation into the fossil-fuel industry to look for tobacco-type fraud.[67] That prompted an outburst of dozens of articles from right-wing editorial pages, fossil-fuel front groups, and various climate-denial outfits. The editorials popped up like mushrooms after rain. Later, at a Senate Judiciary hearing,[68] I asked Attorney General Lynch about a civil fraud investigation into the denial operation of the fossil-fuel industry, and in the following days there was another outburst of dozens more articles. These outbursts against any fossil-fuel fraud investigation were notable for the homogeneity of the message. You could mix and match the dozens of articles virtually interchangeably. Some were actually written by the same people. If you looked at the authors and the outlets, and knew the players, you could inevitably find a link back to the fossil-fuel industry.

The core common argument in these two outbursts was that any investigation would be a terrible infringement on corporate free speech rights protected by the First Amendment. Someone very much wanted to protect any fossil-fuel industry misdeeds from investigation, hiding them under the skirts of the First Amendment. So let's take a look at the merits of the "First Amendment" argument that was at the core of this barrage.

Robert Post is the dean of the Yale Law School, arguably America's most renowned and prestigious law school. In response to the barrage of editorial argument I have described, Dean Post wrote an article titled "ExxonMobil Is Abusing the First Amendment," which ran in the *Washington Post* on June 24, 2016.[69] I will quote a full section of his article.

> Global warming is perhaps the single most significant threat facing the future of humanity on this planet. It is likely to wreak havoc on the economy, including, most especially, on the stocks of companies that sell hydrocarbon energy products. If large oil companies have deliberately misinformed investors about their

knowledge of global warming, they may have committed serious commercial fraud.

A potentially analogous instance of fraud occurred when tobacco companies were found to have deliberately misled their customers about the dangers of smoking. The safety of nicotine was at the time fiercely debated, just as the threat of global warming is now vigorously contested. Because tobacco companies were found to have known about the risks of smoking, even as they sought to convince their customers otherwise, they were held liable for fraud. Despite the efforts of tobacco companies to invoke First Amendment protections for their contributions to public debate, the U.S. Court of Appeals for the D.C. Circuit found: "Of course it is well settled that the First Amendment does not protect fraud."

The point is a simple one. If large corporations were free to mislead deliberately the consuming public, we would live in a jungle rather than in an orderly and stable market.

ExxonMobil and its supporters are now eliding the essential difference between fraud and public debate.

Dean Post's reminder—which most lawyers know—that " 'it is well settled that the First Amendment does not protect fraud' " illustrates a big logical flaw in the fossil-fuel front groups' First Amendment argument. It is not logical to presume the propriety of the fossil-fuel industry's climate denial operation, when that would be the very question at issue in an investigation. If in fact there is "serious commercial fraud" at the core of the fossil-fuel industry's climate denial operation, the First Amendment argument evaporates, since fraud is not protected free speech. To assert freedom of speech as the reason there should be no investigations is to prejudge the answer that the investigations would ultimately determine: was there fraud, or was it just public debate? Courts figure that distinction out all the time.

I was the subject of these outbursts, and I couldn't help noticing their very high emotional tone. The insults were bitter ones, with language sometimes veering into hysteria. I was the terrible inquisitor Torquemada, for instance, and mighty ExxonMobil was the lonely Galileo in his cell.[70] The outbursts' high moral dudgeon ran into some ironies, however. The attorney general of Virginia once harassed a climate scientist at the University of Virginia so vilely that the university had to take the attorney general all the way to the Virginia Supreme Court to make the attorney general knock it off.[71] Where was these groups' outrage about the scientist's free speech then? When a U.S. senator called for criminal prosecution of named climate scientists a few years back, where was their outrage over the scientists' freedom of speech? (For whatever it's worth, I had called for a civil investigation of corporate entities, not criminal prosecution of scientists.) Climate scientists are still regularly bombarded with Freedom of Information Act requests for their university emails, and often threatened with physical harm. Where are the outbursts of outrage about such harassment? There is none. The outrage animating these editorial outbursts is an outrage of convenience, appearing only when the target of a proposed investigation is the fossil-fuel industry; when the target of an investigation actually is an individual scientist, not a peep out of them.

These editorial outbursts were presumably intended to shove a phony First Amendment argument into the public debate, to help the fossil-fuel industry defend against any investigation. Ironically, with their nearly identical message, the same logical fallacy, and the falsely histrionic tones, they actually highlighted a network of mouthpieces linked to the fossil-fuel industry. This was no sincere expression of concern about rights of free speech protected by the First Amendment. It was an elaborate sham, an effort in masquerade and misdirection supporting the fossil-fuel interests who erected the front group screen in the first place, to discourage any fair and proper investigation into possible fraud at the heart of the denial machine.

But if you weren't a United States senator who gets a lot of news clips, if you were just an ordinary citizen reading only one or two of these editorials, you might not see the pattern. You might think the argument was honest, or well-founded. You would not notice any links to the fossil-fuel industry. ExxonMobil had its name on none of the editorials in these outbursts.

As we leave the fossil-fuel groups' First Amendment argument, consider what would happen if their argument were actually to succeed. If even fraudulent corporate speech were protected by the First

Amendment, out would go decades of legal precedent allowing regulation of corporate commercial speech to protect consumers and honest markets. Out would go state and federal consumer protection laws protecting individuals from corporate misrepresentations. It would be open season on the consumer. That's a ludicrous world to envision, but it's the world that would result if the First Amendment "outburst" argument actually became the law. It's a world these forces are willing to contemplate, if it would help protect the fossil-fuel industry against the risk that a court might find they crossed the line into fraud.

CHAPTER ELEVEN

Climate Change and the "Flies of Summer"

THE PROBLEM OF CORPORATE CONTROL OF OUR POLITICS is correctable. We can stand up, push back, and make it right. Teddy Roosevelt did; we can, too. However, there is one place where this corporate power can push us over a tipping point that is not correctable. That is climate change.

In a Vatican Radio speech, Pope Francis quoted the old warning "God always forgives, we men forgive sometimes, but Nature never forgives," and added his own admonition: "If you give her a slap, she will give you one."[1] We are giving Nature a hell of a slap. As noted essayist and Kentucky farmer Wendell Berry wrote: "Whether we and our politicians know it or not, Nature is a party to all our deals and decisions, and she has more votes, a longer memory, and a sterner sense of justice than we do."[2]

For as long as our species has been on planet Earth, the amount of carbon dioxide in the atmosphere has fluctuated between 170 and 300 parts per million. In 2015, the amount of carbon dioxide in the earth's atmosphere blew through 400 parts per million, for the first time in human history.[3] That's a measurement, not a theory. There's no dispute.

The science linking carbon pollution to global warming is nothing new. It dates back to the time of President Lincoln, when Irish physicist John Tyndall first measured how different gases in the atmosphere absorbed heat to varying degrees, essentially predicting the atmospheric warming that excess carbon dioxide would cause.[4] In the century and a half since, we have measured changes in the climate and oceans that legitimate scientists conclude, with virtual unanimity, are caused by our burning of fossil fuels.

Our oceans are warming and acidifying. Those are measurements. Every legitimate scientist concurs that the oceans acidify because they absorb carbon dioxide and it changes their chemistry, and they warm because oceans have absorbed so much of the excess heat from global warming—more than 90 percent of it is the prevailing measure.[5] The chemistry change in the oceans is science you can replicate in a high school science lab. The warming of the oceans is something we measure with thermometers.

The rate of the warming and acidifying of the ocean is the fastest in human history.[6] We measure that, too. We are experiencing the warmest years ever recorded.[7] That's more measurement. Measurements show rising seas lapping at our shores. Rhode Island has measured nearly ten inches of sea level rise since the 1930s.[8]

These are all measurements, not projections. These are facts, not theories. They portend dire consequences for coastal flooding, dying timber forests, farmland drought, shifts in fisheries, and weather emergencies.

Unbelievably, scientists for the fossil-fuel industry have known about the threat of global warming for nearly *fifty years*. A 1968 report commissioned by the American Petroleum Institute noted that the "greenhouse effect" was likely due to carbon dioxide emissions and that significant global warming would likely cause "the melting of the Antarctic ice cap, a rise in sea levels, warming of the oceans, and an increase in photosynthesis." They concluded: "Even the remote possibility of such an occurrence justifies concern."[9]

Even scientists within ExxonMobil concurred. As early as 1979, Exxon scientists wrote in an internal memo:

> The CO_2 concentration in the atmosphere has increased since the beginning of the world industrialization. It is now 15% greater than it was in 1850 and the rate of CO_2 release from anthropogenic sources appears to be doubling every 15 years. The most widely held theory is that:

- The increase is due to fossil-fuel combustion
- Increasing CO_2 concentration will cause a warming of the earth's surface
- The present trend of fossil-fuel consumption will cause dramatic environmental effects before the year 2050.

The memo went on to predict "dramatic world climate changes within the next 75 years, according to many present climatic models."[10] That memo was produced thirty-eight years ago. We are halfway there.

In a 1982 internal memo, Exxon scientists wrote again:

> Over the past several years a clear scientific consensus has emerged regarding the expected climatic effects of increased atmospheric CO_2. The consensus is that a doubling of atmospheric CO_2 from its pre–industrial revolution value would result in an average global temperature rise of (3.0 ± 1.5) degrees C. . . . There is unanimous agreement in the scientific community that a temperature increase of this magnitude would bring about significant changes in the earth's climate.[11]

Thirty-five years ago they admitted that "a clear scientific consensus has emerged."

Exxon science memos also pointed out the "possibility that an atmospheric CO_2 buildup will cause adverse environmental effects in enough areas of the world to consider limiting the future use of fossil fuels as major energy sources"[12] and that "mitigation of the 'greenhouse effect' would require major reductions in fossil-fuel combustion."[13] For the biggest fossil-fuel company in the world, this was serious.

Instead of going into high gear to try to mitigate or reverse some of the effects of its corporate behavior, Exxon chose to dedicate itself to spouting denial and funding the denial machinery. In 2005 the *Wall Street Journal* reported, "Openly and unapologetically, the world's No. 1 oil company disputes the notion that fossil fuels are the main cause of global warming."[14] Assessing Exxon's track record, Naomi Oreskes, a Harvard professor and author of *Merchants of Doubt*, and Congressman Ted Lieu wrote in an opinion piece in *The Hill*,

"A new word needs to be invented in the English language for what ExxonMobil has done. The level of corporate hypocrisy and the potential consequences are staggering, as is their blatant denial of both the facts of science and of their own shameful history."[15] As Shawn Otto summarizes in *The War on Science*, fossil fuel, "the world's most powerful industry," launched "an industrial war on science the likes of which the world has never seen."[16]

Exxon even went so far as to coach its CEO to cite a bogus "petition" of seventeen thousand scientists asserting, in the CEO's words, that there is "no convincing scientific evidence that any release of carbon dioxide, methane or other greenhouse gases is causing or will in the foreseeable future cause catastrophic heating of the earth's atmosphere and disruption of the earth's climate."[17] The CEO omitted to mention to his shareholders that the "petition" was put together by a climate denier named Fred Seitz, who has worked in Exxon-funded climate denial fronts and whose former job was to refute the criticisms of cigarettes on behalf of tobacco giant R.J. Reynolds.[18] Nor did he mention that signatories on the "petition" included imaginary TV and cartoon characters.[19]

The path Exxon chose was well described by Steve Coll in his prize-winning investigative book *Private Empire: ExxonMobil and American Power*: "a kaleidoscope of overlapping and competing influence campaigns, some open, some conducted by front organizations, and some entirely clandestine. Strategists created layers of disguise, subtlety, and subterfuge—corporate-funded 'grassroots' programs and purpose-built think tanks, as fingerprint-free as possible. In such an opaque and untrustworthy atmosphere, the ultimate advantage lay with any lobbyist whose goal was to manufacture confusion and perpetual controversy. On climate, this happened to be the oil industry's position."[20]

Conservation and stewardship were once fundamental principles of American conservatism. From seminal thinkers of the conservative movement to great Republican leaders of the twentieth century, the conservative ideal included a commitment to the interests of future generations, and the conservation that honored that commitment.

Edmund Burke, an Irish-born member of Britain's Parliament, is considered by many the father of modern conservatism. His 1790 conservative pamphlet, "Reflections on the Revolution in France," cautioned that we are but "temporary possessors" of our society. If individuals are "unmindful of what they have received from their ancestors, or what is due to their posterity," he wrote, "no one generation could link with the other. Men would become little better than the flies of a summer."[21] In our case, flies of a carbon-fueled summer.

A Distinguished Scholar at the Heritage Foundation, Russell Kirk was dubbed by President Ronald Reagan "the prophet of American conservatism."[22] In a 1970 piece in the *Baltimore Sun*, "Conservation Activism Is a Healthy Sign," Kirk wrote, "There is nothing more conservative than conservation."[23]

President Dwight Eisenhower's 1961 farewell address invoked our national legacy: "As we peer into society's future, we—you and I, and our government—must avoid the impulse to live only for today, plundering, for our own ease and convenience, the precious resources of tomorrow. We cannot mortgage the material assets of our grandchildren without risking the loss also of their political and spiritual heritage."[24]

President Gerald Ford, who once worked as a national park ranger, said in 1975: "We have too long treated the natural world as an adversary rather than as a life-sustaining gift from the Almighty. If man has the genius to build, which he has, he must also have the ability and the responsibility to preserve."[25]

In 1984, President Ronald Reagan, perhaps the figure most revered by today's Republican Party, put this question to his fellow Republicans: "What is a conservative after all but one who conserves, one who is committed to protecting and holding close the things by which we live. . . . And we want to protect and conserve the land on which we live—our countryside, our rivers and mountains, our plains and meadows and forests. This is our patrimony. This is what we leave to our children. And our great moral responsibility is to leave it to them either as we found it or better than we found it."[26] President Reagan's conservative credentials are unassailable, and GOP candidates for elected office strive mightily to out-Reagan each other at every turn, but those words would make Reagan a fringe liberal candidate in today's corporate/conservative movement.

Even the National Association of Evangelicals has said: "Christians must care about climate change because we love God the Creator and

Jesus our Lord, through whom and for whom the creation was made. This is God's world, and any damage that we do to God's world is an offense against God Himself."[27]

The long lineage of conservative thinkers and politicians who felt a duty to protect the environment did not end with Reagan. There was a steady, healthy heartbeat of Republican support for major U.S. legislation to address carbon pollution, all the way through the first decade of this century. In 2003, Senator John McCain was the lead Republican co-sponsor of the Climate Stewardship Act, which would have created a market-based emissions cap-and-trade program to reduce carbon dioxide and other heat-trapping pollutants from the biggest U.S. sources. At the time, McCain said: "While we cannot say with 100 percent confidence what will happen in the future, we do know the emission of greenhouse gases is not healthy for the environment. As many of the top scientists through the world have stated, the sooner we start to reduce these emissions, the better off we will be in the future."[28] McCain's Climate Stewardship Act then actually got to a vote. And when it did not prevail, McCain reintroduced the measure himself in the following Congress. Republican senators Olympia Snowe of Maine and Lincoln Chafee of Rhode Island—my predecessor—were among that bill's co-sponsors.

Other Republicans got behind other cap-and-trade proposals: Senator Tom Carper's Clean Air Planning Act at one time or another counted Senator Lamar Alexander of Tennessee, Senator Lindsey Graham of South Carolina, and Senator Susan Collins of Maine among its supporters. In 2007, Republican senator Olympia Snowe was a lead co-sponsor of Senator John Kerry's Global Warming Reduction Act. Senators Lisa Murkowski and Ted Stevens from Alaska, and Senator Arlen Specter of Pennsylvania, then a Republican, were original co-sponsors of the Low Carbon Economy Act. And that same year, Alexander introduced the Clean Air/Climate Change Act. Each of these bills sought to reduce carbon emissions through a cap-and-trade mechanism. Said Alexander in 2007: "It is also time to acknowledge that climate change is real, human activity is a big part of the problem, and it is up to us to act."[29]

That bipartisan heartbeat remained alive in 2009. Senator Mark Kirk of Illinois, while he served in the House of Representatives, was one of eight Republicans to vote for the Waxman-Markey cap-and-trade proposal. In that same year, Senator Jeff Flake of Arizona, then representing Arizona in the House, was an original co-sponsor of the Raise Wages, Cut Carbon Act, to reduce payroll taxes for employers and employees in exchange for equal revenue from a carbon tax. On the House floor, Flake argued the virtues of this approach: "If we want to be honest about helping the environment, then just impose a carbon tax and make it revenue neutral, give commensurate tax relief on the other side. . . . Let's have an honest debate about whether or not we want to help the environment by actually having something that is revenue neutral where you tax consumption as opposed to income."[30]

Those words were echoed in the Senate by Susan Collins, a lead co-sponsor of the Carbon Limits and Energy for America's Renewal Act, a carbon fee bill she sponsored with Senator Maria Cantwell. "In the United States alone," said Collins, "emissions of the primary greenhouse gas, carbon dioxide, have risen more than 20 percent since 1990. Climate change is the most daunting environmental challenge we face and we must develop reasonable solutions to reduce our greenhouse gas emissions."[31]

As recently as 2009, there was clear and forceful acknowledgment from leading Republican voices of the real danger posed by climate change, and of Congress's responsibility to act.

Then came 2010, the year of *Citizens United*.

As *Citizens United* unleashed its torrent of corporate money into our elections, Republicans were the initial targets of the fossil-fuel industry's onslaught, and Republican interest in climate change suddenly disappeared from Congress. One of the lessons learned by the fossil-fuel industry from David Koch's quixotic bid for the vice presidency in 1980 was that third parties are a fool's errand: they tend to steal voters from the party they most resemble, helping the adversary. So instead of running their own candidate, the industry decided it would be more effective to co-opt one of the existing parties. The chief climate deniers are the Koch brothers, and they and the fossil-fuel industry have captured the Republican Party, through *Citizens United* money and the Tea Party apparatus. One of my Republican colleagues said to me after a speech I gave on the Senate floor slamming the Koch brothers: "What are you complaining about? They're spending more against us than they are against you!"

By capturing the Republican Party on climate change, the fossil-fuel industry has been able to disguise what is basically special-interest special pleading as a partisan contest, tangling their pollution up in our culture wars.

As the fossil-fuel industry tightened the screws on the Republican Party after *Citizens United*, the climate evidence only became stronger. NASA and NOAA officially declared 2014 and 2015 the hottest years ever recorded, "easily breaking the previous records."[32] Yet in Washington, no Republican would step forward. *Citizens United* had uncorked all that vicious dark money to cast its shadow of intimidation over our democracy, the industry brought that brute force to bear on the Republican Party, and Republicans had to walk back from any major climate legislation. Even colleagues who know this is real and who privately encourage me to keep fighting went silent after *Citizens United*. I have been told by Republican colleagues, "Keep working on your carbon fee bill; I can't be with you yet but it's the right thing and I'll get there." I've been told, "I know I need to do the right thing on this, but I've got to be *so* deft about how I do it." I've been told, "Let's keep talking—but don't tell my staff. Nobody else can know."

Talking to these Republican senators about climate change is like talking to prisoners about escape. Political attacks funded by *Citizens United* money, and the very real threat of those attacks if you don't behave, loom over Republicans who might work with Democrats on curbing carbon pollution. These threats are particularly concrete and potent when it comes to the primary process: the Koch network has made plain that any Republican lawmaker who goes against the corporate line on climate change will be at a "severe disadvantage in the nominating process."[33] If a Republican in Congress were to publicly acknowledge the reality of climate change and try to do something about it, the fossil-fuel industry could handpick a Tea Party candidate and throw millions of dollars her way from behind innumerable masks to take that Republican out in the next primary.

We have Republican senators who represent historic native villages that are now washing into the sea and need relocation because of climate change and sea level rise. We have Republican senators who represent great American coastal cities now flooded by high tides on sunny days because of climate change. We have Republican senators representing states swept by drought and wildfire. We have Republican senators whose home-state forests are being killed in the hundreds of square miles by the marauding pine beetle, whose range has expanded due to the warming climate.[34] We have Republican senators whose home states' glaciers are disappearing before their very eyes. We have Republican senators whose states are having to raise offshore bridges and coastal highways before rising seas. We have Republican senators whose emblematic home state species are dying off or migrating away. Yet none will work on a major climate bill. None will place a price on carbon. It's simply not safe, not since *Citizens United* allowed special interests to bombard our elections—and threaten and promise to bombard our elections—with their attack ads. *Citizens United* did not enhance speech in our democracy; instead it allowed wealthy special interests to suppress and silence real debate.

Outside the walls of Congress, where *Citizens United* money holds less sway, the situation is very different. Responsible Republican voices outside of Congress more and more acknowledge the threat of climate change and call for responsible solutions. Many want to correct the market failure that aids and abets the fossil-fuel industry's irresponsible practices. These Republicans don't face the political threat of *Citizens United*. They're not prisoners.

Former members of Congress, for example, are free now from the polluters' thrall, and implore their colleagues to take on climate change. Bob Inglis, the former Republican representative from South Carolina, who was bombarded in the primaries by outside money for supporting climate action, invokes the tenets of conservative economics. "If you're a conservative, it is time to step forward and engage in the climate and energy debate because we have the answer—free enterprise," he argues. "Conservatives understand that we must set the correct incentives, and this should include internalizing pollution and other environmental costs in our market system. We tax income but we don't tax emissions. It makes sense to conservatives to take the tax off something you want more of, income, and shift the tax to something you want less of, emissions."[35]

Sherwood Boehlert and Wayne Gilchrest, former Republican

representatives from New York and Maryland, respectively, in a joint February 2012 *Washington Post* op-ed with Representative Henry Waxman and Senator Ed Markey, both Democrats, made the fiscal case for a carbon fee: "The debate over how to reduce our nation's debt has been presented as a dilemma between cutting spending on programs Americans cherish or raising taxes on American job creators. But there is a better way: We could slash our debt by making power plants and oil refineries pay for the carbon emissions that endanger our health and environment. This policy would strengthen our economy, lessen our dependence on foreign oil, keep our skies clean—and raise a lot of revenue. The best approach would be to use a market mechanism such as the sale of carbon allowances or a fee on carbon pollution to lower emissions and increase revenue."[36]

Top advisors to former Republican presidents have joined the chorus. William D. Ruckelshaus, Lee M. Thomas, William K. Reilly, and Christine Todd Whitman wrote in a *New York Times* op-ed: "As administrators of the E.P.A. under Presidents Richard M. Nixon, Ronald Reagan, George Bush and George W. Bush, we held fast to commonsense conservative principles—protecting the health of the American people, working with the best technology available and trusting in the innovation of American business and in the market to find the best solutions for the least cost."[37] These Republican officials recognize that a "market-based approach, like a carbon tax, would be the best path to reducing greenhouse-gas emissions," and urge, "[w]e must continue efforts to reduce the climate-altering pollutants that threaten our planet. The only uncertainty about our warming world is how bad the changes will get, and how soon. What is most clear is that there is no time to waste."[38]

For one former Republican member of the Senate, the threat of climate change had serious professional implications. As secretary of defense, Chuck Hagel was responsible for accounting for all hazards to our national security and our interests in the world. He gave this clear-eyed assessment at the Halifax International Security Forum: "Climate change does not directly cause conflict, but it can significantly add to the challenges of global instability, hunger, poverty, and conflict. Food and water shortages, pandemic disease, disputes over refugees and resources, more severe natural disasters—all place additional burdens on economies, societies, and institutions around the world. . . . The effects of climate change and new energy resources are far-reaching and unpredictable . . . demanding our attention and strategic thinking."[39] Hagel joined twenty-two other Republican former national security officials and Republican former members of Congress, along with ten senior retired military officers, in taking out a full-page ad in the *Wall Street Journal* on October 22, 2015, under the blaring headline "Republicans and Democrats Agree: U.S. Security Demands Global Climate Action."

George Schultz served as secretary of both labor and treasury under President Nixon, and as secretary of state under President Reagan. In a 2013 *Wall Street Journal* op-ed written with Nobel Prize–winning economist Gary Becker, Schultz appealed to our American sense of fairness, writing: "Americans like to compete on a level playing field. All the players should have an equal opportunity to win based on their competitive merits, not on some artificial imbalance that gives someone or some group a special advantage. We think this idea should be applied to energy producers. They all should bear the full costs of the use of the energy they provide. . . . Clearly a revenue-neutral carbon tax would benefit all Americans by eliminating the need for costly energy subsidies while promoting a level playing field for energy producers."[40]

David Frum, speechwriter to George W. Bush, wrote in a December 2012 CNN.com op-ed that a carbon fee could help address a number of pressing national issues: "Take three worrying long-term challenges: climate change, the weak economic recovery, and America's chronic budget deficits. Combine them into one. And suddenly three tough problems become one attractive solution. Tax carbon. . . . The revenues from a carbon tax could be used to reduce the deficit while also extending new forms of payroll tax relief to middle-class families, thus supporting middle-class family incomes."[41] Gregory Mankiw, economic advisor to George W. Bush and Mitt Romney, specifically highlighted a Senate carbon fee proposal in an August 2013 op-ed in the *New York Times*. The bill, he wrote, "is more effective and less invasive than the regulatory approach that the federal government has traditionally pursued. . . . [I]f the Democratic sponsors conceded to using the new revenue to reduce personal and corporate income tax rates, a bipartisan compromise is possible to imagine. Among economists the issue is largely a no-brainer."[42]

Jim Brainard, five-term Republican mayor of Carmel, Indiana, implored in an *Indianapolis Star* op-ed, "This issue isn't just about saving polar bears. It's about saving our cities. No matter your politics, there is overwhelming evidence of climate change and we as a nation have a moral obligation to address these issues."[43]

The contrast is plain. Republican leaders who are not captive to the *Citizens United* threats and bullying of the big polluters are ready to get to work on climate change. The problem is not Republicans, but abuse post–*Citizens United* by the fossil-fuel industry of corporate political power.

How exactly does one narrow slice of the country—namely, the fossil-fuel industry—silence an entire political party in Congress on what is perhaps the single most consequential issue facing Americans today? Much of the action has got to be in behind-the-scenes threats that we can never fully appreciate. But some lobbying groups are bolder, and their boldness gives us a window into what must be taking place behind closed doors.

There's the striking example of the Koch-backed Americans for Prosperity openly promising to wipe out candidates who support any curbs on carbon pollution. The group's president said that if Republicans supported a carbon tax or climate regulations, they'd "be at a severe disadvantage in the Republican nomination process. . . . We would absolutely make that a crucial issue."[44] The threat is plain: step out of line, and here come the attack ads and the primary challengers—all funded by the deep pockets of the fossil-fuel industry, enabled by *Citizens United*, and largely protected from disclosure. It's a modern political version of the ancient threat from Shakespeare's evil Richard III: "I'll make a corpse of him that disobeys."[45]

It worked. And Americans for Prosperity is happy to claim credit. As its president, Tim Phillips, told the *National Journal*, according to author Jane Mayer, "If you look at where the situation was three years ago and where it is today, there's been a dramatic turnaround. . . . We've made great headway. What it means for candidates on the Republican side is, if you buy into green energy or you play footsie on this issue, you do so at your political peril. The vast majority of the people who are involved in the nominating process—the conventions and the primaries—are suspect of the science. And that's our influence. Groups like Americans for Prosperity have done it."[46]

The political primary process is key to understanding how Republicans in Congress are put in "political peril." If you look at who is scared of whom and who is angry at whom in Congress, you will see that most Democrats and Republicans (at least in the Senate) actually get along rather well. We're policy adversaries on many things, but we've been policy adversaries for decades. Democrat versus Republican is old news. It doesn't explain the new weirdness of Congress.

The new factor in this equation is the Tea Party. The real fear and the real anger around Congress, at least from my vantage point in the Senate, has been between the mainstream Republicans and the Tea Party extremists. Where do emotions run the highest? Where are the shouting matches? Where are insults hurled? Where are senators heckled by their colleagues? The worst of it is not between Democrat and Republican; it's between Tea Party Republican and mainstream Republican. Who is being told how they can and cannot vote and what they can and cannot say? Who is being bullied and punished when they don't follow the party line—the Tea Party line? Not Democrats. It is regular Republicans.

But I've got news. It's not the irrefutable logic of Tea Party argument that convinces regular Republicans. Logic is not the Tea Party's strong suit. It's not the clear grasp by the Tea Party of modern economic, cultural, and scientific realities that convinces regular Republicans. The Tea Party exists in an angry, white, elderly, predominantly southern bubble. Extremists everywhere share telltale clues: the phony facts they rely on, the conspiracy theories they believe, their scorn of compromise, their visceral anger and impatient simple-mindedness. They do not seek policy solutions, but instead relish the feverish role of aggrieved victims. They'd rather yell than listen. Anger is not a cure for ignorance, but extremism doesn't know that.

Extreme views are not a new thing in politics, not even in American politics. Ordinarily, though, the political system adapts: a coalition of grown-ups comes together and forms a working majority, the majority rules, and the cranky extremists hoot and holler and jump up and down in the back benches. So why is it in this particular era that Congress has not adapted? The problem of cranks and extremists in a legislative body isn't new with the Tea Party; it's as old as legislative bodies. Back in 1932 Duff Cooper wrote in his biography of Talleyrand that extremists "are the disease germs in the body politic. They can never create, but when the general health of the body is weak, they can bring destruction."[47] So why has a simple political solution to this recurring political problem eluded us in Congress?

The thing that scares regular Republicans about challenging the Tea Party is the big money—the big corporate money, the billionaire money—behind the Tea Party. The Tea Party would ordinarily be a fringe group of outliers in Congress, and a centrist governing coalition of regular Republicans and Democrats would ordinarily have emerged, except for the threat of massive *Citizens United* money.

A lot of the right-wing special-interest money has actually been spent against Republicans. Remember what my Republican friend said to me about the Koch brothers: "What are you complaining about? They're spending more against us than against you!" And when the Koch brothers' big money comes in and bombs you in a small Republican primary election, it's pretty scary. When the paid-for right-wing attack machine turns its chatter-guns on you in your Republican primary, that can be pretty scary.

The gridlock and silence we see on climate change are the result. Republicans won't work with Democrats on serious climate legislation, not because Democrats don't make sense, and not because most Republicans don't want to make sense, but because they're scared of Tea Party attacks funded by *Citizens United* money out of the fossil-fuel industry. That's how they became, in Peggy Noonan's great phrase, "the party of Donor's Policy Preferences."[48] Yes, some senators actually believe that climate change is a liberal fabrication, and some have state industries and state economies so dependent on fossil fuels that they have a real constituent problem if they try to address climate change. But that's not all of them. It's not even most of them.

Think of Republican senators in a corral, fenced in. Think of the fences as high and barbed. Think of gun towers at the corners, and signs on the fence warning "Political Peril." Imagine bullhorn-amplified voices warning, "Nobody leaves the corral. Try to leave and we're going to 'severely disadvantage' you!" That's not a bad analogy. There are mutinous rumblings in the corral—a lot of the inmates are restless. The corral is not a great place to be. Nobody likes to be threatened and bossed around. Nobody likes having to play the fool or cater to someone else's whims. Nobody likes having to go against what so many respected voices, and their own consciences and home state universities, are telling them. NASA is driving a rover around on Mars right now; when NASA warns us about climate change, most colleagues understand that these are scientists who know what they're talking about. But nobody wants to be the first one to take a run at the fence.

Take away *Citizens United*, and the fence loses its barbs. The fossil-fuel guns disappear from the guard tower. Maybe the fence just becomes a chalk line, and all the guards can do is blow whistles when you cross it. They may blow their whistles and be angry, but without *Citizens United*, they neither have the tools to do worse nor a credible threat to do worse.

Look again at Americans for Prosperity, the Koch brothers venture that openly threatened to take out pro-climate Republicans in the primaries and that so publicly threatened to spend $750 million in the 2016 elections. This is the group that rivals or exceeds the Republican National Committee. Small wonder that it is hard to have an honest conversation with Republicans about carbon pollution in the Senate when the anti-climate big spenders have more muscle come election time than their own political party.

Put simply, the U.S. Congress has lost the ability to address climate change in a bipartisan way because of the evils of the Supreme Court's *Citizens United* decision. And the fossil-fuel industry couldn't be happier. *Citizens United* allowed this bullying, wealthy special interest to quash real debate.

In the silence of regular Republican voices in Congress, the voices you hear are the extreme ones; the message you hear is denial. What do Republicans in Congress today have to say to our heirs, to our children and grandchildren, about the looming threat of climate change? "Catastrophic global warming is a hoax," says Republican senator James Inhofe of Oklahoma.[49] (He's so extreme, he's even listed as "extreme" in University of Oklahoma presentations by the state of Oklahoma's own climatologists.)[50] "It's not proven by any stretch of the imagination," says Republican senator Ron Johnson of Wisconsin.[51] He's so extreme, he's been called out by Wisconsin's largest newspaper, which noted that his practice of "stubbornly denying the facts on climate change may be akin to denying the facts on evolution or whether the Earth is flat."[52] "A lot of this is condescending elitism," says Republican senator Pat Roberts of Kansas, while Kansas State University researchers project the effect of climate change on Kansas wheat production as "pretty severe."[53] That's the captive voice of today's Republican Party.

According to one analysis, 56 percent of congressional Republicans in the 113th Congress have denied or questioned the overwhelming scientific consensus that the Earth's oceans and atmosphere are changing in unprecedented ways, driven by carbon pollution. This includes every single Republican member of the Senate Committee on Environment and Public Works.[54]

That is not the message from mainstream Republicans voters. Sixty-one percent of non–Tea Party Republicans say there is "solid evidence the earth is warming."[55] And a survey conducted for the League of Conservation Voters found that more than half of young Republican voters—53 percent of Republicans under the age of thirty-five—describe a politician who denies that climate change is happening as "ignorant," "out-of-touch," or "crazy."[56] Former Republican senator Judd Gregg of New Hampshire, who also served his state as governor, has warned of the political consequences in New Hampshire of ignoring climate change. "Anybody who says science doesn't support it is going to have a hard time making that case in New Hampshire," said Gregg, adding, "That's just not going to fly. Most Republicans in New Hampshire are very environmentally focused."[57]

On climate change, it's not so much Republican Party voters as it is Tea Party voters that are the deniers. Is there "solid evidence the earth is warming"? Only 25 percent of Tea Partiers say yes, while 61 percent of Republicans do—a thirty-six-point swing. And 41 percent of Tea Partiers assert that warming is "just not happening." Not "we don't have enough information yet"—it is "just not happening."[58]

"Just not happening"? Regardless of what you think causes climate change, there are independent measurements from all over the Earth that it is happening. This isn't a theory. We measure the rise in the temperature of the atmosphere and oceans. We measure the rate at which ice caps and glaciers are melting. We measure the rise of the seas. We measure the shifting of the very seasons. It is one thing to be the party that's against scientific modeling, but the Tea Partiers would turn the great and historic Republican Party into a party that is against measurement. The Tea Party wants to lead the Republican Party off the climate cliff. And *Citizens United* money gives them and their corporate industry backers the weaponry to do it. Without *Citizens United,* they would be a crank caucus that responsible members of both parties would simply ignore or work around.

For a country that prides itself on its democracy and offers its example of democracy to the world, this has ramifications beyond climate change.

CHAPTER TWELVE

America's Lamp in Peril

AMERICA HAS LONG STOOD BEFORE THE WORLD as an exceptional country, and deservedly so. We proved the case for popular sovereignty, with no need of kings or crowns. We rode our balanced market capitalism (and the safety of two oceans) to international economic dominance. We have long been the vanguard of civil and human rights for our people and for people around the globe. When we must use our military power, we don't conquer and rule, we come home. Where we have succeeded, we have left freedom in our wake.

Across our small globe dawn sweeps each morning, lighting cities and cottages, farms and barrios and villages. The poorest and most brutalized people can come out of their homes and huts and tenements into each new morning's sun and know from our American example that life does not have to be the way it now is for them. Each can know that an example of liberty and self-government stands free before them as a rebuke to the tyranny, corruption, and injustice they may suffer every day.

This exceptional nature of America confers upon us a responsibility. It also confers on us a gravitational power that allows us influence by our example. That power of example draws people to our country. It draws people to our ideals, and it draws people to free and democratic government. These are tidal forces, pulled by the gravity of our good example, and they have flooded in our favor for generations. They have helped make America "the essential nation." No edict makes that so. Generation by generation, Americans must earn that standing.

Years ago, Daniel Webster described the work of our American

Founders as having "set the world an example."[1] This was not a unique vision of America. From Jonathan Winthrop[2] to Ronald Reagan,[3] we have called ourselves "a city upon a hill," set high for the world to witness. From President John F. Kennedy[4] to President Obama,[5] inaugural addresses have noted that the glow of our ideals "light[s] the world." We Americans see our nation as a beacon of hope, as a light in the darkness. Our lamp is lifted up in welcome and in example. President Bill Clinton has argued that "people the world over have always been more impressed by the power of our example than the example of our power."[6]

Each American generation receives this precious inheritance from generations that fought, bled, and died to put it safely in our hands. When Daniel Webster said that our Founding Fathers had set the world an example, he went on to say this: "The last hopes of mankind, therefore, rest with us; and if it should be proclaimed, that our example had become an argument against the experiment, the knell of popular liberty would be sounded throughout the earth."[7]

It is not ordained that the rest of the world must be proud of us. We have to earn it by our example. In response to the damage done to America's image by the Wall Street bailout, Joseph Stiglitz, Nobel Prize–winning economist and former chief economist of the World Bank, wrote: "In the developing world people look at Washington and see a system of government that allowed Wall Street to write self-serving rules, which put at risk the entire global economy, and then when the day of reckoning came, Washington turned to those from Wall Street and their cronies to manage the recovery—in ways that gave Wall Street amounts of money that would be beyond the wildest dreams of the most corrupt in the developing world. They see corruption American-style as perhaps more sophisticated—bags of money don't change hands in dark corners—but just as nefarious."[8] And the Wall Street meltdown was a lesser day of reckoning than the climate crisis portends.

We are in a period of political crisis at home. It sounds harsh to say these things, but the truth is harsh: corporate money is calling the tune in Congress; Congress is unwilling or unable to stand up to corporate power (indeed, Congress is often its agent); and a massive propaganda effort is churning full steam to deny the facts of major policy issues wherever those facts are contrary to corporate interests. In Federalist No. 63, James Madison (or perhaps Alexander Hamilton; authorship is debated) warned of "moments in public affairs when the people . . . misled by the artful misrepresentations of interested men, may call for measures which they themselves will afterwards be the most ready to lament and condemn."[9] We are aswarm now in "artful misrepresentations" and "misled by interested men" gathered and organized in corporate form; the result has been both action and inaction that our descendants will surely "lament and condemn."

Lord Acton urged historians "to suffer no man and no cause to escape the undying penalty which history has the power to inflict on wrong."[10] Those dishonorable corporations and their allies will be judged harshly by history for what they are doing, as they infiltrate our democracy and exert their wicked influence. Their success, however, is also our failure—a failure to defend the American democracy that we inherited. That failure too will be judged harshly.

My father was a member of the Greatest Generation. He was a Marine in the Pacific Islands campaign in World War II. He lost his only brother in that war, a Navy fighter pilot killed over Legaspi in the Philippines. He dedicated the rest of his life to his country's service, serving in faraway places, often at great personal danger. His last task for his country was to come out of retirement to set up Special Operations Command in the Pentagon for President Reagan. He is representative of thousands and thousands of Americans who went in harm's way against the great Axis powers to protect democracy for us and for people all over the globe, and then went on to build the American Century. American cemeteries in Normandy and Manila tell mutely of that generation's willingness, their bravery, and their sacrifice. In light of that sacrifice, it does not seem too much to ask of this generation that we be willing to stand up to the "resolute enemy within our gates"[11] and win in our time the "trial of strength"[12] that Jefferson foretold.

If you believe that the world needs America, if you believe that America is to be the essential and exceptional nation, then it matters that we do right. It matters that we get these issues, such as climate change, right—even when the conflict pits "We the People" against mighty corporations. A world fouled and impoverished by carbon pollution will want to know why. We will be held to account: a democracy disabled by special interests, a democracy that knew what carbon pollution was doing to our atmosphere and our oceans but could not rouse itself to do what was required. Failing to lead at this moment of necessity will soon and long darken the lamp America holds up to the world, and it will make a powerful argument for our adversaries against our democratic experiment. We must not be the generation that failed at our duty. We can still leave an honorable legacy of our own, one that will echo down the corridors of history and justly earn the wholehearted admiration of future generations.

The historian David McCullough spoke recently to a group of us at the Library of Congress about John Adams and America's Founding generation. He reminded us that when those men pledged their lives, their fortunes, and their sacred honor to this cause, it was not mere words. When they signed the Declaration of Independence, he said, they were signing their own death warrants. Asked how they found the courage to do this, David McCullough explained, "It was a courageous time."[13]

It just takes courage to make this our own courageous time.

Postscript

THE 2016 CAMPAIGN IS OVER. This postscript looks back at the lessons for this book from a boisterous, bizarre, and joyless American election. The focus of the 2016 presidential campaign was on personalities, whether the relentless personal smearing of Hillary Clinton as "Crooked Hillary" who should be "locked up," or the boastful antics and crude personal behavior of Donald Trump. Behind the distracting dazzle of that contest of personalities, however, the constant, intrusive forces I describe in this book remained at play and often showed their heads. The media are easily distracted by a shiny object, and Donald Trump was the ultimate shiny object. As president, he will likely continue to occupy the center of the media's attention. That makes paying attention to these more silent and surreptitious forces all the more important.

One of the major topics of this book has been the underlying problem of secret and unlimited money in our politics. This problem persisted throughout the election, and in one important sense, it worsened: Democrats overcame their distaste for secret money and big donors. This allowed Democrats, particularly Secretary Clinton, to compete more effectively in the new, post–*Citizens United*, political bizarro-world the Supreme Court has made. As the *New York Times* reported, "Democrats have built the largest and best-coordinated apparatus of outside groups operating in the 2016 presidential campaign, defying expectations that conservative and corporate wealth would dominate the race."[1]

This otherwise bad news actually gives me some faint hope that with sufficient public pressure Congress may be able to drain the big-donor, "dark-money" swamp. I remember talking with a Republican colleague on the Senate floor as the 2016 political season was gearing up, seeking some bipartisan support for my campaign spending disclosure bill (requiring transparency for all political spending over $10,000, whether corporate, individual, or union) and telling him, "you guys have got to hate this, too. It's bad for everyone." He replied, "Yeah, but you Democrats have got to start raising some real money of your own this way. Then we might be able to get rid of the stuff. You can't expect us to give it up while so much of it is coming our way."

Well, it sure looks like we Democrats got into the big donor game in this election. In an article titled "How Democrats Stopped Worrying and Learned to Love Big Donor Money," Nicholas Confessore and Rachel Shorey reported that "just 250 donors have accounted for about $44 million in contributions to the Hillary Victory Fund," through a "legal end-run around contribution limits, allowing wealthy donors to give far more."[2] The device for that legal end-run was a one-stop-shopping campaign account that allowed big donors to consolidate into one check donations to Hillary Clinton's campaign and to all the Democratic state party committees around the country, many of which then cycled some or all of the funds back into the account, to go to key battleground states. The result "def[ied] expectations at the beginning of the campaign that Republicans would dominate the money chase."[3] And that didn't count super PACs or dark money.

On the super PAC front, big money continued to rule in 2016, as super PAC donations blew through the billion-dollar mark. And independence of the super PACs was a joke: as the *Washington Post* reported, "personalized super PACs became the norm in a presidential campaign, run by the candidates' close advisers."[4] Over half a billion dollars came in to the super PACs from just sixty-two individuals, corporations, and unions, with the big-money parade led by a few mega-donors.[5] As of the beginning of November, the top ten mega-donors had given a grand total of more than $300 million to super PACs; the number ten donor alone gave $17 million—a retire-in-style, won-the-lottery fortune for most Americans.[6] Put another way, if you had written million-dollar checks to sixteen of your favorite candidates' super PACs in the last election, you wouldn't even have made the Top 10 list! And this sum only counts the disclosed super PAC contributions, not the dark money.

A good deal of this Democratic funding reflected what the *New York Times* described as "Mrs. Clinton's close personal ties to her party's elite donors and her allies' willingness to exploit the 2010 ruling in the *Citizens United* case far more aggressively than President Obama did," but there's also a Trump factor.[7] His "provocations and tirades—along with a loud crusade against his own party's donors—have virtually shut off what once promised to be a half-billion-dollar spigot of outside money."[8] Democrats should not expect this big money shift to persist, however, and Republicans can read the same tea leaves.

All this big money on the Democratic side creates a slim opening for Republicans, without undue political sacrifice, to help us clear mega-donors and dark money out of politics. It was, after all, Republican Teddy Roosevelt who said, "If our political institutions were perfect, they would absolutely prevent the political domination of money in any part of our affairs."[9] Those who profit by the political domination of money in our affairs, however, will vigorously defend the present system. The ability to threaten and promise unlimited political spending is a massive political weapon in the hands of the corporate donor class, a weapon regular people don't enjoy. And the ability to do it anonymously makes it even more formidable.

The machinations to hide identities remained creepy. Here's one example, reported by BNA, Inc.'s *Money and Politics Report* (yes, political spending has gotten so weird there is such a thing): Republican Senate Leader Mitch McConnell has a super PAC called the Senate Leadership Fund. The Senate Leadership Fund shares an address with a 501(c)(4) organization called One Nation. They are run by the same person, who, by the way, also heads American Crossroads and Crossroads GPS, set up by Karl Rove. The 501(c)(4) hides donor identities, so someone gave $11 million to One Nation anonymously, One Nation gave $11 million to McConnell's Senate Leadership Fund, and the Fund spent the $11 million defending GOP Senate seats.[10] Don't tell me Mitch McConnell won't know who's behind the $11 million and all the other dark money that helped save his job as majority leader; we just won't.

Donald Trump's flamboyant personality became a media fixation, allowing Trump to jump the usual fundraising rails and provoke free media attention, where his rivals had to buy airtime for ads. But let's remember how this season started and how it ended. "The hunt for big dollars began in January 2015 outside Palm Springs at a luxury hillside resort," wrote *Washington Post* political correspondent Matea Gold. "There the emerging crop of Republican presidential candidates jockeyed to impress the millionaires and billionaires who make up the Koch political network."[11] Donald Trump ridiculed them as "puppets" of the Kochs and other big donors, and differentiated himself from the Republican pack right away. Sure enough, the other candidates' "all-consuming pursuit of mega-donors . . . drew them away from the campaign trail, leaving them vulnerable to the fiercely populist mood gripping voters—and to a candidate on the GOP side, Donald Trump, uniquely positioned to harness that anger."[12] Trump commanded enough media attention not to need the usual advertising barrage, and enough personal wealth to scorn the big donors for a while.

But at the end, he reverted to form, with "his own billionaire backers," and an "array of superPACs that cropped up to support his campaign."[13] As *The Guardian* reported, "Rich Republicans may have initially balked at Donald Trump, but pro-Trump billionaires [left] the sidelines in the last week of the election to dump cash directly into crucial counties and swing states."[14] The *Wall Street Journal* reported that five billionaires "poured at least $24 million into groups backing Donald Trump."[15] And after the election, the *New York Times* reported, "President-elect Donald J. Trump, who campaigned against the corrupt power of special interests, is filling his transition team with some of the very sort of people who he has complained have too much clout in Washington: corporate consultants and lobbyists."[16] Corporate money is relentless; money still matters, a lot; and the influencers are already crawling in.

One last secret-money consideration from the 2016 presidential scrum was a new rationale for secret political donations: embarrassment. Said one big fundraiser: "There is a substantial appetite for a non-disclosing vehicle [to give money through], because it's embarrassing to support Trump."[17] Indeed, this was the actual fundraising pitch of a pro-Trump super PAC.[18]

Whatever its reason, no good can come from secret money and unlimited money in our elections. It gives too much power to a donor class and the corporate political machine. It lets them hide their hands, and the result is that regular people lose out even more to the big influencers seeking control in our democracy.

Another focus of this book has been the relentless efforts at political manipulation by the Koch brothers on behalf of the fossil-fuel industry their corporation inhabits. One unexpected development in the 2016 race was the Koch brothers' political machine getting thrown off course by the Great Trump Disruption within the Republican Party, and turning its focus away from the presidential race to the 2016 Senate races. It was effective in inundating the Senate races with political spending, mostly on attack ads, limiting Democrats to two gained seats and no majority, in what had been a promising year to take five or more seats and regain a Democratic majority. The Republican Senate majority can be expected to be a bastion of corporate, billionaire influence after this dark-money, big-money deluge.

The Koch machine continued to grow and develop its database, expanding "the vast trove of voter information the Kochs are building. . . . Its database is a vault of voting records, consumer data, census information and social media profiles on more than 250 million adults."[19] (If you're worried about the government knowing too much about you, you might want to expand your orbit of concern.) The Koch machine continues to plan for the future. With the machine having time in this election cycle "to further build up its ground game and data operations" as the Kochs' distaste for Trump kept them largely out of the 2016 presidential race, "the Koch network leaders are focusing on 2020 and 2024."[20]

Secrecy remained the Kochs' political hallmark. "The Kochs have gone to great lengths over the years to conceal the nature of their vast political operations," *Newsweek* reported, and the Kochs' political network "is made up almost entirely of 501(c)(3) and 501(c)(4) nonprofit organizations that can accept unlimited funds and do not have to disclose their donors."[21] That won't change. And Republican bullying of the IRS to keep the agency ineffectual in enforcing the laws against dark money persisted. (Or, as Koch Companies' operative Phillip

Ellender calls enforcing the dark money laws, "targeting of non-profit organizations by the Internal Revenue Service (IRS) to limit free speech."[22] Yeah, right.)

Cut to Florida, where the Kochs were very active, with fourteen field offices in that one state (small wonder that Senator Rubio remains opposed to climate legislation even as his state sinks under sea level rise). The head of the Florida Chamber of Commerce has a close-up view there of the Kochs' methods and aspirations. "They've been very transparent about what they're trying to do," he said, "and I think a lot of people don't believe them. They want to replace political parties."[23]

The muscle and threats that are the Koch brothers' other hallmark also persisted. *USA Today* reported, "Conservative billionaire Charles Koch and his allies celebrated Republicans retaining their grip on Congress this week and signaled that his powerful political network plans to play a larger role in policy as the nation prepares for a GOP-controlled capital."[24] Move aside, Trump. In a rare public letter to his network, Koch touted wins by "pro-freedom" (pro-freedom-to-pollute is what that means) candidates in the Senate and voter anger about a "rigged economy" and urged that his orthodoxies offered "something to unite behind"; that it is his network that "offers that vision," not Donald Trump.[25]

USA Today reported that the Kochs' network "deployed big sums in Senate races" and racked up Republican wins in most targeted states. "In all, the network spent about $250 million on its political and policy programs this year, including $42.1 million in advertising to shape Senate contests in states. Activists and staffers knocked on four million doors, made 33 million calls and sent out 37 million pieces of mail to sway voters in key states. . . . The network regularly touts its standing force of 2.8 million activists who are willing to engage in policy fights even in non-election years."[26]

All that political muscle emboldens the Koch apparatus to make big threats. Koch network officials, *USA Today* reported, "will aggressively fight efforts in Washington to increase government spending, even if the push comes from the nation's most powerful Republican himself, President-elect Donald Trump."[27] James Davis is the spokesman for the Koch brothers' front group Freedom Partners Chamber of Commerce. As *USA Today* reported, "If senators veer 'off course,' Davis said, 'we can hold them accountable and turn up the heat from the people to change the policy.'"[28] It will get interesting if what the Kochs deem "off course" for senators they manipulate is actually something "on course" for President Trump: for instance, things he campaigned on such as infrastructure investments, paid family leave, and closing the carried interest tax loophole.

Another telling comment by a Koch operative helps clarify the control relationship between the Kochs' big money operation and the conservative base it supports and manages. The Kochs' lead front group is Americans for Prosperity. Its president, Tim Phillips, reflected in late 2016 on Donald Trump's success in engaging the Republican base voters' support for Medicare and Social Security (there are many signals that the Republican base's support for Medicare is strong, including anti-Obamacare protesters during the fights over that law telling us to "keep your government hands off our Medicare"). Phillips also spoke of Trump's success in animating the populist Republican voter's distaste for "free trade." Phillips was distressed, because antagonism to Medicare and Social Security and support for free trade are Koch political dogma. "Just when you think you've won an issue within the base, you realize no issue is really ever won," he said. "We thought it was settled orthodoxy; suddenly, it's not anymore."[29]

This is a candid admission that the Koch operation is out to drive its "orthodoxies" into the Republican base to suit the Kochs' agenda, rather than listening to and reflecting what working-class Republicans actually want. The Kochs manufacture and control a big-money, pro-polluter, "settled orthodoxy" to sell to the base like soap. Without Trump coming in and unsettling their orthodoxy, it probably would have worked. Now they may even have to fight President Trump, and they have signaled their willingness to do so.

The anguish of Republicans who expected a Trump defeat opened other telling glimpses of candor. A striking admission of how this big-money fixery works was written by *Business Insider*'s Josh Barro, a Republican who interned for Grover Norquist, worked at the conservative Manhattan Institute for Policy Research, and left the party in disgust over Trump. Just before the election, Barro wrote, "If [conservatives] look honestly enough, they will realize the conservative information sphere has long been full of lies. The reason for this is that lying has been the most effective way to promote many of the policies favored by donor-class conservatives, and so they built an apparatus to invent and spread the best lies."[30] Barro uses as one example that "wealthy conservatives favor lower taxes on themselves for the obvious reason," but since billionaires keeping more money and paying less taxes is, to put it mildly, "not a compelling electoral argument," they have "built a network of think tanks and magazines and pressure groups funded by wealthy donors whose job was to come up with arguments that would sell the donor-class agenda to the masses."[31] Similarly, conservative commentator and author Jamie Weinstein wrote on election day, "As for the Republican primary electorate, we learned that perhaps they don't care so much about conservative principles after all—that the conservative movement may be nothing more than a collection of magazine offices and think tanks in Manhattan and Washington, DC."[32] This collection, I would add, is funded, run, and controlled by big money, not by little voters, so pushing the big-money corporate agenda is easy to do. (Another glimpse of candor came from Romney chief campaign strategist Stuart Stevens, about the role of "angry rich media figures" such as Sean Hannity and Rush Limbaugh in selling nonsense to the Republican base: "they have made fortunes peddling bile and prejudice"; "even if they are wrong, there is a lot of money to be made denying reality."[33])

Much of the fodder that is fed to irate right-wingers by this apparatus is a corporate product designed to trick them. It's an ideological form of consumer fraud on the Republican voter. Other candidates sought the political blessing of the right-wing corporate intermediaries and the political backing of the big-money influencers behind them, and paid the price of signing on to their corporate, big-money agenda. Trump blew all this up by taking his message directly from what he heard in voters' anger, rather than joining in on the corporate intermediaries' plan to fool them. This disruption may explain much of the distaste for Trump in certain Republican establishment quarters, in particular from the Koch brothers.

Although Trump blew up the selfish "settled orthodoxy" the Koch political machine thought it had sold to Republican voters, the Kochs will assuredly be back, with billions in secret money to manipulate the public and press their pro-corporate agenda. The big, behind-the-scenes battle of the Trump presidency will be how—or whether—Trump fends off the billionaire agenda and what the terms are of any quiet reconciliation reached between him and the corporatist Kochs. Clearly, the Koch operation wants to stamp out the populist agenda of Donald Trump and restore the corporate "settled orthodoxy" he disrupted.

The player to watch in this battle is Vice President–elect Mike Pence. Early on in the election cycle, before he disqualified himself as a presidential candidate with his harsh stand against gay rights (before Donald Trump made harsh stands a new political art form), Pence was seen by many Republican colleagues in the Senate as the likeliest candidate to become their nominee, because he was so close to the Koch brothers and their dark money operation. Such is the power of the Kochs: as their guy, he was seen as the likely Republican nominee. He probably still is their guy, so President Trump and his voters need to watch Vice President Pence closely.

This book's point about the power of the fossil-fuel industry over the Republican Party became more and more evident through the election: "an overwhelming 91 percent of fossil fuel industry campaign donations now flow to Republican candidates," one report calculated.[34] The disclosed campaign contributions in this election cycle exceeded $37 million.[35] That does not even count super PAC or dark money. Oklahoma State University sociologist Riley Dunlap reported that the environmental voting record of the Republican Party in Congress has fallen to a nearly exact reciprocal of its fossil-fuel money share. Measured by the League of Conservation Voters' environmental votes tally, Democrats average about 90 percent, and Republicans have fallen into single digits.[36] For me, a senator from Rhode Island, which has a history of environmental Republicans such as Senator John Chafee and his son Lincoln, this is a harsh fact to have to report. The fossil-fuel industry has taken over and now occupies the Republican Party, much as that *Men in Black* alien dressed itself in the clothing and skin of the unfortunate farmer.

My point about this occupation of the party by fossil-fuel interests was underscored by President-elect Trump's appointment of militant climate denier Myron Ebell (who has cycled through several

Koch-funded front groups) to lead his EPA transition team. *Politico* reported that Ebell "has largely been an outside agitator attacking politicians who look like they may be going soft on environmental issues—especially Republicans."[37] Conservative economist Jerry Taylor, who worked with Ebell at the Koch-funded Cato Institute, writes that Ebell was involved in "building a skeptic movement and enforcing that political orthodoxy as best he could in the Republican Party."[38] What one environmentalist gave Ebell credit for was "taking the tobacco playbook and applying it to climate change."[39]

With Trump having reached his new, ill-considered, campaign conclusion that climate change is a "hoax," another Republican obstacle now exists to responsible climate policies. I say "new" because of the full-page ad he signed in the *New York Times* in 2009 calling for strong climate action. "We support your effort," the ad said to the Obama administration, "to ensure meaningful and effective measures to control climate change, an immediate challenge facing the United States and the world today. Please don't postpone the Earth. If we fail to act now, it is scientifically irrefutable that there will be catastrophic and irreversible consequences for humanity and our planet."[40] Signatories were Donald Trump, his son Donald Jr., his son Eric, and his daughter Ivanka. That was then.

We heard in 2016 the oil company CEOs' statements that climate change is real, that fossil fuels are causing most of it, and that they would support a carbon price as a remedy.[41] To be clear, all of that is window dressing. The CEOs may be wildly ignorant of their own lobbying operation, but all their lobbying muscle is still exerted to push Congress in the exact opposite direction. The fossil-fuel machine exerts its own lobbying force through groups such as the American Petroleum Institute, but it also controls the climate agenda of the big business lobbying organizations (notwithstanding the good climate positions of most of those organizations' members), so all that big business lobbying muscle gets added to the fossil-fuel industry's direct lobbying against any climate action. Unless and until the rest of America's corporate community takes an interest in Congress doing something on climate change (which now they do not, I know from firsthand experience[42]), the fossil-fuel machine will continue to bully Republicans, lie to the public, and shut down progress. With Republicans controlling the

House, Senate, and White House, the mainstream American corporate community can no longer look to those institutions of government for leadership. The corporate community will need to step up.

The best-case industry scenario is that the fossil-fuel industry has been dragging its heels to put counterpressure against President Obama's climate program, and to gain time to figure out how to address the clean power revolution quaking the energy industry, all the while knowing and accepting that progress was being made and actually needed to be made. In effect, they were braking the carriage so it didn't careen downhill, but they didn't want the carriage to come to a halt. The best-case political scenario is that Republican opposition to clean power and to Obama worked for them politically and kept their fossil-fuel money flowing. But it worked politically so long as progress was actually being made anyway—so long as the carriage was moving. If the carriage were actually to grind to a halt, a whole new array of forces and consequences could emerge.

Now that Republicans own accountability for what happens and know they will pay the price of America failing at this, they may decide they have to figure something out. The Republican Party is nowadays by its nature happier as an opposition party: complaining rather than governing, criticizing rather than compromising, and scorning rather than working. Once you've got all the elements of government under your control, however, there's no refuge left in complaining, criticizing, and scorning.

It's a hell of a dangerous bet for them and for the industry that funds them to actually halt the carriage on climate; it's much safer to drag their heels and complain as the carriage moves. If the fossil-fuel industry and the Republicans come to this realization, we can do great things and they will be surprise heroes. Or they can drive us off the climate cliff. And own that.

This book lays out how the Supreme Court conservative bloc has become a vital political tool for Republican and corporatist forces. This point was confirmed by the end-of-campaign comments from some Republican senators that they thought the Senate should block any Supreme Court appointees of President Hillary Clinton, for her whole term, if necessary. Political control of the institution is so important to them that they'd rather break the Court than lose control of it.[43] With control of the presidency and the Senate now in Republican hands, it will be up to the Court itself to assert its independence from the forces that secure conservative justices' nominations, and from the crowded array of corporate-funded courtier groups that pile together to signal the corporate agenda to the conservatives. The decision to step free from their influence is a decision that cannot be made by all the members of the Court. It will take the conservative justices themselves to break the link I have described between their decisions and the wishes of the corporate establishment. It is out of anyone else's hands now. History will be watching. I'm sorry to be pessimistic, but I suspect they'll keep dancing with the guys that brung them.

My point that the tentacles of corporate power reach into government in ways we don't expect was demonstrated by recent reporting about political influence being exerted down into the offices of secretaries of state, the officials who ordinarily manage the election apparatus in the states. You may not even know who your secretary of state is, but they do. As the *New York Times* disclosed, "the targeting of secretaries of state with campaign donations, corporate-funded weekend outings and secret meetings with industry lobbyists reflects an intense focus on often overlooked ballot questions, which the secretaries frequently help write."[44] If corporate forces can get a local secretary of state to put the fix in on the language of a ballot referendum, they can limit the voter's options before he or she ever gets the chance to vote. They win the battle before it even starts. It is just one more example of the ardent pursuit by corporatist forces, at least those that have chosen political influence as a profit-making enterprise, to find new, clever, quiet ways to exert that political influence.

The ultimate goal I have in this book is that you, the reader, consider what role our Founders expected corporations to have in the political operation of our American democracy (no political role at all, I believe); and that you consider the astounding number of ways corporate influence exerts itself today. I say again: it is not always corporations themselves that do this directly. It can be corporate billionaires, or the foundations and front groups they have thrown up to do their dirty work, or the big business lobbies they direct and control. But the corporate political machinery is infiltrating everywhere.

Corporate dark money and corporate billionaire big money dominate our election spending. Behind all that actual corporate political spending lurks its shadow twin: the quiet, private threat or promise to engage in massive election spending. Reported corporate lobbying of Congress dominates by thirty to one all other lobbying of Congress combined. Corporate control and manipulation of regulatory agencies is so pervasive that it has coined the term "regulatory capture." The corporate alternate-reality machine is up and running, prepared to react with calculated misinformation and denial whenever science begins to warn of a danger associated with a profitable corporate product. Its phony alt-science then gets propagated by an array of corporate right-wing media outlets. Corporate power captured the Supreme Court, lost that majority control with Justice Scalia's death, freaked out and caused the Senate to disrupt constitutional norms by refusing to give even a hearing to the sitting president's nominee, and now looks ready (with a sigh of corporate relief) to recapture the Court. The Supreme Court's conservative majority has obediently repaid the corporate powers by changing the basic operating systems of our democracy in ways that consistently give big corporate powers even more power in our process of government, rewiring our democracy to corporate advantage. Corporate power even seeks to crush a constitutional element of our government: the civil jury, which is (not coincidentally) the one element designed to protect us against concentrations of private wealth and power.

We can be dazzled by the outlandish behavior of candidates, or distracted by the personal smears and character assassination that pervade our politics, and never notice the real danger to the republic: the quiet infiltration throughout our government of corporate forces. These forces are only too pleased for us to look elsewhere. They don't want to be the center of attention, and an election that became a soap-opera slugfest was a dazzling distraction. But they are infiltrating everywhere, their tentacles constantly creeping and grasping. They often have virtually unlimited money and usually enjoy the remorseless staying power that comes from this effort being a profitable exercise. They seek power, and they seek power over us. Their behavior on climate change, civil juries, and election corruption shows they are willing to drag America down as long as it helps them get their way. We'd be fools to be distracted by all the dazzle and not see the real menace.

So please, let's wake up and get off the couch. There are plenty of groups out there that want your participation. There are plenty of issues out there that need your voice. There are plenty of tentacles creeping around that need to be spotlighted and driven out. Find the ones that move you, and engage.

Sheldon Whitehouse, Newport, Rhode Island
November 17, 2016

Author's Note

THIS BOOK IS ROOTED IN MY LIFELONG EXPERIENCE in government and politics. Without that experience, there'd be no book. More than anyone, I want to dedicate this book to my family—to Sandra and Molly and Alexander—and to acknowledge what they did to make this book possible.

A life in government and politics has its joys and it has its woes. The problem for families is that those joys and woes are not fairly distributed between the politician and his family. I got more of the joys; they got more of the woes. I got the feelings of accomplishment at things done well. I got the camaraderie of politics. I got the exposure to people I might not otherwise have known, and ideas I might not otherwise have considered. I got the attention. They didn't get as much of any of that.

Whether I would have made more money had I pursued a more lucrative career is an unknown. What is a known is that I didn't.

Another known is the time my work in government has required. There were many years of very long hours away from home. Often being home meant bringing work home. Sometimes there were surges of effort where I barely saw my family at all. At one point I was going to work so early and coming home so late that all I could do was kiss my little daughter while she was sleeping. I was in the press a lot at the time, and one evening when she saw me on the news, she asked my wife why I had gone away to the TV, and would I come back.

They have had to endure my defeats and failures, many of which were very public. They have had to console me and buck me up and keep a brave face through their own disappointment for me. They have had to endure harsh political criticisms of me. We all went without TV for a while because the political attack ads against me on the television were so unpleasant, and it wasn't worth explaining it to the kids. Thank goodness it was the time of the VCR—we watched lots of movies. They had to cope with the uncertainty and stress of campaigning, of press attention, of debates, and of election night. They showed amazing resilience: my son kept his close friendship with the son of a political opponent all the way through our demanding race, and they have remained close friends to this day. I'm proud of him for that.

My family members have often lost the chance to make a clean first impression with people, bearing whatever impression their relation with me imposes. Some of their friends may not like my politics, and that can shadow their friendship. Some people may not want to be friends of theirs at all, just for that reason. And it's not offset by the people who want to be their friends just because of my position—those are never real friends.

My family's mistakes have been amplified, and their achievements have been diminished, as a result of my career. My wife is a published, Ivy League–educated doctor of marine science, with a specialty in coastal biology; her appointment as an unpaid board member to our state coastal resources agency was announced by the local newspaper with the headline "Wife of Aide Gets Job." Other staffers in that administration years ago have the right to this day to refer to Sandra as "Wife of Aide"; it was so unfair, it became a thing among us all—a wry, New England way of bonding and standing with her.

I have been really stressed at times. I've tried my best to be a good husband and father, but all that stress couldn't have helped. At one point, after a particularly strenuous ordeal, I went to my doctor for a checkup, and he gave me a surprising diagnosis. Evidently, when one is under a lot of stress, the digestive process can slow down. That produced the memorable diagnosis (which had to be a joyous opportunity for a doctor to deliver, speaking to a politician): "Well, Sheldon, I can tell you that as a medical matter, you are officially F.O.S." I was not too stressed to figure out what that stood for. To those readers who may suspect this of me already—well, you have at least one medical diagnosis in your corner.

The upshot of all of this is that my family has put up with a lot. I expect most political and government families have to put up with a lot. It's not really their fault that they got dragged into this life. So reader, be kind, if you can, to the families.

Acknowledgments

DIANE WACHTELL APPROACHED ME ABOUT WRITING A BOOK, and that invitation launched the thought process about how disparate issues I was working on shared a common theme. I am grateful for her confidence and guidance, and glad that The New Press exists to make this kind of book happen. Melanie Wachtell Stinnett played an important role in this book. She ran down innumerable sources, edited choppy or turgid parts of the book, added additional research and text in various areas, kept me on schedule, patiently coped with my edits, re-edits, and re-re-edits, and organized reviews of drafts by other talented people who all helped make this a better book. My only other book was an assembly of quotations, so this was the first book I have written rather than just compiled. This was Melanie's first effort as a co-author/editor /researcher. It was a pleasure to learn from each other.

—S.W.

THIS BOOK WOULD NOT BE POSSIBLE WITHOUT THE dedicated efforts of The New Press's editors and staff, particularly Carl Bromley, Jed Bickman, and Maury Botton. We are grateful to the whole New Press team. We would also like to thank those who reviewed early drafts of the manuscript: Bill Novak, Trevor Potter, Steven Nightingale, Sabeel Rahman, and Tom Goldstein.

—S.W. & M.W.S.

Notes

Introduction

1. William S. White, *Citadel: The Story of the U.S. Senate* (New York: Harper, 1957), 135.

2. "Satisfaction with the United States," Gallup, February 3–7, 2016, www.gallup.com/poll/1669/general-mood-country.aspx.

3. Abraham Lincoln, "Gettysburg Address," November 19, 1863, http://avalon.law.yale.edu/19th_century/gettyb.asp.

4. Lee Drutman, "How Corporate Lobbyists Conquered American Democracy," *The Atlantic*, April 20, 2015.

5. James Madison, *The Debates in the Several State Conventions of the Adoption of the Federal Constitution*, ed. Jonathan Elliot (Virginia: Collected and revised from contemporary publishers, 1836), 3:87.

Chapter One: The Constitution's Blind Spot

1. "Declaration of Independence," www.archives.gov/exhibits/charters/declaration_transcript.html.

2. Naomi Lamoreaux and William J. Novak, "Corporations and American Democracy: An Introduction," in *Corporations and American Democracy*, ed. Naomi Lamoreaux and William J. Novak (Harvard University Press, forthcoming: 2017), available at http://tobinproject.org/books-papers/corporations-american-democracy.

3. 1 *Fletcher Cyc. Corp.* § 2, n. 12.

4. *Encyclopaedia Britannica Online*, s.v. "Massachusetts Bay Colony."

5. Horace Walpole, quoted in William Dalrymple, "The East Indian Company: The Original Corporate Raiders," *The Guardian*, March 4, 2015.

6. John Francis, "Chronicles and Characters of the Stock Exchange" (London: Willoughby, 1849), reprinted in *The Church of England, Quarterly Review* 27 (1850): 142.

7. *Journals of the House of Commons, Volumes 18–34* (reprint; London, 1805), 110.

8. *Encyclopedia Britannica*, s.v. "Bank of the United States."

9. *The Federalist Papers*, www.congress.gov/resources/display/content/The+Federalist+Papers.

10. James Madison, "Detached Memoranda," ca. 1817, http://press-pubs.uchicago.edu/founders/documents/amendI_religions64.html.

11. Thomas Jefferson, letter to George Logan, November 12, 1816, http://tjrs.monticello.org/letter/1392.

12. Eric Hilt, "Early American Corporations and the State," in *Corporations and American Democracy*, ed. Naomi Lamoreaux and William J. Novak (Harvard University Press, forthcoming: 2017), 5–6, available at http://tobinproject.org/books-papers/corporations-american-democracy.

13. Ibid.

14. *Citizens United v. FEC*, 558 U.S. 310, 430 (2010) (Stevens, J., dissenting).

15. Ibid., 479 (Stevens, J., dissenting).

16. Rick Unger, "The Founding Fathers and Occupy Wall Street," *Washington Monthly*, October 28, 2011.

17. William Novak, email message to the author, March 9, 2016.

18. See Robert C. Hinkley, "How Corporate Law Inhibits Social Responsibility," *CommonDreams*, January 29, 2002.

19. *In re Indiana Brewing Co.'s License*, 75 A. 29, 30.

20. *Peasley v. Producers' Market Co.*, 261 P. 733, 736 (1927).

21. *Hannibal Inv. Co. v. Schmidt*, 113 S.W.2d 1048, 1052 (Mo. App. 1938).

22. 1 *Fletcher Cyc. Corp.* § 7.

23. Lee R. Raymond, quoted in Steve Coll, *Private Empire: ExxonMobil and American Power* (New York: Penguin, 2012), 71.

24. 1 *Fletcher Cyc. Corp.* § 6, citing *Gast Monuments, Inc. v. Rosehill Cemetery Co.*, 207 Ill. App. 3d 901 (1st Dist. 1990).

25. 18 C.J.S. Corporations § 2, "Corporation as person" (2015), citing *Matter of Estate of Cooper*, 1992 OK CIV APP 90, 838 P.2d 40 (Ct. App. Div. 2 1992).

26. Jesse Unruh, quoted in Mark A. Uhlig, "Jesse Unruh, A California Political Power, Dies," *New York Times*, August 6, 1987.

27. *Bank of the United States v. Deveaux*, 9 U.S. 61, 86 (1809), cited in "Brief of Amici Curiae Historians and Legal Scholars Supporting Neither Party," Jonathan Massey, in the Supreme Court of the United States in *Hobby Lobby*, January 28, 2014.

28. Burt Neuborne, *Madison's Music: On Reading the First Amendment* (New York: The New Press, 2015), 70.

29. *Citizens United*, 558 U.S. at 465–6 (Stevens, J., dissenting).

30. Ibid.

31. *The Voice of Madison* (from "The Nationalist," Boston, August 1889), www.slp.org/pdf/de_leon/eds1889/1889_aug.pdf.

32. See David Michaels, *Doubt Is Their Product: How Industry's Assault on Science Threatens Your Health* (New York: Oxford University Press, 2006).

33. Catherine Greene, "Consumer Demand Bolstering Organic Production and Markets in the U.S.," *USDA Blog*, February 26, 2016.

34. Franklin Roosevelt's Address at Madison Square Garden, New York City, October 31, 1936, American Presidency Project, www.presidency.ucsb.edu/ws/?pid=15219.

35. Franklin Delano Roosevelt, "Acceptance Speech for the Re-nomination for the Presidency," June 27, 1936, American Presidency Project, www.presidency.ucsb.edu/ws/?pid=15314.

36. Franklin Roosevelt's Address at Madison Square Garden.

37. This language appears in Theodore Roosevelt's Progressive Party Platform of 1912, available at www.pbs.org/wgbh/americanexperience/features/primary-resources/tr-progressive.

38. Theodore Roosevelt, speech delivered at Osawatomie, KS, August 31, 1910, www.whitehouse.gov/blog/2011/12/06/archives-president-teddy-roosevelts-new-nationalism-speech.

39. Ibid.

Chapter Two: The Growth of Corporate Power

1. "What Is the Greatest Collaboration of All Time?" *The Atlantic*, Jan./Feb. 2016.

2. 1 *Fletcher Cyc. Corp.* § 1.

3. Ibid.

4. Ibid.

5. 1 *Fletcher Cyc. Corp.* § 2.

6. *Trustees of Dartmouth College v. Woodward*, 17 U.S. 518 (1819).

7. Ibid., 636.

8. *Bank of the United States v. Deveaux*, 9 U.S. 61, 88 (1809).

9. *People v. Knapp*, 206 N.Y. 373, 381 (N.Y. 1912).

10. *Matter of American Fibre Chair Seat Corporation*, 265 N.Y. 416, 420 (N.Y. 1934).

11. *Fairhope Single Tax Corporation v. Melville*, 69 South. 466, 471 (1915).

12. *Dartmouth College*, 17 U.S. at 650.

13. "Appendix: Speech of Charles J. Ingersoll," *United States Democratic Review* 5, no. 13 (January 1839): 99–144.

14. Eric Hilt, "Early American Corporations and the State," in *Corporations and American Democracy*, ed. Naomi Lamoreaux and William J. Novak (Harvard University Press, forthcoming: 2017), available at http://tobinproject.org/books-papers/corporations-american-democracy, 25–26.

15. "Appendix: Speech of Charles J. Ingersoll."

16. Thomas Jefferson, letter to George Logan, November 12, 1816, http://tjrs.monticello.org/letter/1392.

17. Charles Perrow, *Organizing America: Wealth, Power, and the Origins of Corporate Capitalism* (Princeton, NJ: Princeton University Press, 2001), 217.

18. Jessica Hennessey and John Wallis, "Corporations and Organizations in the U.S. After 1840," in *Corporations and American Democracy*, 23.

19. Perrow, *Organizing America*, 217.

20. Hennessey and Wallis, "Corporations and Organizations in the U.S. After 1840," 2.

21. Hilt, "Early American Corporations and the State," 5.

22. H.W. Brands, *American Colossus: The Triumph of Capitalism (1865–1900)* (New York: Anchor Doubleday, 2011), 7.

23. Daniel A. Crane, "The Dissociation of Corporation and Regulation in the Progressive Era and the New Deal," in *Corporations and American Democracy*, 3.

24. Robert C. Post, *Citizens Divided: Campaign Finance Reform and the Constitution* (Cambridge, MA: Harvard University Press, 2014), 28.

25. Doris Kearns Goodwin, *The Bully Pulpit: Theodore Roosevelt, William Howard Taft, and the Golden Age of Journalism* (New York: Simon & Schuster, 2013), 324.

26. Ibid., 338.

27. William J. Novak, "A Revisionist History of Regulatory Capture," in *Preventing Regulatory Capture: Special Interest Influence and How to Limit It*, ed. Daniel Carpenter and David Moss (New York: Cambridge University Press, 2014), 41 (italics added).

28. 1 *Fletcher Cyc. Corp.* § 2.

29. Ibid.

30. *Del Monte Light and Power Co. v. Jordan*, 196 Cal. 488, 495 (Cal. 1925).

31. 1 *Fletcher Cyc. Corp.* § 2.

32. *Louis K. Liggett Co. v. Lee*, 288 U.S. 517, 555 (1933) (Brandeis, J., dissenting).

33. Ibid., 557.

34. Crane, "Dissociation," 4.

35. Ibid.

36. Ibid.

37. *Standard Oil Company of New Jersey v. United States*, 221 U.S. 1, 83 (1901) (Harlan, J., concurring in part and dissenting in part).

38. *Louis K. Liggett Co. v. Lee*, 288 U.S. 517, 549 (1933) (Brandeis, J., dissenting).

39. Crane, "Dissociation," 4, citing Thomas Cooley, A *Treatise on the Constitutional Limitations Which Rest upon the Legislative Power of the United States of the American Union*, 279 n. 2 (3rd ed., 1874).

40. Jacob S. Hacker and Paul Pierson, *Winner-Take-All Politics: How Washington Made the Rich Richer and Turned Its Back on the Middle Class* (New York: Simon & Schuster, 2011), 79.

41. Charles Francis Adams Jr., "The Railroad System," 427, cited in Novak, "Revisionist History."

42. Larry Lessig, *Republic, Lost: How Money Corrupts Congress—and a Plan to Stop It* (New York: Twelve Books, 2011), 5.

43. Goodwin, *Bully Pulpit*, 372.

44. Post, *Citizens Divided*, 28.

45. Goodwin, *Bully Pulpit*, 467.

46. Grover Cleveland, State of the Union address, 1888, American Presidency Project, www.presidency.ucsb.edu/ws/index.php?pid=29529.

47. Adam Winkler, "*Citizens United*, Personhood, and the Corporation in Politics," *Corporations and American Democracy* (Cambridge, MA: Harvard University Press, forthcoming), 7–8.

48. Ibid., 8.

49. Post, *Citizens Divided*, 28, quoting Elihu Root.

50. Ibid.

51. Zephyr Teachout, *Corruption in America* (Cambridge, MA: Harvard University Press, 2014), 181.

52. Ibid., 182.

53. Theodore Roosevelt, speech delivered at the dedication of the John Brown Memorial Park in Osawatomie, Kansas, August 31, 1910, www.whitehouse.gov/blog/2011/12/06/archives-president-teddy-roosevelts-new-nationalism-speech.

54. Post, *Citizens Divided*, 28–29.

55. Theodore Roosevelt, "Nationalism and Popular Rule," *The Outlook*, January 21, 1911, 96, available at http://www.unz.org/Pub/Outlook-1911jan21-00096.

56. A Charter of Democracy speech before the Ohio Constitutional Convention, February 1912, Theodore Roosevelt Collection, MS Am 1454.50 (139), Harvard College Library, www.theodorerooseveltcenter.org/Research/Digital-Library/Record.aspx?libID=o285145.

57. Goodwin, *Bully Pulpit*, 298, quoting Mark Sullivan.

58. Theodore Roosevelt, speech on August 31, 1910.

59. Theodore Roosevelt, State of the Union address, December 3, 1906, www.let.rug.nl/usa/presidents/theodore-roosevelt/state-of-the-union-1906.php.

60 Trevor Potter, "Introduction," January 21, 2016, www.brookings.edu/wp-content/uploads/2016/01/20160121_campaign_finance_summit_transcript.pdf.

61. Franklin Delano Roosevelt, "Acceptance Speech for the Re-nomination for the Presidency," June 27, 1936, American Presidency Project, www.presidency.ucsb.edu/ws/?pid=15314.

62. "The Annual Message of the President Transmitted to Congress, December 3, 1907," *Papers Relating to the Foreign Relations of the United States*, congressional ed. (Washington, DC: Government Printing Office, 1910), vol. 5270, issue 1, ix.

63. S. Rep. No. 3056, 59th Cong., 1st Sess., 2 (1906), cited in *Citizens United v. Fed. Election Comm'n*, 558 U.S. 310, 433 (2010) (Stevens, J., dissenting).

64. Teachout, *Corruption*, 188.

65. Post, *Citizens Divided*, 28–29.

Chapter Three: Where We Are Now

1. Zephyr Teachout, *Corruption in America* (Cambridge, MA: Harvard University Press, 2014), 311–12.

2. Federal Election Commission, "The Federal Election Campaign Laws: A Short History," www.fec.gov/info/appfour.htm.

3. Teachout, *Corruption*, 206–7.

4. Lee Drutman, *The Business of America Is Lobbying: How Corporations Became Politicized and Politics Became More Corporate* (New York: Oxford University Press, 2015), 3.

5. Lewis F. Powell Jr., "Confidential Memorandum: Attack on American Free Enterprise System," August 23, 1971, available at http://law2.wlu.edu/deptimages/Powell%20Archives/PowellMemorandumTypescript.pdf.

6. Elizabeth Drew, *Citizen McCain* (New York: Simon & Schuster, 2002), 13.

7. Ibid., 3.

8. Ibid., 34.

9. David Rothkopf, *Power, Inc.: The Epic Rivalry Between Big Business and Government—and the Reckoning That Lies Ahead* (New York: Farrar, Straus, & Giroux, 2013), 201.

10. Ibid.

11. Ibid., 311.

12. Ibid.

13. James Kirkup, "Sony vs North Korea: Some Companies Are Bigger than Countries. So What?" *The Telegraph*, December 18, 2014.

14. Rothkopf, *Power Inc.*, 314.

15. Ibid., 315.

16. "Super PACs, Nonprofits Favored Romney over Obama: Citizens United Decision Helped Romney Neutralize Obama's Fundraising Advantage," Center for Responsive Politics, October 30, 2012

17. Ibid.

18. Michael Beckel and Russ Choma, "Super PACs, Nonprofits Favored Romney over Obama," Center for Responsive Politics, October 30, 2012.

19. Nicholas Confessore, "Koch Brothers' Budget of $889 Million for 2016 Is on Par with Both Parties' Spending," *New York Times*, January 26, 2015.

20. Michael Beckel, "Super PAC Doppelgangers Eclipse Candidates in Campaign Money Chase," Center for Public Integrity, August 1, 2015.

21. Kenneth Vogel, "Democrats Win PACs, Lose Money War," *Politico*, December 6, 2014.

22. Kenneth Vogel, "Koch brothers' Americans for Prosperity plans $125 million spending spree," *Politico*, May 9, 2014.

23. Rebecca Ballhaus, "Koch Brothers Nonprofits' Spending Surged in 2014," *Wall Street Journal*, November 18, 2015.

24. "Koch Industries," Center for Responsive Politics, www.opensecrets.org/lobby/clientsum.php?id=D000000186.

25. Confessore, "Koch Brothers' Budget."

26. Nicholas Confessore, "Koch Political Group Spent $400 Million in 2015, Officials Say," *New York Times*, January 31, 2016.

27. Kenneth P. Vogel, "How the Koch Network Rivals the GOP," *Politico*, December 30, 2015.

28. Riley E. Dunlap, Aaron M. McCright, and Jerrod H. Yarosh, "The Political

Divide on Climate Change: Partisan Polarization Widens in the U.S.," *Environment* 58 no. 5.

29. Mike Allen and Kenneth P. Vogel, "Inside the Koch Data Mine," *Politico*, December 8, 2014; Kenneth P. Vogel, "The Koch Intelligence Agency," *Politico*, November 18, 2015.

30. Kenneth P. Vogel, "How the Kochs Launched Joni Ernst," *Politico*, November 12, 2015.

31. Claire Moser and Matt Lee-Ashley, "The Fossil-Fuel Industry Spent Big to Set the Anti-Environment Agenda of the Next Congress," Center for American Progress, December 22, 2014.

32. Ibid.

33. Nicholas Confessore, "Charles Koch Defends Big-Money Campaign Contributions," *New York Times*, November 3, 2015.

34. Zephyr Teachout, *Corruption in America: From Benjamin Franklin's Snuff Box to Citizens United* (Cambridge, MA: Harvard University Press, 2014), 246.

35. Lee Drutman, "How Corporate Lobbyists Conquered American Democracy," *The Atlantic*, April 20, 2015. For those interested further I recommend Lee Drutman's excellent *The Business of America Is Lobbying: How Corporations Became Politicized and Politics Became More Corporate* (New York: Oxford University Press, 2015).

36. "Money in Politics Factsheet," Issue One, www.issueone.org/wp-content/uploads/2016/03/gee-whiz-factsheet-sources.pdf.

37. Ibid.

38. "Contribution Limits for 2009–2010," Federal Election Commission, www.fec.gov/info/contriblimits0910.pdf.

39. "The Soaring Price of Political Access," editorial, *New York Times*, September 26, 2015, citing Matea Gold and Tom Hamburger, "Political Parties Go After Million-Dollar Donors in Wake of Looser Rules," *Washington Post*, September 19, 2015.

40. Peter Olsen-Phillips, Russ Choma, Sarah Bryner, and Doug Weber, "The Political One Percent of the One Percent in 2014: Mega Donors Fuel Rising Cost of Elections," Center for Responsive Politics, April 30, 2015.

41. Kenneth P. Vogel and Isaac Arnsdorf, "The Politico 100: Billionaires Dominate 2016," *Politico*, February 8, 2016.

42. "The Soaring Price of Political Access."

43. Nicholas Confessore, Sarah Cohen, and Karen Yourish, "The Families Funding the 2016 Presidential Election," *New York Times*, October 10, 2015.

44. "The Legacy of 'Citizens United' Strays from the Supreme Court's Vision," editorial, *Washington Post*, January 20, 2015.

45. "Policy Basics: Where Do Federal Tax Revenues Come From?", Center on Budget and Policy Priorities, http://www.cbpp.org/research/policy-basics-where-do-federal-tax-revenues-come-from.

46. Ibid.

47. Editorial, "Apple, Congress and the Missing Taxes," *New York Times*, August 30, 2016.

48. Mike McIntire and Nicholas Confessore, "Tax-Exempt Groups Shield Political Gifts of Businesses," *New York Times*, July 7, 2012.

49. Kennedy Elliot, Matea Gold, and Tim Farnam, "Dark Money in the Midterm Elections," *Washington Post*, November 29, 2014.

50. "Money in Politics Factsheet."

51. Paul Blumenthal, "Yes, Citizens United And Other Court Rulings Led To A Rise In Dark Money," *Huffington Post*, August 26, 2016.

52. Ibid.

53. "Why Senator McConnell Is So Nervous," editorial, *New York Times*, July 7, 2012.

54. Anna Palmer and Abby Phillip, "Corporations Not Funding Super PACS," *Politico*, March 8, 2012.

55. Burt Neuborne, *Madison's Music: On Reading the First Amendment* (New York: The New Press, 2015), 22.

56. Rebecca Ballhaus, "New Path for Masking Super PAC Donors," *Wall Street Journal*, February 3, 2016.

57. Joe Hagan, "The Coming Tsunami of Slime," *New York Magazine*, January 22, 2012.

58. "Presidential Ads 70% Negative in 2012, Up from 9% in 2008," Wesleyan Media Project Advertising Analysis press release, May 2, 2012, http://mediaproject.wesleyan.edu/releases/jump-in-negativity-2.

59. E.J. Dionne Jr., "'Citizens United' Is Turning More Americans into Bystanders," *Washington Post*, October 12, 2014.

60. Alex Seitz-Wald, "Huckabee: Super PACs Are 'One of the Worst Things That Ever Happened in American Politics,'" *ThinkProgress*, January 3, 2012.

61. "Annenberg Public Policy Center Calculates Dollars Spent by Third-Party Groups on Deceptive TV Ads Attacking or Supporting the Presidential Candidates," Annenberg Public Policy Center, University of Pennsylvania, September 25, 2012.

62. Benjamin H. Barton, "An Empirical Study of Supreme Court Justice Pre-Appointment Experience," *Florida Law Review* 64 (2012): 1155.

63. Jonathan Weisman, "Tax-Exempt Group's Election Activity Highlights Limits of Campaign Finance Rules," *New York Times*, July 16, 2012.

64. Peter Overby and Andrea Seabrook, "Question Marks Surround Key Election Advertiser," *All Things Considered*, NPR, October 27, 2010.

65. "Hit And Run: How One Supposed Non-Profit Spent Millions On Campaign Ads, Broke The Law, Then Disappeared," *Center for Responsibility and Ethics in Washington*, July 17, 2012, available at http://s3.amazonaws.com/storage.citizensforethics.org/wp-content/uploads/2016/07/20022714/CHGO%20Final%20Report%207%2013%2012.pdf.

66. Weisman, "Tax-Exempt."

67. Trip Gabriel and Ashley Parker, "Republican 'Super PACs' Turn to TV Ads for High-Stakes Primaries," *New York Times*, September 24, 2015.

68. Ibid.

69. Ibid.

70. Ibid.

71. Eric Lichtblau, "Reclusive Media Mogul Stands Firmly in Carly Fiorina's Corner," *New York Times*, October, 8, 2015.

72. Beth Rienhard, "Hank Greenberg Gives $10 Million to Super PAC Backing Jeb Bush," *Wall Street Journal*, January 7, 2016.

73. Julie Bykowicz and Jack Gillum, "Data: Nearly 5 Dozen Give a Third of All '16 Campaign Cash," Associated Press, August 1, 2015.

74. Ibid.

75. Ibid.

76. See *Citizens United*, 558 U.S. at 360.

77. Beth Reinhard and Christopher S. Stewart, "Some Candidates, Super PACs Draw Closer," *Wall Street Journal*, October 25, 2015.

78. Nick Gass, "Jeb Bush Recounts Conversation with Mitt Romney," *Politico*, January 5, 2016.

79. Seth McLaughlin, "Candidates' Super PAC Footage Tests Spirit of Campaign Finance Laws," *Washington Times*, September 21, 2015.

80. Reinhard and Stewart, "Some Candidates."

81. Ibid.

82. Nick Corasaniti, "Carly Fiorina's 'Super PAC' Aids Her Campaign, in Plain Sight," *New York Times*, September 30, 2015.

83. Eric Lichtblau, "Reclusive Media Mogul Stands Firmly in Carly Fiorina's Corner," *New York Times*, October, 8, 2015.

84. Corasaniti, "Carly Fiorina's 'Super PAC.'"

85. Ibid.

86. Julie Bykowicz, "Rubio's Presidential Bid Boosted by Secret-Money Commercials," Associated Press, October 8, 2015.

87. Ibid.

88. Jonathan Martin and Nicholas Confessore, "Nonprofit Masks Source of Ads Backing Rubio," *New York Times*, October 11, 2015.

89. Ibid.

90. Ibid.

91. Ibid.

92. Ibid.

93. Ibid.

94. Bykowicz and Gillum, "Data."

95. Trevor Potter, "A Republic If You Can Keep It," presented July 4, 2016, to The Chautauqua Institution, http://www.campaignlegalcenter.org/sites/default/files/Chautauqua%202016%20Final.pdf.

96. Marc Caputo and Kenneth P. Vogel, "Pro-Rubio super PAC raised $14.4 million in second half of 2015," *Politico*, January 31, 2016; Will Tucker, "Super PACs allow Wall Street to dominate presidential giving in 2015," OpenSecrets.org, February 2, 2016.

97. Josh Barro, "Rubio's Call for No Capital Gains Tax Is a Break with the G.O.P.," *New York Times*, February 4, 2016.

98. Ben Jacobs and David Smith, "'Politics Are Corrupt': Fears About Money and Its Influence on Elections Loom Large," *The Guardian*, July 8, 2016.

99. Kenneth P. Vogel, "The Koch ATM," *Politico*, November 17, 2015.

100. Brendan Fischer, "Kochs' Freedom Partners Spent $129M in 2014, Invested Massively in Voter Data Lists," *PR Watch*, Center for Media and Democracy, November 18, 2015.

101. "Trees of Liberty," Conservative Transparency, accessed January 4, 2016, http://conservativetransparency.org/org/trees-of-liberty.

102. Vogel, "Koch ATM."

103. Vogel, "How the Kochs Launched."

104. Vogel, "Koch ATM."

105. Vogel, "How the Kochs Launched."

106. Ibid.

107. Vogel, "Koch ATM."

108. Vogel, "How the Kochs Launched."

109. Matea Gold and Anu Narayanswamy, "How 'Ghost Corporations' Are Funding the 2016 Election," *Washington Post*, March 28, 2016.

110. Alex Isenstadt and Kenneth P. Vogel, "Trump blesses major super PAC effort," *Politico*, July 20, 2016.

111. Shane Goldmacher, "Trump's economic advisors are also his biggest donors," *Politico*, August 7, 2016.

112. Ibid.

113. Ibid.

114. Peggy Noonan, "America Is So in Play," *Wall Street Journal*, August 27, 2015 (80 percent of Americans think the system is rigged for the wealthy); "Super PACs Having Negative Impact, Say Voters Aware of 'Citizens United' Ruling," Pew Research Center, January 17, 2012 (60 percent of Republicans, 63 percent of Democrats, and 67 percent of independents who had heard of the decision believed *Citizens United* had a negative effect on the campaigns); "Bloomberg Politics National Poll," *Bloomberg BusinessWeek*, September 18–21, 2015 (78 percent of voters say *Citizens United* should be overturned and 87 percent say campaign finance rules should be reformed so the rich don't outinfluence the poor); "National Survey: Super PACs, Corruption, and Democracy," Brennan Center for Justice, April 24, 2012 (one in four Americans less likely to vote because super PACs have so much influence).

115. Martin Gilens and Benjamin I. Page, "Testing Theories of American Politics: Elites, Interest Groups, and Average Citizens" (abstract), *Perspectives on Politics* 12, no. 3 (September 2014): 564.

116. Ibid., 564.

117. Ibid., 565.

118. Ibid., 563.

119. Ibid., 576.

120. Ibid., 577.

121. Geoffrey Wood, "Business and Politics in a Criminal State: The Case of Equatorial Guinea," *African Affairs* 103, no. 413 (2004): 547–67, quoting J.-F.

Bayart, S. Ellis, and B. Hibou, *The Criminalization of the State in Africa* (Bloomington, IN: James Currey, 1999), 25–26.

122. Ken Silverstein, *The Secret World of Oil* (London: Verso, 2014), 107.

123. Ibid., at 119.

124. Ibid., at 175.

Chapter Four: What the Machine Wants

1. "Opportunity Denied: How Overregulation Harms Minorities," Subcommittee on Oversight, Agency Action, Federal Rights and Federal Courts, U.S. Senate, October 6, 2015, www.judiciary.senate.gov/meetings/opportunity-denied_how-overregulation-harms-minorities.

2. Per review on file with author, conducted November 3, 2015.

3. Rebecca Leber and Adam Peck, "House Republicans Voted Against the Environment More Than 500 Times in the Past Four Years," *The New Republic*, December 10, 2014.

4. See, generally, Kevin Cerilli and Christina Marcos, "House Passes Dodd-Frank Changes," *The Hill*, January 14, 2015; Simon Johnson, "The Republican Strategy to Repeal Dodd-Frank," *Baseline Scenario* (blog), January 7, 2015.

5. "Red Tape, Hidden Taxes and Regulation," FreedomWorks, accessed January 5, 2016, www.freedomworks.org/issue/red-tape-hidden-taxes-regulation.

6. "Overregulation," Libre Initiative, accessed January 5, 2016, http://thelibreinitiative.com/issue/overregulation.

7. Burgess Everett and Seung Min Kim, "GOP Readying for End-of-Year Spending Fights," *Politico*, November 5, 2015.

8. Tyson Slocum, "Electric Utility Deregulation and the Myths of the Energy Crisis," *Bulletin of Science, Technology and Society* 21, no. 6 (December 2001) .

9. See Marc Gunther, "With Rooftop Solar on the Rise, U.S. Utilities Are Striking Back," *Yale Environment* 360, September 3, 2013; Joby Warrick, "Utilities Fight Rise in Home Solar Power," *Boston Globe*, March 15, 2015.

10. Carolyn Korman, "Greening the Tea Party," *New Yorker*, February 17, 2015; Edward Humes, "Throwing Shade: How the Nation's Investor-Owned Utilities Are Moving to Blot Out the Solar Revolution," *Sierra Magazine*, May/June 2014.

11. Chye-Ching Huang and Brandon Debot, "Ten Facts You Should Know About the Federal Estate Tax," Center on Budget and Policy Priorities, March 25, 2015.

12. For background on "carried interest," see "Business Taxation: What Is Carried Interest and How Should It Be Taxed?" Tax Policy Center, Urban Institute and Brookings Institution, www.taxpolicycenter.org/briefing-book/key-elements/business/carried-interest.cfm.

13. See Paul Solman, "Is Carried Interest Simply a Tax Break for the Ultra-Rich?" *PBS NewsHour*, October 29, 2015.

14. Catherine Rampell, "The Little People Pay Taxes," *New York Times*, *Economix* blog, February 23, 2011.

15. Ibid.

16. Associated Press, "Maid Testifies Helmsley Denied Paying Taxes," *New York Times*, July 12, 1989.

17. Jane Mayer, *Dark Money: The Hidden History of the Billionaires Behind the Rise of the Radical Right* (New York: Knopf Doubleday, 2016), 57.

18. "What Do the Koch Brothers Want?" Sen. Bernie Sanders website, www.sanders.senate.gov/koch-brothers, accessed January 5, 2016; "1980 Libertarian Party Platform," *LPedia: A Collaborative History of the Libertarian Party*, www.lpedia.org/1980_Libertarian_Party_Platform#2._Taxation, accessed January 5, 2016.

19. Jane Mayer, "New Koch," *New Yorker*, January 25, 2016.

20. See, e.g., Sari Horwitz, "Unlikely Allies," *Washington Post*, August 15, 2015.

21. See, e.g., "Not So Guilty as Charged," editorial, *Wall Street Journal*, December 4, 2015.

22. *People v. Roby*, 52 Mich. 577, 579 (1884).

23. Mayer, "New Koch."

24. Danny Hakim, "U.S. Chamber Out of Step with Its Board, Report Finds," *New York Times*, June 14, 2016; Sheldon Whitehouse, Elizabeth Warren, Barbara Boxer, Bernard Sanders, Sherrod Brown, Jeff Merkley, Richard Blumenthal, and Edward Markey, "The U.S. Chamber of Commerce: Out of Step with the American People and Its Members," June 14, 2016, available at www.whitehouse.senate.gov/news/release/senators-issue-report-on-us-chamber-of-commerce-lobbying.

25. Whitehouse, Warren, et al., "U.S. Chamber of Commerce," 13.

26. Paul Hodgson, "Top CEOs Make More than 300 Times the Average Worker," *Fortune*, June 22, 2015.

27. Benjamin I. Page, Larry M. Bartels, and Jason Seawright, "Democracy and the Policy Preferences of Wealthy Americans," *Perspectives on Politics* 11, no. 1 (March 2013): 51.

28. David Callahan and J. Mijin Cha, "Stacked Deck: How the Dominance of Politics by the Affluent and Business Undermines Economic Mobility in America," *Dēmos*, February 2013, 5–6, table 1.

29. Page, Bartels, and Seawright, "Democracy."

30. Ibid.

31. Ibid.

32. Ibid.

33. Peggy Noonan, "A Party Divided, and None Too Soon," *Wall Street Journal*, June 2, 2016.

Chapter Five: The Powell Memo and the Corporate Strategy

1. S. Rep. No. 3056, 59th Cong., 1st Sess., 2 (1906), cited in *Citizens United v. Fed. Election Comm'n*, 558 U.S. 310, 433 (2010) (Stevens, J., dissenting).

2. Lewis F. Powell Jr., "Confidential Memorandum: Attack on American Free Enterprise System," August 23, 1971, available at http://law2.wlu.edu/deptimages/Powell%20Archives/PowellMemorandumTypescript.pdf.

3. Joan Biskupic and Fred Barbash, "Retired Justice Lewis Powell Dies at 90," *New York Times*, August 26, 1998.

4. Jane Mayer, *Dark Money: The Hidden History of the Billionaires Behind the Rise of the Radical Right* (New York: Knopf Doubleday, 2016), 61.

5. Powell, "Confidential Memorandum."

6. Ryan Grim and Lucia Graves, "GOP, U.S. Chamber of Commerce Beat Back Bill to Combat Outsourcing," *Huffington Post*, September 28, 2010 .

7. Eric Lipton, Mike McIntire, and Don Van Natta Jr., "Top Corporations Aid U.S. Chamber of Commerce Campaign," *New York Times*, October 21, 2010.

8. Lee Drutman, *The Business of America Is Lobbying: How Corporations Became Politicized and Politics Became More Corporate* (New York: Oxford University Press, 2015), 3.

9. Powell, "Confidential Memorandum."

10. Ibid.

11. Ibid.

12. Ibid.

13. See "Public Comment to the Advisory Committee on the Civil Rules," U.S. Chamber Institute for Legal Reform, November 7, 2013, www.instituteforlegalreform.com/uploads/sites/1/FRCP_Submission_Nov.7.2013.pdf.

14. Richard Nixon, "Address to the Nation Announcing Intention to Nominate Lewis F. Powell, Jr., and William H. Rehnquist to be Associate Justices of the Supreme Court of the United States," October 21, 2971, American Presidency Project, www.presidency.ucsb.edu/ws/?pid=3196.

15. John Calvin Jeffries, *Justice Lewis F. Powell, Jr.* (New York: Fordham University Press, 2001), 1.

16. Jacob S. Hacker and Paul Pierson, *Winner-Take-All Politics: How Washington Made the Rich Richer and Turned Its Back on the Middle Class* (New York: Simon & Schuster, 2011), 118.

17. Ibid., 119–20.

18. Ibid., 121.

19. *First National Bank of Boston v. Bellotti*, 435 US 765 (1978).

20. Steven M. Teles, *The Rise of the Conservative Legal Movement: The Battle for Control of the Law* (Princeton, NJ: Princeton University Press, 2008), 142 (internal citation omitted).

21. *Palazzolo v. Rhode Island*, 533 U.S. 606 (2001).

22. Ibid.

23. Adam Liptak, "With Subtle Signals, Supreme Court Justices Request the Cases They Want to Hear," *New York Times*, July 6, 2015.

24. Adam Liptak, "Victory for Unions as Supreme Court, Scalia Gone, Ties 4–4," *New York Times*, March 29, 2016.

25. Jess Bravin, "Supreme Court's Term Disappoints Conservatives and Businesses," *Wall Street Journal*, June 28, 2016, quoting Florida State University law professor Mary Ziegler.

26. Ibid.

27. Robert Barnes, "For Conservatives, High Court's Term Was a Letdown," *Washington Post*, June 28, 2016, quoting Stanford Law Professor Pamela S. Karlan.

28. Adam Liptak, "The Right-Wing Supreme Court That Wasn't," *New York Times*, June 28, 2016.

29. Ibid.

30. Ibid.

31. Barnes, "For Conservatives."

32. Bravin, "Supreme Court's Term."

33. Community Rights Counsel, "Nothing for Free," July 24, 2000, 94, http://communityrights.org/NothingForFREE/NFFmain.php.

34. Ibid., 20.

35. Ibid., 14.

36. Ibid., 12.

37. Bob Sloan, "ALEC's Koch Funded Cabal 'Educating' Our State and Federal Judges," *Daily Kos*, August 20, 2012.

38. Community Rights Counsel, "Nothing for Free," 12.

39. Ibid.; Mayer, *Dark Money*, 110.

40. Chris Young, Reity O'Brien, and Andrea Fuller, "Corporations, pro-business nonprofits foot bill for judicial seminars," *Center for Public Integrity*, March 28, 2013.

41. Ibid., 15.

42. Ibid., 17.

43. Ibid., 79.

44. Ibid., 9.

45. Ibid., 29.

46. Ibid., 31.

47. Sloan, "ALEC's Koch Funded Cabal."

48. Community Rights Counsel, "Nothing for Free," 34.

49. Ibid., 37.

50. Ibid., 39.

51. Ibid., 54 n. 68.

52. Ibid., 62.

53. Ibid., 62.

54. Ibid., 79.

55. Sloan, "ALEC's Koch Funded Cabal."

56. Community Rights Counsel, "Nothing for Free," 8, citing *Ft. Lauderdale Sun-Sentinel*, April 18, 1998, 18A.

57. Ibid., citing *Louisville Courier Journal*, June 19, 1998.

58. Ibid., citing *San Antonio Express-News*, April 19, 1998, 9.

59. Mayer, *Dark Money*, 110.

60. *State of Rhode Island v. Lead Industries Association, et al.*, Civil Action No: PB/99-5226, Superior Court, State of Rhode Island and Providence Plantations Providence, Sc., (2002/09/17, 5:23-6:12).

61. *State of Rhode Island v. Lead Paint Assoc. et al.*, 951 A.2d 428, 443, 444, 448, 449, 450, 454 (R.I. 2008), citing Donald G. Gifford, "Public Nuisance as a Mass Products Liability," *University of Cincinnati Law Review* 71 (2003): 790–91, 794. See also Fidelma Fitzpatrick, "Painting over Long-Standing Precedent: How the

Rhode Island Supreme Court Misapplied Public Nuisance Law in *State v. Lead Industries Association*," *Roger Williams University Law Review* 15 (2010): 448 n. 32 (describing the court's citations of Gifford).

62. Powell, "Confidential Memorandum."

Chapter Six: Capture of the Court

1. I have previously published on the ideas presented here in Sheldon Whitehouse, "Conservative Judicial Activism: The Politicization of the Court Under Justice John Roberts," *Harvard Law and Policy Review* 9 (Winter 2015): 195.

2. "Transcript: Day One of the Roberts Hearings," *Washington Post*, September 13, 2005.

3. Adam Liptak, "Corporations Find a Friend in the Supreme Court," *New York Times*, May 4, 2013, citing Lee Epstein, William M. Landes, and Richard A. Posner, "How Business Fares in the Supreme Court," *Minnesota Law Review* 97 (2013): 1434.

4. Liptak, "Corporations.".

5. Jeffrey Toobin, "No More Mr. Nice Guy: The Supreme Court's Stealth Hard-liner," *New Yorker*, May 25, 2009.

6. *Trop v. Dulles*, 356 U.S. 86, 120 (1958) (J. Frankfurter, dissenting).

7. Adam Liptak, "Chief Justice John Roberts Amasses a Conservative Record, and Wrath from the Right," *New York Times*, September 18, 2015, citing Lee Epstein, William M. Landes, and Richard A. Posner, "Revisiting the Ideology Rankings of Supreme Court Justices," *Journal of Legal Studies* 44 (2015): S295–S317.

8. Epstein, Landes, and Posner, "Revisiting."

9. Jeffrey M. Jones, "Confidence in U.S. Institutions Still Below Historical Norms," Gallup, June 15, 2015, www.gallup.com/poll/183593/confidence-institutions-below-historical-norms.aspx.

10. Greenberg Quinlan Rosner Research, "Democracy Corps Supreme Court Project: Frequency Questionnaire," April 16–21, 2014, www.democracycorps.com/attachments/article/979/042214%20DCORPS%20SCOTUS%20FQ.pdf.

11. Ibid.

12. The Mellman Group, "Findings From Recent Polling On The Supreme Court," May 19, 2014, https://perma.cc/X2HA-BCXT.

13. Linda Greenhouse, "Polar Vision," *New York Times*, May 28, 2014.

14. Norm Ornstein, "Why the Supreme Court Needs Term Limits," *The Atlantic*, May 22, 2014; Jeffrey Toobin, "Five to Four," *New Yorker*, June 25, 2007.

15. Dana Milbank, "The Roberts Court Finds a New Way to Stack the Deck in Favor of the Rich," *Washington Post*, January 11, 2016.

16. *National Federation of Independent Business v. Sebelius*, 567 U.S. ___ (2012).

17. Ibid., 39.

18. Ibid., 20.

19. Ibid., 52.

20. "Republican Party Platform of 2000," July 31, 2000, American Presidency Project, /www.presidency.ucsb.edu/ws/?pid=25849.

21. "No More Souters," editorial, *Wall Street Journal*, July 19, 2005.

22. *Brown v. Board of Education of Topeka*, 347 U.S. 483 (1954); Harry Flood Byrd, 1954, quoted in "Brown at 60: The Southern Manifesto and 'Massive Resistance' to Brown," NAACP Legal Defense and Educational Fund, www.naacpldf.org/brown-at-60-southern-manifesto-and-massive-resistance-brown.

23. *Roe v. Wade*, 410 U.S. 113 (1973).

24. *Miranda v. Arizona*, 384 U.S. 436, 468 (1966).

25. *Texas v. Johnson*, 491 U.S. 397 (1989).

26. In a March 22, 2016, CBS/*New York Times* poll, when asked "How important to you is who sits on the Supreme Court?," 49 percent of Republicans answered "Very important," while only 34 percent of Democrats gave the same answer; www.scribd.com/doc/305599300/NYT-CBS-poll-on-Supreme-Court-Mar16d-scotus.

27. Akhil Amar, "Should We Trust Judges?", *Los Angeles Times*, December 17, 2000.

28. *Shelby County v. Holder*, 133 S. Ct. 2612 (2013).

29. Tomas Lopez, "Shelby County: One Year Later," Brennan Center for Justice, June 24, 2014.

30. "North Carolina's Voter ID Shenanigans," editorial, *Washington Post*, January 31, 2016.

31. Anne Blythe, "4th U.S. Circuit Judges Overturn North Carolina's Voter ID Law," *Charlotte Observer*, July 29, 2016.

32. Fifteenth Amendment, United States Constitution.

33. Oral Argument at 16:14–17:7, *Shelby County v. Holder*.

34. *Northwest Austin Municipal Utility District No. 1 v. Holder*, 557 U.S. 193, 203 (2009).

35 *Shelby County*, 133 S. Ct. at 2621.

36. "Transcript: Day One of the Roberts Hearings," *Washington Post*, September 13, 2005.

37. Richard A. Posner, "The Voter Rights Act Ruling Is About the Conservative Imagination," *Slate*, June 26, 2013.

38. See Christopher Klein, "'A New Species of Monster': How Massachusetts Spawned the Gerrymander," *Boston Globe*, September 11, 2011.

39. Christopher Ingraham, "This Is the Best Explanation of Gerrymandering You Will Ever See," *Washington Post, Wonkblog*, March 1, 2015.

40. Olga Pierce, Justin Elliott, and Theodoric Meyer, "How Dark Money Helped Republicans Hold the House and Hurt Voters," ProPublica, December 21, 2012.

41. "2012 REDMAP Summary Report," The Redistricting Majority Project, January 4, 2013, www.redistrictingmajorityproject.com/?p=646.

42. Karen L. Haas, Clerk of the House of Representatives, "Statistics of the Presidential and Congressional Election of November 6, 2012," February 28, 2013, http://clerk.house.gov/member_info/electionInfo/2012election.pdf.

43. Ibid.

44. "2012 REDMAP Summary Report."

45. Ibid.

46. Sam Wang, "Let Math Save Our Democracy," *New York Times*, December 5, 2015.

47. "2012 REDMAP Summary Report."

48. Karen L. Haas, Clerk of the House of Representatives, "Statistics of the Presidential and Congressional Election of November 6, 2012," February 28, 2013, http://clerk.house.gov/member_info/electionInfo/2012election.pdf.

49. Ibid.

50. "2012 REDMAP Summary Report."

51. Ibid.

52. *Vieth v. Jubelirer*, 541 U.S. 267 (2004).

53. J. Gerald Hebert, Paul M. Smith, Martina E. Vandenberg, and Michael B. DeSanctis, *The Realist's Guide to Redistricting: Avoiding the Legal Pitfalls*, 2nd ed. (Chicago: American Bar Association, 2011).

54. *First National Bank of Boston v. Bellotti*, 435 U.S. 765 (1978).

55. Joe Hagan, "The Coming Tsunami of Slime," *New York*, January 22, 2012.

56. William F. Buckley Jr., "Our Mission Statement," *National Review*, November 19, 1955.

57. *District of Columbia v. Heller*, 554 U.S. 570 (2008).

58. Interview by Charlayne Hunter-Gault with Warren Burger, *MacNeil/Lehrer NewsHour*, PBS, December 16, 1991 (Monday transcript # 4226), cited in Joan Biskupic, "Guns: A Second (Amendment) Look," *Washington Post*, May 10, 1995.

59. Richard A. Posner, "In Defense of Looseness," *New Republic*, August 27, 2008.

60. Amanda Hollis-Brusky, *Ideas with Consequences: The Federalist Society and the Conservative Counterrevolution* (New York: Oxford University Press, 2015), 148.

61. Adam Liptak, "Supreme Court Prepares to Take On Politically Charged Cases," *New York Times*, October 4, 2015.

62. *Citizens United*, 558 U.S. at 379.

63. Ibid. at 380.

64. "A Corporate Court? Tracking the U.S. Chamber of Commerce and the Roberts Court: Current Term (OT 2015)," Constitutional Accountability Center, accessed March 31, 2016, http://theusconstitution.org/corporate-court.

65. Ibid.

66. *Ledbetter v. Goodyear Tire and Rubber Company*, 550 U.S. 618 (2007).

67. *Leegin Creative Leather Products, Inc. v. PSKS, Inc.*, 551 U.S. 877 (2007).

68. *Janus Capital Group, Inc. v. First Derivative Traders*, 564 U.S. ___ (2011).

69. *Gross v. FBL Financial Services, Inc.*, 557 U.S. ___ (2009).

70. *Ashcroft v. Iqbal*, 556 U.S. 662 (2009); *Bell Atlantic Corp. v. Twombly*, 550 U.S. 544 (2007).

71. *Rent-A-Center West, Inc. v. Jackson*, 561 U.S. 63 (2010).

72. *Wal-Mart Stores, Inc. v. Dukes*, 564 U.S. ___ (2011); *AT&T Mobility LLC v. Concepcion*, 563 U.S. 333 (2011).

73. *DirecTV Inc. v. Imburgia*, 577 U.S. ___ (2015).

74. *Vance v. Ball State University*, 570 U.S. __ (2013); *Mutual Pharmaceutical Co. v. Bartlett*, 570 U.S. ___ (2013); *Comcast v. Behrend*, 569 U.S. ___ (2013).

75. *Burwell v. Hobby Lobby Stores* 573 U.S. ___ (2014); *Harris v. Quinn*, 573 U.S. ___ (2014).

76. "Transcript: Day One of the Roberts Hearings," *Washington Post*, September 13, 2005.

Chapter Seven: Capture of Elections: *Citizens United*

1. *Marshall v. Baltimore & Ohio Railroad Company*, 57 U.S. 314, 335 (1853).

2. I have previously published on the ideas presented here in: Sheldon Whitehouse, "Conservative Judicial Activism: The Politicization of the Court Under Justice John Roberts," *Harvard Law and Policy Review* 9 (Winter 2015): 195.

3. "McCain: Supreme Court Ignorant on Politics," CBS News, January 5, 2012.

4. Fred Wertheimer, "How Chief Justice Roberts and Four Supreme Court Colleagues Gave the Nation a System of Legalized Bribery," *Huffington Post*, October 6, 2015, citing Nina Totenberg, "Federal Judge Richard Posner: The GOP Has Made Me Less Conservative," NPR, June 5, 2012.

5. James Vicini, "Landmark Supreme Court Ruling Allows Corporate Political Cash," Reuters, January 21, 2010.

6. Alan Simpson, Bill Bradley, and Bob Kerrey, "How to Make Our Democracy Work for Everyone," *Roll Call*, January 21, 2015.

7. Connie Morella and Dan Glickman, "We Are Gyrocopter," *Roll Call*, May 22, 2015.

8. Mark McKinnon, "Why We Won't Stop Fighting Corruption," *Daily Beast*, November 11, 2014.

9. *Citizens United*, 558 U.S. at 428–29 (Stevens, J., dissenting), citing *Trustees of Dartmouth College v. Woodward*, 4 Wheat. 518, 636, 4 L.Ed. 629 (1819) (Marshall, C.J.)

10. Ibid. at 466.

11. Burt Neuborne, *Madison's Music: On Reading the First Amendment* (New York: The New Press, 2015), 79–80.

12. See "Warren Buffett: Citizens United Pushes U.S. Toward a Plutocracy," People for the American Way, quoting CNN:Money interview with Buffett, April 3, 2015, http://blog.pfaw.org/content/warren-buffett-citizens-united-pushes-us-toward-plutocracy.

13. Adam Liptak, "Justices, 5–4, Reject Corporate Spending Limit," *New York Times*, January 21, 2010.

14. Jane Mayer, *Dark Money: The Hidden History of the Billionaires Behind the Rise of the Radical Right* (New York: Knopf Doubleday, 2016), 252.

15. *Citizens United*, 558 U.S. at 354–5.

16. Neuborne, *Madison's Music*, 102.

17 Robert Barnes and Dan Eggen, "Supreme Court Rejects Limits on Corporate Spending on Political Campaigns," *Washington Post*, January 22, 2010.

18. Sam Jewler, "The Dark Side of Citizens United," Public Citizen Report,

October 29, 2014, www.citizen.org/documents/us-chamber-of-commerce-dark-money-spending-report.pdf.

19. Robert Barnes and Dan Eggen, "Supreme Court Rejects Limits on Corporate Spending on Political Campaigns," *Washington Post*, January 22, 2010.

20. Tilman Klumpp, Hugo M. Mialon, and Michael A. Williams, "Yes, 'Citizens United' Gives Republicans an Electoral Edge. Here's Proof," *Washington Post*, April 7, 2016.

21. See *Citizens United*, 558 U.S. at 358.

22. Voltaire, *Candide*, trans. Lowell Bair (New York: Bantam Books, 1959), 87.

23. Nicholas Confessore, "Koch Brothers' Budget of $889 Million for 2016 Is on Par with Both Parties' Spending," *New York Times*, January 26, 2015; Matea Gold, "Charles Koch Downgrades His Political Network's Projected 2016 Spending from $889 Million to $750 Million," *Washington Post*, October 21, 2015; Coral Davenport, "Why Republicans Keep Telling Everyone They're Not Scientists," *New York Times*, October 30, 2014.

24. Coral Davenport, "Many Conservative Republicans Believe Climate Change Is a Real Threat," *New York Times*, September 28, 2015.

25. Kenneth P. Vogel and Burgess Everett, "How the Koch Network Created the Ex-Im Fight," *Politico*, December 3, 2015.

26. Sarah Karlin-Smith, "Drug lobby plans counterattack on prices," *Politico*, August 4, 2016.

27. Alex Altman, "Silent Partners," *Time*, October 10, 2016.

28. *Caperton v. A.T. Massey Coal Co*, 556 U.S. 868 (2009).

29. Ibid. at 868, 884.

30. Trevor Potter, "The Supreme Court Needs to Get Smarter About Politics," *Washington Post*, October 11, 2013.

31. Kenneth P. Vogel, "Undisclosed Dollars Dominate Campaign Spending," *Politico*, January 12, 2016.

32. *Citizens United v. FEC*, 558 U.S. 310, 358 (2010).

33. Ibid. at 360.

34. *Marbury v. Madison*, 5 U.S. 137, 177 (1803).

35. Benjamin Cardozo, *The Nature of the Judicial Process* (New Haven, CT: Yale University Press, 1921), 141.

36. *Citizens United*, 558 U.S. at 400 (Stevens, J., dissenting).

37. See "08-205 Citizens United v. Federal Election Commission," Supreme Court Docket, accessed March 2, 2016, www.supremecourt.gov/qp/08-00205qp.pdf.

38. See ibid., order of June 29, 2009; see generally *Citizens United*, 558 U.S. at 396-98 (Stevens, J., dissenting).

39. *Citizens United*, 538 U.S. at 398 (Stevens, J., dissenting).

40. *Citizens United*, 558 U.S. at 345 (slip op at 40), citing *Buckley v. Valeo*, 424 U.S. 1, 25 (1976).

41. Ibid.

42. *Citizens United*, 558 U.S. at 358.

43. "National Survey: Super PACs, Corruption, and Democracy," Brennan Center for Justice, April 24, 2012.

44. Ibid.

45. "Americans' Views on Money in Politics," *New York Times*, June 2, 2015.

46. Harold Meyerson, "Americans See a Government of, by and for the Rich," *Washington Post*, November 18, 2015, citing "Survey: Anxiety, Nostalgia, and Mistrust: Findings from the 2015 American Values Survey," Public Religion Research Institute, November 17, 2015.

47. Patrick O'Connor and Janet Hook, "WSJ/NBC Poll Finds Anger at Political System," *Wall Street Journal*, November 3, 2015.

48. Greg Stohr, "Bloomberg Poll: Americans Want Supreme Court to Turn Off Political Spending Spigot," *Bloomberg Politics*, September 28, 2015.

49. *Citizens United*, 558 U.S. at 425–30 (Stevens, J. dissenting).

50. Ibid. at 429.

51. *Citizens United*, 558 U.S. at 319.

52. *Citizens United*, 558 U.S. at 414 (Stevens, J., dissenting) (quoting *Vasquez v. Hillery*, 474 U.S. 254, 265 [1986]).

53. Ibid. at 414 (Stevens, J., dissenting).

54. "2012 Presidential Race: Candidates Opposed/Supported by Outside Groups and Party Committees," OpenSecrets.org, https://www.opensecrets.org/pres12/indexp.php.

55. WSJ News Graphics, "Super PAC Contributions for the 2016 Presidential Campaign," *Wall Street Journal*, July 31, 2015, http://graphics.wsj.com/elections/2016/campaign-super-pacs/.

56. The Mellman Group, "Findings From Recent Polling On The Supreme Court."

57. *Citizens United*, 558 U.S. at 370–71.

58. *American Tradition Partnership v Bullock*, 567 U.S. ___ (2012).

59. *Western Tradition Partn. v. Attorney General*, 2011 MT 328 (2011).

60. *Western Tradition Partn. v. Attorney General*, 363 Mont. 220, 230–33 (2011).

61. Ibid.

62. Matt Schudel, "Huguette Clark, Copper Heiress and Recluse, Dies at 104," *Washington Post*, May 24, 2011.

63. *Western Tradition Partn. v. Attorney General*, 363 Mont. at 228.

64. Brief of United States Senators Sheldon Whitehouse and John McCain as Amici Curiae in Support of Respondents, *American Tradition Partnership, Inc. v. Bullock*, No. 11-1179, May 2012.

65. See generally *Western Tradition Partn. v. Attorney General*, 363 Mont. 220 (2011).

66. *American Tradition Partnership v. Bullock*, 567 U.S. ___ (2012).

67. *McCutcheon v. FEC*, 572 U.S. ___ (2014).

68. Ibid.

69. Marcia Coyle, "Justice Anthony Kennedy Loathes the Term 'Swing-Vote,'" *National Law Journal*, October 27, 2015.

70. "Scalia on Unlimited Political Ads: Turn Off TV," CBS News, January 21, 2012.

Chapter Eight: Capture of Regulatory Agencies

1. Shawn Otto, *The War on Science* (Milkweed Editions, 2016), 350.

2. See, e.g., Daniel Carpenter and David Moss, eds., *Preventing Regulatory Capture: Special Interest Influence and How to Limit It* (New York: Cambridge University Press, 2014).

3. Charlie Savage, "Sex, Drugs, and Graft Cited in Interior Department," *New York Times*, September 10, 2008.

4. "Gulf Oil Industry, Government Ties Persist," *USA Today*, July 26, 2011.

5. "Investigative Report: Island Operating Company et al.," Inspector General, Department of the Interior, March 31, 2010, 3, http://www.govexec.com/pdfs/052510ts1.pdf.

6. Savage, "Sex, Drugs, and Graft Cited in Interior Department."

7. Ibid., 7.

8. Ibid.

9. Gerald P. O'Driscoll Jr., "The Gulf Spill, the Financial Crisis and Government Failure," *Wall Street Journal*, June 12, 2010.

10. "Editorial: The mess at MMS," *Providence Journal*, May 30, 2010.

11. Stephen Labton, "Agency's '04 Rule Let Banks Pile Up New Debt," *New York Times*, October 2, 2008.

12. Thomas Frank, "Obama and 'Regulatory Capture,'" *Wall Street Journal*, June 24, 2009.

13. Woodrow Wilson, *The New Freedom* (New York: Doubleday, Page, 1913).

14. Marver H. Bernstein, *Regulating Business by Independent Commission* (Princeton, NJ: Princeton University Press, 1955), 87, 90.

15. Ibid., 88.

16. Ibid., 88–89.

17. See "Legislation," U.S. Food and Drug Administration, last updated July 2, 2015, at www.fda.gov/RegulatoryInformation/Legislation.

18. "Famous Cases and Criminals: Willie Sutton," Federal Bureau of Investigation, accessed January 26, 2016, www.fbi.gov/history/famous-cases/willie-sutton.

19. "GDP (Current US$)," World Bank, accessed July 30, 2016, http://data.worldbank.org/indicator/NY.GDP.MKTP.CD; "OTC Derivatives Statistics at End-June 2015," Bank for International Settlements, accessed July 30, 2016, www.bis.org/publ/otc_hy1511.htm.

20. Russell Baker, "Dirksen, Reagan and Real Money," *Chicago Tribune*, October 5, 1985.

21. James Kwak, "Cultural Capture and the Financial Crisis," in *Preventing Regulatory Capture: Special Interest Influence and How to Limit It*, ed. Daniel Carpenter and David Moss (New York: Cambridge University Press, 2014), 92.

22. Luigi Zingales, "Preventing Economists' Capture," in *Preventing Regulatory Capture: Special Interest Influence and How to Limit It*, ed. Daniel Carpenter and David Moss (New York: Cambridge University Press, 2014), 127.

23. Ibid.

24. "BP Found 'Grossly Negligent' in Gulf of Mexico Oil Spill," *New Orleans Sun*, September 5, 2014.

25. Michael Cooper, Gardiner Harris, and Eric Lipton, "In Mine Safety, a Meek Watchdog," *New York Times*, April 10, 2010.

26. "Protecting the Public Interest: Understanding the Threat of Agency Capture," Hearing Before the Subcommittee on Administrative Oversight and the Courts of the Committee on the Judiciary, United States Senate, August 3, 2010.

27. Ibid., statement of Nicholas Bagley.

28. Barbara W. Tuchman, *The March of Folly: From Troy to Vietnam* (New York: Random House, 1985), 382.

29. James Madison, "The Same Subject Continued: The Union as a Safeguard Against Domestic Faction and Insurrection," Federalist No. 10, November 23, 1787, www.congress.gov/resources/display/content/The+Federalist+Papers#TheFederalistPapers-10.

30. Kie Relyea, "Ten Years After Pipeline Explosion, Kings Learn to Feel Joy Again," *Bellingham Herald*, June 7, 2009.

31. "Pipeline Accident Report: Pipeline Rupture and Subsequent Fire in Bellingham, Washington," National Transportation Safety Board, June 10, 1999, 11.

32. Ibid., 8.

33. Ibid.

34. Ibid., 11.

35. Keiko Morris, Janet Burkitt, Jim Brunner, and Jack Broom, "Fire Takes Young Lives—Cause Investigated; Pipeline Has Anacortes Refinery Tie," *Seattle Times*, June 11, 1999.

36. "Pipeline Accident Report," 11.

37. Ibid.

38. Ibid.

39. Morris et al., "Fire"; "Pipeline Accident Report," 11.

40. Andrew Restuccia and Elana Schorr, "Pipelines Blow Up and People Die," *Politico*, April 21, 2015.

41. "Pipeline Accident Report," v.

42. Restuccia and Schorr, "Pipelines."

43. Ibid.

44. Ibid.

45. Ibid.

46. Ibid.

47. Ibid.

48. Ibid.

49. A bill I have proposed to create a "regulatory capture cop" has consistently gone nowhere. Maybe it will take yet another disaster to pass it.

50. Restuccia and Schorr, "Pipelines."

51. Relyea, "Ten Years."

52. Ibid.

53. "About the FEC," Federal Election Commission, accessed March 6, 2016, www.fec.gov/about.shtml.

54. 52 U.S.C. Section 301, Federal Election Campaign Act.

55. Mike McIntire and Michael Luo, "Fine Line Between 'Super PACs' and Campaigns," *New York Times*, February 25, 2012.

56. Statement of Reasons Of Chair Ellen L. Weintraub and Commissioners Cynthia L. Bauerly and Steven T. Walther, Before the Federal Election Commission, *In the Matter of Friends of Laura Ruderman, et al.*, MUR 6611, at 3, available at http://eqs.fec.gov/eqsdocsMUR/13044330712.pdf.

57. Statement of Lawrence M. Noble, President and CEO, Americans for Campaign Reform, Before the Subcommittee on Crime and Terrorism Senate Committee on the Judiciary, "Current Issues in Campaign Finance Law Enforcement," April 9, 2013, www.judiciary.senate.gov/imo/media/doc/4-09-13NobleTestimony.pdf.

58. Paul Blumenthal, "How SuperPACs and Campaigns Are Coordinating in 2016," *Huffington Post*, November 14, 2015.

59. *Citizens United*, 558 U.S. at 370–71.

60. 52 U.S.C. Section 30104.

61. Statement of Lawrence M. Noble; see generally, "The Federal Election Commission Is Worse than Useless," editorial, *Los Angeles Times*, March 31, 2016. See also T.W. Farnam, "Despite Supreme Court support, disclosure of funding for 'issue ads' has decreased," *Washington Post*, September 15, 2010.

62. Statement of Lawrence M. Noble.

63. 2 U.S.C. Section 441f.

64. Statement of Lawrence M. Noble.

65. Ibid., 3.

66. Ellen Killoran, "Phantom Company Donates $1 Million to Romney Group," *International Business Times*, August 4, 2011.

67. See generally Internal Revenue Service, "Social Welfare Organizations," www.irs.gov/Charities-&-Non-Profits/Other-Non-Profits/Social-Welfare-Organizations, accessed March 6, 2016.

68. Internal Revenue Code 501(c)(4).

69. See Internal Revenue Service, "Social Welfare Organizations."

70. Kim Barker, "How Nonprofits Spend Millions on Elections and Call it Public Welfare," ProPublica, August 18, 2012.

71. Ibid.

72. See generally ibid.

73. Internal Revenue Service, "Social Welfare Organizations."

74. Americans for Prosperity, IRS Form 1024, Question 15, Page 4, filed August 4, 2004; Americans for Prosperity, IRS Form 990, November 8, 2013, see Question 3, page 3, and see page 59.

75. Barker, "How Nonprofits Spend."

76. Ibid.

77. Ibid.

78. Ibid.

79. Ibid.

80. Ibid.

81. Justin Elliot, "Watchdogs to IRS: Reject Rove Group's Tax Application," ProPublica, January 2, 2013.

82. Barker, "How Nonprofits Spend."

83. Ibid.

84. Kim Barker, "Controversial Dark Money Group Among Five That Told IRS They Would Stay Out of Politics, Then Didn't," ProPublica, January 2, 2013.

85. Eric Lichtblau, "FEC Can't Curb 2016 Election Abuse, Commission Chief Says," *New York Times*, May 3, 2015.

86. Matea Gold and Anu Narayanswamy, "How 'Ghost Corporations' Are Funding the 2016 Election," *Washington Post*, March 18, 2016.

87. "The Federal Election Commission Is Worse than Useless," editorial, *Los Angeles Times*, March 31, 2016.

88. See generally Statement of Lawrence M. Noble.

Chapter Nine: Capture of the Civil Jury

1. I have previously published on the ideas presented in this chapter in: Sheldon Whitehouse, "Restoring the Civil Jury's Role in the Structure of Our Government," *William and Mary Law Review* 55 (2014): 1241; Sheldon Whitehouse, "Opening Address," *University of Pennsylvania Law Review* 162 (2013–2014): 1517.

2. Alexis de Tocqueville, *Democracy in America*, trans. Arthur Goldhammer (New York: Penguin Putnam, 2004) , 283.

3. There are some social ills that juries can't cure, as the injustices wrought by all-white juries in the South remind us. There are some conditions that some medicines just can't cure. But they are still good medicine for what they can cure.

4. John H. Langbein et al., *History of the Common Law: The Development of Anglo-American Legal Institutions* (New York: Aspen, 2009), 100 (alteration in original), quoting F.W. Maitland, *The Forms of Action at Common Law*, ed. A.H. Chaytor and W. Whittaker (1909), 22 (internal quotation marks omitted).

5. Ibid., 100, 244–45.

6. Stephan Landsman, "The Civil Jury in America: Scenes from an Underappreciated History," *Hastings Law Journal* 44 (1993): 592 (footnotes omitted), citing Harold M. Hyman and Catherine M. Tarrant, "Aspects of American Trial Jury History," in *The Jury System in America*, ed. Rita J. Simon (Beverly Hills, CA: Sage, 1975), 24–25; Massachusetts Body of Liberties para. 29 (1641), reprinted in *Sources of Our Liberties*, ed. Richard L. Perry and John C. Cooper (Chicago: American Bar Foundation, 1952), 151.

7. Akhil Reed Amar, *America's Constitution: A Biography* (New York: Random House, 2005), 233.

8. Landsman, "Civil Jury," 595.

9. Declaration of Independence.

10. U.S. Constitution, Amendment VII.

11. Alexander Hamilton, "The Judiciary Continued in Relation to Trial by

Jury," Federalist No. 83, www.congress.gov/resources/display/content/The+Federalist+Papers#TheFederalistPapers-83.

12. See Thomas J. Methvin, Alabama—The Arbitration State, 62 ALA. LAW. 48, 49 (2001) ("In 1774, John Adams stated: 'Representative government and trial by jury are the heart and lungs of liberty. Without them, we have no other fortification against being ridden like horses, fleeced like sheep, worked like cattle, and fed and clothed like swines and hounds.'").

13. William Blackstone, *Commentaries* (London: Collins and Hannay, 1832), vol. 2, book 3, 380.

14. Ibid.

15. Ibid.

16. Nathan S. Chapman, "The Jury's Constitutional Judgment," *Alabama Law Review* 67 (2015): 207.

17. 18 U.S.C. Section 1503 (influencing or injuring officer or juror generally); 18 U.S.C. Section 1504 (influencing juror by writing).

18. Blackstone, *Commentaries*, 294.

19. David Marcus, "Finding the Civil Trial's Democratic Future After Its Demise," *Nevada Law Journal* 15 (2015): 1524.

20. John H. Langbein, "The Disappearance of Civil Trial in the United States," *Yale Law Journal* 122 (2012): 524 (arguing that an increase in pretrial discovery has eliminated the need for a fact-finding jury).

21. Ibid.

22. *Bell Atl. Corp. v. Twombly*, 550 U.S. 544, 575 (2007) (Stevens, J., dissenting).

23. See, e.g., *Comcast v. Behrend*, 569 U.S. ___ (2013).

24. *Celotex Corp. v. Catrett*, 477 U.S. 317 (1986); *Anderson v. Liberty Lobby, Inc.*, 477 U.S. 242 (1986); *Matsushita Elec. Indus. Co. v. Zenith Radio Corp.*, 475 U.S. 574 (1986).

25. Per Westlaw search, March 7, 2016, conducted by Rachel Craft, student, Harvard Law School.

26. *DirecTV v. Imburgio*, 577 U.S. ____ (2015) (Ginsburg, J., dissenting.).

27. Jessica Silver-Greenberg and Robert Gebeloff, "Arbitration Everywhere, Stacking the Deck of Justice," *New York Times*, October 31, 2015.

28. Associated Press, "Firm Agrees to End Role in Arbitrating Credit Card Debt," *New York Times*, April 19, 2009.

29. Henry Farrell, "People Are Freaking Out About the Trans Pacific Partnership's Investor Dispute Settlement System. Why Should You Care?" *Washington Post*, March 26, 2015.

30. Jackie Calmes and Sabrina Tavernise, "U.S. Proposes Provision on Tobacco in Trade Pact," *New York Times*, October 1, 2015 (Philip Morris International net revenues for 2015: $74 billion; Togo GDP [PPP]: $11 billion).

31. Christ Hamby, "The Court That Rules The World," *BuzzFeed*, August 28, 2016.

32. Ibid.

33. Abe Fortas, *Concerning Dissent and Disobedience* (New York: New American Library, 1968), 60.

34. Blackstone, *Commentaries*, 380.

35. Gordon Wood, *The Radicalism of the American Revolution* (New York: Knopf Doubleday, 2011), 174–75.

36. Ibid.

37. Larry Lessig, *Republic, Lost: How Money Corrupts Congress—and a Plan to Stop It* (New York: Twelve Books, 2011).

38. Alexander Hamilton, "Objections to the Power of the Senate to Set as a Court for Impeachments Further Considered," Federalist No. 66, https://www.congress.gov/resources/display/content/The+Federalist+Papers#TheFederalistPapers-66, and "The Mode of Electing the President," Federalist No. 68, https://www.congress.gov/resources/display/content/The+Federalist+Papers#TheFederalistPapers-68.

39. Zephyr Teachout, *Corruption in America* (Cambridge, MA: Harvard University Press, 2014), 38.

40. Ibid., 7.

41. William Novak, "A Revisionist History of Regulatory Capture," in *Preventing Regulatory Capture: Special Interest Influence and How to Limit It*, ed. Daniel Carpenter and David Moss (New York: Cambridge University Press, 2014), 39.

42. Ibid.

43. Teachout, *Corruption*, 167, citing *Mills v. Mills*, 40 N.Y. 543, 546.

44. Teachout, *Corruption*, 191–92, *citing United States v. Classic*, 313 U.S. 299 (1941) (Douglas, J., dissenting).

45. Niccolò Machiavelli, *The Prince*, ch. IX: "Concerning a Civil Principality" (1513).

46. Andrew Jackson, "President Jackson's Veto Message Regarding the Bank of the United States," July 10, 1832, available at http://avalon.law.yale.edu/19th_century/ajveto01.asp.

47. *McCutcheon v. Federal Election Commission*, 572 U.S. ___ (2014), slip op. at 39, quoting *The Speeches of the Right Hon. Edmund Burke*, 129–130 (J. Burke ed. 1867).

48. *United States v. Sun-Diamond Growers of Cal.*, 526 U.S. 398 (1999) (quoting, and rejecting, an argument made by the Independent Counsel on behalf of the United States) (emphasis added by Justice Scalia).

49. *McDonnell v. United States*, 579 U.S. __ (2016), slip op at 4.

50. Editorial, "Robert McDonnell gets freedom from jail—but not from disgrace," *The Washington Post*, September 9, 2016.

51. *McDonnell*, slip op. at 21–22.

52. Editorial, "Robert McDonnell gets freedom from jail—but not from disgrace."

53. Robert Barnes, "Supreme Court Overturns Corruption Conviction of Former Va. Governor McDonnell," *Washington Post*, June 27, 2016.

54. *McDonnell*, slip op at 28.

55. Carl Hulse, "Is the Supreme Court Clueless About Corruption? Ask Jack Abramoff," *New York Times*, July 5, 2016.

56. Rebecca Leber and Adam Peck, "House Republicans Voted Against the

Environment More Than 500 Times in the Past Four Years," *The New Republic*, December 10, 2014.

57. Gordon Wood, *The Radicalism of the American Revolution* (New York: Knopf Doubleday, 2011), 174–75.

Chapter Ten: The Denial Machine

1. Edward L. Bernays, *Propaganda* (Brooklyn, New York: Ig Publishing, 1928).

2. John Stauber, quoted in Shawn Otto, *The War on Science* (Milkweed Editions, 2016), 264–5.

3. Robert J. Brulle, "Institutionalizing Delay: Foundation Funding and the Creation of U.S. Climate Change Counter-Movement Organizations," *Springer Science and Business Media Dordrecht* 2013, November 19, 2013, 2, citing National Research Council, *America's Climate Choices* (Washington, DC: National Academies Press, 2011).

4. *United States v. Philip Morris USA Inc.*, 449 F. Supp. 2d 1 (D.D.C. 2006), *aff'd in part & vacated in part*, 566 F. 3d 1095 (D.C. Cir. 2009 (*per curiam*), *cert. denied*, 561 U.S. ___, 130 S. Ct. 3501 (2010).

5. Bernays, *Propaganda*, 50.

6. Steve Coll, *Private Empire: ExxonMobil and American Power* (New York: Penguin, 2012), 134.

7. Brown and Williamson, *Smoking and Health Proposal*, Brown and Williamson document no. 680561778-1786, 1969, https://industrydocuments.library.ucsf.edu/tobacco/docs/#id=jryf0138, cited in David Michael, *Doubt Is Their Product: How Industry's Assault on Science Threatens Your Health* (New York: Oxford University Press, 2008), x.

8. Jason M. Breslow, "Robert Brulle: Inside the Climate Change 'Countermovement,'" *PBS Frontline*, October 23, 2012.

9. Brulle, "Institutionalizing Delay."

10. Justin Gillis and John Schwartz, "Deeper Ties to Corporate Cash for Doubtful Climate Researcher," *New York Times*, February 21, 2015.

11. Jeremiah Bohr, "The 'climatism' cartel: why climate change deniers oppose market-based mitigation policy," *Environmental Politics* 25, no. 5 (2016), 813.

12. David Edelstein, "Devastating in Its Implications," *New York Magazine*, June 5, 2006.

13. Naomi Oreskes, "Beyond the Ivory Tower: The Scientific Consensus on Climate Change," *Science* 306, no. 5702 (2004): 1686.

14. Justin Farrell, "Network Structure and Influence of the Climate Change Counter-Movement," *Nature Climate Change*, November 30, 2015, doi: 10.1038/NCLIMATE2875.

15. Justin Farrell, "Corporate Funding and Ideological Polarization About Climate Change," *PNAS* 113, no. 1 (January 5, 2016): 92.

16. Ibid., 95–96.

17. Leo Hickman, "Heartland Institute Compares Belief in Global Warming to Mass Murder," *The Guardian*, May 4, 2012.

18. John M. Carroll, "Review: Marshall and Military Victory, 1943–1945," *The Review of Politics* 35, no. 4 (October 1973): 585.

19. Jane Mayer, *Dark Money: The Hidden History of the Billionaires Behind the Rise of the Radical Right* (New York: Knopf Doubleday, 2016), 79.

20. Brulle, "Institutionalizing Delay."

21. Ibid.

22. Otto, *The War on Science*, 130.

23. Ibid.

24. Ibid. at 292.

25. Ibid. at 232.

26. Ibid. at 292.

27. Ibid.

28. Ibid. at 293.

29. Ibid.

30. Ibid.

31. Ibid. at 293–4.

32. Brulle, "Institutionalizing Delay."

33. Mayer, *Dark Money*, 204.

34. Otto, *The War on Science*, 350.

35. Ibid., 352.

36. "Sources of Greenhouse Gas Emissions," EPA, www.epa.gov/ghgemissions /sources-greenhouse-gas-emissions.

37. The Office of Management and Budget provides a range of Social Cost of Carbon estimates, which vary based on the assumed discount rates used to monetize future harms. The central range price, which uses a 3 percent discount rate, is $38 in 2016 in 2007 dollars, which equals $45 in inflation-adjusted nominal dollars (rounded up to the nearest dollar). See Appendix A in "Technical Support Document: Technical Update of the Social Cost of Carbon for Regulatory Impact Analysis—Under Executive Order 12866," May 2013, Revised July 2015, https://www.whitehouse.gov/sites/default/files/omb/inforeg/scc-tsd-final-july -2015.pdf.

38. "Counting the Cost of Energy Subsidies, IMF Survey," International Monetary Fund, July 17, 2015, www.imf.org/external/pubs/ft/survey/so/2015/new 070215a.htm.

39. Mayer, *Dark Money*, 206.

40. Ibid.

41. Brulle, "Institutionalizing Delay," 8, fig. 2.

42. Ibid., 10.

43. Ibid.

44. Ibid.

45. Farrell, "Corporate Funding," 92.

46. Alex McKechnie, "Not Just the Koch Brothers: New Drexel Study Reveals Funders Behind the Climate Change Denial Effort," *Drexel*NOW, December 20, 2013, http://drexel.edu/now/archive/2013/December/Climate-Change.

47. Otto, *The War on Science*, 342.

48. Ibid, 152.

49. Jill Fitzsimmons and Jocelyn Fong, "*The Wall Street Journal*: Dismissing Environmental Threats Since 1976," Media Matters for America, August 2, 2012.

50. Ibid.

51. Ibid., quoting *Wall Street Journal*, "A Bit of Prudence at the CPSC," January 6, 1976, via Factiva.

52. Ibid., quoting *Wall Street Journal*, "Ozone Re-Examined," May 15, 1979, via Factiva.

53. Ibid., quoting *Wall Street Journal*, "Heads in the Ozone," March 5, 1984, via Factiva.

54. Ibid., quoting *Wall Street Journal*, "Ozone Chicken Littles Are at It Again," March 23, 1989, via Factiva.

55. Ibid., quoting *Wall Street Journal*, "Press-Release Ozone Hole," February 28, 1992, via Factiva.

56. Ibid., quoting *Wall Street Journal*, "Heads in the Ozone."

57. Ibid., quoting *Wall Street Journal*, "Clean Air Revisited," August 29, 1990, via Factiva.

58. Ibid.

59. Ibid., quoting *Wall Street Journal*, "Asides: Middle-Class Payments," February 14, 1992, via Factiva.

60. Environmental Protection Agency, "Progress Cleaning the Air and Improving People's Health," citing "The Benefits and Costs of the Clean Air Act 190 to 2010," November 1999, www.epa.gov/clean-air-act-overview/progress-cleaning-air-and-improving-peoples-health.

61. Fitzsimmons and Fong, "*The Wall Street Journal*."

62. Ibid.

63. "Climate of Uncertainty," editorial, *Wall Street Journal*, October 1, 2013.

64. Ibid.

65. "Analysis: How the *Wall Street Journal* Opinion Section Presents Climate Change," Climate Nexus, 2016, available at http://static1.squarespace.com/static/534ec657e4b03c887dde2641/t/575f6edd20c647ff95c170a0/1465872094069/FINAL_CN_WSJ_white_paper-0613.pdf.

66. *Major Campaign Speeches of Adlai E. Stevenson* (New York: Random House, 1952), 130.

67. Sheldon Whitehouse, "The Fossil-Fuel Industry's Campaign to Mislead the American People," *Washington Post*, May 29, 2015.

68. Oversight of the U.S. Department of Justice, Senate Judiciary Committee, March 9, 2016.

69. Robert Post, "Exxon-Mobil is abusing the first amendment," *The Washington Post*, June 24, 2016.

70. See, e.g., Paul Dresser, "RICO for Government Climate Deniers?" *Townhall*, April 16, 2016, http://townhall.com/columnists/pauldriessen/2016/04/16/rico-for-government-climate-deniers-n2149120.

71. See generally, "Timeline: Legal Harassment of Climate Scientist Michael Mann," Union of Concerned Scientists, http://www.ucsusa.org/our-work/center

-science-and-democracy/protecting-scientists-harassment/va-ag-timeline.html#.WAfuhvkrIdU.

Chapter Eleven: Climate Change and the "Flies of Summer"

1. "Pope Francis Says There Are Limits to Freedom of Expression," Vatican Radio, January 16, 2015.

2. Wendell Berry, "Praise for *The Dying of the Trees: The Pandemic of America's Forests* by Charles E. Little," 1997, available at www.ecobooks.com/books/dying.htm.

3. Brian Kahn, "The World Passes 400 PPM Threshold. Permanently," *Climate Central*, September 27, 2016, http://www.climatecentral.org/news/world-passes-400-ppm-threshold-permanently-20738.

4. Steve Graham, "John Tyndall (1820–1893)," NASA: *Earth Observatory*, October 8, 1999, http://earthobservatory.nasa.gov/Features/Tyndall.

5. "Climate Change Indicators: Ocean Heat," US Environmental Protection Agency, https://www.epa.gov/climate-indicators/climate-change-indicators-ocean-heat.

6. Brad Plumer, "The Oceans Are Acidifying at the Fastest Rate in 300 Million Years. How Worried Should We Be?" *Washington Post*, August 31, 2013; Oliver Milman, "World's Oceans Warming at Increasingly Faster Rate, New Study Find," *The Guardian*, January 18, 2016.

7. National Centers for Environmental Information, "Global Analysis—Annual 2015," National Oceanic and Atmospheric Administration, January 2016, https://www.ncdc.noaa.gov/sotc/global/201513.

8. James Boyd, "CRMC Climate Change Adaptation Actions," Rhode Island Coastal Resources Management Council, http://www.crmc.ri.gov/news/2013_0201_climate.html.

9. Benjamin Hulac, "Tobacco and Oil Industries Used Same Researchers to Sway Public," *Scientific American: ClimateWire*, July 20, 2016.

10. Steve Knisely, Planning Engineering Division, "Controlling the CO_2 Concentration in the Atmosphere," October 16, 1979, with memo to R.L. Hirsch, accessed January 16, 2016, http://insideclimatenews.org/sites/default/files/documents/CO2%20and%20Fuel%20Use%20Projections.pdf.

11. Roger W. Cohen, Director, Theoretical and Mathematical Sciences Laboratory, Exxon, "Memo to: Mr. A.M. Natkin, Office of Science and Technology, Exxon Corporation," September 2, 1982, accessed January 16, 2016, http://insideclimatenews.org/sites/default/files/documents/%2522Consensus%2522%20on%20CO2%20Impacts%20%281982%29.pdf.

12. Knisely, "Controlling."

13. M.B. Glaser, Manager, Environmental Affairs Program, "CO_2 'Greenhouse Effect,'" November 12, 1982, http://insideclimatenews.org/sites/default/files/documents/1982%20Exxon%20Primer%20on%20CO2%20Greenhouse%20Effect.pdf#page=5.

14. Jeffrey Ball, "Exxon Chief Makes a Cold Calculation on Global Warming," *Wall Street Journal*, June 14, 2005.

15. Naomi Oreskes and Ted Lieu, "The Harm Exxon Mobil Has Done," *The Hill*, November 4, 2015.

16. Shawn Otto, *The War on Science* (Milkweed Editions, 2016), 269.

17. Steve Coll, *Private Empire: ExxonMobil and American Power* (New York: Penguin, 2012), 88.

18. George Monbiot, "The Denial Industry," *The Guardian*, September 19, 2006; Dennis Hevesi, "Frederick Seitz, Physicist Who Led Skeptics of Global Warming, Dies at 96," *New York Times*, March 6, 2008. Whether Exxon paid for this "petition" is unknown.

19. Coll, *Private Empire*.

20. Ibid., 96.

21. Edmund Burke, "Reflections on the Revolution in France," in *The British Prose Writers* (London: Piccadilly, 1819–21), 21:132–33.

22. Peter Schweizer, "Introduction," *Landmark Speeches of the American Conservative Movement* (College Station: Texas A&M University Press, 2007), 3.

23. "Conservation Activism Is a Healthy Sign," *The Sun* (Baltimore), May 4, 1970, A17, cited in James E. Person Jr., *Russell Kirk: A Critical Biography of a Conservative Mind* (Lanham, MD: Madison Books, 1999), 27.

24. Dwight D. Eisenhower, "Transcript of President Dwight D. Eisenhower's Farewell Address, 1961," www.ourdocuments.gov/doc.php?flash=false&doc=90&page=transcript.

25. Gerald Ford, "Remarks at Dedication Ceremonies for the National Environmental Research Center, Cincinnati, Ohio, July 3, 1975," American Presidency Project, www.presidency.ucsb.edu/ws/?pid=5042.

26. Ronald Reagan, "Remarks at Dedication Ceremonies for the New Building of the National Geographic Society," June 19, 1984, https://reaganlibrary.archives.gov/archives/speeches/1984/61984a.htm.

27. Mitch Hescox and Paul Douglas, *Caring for Creation: The Evangelical's Guide to Climate Change and a Healthy Environment* (Ada, MI: Baker Publishing Group, 2016), 51.

28. *Congressional Record*, vol. 149, part 1, January 9, 2003, 379.

29. Ibid., vol. 153, part 7, April 19, 2007, 9342.

30. Ibid., vol. 155, no. 82, June 3, 2009, H6088.

31. Ibid., vol. 154, no. 91, June 4, 2008, S5019.

32. "Global Analysis—Annual 2014," National Centers for Environmental Information, National Oceanic and Atmospheric Administration, www.ncdc.noaa.gov/sotc/global/201413.

33. Coral Davenport, "Why Republicans Keep Telling Everyone They're Not Scientists," *New York Times*, October 30, 2014.

34. Andrew Nikiforuk, "Bark Beetles, Aided by Climate Change, Are Devastating U.S. Pine Forests," *Washington Post*, December 5, 2011.

35. Bob Inglis, "Putting Free Enterprise to Work: A Conservative Vision of

Our Environmental Future," *Duke Environmental Law and Policy Forum* 23 (Spring 2013): 248–249.

36. Henry A. Waxman, Sherwood Boehlert, Wedward J. Markey, and Wayne Gilchrest, "Carbon Emission Policy Could Slash Debt, Improve Environment," *Washington Post*, February 23, 2012.

37. William D. Ruckelshaus, Lee M. Thomas, William K. Reilly, and Christine Todd Whitman, "A Republican Case for Climate Action," *New York Times*, August 1, 2013.

38. Ibid.

39. Chuck Hagel, "Secretary of Defense Speech," Halifax International Security Forum, November 22, 2013, http://archive.defense.gov/speeches/speech.aspx?speechid=1821.

40. George P. Shultz and Gary S. Becker, "Why We Support a Revenue-Neutral Carbon Tax," *Wall Street Journal*, April 7, 2013.

41. David Frum, "A Tax We Could Learn to Love," CNN, December 3, 2012.

42. N. Gregory Mankiw, "A Carbon Tax That America Could Live With," *New York Times*, August 31, 2013.

43. Jim Brainard, "Cities Must Take Action on Global Warming," *Indystar*, December 11, 2013.

44. Davenport, "Why Republicans Keep Telling."

45. William Shakespeare, *Richard III*, Act 1, Scene 2.

46. Jane Mayer, *Dark Money: The Hidden History of the Billionaires Behind the Rise of the Radical Right* (New York: Knopf Doubleday, 2016), 278.

47. Duff Cooper, *Talleyrand* (New York: Grove Press, 2010 [1932]), 313.

48. Peggy Noonan, "A Party Divided, and None Too Soon," *Wall Street Journal*, June 2, 2016.

49. "Sen. Inhofe Delivers Major Speech on the Science of Climate Change," July 29, 2003, www.inhofe.senate.gov/epw-archive/press/bsen-inhofe-delivers-major-speech-on-the-science-of-climate-change/b-icatastrophic-global-warming-alarmism-not-based-on-objective-sciencei-ipart-2/i; see also James Inhofe, *The Greatest Hoax: How the Global Warming Conspiracy Threatens Your Future* (Washington, DC: WND Books, 2012).

50. Gary McManus, "Global Climate Change and the Implications for Oklahoma," Oklahoma Climatological Survey, April 2010.

51. "Study Finds Climate Change May Dramatically Reduce Wheat Production," Kansas State University News and Communications Service, February 18, 2015, www.k-state.edu/media/newsreleases/feb15/climatewheat21815.html.

52. "Ron Johnson's Climate Change Denials May Not Fly with Voters," editorial, *Milwaukee Journal Sentinel*, October 22, 2013.

53. Tim Carpenter, "Oil, Gas Industry: It's not our fault," *Topeka Capital-Journal*, August 24, 2010.

54. Tiffany Germain, Ryan Koronowski, and Jeff Spross, "The Anti-Science Climate Denier Caucus: 113th Congress Edition," *ThinkProgress*, June 26, 2013.

55. "GOP Deeply Divided over Climate Change," Pew Research Center, No-

vember 1, 2013, www.people-press.org/2013/11/01/gop-deeply-divided-over-climate-change.

56. Amy Levin and Greg Strimple, "Recent Polling on Youth Voters," Memo to League of Conservative Voters, July 24, 2013, http://www.lcv.org/issues/polling/recent-polling-on-youth.pdf.

57. Matt Viser, "GOP Hopefuls Not Embracing Climate Change," *Boston Globe*, August 1, 2015.

58. "GOP Deeply Divided over Climate Change."

Chapter Twelve: America's Lamp in Peril

1. Daniel Webster, "The Bunker Hill Monument," address delivered at the laying of the cornerstone of the Bunker Hill Monument in Charlestown, MA, June 16, 1825, in *The Writings and Speeches of Daniel Webster* (Boston: Little, Brown, 1903), 1:235.

2. John Winthrop, "A Model of Christian Charity," 1630, in *Collections of the Massachusetts Historical Society*, 3rd series, 7 (1838), 31–48.

3. Ronald Reagan, "Reagan's Farewell Speech," 1988, www.pbs.org/wgbh/americanexperience/features/primary-resources/reagan-farewell.

4. John F. Kennedy, "Inaugural Address of President John F. Kennedy," January 20, 1961, www.jfklibrary.org/Research/Research-Aids/Ready-Reference/JFK-Quotations/Inaugural-Address.aspx.

5. Barack Obama, "President Barack Obama's Inaugural Address," January 21, 2009, www.whitehouse.gov/blog/2009/01/21/president-barack-obamas-inaugural-address.

6. William Clinton, "Bill Clinton's Prime-Time Speech," Democratic National Convention, August 27, 2008, www.npr.org/templates/story/story.php?storyId=94045962.

7. Webster, "Bunker Hill Monument."

8. Joseph E. Stiglitz, *Freefall: America, Free Markets, and the Sinking of the World Economy* (New York: W.W. Norton, 2010), 225–26.

9. Alexander Hamilton or James Madison, "The Senate Continued," Federalist No. 63, www.congress.gov/resources/display/content/The+Federalist+Papers#TheFederalistPapers-63.

10. Right Hon. John Edward Emerich, First Baron Acton, "Inaugural Lecture," in *Lectures on Modern History*, ed. John Neville Figgis and Reginald Vere Laurence (London: Macmillan, 1906), 24.

11. Franklin Delano Roosevelt, "Acceptance Speech for the Renomination for the Presidency," American Presidency Project, www.presidency.ucsb.edu/ws/?pid=15314_.

12. Thomas Jefferson, letter to George Logan, November 12, 1816, http://tjrs.monticello.org/letter/1392.

13. David McCullough, "On John Adams" (notes on file with author from Q&A session), Library of Congress, February 14, 2014, www.loc.gov/today/cyberlc/transcripts/2014/140212lib1200.txt.

Postscript

1. Nicholas Confessore and Rachel Shorey, "Outside Money Favors Hillary Clinton at a 2-to-1 Rate Over Donald Trump," *New York Times*, October 22, 2016.
2. Nicholas Confessore and Rachel Shorey, "How Democrats Stopped Worrying and Learned to Love Big Donor Money," *New York Times*, September 30, 2016.
3. Ibid.
4. Matea Gold, "How the Stampede for Big Money Enabled Donald Trump's Rise," *Washington Post*, November 8, 2016.
5. Fredreka Schouten and Christopher Schnaars, "Super PAC Donations Surge Past $1 Billion," *USA Today*, September 21, 2016.
6. Matea Gold and Anu Narayanswamy, "How 10 Mega-donors Already Helped Pour a Record $1.1 Billion into Super PACs," *Washington Post*, October 15, 2016, updated November 2, 2016.
7. Confessore and Shorey, "Outside Money Favors Hillary Clinton at a 2-to-1 Rate Over Donald Trump."
8. Ibid.
9. Theodore Roosevelt, speech delivered at the dedication of the John Brown Memorial Park in Osawatomie, Kansas, August 31, 1910, www.whitehouse.gov/blog/2011/12/06/archives-president-teddy-roosevelts-new-nationalism-speech.
10. "Senate GOP Super PAC Gets $11M from Undisclosed Donors," *BNA, Inc. Money and Politics Report*, October 28, 2016.
11. Gold, "How the Stampede for Big Money Enabled Donald Trump's Rise."
12. Ibid.
13. Ibid.
14. Sam Thielman, "Pro-Trump Billionaires Pour Money into Last-Minute Bid for Swing States," *The Guardian*, November 4, 2016.
15. Rebecca Ballhaus, "Five Big GOP Donors Added at Least $24 Million to Trump Groups in Recent Months," *Wall Street Journal*, October 16, 2016.
16. Eric Lipton, "Trump Campaigned Against Lobbyists, but Now They're on His Transition Team," *New York Times*, November 11, 2016.
17. Kenneth Vogel and Alex Isenstadt, "Secret Money to Boost Trump," *Politico*, September 28, 2016.
18. Ibid.
19. Emily Cadei, "How Charles and David Koch Plan to Remake the Republican Party," *Newsweek*, September 28, 2016.
20. Ibid.
21. Ibid.
22. "Koch Brothers Push Forward Efforts to Hide Nonprofit Donors' Identities," *CBS SF Bay Area*, April 29, 2016.
23. Cadei, "How Charles and David Koch Plan to Remake the Republican Party."
24. Fredreka Schouten, "Charles Koch Say His Network Offers 'Vision' for a Divided Nation," *USA Today*, November 11, 2016.
25. Ibid.

26. Ibid.
27. Ibid.
28. Ibid.
29. Cadei, "How Charles and David Koch Plan to Remake the Republican Party."
30. Josh Barro, "Fact-Free Conservative Media Is a Symptom of GOP Troubles, Not a Cause," *Business Insider*, October 24, 2016.
31. Ibid.
32. Jamie Weinstein, "This Election Was a Great Opportunity for Republicans. Instead, the GOP Lies Broken," *The Guardian*, November 8, 2016.
33. Stuart Stevens, "The Flat-Earth Set Helped Donald Trump Hijack the GOP and Crash It into the Ground," *The Daily Beast*, November 7, 2016.
34. Marianne Lavelle, "Fossil Fuel Money to GOP Grows, and So Does Climate Divide," *Inside Climate News*, September 15, 2016.
35. Ibid.
36. Ibid.
37. Danny Vinik, "Trump's Attack Dog on Climate," *Politico*, November 14, 2016.
38. Ibid.
39. Ibid.
40. For an image of the advertisement, see Ben Adler and Rebecca Leber, "Donald Trump Once Backed Urgent Climate Action. Wait, What?" Grist, June 8, 2016.
41. See Andrew Ward, "Exxon Backs 'Serious Action' on Climate Change," *Financial Times*, October 19, 2016; Stanley Reed, "Oil and Gas Companies Make Statement in Support of U.N. Climate Goals," *New York Times*, October 16, 2015.
42. See Sheldon Whitehouse, "Why Isn't Anyone Lobbying For Climate Change?" *Forbes*, June 7, 2016; Sheldon Whitehouse, "The Climate Movement Needs More Corporate Lobbyists," *Harvard Business Review*, February 25, 2016.
43. Carl Hulse, "Supreme Court Stonewall May Not Crumble Anytime Soon," *New York Times*, November 3, 2016.
44. Eric Lipton and Robert Faturechi, "These Officials Help Write Ballot Questions. Companies Write Them Checks," *New York Times*, November 4, 2016.

Index

About the Authors

Senator Sheldon Whitehouse represents Rhode Island in the U.S. Senate. He has served as his state's United States Attorney and as the state Attorney General, as well as its top business regulator. He is the author of *On Virtues: Quotations and Insight to Live a Full, Honorable, and Truly American Life*, and has written opinion pieces for the *New York Times*, the *Columbia Journalism Review*, and *U.S. News & World Report*, among other outlets. He lives in Newport, Rhode Island, with his wife, a marine scientist, and his grown children when they visit.

Melanie Wachtell Stinnett is a Boston-based writer and former Director of Policy and Communications at the Tobin Project. She has previously published on regulatory policy and Supreme Court litigation trends.

Celebrating 25 Years of Independent Publishing

Thank you for reading this book published by The New Press. The New Press is a nonprofit, public interest publisher celebrating its twenty-fifth anniversary in 2017. New Press books and authors play a crucial role in sparking conversations about the key political and social issues of our day.

We hope you enjoyed this book and that you will stay in touch with The New Press. Here are a few ways to stay up to date with our books, events, and the issues we cover:

- Sign up at www.thenewpress.com/subscribe to receive updates on New Press authors and issues and to be notified about local events
- Like us on Facebook: www.facebook.com/newpressbooks
- Follow us on Twitter: www.twitter.com/thenewpress

Please consider buying New Press books for yourself; for friends and family; and to donate to schools, libraries, community centers, prison libraries, and other organizations involved with the issues our authors write about.

The New Press is a 501(c)(3) nonprofit organization. You can also support our work with a tax-deductible gift by visiting www.thenewpress.com/donate.